Critical Acclaim for
CLIVE BARKER
AND HIS NOVELS

"Mesmerizing invention."
—*Publishers Weekly*

"[A] dazzling metaphysical epic-adventure
. . . an astonishing feat of imagination. . . .
Barker's best yet."
—*Kirkus Reviews*

"Spellbinding."
—*Atlanta Journal*

"Barker's most ambitious work to date. . . .
Rapturously full of emotions."
—*L.A. Life*

"Rich in plot twists, byzantine intrigues and
hidden secrets, *Imajica* is a Chinese puzzle
box constructed on a universal scale. . . .
Barker has an unparalleled talent for
envisioning other worlds."
—*Washington Post Book World*

THE THIEF OF ALWAYS

"A welcome modern-day return to a classic form, this fable lives up to the publisher's billing as a tale for all ages."
—*Publishers Weekly*

"Taut pacing and sound structure. . . . None of Clive Barker's admirers are likely to go away disappointed."
—*New York Newsday*

"A wonderful story for adults and teenagers, profusely illustrated by the author."
—*Denver Post*

"Menacing demons, wondrous miracles, sinister magic, and vivid characters make *Thief* a compulsive, lightning-paced tale that almost begs to be read aloud."
—*Miami Herald*

"Certain to satisfy anyone who just wants to take a fun little trip into one of Barker's worlds."
—*Virginia Pilot/Ledger Star*

"An impressive piece of storytelling."
—*Midweek*

THE GREAT AND SECRET SHOW

Books by Clive Barker

http://www.clivebarker.com

—THE FIFTH DOMINION—

IMAJICA I

CLIVE BARKER

HarperTorch
An Imprint of HarperCollinsPublishers

HARPERTORCH
An Imprint of HarperCollins*Publishers*
10 East 53rd Street
New York, New York 10022-5299

Copyright © 1991, 1995 by Clive Barker
Cover illustration by Jim Burns
ISBN: 0-06-109414-5

First HarperTorch paperback printing: August 2001
First HarperPaperbacks printing: June 1995
First HarperCollins hardcover printing: September 1991
A single volume edition of *Imajica* was published in 1992 by HarperPaperbacks.

HarperCollins®, HarperTorch™, and ♦™ are trademarks of HarperCollins Publishers Inc.
Avon Trademark Reg. U.S. Pat. Off. and in Other Countries, Marca Registrada, Hecho en U.S.A.

Printed in the United States of America

Visit HarperTorch on the World Wide Web at
www.harpercollins.com

20 19 18 17 16 15 14 13 12 11

Back and back we go, searching for reasons; scrutinizing the past in the hope that we'll turn up some fragment of an explanation to help us better understand ourselves and our condition.

For the psychologist, this quest is perhaps at root a pursuit of primal pain. For the physicist, a sniffing after evidence of the First Cause. For the theologian, of course, a hunt for God's fingermarks on Creation.

And for a storyteller—particularly for a fabulist, a writer of *fantastiques* like myself—it may very well be a search for all three, motivated by the vague suspicion that they are inextricably linked.

Imajica was an attempt to weave these quests into a single narrative, folding my dilettante's grasp of this trio of disciplines—psychology, physics, and theology—into an interdimensional adventure. The resulting novel sprawls, no doubt of that. The book is simply too cumbersome and too diverse in its concerns for the tastes of some. For others, however, *Imajica*'s absurd ambition is part of its appeal. These readers forgive the inelegance of the novel's structure and allow that while it undoubtedly has its rocky roads and its cul-de-sacs, all in all the journey is worth the shoe-leather.

For my publishers, however, a more practical problem became apparent when the book was prepared for its paperback edition. If the volume was not to be so thick that it would drop off a bookstore shelf, then the type had to be reduced to a size that several people, myself included, thought less than ideal. When I received my author's copies I was put in mind of a pocket-sized Bible my grandmother gave me for my eighth birthday, the words set so densely that the verses swam before my then healthy eyes. It was not—I will admit—an entirely unpleasant association, given that the roots of Imajica's strange blossom lay in the poetry of Ezekiel, Matthew, and Revelations, but I was well aware, as were my editors, that the book was not as reader-friendly as we all wished it was.

From those early misgivings springs this new, two-volume edition. Let me admit, in all honesty, that the book was not conceived to be thus divided. The place we have elected to split the story has no particular significance. It is simply halfway through the text, or thereabouts: a spot where you can put down one volume and—if the story has worked its magic—pick up the next. Other than the larger type, and the addition of these words of explanation, the novel itself remains unaltered.

Personally, I've never much cared about the details of one edition over another. While it's very pleasurable to turn the pages of a beautifully bound book, immaculately printed on acid-free paper, the words are what count. The first copy of Poe's short stories I ever read was a cheap, gaudily covered paperback; my first *Moby Dick* the same. *A Midsummer Night's Dream* and *The Duchess of Malfi* were first encountered in dog-eared school editions. It mattered not at all that these enchantments were printed on coarse, stained paper. Their potency was undimmed. I hope the same will prove true for the tale you now hold: that the form it comes in is finally irrelevant.

With that matter addressed, might I delay you a little longer with a few thoughts about the story itself? At signings and conventions I am repeatedly asked a number of questions about the book, and this seems as good a place as any to briefly answer them.

Firstly, the question of pronunciation. *Imajica* is full of invented names and terms, some of which are puzzlers: Yzorddorex, Patashoqua, Hapexamendios, and so forth. There is no absolute hard and fast rule as to how these should trip, or stumble, off the tongue. After all, I come from a very small country where you can hike over a modest range of hills and find that the people you encounter on the far side use language in a completely different way to those whose company you left minutes before. There is no right or wrong in this. Language isn't a fascist regime. It's protean, and effortlessly defies all attempts to regulate or confine it. While it's true that I have my own pronunciations of the words I've turned in the book, even those undergo modifications when—as has happened several times—people I meet offer more interesting variations. A book belongs at least as much to its readers as to its author, so please find the way the words sound most inviting to you and take pleasure in them.

The other matter I'd like to address is my motivation for writing the novel. Of course there is no simply encapsulated answer to that question, but I will offer here what clues I can. To begin with, I have an abiding interest in the notion of parallel dimensions, and the influence they may exercise over the lives we live in this world. I don't doubt that the reality we occupy is but one of many; that a lateral step would deliver us into a place quite other. Perhaps our lives are also going on in these other dimensions, changed in vast or subtle ways. Or perhaps these other places will be unrecognizable to us: they'll be realms of spirit, or wonderlands, or hells. Perhaps all of the above. *Imajica* is an attempt to create a narrative which explores those possibilities.

It is also a book about Christ. People are constantly surprised that the figure of Jesus is of such importance to me. They look at *The Hellbound Heart* or at some of the stories in The Books of Blood and take me for a pagan who views Christianity as a pretty distraction from the business of suffering and dying. There is some truth in this. I certainly find the hypocritical cant and derisive dogmas of organized religion grotesque and oftentimes inhumane. Plainly the Vatican, for instance, cares more for its own authority than for the planet and the flock that grazes upon it. But the mythology that is still barely visible beneath the centuries-old encrustation of power plays and rituals—the story of Jesus the crucified and resurrected; the shaman healer who walked on water and raised Lazarus—is as moving to me as any story I have ever heard.

I found Christ as I found Dionysus or Coyote, through art. Blake showed him to me; so did Bellini and Gerard

Manley Hopkins, and half a hundred others, each artist offering his or her own particular interpretation. And from very early on I wanted to find a way to write about Jesus myself; to fold his presence into a story of my own invention. It proved difficult. Most *fantastique* fiction has drawn inspiration from a pre-Christian world, retrieving from Faery, or Atlantis, or dreams of a Celtic twilight creatures that never heard of Communion. There's nothing wrong with that, of course, but it always left me wondering if these authors weren't willfully denying their Christian roots out of frustration or disappointment. Having had no religious education, I harbored no such disappointment: I was drawn to the Christ figure as I was to Pan or Shiva, because the stories and images enlightened and enriched me. Christ is, after all, the central figure of Western mythology. I wanted to feel that my self-created pantheon could accomodate him, that my inventions were not too brittle to bear the weight of his presence.

I was further motivated by a desire to snatch this most complex and contradictory mystery from the clammy hands of the men who have claimed it for their own in recent years, especially here in America. The Falwells and the Robertsons, who, mouthing piety and sowing hatred, use the Bible to justify their plots against our self-discovery. Jesus does not belong to them. And it pains me that many imaginative people are so persuaded by these claims to possession that they turn their backs on the body of Western mysticism instead of *reclaiming* Christ for themselves. I said in an interview once (and meant it) that the Pope, or Falwell, or a thousand others, may announce that God talks to them, instructs them, shows them the Grand Plan, but that the Creator talks to me just as loudly, just as cogently, through the images and ideas He, She, or It has seeded in my imagination.

That said, I must tell you that the deeper I got into writing *Imajica,* the more certain I became that completing it was beyond me. I have never come closer to giving up as I came on this book, never doubted more deeply my skills as a storyteller, was never more lost, never more afraid. But nor was I ever more obsessed. I became so thoroughly immersed in the narrative that for a period of several weeks toward the end of the final draft a kind of benign insanity settled upon me. I woke from dreams of the Dominions only to write about them until I crept back to bed to dream them again. My ordinary life—what little I had—came to seem banal and featureless by contrast with what was happening to me—I should say Gentle, but I *mean* me—as we made our journey toward revelation. It's no accident that the book was finished as I prepared to leave England for America. By the time I came to write the final pages my house in Wimpole Street had been sold, its contents boxed up and sent on to Los Angeles, so that all I had that I took comfort in had gone from around me. It was in some ways a perfect way to finish the novel: like Gentle, I was embarking on another kind of life, and in so doing leaving the country in which I had spent almost forty years. In a sense, *Imajica* became a compendium of locations I had known and felt strongly about: Highgate and Crouch End, where I had spent a decade or more, writing plays, then short stories, then *Weaveworld;* Central London, where I lived for a little time in a splendid Georgian house. There on the page I put the summers of my childhood, and my fantasies of aristocracy. I put my love of a peculiar English apocalyptic: the visions of Stanley Spencer and John Martin and William Blake, dreams of domestic resurrection and Christ upon the doorstep some summer morning. Gamut Street I placed in Clerkenwell, which has always seemed haunted to me. The scenes with the returned Gentle I set on the South Bank, where I had spent many blissful evenings. In short, the book became my farewell to England.

I do not discount the possibility that I will one day return there, of course, but for now, in the smog and sun of Los Angeles, that world seems very remote. It's extraordinary how divided it can make you feel, having been brought up in one country and coming to live in another. For a writer such as myself, who is much concerned with journeys into the strange, and the melancholia and joy of such journeys, it's proved an educative experience.

I offer these scraps of biography in the hope that they illuminate the story that follows, and that some of the feelings that brought me to this novel will be left with you when it's finished. Christ and England have not left my heart of course—they never will—but writing about a subject works an extraordinary magic. It magnifies the passions that inspired the story, and then—with the work finished—buries them, out of sight and mind, so as to allow the writer to move on to another place. I still dream of England, now and then, and I last wrote of Jesus walking on Quiddity's waters in *Everville,* telling Tesla Bombeck that "lives are leaves on the story-tree." But I will never again feel about them as I did when I wrote *Imajica.* Those particular forms and emotions have disappeared into the pages, to be rediscovered there by somebody who wants to find them. If it pleases you to do so, make them your own.

Clive Barker
Los Angeles, 1994

—THE FIFTH DOMINION—
IMAJICA I

I

IT WAS THE PIVOTAL TEACHING of Pluthero Quexos, the most celebrated dramatist of the Second Dominion, that in any fiction, no matter how ambitious its scope or profound its theme, there was only ever room for three players. Between warring kings, a peacemaker; between adoring spouses, a seducer or a child. Between twins, the spirit of the womb. Between lovers, Death. Greater numbers might drift through the drama, of course—thousands in fact—but they could only ever be phantoms, agents, or, on rare occasions, reflections of the three real and self-willed beings who stood at the center. And even this essential trio would not remain intact; or so he taught. It would steadily diminish as the story unfolded, three becoming two, two becoming one, until the stage was left deserted.

Needless to say, this dogma did not go unchallenged. The writers of fables and comedies were particularly vociferous in their scorn, reminding the worthy Quexos that they invariably ended their own tales with a marriage and a feast. He was unrepentant. He dubbed them cheats and told them they were swindling their audiences out of what he called the last great procession, when, after the wedding songs had been sung and the dances danced, the characters took their melancholy way off into darkness, following each other into oblivion.

It was a hard philosophy, but he claimed it was both immutable and universal, as true in the Fifth Dominion, called Earth, as it was in the Second.

And more significantly, as certain in life as it was in art.

Being a man of contained emotion, Charlie Estabrook had little patience with the theater. It was, in his bluntly stated opinion, a waste of breath: indulgence, flummery, lies. But had some student recited Quexos' First Law of Drama to him this cold November night he would have nodded grimly and said: All true, all true. It was his experience precisely. Just as Quexos' Law required, his story had begun with a trio: himself, John Furie Zacharias, and, between them, Judith. That arrangement hadn't lasted very long. Within a few weeks of setting eyes on Judith he had managed to supersede Zacharias in her affections, and the three had dwindled to a blissful two. He and Judith had married and lived happily for five years, until, for reasons he still didn't understand, their joy had foundered, and the two had become one.

He was that one, of course, and the night found him sitting in the back of a purring car being driven around the frosty streets of London in search of somebody to help him finish the story. Not, perhaps, in a fashion Quexos would have approved of—the stage would not be left entirely empty—but one which would salve Estabrook's hurt.

He wasn't alone in his search. He had the company of one half-trusted soul tonight: his driver, guide, and procurer, the ambiguous Mr. Chant. But despite Chant's shows of empathy, he was still just another servant, content to attend upon his master as long as he was promptly paid. He didn't understand the profundity of Estabrook's pain; he was too chilly, too remote. Nor, for all the length of his family history, could Estabrook turn to his lineage for comfort. Although he could trace his ancestors back to the reign of James the First, he had not been able to find a single man on that tree of immoralities—even to the bloodiest root—who had caused, either by his hand or hiring, what he, Estabrook, was out this midnight to contrive: the murder of his wife.

When he thought of her (when didn't he?) his mouth was dry and his palms were wet; he sighed; he shook. She was in his mind's eye now, like a fugitive from some more perfect place. Her skin was flawless and always cool, always pale; her body was long, like her hair, like her fingers, like her laughter; and her eyes, oh, her eyes, had every season of leaf in them: the twin greens of spring and high summer, the golds of autumn, and, in her rages, black midwinter rot.

He was, by contrast, a plain man: well scrubbed but plain. He'd made his fortune selling baths, bidets and toilets, which lent him little by way of mystique. So, when he'd first laid eyes on Judith—she'd been sitting behind a desk at his accountant's office, her beauty all the more luminous for its drab setting—his first thought was: I want this woman; his second: She won't want me. There was, however, an instinct in him when it came to Judith that he'd never experienced with any other woman. Quite simply, he felt she *belonged* to him, and that if he turned his wit to it, he could win her.

His courtship had begun the day they'd met, with the first of many small tokens of affection delivered to her desk. But he sooned learned that such bribes and blandishments would not help his case. She politely thanked him but told him they weren't welcome. He dutifully ceased to send presents and, instead, began a systematic investigation of her circumstances. There was precious little to learn. She lived simply, her small circle vaguely bohemian. But among that circle he discovered a man whose claim upon her preceded his own, and to whom she was apparently devoted. That man was John Furie Zacharias, known universally as Gentle, and he had a reputation as a lover that would have driven Estabrook from the field had that strange certainty not been upon him. He decided to be patient and await his moment. It would come.

Meanwhile he watched his beloved from afar, conspiring to encounter her accidentally now and again, and researching his antagonist's history. Again, there was little to learn. Zacharias was a minor painter, when he wasn't living off his mistresses, and reputedly a dissolute. Of this Estabrook had perfect proof when, by chance, he met the fellow. Gentle was as handsome as his legends suggested, but looked, Charlie thought, like a man just risen from a fever. There was something raw about him—his body sweated to its essence, his face betraying a hunger behind its symmetry—that lent him a bedeviled look.

Half a week after that encounter, Charlie had heard that

his beloved had parted from the man with great grief and was in need of tender care. He'd been quick to supply it, and she'd come into the comfort of his devotion with an ease that suggested his dreams of possession had been well founded.

His memories of that triumph had, of course, been soured by her departure, and now it was he who wore the hungry, yearning look he'd first seen on Furie's face. It suited him less well than it had Zacharias. His was not a head made for haunting. At fifty-six, he looked sixty or more, his features as solid as Gentle's were spare, as pragmatic as Gentle's were rarefied. His only concession to vanity was the delicately curled mustache beneath his patrician nose, which concealed an upper lip he'd thought dubiously ripe in his youth, leaving the lower to jut in lieu of a chin.

Now, as he rode through the darkened streets, he caught sight of that face in the window and perused it ruefully. What a mockery he was! He blushed to think of how shamelessly he'd paraded himself when he'd had Judith on his arm; how he'd joked that she loved him for his cleanliness, and for his taste in bidets. The same people who'd listened to those jokes were laughing in earnest now, were calling him ridiculous. It was unbearable. The only way he knew to heal the pain of his humiliation was to punish her for the crime of leaving him.

He rubbed the heel of his hand against the window and peered out.

"Where are we?" he asked Chant.

"South of the river, sir."

"Yes, but where?"

"Streatham."

Though he'd driven through this area many times—he had a warehouse in the neighborhood—he recognized none of it. The city had never looked more foreign or more unlovely.

"What sex is London, do you suppose?" he mused.

"I hadn't ever thought," Chant said.

"It was a woman once," Estabrook went on. "One calls

a city *she*, yes? But it doesn't seem very feminine any more."

"She'll be a lady again in spring," Chant replied.

"I don't think a few crocuses in Hyde Park are going to make much difference," Estabrook said. "The charm's gone out of it." He sighed. "How far now?"

"Maybe another mile."

"Are you sure your man's going to be there?"

"Of course."

"You've done this a lot, have you? Been a go-between, I mean. What did you call it . . . a *facilitator?*"

"Oh, yes," Chant said. "It's in my blood." That blood was not entirely English. Chant's skin and syntax carried traces of the immigrant. But Estabrook had grown to trust him a little, even so.

"Aren't you curious about all of this?" he asked the man.

"It's not my business, sir. You're paying for the service, and I provide it. If you wanted to tell me your reasons—"

"As it happens, I don't."

"I understand. So it would be useless for me to be curious, yes?"

That was neat enough, Estabrook thought. Not to want what couldn't be had no doubt took the sting from things. He might need to learn the trick of that before he got too much older; before he wanted time he couldn't have. Not that he demanded much in the way of satisfactions. He'd not been sexually insistent with Judith, for instance. Indeed, he'd taken as much pleasure in the simple sight of her as he'd taken in the act of love. The sight of her had pierced him, making her the enterer, had she but known it, and him the entered. Perhaps she had known, on reflection. Perhaps she'd fled from his passivity, from his ease beneath the spike of her beauty. If so, he would undo her revulsion with tonight's business. Here, in the hiring of the assassin, he would prove himself. And, dying, she would realize her error. The thought pleased him. He allowed himself a little smile, which vanished from his face when he felt the car slowing and glimpsed, through the misted window, the place the facilitator had brought him to.

A wall of corrugated iron lay before them, its length daubed with graffiti. Beyond it, visible through gaps where the iron had been torn into ragged wings and beaten back, was a junkyard in which trailers were parked. This was apparently their destination.

"Are you out of your mind?" he said, leaning forward to take hold of Chant's shoulder. "We're not safe here."

"I promised you the best assassin in England, Mr. Estabrook, and he's here. Trust me, he's here."

Estabrook growled in fury and frustration. He'd expected a clandestine rendezvous—curtained windows, locked doors—not a gypsy encampment. This was altogether too public and too dangerous. Would it not be the perfect irony to be murdered in the middle of an assignation with an assassin?

He leaned back against the creaking leather of his seat and said, "You've let me down."

"I promise you this man is a most extraordinary individual," Chant said. "Nobody in Europe comes remotely close. I've worked with him before."

"Would you care to name the victims?"

Chant looked around at his employer and, in faintly admonishing tones, said, "I haven't presumed upon *your* privacy, Mr. Estabrook. Please don't presume upon mine."

Estabrook gave a chastened grunt.

"Would you prefer we go back to Chelsea?" Chant went on. "I can find somebody else for you. Not as good, perhaps, but in more congenial surroundings."

Chant's sarcasm wasn't lost on Estabrook, nor could he resist the recognition that this was not a game he should have entered if he'd hoped to stay lily-white. "No, no," he said. "We're here, and I may as well see him. What's his name?"

"I only know him as Pie," Chant said.

"Pie? Pie what?"

"Just Pie."

Chant got out of the car and opened Estabrook's door.

Icy air swirled in, bearing a few flakes of sleet. Winter was eager this year. Pulling his coat collar up around his nape and plunging his hands into the minty depths of his pockets, Estabrook followed his guide through the nearest gap in the corrugated wall. The wind carried the tang of burning timber from an almost spent bonfire set among the trailers: that, and the smell of rancid fat.

"Keep close," Chant advised, "walk briskly, and don't show too much interest. These are very private people."

"What's your man doing here?" Estabrook demanded to know. "Is he on the run?"

"You said you wanted somebody who couldn't be traced. 'Invisible' was the word you used. Pie's that man. He's on no files of any kind. Not the police, not the Social Security. He's not even registered as born."

"I find that unlikely."

"I specialize in the unlikely," Chant replied.

Until this exchange the violent turn in Chant's eye had never unsettled Estabrook, but it did now, preventing him as it did from meeting the other man's gaze directly. This tale he was telling was surely a lie. Who these days got to adulthood without appearing on a file somewhere? But the thought of meeting a man who even believed himself undocumented intrigued Estabrook. He nodded Chant on, and together they headed over the ill-lit and squalid ground.

There was debris dumped every side: the skeletal hulks of rusted vehicles; heaps of rotted household refuse, the stench of which the cold could not subdue; innumerable dead bonfires. The presence of trespassers had attracted some attention. A dog with more breeds in its blood than hairs on its back foamed and yapped at them from the limit of its rope; the curtains of several trailers were drawn back by shadowy witnesses; two girls in early adolescence, both with hair so long and blond they looked to have been baptized in gold (unlikely beauty, in such a place) rose from beside the fire, one running as if to alert guards, the other watching the newcomers with a smile somewhere between the seraphic and the cretinous.

"Don't stare," Chant reminded him as he hurried on, but Estabrook couldn't help himself.

An albino with white dreadlocks had appeared from one of the trailers with the blond girl in tow. Seeing the strangers he let out a shout and headed towards them.

Two more doors now opened, and others emerged from their trailers, but Estabrook had no chance to either see who they were or whether they were armed because Chant again said, "Just walk, don't look. We're heading for the caravan with the sun painted on it. See it?"

"I see it."

There were twenty yards still to cover. Dreadlocks was delivering a stream of orders now, most of them incoherent but surely intended to stop them in their tracks. Estabrook glanced across at Chant, who had his gaze fixed on their destination and his teeth clenched. The sound of footsteps grew louder behind them. A blow on the head or a knife in the ribs couldn't be far off.

"We're not going to make it," Estabrook said.

Within ten yards of the trailer—the albino at their shoulders—the door ahead opened, and a woman in a dressing gown, with a baby in her arms, peered out. She was small and looked so frail it was a wonder she could hold the child, who began bawling as soon as the cold found it. The ache of its complaint drove their pursuers to action. Dreadlocks took hold of Estabrook's shoulder and stopped him dead. Chant—wretched coward that he was—didn't slow his pace by a beat but strode on towards the trailer as Estabrook was swung around to face the albino. This was his perfect nightmare, to be facing scabby, pockmarked men like these, who had nothing to lose if they gutted him on the spot. While Dreadlocks held him hard, another man—gold incisors glinting—stepped in and pulled open Estabrook's coat, then reached in to empty his pockets with the speed of an illusionist. This was not simply professionalism. They wanted their business done before they were stopped.

As the pickpocket's hand pulled out his victim's wallet, a voice came from the trailer behind Estabrook: "Let the Mister go. He's real."

Whatever the latter meant, the order was instantly obeyed, but by that time the thief had whipped Estabrook's wallet into his own pocket and had stepped back, hands raised to show them empty. Nor, despite the fact that the speaker—presumably Pie—was extending his protection to his guest, did it seem circumspect to try and reclaim the wallet. Estabrook retreated from the thieves, lighter in step and cash but glad to be doing so at all.

Turning, he saw Chant at the trailer door, which was open. The woman, the baby, and the speaker had already gone back inside.

"They didn't hurt you, did they?" Chant said.

Estabrook glanced back over his shoulder at the thugs, who had gone to the fire, presumably to divide the loot by its light. "No," he said. "But you'd better go and check the car, or they'll have it stripped."

"First I'd like to introduce you—"

"Just check the car," Estabrook said, taking some satisfaction in the thought of sending Chant back across the no-man's-land between here and the perimeter. "I can introduce myself."

"As you like."

Chant went off, and Estabrook climbed the steps into the trailer. A scent and a sound met him, both sweet. Oranges had been peeled, and their dew was in the air. So was a lullaby, played on a guitar. The player, a black man, sat in the farthest corner, in a shadowy place beside a sleeping child. The babe lay to his other side, gurgling softly in a simple cot, its fat arms raised as if to pluck the music from the air with its tiny hands. The woman was at a table at the other end of the vehicle, tidying away the orange peel. The whole interior was marked by the same fastidiousness she was applying to this task, every surface neat and polished.

"You must be Pie," Estabrook said.

"Please close the door," the guitar player said. Estabrook did so. "And sit down. Theresa? Something for the gentleman. You must be cold."

The china cup of brandy set before him was like nectar. He downed it in two throatfuls, and Theresa instantly replenished it. He drank again with the same speed, only to have his cup furnished with a further draft. By the time Pie had played both the children to sleep and rose to come and join his guest at the table, the liquor had brought a pleasant buzz to Estabrook's head.

In his life Estabrook had known only two other black men by name. One was the manager of a tiling manufacturer in Swindon, the other a colleague of his brother's: neither of them men he'd wished to know better. He was of an age and class that still swilled the dregs of colonialism at two in the morning, and the fact this man had black blood in him (and, he guessed, much else besides) counted as another mark against Chant's judgment. And yet—perhaps it was the brandy—he found the fellow opposite him intriguing. Pie didn't have the face of an assassin. It wasn't dispassionate, but distressingly vulnerable; even (though Estabrook would never have breathed this aloud) beautiful. Cheeks high, lips full, eyes heavily lidded. His hair, mingled black and blond, fell in Italianate profusion, knotted ringlets to his shoulders. He looked older than Estabrook would have expected, given the age of his children. Perhaps only thirty, but wearied by some excess or other, the burnished sepia of his skin barely concealing a sickly iridescence, as though there were a mercurial taint in his cells. It made him difficult to fix, especially for eyes awash with brandy, the merest motion of his head breaking subtle waves against his bones, their spume draining back into his skin trailing colors Estabrook had never seen in flesh before.

Theresa left them to their business and retired to sit beside the cot. In part out of deference to the sleepers and in part from his own unease at saying aloud what was on his mind, Estabrook spoke in whispers.

"Did Chant tell you why I'm here?"

"Of course," said Pie. "You want somebody murdered." He pulled a pack of cigarettes from the breast pocket of his denim shirt and offered one to Estabrook, who declined with a shake of his head. "That *is* why you're here, isn't it?"

"Yes," Estabrook replied. "Only—"

"You're looking at me and thinking I'm not the one to do it," Pie prompted. He put a cigarette to his lips. "Be honest."

"You're not exactly as I imagined," Estabrook replied.

"So, this is good," Pie said, applying a light to the cigarette. "If I had been what you'd imagined, I'd look like an assassin, and you'd say I was too obvious."

"Maybe."

"If you don't want to hire me, that's fine. I'm sure Chant can find you somebody else. If you *do* want to hire me, then you'd better tell me what you need."

Estabrook watched the smoke drift up over the assassin's gray eyes, and before he could prevent himself he was telling his story, the rules he'd drawn for this exchange forgotten. Instead of questioning the man closely, concealing his own biography so that the other would have as little hold on him as possible, he spilled the tragedy in every unflattering detail. Several times he almost stopped himself, but it felt so good to be unburdened that he let his tongue defy his better judgment. Not once did the other man interrupt the litany, and it was only when a rapping on the door, announcing Chant's return, interrupted the flow that Estabrook remembered there was anyone else alive in the world tonight besides himself and his confessor. And by that time the tale was told.

Pie opened the door but didn't let Chant in. "We'll wander over to the car when we've finished," he told the driver. "We won't be long." Then he closed the door again and returned to the table. "Something more to drink?" he asked.

Estabrook declined, but accepted a cigarette as they talked on, Pie requesting details of Judith's whereabouts and movements, Estabrook supplying the answers in a monotone. Finally, the issue of payment. Ten thousand pounds, to be paid in two halves, the first upon agreement of the contract, the second after its completion.

"Chant has the money," Estabrook said.

"Shall we walk, then?" Pie said.

Before they left the trailer, Estabrook looked into the cot. "You have beautiful children," he said when they were out in the cold.

"They're not mine," Pie replied. "Their father died a year ago this Christmas."

"Tragic," Estabrook said.

"It was quick," Pie said, glancing across at Estabrook and confirming in his glance the suspicion that he was the orphan maker. "Are you quite certain you want this woman dead?" Pie said. "Doubt's bad in a business like this. If there's any part of you that hesitates—"

"There's none," Estabrook said. "I came here to find a man to kill my wife. You're that man."

"You still love her, don't you?" Pie said, once they were out and walking.

"Of course I love her," Estabrook said. "That's why I want her dead."

"There's no Resurrection, Mr. Estabrook. Not for you, at least."

"It's not me who's dying," he said.

"I think it is," came the reply. They were at the fire, now untended. "A man kills the thing he loves, and he must die a little himself. That's plain, yes?"

"If I die, I die," was Estabrook's response. "As long as she goes first. I'd like it done as quickly as possible."

"You said she's in New York. Do you want me to follow her there?"

"Are you familiar with the city?"

"Yes."

"Then do it there and do it soon. I'll have Chant supply extra funds to cover the flight. And that's that. We shan't see each other again."

Chant was waiting at the perimeter and fished the envelope containing the payment from his inside pocket. Pie accepted it without question or thanks, then shook Estabrook's hand and left the trespassers to return to the safety of their car. As he settled into the comfort of the leather seat, Estabrook realized the palm he'd pressed against Pie's was trembling. He knitted its fingers with those of his other hand, and there they remained, white-knuckled, for the length of the journey home.

2

DO THIS FOR THE WOMEN OF THE WORLD, read the note John Furie Zacharias held. *Slit your lying throat.*

Beside the note, lying on the bare boards, Vanessa and her cohorts (she had two brothers; it was probably they who'd come with her to empty the house) had left a neat pile of broken glass, in case he was sufficiently moved by her entreaty to end his life there and then. He stared at the note in something of a stupor, reading it over and over, looking—vainly, of course—for some small consolation in it. Beneath the tick and scrawl that made her name, the paper was lightly wrinkled. Had tears fallen there while she'd written her goodbye, he wondered? Small comfort if they had, and a smaller likelihood still. Vanessa was not one for crying. Nor could he imagine a woman with the least ambiguity of feeling so comprehensively stripping him of possessions. True, neither the mews house nor any stick of furniture in it had been his by law, but they had chosen many of the items together—she relying upon his artist's eye, he upon her money to purchase whatever his gaze admired. Now it was all gone, to the last Persian rug and Deco lamp. The home they'd made together, and enjoyed for a year and two months, was stripped bare. And so indeed was he: to the nerve, to the bone. He had nothing.

It wasn't calamitous. Vanessa hadn't been the first woman to indulge his taste in handmade shirts and silk waistcoats, nor would she be the last. But she was the first in recent memory—for Gentle the past had a way of evaporating after about ten years—who had conspired to remove everything from him in the space of half a day. His error was plain enough. He'd woken that morning, lying beside Vanessa with a hard-on she'd wanted him to pleasure her with, and had stupidly refused her, knowing he had a liaison with Martine that afternoon. How she'd discovered where he was unloading his balls was academic. She had, and that was that. He'd stepped out of the house at noon, believing the woman he'd left was devoted to him, and come home five hours later to find the house as it was now.

He could be sentimental at the strangest times. As now, for instance, wandering through the empty rooms, collecting up the belongings she had felt obliged to leave for him: his address book, the clothes he'd bought with his own money as opposed to hers, his spare spectacles, his cigarettes. He hadn't loved Vanessa, but he had enjoyed the fourteen months they'd spent together here. She'd left a few more pieces of trash on the dining room floor, reminders of that time: a cluster of keys they'd never found doors to fit, instruction documents for a blender he'd burned out making midnight margaritas, a plastic bottle of massage oil. All in all, a pitiful collection, but he wasn't so self-deceiving as to believe their relationship had been much more than a sum of those parts. The question was—now that it was over—where was he to go and what was he to do? Martine was a middle-aged married woman, her husband a banker who spent three days of every week in Luxembourg, leaving her time to philander. She professed love for Gentle at intervals, but not with sufficient consistency to make him think he could prize her from her husband, even if he wanted to, which he was by no means certain he did. He'd known her eight months—met her, in fact, at a dinner party hosted by Vanessa's elder brother, William—and they had only argued once, but it had been a telling exchange. She'd accused him of always looking at other women; looking, looking, as though for the next conquest. Perhaps because he didn't care for her too much, he'd replied honestly and told her she was right. He was stupid for her sex. Sickened in their absence, blissful in their company: love's fool. She'd replied that while his obsession might be healthier than her husband's—which was money and its manipulation—his behavior was still neurotic. Why this endless hunt? she'd asked him. He'd answered with some folderol about seeking the ideal woman, but he'd known the truth even as he was spinning her this tosh, and it was a bitter thing. Too bitter, in fact, to be put on his tongue. In essence, it came down to this: he felt meaningless, empty, almost invisible unless one or more of her sex were doting on him. Yes, he knew his face was finely made, his forehead broad, his gaze haunting, his lips sculpted so that even a sneer looked fetching on them, but he needed a living mirror to tell him so. More, he lived in hope that one such mirror would find something behind his looks only another pair of eyes could see: some undiscovered self that would free him from being Gentle.

As always when he felt deserted, he went to see Chester Klein, patron of the arts by diverse hands, a man who claimed to have been excised by fretful lawyers from more biographies than any other man since Byron. He lived in Notting Hill Gate, in a house he'd bought cheaply in the late fifties, which he now seldom left, touched as he was by agoraphobia or, as he preferred it, "a perfectly rational fear of anyone I can't blackmail."

From this small dukedom he managed to prosper, employed as he was in a business which required a few choice contacts, a nose for the changing taste of his market, and an ability to conceal his pleasure at his achievements. In short, he dealt in fakes, and it was this latter quality he was most deficient in. There were those among his small circle of intimates who said it would be his undoing, but they or their predecessors had been prophesying the same for three decades, and Klein had outprospered every one of them. The luminaries he'd entertained over the decades—the defecting dancers and minor spies, the addicted debutantes, the rock stars with messianic leanings, the bishops who made idols of barrow boys—they'd all had their moments of glory, then fallen. But Klein went on to tell the tale. And when, on occasion, his name did creep into a scandal sheet or a confessional biography, he was invariably painted as the patron saint of lost souls.

It wasn't only the knowledge that, being such a soul,

Gentle would be welcomed at the Klein residence, that took him there. He'd never known a time when Klein didn't need money for some gambit or other, and that meant he needed painters. There was more than comfort to be found in the house at Ladbroke Grove; there was employment. It had been eleven months since he'd seen or spoken to Chester, but he was greeted as effusively as ever and ushered in.

"Quickly! Quickly!" Klein said. "Gloriana's in heat again!" He managed to slam the door before the obese Gloriana, one of his five cats, escaped in search of a mate. "Too slow, sweetie!" he told her. She yowled at him in complaint. "I keep her fat so she's slow," he said. "And I don't feel so piggy myself."

He patted a paunch that had swelled considerably since Gentle had last seen him and was testing the seams of his shirt, which, like him, was florid and had seen better years. He still wore his hair in a ponytail, complete with ribbon, and wore an ankh on a chain around his neck, but beneath the veneer of a harmless flower child gone to seed he was as acquisitive as a bowerbird. Even the vestibule in which they embraced was overflowing with collectibles: a wooden dog, plastic roses in psychedelic profusion, sugar skulls on plates.

"My God, you're cold," he said to Gentle. "And you look wretched. Who's been beating you about the head?"

"Nobody."

"You're bruised."

"I'm tired, that's all."

Gentle took off his heavy coat and laid it on the chair by the door, knowing when he returned it would be warm and covered with cat hairs. Klein was already in the living room, pouring wine. Always red.

"Don't mind the television," he said. "I never turn it off these days. The trick is not to turn up the sound. It's much more entertaining mute."

This was a new habit, and a distracting one. Gentle accepted the wine and sat down in the corner of the ill-sprung couch, where it was easiest to ignore the demands of the screen. Even there, he was tempted.

"So now, my Bastard Boy," Klein said, "to what disaster do I owe the honor?"

"It's not really a disaster. I've just had a bad time. I wanted some cheery company."

"Give them up, Gentle," Klein said.

"Give what up?"

"You know what. The fair sex. Give them up. I have. It's such a relief. All those desperate seductions. All that time wasted meditating on death to keep yourself from coming too soon. I tell you, it's like a burden gone from my shoulders."

"How old are you?"

"Age has got fuck-all to do with it. I gave up women because they were breaking my heart."

"What heart's that?"

"I might ask you the same thing. Yes, you whine and you wring your hands, but then you go back and make the same mistakes. It's tedious. *They're* tedious."

"So save me."

"Oh, now here it comes."

"I don't have any money."

"Neither do I."

"So we'll make some together. Then I won't have to be a kept man. I'm going back to live in the studio, Klein. I'll paint whatever you need."

"The Bastard Boy speaks."

"I wish you wouldn't call me that."

"It's what you are. You haven't changed in eight years. The world grows old, but the Bastard Boy keeps his perfection. Speaking of which—"

"Employ me."

"Don't interrupt me when I'm gossiping. Speaking of which, I saw Clem the Sunday before last. He asked after you. He's put on a lot of weight. And his love life's almost as disastrous as yours. Taylor's sick with the plague. I tell you, Gentle, celibacy's the thing."

"So employ me."

"It's not as easy as that. The market's soft at the moment. And, well, let me be brutal: I have a new *wunderkind.*" He got up. "Let me show you." He led Gentle through the house to the study. "The fellow's twenty-two, and I swear if he had an idea in his head he'd be a great painter. But he's like you; he's got the talent but nothing to say."

"Thanks," said Gentle sourly.

"You know it's true." Klein switched on the light. There were three canvases, all unframed, in the room. One, a nude woman after the style of Modigliani. Beside it, a small landscape after Corot. But the third, and largest of the three, was the *coup.* It was a pastoral scene, depicting classically garbed shepherds standing, in awe, before a tree in the trunk of which a human face was visible.

"Would you know it from a real Poussin?"

"Is it still wet?" Gentle asked.

"Such a wit."

Gentle went to give the painting a more intimate examination. This period was not one he was particularly expert in, but he knew enough to be impressed by the handiwork. The canvas was a close weave, the paint laid upon it in careful regular strokes, the tones built up, it seemed, in glazes.

"Meticulous, eh?" said Klein.

"To the point of being mechanical."

"Now, now, no sour grapes."

"I mean it. It's just too perfect for words. You put this in the market and the game's up. Now, the Modigliani's another matter—"

"That was a technical exercise," Klein said. "I can't sell that. The man only painted a dozen pictures. It's the Poussin I'm betting on."

"Don't. You'll get stung. Mind if I get another drink?"

Gentle headed back through the house to the lounge, Klein following, muttering to himself.

"You've got a good eye, Gentle," he said, "but you're unreliable. You'll find another woman and off you'll go."

"Not this time."

"And I wasn't kidding about the market. There's no room for bullshit."

"Did you ever have a problem with a piece I painted?" Klein mused on this. "No," he admitted.

"I've got a Gauguin in New York. Those Fuseli sketches I did—"

"Berlin. Oh, yes, you've made your little mark."

"Nobody's ever going to know it, of course."

"They will. In a hundred years' time your Fuselis will look as old as they are, not as old as they should be. People will start to investigate, and you, my Bastard Boy, will be discovered. And so will Kenny Soames and Gideon: all my deceivers."

"And you'll be vilified for bribing us. Denying the twentieth century all that originality."

"Originality, shit. It's an overrated commodity, you know that. You can be a visionary painting Virgins."

"That's what I'll do, then. Virgins in any style. I'll be celibate, and I'll paint Madonnas all day. With child. Without child. Weeping. Blissful. I'll work my balls off, Kleiny, which'll be fine because I won't need them."

"Forget the Virgins. They're out of fashion."

"They're forgotten."

"Decadence is your strongest suit."

"Whatever you want. Say the word."

"But don't fuck with me. If I find a client and promise something to him, it's up to you to produce it."

"I'm going back to the studio tonight. I'm starting over. Just do one thing for me?"

"What's that?"

"Burn the Poussin."

He had visited the studio on and off through his time with Vanessa—he'd even met Martine there on two occasions when her husband had canceled a Luxembourg trip and she'd been too heated to miss a liaison—but it was charmless and cheerless, and he'd returned happily to the house in Wimpole Mews. Now, however, he welcomed the studio's austerity. He turned on the little electric fire, made himself a cup of fake coffee with fake milk, and, under its influence, thought about deception.

The last six years of his life—since Judith, in fact—had been a series of duplicities. This was not of itself disastrous—after tonight it would once more be his profession—but whereas painting had a tangible end result (two, if he included the recompense), pursuit and seduction always left him naked and empty-handed. An end to that, tonight. He made a vow, toasted in bad coffee, to the God of Forgers, whoever he was, to become great. If duplicity was his genius, why waste it on deceiving husbands and mistresses? He should turn it to a profounder end, producing masterpieces in another man's name. Time would validate him, the way Klein had said it would: uncover his many works and show him, at last, as the visionary he was about to become. And if it didn't—if Klein was wrong and his handiwork remained undiscovered forever—then that was the truest vision of all. Invisible, he would be seen; unknown, he'd be influential. It was enough to make him forget women entirely. At least for tonight.

3

AT DUSK THE CLOUDS OVER MANHATTAN, which had threatened snow all day, cleared and revealed a pristine sky, its color so ambiguous it might have fueled a philosophical debate as to the nature of blue. Laden as she was with her day's purchases, Jude chose to walk back to Marlin's apartment at Park Avenue and 80th. Her arms ached, but it gave her time to turn over in her head the encounter which had marked the day and decide whether she wanted to share it with Marlin or not. Unfortunately, he had a lawyer's mind: at best, cool and analytical; at worst, reductionist. She knew herself well enough to know that if he challenged her account in the latter mode she'd almost certainly lose her temper with him, and then the atmosphere between them, which had been (with the exception of his overtures) so easy and undemanding, would be spoiled. It was better to work out what she believed about the events of the previous two hours before she shared it with Marlin. Then he could dissect it at will.

Already, after going over the encounter a few times, it was becoming, like the blue overhead, ambiguous. But she held on hard to the facts of the matter. She'd been in the menswear department of Bloomingdale's, looking for a sweater for Marlin. It was crowded, and there was nothing on display that she thought appropriate. She'd started to pick up the purchases at her feet when she'd caught sight of a face she knew, looking straight at her through the moving mesh of people. How long had she seen the face for? A second, two at most? Long enough for her heart to jump and her face to flush; long enough for her mouth to open and shape the word *Gentle*. Then the traffic between them had thickened, and he'd disappeared. She'd fixed the place where he'd been, stooped to pick up her baggage, and gone after him, not doubting that it was he.

The crowd slowed her progress, but she soon caught sight of him again, heading towards the door. This time she yelled his name, not giving a damn if she looked a fool, and dove after him. She was impressive in full flight, and the crowd yielded, so that by the time she reached the door he was only yards away. Third Avenue was as thronged as the store, but there he was, heading across the street. The lights changed as she got to the curb. She went after him anyway, daring the traffic. As she yelled again he was buffeted by a shopper, on some business as urgent as hers, and he turned as he was struck, giving her a second glimpse of him. She might have laughed out loud at the absurdity of her error had it not disturbed her so. Either she was losing her mind, or she'd followed the wrong man. Either way, this black man, his ringleted hair gleaming on his shoulders, was not Gentle. Momentarily undecided as to whether to go on looking or to give up the chase there and then, her eyes lingered on the stranger's face, and for a heartbeat or less his features blurred and in their flux, caught as if by the sun off a wing in the stratosphere, she saw Gentle, his hair swept back from his high forehead, his gray eyes all yearning, his mouth, which she'd not known she missed till now, ready to break into a smile. It never came. The wing dipped; the stranger turned; Gentle was gone. She stood in the throng for several seconds while he disappeared downtown. Then, gathering herself together, she turned her back on the mystery and started home.

It didn't leave her thoughts, of course. She was a woman who trusted her senses, and to discover them so deceptive distressed her. But more vexing still was why it should be that particular face, of all those in her memory's catalogue, she'd chosen to configure from that of a perfect stranger. Klein's Bastard Boy was out of her life, and she out of his. It was six years since she'd crossed the bridge from where they'd stood together, and the river that flowed between was a torrent. Her marriage to Estabrook had come and gone along that river, and a good deal of pain with it. Gentle was still on the other shore, part of her history: irretrievable. So why had she conjured him now?

As she came within a block of Marlin's building she remembered something she'd utterly put out of her head for that six-year span. It had been a glimpse of Gentle, not so unlike the one she'd just had, that had propelled her into her near-suicidal affair with him. She'd met him at one of Klein's parties—a casual encounter—and had given him very little conscious thought subsequently. Then, three nights later, she'd been visited by an erotic dream that regularly haunted her. The scenario was always the same. She was lying naked on bare boards in an empty room, not bound but somehow bounded, and a man whose face she could never see, his mouth so sweet it was like eating candy to kiss him, made violent love to her. Only this time the fire that burned in the grate close by showed her the face of her dream lover, and it had been Gentle's face. The shock, after so many years of never knowing who the man was, woke her, but with such a sense of loss at this interrupted coitus she couldn't sleep again for mourning it. The next day she'd discovered his whereabouts from Klein, who'd warned her in no uncertain manner that John Zacharias was bad news for tender hearts. She'd ignored the warning and gone to see him that very afternoon, in the studio off the Edgware Road. They scarcely left it for the next two weeks, their passion putting her dreams to shame.

Only later, when she was in love with him and it was too late for common sense to qualify her feelings, did she learn more about him. He trailed a reputation for womanizing that, even if it was ninety percent invention, as she assumed, was still prodigious. If she mentioned his name in any circle, however jaded it was by gossip, there was always somebody who had some tidbit about him. He even went by a variety of names. Some referred to him as the Furie; some as Zach or Zacho, or Mr. Zee; others called him Gentle, which was the name she knew him by, of course; still others, John the Divine. Enough names for half a dozen lifetimes. She wasn't so blindly devoted to him that she didn't accept there was truth in these rumors. Nor did he do much to temper them. He liked the air of legend that hung about his head. He claimed, for instance, not to know how old he was. Like herself, he had a very slippery grasp on the past. And he frankly admitted to being obsessed with her sex. Some of the talk she'd heard was of cradle-snatching; some of deathbed fucks: he played no favorites.

So, here was her Gentle: a man known to the doormen of every exclusive club and hotel in the city; who, after ten years of high living had survived the ravages of every excess; who was still lucid, still handsome, still alive. And this same man, this Gentle, told her he was in love with her and put the words together so perfectly she disregarded all she'd heard but those he spoke.

She might have gone on listening forever but for her rage, which was the legend *she* trailed. A volatile thing, apt to ferment in her without her even being aware of it. That had been the case with Gentle. After half a year of their affair, she'd begun to wonder, wallowing in his affection, how a man whose history had been one infidelity after another had mended his ways; which thought led to the possibility that perhaps he hadn't. In fact she had no reason to suspect him. His devotion bordered on the obsessive in some moods, as though he saw in her a woman she didn't

even know herself, an ancient soul mate. She was, she
began to think, unlike any other woman he'd ever met, the
love that had changed his life. When they were so inti-
mately joined, how would she not know if he was cheating
on her? She'd have surely sensed the other woman. Tasted
her on his tongue, or smelled her on his skin. And if not
there, then in the subtleties of their exchanges. But she'd
underestimated him. When, by the sheerest fluke, she'd
discovered he had not one other woman on the side but
two, it drove her to near insanity. She began by destroying
the contents of the studio, slashing all his canvases, painted
or not, then tracking the felon himself and mounting an assault that literally brought him to his knees, in fear for his
balls.

The rage burned a week, after which she fell totally silent for three days: a silence broken by a grief like nothing
she'd ever experienced before. Had it not been for her
chance meeting with Estabrook—who saw through her
tumbling, distracted manner to the woman she was—she
might well have taken her own life.

Thus the tale of Judith and Gentle: one death short of
tragedy, and a marriage short of farce.

She found Marlin already home, uncharacteristically agitated.

"Where have you been?" he wanted to know. "It's six-
thirty-nine."

She instantly knew this was no time to be telling him
what her trip to Bloomingdale's had cost her in peace of
mind. Instead she lied. "I couldn't get a cab. I had to walk."

"If that happens again, just call me. I'll have you picked
up by one of our limos. I don't want you wandering the
streets. It's not safe. Anyhow, we're late. We'll have to eat
after the performance."

"What performance?"

"The show in the Village that Troy was yabbering about
last night, remember? The Neo-Nativity? He said it was the
best thing since Bethlehem."

"It's sold out."

"I have my connections." He gleamed.

"We're going tonight?"

"Not if you don't move your ass."

"Marlin, sometimes you're sublime," she said, dumping her purchases and racing to change.

"What about the rest of the time?" he hollered after her. "Sexy? Irresistible? Beddable?"

If indeed he'd secured the tickets as a way of bribing her between the sheets, he suffered for his lust. He concealed his boredom through the first act, but by intermission he was itching to be away to claim his prize.

"Do we really need to stay for the rest?" he asked her as they sipped coffee in the tiny foyer. "I mean, it's not like there's any mystery about it. The kid gets born, the kid grows up, the kid gets crucified."

"I'm enjoying it."

"But it doesn't make any sense," he complained, in deadly earnest. The show's eclecticism offended his rationalism deeply. "Why were the angels playing jazz?"

"Who knows what angels do?"

He shook his head. "I don't know whether it's a comedy or a satire or what the hell it is," he said. "Do you know what it is?"

"I think it's very funny."

"So you'd like to stay?"

"I'd like to stay."

The second half was even more of a grab bag than the first, the suspicion growing in Jude as she watched that the parody and pastiche was a smokescreen put up to cover the creators' embarrassment at their own sincerity. In the end, with Charlie Parker angels wailing on the stable roof and Santa crooning at the manger, the piece collapsed into high camp. But even that was oddly moving. The child was born. Light had come into the world again, even if it was to the accompaniment of tap-dancing elves.

When they exited, there was sleet in the wind.

"Cold, cold, cold," Marlin said. "I'd better take a leak."

He went back inside to join the line for the toilets, leaving Jude at the door, watching the blobs of wet snow pass through the lamplight. The theater was not large, and the bulk of the audience was out in a couple of minutes, umbrellas raised, heads dropped, darting off into the Village to look for their cars, or a place where they could put some drink in their systems and play critic. The light above the front door was switched off, and a cleaner emerged from the theater with a black plastic bag of rubbish and a broom and began to brush the foyer, ignoring Jude—who was the last visible occupant—until he reached her, when he gave her a glance of such venom she decided to put up her umbrella and stand on the darkened step. Marlin was taking his time emptying his bladder. She only hoped he wasn't titivating himself, slicking his hair and freshening his breath in the hope of talking her into bed.

The first she knew of the assault was a motion glimpsed from the corner of her eye: a blurred form approaching her at speed through the thickening sleet. Alarmed, she turned towards her attacker. She had time to recognize the face on Third Avenue; then the man was upon her.

She opened her mouth to yell, turning to retreat into the theater as she did so. The cleaner had gone. So had her shout, caught in her throat by the stranger's hands. They were expert. They hurt brutally, stopping every breath from being drawn. She panicked; flailed; toppled. He took her weight, controlling her motion. In desperation she threw the umbrella into the foyer, hoping there was somebody out of sight in the box office who'd be alerted to her jeopardy. Then she was wrenched out of shadow into heavier shadow still and realized it was almost too late already. She was becoming light-headed, her leaden limbs no longer hers. In the murk her assassin's face was once more a blur, with two dark holes bored in it. She fell towards them, wishing she had the energy to turn her gaze away from this blankness, but as he moved closer to her a little light caught his cheek and she saw, or thought she saw, tears there, spilling from those dark eyes. Then the light went, not just from his cheek but from the whole world. And as everything slipped away, she could only hold on to the thought that somehow her murderer knew who she was. . . .

"Judith?"

Somebody was holding her. Somebody was shouting to her. Not the assassin but Marlin. She sagged in his arms, catching dizzied sight of the assailant running across the pavement, with another man in pursuit. Her eyes swung back to Marlin, who was asking her if she was all right, then back to the street as brakes shrieked and the failed assassin was struck squarely by a speeding car, which reeled around, wheels locked and sliding over the sleet-greased street, throwing the man's body off the hood and over a parked car. The pursuer threw himself aside as the vehicle mounted the pavement, slamming into a lamppost.

Jude put her arm out for some support other than Marlin, her fingers finding the wall. Ignoring his advice that she stay still, she started to stumble towards the place where her assassin had fallen. The driver was being helped from his smashed vehicle, unleashing a stream of obscenities as he emerged. Others were appearing on the scene to lend help in forming a crowd, but Jude ignored their stares and headed across the street, Marlin at her side. She was determined to reach the body before anybody else. She wanted to see it before it was touched; wanted to meet its open eyes and fix its dead expression; know it, for memory's sake.

She found his blood first, spattered in the gray slush underfoot, and then, a little way beyond, the assassin himself, reduced to a lumpen form in the gutter. As she came within a few yards of it, however, a shudder passed down its spine and it rolled over, showing its face to the sleet. Then, impossible though this seemed, given the blow it had been struck, the form started to haul itself to its feet. She saw how bloodied it was, but she saw also that it was still essentially whole. It's not human, she thought, as it stood upright; whatever it is, it's not human. Marlin groaned with revulsion behind her, and a woman on the pavement screamed. The man's gaze went to the screamer, wavered, then returned to Jude.

It wasn't an assassin any longer. Nor was it Gentle. If it had a self, perhaps this was its face: split by wounds and doubt; pitiful; lost. She saw its mouth open and close as if it was attempting to address her. Then Marlin made a move to pursue it, and it ran. How, after such an accident, its limbs managed any speed at all was a miracle, but it was off at a pace that Marlin couldn't hope to match. He made a show of pursuit but gave up at the first intersection, returning to Jude breathless.

"Drugs," he said, clearly angered to have missed his chance at heroism. "Fucker's on drugs. He's not feeling any pain. Wait till he comes down, he'll drop dead. Fucker! How did he know you?"

"Did he?" she said, her whole body trembling now, as relief at her escape and terror at how close she'd come to losing her life both stung tears from her.

"He called you Judith," Marlin said.

In her mind's eye she saw the assassin's mouth open and close and on them read the syllables of her name.

"Drugs," Marlin was saying again, and she didn't waste words arguing, though she was certain he was wrong. The only drug in the assassin's system had been purpose, and that would not lay him low, tonight or any other.

Eleven days after he had taken Estabrook to the encampment in Streatham, Chant realized he would soon be having a visitor. He lived alone, and anonymously, in a one-room flat on a soon-to-be-condemned estate close to the Elephant and Castle, an address he had given to nobody, not even his employer. Not that his pursuers would be distracted from finding him by such petty secrecy. Unlike *Homo sapiens,* the species his long-dead master Sartori had been wont to call *the blossom on the simian tree,*

Chant's kind could not hide themselves from oblivion's agents by closing a door and drawing the blinds. They were like beacons to those that preyed on them.

Men had it so much easier. The creatures that had made meat of them in earlier ages were zoo specimens now, brooding behind bars for the entertainment of the victorious ape. They had no grasp, those apes, of how close they lay to a state where the devouring beasts of Earth's infancy would be little more than fleas. That state was called the In Ovo, and on the other side of it lay four worlds, the so-called Reconciled Dominions. They teemed with wonders: individuals blessed with attributes that would have made them, in this, the Fifth Dominion, fit for sainthood or burning, or both; cults possessed of secrets that would overturn in a moment the dogmas of faith and physics alike; beauty that might blind the sun or set the moon dreaming of fertility. All this, separated from Earth—the unreconciled Fifth—by the abyss of the In Ovo.

It was not, of course, an impossible journey to make. But the power to do so, which was usually—and contemptuously—referred to as magic, had been waning in the Fifth since Chant had first arrived. He'd seen the walls of reason built against it, brick by brick. He'd seen its practitioners hounded and mocked; seen its theories decay into decadence and parody; seen its purpose steadily forgotten. The Fifth was choking in its own certainties, and though he took no pleasure in the thought of losing his life, he would not mourn his removal from this hard and unpoetic Dominion.

He went to his window and looked down the five stories into the courtyard. It was empty. He had a few minutes yet, to compose his missive to Estabrook. Returning to his table, he began it again, for the ninth or tenth time. There was so much he wanted to communicate, but he knew that Estabrook was utterly ignorant of the involvement of his family, whose name he'd abandoned, with the fate of the Dominions. It was too late now to educate him. A warning would have to suffice. But how to word it so it didn't sound like the rambling of a wild man? He set to again, putting the facts as plainly as he could, though doubting that these words would save Estabrook's life. If the powers that prowled this world tonight wanted him dispatched, nothing short of intervention from the Unbeheld Himself, Hapexamendios, the all-powerful occupant of the First Dominion, would save him.

With the note finished, Chant pocketed it and headed out into the darkness. Not a moment too soon. In the frosty quiet he heard the sound of an engine too suave to belong to a resident and peered over the parapet to see the men getting out the car below. He didn't doubt that these were his visitors. The only vehicles he'd seen here so polished were hearses. He cursed himself. Fatigue had made him slothful, and now he'd let his enemies get dangerously close. He ducked down the back stairs—glad, for once, that there were so few lights working along the landings—as his visitors strode towards the front. From the flats he passed, the sound of lives: Christmas pops on the radio, argument, a baby laughing, which became tears, as though it sensed there was danger near. Chant knew none of his neighbors, except as furtive faces glimpsed at windows, and now— though it was too late to change that—he regretted it.

He reached ground level unharmed, and discounting the thought of trying to retrieve his car from the courtyard he headed off towards the street most heavily trafficked at this time of night, which was Kennington Park Road. If he was lucky he'd find a cab there, though at this time of night they weren't frequent. Fares were harder to pick up in this area than in Covent Garden or Oxford Street, and more likely to prove unruly. He allowed himself one backward glance, then turned his heels to the task of flight.

2

Though classically it was the light of day which showed a painter the deepest flaws in his handiwork, Gentle worked best at night: the instincts of a lover brought to a simpler art. In the week or so since he'd returned to his studio it had once again become a place of work: the air pungent with the smell of paint and turpentine, the burned-down butts of cigarettes left on every available shelf and plate. Though he'd spoken with Klein daily there was no sign of a commission yet, so he had spent the time reeducating himself. As Klein had so cruelly observed, he was a technician without a vision, and that made these days of meandering difficult. Until he had a style to forge, he felt listless, like some latter day Adam, born with the power to impersonate but bereft of subjects. So he set himself an exercise. He would paint a canvas in four radically different styles: a cubist North, an impressionist South, an East after Van Gogh, a West after Dali. As his subject he took Caravaggio's *Supper at Emmaus*. The challenge drove him to a healthy distraction, and he was still occupied with it at three-thirty in the morning, when the telephone rang. The line was watery, and the voice at the other end pained and raw, but it was unmistakably Judith.

"Is that you, Gentle?"

"It's me." He was glad the line was so bad. The sound of her voice had shaken him, and he didn't want her to know. "Where are you calling from?"

"New York. I'm just visiting for a few days."

"It's good to hear from you."

"I'm not sure why I'm calling. It's just that today's been strange and I thought maybe, oh—" She stopped. Laughed at herself, perhaps a little drunkenly. "I don't know what I thought," she went on. "It's stupid. I'm sorry."

"When are you coming back?"

"I don't know that either."

"Maybe we could get together?"

"I don't think so, Gentle."

"Just to talk."

"This line's getting worse. I'm sorry I woke you."

"You didn't—"

"Keep warm, huh?"

"Judith—"

"Sorry, Gentle."

The line went dead. But the water she'd spoken through

gurgled on, like the noise in a seashell. Not the ocean at all, of course; just illusion. He put the receiver down and— knowing he'd never sleep now—squeezed out some fresh bright worms of paint to work with, and set to.

3

It was the whistle from the gloom behind him that alerted Chant to the fact that his escape had not gone unnoticed. It was not a whistle that could have come from human lips, but a chilling scalpel shriek he had heard only once before in the Fifth Dominion, when, some two hundred years past, his then possessor, the Maestro Sartori, had conjured from the In Ovo a familiar which had made such a whistle. It had brought bloody tears to its summoner's eyes, obliging Sartori to relinquish it posthaste. Later Chant and the Maestro had spoken of the event, and Chant had identified the creature. It was known in the Reconciled Dominions as a voider, one of a brutal species that haunted the wastes north of the Lenten Way. Voiders came in many shapes, being made, some said, from collective desire, which fact seemed to move Sartori profoundly.

"I must summon one again," he'd said, "and speak with it," to which Chant had replied that if they were to attempt such a summoning they had to be ready next time, for voiders were lethal and could not be tamed except by Maestros of inordinate power.

The proposed conjuring had never taken place. Sartori had disappeared a short time later. In all the intervening years Chant had wondered if he had attempted a second summoning alone and been the voiders' victim. Perhaps the creature now coming after Chant had been responsible. Though Sartori had disappeared two hundred years ago, the lives of voiders, like those of so many species from the other Dominions, were longer than the longest human span.

Chant glanced over his shoulder. The whistler was in sight. It looked perfectly human, dressed in a gray, well-cut suit and black tie, its collar turned up against the cold, its

hands thrust into its pockets. It didn't run but almost idled
as it came, the whistle confounding Chant's thoughts and
making him stumble. As he turned away the second of his
pursuers appeared on the pavement in front of him, drawing a hand from its pocket. A gun? No. A knife? No. Something tiny crawled in the voider's palm, like a flea. Chant
had no sooner focused upon it than it leapt towards his
face. Repulsed, he raised his arm to keep it from his eyes or
mouth, and the flea landed upon his hand. He slapped at it
with his other hand, but it was beneath his thumbnail
before he could get to it. He raised his arm to see its motion
in the flesh of his thumb and clamped his other hand
around the base of the digit, in the hope of stopping its further advance, gasping as though doused with icewater. The
pain was out of all proportion to the mite's size, but he held
both thumb and sobs hard, determined not to lose all dignity in front of his executioners. Then he staggered off the
pavement into the street, throwing a glance down towards
the brighter lights at the junction. What safety they offered
was debatable, but if worst came to worst he would throw
himself beneath a car and deny the voiders the entertainment of his slow demise. He began to run again, still clutching his hand. This time he didn't glance back. He didn't
need to. The sound of the whistling faded, and the purr of
the car replaced it. He threw every ounce of his energy into
the run, reaching the bright street to find it deserted by
traffic. He turned north, racing past the underground station towards the Elephant and Castle. Now he did glance
behind, to see the car following steadily. It had three occupants: the voiders and another, sitting in the back seat. Sobbing with breathlessness he ran on, and—Lord love it!—a
taxi appeared around the next corner, its yellow light announcing its availability. Concealing his pain as best he
could, knowing the driver might pass on by if he thought
the hailer was wounded, he stepped out into the street and
raised his hand to wave the driver down. This meant un-
clasping one hand from the other, and the mite took instant
advantage, working its way up into his wrist. But the vehicle slowed.

"Where to, mate?"

He astonished himself with the reply, giving not Estabrook's address but that of another place entirely.

"Clerkenwell," he said. "Gamut Street."

"Don't know it," the cabbie replied, and for one heartstopping moment Chant thought he was going to drive on.

"I'll direct you," he said.

"Get in, then."

Chant did so, slamming the cab door with no little satisfaction and barely managing to reach the seat before the cab picked up speed.

Why had he named Gamut Street? There was nothing there that would heal him. Nothing could. The flea—or whatever variation in that species it was that crawled in him—had reached his elbow, and his arm below that pain was now completely numb, the skin of his hand wrinkled and flaky. But the house in Gamut Street had been a place of miracles once. Men and women of great authority had walked in it and perhaps left some ghost of themselves to calm him in extremis. No creature, Sartori had taught, passed through this Dominion unrecorded, even to the least—to the child that perished a heartbeat after it opened its eyes, the child that died in the womb, drowned in its mother's waters—even that unnamed thing had its record and its consequence. So how much more might the oncepowerful of Gamut Street have left, by way of echoes?

His heart was palpitating, and his body full of jitters. Fearing he'd soon lose control of his functions, he pulled the letter to Estabrook from his pocket and leaned forward to slide the half window between himself and the driver aside.

"When you've dropped me in Clerkenwell I'd like you to deliver a letter for me. Would you be so kind?"

"Sorry, mate," the driver said. "I'm going home after this. I've a wife waiting for me."

Chant dug in his inside pocket and pulled out his wallet, then passed it through the window, letting it drop on the seat beside the driver.

"What's this?"

"All the money I've got. This letter has to be delivered."

"All the money you've got, eh?"

The driver picked up the wallet and flicked it open, his gaze going between its contents and the road.

"There's a lot of dosh in here."

"Have it. It's no good to me."

"Are you sick?"

"And tired," Chant said. "Take it, why don't you? Enjoy it."

"There's a Daimler been following us. Somebody you know?"

There was no purpose served by lying to the man. "Yes," Chant said. "I don't suppose you could put some distance between them and us?"

The man pocketed the wallet and jabbed his foot down on the accelerator. The cab leapt forward like a racehorse from the gate, its jockey's laugh rising above the guttural din of the engine. Whether it was the cash he was now heavy with or the challenge of outrunning a Daimler that motivated him, he put his cab through its paces, proving it more mobile than its bulk would have suggested. In under a minute they'd made two sharp lefts and a squealing right and were roaring down a back street so narrow the least miscalculation would have taken off handles, hubs, and mirrors. The mazing didn't stop there. They made another turn, and another, bringing them in a short time to South-wark Bridge. Somewhere along the way, they'd lost the Daimler. Chant might have applauded had he possessed two workable hands, but the flea's message of corruption was spreading with agonizing speed. While he still had five fingers under his command he went back to the window and dropped Estabrook's letter through, murmuring the address with a tongue that felt disfigured in his mouth.

"What's wrong with you?" the cabbie said. "It's not fucking contagious, is it, 'cause if it is—"

". . . not . . ." Chant said.

"You look fucking awful," the cabbie said, glancing in the mirror. "Sure you don't want a hospital?"

"No. Gamut Street. I want Gamut Street."

"You'll have to direct me from here."

The streets had all changed. Trees gone; rows demolished; austerity in place of elegance, function in place of beauty; the new for old, however poor the exchange rate. It was a decade and more since he'd come here last. Had Gamut Street fallen and a steel phallus risen in its place?

"Where are we?" he asked the driver.

"Clerkenwell. That's where you wanted, isn't it?"

"I mean the precise place."

The driver looked for a sign. "Flaxen Street. Does it ring a bell?"

Chant peered out of the window. "Yes! Yes! Go down to the end and turn right."

"Used to live around here, did you?"

"A long time ago."

"It's seen better days." He turned right. "Now where?"

"First on the left."

"Here it is," the man said. "Gamut Street. What number was it?"

"Twenty-eight."

The cab drew up at the curb. Chant fumbled for the handle, opened the door, and all but fell out onto the pavement. Staggering, he put his weight against the door to close it, and for the first time he and the driver came face to face. Whatever the flea was doing to his system, it must have been horribly apparent, to judge by the look of repugnance on the man's face.

"You *will* deliver the letter?" Chant said.

"You can trust me, mate."

"When you've done it, you should go home," Chant said. "Tell your wife you love her. Give a prayer of thanks."

"What for?"

"That you're human," Chant said.

The cabbie didn't question this little lunacy. "Whatever you say, mate," he replied. "I'll give the missus one and give thanks at the same time, how's that? Now don't do anything I wouldn't do, eh?"

This advice given, he drove off, leaving his passenger to the silence of the street.

With failing eyes, Chant scanned the gloom. The houses, built in the middle of Sartori's century, looked to be mostly deserted; primed for demolition, perhaps. But then Chant knew that sacred places—and Gamut Street was sacred in its way—survived on occasion because they went unseen, even in plain sight. Burnished by magic, they deflected the threatening eye and found unwitting allies in men and women who, all unknowing, knew holiness; became sanctuaries for a secret few.

He climbed the three steps to the door and pushed at it, but it was securely locked, so he went to the nearest window. There was a filthy shroud of cobweb across it but no curtain beyond. He pressed his face to the glass. Though his eyes were weakening by the moment, his gaze was still more acute than that of the blossoming ape. The room he looked into was stripped of all furniture and decoration; if anybody had occupied this house since Sartori's time—and it surely hadn't stood empty for two hundred years—they had gone, taking every trace of their presence. He raised his good arm and struck the glass with his elbow, a single jab which shattered the window. Then, careless of the damage he did himself, he hoisted his bulk onto the sill, beat out the rest of the pieces of glass with his hand, and dropped down into the room on the other side.

The layout of the house was still clear in his mind. In dreams he'd drifted through these rooms and heard the Maestro's voice summoning him up the stairs—up! up!—to the room at the top where Sartori had worked his work. It was there Chant wanted to go now, but there were new signs of atrophy in his body with every heartbeat. The hand first invaded by the flea was withered, its nails dropped from their place, its bone showing at the knuckles and wrist. Beneath his jacket he knew his torso to the hip was similarly unmade; he felt pieces of his flesh falling inside his shirt as he moved. He would not be moving for much longer. His legs were increasingly unwilling to bear him up, and his senses were close to flickering out. Like a man whose children were leaving him, he begged as he climbed the stairs.

"Stay with me. Just a little longer. *Please. . . .*"

His cajoling got him as far as the first landing, but then his legs all but gave out, and thereafter he had to climb using his one good arm to haul him onward.

He was halfway up the final flight when he heard the voiders' whistle in the street outside, its piercing din unmistakable. They had found him quicker than he'd anticipated, sniffing him out through the darkened streets. The fear that he'd be denied sight of the sanctum at the top of the stairs spurred him on, his body doing its ragged best to accommodate his ambition.

From below, he heard the door being forced open. Then the whistle again, harder than before, as his pursuers stepped into the house. He began to berate his limbs, his tongue barely able to shape the words.

"Don't let me down! Work, will you? *Work!*"

And they obliged. He scaled the last few stairs in a spastic fashion, but reached the top flight as he heard the voiders' soles at the bottom. It was dark up here, though how much of that was blindness and how much night he didn't know. It scarcely mattered. The route to the door of the sanctum was as familiar to him as the limbs he'd lost. He crawled on hands and knees across the landing, the ancient boards creaking beneath him. A sudden fear seized him: that the door would be locked, and he'd beat his weakness against it and fail to gain access. He reached up for the handle, grasped it, tried to turn it once, failed, tried again, and this time dropped face down over the threshold as the door swung open.

There was food for his enfeebled eyes. Shafts of moonlight spilled from the windows in the roof. Though he'd dimly thought it was sentiment that had driven him back here, he saw now it was not. In returning here he came full circle, back to the room which had been his first glimpse of the Fifth Dominion. This was his cradle and his tutoring room. Here he'd smelled the air of England for the first time, the crisp October air; here he'd fed first, drunk first;

first had cause for laughter and, later, for tears. Unlike the lower rooms, whose emptiness was a sign of desertion, this space had always been sparely furnished, and sometimes completely empty. He'd danced here on the same legs that now lay dead beneath him, while Sartori had told him how he planned to take this wretched Dominion and build in its midst a city that would shame Babylon; danced for sheer exuberance, knowing his Maestro was a great man and had it in his power to change the world.

Lost ambition; all lost. Before that October had become November Sartori had gone, flitted in the night or murdered by his enemies. Gone, and left his servant stranded in a city he barely knew. How Chant had longed then to return to the ether from where he'd been summoned, to shrug off the body which Sartori had congealed around him and be gone out of this Dominion. But the only voice capable of ordering such a release was that which had conjured him, and with Sartori gone he was exiled on earth forever. He hadn't hated his summoner for that. Sartori had been indulgent for the weeks they'd been together. Were he to appear now, in the moonlit room, Chant would not have accused him of negligence but made proper obeisances and been glad that his inspiration had returned.

"Maestro . . ." he murmured, face to the musty boards.

"Not here," came a voice from behind him. It was not, he knew, one of the voiders. They could whistle but not speak. "You were Sartori's creature, were you? I don't remember that."

The speaker was precise, cautious and smug. Unable to turn, Chant had to wait until the man walked past his supine body to get a sight of him. He knew better than to judge by appearances: he, whose flesh was not his own but of the Maestro's sculpting. Though the man in front of him looked human enough, he had the voiders in tow and spoke with knowledge of things few humans had access to. His face was an overripe cheese, drooping with jowls and weary folds around the eyes, his expression that of a funereal comic. The smugness in his voice was here too, in the studied way he licked upper and lower lips with his tongue before he spoke, and tapped the fingertips of each hand together as he judged the broken man at his feet. He wore an immaculately tailored three-piece suit, cut from a cloth of apricot cream. Chant would have given a good deal to break the bastard's nose so he bled on it.

"I never did meet Sartori," he said. "Whatever happened to him?"

The man went down on his haunches in front of Chant and suddenly snatched hold of a handful of his hair.

"I asked you what happened to your Maestro," he said. "I'm Dowd, by the way. You never knew *my* master, the Lord Godolphin, and I never knew yours. But they're gone, and you're scrabbling around for work. Well, you won't have to do it any longer, if you take my meaning."

"Did you . . . did you send him to me?"

"It would help my comprehension if you could be more specific."

"Estabrook."

"Oh, yes. Him."

"You did. Why?"

"Wheels within wheels, my dove," Dowd said. "I'd tell you the whole bitter story, but you don't have the time to listen and I don't have the patience to explain. I knew of a man who needed an assassin. I knew of another man who dealt in them. Let's leave it at that."

"But how did you know about me?"

"You're not discreet," Dowd replied. "You get drunk on the Queen's birthday, and you gab like an Irishman at a wake. Lovey, it draws attention sooner or later."

"Once in a while—"

"I know, you get melancholy. We all do, lovey, we all do. But some of us do our weeping in private, and some of us"—he let Chant's head drop—"make fucking public spectacles of ourselves. There are *consequences,* lovey, didn't Sartori tell you that? There are always *consequences.* You've begun something with this Estabrook business, for instance, and I'll need to watch it closely, or before we know it there'll be ripples spreading through the Imajica."

"The Imajica . . ."

"That's right. From here to the margin of the First Dominion. To the region of the Unbeheld Himself."

Chant began to gasp, and Dowd—realizing he'd hit a nerve—leaned towards his victim.

"Do I detect a little anxiety?" he said. "Are you afraid of going into the glory of our Lord Hapexamendios?"

Chant's voice was frail now. "Yes . . ." he murmured.

"Why?" Dowd wanted to know. "Because of your crimes?"

"Yes."

"What *are* your crimes? Do tell me. We needn't bother with the little things. Just the really shameful stuff'll do."

"I've had dealings with a Eurhetemec."

"Have you indeed?" Dowd said. "However did you get back to Yzorderrex to do that?"

"I didn't," Chant replied. "My dealings . . . were here, in the Fifth."

"Really," said Dowd softly. "I didn't know there were Eurhetemecs here. You learn something new every day. But, lovey, that's no great crime. The Unbeheld's going to forgive a poxy little trespass like that. Unless . . ." He stopped for a moment, turning over a new possibility. "Unless, the Eurhetemec was a mystif. . . ." He trailed the thought, but Chant remained silent. "Oh, my dove," Dowd said. "It *wasn't*, was it?" Another pause. "Oh, it *was*. It *was*." He sounded almost enchanted. "There's a mystif in the Fifth and—what? You're in love with it? You'd better tell me before you run out of breath, lovey. In a few minutes your eternal soul will be waiting at Hapexamendios' door."

Chant shuddered. "The assassin . . ." he said.

"What *about* the assassin?" came the reply. Then, realizing what he'd just heard, Dowd drew a long, slow breath. "The *assassin* is a mystif?" he said.

"Yes."

"Oh, my sweet Hyo!" he exclaimed. "A mystif!" The enchantment had vanished from his voice now. He was hard and dry. "Do you know what they can do? The deceits they've got at their disposal? This was supposed to be an anonymous piece of shit-stirring, and look what you've done!" His voice softened again. "Was it beautiful?" he asked. "No, no. Don't tell me. Let me have the surprise, when I see it face to face." He turned to the voiders. "Pick the fucker up," he said.

They stepped forward and raised Chant by his broken arms. There was no strength left in his neck, and his head lolled forward, a solid stream of bilious fluid running from his mouth and nostrils. "How often does the Eurhetemec tribe produce a mystif?" Dowd mused, half to himself. "Every ten years? Every fifty? They're certainly rare. And there you are, blithely hiring one of these little divinities as an assassin. Imagine! How pitiful, that it had fallen so low. I must ask it how that came about." He stepped towards Chant, and at Dowd's order one of the voiders raised Chant's head by the hair. "I need the mystif's where-abouts," Dowd said. "And its name."

Chant sobbed through his bile. "Please," he said. "I meant . . . I . . . meant—"

"Yes, yes. No harm. You were just doing your duty. The Unbeheld will forgive you, I guarantee it. But the *mystif,* lovey, I need you to tell me about the mystif. Where can I find it? Just speak the words, and you won't ever have to think about it again. You'll go into the presence of the Un-beheld like a babe."

"I will?"

"You will. Trust me. Just give me its name and tell me the place where I can find it."

"Name . . . and . . . place."

"That's right. But get to it, lovey, before it's too late!"

Chant took as deep a breath as his collapsing lungs allowed. "It's called Pie 'oh' pah," he said.

Dowd stepped back from the dying man as if slapped. "Pie 'oh' pah? Are you sure?"

"I'm sure. . . ."

"Pie 'oh' pah is alive? And Estabrook hired it?"

"Yes."

Dowd threw off his imitation of a Father Confessor and

murmured a fretful question of himself. "What does this mean?" he said.

Chant made a pained little moan, his system racked by further waves of dissolution. Realizing that time was now very short, Dowd pressed the man afresh.

"Where *is* this mystif? Quickly, now! *Quickly!*"

Chant's face was decaying, cobs of withered flesh sliding off the slickened bone. When he answered, it was with half a mouth. But answer he did, to be unburdened.

"I thank you," Dowd said to him, when all the information had been supplied. "I thank you." Then, to the voiders, "Let him go."

They dropped Chant without ceremony. When he hit the floor his face broke, pieces spattering Dowd's shoe. He viewed the mess with disgust.

"Clean it off," he said.

The voiders were at his feet in moments, dutifully removing the scraps of matter from Dowd's handmade shoes.

"What does this mean?" Dowd murmured again. There was surely synchronicity in this turn of events. In a little over half a year's time the anniversary of the Reconciliation would be upon the Imajica. Two hundred years would have passed since the Maestro Sartori had attempted, and failed, to perform the greatest act of magic known to this or any other Dominion. The plans for that ceremony had been laid here, at number 28 Gamut Street, and the mystif, among others, had been there to witness the preparations.

The ambition of those heady days had ended in tragedy, of course. Rites intended to heal the rift in the Imajica, and reconcile the Fifth Dominion with the other four, had gone disastrously awry. Many great theurgists, shamans, and theologians had been killed. Determined that such a calamity never be repeated, several of the survivors had banded together in order to cleanse the Fifth of all magical knowledge. But however much they scrubbed to erase the past, the slate could never be entirely cleansed. Traces of what had been dreamed and hoped for remained; fragments of poems to Union, written by men whose names had been systematically removed from all record. And as long as

such scraps remained, the spirit of the Reconciliation
would survive.

But spirit was not enough. A Maestro was needed, a magician arrogant enough to believe that he could succeed
where Christos and innumerable other sorcerers, most lost
to history, had failed. Though these were blissless times,
Dowd didn't discount the possibility of such a soul appearing. He still encountered in his daily life a few who looked
past the empty gaud that distracted lesser minds and
longed for a revelation that would burn the tinsel away, an
Apocalypse that would show the Fifth the glories it
yearned for in its sleep.

If a Maestro was going to appear, however, he would
need to be swift. Another attempt at Reconciliation
couldn't be planned overnight, and if the next midsummer
went unused, the Imajica would pass another two centuries
divided: time enough for the Fifth Dominion to destroy itself out of boredom or frustration and prevent the Reconciliation from ever taking place.

Dowd perused his newly polished shoes. "Perfect," he
said. "Which is more than I can say for the rest of this
wretched world."

He crossed to the door. The voiders lingered by the
body, however, bright enough to know they still had some
duty to perform with it. But Dowd called them away.

"We'll leave it here," he said. "Who knows? It may stir
a few ghosts."

Two days after the predawn call from Judith—days in
which the water heater in the studio had failed, leaving
Gentle the option of bathing in polar waters or not at all
(he chose the latter)—Klein summoned him to the house.
He had good news. He'd heard of a buyer with a hunger

that was not being satisfied through conventional markets, and Klein had allowed it to be known that he might be able to lay his hands on something attractive. Gentle had successfully re-created one Gauguin previously, a small picture which had gone onto the open market and been consumed without any questions being asked. Could he do it again? Gentle replied that he would make a Gauguin so fine the artist himself would have wept to see it. Klein advanced Gentle five hundred pounds to pay the rent on the studio and left him to it, remarking only that Gentle was looking a good deal better than he'd looked previously, though he smelled a good deal worse.

Gentle didn't much care. Not bathing for two days was no great inconvenience when he only had himself for company; not shaving suited him fine when there was no woman to complain of beard burns. And he'd rediscovered the old private erotics: spit, palm, and fantasy. It sufficed. A man might get used to living this way; might get to like his gut a little ample, his armpits sweaty, his balls the same. It wasn't until the weekend that he started to pine for some entertainment other than the sight of himself in the bathroom mirror. There hadn't been a Friday or Saturday in the last year which hadn't been occupied by some social gathering, where he'd mingled with Vanessa's friends. Their numbers were still listed in his address book, just a phone call away, but he felt squeamish about making contact. However much he may have charmed them, they were her friends, not his, and they'd have inevitably sided with her in this fiasco.

As for his own peers—the friends he'd had before Vanessa—most had faded. They were a part of his past and, like so many other memories, slippery. While people like Klein recalled events thirty years old in crystalline detail, Gentle had difficulty remembering where he was and with whom even ten years before. Earlier than that still, and his memory banks were empty. It was as though his mind was disposed only to preserve enough details of his history to make the present plausible. The rest it disregarded. He kept this strange fallibility from almost everybody he knew, concocting details if pressed hard. It didn't much bother him. Not knowing what it meant to have a past, he didn't miss it. And he construed from exchanges with others that though they might talk confidentially about their childhood and adolescence, much of it was rumor and conjecture, some of it pure fabrication.

Nor was he alone in his ignorance. Judith had once confided that she too had an uncertain grasp of the past, though she'd been drunk at the time and had denied it vehemently when he'd raised the subject again. So, between friends lost and friends forgotten, he was very much alone this Saturday night, and he picked up the phone when it rang with some gratitude.

"Furie here," he said. He felt like a Furie tonight. The line was live, but there was no answer. "Who's there?" he said. Still, silence. Irritated, he put down the receiver. Seconds later, the phone rang again. "Who the hell *is* this?" he demanded, and this time an impeccably spoken man replied, albeit with another question.

"Am I speaking to John Zacharias?"

Gentle didn't hear himself called that too often. "Who is this?" he said again.

"We've only met once. You probably don't remember me. Charles Estabrook?"

Some people lingered longer in the memory than others. Estabrook was one. The man who'd caught Jude when she'd dropped from the high wire. A classic inbred Englishman, member of the minor aristocracy, pompous, condescending and—

"I'd like very much to meet with you, if that's possible."

"I don't think we've got anything to say to each other."

"It's about Judith, Mr. Zacharias. A matter I'm obliged to keep in the strictest confidence but is, I cannot stress too strongly, of the profoundest importance."

The tortured syntax made Gentle blunt. "Spit it out, then," he said.

"Not on the telephone. I realize this request comes without warning, but I beg you to consider it."

"I have. And no. I'm not interested in meeting you."

"Even to gloat?"

"Over what?"

"Over the fact that I've lost her," Estabrook said. "She left me, Mr. Zacharias, just as she left you. Thirty-three days ago." The precision of that spoke volumes. Was he counting the hours as well as the days? Perhaps the minutes too? "You needn't come to the house if you don't wish to. In fact, to be honest, I'd be happier if you didn't."

He was speaking as if Gentle would agree to the rendezvous, which, though he hadn't said so yet, he would.

2

It was cruel, of course, to bring someone of Estabrook's age out on a cold day and make him climb a hill, but Gentle knew from experience you took whatever satisfactions you could along the way. And Parliament Hill had a fine view of London, even on a day of lowering cloud. The wind was brisk, and as usual on a Sunday the hill had a host of kite flyers on its back, their toys like multicolored candies suspended in the wintry sky. The hike made Estabrook breathless, but he seemed glad that Gentle had picked the spot.

"I haven't been up here in years. My first wife used to like coming here to see the kites."

He brought a brandy flask from his pocket, proffering it first to Gentle. Gentle declined.

"The cold never leaves one's marrow these days. One of the penalties of age. I've yet to discover the advantages. How old are you?"

Rather than confess to not knowing, Gentle said, "Almost forty."

"You look younger. In fact, you've scarcely changed since we first met. Do you remember? At the auction? You were with her. I wasn't. That was the world of difference between us. With; without. I envied you that day the way I'd never envied any other man, just for having her beside you. Later, of course, I saw the same look on other men's faces—"

"I didn't come here to hear this," Gentle said.

"No, I realize that. It's just necessary for me to express how very precious she was to me. I count the years I had with her as the best of my life. But of course the best can't go on forever, can they, or how are they the best?" He drank again. "You know, she *never* talked about you," he said. "I tried to provoke her into doing so, but she said she'd put you out of her mind completely—she'd forgotten you, she said—which is nonsense, of course."

"I believe it."

"Don't," Estabrook said quickly. "You were her guilty secret."

"Why are you trying to flatter me?"

"It's the truth. She still loved you, all through the time she was with me. That's why we're talking now. Because I know it, and I think you do too."

Not once so far had they mentioned her by name, almost as though from some superstition. She was *she,* her, the woman: an absolute and invisible power. Her men seemed to have their feet on solid ground, but in truth they drifted like the kites, tethered to reality only by the memory of her.

"I've done a terrible thing, John," Estabrook said. The flask was at his lips again. He took several gulps before sealing it and pocketing it. "And I regret it bitterly."

"What?"

"May we walk a little way?" Estabrook said, glancing towards the kite flyers, who were both too distant and too involved in their sport to be eavesdropping. But he was not comfortable with sharing his secret until he'd put twice the distance between his confession and their ears. When he had, he made it simply and plainly. "I don't know what kind of madness overtook me," he said, "but a little while ago I made a contract with somebody to have her killed."

"You did *what?*"

"Does it appall you?"

"What do you think? Of course it appalls me."

"It's the highest form of devotion, you know, to want to

end somebody's existence rather than let them live on without you. It's love of the highest order."

"It's a fucking obscenity."

"Oh, yes, it's that too. But I couldn't bear . . . just couldn't *bear* . . . the idea of her being alive and me not being with her. . . ." His delivery was now deteriorating, the words becoming tears. "She was so dear to me. . . ."

Gentle's thoughts were of his last exchange with Judith: the half-drowned telephone call from New York, which had ended with nothing said. Had she known then that her life was in jeopardy? If not, did she now? My God, was she even alive? He took hold of Estabrook's lapel with the same force that the fear took hold of him.

"You haven't brought me here to tell me she's dead."

"No. *No,*" he protested, making no attempt to disengage Gentle's hold. "I hired this man, and I want to call him off."

"So do it," Gentle said, letting the coat go.

"I can't."

Estabrook reached into his pocket and pulled out a sheet of paper. To judge by its crumpled state it had been thrown away, then reclaimed.

"This came from the man who found me the assassin," he went on. "It was delivered to my home two nights ago. He was obviously drunk or drugged when he wrote it, but it indicates that he expects to be dead by the time I read it. I'm assuming he's correct. He hasn't made contact. He was my only route to the assassin."

"Where did you meet this man?"

"He found me."

"And the assassin?"

"I met him somewhere south of the river, I don't know where. It was dark. I was lost. Besides, he won't be there. He's gone after her."

"So warn her."

"I've tried. She won't accept my calls. She's got another lover now. He's being covetous the way I was. My letters, my telegrams, they're all sent back unopened. But he won't be able to save her. This man I hired, his name's Pie—"

"What's that, some kind of code?"

"I don't know," Estabrook said. "I don't know anything except I've done something unforgivable and you have to help me undo it. *You have to.* This man Pie is lethal."

"What makes you think she'll see me when she won't see you?"

"There's no guarantee. But you're a younger, fitter man, and you've had some . . . experience of the criminal mind. You've a better chance of coming between her and Pie than I have. I'll give you money for the assassin. You can pay him off. And I'll pay whatever you ask. I'm rich. Just warn her, Zacharias, and get her to come home. I can't have her death on my conscience."

"It's a little late to think about that."

"I'm making what amends I can. Do we have a deal?" He took off his leather glove in preparation for shaking Gentle's hand.

"I'd like the letter from your contact," Gentle said.

"It barely makes any sense," Estabrook said.

"If he *is* dead, and she dies too, that letter's evidence whether it makes sense or not. Hand it over, or no deal."

Estabrook reached into his inside pocket, as if to pull out the letter, but with his fingers upon it he hesitated. Despite all his talk about having a clear conscience, about Gentle being the man to save her, he was deeply reluctant to part with the letter.

"I thought so," Gentle said. "You want to make sure I look like the guilty party if anything goes wrong. Well, go fuck yourself."

He turned from Estabrook and started down the hill. Estabrook came after him, calling his name, but Gentle didn't slow his pace. He let the man run.

"All right!" he heard behind him. "All right, have it! Have it!"

Gentle slowed but didn't stop. Gray with exertion, Estabrook caught up with him.

"The letter's yours," he said.

Gentle took it, pocketing it without unfolding it. There'd be plenty of time to study it on the flight.

6

I

Chant's body was discovered the following day by ninety-three-year-old Albert Burke, who found it while looking for his errant mongrel, Kipper. The animal had sniffed from the street what its owner only began to nose as he climbed the stairs, whistling for his hound between curses: the rotting tissue at the top. In the autumn of 1916, Albert had fought for his country at the Somme, sharing trenches with dead companions for days at a time. The sights and smells of death didn't much distress him. Indeed, his sanguine response to his discovery lent color to the story, when it reached the evening news, and assured it of greater coverage than it might otherwise have merited, that focus in turn bringing a penetrating eye to bear on the identity of the dead man. Within a day a portrait of the deceased as he might have looked in life had been produced, and by Wednesday a woman living on a council estate south of the river had identified him as her next-door neighbor, Mr. Chant.

An examination of his flat turned up a second picture, not of Chant's flesh, this time, but of his life. It was the conclusion of the police that the dead man was a practitioner of some obscure religion. It was reported that a small altar dominated his room, decorated with the withered heads of animals that forensics could not identify, its centerpiece an idol of so explicitly sexual a nature no newspaper dared publish a sketch of it, let alone a photograph. The gutter press particularly enjoyed the story, especially as the artifacts had belonged to a man now thought to have been murdered. They editorialized with barely concealed racism on the influx of perverted foreign religions. Between this and stories on Burke of the Somme, Chant's death attracted a lot of column inches. That fact had several consequences. It brought a rash of right-wing attacks on mosques

in greater London, it brought a call for the demolition of
the estate where Chant had lived, and it brought Dowd up
to a certain tower in Highgate, where he was summoned in
lieu of his absentee master, Estabrook's brother, Oscar
Godolphin.

2

In the 1780s, when Highgate Hill was so steep and deeply
rutted that carriages regularly failed to make the grade and
the drive to town was sufficiently dangerous that a wise
man went with pistols, a merchant called Thomas Roxborough had constructed a handsome house on Hornsey
Lane, designed for him by one Henry Holland. At that time
it had commanded fine views: south all the way to the river;
north and west over the lush pastures of the region towards
the tiny village of Hampstead. The former view was still
available to the tourist, from the bridge that spanned the
Archway Road, but Roxborough's fine house had gone, replaced in the late thirties with an anonymous ten-story
tower, set back from the street. There was a screen of well-
tended trees between tower and road, not sufficiently thick
to conceal the building entirely, but enough to render what
was already an undistinguished building virtually invisible.
The only mail that was delivered there was circulars and
official paperwork of one kind or another. There were no
tenants, either individuals or businesses. Yet Roxborough
Tower was kept well by its owners, who once every month
or so gathered in the single room which occupied the top
floor of the building, in the name of the man who had
owned this plot of land two hundred years before and who
had left it to the society he founded. The men and women
(eleven in all) who met here and talked for a few hours and
went their unremarkable ways were the descendants of the
impassioned few Roxborough had gathered around him in
the dark days following the failure of the Reconciliation.
There was no passion among them now, nor more than a
vague comprehension of Roxborough's purpose in forming
what he'd called the Society of the Tabula Rasa, or the

Clean Slate. But they met anyway, in part because in their early childhood one or other of their parents, usually but not always the father, had taken them aside and told them a great responsibility would fall to them—the carrying forward of a hermetically protected family secret—and in part because the Society looked after its own. Roxborough had been a man of wealth and insight. He'd purchased considerable tracts of land during his lifetime, and the profits that accrued from that investment had ballooned as London grew. The sole recipient of those monies was the Society, though the funds were so ingeniously routed, through companies and agents who were unaware of their place in the system, that nobody who serviced the Society in any capacity whatsoever knew of its existence.

Thus the Tabula Rasa flourished in its peculiar, purposeless way, gathering to talk about the secrets it kept, as Roxborough had decreed, and enjoying the sight of the city from its place on Highgate Hill.

Kuttner Dowd had been here several times, though never when the Society was assembled, as it was tonight. His employer, Oscar Godolphin, was one of the eleven to whom the flame of Roxborough's intent had been passed, though of all of them surely none was so perfect a hypocrite as Godolphin, who was both a member of a Society committed to the repression of all magical activity, and the employer (Godolphin would have said *owner*) of a creature summoned by magic in the very year of the tragedy that had brought the Society into being.

That creature was of course Dowd, whose existence was known to the Society's members but whose origins were not. If it had been, they would never have summoned him here and allowed him access to the hallowed tower. Rather, they would have been bound by Roxborough's edict to destroy him at whatever cost to their bodies, souls, or sanity that might entail. Certainly they had the expertise, or at least the means to gain it. The tower reputedly housed a library of treatises, grimoires, cyclopedias, and symposia second to none, collected by Roxborough and the group of Fifth Dominion magi who'd first supported the attempt at the Reconciliation. One of those men had been Joshua Godolphin, Earl of Bellingham. He and Roxborough had survived the calamitous events of that midsummer almost two hundred years ago, but most of their dearest friends had not. The story went that after the tragedy Godolphin had retired to his country estate and never again ventured beyond its perimeters. Roxborough, on the other hand, ever the most pragmatic of the group, had within days of the cataclysm secured the occult libraries of his dead colleagues, hiding the thousands of volumes in the cellar of his house where they could, in the words of a letter to the Earl, *no longer taint with un-Christian ambition the minds of good men like our dear friends. We must hereafter keep the doing of this damnable magic from our shores.* That he had not destroyed the books, but merely locked them away, was testament to some ambiguity in him, however. Despite the horrors he'd seen, and the fierceness of his revulsion, some small part of him retained the fascination that had drawn him, Godolphin, and their fellow experimenters together in the first place.

Dowd shivered with unease as he stood in the plain hallway of the tower, knowing that somewhere nearby was the largest collection of magical writings gathered in one place outside the Vatican, and that among them would be many rituals for the raising and dispatching of creatures like himself. He was not the conventional stuff of which familiars were made, of course. Most were simpering, mindless functionaries, plucked by their summoners from the In Ovo—the space between the Fifth and the Reconciled Dominions—like lobsters from a restaurant tank. He, on the other hand, had been a professional actor in his time, and fêted for it. It wasn't congenital stupidity that had made him susceptible to human jurisdiction, it was anguish. He'd seen the face of Hapexamendios Himself and, half-crazed by the sight, had been unable to resist the summons, and the binding, when it came. His invoker had of course been Joshua Godolphin, and he'd commanded Dowd to serve his line until the end of time. In fact, Joshua's retirement to the safety of his estate had freed Dowd to wander until the old man's demise, when he was drawn back to offer his services to Joshua's son Nathaniel, only revealing his true nature once he'd made himself indispensable, for fear he was trapped between his bounden duty and the zeal of a Christian.

In fact, Nathaniel had grown into a dissolute of considerable proportions by the time Dowd entered his employ, and could not have cared less what kind of creature Dowd was as long as he procured the right kind of company. And so it had gone on, generation after generation, Dowd changing his face on occasion (a simple trick, or feit) so as to conceal his longevity from the withering human world. But the possibility that one day his double-dealing would be discovered by the Tabula Rasa, and they would search through their library and find some vicious sway to destroy him, never entirely left his calculations: especially now, waiting for the call into their presence.

That call was an hour and a half in coming, during which time he distracted himself thinking about the shows that were opening in the coming week. Theater remained his great love, and there was scarcely a production of any significance he failed to see. On the following Tuesday he had tickets for the much-acclaimed *Lear* at the National and then, two days later, a seat in the stalls for the revival of *Turandot* at the Coliseum. Much to look forward to, once this wretched interview was over.

At last the lift hummed into life and one of the Society's younger members, Giles Bloxham, appeared. At forty, Bloxham looked twice that age. It took a kind of genius, Godolphin had once remarked when talking about Bloxham (he liked to report on the absurdities of the Society, particularly when he was in his cups), to look so dissipated and have nothing to regret for it.

"We're ready for you now," Bloxham said, indicating that Dowd should join him in the lift. "You realize," he said as they ascended, "that if you're ever tempted to breathe a word of what you see here, the Society will eradicate you so quickly and so thoroughly your mother won't even know you existed?"

This overheated threat sounded ludicrous delivered in Bloxham's nasal whine, but Dowd played the chastened functionary. "I perfectly understand," he said.

"It's an extraordinary step," Bloxham continued, "calling anyone who isn't a member to a meeting. But these are extraordinary times. Not that it's any of your business."

"Quite so," Dowd said, all innocence.

Tonight he'd take their condescension without argument, he thought, more confident by the day that something was coming that would rock this tower to its foundations. When it did, he'd have his revenge.

The lift door opened, and Bloxham ordered Dowd to follow him. The passages that led to the main suite were stark and uncarpeted; the room he was led into, the same. The drapes were drawn over all the windows; the enormous marble-topped table that dominated the room was lit by overhead lamps, the wash of their light thrown up on the five members, two of them women, sitting around it. To judge by the clutter of bottles, glasses, and overfilled ashtrays, and the brooding, weary faces, they had been debating for many hours. Bloxham poured himself a glass of water and took his place. There was one empty seat: Godolphin's. Dowd was not invited to occupy it but stood at the end of the table, mildly discomfited by the stares of his interrogators. Not one face among them would have been known by the populace at large. Though all of them had descended from families of wealth and influence, these were not public powers. The Society forbade any member to hold office or take as a spouse an individual who might invite or arouse the curiosity of the press. It worked in mystery, for the demise of mystery. Perhaps it was that paradox—more than any other aspect of its nature—which would finally undo it.

At the other end of the table from Dowd, sitting in front of a heap of newspapers doubtless carrying the Burke reports, sat a professorial man in his sixties, white hair oiled to his scalp. Dowd knew his name from Godolphin's description: Hubert Shales, dubbed The Sloth by Oscar. He moved and spoke with the caution of a glass-boned theologian.

"You know why you're here?" he said.

"He knows," Bloxham put in.

"Some problem with Mr. Godolphin?" Dowd ventured.

"He's not here," said one of the women to Dowd's right, her face emaciated beneath a confection of dyed black hair. Alice Tyrwhitt, Dowd guessed. "That's the problem."

"So I see," Dowd said.

"Where the hell is he?" Bloxham demanded.

"He's traveling," Dowd replied. "I don't think he anticipated a meeting."

"Neither did we," said Lionel Wakeman, flushed with the Scotch he'd imbibed, the bottle lying in the crook of his arm.

"Where's he traveling?" Tyrwhitt asked. "It's imperative we find him."

"I'm afraid I don't know," Dowd said. "His business takes him all over the world."

"Anything respectable?" Wakeman slurred.

"He's got a number of investments in Singapore," Dowd replied. "And in India. Would you like me to prepare a dossier? I'm sure he'd be—"

"Bugger the dossier!" Bloxham said. "We want him here! Now!"

"I'm afraid I don't know his precise whereabouts. Somewhere in the Far East."

The severe but not unalluring woman to Wakeman's left now entered the exchange, stabbing her cigarette in the ashtray as she spoke. This could only be Charlotte Feaver: Charlotte the Scarlet, as Oscar called her. She was the last of the Roxborough line, he'd said, unless she found a way to fertilize one of her girlfriends.

"This isn't some damn club he can visit when it fucking well suits him," she said.

"That's right," Wakeman put in. "It's a damn poor show."

Shales picked up one of the newspapers in front of him and pitched it down the table in Dowd's direction.

"I presume you've read about this body they found in Clerkenwell?" he said.

"Yes. I believe so."

Shales paused for several seconds, his sparrow eyes going from one member to another. Whatever he was about to say, its broaching had been debated before Dowd entered.

"We have reason to believe that this man Chant did not originate in this Dominion."

"I'm sorry?" Dowd said, feigning confusion. "I don't follow. Dominion?"

"Spare us your discretion," Charlotte Feaver said. "You know what we're talking about. Oscar hasn't employed you for twenty-five years and kept his counsel."

"I know very little," Dowd protested.

"But enough to know there's an anniversary imminent," Shales said.

My, my, Dowd thought, they're not as stupid as they look.

"You mean the Reconciliation?" he said.

"That's exactly what I mean. This coming mid-summer—"

"Do we have to spell it out?" Bloxham said. "He already knows more than he should."

Shales ignored the interruption and was beginning again when a voice so far unheard, emanating from a bulky figure sitting beyond the reach of the light, broke in. Dowd had been waiting for this man, Matthias McGann, to say his piece. If the Tabula Rasa had a leader, this was he.

"Hubert?" he said. "May I?"

Shales murmured, "Of course."

"Mr. Dowd," said McGann, "I don't doubt that Oscar has been indiscreet. We all have our weaknesses. You must be his. Nobody here blames you for listening. But this Society was created for a very specific purpose and on occasion has been obliged to act with extreme severity in the pursuit of that purpose. I won't go into details. As Giles says, you're already wiser than any of us would like. But believe me, we will silence any and all who put this Dominion at risk."

He leaned forward. His face announced a man of good humor, presently unhappy with his lot.

"Hubert mentioned that an anniversary is imminent. So it is. And forces with an interest in subverting the sanity of this Dominion may be readying themselves to celebrate that anniversary. So far, this"—he pointed to the newspaper—"is the only evidence we'd found of such preparations, but if there are others they will be swiftly terminated by this Society and its agents. Do you understand?"

He didn't wait for an answer.

"This sort of thing is very dangerous," he went on. "People start to investigate. Academics. Esoterics. They start to question, and they start to dream."

"I could see how that would be dangerous," Dowd said.

"Don't smarm, you smug little bastard," Bloxham burst out. "We all know what you and Godolphin have been doing. Tell him, Hubert!"

"I've traced some artifacts of . . . nonterrestrial origin . . . that came my way. The trail, as it were, leads back to Oscar Godolphin."

"We don't know that," Lionel put in. "These buggers lie."

"I'm satisfied Godolphin's guilty," Alice Tyrwhitt said. "And this one with him."

"I protest," Dowd said.

"You've been dealing in magic," Bloxham hollered. "Admit it!" He rose and slammed the table. *"Admit it!"*

"Sit down, Giles," McGann said.

"Look at him," Bloxham went on, jabbing his thumb in Dowd's direction. "He's guilty as hell."

"I said *sit down,*" McGann replied, raising his voice ever so slightly. Cowed, Bloxham sat. "You're not on trial here," McGann said to Dowd. "It's Godolphin we want."

"So find him," Feaver said.

"And when you do," Shales said, "tell him I've got a few items he may recognize."

The table fell silent. Several heads turned in Matthias McGann's direction. "I think that's it," he said. "Unless you have any remarks to make?"

"I don't believe so," Dowd replied.

"Then you may go."

Dowd took his leave without further exchange, escorted as far as the lift by Charlotte Feaver and left to make the descent alone. They were better informed than he'd imagined, but they were some way from guessing the truth. He turned over passages of the interview as he drove back to Regent's Park Road, committing them to memory for later recitation. Wakeman's drunken irrelevancies; Shales's indiscretion; McGann, smooth as a velvet scabbard. He'd repeat it all for Godolphin's edification, especially the cross-questioning about the absentee's whereabouts.

Somewhere in the East, Dowd had said. East Yzordderrex, maybe, in the Kesparates built close to the harbor where Oscar liked to bargain for contraband brought back from Hakaridek or the islands. Whether he was there or some other place, Dowd had no way of fetching him back. He would come when he would come, and the Tabula Rasa would have to bide its time, though the longer he was away the more the likelihood grew of one of their number voicing the suspicion some of them surely nurtured: that Godolphin's dealings in talismans and wantons were only the tip of the iceberg. Perhaps they even suspected he took trips.

He wasn't the only Fifther who'd jaunted between Dominions, of course. There were many routes from Earth to the Reconciled Dominions, some safer than others but all used at one time or another, and not always by magicians. Poets had found their way over (and sometimes back, to tell the tale); so had a good number of priests over the centuries, and hermits, meditating on their essence so hard the In Ovo enveloped them and spat them into another world. Any soul despairing or inspired enough could get access. But few in Dowd's experience had made such a commonplace of it as Godolphin.

These were dangerous times for such jaunts, both here

and there. The Reconciled Dominions had been under the control of Yzordderrex's Autarch for over a century, and every time Godolphin returned from a trip he had new signs of unrest to report. From the margins of the First Dominion to Patashoqua and its satellite cities in the Fourth, voices were raised to stir rebellion. There was as yet no consensus on how best to overcome the Autarch's tyranny, only a simmering unrest which regularly erupted in riots or strikes, the leaders of such mutinies invariably found and executed. In fact, on occasion the Autarch's suppressions had been more Draconian still. Entire communities had been destroyed in the name of the Yzordderrexian Empire: tribes and small nations deprived of their gods, their lands, and their right to procreate, others, simply eradicated by pogroms the Autarch personally supervised. But none of these horrors had dissuaded Godolphin from traveling in the Reconciled Dominions. Perhaps tonight's events would, however, at least until the Society's suspicions had been allayed.

Tiresome as it was, Dowd knew he had no choice as to where he went tonight: to the Godolphin estate and the folly in its deserted grounds which was Oscar's departure place. There he would wait, like a dog grown lonely at its master's absence, until Godolphin's return. Oscar was not the only one who would have to muster some excuses in the near future; so would he. Killing Chant had seemed like a wise maneuver at the time—and, of course, an agreeable diversion on a night without a show to go to—but Dowd hadn't predicted the furor it would cause. With hindsight, that had been naïve. England loved murder, preferably with diagrams. And he'd been unlucky, what with the ubiquitous Mr. Burke of the Somme and a low quota of political scandals conspiring to make Chant posthumously famous. He would have to be prepared for Godolphin's wrath. But hopefully it would be subsumed in the larger anxiety of the Society's suspicions. Godolphin would need Dowd to help him calm these suspicions, and a man who needed his dog knew not to kick it too hard.

Gentle called Klein from the airport, minutes before he caught his flight. He presented Chester with a severely edited version of the truth, making no mention of Estabrook's murder plot but explaining that Jude was ill and had requested his presence. Klein didn't deliver the tirade that Gentle had anticipated. He simply observed, rather wearily, that if Gentle's word was worth so little after all the effort he, Klein, had put into finding work for him, it was perhaps best that they end their business relationship now. Gentle begged him to be a little more lenient, to which Klein said he'd call Gentle's studio in two days' time and, if he received no answer, would assume their deal was no longer valid.

"Your dick'll be the death of you," he commented as he signed off.

The flight gave Gentle time to think about both that remark and the conversation on Kite Hill, the memory of which still vexed him. During the exchange itself he'd moved from suspicion to disbelief to disgust and finally to acceptance of Estabrook's proposal. But despite the fact that the man had been as good as his word, providing ample funds for the trip, the more Gentle returned to the conversation in memory, the more that first response—suspicion—was reawakened. His doubts circled around two elements of Estabrook's story: the assassin himself (this Mr. Pie, hired out of nowhere) and, more particularly, around the man who'd introduced Estabrook to his hired hand: Chant, whose death had been media fodder for the past several days.

The dead man's letter was virtually incomprehensible, as Estabrook had warned, veering from pulpit rhetoric to opiate invention. The fact that Chant, knowing he was going to be murdered (that much *was* cogent), should have chosen to set these nonsenses down as vital information was proof of significant derangement. How much more deranged, then, a man like Estabrook, who did business with this crazy? And by the same token was Gentle not crazier still, employed by the lunatic's employer?

Amid all these fantasies and equivocations, however, there were two irreducible facts: death and Judith. The former had come to Chant in a derelict house in Clerkenwell; about that there was no ambiguity. The latter, innocent of her husband's malice, was probably its next target. His task was simple: to come between the two.

He checked into his hotel at 52nd and Madison a little after five in the afternoon, New York time. From his window on the fourteenth floor he had a view downtown, but the scene was far from welcoming. A gruel of rain, threatening to thicken into snow, had begun to fall as he journeyed in from Kennedy, and the weather reports promised cold and more cold. It suited him, however. The gray darkness, together with the horn and brake squeals rising from the intersection below, fitted his mood of dislocation. As with London, New York was a city in which he'd had friends once, but lost them. The only face he would seek out here was Judith's.

There was no purpose in delaying that search. He ordered coffee from Room Service, showered, drank, dressed in his thickest sweater, leather jacket, corduroys, and heavy boots, and headed out. Cabs were hard to come by, and after ten minutes of waiting in line beneath the hotel canopy, he decided to walk uptown a few blocks and catch a passing cab if he got lucky. If not, the cold would clear his head. By the time he'd reached 70th Street the sleet had become a drizzle, and there was a spring in his step. Ten blocks from here Judith was about some early evening occupation: bathing, perhaps, or dressing for an evening on the town. Ten blocks, at a minute a block. Ten minutes until he was standing outside the place where she was.

2

Marlin had been as solicitous as an erring husband since the attack, calling her from his office every hour or so, and several times suggesting that she might want to talk with an analyst, or at very least with one of his many friends who'd been assaulted or mugged on the streets of Manhattan. She declined the offer. Physically, she was quite well. Psychologically too. Though she'd heard that victims of attack often suffered from delayed repercussions—depression and sleeplessness among them—neither had struck her yet. It was the mystery of what had happened that kept her awake at night. Who was he, this man who knew her name, who got up from a collision that should have killed him outright and still managed to outrun a healthy man? And why had she projected upon his face the likeness of John Zacharias? Twice she'd begun to tell Marlin about the meeting in and outside Bloomingdale's; twice she'd rechanneled the conversation at the last moment, unable to face his benign condescension. This enigma was hers to unravel, and sharing it too soon, perhaps at all, might make the solving impossible.

In the meantime, Marlin's apartment felt very secure. There were two doormen: Sergio by day and Freddy by night. Marlin had given them both a detailed description of the assailant, and instructions to let nobody up to the second floor without Ms. Odell's permission, and even then they were to accompany visitors to the apartment door and escort them out if his guest chose not to see them. Nothing could harm her as long as she stayed behind closed doors. Tonight, with Marlin working until nine and a late dinner planned, she'd decided to spend the early evening assigning and wrapping the presents she'd accumulated on her various Fifth Avenue sorties, sweetening her labors with wine and music. Marlin's record collection was chiefly seduction songs of his sixties adolescence, which suited her fine. She played smoochy soul and sipped well-chilled Sauvignon as

she pottered, more than content with her own company.
Once in a while she'd get up from the chaos of ribbons and
tissue and go to the window to watch the cold. The glass
was misting. She didn't clear it. Let the world lose focus.
She had no taste for it tonight.

There was a woman standing at one of the third-story windows when Gentle reached the intersection, just gazing out
at the street. He watched her for several seconds before the
casual motion of a hand raised to the back of her neck and
run up through her long hair identified the silhouette as Judith. She made no backward glance to signify the presence
of anyone else in the room. She simply sipped from her
glass, and stroked her scalp, and watched the murky night.
He had thought it would be easy to approach her, but now,
watching her remotely like this, he knew otherwise.

The first time he'd seen her—all those years ago—he'd
felt something close to panic. His whole system had been
stirred to nausea as he relinquished power to the sight of
her. The seduction that had followed had been both an
homage and a revenge: an attempt to control someone who
exercised an authority over him that defied analysis. To
this day he didn't understand that authority. She was certainly a bewitching woman, but then he'd known others
every bit as bewitching and not been panicked by them.
What was it about Judith that threw him into such confusion now, as then? He watched her until she left the window; then he watched the window where she'd been; but he
wearied of that, finally, and of the chill in his feet. He
needed fortification: against the cold, against the woman.
He left the corner and trekked a few blocks east until he
found a bar, where he put two bourbons down his throat
and wished to his core that alcohol had been his addiction
instead of the opposite sex.

At the sound of the stranger's voice, Freddy, the night
doorman, rose muttering from his seat in the nook beside
the elevator. There was a shadowy figure visible through
the ironwork filigree and bulletproof glass of the front

door. He couldn't quite make out the face, but he was certain he didn't know the caller, which was unusual. He'd worked in the building for five years and knew the names of most of the occupants' visitors. Grumbling, he crossed the mirrored lobby, sucking in his paunch as he caught sight of himself. Then, with chilled fingers, he unlocked the door. As he opened it he realized his mistake. Though a gust of icy wind made his eyes water, blurring the caller's features, he knew them well enough. How could he not recognize his own brother? He'd been about to call him and find out what was going on in Brooklyn when he'd heard the voice and the rapping on the door.

"What are you doing here, Fly?"

Fly smiled his missing-toothed smile. "Thought I'd just drop in," he said.

"You got some problem?"

"No, everything's fine," Fly said. Despite all the evidence of his senses, Freddy was uneasy. The shadow on the step, the wind in his eye, the very fact that Fly was here when he never came into the city on weekdays: it all added up to something he couldn't quite catch hold of.

"What you want?" he said. "You shouldn't be here."

"Here I am, anyway," Fly said, stepping past Freddy into the foyer. "I thought you'd be pleased to see me."

Freddy let the door swing closed, still wrestling with his thoughts. But they went from him the way they did in dreams. He couldn't string Fly's presence and his doubts together long enough to know what one had to do with the other.

"I think I'll take a look around," Fly was saying, heading towards the elevator.

"Wait up! You can't do that."

"What am I going to do? Set fire to the place?"

"I said *no*!" Freddy replied and, blurred vision notwithstanding, went after Fly, overtaking him to stand between his brother and the elevator. His motion dashed the tears from his eyes, and as he came to a halt he saw the visitor plainly. "You're not Fly!" he said.

He backed away towards the nook beside the elevator,

where he kept his gun, but the stranger was too quick. He reached for Freddy and, with what seemed no more than a flick of his wrist, pitched him across the foyer. Freddy let out a yell, but who was going to come and help? There was nobody to guard the guard. He was a dead man.

Across the street, sheltering as best he could from the blasts of wind down Park Avenue, Gentle—who'd returned to his station barely a minute before—caught sight of the doorman scrabbling on the foyer floor. He crossed the street, dodging the traffic, reaching the door in time to see a second figure stepping into the elevator. He slammed his fist on the door, yelling to stir the doorman from his stupor.

"Let me in! For God's sake, let me in!"

Two floors above, Jude heard what she took to be a domestic argument and, not wanting somebody else's marital strife to sour her fine mood, was crossing to turn up the soul song on the turntable when somebody knocked on the door.

"Who's there?" she said.

The summons came again, not accompanied by any reply. She turned the volume down instead of up and went to the door, which she'd dutifully bolted and chained. But the wine in her system made her incautious; she fumbled with the chain and was in the act of opening the door when doubt entered her head. Too late. The man on the other side took instant advantage. The door was slammed wide, and he came at her with the speed of the vehicle that should have killed him two nights before. There were only phantom traces of the lacerations that had made his face scarlet and no hint in his motion of any bodily harm. He had healed miraculously. Only the expression bore an echo of that night. It was as pained and as lost—even now, as he came to kill her—as it had been when they'd faced each other in the street. His hands reached for her, silencing her scream behind his palm.

"Please," he said.

If he was asking her to die quietly, he was out of luck.

She raised her glass to break it against his face but he intercepted her, snatching it from her hand.

"Judith!" he said.

She stopped struggling at the sound of her name, and his hand dropped from her face.

"How the fuck do you know who I am?"

"I don't want to hurt you," he said. His voice was downy, his breath orange-scented. The perversest desire came into her head, and she cast it out instantly. This man had tried to kill her, and this talk now was just an attempt to quiet her till he tried again.

"Get away from me."

"I have to tell you—"

He didn't step away, nor did he finish. She glimpsed a movement behind him, and he saw her look, turning his head in time to meet a blow. He stumbled but didn't fall, turning his motion to an attack with balletic ease and coming back at the other man with tremendous force.

It wasn't Freddy, she saw. It was Gentle, of all people. The assassin's blow threw him back against the wall, hitting it so hard he brought books tumbling from the shelves, but before the assassin's fingers found his throat he delivered a punch to the man's belly that must have touched some tender place, because the assault ceased, and the attacker let him go, his eyes fixing for the first time on Gentle's face.

The expression of pain in his face became something else entirely: in some part horror, in some part awe, but in the greatest part some sentiment for which she knew no word. Gasping for breath, Gentle registered little or none of this but pushed himself up from the wall to relaunch his attack. The assassin was quick, however. He was at the door and out through it before Gentle could lay hands on him. Gentle took a moment to ask if Judith was all right—which she was—then raced in pursuit.

The snow had come again, its veil dropping between Gentle and Pie. The assassin was fast, despite the hurt done him, but Gentle was determined not to let the bastard slip. He chased Pie across Park Avenue and west on 80th, his heels sliding on the sleet-slickened ground. Twice his quarry threw him backward glances, and on the second occasion seemed to slow his pace, as if he might stop and attempt a truce, but then thought better of it and put on an extra turn of speed. It carried him over Madison towards Central Park. If he reached its sanctuary, Gentle knew, he'd be gone. Throwing every last ounce of energy into the pursuit, Gentle came within snatching distance. But even as he reached for the man he lost his footing. He fell headlong, his arms flailing, and struck the street hard enough to lose consciousness for a few seconds. When he opened his eyes, the taste of blood sharp in his mouth, he expected to see the assassin disappearing into the shadows of the park, but the bizarre Mr. Pie was standing at the curb, looking back at him. He continued to watch as Gentle got up, his face betraying a mournful empathy with Gentle's bruising. Before the chase could begin again he spoke, his voice as soft and melting as the sleet.

"Don't follow me," he said.

"You leave her . . . the fuck . . . alone," Gentle gasped, knowing even as he spoke he had no way of enforcing this edict in his present state.

But the man's reply was affirmation. "I will," he said. "But please, I beg you . . . forget you ever set eyes on me."

As he spoke he began to take a backward step, and for an instant Gentle's dizzied brain almost thought it possible the man would retreat into nothingness: be proved spirit rather than substance.

"Who are you?" he found himself asking.

"Pie 'oh' pah," the man returned, his voice perfectly matched to the soft expellations of those syllables.

"But who?"

"Nobody and nothing," came the second reply, accompanied by a backward step.

He took another and another, each pace putting further layers of sleet between them. Gentle began to follow, but the fall had left him aching in every joint, and he knew the chase was lost before he'd hobbled three yards. He pushed himself on, however, reaching one side of Fifth Avenue as Pie 'oh' pah made the other. The street between them was empty, but the assassin spoke across it as if across a raging river.

"Go back," he said. "Or if you come, be prepared. . . ."

Absurd as it was, Gentle answered as if there were white waters between them. "Prepared for what?" he shouted.

The man shook his head, and even across the street, with the sleet between them, Gentle could see how much despair and confusion there was on his face. He wasn't certain why the expression made his stomach churn, but churn it did. He started to cross the street, plunging a foot into the imaginary flood. The expression on the assassin's face changed: despair gave way to disbelief, and disbelief to a kind of terror, as though this fording was unthinkable, unbearable. With Gentle halfway across the street the man's courage broke. The shaking of the head became a violent fit of denial, and he let out a strange sob, throwing back his head as he did so. Then he retreated, as he had before, stepping away from the object of his terror—Gentle—as though expecting to forfeit his visibility. If there was such magic in the world—and tonight Gentle could believe it—the assassin was not an adept. But his feet could do what magic could not. As Gentle reached the river's other bank Pie 'oh' pah turned and fled, throwing himself over the wall into the park without seeming to care what lay on the other side: anything to be out of Gentle's sight.

There was no purpose in following any further. The cold was already making Gentle's bruised bones ache fiercely, and in such a condition the two blocks back to Jude's apartment would be a long and painful trek. By the time he made it the sleet had soaked through every layer of his clothing. With his teeth chattering, his mouth bleeding, and his hair flattened to his skull he could not have looked less appealing as he presented himself at the front door. Jude was waiting in the lobby, with the shame-faced doorman. She came to Gentle's aid as soon as he appeared, the exchange between them short and functional: Was he badly hurt? No. Did the man get away? Yes.

"Come upstairs," she said. "You need some medical attention."

3

There had been too much drama in Jude and Gentle's reunion already tonight for them to add more to it, so there was no gushing forth of sentiment on either side. Jude attended to Gentle with her usual pragmatism. He declined a shower but bathed his face and wounded extremities, delicately sluicing the grit from the palms of his hands. Then he changed into a selection of dry clothes she'd found in Marlin's wardrobe, though Gentle was both taller and leaner than the absent lender. As he did so, Jude asked if he wanted to have a doctor examine him. He thanked her but said no, he'd be fine. And so he was, once dry and clean: aching, but fine.

"Did you call the police?" he asked, as he stood at the kitchen door watching her brew Darjeeling.

"It's not worth it," she said. "They already know about this guy from the last time. Maybe I'll get Marlin to call them later."

"This is his second try?" She nodded. "Well, if it's any comfort, I don't think he'll try again."

"What makes you say that?"

"Because he looked about ready to throw himself under a car."

"I don't think that'd do him much harm," she said, and went on to tell him about the incident in the Village, finishing up with the assassin's miraculous recovery.

"He should be dead," she said. "His face was smashed up . . . it was a wonder he could even stand. Do you want sugar or milk?"

"Maybe a dash of Scotch. Does Marlin drink?"

"He's not a connoisseur like you."

Gentle laughed. "Is that how you describe me? The alcoholic Gentle?"

"No. To tell the truth, I don't really describe you at all," she said, slightly abashed. "I mean I'm sure I've mentioned you to Marlin in passing, but you're . . . I don't know . . . you're a guilty secret."

This echo of Kite Hill brought his hirer to mind. "Have you spoken to Estabrook?" he said.

"Why should I do that?"

"He's been trying to contact you."

"I don't want to talk to him."

She put his tea down on the table in the living room, sought out the Scotch, and set it beside the cup.

"Help yourself," she said.

"You're not having a dram?"

"Tea, but no whisky. My brain's crazed enough as it is." She crossed back to the window, taking her tea. "There's so much I don't understand about all of this," she said. "To start with, why are you here?"

"I hate to sound melodramatic, but I really think you should sit down before we have this discussion."

"Just tell me what's going on," she said, her voice tainted with accusation. "How long have you been watching me?"

"Just a few hours."

"I thought I saw you following me a couple of days ago."

"Not me. I was in London until this morning."

She looked puzzled at this. "So what do you know about this man who's trying to kill me?"

"He said his name was Pie 'oh' pah."

"I don't give a fuck what his name is," she said, her show of detachment finally dropping away. "Who is he? Why does he want to hurt me?"

"Because he was hired."

"He was *what?*"

"He was hired. By Estabrook."

Tea slopped from her cup as a shudder passed through her. "To kill me?" she said. "He hired someone to kill me? I don't believe you. That's crazy."

"He's obsessed with you, Jude. It's his way of making sure you don't belong to anybody else."

She drew the cup up to her face, both hands clutched around it, the knuckles so white it was a wonder the china didn't crack like an egg. She sipped, her face obscured. Then, the same denial, but more flatly: "I don't believe you."

"He's been trying to speak to you to warn you. He hired this man, then changed his mind."

"How do you know all of this?" Again, the accusation.

"He sent me to stop it."

"Hired you too?"

It wasn't pleasant to hear it from her lips, but yes, he said, he was just another hireling. It was as though Estabrook had set two dogs on Judith's heels—one bringing death, the other life—and let fate decide which caught up with her first.

"Maybe I will have some booze," she said, and crossed to the table to pick up the bottle.

He stood to pour for her but his motion was enough to stop her in her tracks, and he realized she was afraid of him. He handed her the bottle at arm's length. She didn't take it.

"I think maybe you should go," she said. "Marlin'll be home soon. I don't want you here. . . ."

He understood her nervousness but felt ill treated by this change of tone. As he'd hobbled back through the sleet a tiny part of him had hoped her gratitude would include an embrace, or at least a few words that would let him know she felt something for him. But he was tarred with Estabrook's guilt. He wasn't her champion, he was her enemy's agent.

"If that's what you want," he said.

"It's what I want."

"Just one request? If you tell the police about Estabrook, will you keep me out of it?"

"Why? Are you back at the old business with Klein?"

"Let's not get into why. Just pretend you never saw me."

She shrugged. "I suppose I can do that."

"Thank you," he said. "Where did you put my clothes?"

"They won't be dry. Why don't you just keep the stuff you're wearing?"

"Better not," he said, unable to resist a tiny jab. "You never know what Marlin might think."

She didn't rise to the remark, but let him go and change. The clothes had been left on the heated towel rack in the bathroom, which had taken some of the chill off them, but insinuating himself into their dampness was almost enough to make him retract his jibe and wear the absent lover's clothes. Almost, but not quite. Changed, he returned to the living room to find her standing at the window again, as if watching for the assassin's return.

"What did you say his name was?" she said.

"Something like Pie 'oh' pah."

"What language is that? Arabic?"

"I don't know."

"Well, did you tell him Estabrook had changed his mind? Did you tell him to leave me alone?"

"I didn't get a chance," he said, lamely.

"So he could still come back and try again?"

"Like I said, I don't think he will."

"He's tried twice. Maybe he's out there thinking, Third time lucky. There's something . . . *unnatural* about him, Gentle. How the hell could he heal so fast?"

"Maybe he wasn't as badly hurt as he looked."

She didn't seem convinced. "A name like that . . . he shouldn't be difficult to trace."

"I don't know, I think men like him . . . they're almost invisible."

"Marlin'll know what to do."

"Good for Marlin."

She drew a deep breath. "I should thank you, though," she said, her tone as far from gratitude as it was possible to get.

"Don't bother," he replied. "I'm just a hired hand. I was only doing it for the money."

4

From the shadows of a doorway on 79th Street, Pie 'oh' pah watched John Furie Zacharias emerge from the apartment building, pull the collar of his jacket up around his bare nape, and scan the street north and south, looking for a cab. It was many years since the assassin's eyes had taken the pleasure they did now, seeing him. In the time between, the world had changed in so many ways. But this man looked unchanged. He was a constant, freed from alteration by his own forgetfulness; always new to himself, and therefore ageless. Pie envied him. For Gentle time was a vapor, dissolving hurt and self-knowledge. For Pie it was a sack into which each day, each hour, dropped another stone, bending the spine until it creaked. Nor, until tonight, had he dared entertain any hope of release. But here, walking away down Park Avenue, was a man in whose power it lay to make whole all broken things, even Pie's wounded spirit. Indeed, especially that. Whether it was chance or the covert workings of the Unbeheld that had brought them together this way, there was surely significance in their reunion.

Minutes before, terrified by the scale of what was unfolding, Pie had attempted to drive Gentle away and, having failed, had fled. Now such fear seemed stupid. What was there to be afraid of? Change? That would be welcome. Revelation? The same. Death? What did an assassin care for death? If it came, it came; it was no reason to turn from opportunity. He shuddered. It was cold here in the doorway; cold in the century too. Especially for a soul like his, that loved the melting season, when the rise of sap and sun made all things seem possible. Until now, he'd given up hope that such a burgeoning time would ever come again. He'd been obliged to commit too many crimes in this joyless world. He'd broken too many hearts. So had they both, most likely. But what if they were obliged to seek that elusive spring for the good of those they'd orphaned and an-

guished? What if it was their *duty* to hope? Then his denying of this near reunion, his fleeing from it, was just another
crime to be laid at his feet. Had these lonely years made
him a coward? Never.

Clearing his tears, he left the doorstep and pursued the
disappearing figure, daring to believe as he went that there
might yet be another spring, and a summer of reconcilia-
tions to follow.

8

WHEN HE GOT BACK TO THE HOTEL, Gentle's first instinct was
to call Jude. She'd made her feelings towards him abun-
dantly clear, of course, and common sense decreed that he
leave this little drama to fizzle out, but he'd glimpsed too
many enigmas tonight to be able to shrug off his unease
and walk away. Though the streets of this city were solid,
their buildings numbered and named, though the avenues
were bright enough even at night to banish ambiguity, he
still felt as though he was on the margin of some unknown
land, in danger of crossing into it without realizing he was
even doing so. And if *he* went, might Jude not also follow?
Determined though she was to divide her life from his, the
obscure suspicion remained in him that their fates were in-
terwoven.

He had no logical explanation for this. The feeling was a
mystery, and mysteries weren't his specialty. They were the
stuff of after-dinner conversation, when—mellowed by
brandy and candlelight—people confessed to fascinations
they wouldn't have broached an hour earlier. Under such
influence he'd heard rationalists confess their devotion to
tabloid astrologies; heard atheists lay claim to heavenly
visitations; heard tales of psychic siblings and prophetic
deathbed pronouncements. They'd all been amusing
enough, in their way. But this was something different. This
was happening to him, and it made him afraid.

He finally gave in to his unease. He located Marlin's
number and called the apartment. The lover boy picked up.

He sounded agitated and became more so when Gentle identified himself.

"I don't know what your goddamn game is," he said.

"It's no game," Gentle told him.

"You just keep away from this apartment—"

"I've no intention—"

"—because if I see your face, I swear—"

"Can I speak to Jude?"

"Judith's not—"

"I'm on the other line," Jude said.

"Judith, put down the phone! You don't want to be talking with this scum."

"Calm down, Marlin."

"You heard her, Mervin. Calm down."

Marlin slammed down the receiver.

"Suspicious, is he?" Gentle said.

"He thinks this is all your doing."

"So you told him about Estabrook?"

"No, not yet."

"You're just going to blame the hired hand, is that it?"

"Look, I'm sorry about some of the things I said. I wasn't thinking straight. If it hadn't been for you maybe I'd be dead by now."

"No maybe about it," Gentle said. "Our friend Pie meant business."

"He meant *something,*" she replied. "But I'm not sure it was murder."

"He was trying to smother you, Jude."

"Was he? Or was he just trying to hush me? He had such a strange look—"

"I think we should talk about this face to face," Gentle said. "Why don't you slip away from lover boy for a late-night drink? I can pick you up right outside your building. You'll be quite safe."

"I don't think that's such a good idea. I've got packing to do. I've decided to go back to London tomorrow."

"Was that planned?"

"No. I'd just feel more secure if I was at home."

"Is Mervin going with you?"

"It's Marlin. And no, he isn't."

"More fool him."

"Look, I'd better go. Thanks for thinking of me."

"It's no hardship," he said. "And if you get lonely between now and tomorrow morning—"

"I won't."

"You never know. I'm at the Omni. Room one-oh-three. There's a double bed."

"You'll have plenty of room, then."

"I'll be thinking of you," he said. He paused, then added, "I'm glad I saw you."

"I'm glad you're glad."

"Does that mean you're not?"

"It means I've got packing to do. Good night, Gentle."

"Good night."

"Have fun."

He did what little packing of his own he had to do, then ordered up a small supper: a club sandwich, ice cream, bourbon, and coffee. The warmth of the room after the icy street and its exertions made him feel sluggish. He undressed and ate his supper naked in front of the television, picking the crumbs from his pubic hair like lice. By the time he got to the ice cream he was too weary to eat, so he downed the bourbon—which instantly took its toll—and retired to bed, leaving the television on in the next room, its sound turned down to a soporific burble.

His body and his mind went about their different businesses. The former, freed from conscious instruction, breathed, rolled, sweated, and digested. The latter went dreaming. First, of Manhattan served on a plate, sculpted in perfect detail. Then of a waiter, speaking in a whisper, asking if sir wanted *night;* and of night coming in the form of a blueberry syrup, poured from high above the plate and falling in viscous folds upon the streets and towers. Then, Gentle walking in those streets, between those towers, hand in hand with a shadow, the company of which he was happy to keep, and which turned when they reached an intersection and laid its feather finger upon the middle of his brow, as though Ash Wednesday were dawning.

He liked the touch and opened his mouth to lightly lick the ball of the shadow's hand. It stroked the place again. He shuddered with pleasure, wishing he could see into the darkness of this other and know its face. In straining to see, he opened his eyes, body and mind converging once again. He was back in his hotel room, the only light the flicker of the television, reflected in the gloss of a half-open door. Though he was awake the sensation continued, and to it was added sound: a milky sigh that excited him. There was a woman in the room.

"Jude?" he said.

She pressed her cool palm against his open mouth, hushing his inquiry even as she answered it. He couldn't distinguish her from the darkness, but any lingering doubt that she might belong to the dream from which he'd risen was dispatched as her hand went from his mouth to his bare chest. He reached up in the darkness to take hold of her face and bring it down to his mouth, glad that the murk concealed the satisfaction he wore. She'd come to him. After all the signals of rejection she'd sent out at the apartment—despite Marlin, despite the dangerous streets, despite the hour, despite their bitter history—she'd come, bearing the gift of her body to his bed.

Though he couldn't see her, the darkness was a black canvas, and he painted her there to perfection, her beauty gazing down on him. His hands found her flawless cheeks. They were cooler than her hands, which were on his belly now, pressing harder as she hoisted herself over him. There was everywhere in their exchange an exquisite synchronicity. He thought of her tongue and tasted it; he imagined her breasts, and she took his hands to them; he wished she would speak, and she spoke (oh, how she spoke), words he hadn't dared admit he'd wanted to hear.

"I had to do this . . ." she said.

"I know. I know."

"Forgive me."

"What's to forgive?"

"I can't be without you, Gentle. We belong to each other, like man and wife."

With her here, so close after such an absence, the idea of marriage didn't seem so preposterous. Why not claim her now and forever?

"You want to marry me?" he murmured.

"Ask me again another night," she replied.

"I'm asking you now."

She put her hand back upon that anointing place in the middle of his brow. "Hush," she said. "What you want now you might not want tomorrow. . . ."

He opened his mouth to disagree, but the thought lost its way between his brain and his tongue, distracted by the small circular motions she was making on his forehead. A calm emanated from the place, moving down through his torso and out to his fingertips. With it, the pain of his bruising faded. He raised his hands above his head, stretching to let bliss run through him freely. Released from aches he'd become accustomed to, his body felt new minted: gleaming invisibly.

"I want to be inside you," he said.

"How far?"

"All the way."

He tried to divide the darkness and catch some glimpse of her response, but his sight was a poor explorer and returned from the unknown without news. Only a flicker from the television, reflected in the gloss of his eye and thrown up against the blank darkness, lent him the illusion of a luster passing through her body, opaline. He started to sit up, seeking her face, but she was already moving down the bed, and moments later he felt her lips on his stomach, and then upon the head of his cock, which she took into her mouth by degrees, her tongue playing on it as she went, until he thought he would lose control. He warned her with a murmur, was released and, a breath later, swallowed again.

The absence of sight lent potency to her touch. He felt every motion of tongue and tooth in play upon him, his prick, particularized by her appetite, becoming vast in his mind's eye until it was his body's size: a veiny torso and a blind head lying on the bed of his belly wet from end to end, straining and shuddering, while she, the darkness, swallowed him utterly. He was only sensation now, and she its supplier, his body enslaved by bliss, unable to remember its making or conceive of its undoing. God, but she knew how he liked to be pleasured, taking care not to stale his nerves with repetition, but cajoling his juice into cells already brimming, until he was ready to come in blood and be murdered by her work, willingly.

Another skitter of light behind his eye broke the hold of sensation, and he was once again entire—his prick its modest length—and she not darkness but a body through which waves of iridescence seemed to pass. Only *seemed*, he knew. This was his sight-starved eyes' invention. Yet it came again, a sinuous light, sleeking her, then going out. Invention or not it made him want her more completely, and he put his arms beneath her shoulders, lifting her up and off him. She rolled over to his side, and he reached across to undress her. Now that she was lying against white sheets her form was visible, albeit vaguely. She moved beneath his hand, raising her body to his touch.

"Inside you . . ." he said, rummaging through the damp folds of her clothes.

Her presence beside him had stilled; her breathing lost its irregularity. He bared her breasts, put his tongue to them as his hands went down to the belt of her skirt, to find that she'd changed for the trip and was wearing jeans. Her hands were on the belt, almost as if to deny him. But he wouldn't be delayed or denied. He pulled the jeans down around her hips, feeling skin so smooth beneath his hands it was almost fluid; her whole body a slow curve, like a wave about to break over him.

For the first time since she'd appeared she said his name, tentatively, as though in this darkness she'd suddenly doubted he was real.

"I'm here," he replied. "Always."

"This is what you want?" she said.

"Of course it is. Of course," he replied, and put his hand on her sex.

This time the iridescence, when it came, was almost bright, and fixed in his head the image of her crotch, his fingers sliding over and between her labia. As the light went, leaving its afterglow on his blind eyes, he was vaguely distracted by a ringing sound, far off at first but closer with every repetition. The telephone, damn it! He did his best to ignore it, failed, and reached out to the bedside table where it sat, throwing the receiver off its cradle and returning to her in one graceless motion. The body beneath him was once again perfectly still. He climbed on top of her and slid inside. It was like being sheathed in silk. She put her hands up around his neck, her fingers strong, and raised her head a little way off the bed to meet his kisses. Though their mouths were clamped together he could hear her saying his name—*"Gentle? Gentle?"*—with that same questioning tone she'd had before. He didn't let memory divert him from his present pleasure, but found his rhythm: long, slow strokes. He remembered her as a woman who liked him to take his time. At the height of their affair they'd made love from dusk to dawn on several occasions, toying and teasing, stopping to bathe so they'd have the bliss of working up a second sweat. But this was an encounter that had none of the froth of those liaisons. Her fingers were digging hard at his back, pulling him onto her with each thrust. And still he heard her voice, dimmed by the veils of his self-consumption: "Gentle? Are you there?"

"I'm here," he murmured.

A fresh tide of light was rising through them both, the erotic becoming a visionary toil as he watched it sweep over their skin, its brightness intensifying with every thrust.

Again she asked him, "Are you there?"

How could she doubt it? He was never more present than in this act, never more comprehending of himself than when buried in the other sex.

"I'm here," he said.

Yet she asked again, and this time, though his mind was stewed in bliss, the tiny voice of reason murmured that it wasn't his lady who was asking the question at all, but the woman on the telephone. He'd thrown the receiver off the hook, but she was haranguing the empty line, demanding he reply. Now he listened. There was no mistaking the voice. It was Jude. And if Jude was on the line, who the fuck was he fucking?

Whoever it was, she knew the deception was over. She dug deeper into the flesh of his lower back and buttocks, raising her hips to press him deeper into her still, her sex tightening around his cock as though to prevent him from leaving her unspent. But he was sufficiently master of himself to resist and pulled out of her, his heart thumping like some crazy locked up in the cell of his chest.

"Who the hell are you?" he yelled.

Her hands were still upon him. Their heat and their demand, which had so aroused him moments before, unnerved him now. He threw her off and started to reach towards the lamp on the bedside table. She took hold of his erection as he did so and slid her palm along the shaft. Her touch was so persuasive he almost succumbed to the idea of entering her again, taking her anonymity as carte blanche and indulging in the darkness every last desire he could dredge up. She was putting her mouth where her hand had been, sucking him into her. He regained in two heartbeats the hardness he'd lost.

Then the whine of the empty line reached his ears. Jude had given up trying to make contact. Perhaps she'd heard his panting and the promises he'd been making in the dark. The thought brought new rage. He took hold of the woman's head and pulled her from his lap. What could have possessed him to want somebody he couldn't even see? And what kind of whore offered herself that way? Diseased? Deformed? Psychotic? He had to see. However repulsive, he had to see!

He reached for the lamp a second time, feeling the bed shake as the harridan prepared to make her escape. Fumbling for the switch, he brought the lamp off its perch. It didn't smash, but its beams were cast up at the ceiling, throwing a gauzy light down on the room below. Suddenly fearful she'd attack him, he turned without picking the lamp up, only to find that the woman had already claimed her clothes from the snarl of sheets and was retreating to the bedroom door. His eyes had been feeding on darkness and projections for too long, and now, presented with solid reality, they were befuddled. Half concealed by shadow the woman was a mire of shifting forms—face blurred, body smeared, pulses of iridescence, slow now, passing from toes to head. The only fixable element in this flux was her eyes, which stared back at him mercilessly. He wiped his hand from brow to chin in the hope of sloughing the illusion off, and in these seconds she opened the door to make her escape. He leapt from the bed, still determined to get past his confusions to the grim truth he'd coupled with, but she was already halfway through the door, and the only way he could stop her was to seize hold of her arm.

Whatever power had deranged his senses, its bluff was called when he made contact with her. The roiling forms of her face resolved themselves like pieces of a multifaceted jigsaw, turning and turning as they found their place, concealing countless other configurations—rare, wretched, bestial, dazzling—behind the shell of a congruous reality. He knew the features, now that they'd come to rest. Here were the ringlets, framing a face of exquisite symmetry. Here were the scars that healed with such unnatural speed. Here were the lips that hours before had described their owner as nothing and nobody. It was a lie! This nothing had two functions at least: assassin and whore. This nobody had a name.

"Pie 'oh' pah!"

Gentle let go of the man's arm as though it were venomous. The form before him didn't redissolve, however, for which fact Gentle was only half glad. That hallucinatory chaos had been distressing, but the solid thing it had concealed appalled him more. Whatever sexual imaginings he'd shaped in the darkness—Judith's face, Judith's breasts, belly, sex—all of them had been an illusion. The creature he'd coupled with, almost shot his load into, didn't even share her sex.

He was neither a hypocrite nor a puritan. He loved sex too much to condemn any expression of lust, and though he'd discouraged the homosexual courtships he'd attracted, it was out of indifference, not revulsion. So the shock he felt now was fueled more by the power of the deceit worked upon him than by the sex of the deceiver.

"What have you done to me?" was all he could say. "What have you done?"

Pie 'oh' pah stood his ground, knowing perhaps that his nakedness was his best defense.

"I wanted to heal you," he said. Though it trembled, there was music in his voice.

"You put some drug in me."

"No!" Pie said.

"Don't give me *no*! I thought you were Judith! You let me think you were Judith!" He looked down at his hands, then up at the hard, lean body in front of him. "I felt *her*, not you." Again, the same complaint. "What have you done to me?"

"I gave you what you wanted," Pie said.

Gentle had no retort to this. In its way, it was the truth. Scowling, he sniffed his palms, thinking there might be traces of some drug in his sweat. But there was only the stench of sex on him, of the heat of the bed behind him.

"You'll sleep it off," Pie said.

"Get the fuck out of here," Gentle replied. "And if you go anywhere near Jude again, I swear . . . I *swear* . . . I'll take you apart."

"You're obsessed with her, aren't you?"

"None of your fucking business."

"It'll do you harm."

"Shut up."

"It will, I'm telling you."

"I told you," Gentle yelled, *"shut the fuck up!"*

"She doesn't belong to you," came the reply.

The words ignited new fury in Gentle. He reached for Pie and took him by the throat. The bundle of clothes dropped from the assassin's arm, leaving him naked. But he put up no defense; he simply raised his hands and laid them lightly on Gentle's shoulders. The gesture only infuriated Gentle further. He let out a stream of invective, but the placid face before him took both spittle and spleen without flinching. Gentle shook him, digging his thumbs into the man's throat to stop his windpipe. Still he neither resisted nor succumbed, but stood in front of his attacker like a saint awaiting martyrdom.

Finally, breathless with rage and exertion, Gentle let go his hold and threw Pie back, stepping away from the creature with a glimmer of superstition in his eyes. Why hadn't the fellow fought back or fallen? Anything but this sickening passivity.

"Get out," Gentle told him.

Pie still stood his ground, watching him with forgiving eyes.

"Will you get out?" Gentle said again, more softly, and this time the martyr replied.

"If you wish."

"I wish."

He watched Pie 'oh' pah stoop to pick up the scattered clothes. Tomorrow, this would all come clear in his head, he thought. He'd have shat this delirium out of his system, and these events—Jude, the chase, his near rape at the hands of the assassin—would be a tale to tell Klein and Clem and Taylor when he got back to London. They'd be entertained. Aware now that he was more naked than the other man, he turned to the bed and dragged a sheet off it to cover himself with.

There was a strange moment then, when he knew the bastard was still in the room, still watching him, and all he could do was wait for him to leave. Strange because it reminded him of other bedroom partings: sheets tangled, sweat cooling, confusion and self-reproach keeping glances at bay. He waited, and waited, and finally heard the door close. Even then he didn't turn, but listened to the room to be certain there was only one breath in it: his own. When he finally looked back and saw that Pie 'oh' pah had gone, he pulled the sheet up around him like a toga, concealing himself from the absence in the room, which stared back at him too much like a reflection for his peace of mind. Then he locked the suite door and stumbled back to bed, listening to his drugged head whine like the empty telephone line.

9

I

Oscar Esmond Godolphin always recited a little prayer in praise of democracy when, after one of his trips to the Dominions, he stepped back onto English soil. Extraordinary as those visits were—and as warmly welcomed as he found himself in the diverse Kesparates of Yzordderrex—the city-state was an autocracy of the most extreme kind, its excesses dwarfing the repressions of the country he'd been born in. Especially of late. Even his great friend and business partner in the Second Dominion, Hebbert Nuits-St.-Georges, called Peccable by those who knew him well, a merchant who had made substantial profit from the superstitious and the woebegone in the Second Dominion, regularly remarked that the order of Yzordderrex was growing less stable by the day and he would soon take his family out of the city, indeed out of the Dominion entirely, and find a new home where he would not have to smell burning bodies when he opened his windows in the morning. So far, it was only talk. Godolphin knew Peccable well enough to be certain that until he'd exhausted his supply of idols, relics, and jujus from the Fifth and could make no more profit, he'd stay put. And given that it was Godolphin himself who supplied these items—most were simply terrestrial trivia, revered in the Dominions because of their place of origin— and given that he would not cease to do so as long as the fever of collection was upon him and he could exchange such items for artifacts from the Imajica, Peccable's business would flourish. It was a trade in talismans, and neither man was likely to tire of it soon.

Nor did Godolphin tire of being an Englishman in that most un-English of cities. He was instantly recognizable in the small but influential circle he kept. A large man in every way, he was tall and big-bellied: bellicose when fondest, hearty when not. At fifty-two he had long ago found his style and was more than comfortable with it. True, he concealed his second and third chins beneath a gray-brown beard that only got an efficient trimming at the hands of Peccable's eldest daughter, Hoi-Polloi. True, he attempted to look a little more learned by wearing silver-rimmed spectacles that were dwarfed by his large face but were, he thought, all the more pedagoguish because they didn't flatter. But these were little deceits. They helped to make him unmistakable, which he liked. He wore his thinning hair short and his collars long, preferring for dress a clash of tweeds and a striped shirt; always a tie; invariably a waistcoat. All in all, a difficult sight to ignore, which suited him fine. Nothing was more likely to bring a smile to his face than being told he was talked about. It was usually with affection.

There was no smile on his face now, however, as he stepped out of the site of the Reconciliation—known euphemistically as the Retreat—to find Dowd sitting perched on a shooting stick a few yards from the door. It was early afternoon but the sun was already low in the sky, the air as chilly as Dowd's welcome. It was almost enough to make him turn around and go back to Yzordderrex, revolution or no.

"Why do I think you haven't come here with sparkling news?" he said.

Dowd rose with his usual theatricality. "I'm afraid you're absolutely correct," he said.

"Let me guess: the government fell! The house burned down." His face dropped. "Not my brother?" he said. "Not Charlie?" He tried to read Dowd's face. "What: dead? A massive coronary. When was the funeral?"

"No, he's alive. But the problem lies with him."

"Always has. Always has. Will you fetch my goods and

chattels out of the folly? We'll talk as we walk. Go on in, will you? There's nothing there that's going to bite."

Dowd had stayed out of the Retreat all the time he'd waited for Godolphin (a wearisome three days), even though it would have given him some measure of protection against the bitter cold. Not that his system was susceptible to such discomforts, but he fancied himself an empathic soul, and his time on Earth had taught him to feel cold as an intellectual concept, if not a physical one, and he might have wished to take shelter. Anywhere other than the Retreat. Not only had many esoterics died there (and he didn't enjoy the proximity of death unless he'd been its bringer), but the Retreat was a passing place between the Fifth Dominion and the other four, including, of course, the home from which he was in permanent exile. To be so close to the door through which his home lay, and be prevented by the conjurations of his first keeper, Joshua Godolphin, from opening that door, was painful. The cold was preferable.

He stepped inside now, however, having no choice in the matter. The Retreat had been built in neoclassical style: twelve marble pillars rising to support a dome that called for decoration but had none. The plainness of the whole lent it gravity and a certain functionalism which was not inappropriate. It was, after all, no more than a station, built to serve countless passengers and now used by only one. On the floor, set in the middle of the elaborate mosaic that appeared to be the building's sole concession to prettification but was in fact the evidence of its true purpose, were the bundles of artifacts Godolphin brought back from his travels, neatly tied up by Hoi-Polloi Nuits-St.-Georges, the knots encrusted with scarlet sealing wax. It was her present delight, this business with the wax, and Dowd cursed it, given that it fell to him to unpack these treasures. He crossed to the center of the mosaic, light on his heels. This was tremulous terrain, and he didn't trust it. But moments later he emerged with his freight, to find that Godolphin was already marching out of the copse that screened the

Retreat from both the house (empty, of course; in ruins) and any casual spy who peered over the wall. He took a deep breath and went after his master, knowing the explanation ahead would not be easy.

2

"So they've *summoned* me, have they?" Oscar said, as they drove back into London, the traffic thickening with the dusk. "Well, let them wait."

"You're not going to tell them you're here?"

"In my time, not in theirs. This is a mess, Dowdy. A wretched mess."

"You told me to help Estabrook if he needed it."

"Helping him hire an assassin isn't what I had in mind."

"Chant was very discreet."

"Death makes you that way, I find. You really have made a pig's ear of the whole thing."

"I protest," said Dowd. "What else was I supposed to do? You knew he wanted the woman dead, and you washed your hands of it."

"All true," said Godolphin. "She *is* dead, I assume?"

"I don't think so. I've been scouring the papers, and there's no mention."

"So why did you have Chant killed?"

Here Dowd was more cautious in his account. If he said too little, Godolphin would suspect him of concealment. Too much, and the larger picture might become apparent. The longer his employer stayed in ignorance of the scale of the stakes, the better. He proffered two explanations, both ready and waiting.

"For one thing, the man was more unreliable than I'd thought. Drunk and maudlin half the time. And I think he knew more than was good for either you or your brother. He might have ended up finding out about your travels."

"Instead it's the Society that's suspicious."

"It's unfortunate the way these things turn out."

"Unfortunate, my arse. A total balls-up is what it is."

"I'm very sorry."

"I know you are, Dowdy," Oscar said. "The point is, where do we find a scapegoat?"

"Your brother?"

"Perhaps," Godolphin replied, cannily concealing the degree to which this suggestion found favor.

"When should I tell them you've come back?" Dowd asked.

"When I've made up a lie I can believe in," came the reply.

Back in the house in Regent's Park Road, Oscar took some time to study the newspaper reports of Chant's death before retiring to his treasure house on the third floor with both his new artifacts and a good deal to think about. A sizable part of him wanted to exit this Dominion once and for all. Take himself off to Yzordderrex and set up business with Peccable; marry Hoi-Polloi despite her crossed eyes; have a litter of kids and retire to the Hills of the Conscious Cloud, in the Third, and raise parrots. But he knew he'd yearn for England sooner or later, and a yearning man could be cruel. He'd end up beating his wife, bullying his kids, and eating the parrots. So, given that he'd always have to keep a foot in England, if only during the cricket season, and given that as long as he kept a presence here he would be answerable to the Society, he had to face them.

He locked the door of his treasure room, sat down amid his collection, and waited for inspiration. The shelves around him, which were built to the ceiling, were bowed beneath the weight of his trove. Here were items gathered from the edge of the Second Dominion to the limits of the Fourth. He had only to pick one of them up to be transported back to the time and place of its acquisition. The statue of the Etook Ha'chiit, he'd bartered for in a little town called Slew, which was now, regrettably, a blasted spot, its citizens the victims of a purge visited upon them for the crime of a song, written in the dialect of their community, suggesting that the Autarch of Yzordderrex lacked testicles.

Another of his treasures, the seventh volume of Gaud

Maybellome's *Encyclopedia of Heavenly Signs,* originally written in the language of Third Dominion academics but widely translated for the delectation of the proletariat, he'd bought from a woman in the city of Jassick, who'd approached him in a gaming room, where he was attempting to explain cricket to a group of the locals, and said she recognized him from stories her husband (who was in the Autarch's army in Yzordderrex) had told.

"You're the English male," she'd said, which didn't seem worth denying.

Then she'd shown him the book: a very rare volume indeed. He'd never ceased to find fascination within its pages, for it was Maybellome's intention to make an encyclopedia listing all the flora, fauna, languages, sciences, ideas, moral perspectives—in short, anything that occurred to her—that had found their way from the Fifth Dominion, the Place of the Succulent Rock, through to the other worlds. It was a herculean task, and she'd died just as she was beginning the nineteenth volume, with no end in sight, but even the one book in Godolphin's possession was enough to guarantee that he would search for the others until his dying day. It was a bizarre, almost surreal volume. Even if only half the entries were true, or nearly true, Earth had influenced just about every aspect of the worlds from which it was divided. Fauna, for instance. There were countless animals listed in the volume which Maybellome claimed to be invaders from the other world. Some clearly were: the zebra, the crocodile, the dog. Others were a mixture of genetic strands, part terrestrial, part not. But many of these species (pictured in the book like fugitives from a medieval bestiary) were so outlandish he doubted their very existence. Here, for instance, were hand-sized wolves with the wings of canaries. Here was an elephant that lived in an enormous conch. Here was a literate worm that wrote omens with its thread-fine half-mile body. Wonderment upon wonderment. Godolphin only had to pick up the encyclopedia and he was ready to put on his boots and set off for the Dominions again.

What was self-evident from even a casual perusal of the

book was how extensively the unreconciled Dominion had influenced the others. The languages of earth—English, Italian, Hindustani, and Chinese particularly—were known in some variation everywhere, though it seemed the Autarch—who had come to power in the confusion following the failed Reconciliation—favored English, which was now the preferred linguistic currency almost everywhere. To name a child with an English word was thought particularly propitious, though there was little or no consideration given to what the word actually meant. Hence Hoi-Polloi, for instance; this one of the less strange namings among the thousands Godolphin had encountered.

He flattered himself that he was in some small part responsible for such blissful bizarrities, given that over the years he'd brought all manner of influences through from the Succulent Rock. There was always a hunger for newspapers and magazines (usually preferred to books), and he'd heard of baptizers in Patashoqua who named children by stabbing a copy of the London *Times* with a pin and bequeathing the first three words they pricked upon the infant, however unmusical the combination. But he was not the only influence. He hadn't brought the crocodile or the zebra or the dog (though he would lay claim to the parrot). No, there had always been routes through from Earth into the Dominions, other than that at the Retreat. Some, no doubt, had been opened by Maestros and esoterics, in all manner of cultures, for the express purpose of their passing to and fro between worlds. Others were conceivably opened by accident, and perhaps remained open, marking the sites as haunted or sacred, shunned or obsessively protected. Yet others, these in the smallest number, had been created by the sciences of the other Dominions, as a means of gaining access to the heaven of the Succulent Rock.

In such a place, this near the walls of the Iahmandhas in the Third Dominion, Godolphin had acquired his most sacred possession: a Boston Bowl, complete with its forty-one colored stones. Though he'd never used it, the bowl was reputedly the most accurate prophetic tool known in the worlds, and now—sitting amid his treasures, with a sense growing in him that events on earth in the last few days were leading to some matter of moment—he brought the bowl down from its place on the highest shelf, unwrapped it, and set it on the table. Then he took the stones from their pouch and laid them at the bottom of the bowl. Truth to tell, the arrangement didn't look particularly promising: the bowl resembled something for kitchen use, plain fired ceramic, large enough to whip eggs for a couple of soufflés. The stones were more colorful, varying in size and shape from tiny flat pebbles to perfect spheres the size of an eyeball.

Having set them out, Godolphin had second thoughts. Did he even believe in prophecy? And if he did, was it wise to know the future? Probably not. Death was bound to be in there somewhere, sooner or later. Only Maestros and deities lived forever, and a man might sour the balance of his span knowing when it was going to end. But then, suppose he found in this bowl some indication as to how the Society might be handled? That would be no small weight off his shoulders.

"Be brave," he told himself, and laid the middle finger of each hand upon the rim, as Peccable, who'd once owned such a bowl and had it smashed by his wife in a domestic row, had instructed.

Nothing happened at first, but Peccable had warned him the bowls usually took some time to start from cold. He waited and waited. The first sight of activation was a rattling from the bottom of the bowl as the stones began to move against each other; the second a distinctly acidic odor rising to jab at his sinuses; the third, and most startling, the sudden ricocheting of one pebble, then two, then a dozen, across the bowl and back, several skipping higher than the rim. Their ambition increased by the movement, until all forty-one were in violent motion, so violent that the bowl began to move across the table, and Oscar had to take a firm hold of it to keep it from turning over. The stones struck his fingers and knuckles with stinging force, but the pain was made sweeter by the success that now followed, as the speed and motion of the multifarious shapes and colors began to describe images in the air above the bowl.

Like all prophecy, the signs were in the eye of the beholder, and perhaps another witness would have seen different forms in the blur. But what Godolphin saw seemed quite plain to him. The Retreat, for one, half hidden in the copse. Then himself, standing in the middle of the mosaic, either coming back from Yzorddderrex or preparing to depart. The images lingered for only a brief time before changing, the Retreat demolished in the storm of stones and a new structure raised in the whirl: the tower of the Tabula Rasa. He fixed his eyes on the prophecy with fresh deliberation, denying himself the comfort of blinking to be certain he missed nothing. The tower as seen from the street gave way to its interior. Here they were, the wise ones, sitting around the table contemplating their divine duty. They were navel defluffers and snot rollers to a man. Not one of them would be capable of surviving an hour in the alleyways of East Yzorddderrex, he thought, down by the harbor where even the cats had pimps. Now he saw himself step into the picture, and something he was doing or saying made the men and women before him jump from their seats, even Lionel.

"What's this?" Oscar murmured.

They had wild expressions on their faces, every one. Were they laughing? What had he done? Cracked a joke? Passed wind? He studied the prophecy more closely. No, it wasn't humor on their faces. It was horror.

"Sir?"

Dowd's voice from outside the door broke his concentration. He looked away from the bowl for a few seconds to snap, "Go away."

But Dowd had urgent news. "McGann's on the telephone," he said.

"Tell him you don't know where I am." Oscar snorted, returning his gaze to the bowl. Something terrible had happened in the time between his looking away and looking back. The horror remained on their faces, but for some reason he'd disappeared from the scene. Had they dispatched

him summarily? God, was he dead on the floor? Maybe.
There was something glistening on the table, like spilled
blood.

"Sir!"

"Fuck off, Dowdy."

"They know you're here, sir."

They knew; *they knew.* The house was being watched,
and they knew.

"All right," he said. "Tell him I'll be down in a moment."

"What did you say, sir?"

Oscar raised his voice over the din of the stones, looking
away again, this time more willingly. "Get his whereabouts.
I'll call him back."

Again, he returned his gaze to the bowl, but his concentration had faltered, and he could no longer interpret the
images concealed in the motion of the stones. Except for
one. As the speed of the display slowed he seemed to
catch—oh, so fleetingly—a woman's face in the mêlée. His
replacement at the Society's table, perhaps; or his dispatcher.

3

He needed a drink before he spoke to McGann. Dowd,
ever the anticipator, had already mixed him a whisky and
soda, but he forsook it for fear it would loosen his tongue.
Paradoxically, what had been half revealed by the Boston
Bowl helped him in his exchange. In extreme circumstances he responded with almost pathological detachment; it was one of his most English traits. He had thus
seldom been cooler or more controlled than now, as he told
McGann that yes, indeed, he had been traveling, and no, it
was none of the Society's business where or about what
pursuit. He would of course be delighted to attend a gathering at the tower the following day, but was McGann
aware (indeed did he care?) that tomorrow was Christmas
Eve?

"I never miss Midnight Mass at St. Martin-in-the-

Fields," Oscar told him, "so I'd appreciate it greatly if the meeting could be concluded quickly enough to allow me time to get there and find a pew with a good view."

He delivered all of this without a tremor in the voice. McGann attempted to press him as to his whereabouts in the last few days, to which Oscar asked why the hell it mattered.

"I don't ask about your private affairs, now, do I?" he said, in a mildly affronted tone. "Nor, by the way, do I spy on your comings and goings. Don't splutter, McGann. You don't trust me and I don't trust you. I will take tomorrow's meeting as a forum to debate the privacy of the Society's members and a chance to remind the gathering that the name of Godolphin is one of the cornerstones of the Society."

"All the more reason for you to be forthright," McGann said.

"I'll be perfectly forthright," was Oscar's reply. "You'll have ample evidence of my innocence." Only now, with the war of wits won, did he accept the whisky and soda Dowd had mixed for him. "Ample and definitive." He silently toasted Dowd as he talked, knowing as he sipped it that there'd be blood shed before Christmas Day dawned. Grim as that prospect was, there was no avoiding it now.

When he put the phone down he said to Dowd, "I think I'll wear the herringbone suit tomorrow. And a plain shirt. White. Starched collar."

"And the tie?" Dowd asked, replacing Oscar's drained glass with a fresh one.

"I'll be going straight on to Midnight Mass," Oscar said.

"Black, then."

"Black."

10

I

The afternoon of the day following the assassin's appearance at Marlin's apartment a blizzard descended upon New York with no little ferocity, conspiring with the inevitable seasonal rush to make finding a flight back to England difficult. But Jude was not easily denied anything, especially when she'd set her mind firmly on an objective; and she was certain—despite Marlin's protestations—that leaving Manhattan was the most sensible thing to do.

She had reason on her side. The assassin had made two attempts upon her life. He was still at large. As long as she stayed in New York she would be under threat. But even if this had not been the case (and there was a part of her that still believed that he'd come that second time to explain, or apologize), she would have found an excuse for returning to England, just to be out of Marlin's company. He had become too cloying in his affections, his talk as saccharine as the dialogue from the Christmas classics on the television, his every gaze mawkish. He'd had this sickness all along, of course, but he'd worsened since the assassin's visit, and her tolerance for its symptoms, braced as she'd been by her encounter with Gentle, had dropped to zero. Once she'd put the phone down on him the previous night she'd regretted her skittish way with him, and after a heart-to-heart with Marlin in which she'd told him she wanted to go back to England, and he'd replied that it would all seem different in the morning and why didn't she just take a pill and lie down, she'd decided to call him back. By this time, Marlin was sound asleep. She'd left her bed, gone through to the living room, put on a single lamp, and made the call. It felt covert, which in a way it was. Marlin had not been pleased to know that one of her ex-lovers had attempted to play hero in his own apartment, and he wouldn't have been happy to find her making contact with Gentle at two in the morning. She still didn't know what had happened when she'd been put through to the room. The receiver had been picked up and then dropped, leaving her to listen with increasing fury and frustration to the sound of Gentle making love. Instead of putting the phone down there and then she'd listened, half wishing she could have joined the escapade. Eventually, after failing to distract Gentle from his labors, she'd hung up and traipsed back to her cold bed in a foul humor.

He'd called the next day, and Marlin had answered. She let him tell Gentle that if he ever saw hide or hair of Gentle in the building again he'd have him arrested as an accomplice to attempted murder.

"What did he say?" she'd asked when the conversation was done.

"Not very much. He sounded drunk."

She had not discussed the matter any further. Marlin was already sullen enough, after her breakfast announcement that she still intended to return to England that day. He'd asked her over and over: why? Was there something he could do to make her stay more comfortable? Extra locks on the doors? A promise that he wouldn't leave her side? None of these, of course, filling her with renewed enthusiasm for staying. If she told him once she told him two dozen times that he was quite the perfect host, and that he wasn't to take this personally, but she wanted to be back in her own house, her own city, where she would feel most protected from the assassin. He'd then offered to come back with her, so she wasn't returning to an empty house alone, at which point—running out of soothing phrases and patience—she'd told him that alone was exactly what she wanted to be.

And so here she was, one snail crawl through the blizzard to Kennedy, a five-hour delay, and a flight in which she was wedged between a nun who prayed aloud every time they hit an air pocket and a child in need of worming, later. Her own sole possessor, in an empty flat on Christmas Eve.

2

The painting in four contrary modes was there to greet Gentle when he got back to the studio. His return had been delayed by the same blizzard that had almost prevented Judith from leaving Manhattan, and put him beyond the deadline Klein had set. But his thoughts had not turned to his business dealings with Klein more than once during the journey. They'd revolved almost entirely around the encounter with the assassin. Whatever mischief Pie 'oh' pah had worked upon his system it had cleared by the following morning—his eyes were operating normally, and he was lucid enough to deal with the practicalities of departure—but the echoes of what he'd experienced still reverberated. Dozing on the plane he felt the smoothness of the assassin's face in his fingertips, the tumble of hair he'd taken to be Jude's over the back of his hands. He could still smell the scent of wet skin and feel the weight of Pie 'oh' pah's body on his hips, this so persuasive he had an erection apparent enough to draw a stare from one of the flight attendants. He reasoned that perhaps he would have to put fresh sensation between these echoes and their origins: fuck them out, sweat himself clean. The thought comforted him. When he dozed again, and the memories returned, he didn't fight them, knowing he had a means of scouring them from his system once he got back to England.

Now he sat in front of the painting in four modes and flipped through his address book looking for a partner for the night. He made a few calls but couldn't have chosen a worse time to be setting up a casual liaison. Husbands were home; family gatherings were in the offing. He was out of season.

He did eventually speak to Klein, who after some persuasion accepted his apologies and then went on to tell him there was to be a party at Taylor and Clem's house the following day, and he was sure Gentle would be welcome if he had no other plans.

"Everyone says it'll be Taylor's last," Chester said. "I know he'd like to see you."

"I suppose I should go, then," Gentle said.

"You should. He's very sick. He's had pneumonia, and now cancer. He was always very fond of you, you know."

The association of ideas made fondness for Gentle sound like another disease, but he didn't comment on it, merely made arrangements to pick up Klein the following evening; and put down the phone, plunged into a deeper trough than ever. He'd known Taylor had the plague but hadn't realized people were counting the days to his demise. Such grim times. Everywhere he looked things were coming apart. There seemed to be only darkness ahead, full of blurred shapes and pitiful glances. The Age of Pie 'oh' pah, perhaps. The time of the assassin.

He didn't sleep, despite being tired, but sat up into the small hours with an object of study that he'd previously dismissed as fanciful nonsense: Chant's final letter. When he'd first read it, on the plane to New York, it had seemed a ludicrous outpouring. But there had been strange times since then, and they'd put Gentle in an apter mood for this study. Pages that had seemed worthless a few days before were now pored over, in the hope they'd yield some clue, encoded in the fanciful excesses of Chant's idiosyncratic and ill-punctuated prose, that would lead him to some fresh comprehension of the times and their movers. Whose god, for instance, was this Hapexamendios that Chant exhorted Estabrook to pray to and praise? He came trailing synonyms: the Unbeheld, the Aboriginal, the Wanderer. And what was the greater plan that Chant hoped in his final hours he was a part of?

I AM ready for death in this DOMINION, he'd written, *if I know that the Unbeheld has used me as His INSTRUMENT. All praise to HAPEXAMENDIOS. For He was in the Place of the Succulent Rock and left His children to SUFFER here, and I have suffered here and AM DONE with suffering.*

That at least was true. The man had known his death

was imminent, which suggested he'd known his murderer too. Was it Pie 'oh' pah he'd been expecting? It seemed not. The assassin was referred to, but not as Chant's executioner. Indeed, in his first reading of the letter Gentle hadn't even realized it was Pie 'oh' pah who was being spoken of in this passage. But on this rereading it was completely apparent.

You have made a covenant with a RARE thing in this DOMINION or any other, and I do not know if this death nearly upon me is my punishment or my reward for my agency in that. But be circumspect in all your dealings with it, for such power is capricious, being a stew of kinds and possibilities, no UTTER thing, in any part of its nature, but pavonine and prismatic, an apostate to its core.

I was never the friend of this power—it has only ADORERS AND UNDOERS—but it trusted me as its representative and I have done it as much harm in these dealings as I have you. More, I think; for it is a lonely thing, and suffers in this DOMINION as I have. You have friends who know you for the man you are and do not have to conceal your TRUE NATURE. Cling to them, and their love for you, for the Place of the Succulent Rock is about to shake and tremble, and in such a time all a soul has is the company of its loving like. I say this having lived in such a time, and am GLAD that if such is coming upon the FIFTH DOMINION again, I will be dead, and my face turned to the glory of the UNBEHELD.

All praise to HAPEXAMENDIOS.

And to you sir, in this moment, I offer my contrition and my prayers.

There was a little more, but both handwriting and the sentence structure deteriorated rapidly thereafter, as though Chant had panicked and scrawled the rest while putting on his coat. The more coherent passages contained enough hints to keep Gentle from sleep, however. The descriptions of Pie 'oh' pah were particularly alarming:

"a RARE thing . . . a stew of kinds and possibilities."

How was that to be interpreted, except as a verification of what Gentle's senses had glimpsed in New York?

If so, what was this creature that had stood before him, naked and singular, but concealed multitudes; this power Chant had said possessed no friends (*it has only ADOR-ERS and UNDOERS,* he'd written) and had been done as much harm in these dealings (again, Chant's words) as Estabrook, to whom Chant had offered his contrition and his prayers? Not human, for certain. Not born of any tribe or nation Gentle was familiar with. He read the letter over and over again, and with each rereading the possibility of belief crept closer. He felt its proximity. It was fresh from the margins of that land he'd first suspected in New York. The thought of being there had made him fearful then. But it no longer did, perhaps because it was Christmas morning, and time for something miraculous to appear and change the world.

The closer they crept—both morning and belief—the more he regretted shunning the assassin when it had so plainly wanted his company. He had no clues to its mystery but those contained in Chant's letter, and after a hundred readings they were exhausted. He wanted more. The only other source was his memory of the creature's jigsaw face, and, knowing his propensity for forgetting, they'd start to fade all too soon. He had to set them down! That was the priority now: to set the vision down before it slipped away!

He threw the letter aside and went to stare at his *Supper at Emmaus.* Was any of those styles capable of capturing what he'd seen? He doubted it. He'd have to invent a new mode. Fired up by that ambition, he turned the *Supper* on end and began to squeeze burnt umber directly onto the canvas, spreading it with a palette knife until the scene beneath was completely obscured. In its place was now a dark ground, into which he started to gouge the outline of a figure. He had never studied anatomy very closely. The male body was of little aesthetic interest to him, and the female was so mutable, so much a function of its own motion, or that of light across it, that all static representation seemed to him doomed from the outset. But he wanted to represent a protean form now, however impossible; wanted to find a way to fix what he'd seen at the door of his hotel room, when Pie 'oh' pah's many faces had been shuffled in front of him like cards in an illusionist's deck. If he could fix that sight, or even begin to do so, he might yet find a way of controlling the thing that had come to haunt him.

He worked in a fair frenzy for two hours, making demands of the paint he'd never made before, plastering it on with palette knife and fingers, attempting to capture at least the shape and proportion of the thing's head and neck. He could see the image clearly enough in his mind's eye (since that night no two rememberings had been more than a minute apart), but even the most basic sketch eluded his hand. He was badly equipped for the task. He'd been a parasite for too long, a mere copier, echoing other men's visions. Now he finally had one of his own—only one, but all the more precious for that—and he simply couldn't set it down. He wanted to weep at this final defeat, but he was too tired. With his hands still covered in paint, he lay down on the chilly sheets and waited for sleep to take his confusions away.

Two thoughts visited him as he slipped into dreams. The first, that with so much burnt umber on his hands he looked as though he'd been playing with his own shit. The second, that the only way to solve the problem on the canvas was to see its subject again in the flesh, which thought he welcomed, and went to dreams relieved of his frauds and pieties, smiling to think of having the rare thing's face before him once again.

THOUGH THE JOURNEY FROM Godolphin's house in Primrose Hill to the Tabula Rasa's tower was short, and Dowd got him up to Highgate on the dot of six, Oscar suggested they drive down through Crouch End, then up through Muswell Hill, and back to the tower, so that they'd arrive ten minutes late.

"We mustn't seem to be too eager to prostrate ourselves," he observed as they approached the tower for a second time. "It'll only make them arrogant."

"Shall I wait down here?"

"Cold and lonely? My dear Dowdy, out of the question. We'll ascend together, bearing gifts."

"What gifts?"

"Our wit, our taste in suits—well, *my* taste—in essence, ourselves."

They got out of the car and went to the porch, their every step monitored by cameras mounted above the door. The lock clicked as they approached, and they stepped inside. As they crossed the foyer to the lift, Godolphin whispered, "Whatever happens tonight, Dowdy, please remember—"

He got no further. The lift doors opened, and Bloxham appeared, as preening as ever.

"Pretty tie," Oscar said to him. "Yellow's your color." The tie was blue. "Don't mind my man Dowd here, will you? I never go anywhere without him."

"He's got no place here tonight," Bloxham said.

Again, Dowd offered to wait below, but Oscar would have none of it. "Heaven forfend," he said. "You can wait upstairs. Enjoy the view."

All this irritated Bloxham mightily, but Oscar was not an easy man to deny. They ascended in silence. Once on the top floor Dowd was left to entertain himself, and Bloxham led Godolphin through to the chamber. They were all waiting, and there was accusation on every face. A few—

Shales, certainly, and Charlotte Feaver—didn't attempt to disguise their pleasure that the Society's most ebullient and unrepentant member was here finally called to heel.

"Oh, I'm sorry," Oscar said, as they closed the doors behind him. "Have you been waiting long?"

Outside, in one of the deserted antechambers, Dowd listened to his tinny little radio and mused. At seven the news bulletin brought a report of a motorway collision which had claimed the lives of an entire family traveling north for Christmas, and of prison riots that had ignited in Bristol and Manchester, with inmates claiming that presents from loved ones had been tampered with and destroyed by prison officers. There was the usual collection of war updates, then the weather report, which promised a gray Christmas, accompanied by a springlike balm. This would on past experience coax the crocuses out in Hyde Park, only to be spiked by frost in a few days' time. At eight, still waiting by the window, he heard a second bulletin correcting one of the reports from the first. A survivor had been claimed from the entangled vehicles on the motorway: a tot of three months, found orphaned but unscathed in the wreckage. Sitting in the cold gloom, Dowd began to weep quietly, which was an experience as far beyond his true emotional capacity as cold was beyond his nerve endings. But he'd trained himself in the craft of grief with the same commitment to feigning humanity as he had learning to shiver: his tutor, the Bard; *Lear* his favorite lesson. He cried for the child, and for the crocuses, and was still moist-eyed when he heard the voices in the chamber suddenly rise up in rage. The door was flung open, and Oscar called him in, despite shouts of complaint from some of the other members.

"This is an outrage, Godolphin!" Bloxham yelped.

"You drive me to it!" was Oscar's reply, his performance at fever pitch. Clearly he'd been having a bad time of it. The sinews in his neck stood out like knotted string; sweat gleamed in the pouches beneath his eyes; every word brought flecks of spittle. "You don't know the half of it!"

he was saying. "Not the half. We're being conspired against, by forces we can barely conceive of. This man Chant was undoubtedly one of their agents. They can take human form!"

"Godolphin, this is absurd," Alice Tyrwhitt said.

"You don't believe me?"

"No, I don't. And I certainly don't want your bum-boy here listening to us debate. Will you please remove him from the chamber?"

"But he has evidence to support my thesis," Oscar insisted.

"Oh, does he?" said Shales.

"He'll have to show you himself," Oscar said, turning to Dowd. "You're going to have to show them, I'm afraid," he said, and as he spoke reached into his jacket.

An instant before the blade emerged, Dowd realized Godolphin's intent and started to turn away, but Oscar had the edge, and it came forth glittering. Dowd felt his master's hand on his neck and heard shouts of horror on all sides. Then he was thrown back across the table, sprawling beneath the lights like an unwilling patient. The surgeon followed through with one swift stab, striking Dowd in the middle of his chest.

"You want proof?" Oscar yelled, through Dowd's screams and the din of shouts around the table. "You want proof? Then here it is!"

His bulk put weight behind the blade, driving it first to the right, then to the left, encountering no obstruction from rib or breastbone. Nor was there blood; only a fluid the color of brackish water, that dribbled from the wounds and ran across the table. Dowd's head thrashed to and fro as this indignity was visited upon him, only once raising his gaze to stare accusingly at Godolphin, who was too busy about this undoing to return the look. Despite protests from all sides he didn't halt his labors until the body before him had been opened from the navel to throat, and Dowd's thrashings had ceased. The stench from the carcass filled the chamber: a pungent mixture of sewage and vanilla. It drove two of the witnesses to the door, one of them Bloxham, whose nausea overtook him before he could reach the corridor. But his gaggings and moans didn't slow Godolphin by a beat. Without hesitation he plunged his arm into the open body and, rummaging there, pulled out a fistful of gut. It was a knotty mass of blue and black tissue—final proof of Dowd's inhumanity. Triumphant, he threw the evidence down on the table beside the body, then stepped away from his handiwork, chucking the knife into the wound it had opened. The whole performance had taken no more than a minute, but in that time he'd succeeded in turning the chamber's table into a fish-market gutter.

"Satisfied?" he said.

All protest had been silenced. The only sound was the rhythmical hiss of fluid escaping an opened artery.

Very quietly McGann said, "You're a fucking maniac."

Oscar reached gingerly into his trouser pocket and teased out a fresh handkerchief. One of poor Dowd's last tasks had been its pressing. It was immaculate. He shook out its scalpel creases and began to clean his hands.

"How else was I going to prove my point?" he said. "You drove me to this. Now there's the evidence, in all its glory. I don't know what happened to Dowd—my bumboy, I think you called him, Alice—but wherever he is this *thing* took his place."

"How long have you known?" Charlotte asked.

"I've suspected for the last two weeks. I was here in the city all the time, watching its every move while it—and you—thought I was disporting myself in sunnier climes."

"What the bugger is it?" Lionel wanted to know, prodding a scrap of alien entrail with his finger.

"God alone knows," Godolphin said. "Something not of this world, clearly."

"What did it want?" Alice said. "That's more to the point."

"At a guess, access to this chamber, which"—he looked at those around the table one by one—"I gather you granted it three days ago. I trust none of you was indiscreet." Furtive glances were exchanged. "Oh, you were," he said. "That's a pity. Let's hope it didn't have time to communicate any of its findings to its overlords."

"What's done's done," McGann said, "and we must all bear some part of the responsibility. Including you, Oscar. You should have shared your suspicions with us."

"Would you have believed me?" Oscar replied. "I didn't believe it myself at first, until I started to notice little changes in Dowd."

"Why you?" Shales said. "That's what I want to know. Why would they target you for this surveillance unless they thought you were more susceptible than the rest of us? Maybe they thought you'd join them. Maybe you *have.*"

"As usual, Hubert, you're too self-righteous to see your own frailties," Godolphin replied. "How do you know I *am* the only one they targeted? Could you swear to me every one of your circle is above suspicion? How closely do you watch your friends? Your family? Any one of them might be a part of this conspiracy."

It gave Oscar a perverse joy to sow these doubts. He saw them taking root already, saw faces that half an hour before had been puffed up with their own infallibility deflated by doubt. It was worth the risk he'd taken with these theatrics, just to see them afraid. But Shales wouldn't leave this bone alone.

"The fact remains this thing was in your employ," he said.

"We've heard enough, Hubert," McGann said softly. "This is no time for divisive talk. We've got a fight on our hands, and whether we agree with Oscar's methods or not—and just for the record, I don't—surely none of us can doubt his integrity." He glanced around the table. There were murmurs of accord on all sides. "God knows what a creature like this might have been capable of had it realized its ruse had been discovered. Godolphin took a very considerable risk on our behalf."

"I agree," Lionel said. He'd come around to Oscar's side of the table and placed a glass of neat malt whisky in the executioner's freshly wiped fingers. "Good man, I say," he remarked. "I'd have done the same. Drink up."

Oscar accepted the glass. *"Salut,"* he said, downing the whisky in one.

"I see nothing to celebrate," said Charlotte Feaver, the first to sit down at the table despite what lay upon it. She lit a fresh cigarette, expelling the smoke through pursed lips. "Assuming Godolphin's right, and this thing *was* attempting to get access to the Society, we have to ask *why*."

"Ask away," Shales said dryly, indicating the corpse. "He's not going to be telling us very much. Which is no doubt convenient for some."

"How much longer do I have to endure this innuendo?" Oscar demanded.

"I said we've heard enough, Hubert," McGann remarked.

"This is a democratic gathering," Shales said, rising to challenge McGann's unspoken authority. "If I've got something to say—"

"You've already said it," Lionel remarked with well-lubricated vim. "Now why don't you just shut up?"

"The point is, what do we do now?" Bloxham said. He'd returned to the table, his chin wiped, and was determined to reassert himself following his unmanly display. "This is a dangerous time."

"That's why they're here," said Alice. "They know the anniversary's coming up, and they want to start the whole damn Reconciliation over again."

"Why try and penetrate the Society?" Bloxham said.

"To put a spoke in our wheels," Lionel said. "If they know what we're planning, they can outmaneuver us. By the way, was the tie furiously expensive?"

Bloxham looked down to see that his silk tie was comprehensively spattered with puke. Casting a rancorous look in Lionel's direction, he tore it from his neck.

"I don't see what they could find out from us anyway," said Charlotte Feaver, in her distracted manner. "We don't even know what the Reconciliation is."

"Yes, we do," Shales said. "Our ancestors were trying to put Earth into the same orbit as Heaven."

"Very poetic," Charlotte remarked. "But what does

that *mean,* in concrete terms? Does anybody know?" There was silence. "I thought not. Here we are, sworn to prevent something we don't even understand."

"It was an experiment of some kind," Bloxham said. "And it failed."

"Were they all insane?" Alice said.

"Let's hope not," Lionel put in. "Insanity usually runs in the family."

"Well, I'm not crazy," Alice said. "And I'm damn sure my friends are as sane and normal and human as I am. If they were anything else, I'd know it."

"Godolphin," McGann said, "you've been uncharacteristically quiet."

"I'm soaking up the wisdom," Oscar replied.

"Have you reached any conclusions?"

"Things go in cycles," he said, taking his time to reply. He was as certain of his audience as any man could ever hope to be. "We're coming to the end of the millennium. Reason'll be supplanted by unreason. Detachment by sentiment. I think if I were a fledgling esoteric with a nose for history, it wouldn't be difficult to turn up details of what was attempted—the experiment, as Bloxham called it— and maybe get it into my head that the time was right to try again."

"Very plausible," said McGann.

"Where would such an adept get the information?" Shales inquired.

"Self-taught."

"From what source? We've got every tome of any value buried in the ground beneath us."

"*Every* one?" said Godolphin. "How can we be so sure?"

"Because there hasn't been a significant act of magic performed on earth in two centuries," was Shales' reply. "The esoterics are powerless; lost. If there'd been the least sign of magical activity we'd know about it."

"We didn't know about Godolphin's little friend," Charlotte pointed out, denying Oscar the pleasure of that irony dropping from his own lips.

"Are we even sure the library's intact?" Charlotte went on. "How do we know books haven't been stolen?"

"Who by?" said Bloxham.

"By Dowd, for one. They've never been properly catalogued. I know that Leash woman attempted it, but we all know what happened to her."

The tale of the Leash woman, who had been a member of the Society, was one of its lesser shames: a catalogue of accidents that had ended in tragedy. In essence, the obsessive Clara Leash had taken it upon herself to make a full account of the volumes in the Society's possession and had suffered a stroke while doing so. She'd lain for three days on the cellar floor. By the time she was discovered, she was barely alive and quite without her wits. She survived, however, and eleven years later was still a resident in a hospice in Sussex, witless as ever.

"It still shouldn't be that difficult to find out if the place has been tampered with," Charlotte said.

Bloxham agreed. "That should be looked into," he said.

"I take it you're volunteering," said McGann.

"And if they didn't get their information from downstairs," Charlotte said, "there are other sources. We don't believe we have every last book dealing with the Imajica in our hands, do we?"

"No, of course not," said McGann. "But the Society's broken the back of the tradition over the years. The cults in this country aren't worth a damn, we all know that. They cobble workings together from whatever they can scrape up. It's all piecemeal. Senseless. None of them have the wherewithal to conceive of a Reconciliation. Most of them don't even know what the Imajica is. They're putting hexes on their bosses at the bank."

Godolphin had heard similar speeches for years. Talk of magic in the Western World as a spent force: self-congratulatory accounts of cults that had been infiltrated and discovered to be groups of pseudo-scientists exchanging arcane theories in a language no two of them agreed upon; or sexual obsessives using the excuse of workings to demand favors they couldn't seduce from their partners; or, most often, crazies in search of some mythology, however ludicrous, to keep them from complete psychosis. But among the fakes, obsessives, and lunatics was there perhaps a man who *instinctively* knew the route to the Imajica? A natural Maestro, born with something in his genes that made him capable of reinventing the workings of the Reconciliation? Until now the possibility hadn't occurred to Godolphin— he'd been too preoccupied by the secret that he'd lived with most of his adult life—but it was an intriguing, and disturbing, thought.

"I believe we should take the risk seriously," he pronounced. "However unlikely we think it is."

"What risk?" McGann said.

"That there *is* a Maestro out there. Somebody who understands our forefathers' ambition and is going to find his own way of repeating the experiment. Maybe he doesn't want the books. Maybe he doesn't *need* the books. Maybe he's sitting at home somewhere, even now, working out the problems for himself."

"So what do we do?" said Charlotte.

"We purge," said Shales. "It pains me to say it, but Godolphin's right. We don't know what's going on out there. We've kept an eye on things from a distance, and occasionally arranged to have somebody put under permanent sedation, but we haven't purged. I think we've got to begin."

"How do we go about that?" Bloxham wanted to know. He had a zealot's gleam in his dishwater eyes.

"We've got our allies. We use them. We turn over every stone, and if we find anything we don't like, we kill it."

"We're not an assassination squad."

"We have the finance to hire one," Shales pointed out. "And the friends to cover the evidence if need be. As I see it, we have one responsibility: to prevent, at all costs, another attempt at Reconciliation. That's what we were *born* to do."

He spoke with a total lack of melodrama, as though he were reciting a shopping list. His detachment impressed the room. So did the last sentiment, however blandly it was presented. Who could fail to be stirred by the thought of such purpose, reaching back over generations to the men who had gathered on this spot two centuries before? A few bloodied survivors, swearing that they, and their children, and their children's children, and so on until the end of the world would live and die with one ambition burning in their hearts: the prevention of another such apocalypse.

At this juncture McGann suggested a vote, and one was taken. There were no dissenting voices. The Society was agreed that the way forward lay in a comprehensive purge of all elements—innocent or not—who might presently be tampering, or tempted to tamper, with rituals intended to gain access to so-called Reconciled Dominions. All conventional religious structures would be excluded from this sanction, as they were utterly ineffectual and presented a useful distraction for some souls who might have been tempted towards esoteric practices. The shams and the profiteers would also be passed over. The pier-end palmists and fake psychics, the spiritualists who wrote new concertos for dead composers and sonnets for poets long since dust—all these would be left untouched. Only those who stood a chance of tripping over something Imajical, and acting upon it, would be rooted out. It would be an extensive and sometimes brutal business, but the Society was the equal of the challenge. This was not the first purge it had masterminded (though it would be the first of this scale); the structure was in place for an invisible but comprehensive cleansing. The cults would be the prime targets: their acolytes would be dispersed, their leaders bought off or incarcerated. It had happened before that England had been sluiced clean of every significant esoteric and thaumaturgist. Now it would happen again.

"Is the business of the day concluded?" Oscar asked. "Only Mass calls me."

"What's to be done with the body?" Alice Tyrwhitt asked.

Godolphin had his answer ready and waiting. "It's my mess and I'll clear it up," he said, with due humility. "I can arrange to have it buried in a motorway tonight, unless anybody has a better idea?"

There were no objections.

"Just as long as it's out of here," Alice said.

"I'll need some help to wrap it up and get it down to the car. Bloxham, would you oblige?"

Reluctant to refuse, Bloxham went in search of something to contain the carcass.

"I see no reason for us to sit and watch," Charlotte said, rising from her seat. "If that's the night's business, I'm going home."

As she headed to the door, Oscar took his cue to sow one last triumphant mischief.

"I suppose we'll be all thinking the same thing tonight," he said.

"What's that?" Lionel asked.

"Oh, just that if these things are as good at imitation as they appear to be, then we can't entirely trust each other from now on. I'm assuming we're all still human at the moment, but who knows what Christmas will bring?"

Half an hour later, Oscar was ready to depart for Mass. For all his earlier squeamishness, Bloxham had done well, returning Dowd's guts into the bowl of the carcass and mummifying the whole sorry slab in plastic and tape. He and Oscar had then lugged the corpse to the lift and, at the bottom, out of the tower to the car. It was a fine night, the moon a virtuous sliver in a sky rife with stars. As ever, Oscar took beauty where he could find it and, before setting off, halted to admire the spectacle.

"Isn't it stupendous, Giles?"

"It is indeed!" Bloxham replied. "It makes my head spin."

"All those worlds."

"Don't worry," Bloxham replied. "We'll make sure it never happens."

Confounded by this reply, Oscar looked across at the other man, to see that he wasn't looking at the stars at all but was still busying himself with the body. It was the thought of the coming purge he found stupendous.

"That should do it," Bloxham said, slamming the trunk and offering his hand for shaking.

Glad that he had the shadows to conceal his distaste, Oscar shook it, and bid the boor good night. Very soon, he knew, he would have to choose sides, and despite the success of tonight's endeavor, and the security he'd won with it, he was by no means sure that he belonged among the ranks of the purgers, even though they were certain to carry the day. But then if his place was not there, where *was* his place? This was a puzzlement, and he was glad he had the soothing spectacle of Midnight Mass to distract him from it.

Twenty-five minutes later, as he climbed the steps of St. Martin-in-the-Fields, he found himself offering up a little prayer, its sentiments not so very different from those of the carols this congregation would presently be singing. He prayed that hope was somewhere out there in the city tonight, and that it might come into his heart and scour him of his doubts and confusions, a light that would not only burn in him but would spread throughout the Dominions and illuminate the Imajica from one end to the other. But if such a divinity was near, he prayed that the songs had it wrong, because sweet as tales of Nativity were, time was short, and if hope was only a babe tonight then by the time it had reached redeeming age the worlds it had come to save would be dead.

12

I

Taylor Briggs had once told Judith that he measured out his life in summers. When his span came to an end, he said, it would be the summers he remembered and, counting them, count himself blessed among them. From the romances of his youth to the days of the last great orgies in the back rooms and bathhouses of New York and San Francisco, he could recall his career in love by sniffing the sweat from his armpits. Judith had envied him at the time. Like Gentle, she had difficulty remembering more than ten years of her past. She had no recollection of her adolescence whatsoever, nor her childhood; could not picture her parents or even name them. This inability to hold on to history didn't much concern her (she knew no other), until she encountered somebody like Taylor, who took such satisfaction from memory. She hoped he still did; it was one of the few pleasures left to him.

She'd first heard news of his sickness the previous July, from his lover, Clem. Despite the fact that he and Taylor had lived the same high life together, the plague had passed Clem by, and Jude had spent several nights with him, talking through the guilt he felt at what he saw as an undeserved escape. Their paths had diverged through the autumn months, however, and she was surprised to find an invitation to their Christmas party awaiting her when she got back from New York. Still feeling delicate after all that had happened, she'd rung up to decline, only to have Clem quietly tell her that Taylor was not expected to see another spring, never mind another summer. Would she not come, for his sake? She of course accepted. If any of her circle could make good times of bad it was Taylor and Clem, and she owed them both her best efforts in that endeavor. Was it perhaps because she'd had so many difficulties with the heterosexual males in her life that she relaxed in the company of men for whom her sex were not contested terrain?

At a little after eight in the evening of Christmas Day, Clem opened the door and ushered her in, claiming a kiss beneath the sprig of mistletoe in the hallway before, as he put it, the barbarians were upon her. The house had been decorated as it might have been a century earlier, tinsel, fake snow, and fairy lights forsaken in favor of evergreen, hung in such abundance around the walls and mantelpieces that the rooms were half forested. Clem, whose youth had outrun the toll of years for so long, was not such a healthy sight. Five months before he'd looked a fleshy thirty in a flattering light. Now he looked ten years older at least, his bright welcome and flattery unable to conceal his fatigue.

"You wore green," he said as he escorted her in to the lounge. "I told Taylor you'd do that. Green eyes, green dress."

"Do you approve?"

"Of course! We're having a pagan Christmas this year. *Dies natalis solis invictus.*"

"What's that?"

"The Birth of the Unconquered Sun," he said. "The Light of the World. We need a little of that right now."

"Do I know many people here?" she said, before they stepped into the hub of the party.

"Everybody knows you, darling," he said fondly. "Even the people who've never met you."

There were many faces she knew awaiting them, and it took her five minutes to get across to where Taylor was sitting, lord of all he surveyed, in a well-cushioned chair close to the roaring fire. She tried not to register the shock she felt at the sight of him. He'd lost almost all of what had once been a leonine head of hair, and every spare ounce of substance from the face beneath. His eyes, which had always been his most penetrating feature (one of the many things they'd had in common), seemed enormous now, as though to devour in the time he had left the sights his demise would deny him. He opened his arms to her.

"Oh, my sweet," he said. "Give me a hug. Excuse me if I don't get up."

She bent and hugged him. He was skin and bone; and cold, despite the fire close by.

"Has Clem got you some punch?"

"I'm on my way," Clem said.

"Get me another vodka while you're at it," Taylor said, imperious as ever.

"I thought we'd agreed—" Clem said.

"I know it's bad for me. But staying sober's worse."

"It's your funeral," Clem said, with a bluntness Jude found shocking. But he and Taylor eyed each other with a kind of adoring ferocity, and she saw in the look how Clem's cruelty was part of their mechanism for dealing with this tragedy.

"You wish," Taylor said. "I'll have an orange juice. No, make that a Virgin Mary. Let's be seasonal about it."

"I thought you were having a pagan celebration," Jude said as Clem headed away to fetch the drinks.

"I don't see why the Christians should have the Holy Mother," Taylor said. "They don't know what to do with her when they've got her. Pull up a chair, sweetie. I heard a rumor you were in foreign climes."

"I was. But I came back at the last minute. I had some problems in New York."

"Whose heart did you break this time?"

"It wasn't that kind of problem."

"Well?" he said. "Be a telltale. Tell Taylor."

This was a bad joke from way back, and it brought a smile to Judith's lips. It also brought the story, which she'd come here swearing she'd keep to herself.

"Somebody tried to murder me," she said.

"You're jesting," he replied.

"I wish I was."

"What happened?" he said. "Spill the beans. I like hearing other people's bad news just at the moment. The worse, the better."

She slid her palm over Taylor's bony hand. "Tell me how *you* are first."

"Grotesque," he said. "Clem's wonderful, of course, but all the tender loving care in the world won't make me healthy. I have bad days and good days. Mostly bad lately. I am, as my ma used to say, not long for this world." He glanced up. "Look out, here comes Saint Clemence of the Bedpan. Change the subject. Clem, did Judy tell you somebody tried to kill her?"

"No. Where was this?"

"In Manhattan."

"A mugger?"

"No."

"Not someone you knew?" Taylor said.

Now she was on the point of telling the whole thing, and she wasn't sure she wanted to. But Taylor had an anticipatory gleam in his eye, and she couldn't bear to disappoint him. She began, her account punctuated by exclamations of delighted incredulity from Taylor, and she found herself rising to her audience as though this story were not the grim truth but a preposterous fiction. Only once did she lose her momentum, when she mentioned Gentle's name, and Clem broke in to say that he'd been invited tonight. Her heart tripped and took a beat to get back into its rhythm.

"Tell the rest," Taylor was exhorting her. "What happened?"

She went on with her story, but now, with her back to the door, she found herself wondering every moment if he was stepping through it. Her distraction took its toll on the narrative. But then perhaps a tale about murder told by the prey was bound to predictability. She wrapped it up with undue haste.

"The point is, I'm alive," she said.

"I'll drink to that," Taylor replied, passing his unsipped Virgin Mary back to Clem. "Maybe just a splash of vodka?" he pleaded. "I'll take the consequences."

Clem made a reluctant shrug and, claiming Jude's empty glass, wended his way back through the crowd to the drinks table, giving Jude an excuse for turning around and scanning the room. Half a dozen new faces had appeared since she'd sat down. Gentle was not among them.

"Looking for Mr. Right?" Taylor said. "He's not here yet."

She looked back to meet his amusement.

"I don't know who you're talking about," she said.

"Mr. Zacharias."

"What's so funny?"

"You and him. The most talked-about affair of the last decade. You know, when you mention him, your voice changes. It gets—"

"Venomous."

"Breathy. Yearning."

"I don't yearn for Gentle."

"My mistake," he said archly. "Was he good in bed?"

"I've had better."

"You want to know something I never told anybody?"

He leaned forward, the smile becoming more pained. She thought it was his aching body that brought the frown to his brow, until she heard his words.

"I was in love with Gentle from the moment I met him. I tried everything to get him into bed. Got him drunk. Got him high. Nothing worked. But I kept at him, and about six years ago—"

Clem appeared at this juncture, supplying Taylor and Jude with replenished glasses before heading off to welcome a fresh influx of guests.

"You slept with Gentle?" Jude said.

"Not exactly. I mean, I sort of talked him into letting me give him a blow job. He was very high. Grinning that grin of his. I used to worship that grin. So there I am," Taylor went on, as lascivious as he'd ever been when recounting his conquests, "trying to get him hard, and he starts . . . I don't know how to explain this . . . I suppose he began speaking in tongues. He was lying back on my bed with his trousers around his ankles, and he just started to talk in some other language. Nothing vaguely recognizable. It wasn't Spanish. It wasn't French. I don't know what it was. And you know what? I lost my hard-on, and he got one." He laughed uproariously, but not for long. The laugh went from his face, as he began again. "You know, I was a little afraid of him suddenly. I was actually afraid. I couldn't finish what I'd started. I got up and left him to it, lying there with his dick sticking up, speaking in tongues." He claimed her drink from her hand and took a throatful. The memory had clearly shaken him. There was a mottled rash on his neck, and his eyes were glistening.

"Did you ever hear anything like that from him?" She shook her head. "I only ask because I know you broke up very quickly. I wondered if he'd freaked you out for some reason."

"No. He just fucked around too much."

Taylor made a noncommittal grunt, then said, "I get these night sweats now, you know, and I have to get up sometimes at three in the morning and let Clem change the sheets. I don't know whether I'm awake or asleep half the time. And all kinds of memories are coming back to me. Things I haven't thought about in years. One of them was that. I can hear him, when I'm standing there in a pool of sweat. Hear him talking like he's possessed."

"And you don't like it?"

"I don't know," he said. "Memories mean different things to me now. I dream about my mother, and it's like I want to crawl back into her and be born all over again. I dream about Gentle, and I wonder why I let all these mysteries in my life go. Things it's too late to solve now. Being in love. Speaking in tongues. It's all one in the end. I haven't understood any of it." He shook his head and shook down tears at the same time. "I'm sorry," he said. "I always get maudlin at Christmas. Will you fetch Clem for me? I need the bathroom."

"Can't I help?"

"There's some things I still need Clem for. Thanks anyway."

"No problem."

"And for listening."

She threaded her way to where Clem was chatting and discreetly informed him of Taylor's request.

"You know Simone, don't you?" Clem said by way of an exit, and left Jude to talk.

She did indeed know Simone, though not well, and after the conversation she'd just had with Taylor, she found it difficult to whip up a social soufflé. But Simone was almost flirtatiously excessive in her responses, unleashing a gurgling laugh at the merest hint of a cue and fingering her neck as though to mark the places she wanted kissed. Jude was silently rehearsing a polite refusal when she caught Simone's glance, ill concealed in a particularly extravagant laugh, flitting towards somebody elsewhere in the crowd. Irritated to be cast as a stooge for the woman's vamping, she said, "Who is he?"

"Who's who?" Simone said, flustered and blushing. "Oh, I'm sorry. It's just some man who keeps staring at me."

Her gaze went back to her admirer, and as it did so Jude was seized by the utter certainty that if she were to turn now it would be Gentle's stare she intercepted. He was here, and up to his stale old tricks, threading himself a little string of gazes, ready to pluck the prettiest when he tired of the game.

"Why don't you just go near and talk to him," she said.

"I don't know if I should."

"You can always change your mind if a better offer comes along."

"Maybe I will," Simone said, and without making any further attempt at conversation she took her laugh elsewhere.

Jude fought the temptation to follow her progress for fully two seconds, then glanced around. Simone's wooer was standing beside the Christmas tree, smiling a welcome at his object of desire as she breasted her way through the crowd towards him. It wasn't Gentle after all, but a man she thought she remembered as Taylor's brother. Oddly relieved, and irritated at herself for being so, she headed towards the drinks table for a refill, then wandered out into the hallway in search of some cooler air. There was a cellist on the half landing, playing *In the Bleak Midwinter,* the melody and the instrument it was being played upon combining to melancholy effect. The front door stood open, and the air through it raised goose bumps. She went to close it, only to have one of the other listeners discreetly whisper, "There's somebody being sick out there."

She glanced into the street. There was indeed somebody sitting on the edge of the pavement, in the posture of one resigned to the dictates of his belly: head down, elbows on his knees, waiting for the next surge. Perhaps she made a sound. Perhaps he simply felt her gaze on him. He raised his head and looked around.

"Gentle. What are you doing out here?"

"What does it look like?" He hadn't looked too pretty last time she'd seen him, but he looked a damn sight worse now: haggard, unshaven, and waxy with nausea.

"There's a bathroom in the house."

"There's a wheelchair up there," Gentle said, with an almost superstitious look. "I'd prefer to be sick out here."

He wiped his mouth with the back of his hand. It was virtually covered in paint. So was the other, she now saw; and his trousers, and his shirt.

"You've been busy."

He misunderstood. "I shouldn't have drunk anything," he said.

"Do you want me to get you some water?"

"No, thanks. I'm going home. Will you say goodbye to Taylor and Clem for me? I can't face going back in. I'll disgrace myself." He got to his feet, stumbling a little. "We don't seem to meet under very pleasant circumstances, do we?" he said.

"I think I should drive you home. You'll either kill yourself or somebody else."

"It's all right," he said, raising his painted hands. "The roads are empty. I'll be fine." He started to rummage in his pocket for his car keys.

"You saved my life; let me return the favor."

He looked up at her, his eyelids drooping. "Maybe it wouldn't be such a bad idea."

She went back inside to say farewell on behalf of herself

and Gentle. Taylor was back in his chair. She caught sight of him before he saw her. He was staring into middle distance, his eyes glazed. It wasn't sorrow she read in his expression, but a fatigue so profound it had wiped all feeling from him except, maybe, regret for unsolved mysteries. She went to him and explained that she'd found Gentle and that he was sick and needed taking home.

"Isn't he going to come and say goodbye?" Taylor said.

"I think he's afraid of throwing up all over the carpet, or you, or both."

"Tell him to call me. Tell him I want to see him soon." He took hold of Jude's hand, holding it with surprising strength. "Soon, tell him."

"I will."

"I want to see that grin of his one more time."

"There'll be lots of times," she said.

He shook his head. "Once will have to do," he replied softly.

She kissed him and promised she'd call to say she got home safely. On her way to the door she met Clem and once again made her apologies and farewells.

"Call me if there's anything I can do," she offered.

"Thanks, but I think it's a waiting game."

"Then we can wait together."

"Better just him and me," Clem said. "But I will call."

He glanced towards Taylor, who was once more staring at nothing.

"He's determined to hold on till spring. One more spring, he keeps saying. He never gave a fuck about crocuses till now." Clem smiled. "You know what's wonderful?" he said. "I've fallen in love with him all over again."

"That *is* wonderful."

"And now I'm going to lose him, just when I realize what he means to me. You won't make that mistake, will you?" He looked at her hard. "You know who I mean."

She nodded.

"Good. Then you'd better take him home."

2

The roads were as empty as he'd predicted, and it took only fifteen minutes to get back to Gentle's studio. He wasn't exactly coherent. On the way, the exchanges between them were full of gaps and discontinuities, as though his mind were running ahead of his tongue, or behind it. Drink wasn't the culprit. Jude had seen Gentle drunk on all forms of alcohol; it made him roaring, randy, and sanctimonious by turns. Never like this, with his head back against the seat, his eyes closed, talking from the bottom of a pit. One moment he was thanking her for looking after him, the next he was telling her not to mistake the paint on his hands for shit. It wasn't shit, he kept saying, it was burnt umber, and prussian blue, and cadmium yellow, but somehow when you mixed colors together, any colors, they always came out looking like shit eventually. This monologue dwindled into silence, from which, a minute or two later, a new subject emerged.

"I can't look at him, you know, the way he is . . ."

"Who?" Jude said.

"Taylor. I can't look at him when he's so sick. You know how much I hate sickness."

She'd forgotten. It amounted to a paranoia with him, fueled perhaps by the fact that though he treated his body with scant regard for its health he not only never sickened but hardly aged. Doubtless the collapse, when it came, would be calamitous: excess, frenzy, and the passage of years taking their toll in one fell swoop. Until that time he wanted no reminders of his physical frailty.

"Taylor's going to die, isn't he?" he said.

"Clem thinks very soon."

Gentle gave a heavy sigh. "I should spend some time with him. We were good friends once."

"There were rumors about you two."

"He spread them, not me."

"Just rumors, were they?"

"What do you think?"

"I think you've probably tried every experience that swam by at least once."

"He's not my type," Gentle said, not opening his eyes.

"You should see him again," she said. "You've got to face up to falling apart sooner or later. It happens to us all."

"Not to me it won't. When I start to decay, I'm going to kill myself. I swear." He made fists of his painted hands and raised them to his face, drawing the knuckles down over his cheeks. "I won't let it happen," he said.

"Good luck," she replied.

They drove the rest of the way without any further exchange between them, his passive presence on the passenger seat beside her making her uneasy. She kept thinking of Taylor's story and expecting him to start talking, unleashing a stream of lunacies. It wasn't until she announced that they'd arrived at the studio that she realized he'd fallen asleep. She stared at him awhile: at the smooth dome of his forehead and the delicate configuration of his lips. It was still in her to dote on him, no question of that. But what lay that way? Disappointment and frustrated rage. Despite Clem's words of encouragement she was almost certain it was a lost cause.

She shook him awake and asked him if she could use his bathroom before going on her way. The punch was heavy in her bladder. He was hesitant, which surprised her. The suspicion dawned that he'd already moved a female companion into the studio, some seasonal bird to be stuffed for Christmas and dumped by New Year. Curiosity made her press to be allowed in. Reluctant as he was, he could scarcely say no, of course, and she traipsed up the stairs after him, wondering as she went what the conquest was going to look like, only to find that the studio was empty. His sole companion was the painting that had so filthied his hands. He seemed genuinely upset that she'd set eyes on it and ushered her to the bathroom, more discomfited than if her first suspicions had been correct and one of his conquests had indeed been disporting herself on the threadbare couch. Poor Gentle. He was getting stranger by the day.

She relieved herself and emerged from the toilet to find the painting covered with a stained sheet and him looking furtive and fidgety, clearly eager to have her out of the place. She saw no reason not to be plain with him, and said, "Working on something new?"

"Nothing much," he said.

"I'd like to see."

"It's not finished."

"It doesn't matter to me if it's a fake," she said. "I know what you and Klein get up to."

"It's not a fake," he said, a fierceness in his voice and face she'd not seen so far tonight. "It's *mine.*"

"An original Zacharias?" she remarked. "This I *have* to see."

She reached for the sheet, before he could stop her, and flipped it up over the top of the canvas. She'd only had a glimpse of the picture as she'd entered, and from some distance. Up close, it was clear he'd worked on the canvas with no little ferocity. There were places where it had been punctured, as though he'd stabbed it with his palette knife or brush; other places where the paint was laid on with glutinous abandon, then thumbed and fingered to drive it before his will. All this to achieve the likeness of what? Two people, it seemed, standing face to face against a brutal sky, their flesh white, but shot through with jabs of livid color.

"Who are they?" she said.

"*They?*" he said, sounding almost surprised that she'd read the image thusly, then covering his response with a shrug. "Nobody," he said, "just an experiment," and pulled the sheet back down over the painting.

"Is it a commission?"

"I'd prefer not to discuss it," he said.

His discomfort was oddly charming. He was like a child who'd been caught about some secret ritual. "You're full of surprises," she said, smiling.

"Nah, not me."

Though the painting was out of sight he continued to look ill at ease, and she realized there was going to be no further discussion of the picture or its import.

"I'll be off, then," she said.

"Thanks for the lift," he replied, escorting her to the door.

"Do you still want to have that drink?" she said.

"You're not going back to New York?"

"Not immediately. I'll call you in a couple of days. Don't forget Taylor."

"What are you, my conscience?" he said, with too small a trace of humor to soften the weight of the reply. "I won't forget."

"You leave marks on people, Gentle. That's a responsibility you can't just shrug off."

"I'll try to be invisible from now on," he replied.

He didn't take her to the front door but let her head down the stairs alone, closing the studio door before she'd taken more than half a dozen steps. As she went, she wondered what misbegotten instinct had made her suggest drinks. Well, it was easily slipped out of, even assuming he remembered the suggestion had been made, which she doubted.

Once out in the street she looked up at the building to see if she could spot him through the window. She had to cross the road to do so, but from the opposite pavement she could see him standing in front of the painting, which he had once again unveiled. He was staring at it with his head slightly cocked. She couldn't be certain, but it looked as though his lips were moving; as though he were talking to the image on the canvas. What was he saying? she wondered. Was he coaxing some image forth from the chaos of paint? And if so, in which of his many tongues was he speaking?

13

I

She had seen two people where he'd painted one. Not a he, a she, or an it, but *they*. She'd looked at the image and seen past his conscious intention to a buried purpose, one he'd hidden even from himself. Now he went back to the canvas and looked at it again, with borrowed eyes, and there they were, the two she'd seen. In his passion to capture some impression of Pie 'oh' pah, he had painted the assassin stepping from shadow (or back into it), a stream of darkness running down the middle of his face and torso. It divided the figure from top to bottom, and its outer edges, ragged and lush, described the reciprocative forms of profiles, etched in white from the halves of what he'd intended to be a single face. They stared at each other like lovers, eyes looking forward in the Egyptian manner, the backs of their heads folded into shadow. The question was: Who *were* these two? What had he been trying to express, setting these faces thus, nose to nose?

He interrogated the painting for several minutes after she'd gone, preparing as he did so to attack the canvas again. But when it came to doing so, he lacked the strength. His hands were trembling, his palms clammy; his eyes could only focus upon the image indifferently well. He retreated from the picture, afraid to touch it in this weakened state for fear he'd undo what little he'd already achieved. A painting could escape so quickly. A few inept strokes and a likeness (to a face, to another painter's work) could flee the canvas and never be recaptured. Better to leave it alone tonight. To rest, and hope he was strong tomorrow.

He dreamed of sickness. Of lying in his bed, naked beneath a thin white sheet, shivering so hard his teeth chattered. Snow fell from the ceiling intermittently and didn't melt when it touched his flesh, because he was colder than the snow. There were visitors in his sickroom, and he tried to tell them how cold he was, but he had no power in his voice, and the words came out as gasps, as though he were struggling for his last breath. He began to fear that this dream condition was fatal; that snow and breathlessness would bury him. He had to act. Rise up from the hard bed and prove these mourners premature.

With painful slowness, he moved his hands to the edge of the mattress in the hope of pulling himself upright, but the sheets were slick with his final sweat, and he couldn't get a firm hold. Fear turned to panic, despair bringing on a new round of gasps, more desperate than the last. He struggled to make his situation plain, but the door of his sickroom stood wide, now, and all the mourners had disappeared through it. He could hear them in another room, talking and laughing. There was a patch of sun on the threshold, he saw. Next door it was summer. Here, there was only the heart-stopping cold, taking a firmer grip on him by the moment. He gave up attempting Lazarus and instead let his palms lie flat on the sheets and his eyes flutter closed. The sound of voices from the next room softened to a murmur. The noise of his heart dwindled. New sounds rose to replace it, however. A wind was gusting outside, and branches thrashed at the windows. Somebody's voice rose in prayer; another simply sobbed. What grief was this? Not his passing, surely. He was too minor to earn such lamentation. He opened his eyes again. The bed had gone; so had the snow. Lightning threw into silhouette a man who stood watching the storm.

"Can you make me forget?" Gentle heard himself saying. "Do you have the trick of that?"

"Of course," came the soft reply. "But you don't want it."

"No, what I want's death, but I'm too afraid of that tonight. That's the real sickness: fear of death. But I can live with forgetfulness, give me that."

"For how long?"

"Until the end of the world."

Another lightning flash burned out the figure in front of

him, and then the whole scene. Gone; forgotten. Gentle blinked the afterimage of window and silhouette out of his eyes and, in doing so, passed between sleep and waking.

The room was cold, but not as icy as his deathbed. He sat upright, staring first at his unclean hands, then at the window. It was still night, but he could hear the sound of vehicles on the Edgware Road, their murmur reassuring. Already—distracted by sound and sight—the nightmare was fading. He was happy to lose it.

He shrugged off the bedclothes and went to the kitchen to find himself something to drink. There was a carton of milk in the refrigerator. He downed its contents—though the milk was ready to turn—aware that his churned system would probably reject it in short order. Quenched, he wiped his mouth and chin and went through to look at the painting again, but the intensity of the dream from which he'd just woken made a mockery of his efforts. He would not conjure the assassin by this crude magic. He could paint a dozen canvases, a hundred, and still not capture the ambiguities of Pie 'oh' pah. He belched, bringing the taste of bad milk back up into his mouth. What was he to do? Lock himself away and let this sickness in him—put there by the sight of the assassin—consume him? Or bathe, sweeten himself, and go out to find some faces to put between him and the memory? Both vain endeavors. Which left a third, distressing route. To find Pie 'oh' pah in the flesh: to face him, question him, have his fill of him, until every ambiguity was scoured away.

He went on staring at the painting while he turned this option over. What would it take to find the assassin? An interrogation of Estabrook, for one. That wouldn't be too onerous a duty. Then a search of the city, to find the place Estabrook had claimed he couldn't recall. Again, no great hardship. Better than sour milk and sourer dreams.

Knowing that in the light of morning he might lose his present clarity of mind, and he was best to close off at least one route of retreat, he went to the paints, squeezed onto his palm a fat worm of cadmium yellow, and worked it into the still-wet canvas. It obliterated the lovers immediately, but he wasn't satisfied until he'd covered the canvas from edge to edge. The color fought for its brilliance, but it soon deteriorated, tainted by the darkness it was trying to obscure. By the time he'd finished, it was as if his attempt to capture Pie 'oh' pah had never been made.

Satisfied, he stood back and belched again. The nausea had gone from him. He felt strangely buoyant. Maybe sour milk suited him.

2

Pie 'oh' pah sat on the step of his trailer and stared up at the night sky. In their beds behind him, his adopted wife and children slept. In the heavens above him, the stars were burning behind a blanket of sodium-tinted cloud. He had seldom felt more alone in his long life than now. Since returning from New York he had been in a state of constant anticipation. Something was going to happen to him and his world, but he didn't know what. His ignorance pained him, not simply because he was helpless in the face of this imminent event, but because his inability to grasp its nature was testament to how his skills had deteriorated. The days when he could read futurities off the air had gone. He was more and more a prisoner of the here and now. That here, the body he occupied, was also less than its former glory. It was so long since he'd corresponded the way he had with Gentle, taking the will of another as the gospel of his flesh, that he'd almost lost the trick of it. But Gentle's desire had been potent enough to remind him, and his body still reverberated with echoes of their time together. Though it had ended badly he didn't regret snatching those minutes. Another such encounter might never come.

He wandered from his trailer towards the perimeter of the encampment. The first light of dawn was beginning to eat at the murk. One of the camp mongrels, back from a night of adventuring, squeezed between two sheets of corrugated iron and came wagging to his side. He stroked the dog's snout and tickled behind its battle-ravaged ears, wishing he could find his way back to his home and master so easily.

3

It was the oft-stated belief of Esmond Bloom Godolphin, the late father of Oscar and Charles, that a man could never have too many bolt holes, and of E.B.G.'s countless saws this was the only one Oscar had been significantly influenced by. He had not less than four places of occupation in London. The house in Primrose Hill was his chief residence, but there was also a pied-à-terre in Maida Vale, a smallish flat in Notting Hill, and the location he was presently occupying: a windowless warehouse concealed in a maze of derelict and near-derelict properties near the river.

It was not a place he was particularly happy to frequent, especially not on the day after Christmas, but over the years it had proved a secure haven for Dowd's two associates, the voiders, and it now served as a Chapel of Rest for Dowd himself. His naked corpse lay beneath a shroud on the cold concrete, with aromatic herbs, picked and dried on the slopes of the Jokalaylau, smoldering in bowls at his head and feet, after the rituals proscribed in that region. The voiders had shown little interest in the arrival of their leader's body. They were functionaries, incapable of anything but the most rudimentary thought processes. They had no physical appetites: no desire, no hunger or thirst, no ambition. They simply sat out the days and nights in the darkness of the warehouse and waited for Dowd to instruct them. Oscar was less than comfortable in their company, but could not bring himself to leave until this business was finished. He'd brought a book to read: a cricket almanac that he found soothing to peruse. Every now and then he'd get up and refuel the bowls. Otherwise there was little to do but wait.

It had already been a day and a half since he'd made such a show of taking Dowd's life: a performance of which he was justly proud. But the casualty that lay before him was a real loss. Dowd had been passed down the line of Godolphins for two centuries, bound to them until the end of time or of Joshua's line, whichever came first. And he had been a fine manservant. Who else could mix a whisky and soda so well? Who else knew to dry and powder between Oscar's toes with special care, because he was prone to fungal infections there? Dowd was irreplaceable, and it had pained Oscar considerably to take the brutal measures circumstance had demanded. But he'd done so knowing that while there was a slim possibility that he would lose his servant forever, an entity such as Dowd could survive a disemboweling as long as the rituals of Resurrection were readily and precisely followed. Oscar was not in ignorance of those rituals. He'd spent many lazy Yzordderrexian evenings on the roof of Peccable's house, watching the tail of the comet disappear behind the towers of the Autarch's palace, talking about the theory and practice of Imajical feits, writs, pneumas, uredos, and the rest. He knew the oils to pour into Dowd's carcass, and what blossoms to burn around the body. He even had in his treasure room a phonetic version of the ritual, set down by Peccable himself, in case Dowd was ever harmed. He had no idea how long the process would take, but he knew better than to peer beneath the sheet to see if the bread of life was rising. He could only bide his time and hope he'd done all that was necessary.

At four minutes past four, he had proof of his precision. A choking breath was drawn beneath the sheet, and a second later Dowd sat up. The motion was so sudden, and—after such a time—so unexpected, Oscar panicked, his chair tipping over as he rose, the almanac flying from his hand. He'd seen much in his time that the people of the Fifth would call miraculous, but not in a dismal room like this, with the commonplace world grinding on its way outside the door. Composing himself, he searched for a word of welcome, but his mouth was so dry he could have blotted a letter with his tongue. He simply stared, gaping and amazed.

Dowd had pulled the sheet off his face and was studying the hand with which he'd done so, his face as empty as the eyes of the voiders sitting against the opposite wall.

I've made a terrible error, Oscar thought. I've brought back the body, but the soul's gone out of him: Oh, Christ, what now?

Dowd stared on, blankly. Then, like a puppet into which a hand has been inserted, bringing the illusion of life and independent purpose to senseless stuff, he raised his head, and his face filled with expression. It was all anger. He narrowed his eyes and bared his teeth as he spoke.

"You did me a great wrong," he said. "A terrible wrong."

Oscar worked up some spittle, thick as mud. "I did what I deemed necessary," he replied, determined not to be cowed by the creature. It had been bound by Joshua never to do a Godolphin harm, much as it might presently wish to.

"What have I ever done to you that you humiliate me that way?" Dowd said.

"I had to prove my allegiance to the Tabula Rasa. You understand why."

"And must I continue to be humiliated?" he said. "Can I not at least have something to wear?"

"Your suit's stained."

"It's better than nothing," Dowd replied.

The garments lay on the floor a few feet from where Dowd sat, but he made no move to pick them up. Aware that Dowd was testing the limits of his master's remorse, but willing to play the game for a while at least, Oscar picked up the clothes and laid them within Dowd's reach.

"I knew a knife wasn't going to kill you," he said.

"It's more than I did," Dowd replied. "But that's not the point. I would have entered the game with you if that's what you'd wanted. Happily; *slavishly*. Entered and died for you." His tone was that of a man deeply and inconsolably affronted. "Instead, you conspire against me. You make me suffer like a common criminal."

"I couldn't afford for it to look like a charade. If they'd suspected it was stage-managed—"

"Oh, I see," Dowd replied. Unwittingly Oscar had caused even greater offense with this justification. "You didn't trust my actorly instincts. I've played every lead Quexos wrote: comedy, tragedy, farce. And you didn't trust me to carry off a petty little death scene!"

"All right, I was mistaken."

"I thought the knife stung badly enough. But *this*—"

"Please, accept my apologies. It was crude and hurtful. What can I do to heal the harm, eh? Name it, Dowdy. I feel I've violated the trust between us and I have to make good. Whatever you want, just name it."

Dowd shook his head. "It's not as easy as that."

"I know. But it's a start. Name it."

Dowd considered the offer for a full minute, staring not at Oscar but the blank wall. Finally, he said, "I'll start with the assassin, Pie 'oh' pah."

"What do you want with a mystif?"

"I want to torment it. I want to humiliate it. And finally, I want to kill it."

"Why?"

"You offered me whatever I wanted. Name it, you said. I've named it."

"Then you have carte blanche to do whatever you wish," Oscar said. "Is that all?"

"For now," Dowd said. "I'm sure something more will occur. Death's put some strange ideas in my head. But I'll name them as time goes by."

14

I

While it was to prove difficult for Gentle to prize from Estabrook the details of the night journey that had taken him to Pie 'oh' pah, it was not as difficult as getting in to see the man in the first place. He went to the house around noon, to find the curtains at all the windows meticulously drawn. He knocked and rang the bell for several minutes, but there was no reply. Assuming Estabrook had gone out for a constitutional, he left off his attempt and went to find something to put into his stomach, which after being so thoroughly scorned the night before was echoing with its own emptiness. It was Boxing Day, of course, and there was no café or restaurant open, but he located a small supermarket managed by a family of Pakistanis, who were doing a fine trade supplying Christians with stale bread to break. Though the stock had disappeared from many of the shelves, the store still had a tempting parade of tooth decayers, and Gentle left with chocolate, biscuits, and cake to satisfy his sweet tooth. He found a bench and sat down to subdue his hunger. The cake was too moist and heavy for his taste, so he broke it up into pieces and threw it to the pigeons his meal had attracted. The news soon spread that there was sustenance to be had, and what had been an intimate picnic quickly turned into a squabbling match. In lieu of loaves and fishes to subdue the mob, Gentle tossed the rest of his biscuits into the midst of the feasters and returned to Estabrook's house content with his chocolate. As he approached he saw a motion at one of the upper windows. He didn't bother to ring and knock this time, but simply called up at the window.

"I want a word, Charlie! I know you're in there. Open up!"

When there was no sign of Estabrook obliging, he let his voice ring out a little louder. There was very little competition from traffic, this being a holiday. His call was a clarion.

"Come on, Charlie, open up, unless you want me to tell the neighbors about our little deal."

The curtain was drawn aside this time, and Gentle had his first sight of Estabrook. A glimpse only, for the curtain was dropped back into place a moment later. Gentle waited, and just as he was about to start his haranguing afresh heard the front door being unbolted. Estabrook appeared, barefoot and bald. The latter was a shock. Gentle hadn't known the man wore a toupée. Without it his face was as round and white as a plate, his features set upon it like a child's breakfast. Eggs for eyes, a tomato nose, sausage lips: all swimming in a grease of fear.

"It's time we talked," Gentle said and, without waiting for an invitation, stepped inside.

He pulled no punches in his interrogation, making it plain from the outset that this was no social call. He needed to know where to find Pie 'oh' pah, and he wasn't going to be fobbed off with excuses. To aid Estabrook's memory he'd brought a battered street map of London. He set it down on the table between them.

"Now," he said. "We sit here until you've told where you went that night. And if you lie to me I swear I'm going to come back and break your neck."

Estabrook didn't attempt any obfuscation. His manner was that of a man who had passed many days in terror of a sound upon his step and was relieved, now that it had come, that his caller was merely human. His egg eyes were perpetually on the verge of breaking, and his hands trembled as he flipped the pages of the gazetteer, murmuring as he did so that he was sure of nothing but he would try to remember. Gentle didn't press too hard, but let the man make the journey again in memory, running his finger back and forth over the map as he did so.

They'd driven through Lambeth, he said, then Kennington and Stockwell. He didn't remember grazing Clapham Common, so he assumed they'd driven to the east of it, towards Streatham Hill. He remembered a church and sought out a cross on the map that would mark the place.

There were several, but only one close to the other land-mark he remembered, the railway line. At this point, he said he could offer nothing more by way of directions, only a description of the place itself: the corrugated iron perimeter, the trailers, the fires.

"You'll find it," he said.

"I'd better," Gentle replied.

He'd so far told Estabrook nothing about the circumstances that had brought him back here, though the man had several times asked if Judith was alive and well. Now he asked again.

"Please tell me," he said. "I've been straight with you, I swear I have. Won't you please tell me how she is?"

"She's alive and kicking," Gentle said.

"Has she mentioned me at all? She must have done. What did she say? Did you tell her I still love her?"

"I'm not your pimp," Gentle said. "Tell her yourself. If you can get her to talk to you."

"What am I going to do?" Estabrook said. He took hold of Gentle's arm. "You're an expert with women, aren't you? Everybody says so. What can I do to make amends?"

"She'd probably be satisfied if you sent her your balls," Gentle said. "Anything less wouldn't be appropriate."

"You think it's funny."

"Trying to have your wife killed? No, I don't think that's very amusing. Changing your mind and wanting everything lovey-dovey again: *that's* hysterical."

"You wait till you love somebody the way I love Judith. If you're capable of that, which I doubt. You wait until you want somebody so badly your sanity hangs on it. You'll learn."

Gentle didn't rise to the remark. It was too close to his present state to be fully confessed, even to himself. But once out of the house, map in hand, he couldn't suppress a smile of pleasure that he had a way forward. It was already getting gloomy, as the midwinter afternoon closed its fist on the city. But darkness loved lovers, even if the world no longer did.

2

At midday, with his unease of the previous night allayed not one jot, Pie 'oh' pah had suggested to Theresa that they should leave the encampment. The suggestion wasn't met with enthusiasm. The baby was sick with sniffles and had not stopped wailing since she'd woken; the other child was feverish too. This was no time to be going away, Theresa said, even if they had somewhere to go, which they didn't. We'll take the trailer with us, Pie replied; we'll just drive out of the city. To the coast, maybe, where the children would benefit from the cleaner air. Theresa liked that idea. Tomorrow, she said, or the day after, but not now.

Pie pressed the case, however, until she asked him what he was so nervous about. He had no answer to give; at least none that she'd care to hear. She understood nothing of his nature, nor questioned him about his past. He was simply a provider, someone who put food in the mouths of her children and his arms around her at night. But her question still hung in the air, so he answered it as best he could.

"I'm afraid for us," he said.

"It's that old man, isn't it?" Theresa replied. "The one who came to see you? Who was he?"

"He wanted a job done."

"And you did it?"

"No."

"So you think he's going to come back?" she said. "We'll set the dogs on him."

It was healthy to hear such plain solutions, even if—as now—they didn't answer the problem at hand. His mystif soul was sometimes too readily drawn to the ambiguities that mirrored his true self. But she chastened him; reminded him that he'd taken a face and a function and, in this human sphere, a sex; that as far as she was concerned he belonged in the fixed world of children, dogs, and orange peel. There was no room for poetry in such straitened

circumstances; no time between hard dawn and uneasy
dusk for the luxury of doubt or speculation.

Now another of those dusks had fallen, and Theresa was
putting her cherished ones to bed in the trailer. They slept
well. He had a spell that he'd kept polished from the days
of his power, a way of speaking prayers into a pillow so
they'd sweeten the sleeper's dreams. His Maestro had
asked for its comfort often, and Pie used it still, two hundred years later. Even now Theresa was laying her children's heads upon down suffused with cradle songs,
secreted there to guide them from the dark world into the
bright.

The mongrel he'd met at the perimeter in the predawn
gloom was barking furiously, and he went out to calm it.
Seeing him approach it pulled on its chain, scrabbling at the
dirt to be closer to him. Its owner was a man Pie had little
contact with, a short-tempered Scot who brutalized the dog
when he could catch it. Pie went down on his haunches to
hush the creature, for fear its din brought the owner out
from his supping. The dog obeyed but continued to paw at
Pie fretfully, clearly wanting to be loosed from its leash.

"What's wrong, buster?" he said to it, scratching behind
its war-torn ears. "Have you got a lady out there?"

He looked up towards the perimeter as he spoke and
caught the fleeting glimpse of a figure stepping into shadow
behind one of the trailers. The dog had seen the interloper
too. It set up a new round of barking. Pie stood up again.

"Who's there?" he demanded.

A sound at the other end of the encampment claimed his
attention momentarily: water splashing on the ground. No,
not water. The stench that reached his nostrils was that of
petrol. He looked back towards his own trailer. Theresa's
shadow was on the blind, her head bowed as she turned off
the nightlight beside the children's bed. The stench was
coming from that direction too. He reached down and released the dog.

"Go, boy! Go! Go!"

It ran barking at a figure slipping out through a gap in

the fence. As it went Pie started towards his trailer, yelling
Theresa's name.

Behind him, somebody shouted for him to shut up out
there, but the curses were unfinished, erased by the boom
and bloom of fire, twin eruptions that lit the encampment
from end to end. He heard Theresa scream, saw flame
surge up and around his trailer. The spilled fuel was only a
fuse. Before he'd covered ten yards the mother lode exploded directly under the vehicle, the force sufficient to lift
it off the ground and pitch it on its side.

Pie was blown over by a solid wave of heat. By the time
he'd scrabbled to his feet the trailer was a solid sheet of
flame. As he pitched himself through the baking air towards the pyre he heard another sobbing cry and realized it
was his own, a sound he'd forgotten his throat could make
but which was always the same, grief on grief.

Gentle had just sighted the church which had been Estabrook's last landmark when a sudden day broke on the
street ahead, as though the sun had come to burn the night
away. The car in front of his veered sharply, and he was
only able to prevent a collision by mounting the pavement,
bringing his own car to a juddering halt inches short of the
church wall.

He got out and headed towards the fire on foot, turning
a corner to head directly into the smoke, which veered and
veered again as he ran, allowing him only glimpses of his
destination. He saw a corrugated iron fence, and beyond it
a host of trailers, most of which were already ablaze. Even
if he'd not had Estabrook's description to confirm that this
was indeed Pie 'oh' pah's home, the fact of its destruction
would have marked it out. Death had preceded him here,
like his shadow, thrown forward by a blaze at his back that
was even brighter than the one that lay ahead. His knowledge of this other cataclysm, the one behind, had been a
part of the business between himself and the assassin from
the beginning. It had flickered in their first exchanges on
Fifth Avenue; it had lit the fury that had sent him to debate
with the canvas; and it had burned brightest in his dreams,

in that room he'd invented (or remembered) where he'd begged Pie for forgetfulness. What had they experienced together that had been so terrible he'd wanted to forget his whole life rather than live with the fact? Whatever it was, it was somehow echoed in this new calamity, and he wished to God he could have his forgetfulness undone and know what crime he'd committed that brought upon innocents such punishment as this.

The encampment was an inferno, wind fanning flames that in turn inspired new wind, with flesh the toy of both. He had only piss and spittle against this conflagration— useless!—but he ran on towards it anyway, his eyes streaming as the smoke bit at them, not knowing what hope of survival he had, only certain that Pie was somewhere in this firestorm and to lose him now would be tantamount to losing himself.

There were some escapees, a pitiful few. He ran past them towards the gap in the fence through which they'd escaped. His route was by turns clear and confounded, as the wind brought choking smoke in his direction, then carried it away again. He pulled off his leather jacket and threw it over his head as primitive protection against the heat, then ducked through the fence. There was solid flame in front of him, making the way forward impassable. He tried to his left and found a gap between two blazing vehicles. Dodging between them, the smell of singeing leather already sharp in his nostrils, he found himself in the middle of the compound, a space relatively free of combustible material, and thus of fire. But on every side, the flames had hold. Only three of the trailers weren't blazing, and the veering wind would soon carry the flame in their direction. How many of the inhabitants had fled before the flames took hold he couldn't know, but it was certain there'd be no further escapees. The heat was nearly unbearable. It beat upon him from every side, cooking his thoughts to incoherence. But he held on to the image of the creature he'd come to find, determined not to desert the pyre until he had that face in his hands or knew beyond doubt it was ash.

A dog appeared from the smoke, barking hysterically.

As it ran past him a fresh eruption of fire drove it back the way it had come, its panic escalating. Having no better route, he chased its tail through the chaos, calling Pie's name as he ran, though each breath he took was hotter than the last, and after a few such shouts the name was a rasp. He'd lost the dog in the smoke, and all sense of direction at the same time. Even if the way was still clear he no longer knew where it lay. The world was fire on every side.

Somewhere up ahead he heard the dog again, and thinking now that maybe the only life he'd claim from this horror was the hound's, he ran in search of it. Tears were pouring from his smoke-stung eyes; he could barely focus on the ground he was stumbling across. The barking stopped again, leaving him without a beacon. There was no way to go but forward, hoping the silence didn't mean the dog had succumbed. It hadn't. He spotted it ahead of him now, cowering in terror.

As he drew a breath to call it to him he saw the figure beyond it, stepping from the smoke. The fire had taken its toll on Pie 'oh' pah, but he was at least alive. His eyes, like Gentle's, streamed. There was blood at his mouth and neck and, in his arms, a forlorn bundle. A child.

"Are there more?" Gentle yelled.

Pie's reply was to glance back over his shoulder, towards a heap of debris that had once been a trailer. Rather than draw another lung-cooking breath to reply, Gentle started towards this bonfire but was intercepted by Pie, who passed over the child in his arms.

"Take her," he said.

Gentle threw aside his jacket and took the child.

"Now get out!" Pie said. *"I'll follow."*

He didn't wait to see his instruction obeyed but turned back towards the debris.

Gentle looked down at the child he was carrying. She was bloody and blackened, surely dead. But perhaps life could be pumped back into her if he was quick. What was the fastest route to safety? The way he'd come was blocked now, and the ground ahead littered with burning wreckage. Between left and right, he chose left, because he heard the incongruous sound of somebody whistling somewhere in the smoke: at least proof that breath could be drawn in that direction.

The dog came with him, but only for a few steps. Then it retreated again, despite the fact that the air was cooler by the step, and a gap in the flames was visible ahead. Visible, but not empty. As Gentle headed for the place a figure stepped out from behind one of the bonfires. It was the whistler, still practicing his craft, though his hair was burning and his hands, raised in front of him, were smoking ruins. He turned his head as he walked and looked at Gentle.

The tune he whistled was charmless, but it was sweet beside the stare he had. His eyes were like mirrors, reflecting the fires: they flared and smoked. This was the fire setter, he realized, or one of them. That was why it whistled as it burned, because this was its paradise. It didn't attempt to lay its carbonized hands on either Gentle or the child but walked on into the smoke, turning its stare back towards the blaze as it did so, leaving Gentle's route to the perimeter clear. The cooler air was heady; it dizzied him, made him stumble. He held on tight to the child, his only thought now to get it out into the street, in which endeavor he was aided by two masked firemen who'd seen his approach and came to meet him now, arms outstretched. One took the child from him; the other bore him up as his legs gave way beneath him.

"There's people alive in there!" he said, looking back towards the fire. "You've got to get them out!"

His rescuer didn't leave his side till he'd got Gentle through the fence and into the street. Then there were other hands to take charge. Ambulance attendants with stretchers and blankets, telling him that he was safe now and everything would be all right. But it wasn't, not as long as Pie was in the fire. He shrugged off the blanket and refused the oxygen mask they were ready to clamp to his face, insisting that he wanted no help. With so many others in need, they didn't waste time attempting to persuade him but went to aid those who were sobbing and shrieking on all sides. They were the lucky ones, who had voices to raise. He saw others being carried past who were too far gone to complain, and still others lying beneath makeshift shrouds on the pavement, blackened limbs jutting out here and there.

He turned his back on this horror and began to make his way around the edge of the encampment. The fence was being torn down to allow the hoses, which thronged the street like mating snakes, access to the fire. The engines pumped and roared, their reeling blue lights no competition for the fierce brightness of the fire itself. By that blaze he saw a substantial crowd had gathered to watch. They raised a cheer as the fence was toppled, sending plagues of fireflies up as it fell. He moved on as the firefighters advanced into the conflagration, bringing their hoses to bear on the heart of the fire. By the time he'd made a half circuit of the site and was standing opposite the breach they'd made, the flames were already in retreat in several places, smoke and steam replacing their fury. He watched them gain ground from his new vantage point, hoping for some glimpse of life, until the appearance of another two machines and a further group of firefighters drove him on around the perimeter, back to the place from which he'd emerged.

There was no sign of Pie 'oh' pah, either being carried from the blaze or standing among those few survivors who, like Gentle, had refused to be taken away to be tended. The smoke issuing from the fire's steady defeat was thickening, and by the time he got back to the row of bodies on the pavement—the number of which had doubled—the whole scene was barely visible through the pall. He looked down at the shrouded forms. Was one of them Pie 'oh' pah? As he approached the nearest of them a hand was laid on his shoulder, and he turned to face a policeman whose features were those of a boy soprano, smooth and troubled.

"Aren't you the one who brought out the kid?" he said.

"Yes. Is she all right?"

"I'm sorry, mate. I'm afraid she's dead. Was she your kid?"

He shook his head. "There was somebody else. A black guy with long curly hair. He had blood on his face. Has he come out of there?"

Formal language now: "I haven't seen anybody of that description."

Gentle looked back towards the bodies on the pavement.

"It's no use looking there," the policeman said. "They're all black now, whatever color they started out."

"I have to look," Gentle said.

"I'm telling you it's no use. You wouldn't recognize them. Why don't you let me put you in an ambulance? You need seeing to."

"No. I have to keep looking," Gentle said, and was about to move off when the policeman took hold of his arm.

"I think you'd be better away from the fence, sir," he said. "There's some danger of explosions."

"But he could still be in there."

"If he is, sir, I think he's gone. There's not much chance of anybody else coming out alive. Let me take you to the police line. You can watch from there."

Gentle shook off the man's hold.

"I'll go," he said. "I don't need an escort."

It took an hour for the fire to be finally brought under control, by which time it had little left to consume. During that hour all Gentle could do was wait behind the cordon and watch as the ambulances came and went, ferrying the last of the injured away and then taking the bodies. As the boy soprano had predicted, no further victims were brought out, dead or alive, though Gentle waited until all but a few late arrivals among the crowd had left, and the fire was almost completely doused. Only when the last of the firefighters emerged from the crematorium, and the hoses were turned off, did he give up hope. It was almost two in the morning. His limbs were burdened with exhaustion, but they were light beside the weight in his chest. To go heavyhearted was no poet's conceit: it felt as though the pump had turned to lead and was bruising the plush meat of his innards.

As he wandered back to his car he heard the whistling again, the same tuneless sound floating on the dirty air. He stopped walking and turned to all compass points, looking for the source, but the whistler was already out of sight, and Gentle was too weary to give chase. Even if he had, he thought, even if he'd caught it by its lapels and threatened to break its burned bones, what purpose would that have served? Assuming it had been moved by his threat (and pain was probably meat and drink to a creature that whistled as it burned) he'd be no more able to comprehend its reply than interpret Chant's letter: and for similar reasons. They were both escapees from the same unknown land, whose borders he'd grazed when he'd gone to New York; the same world that held the God Hapexamendios and had given birth to Pie 'oh' pah. Sooner or later he'd find a way to gain access to that state, and when he did all the mysteries would come clear: the whistler, the letter, the lover. He might even solve the mystery that he met most mornings in the shaving mirror: the face he thought he'd known well enough until recently, but whose code he now realized he'd forgotten and would not now remember without the help of the undiscovered God.

3

Back in the house in Primrose Hill, Godolphin sat up through the night and listened to the news bulletins reporting the tragedy. The number of dead rose every hour; two more victims had already perished in the hospital. Theories were being advanced everywhere as to the cause of the fire; pundits used the event to comment on the lax safety standards applied to sites where itinerants camped and demanded a full Parliamentary inquiry to prevent a repeat of such a conflagration.

The reports appalled him. Though he'd given Dowd leash enough to dispatch the mystif—and who knew what hidden agenda lay there?—the creature had abused the freedom he'd been granted. There would have to be punishment meted out for such abuse, though Godolphin was in no mood to plot that now. He'd bide his time, choose his moment. It would come. Meanwhile, Dowd's violence seemed to him further evidence of a disturbing pattern. Things he'd thought immutable were changing. Power was slipping from the possession of those who'd traditionally held it into the hands of underlings—fixers, familiars, and functionaries—who were ill equipped to use it. Tonight's disaster was symptomatic of that. But the disease had barely begun to take hold. Once it spread through the Dominions there'd be no stopping it. There had already been uprisings in Vanaeph and L'Himby, there were mutterings of rebellion in Yzordderrex; now there was to be a purge here in the Fifth Dominion, organized by the Tabula Rasa, a perfect background to Dowd's vendetta and its bloody consequences. Everywhere, signs of disintegration.

Paradoxically the most chilling of those signs was superficially an image of reconstruction: that of Dowd re-creating his face so that if he was seen by any member of the Society he'd not be recognized. It was a process he'd undertaken with each generation, but this was the first time any Godolphin had witnessed said process. Now Oscar thought back on it, he suspected Dowd had deliberately displayed his transformative powers, as further evidence of his newfound authority. It had worked. Seeing the face he'd grown so used to soften and shift at the will of its possessor was one of the most distressing spectacles Oscar had set eyes upon. The face Dowd had finally fixed was *sans* mustache and eyebrows, the head sleeker than his other, and younger: the face that of an ideal National Socialist. Dowd must also have caught that echo, because he later bleached his hair and bought several new suits, all apricot but of a much severer cut than those he'd worn in his earlier incarnation. He sensed the instabilities ahead as well as Oscar; he felt the rot in the body politic and was readying himself for a New Austerity.

And what more perfect tool than fire, the book burner's joy, the soul cleanser's bliss? Oscar shuddered to contemplate the pleasure Dowd had taken from his night's work, callously murdering innocent human families in pursuit of the mystif. He would return to the house, no doubt, with tears on his face and say he regretted the hurt he'd done to the children. But it would be a performance, a sham. There was no true capacity for grief or regret in the creature, and Oscar knew it. Dowd was deceit incarnate, and from now on Oscar knew he had to be on his guard. The comfortable years were over. Hereafter he would sleep with his bedroom door locked.

15

I

In her rage at his conspiracies Jude had contemplated several possible ways to revenge herself upon Estabrook, ranging from the bloodily intimate to the classically detached. But her nature never ceased to surprise her. All thoughts of garden shears and prosecutions dimmed in a short time, and she came to realize that the worst harm she could do him—given that the harm he'd intended to do her had been stopped in its tracks—was to ignore him. Why give him the satisfaction of her least interest in him? From now on he would be so far beneath her contempt as to be invisible. Having unburdened herself of her story to Taylor and Clem, she sought no further audience. From now on she wouldn't sully her lips with his name or let her thoughts dally with him for two consecutive seconds. At least, that was the pact she made with herself. It proved difficult to keep.

On Boxing Day she received the first of what were to be many calls from him, which she resolutely cut short the instant she recognized his voice. It wasn't the authoritative Estabrook she'd been used to hearing, and it took her three exchanges before she realized who was on the other end of the line, at which point she put down the receiver and let it

lie uncradled for the rest of the day. The following morning
he called again, and this time, just in case he was in any
doubt, she told him, "I don't ever want to hear your voice
again," and once more cut him off.

When she'd done so she realized he'd been sobbing as
he spoke, which gave her no little satisfaction, and the hope
that he wouldn't try again. A frail hope; he called twice that
evening, leaving messages on her answering machine while
she was out at a party flung by Chester Klein. There she
heard news of Gentle, to whom she hadn't spoken since
their odd parting at the studio. Chester, who was much the
worse for vodka, told her plainly he expected Gentle to
have a full-blown nervous breakdown in a short time. He'd
spoken to the Bastard Boy twice since Christmas, and he
was increasingly incoherent.

"What is it about all you men?" she found herself saying. "You fall apart so easily."

"That's because we're the more tragic of the sexes,"
Chester returned. "God, woman, can't you see how we *suffer?*"

"Frankly, no."

"Well, we do. Take it from me. We do."

"Is there any particular reason, or is it just free-form suffering?"

"We're all sealed up," Klein said. "Nothing can get in."

"So are women. What's the—"

"Women get *fucked,*" Klein interrupted, pronouncing
the word with a drunken ripeness. "Oh, you bitch about it,
but you love it. Go on, admit it. You love it."

"So all men really want is to get fucked, is that it?" Jude
said. "Or are you just talking personally?"

This brought a ripple of laughter from those who'd
given up their chitchat to watch the fireworks.

"Not literally," Klein spat back. "You're not listening to
me."

"I'm listening. You're just not making any sense."

"Take the church—"

"Fuck the church!"

"No, *listen!*" Klein said, teeth clenched. "I'm telling

God's honest fucking truth here. Why do you think men invented the church, huh? *Huh?*"

His bombast had infuriated Jude to the point where she refused to reply. He went on, unperturbed, talking pedantically, as if to a slow student.

"Men invented the church so they could bleed for Christ. So they could be entered by the Holy Spirit. So they could be saved from being sealed up." His lesson finished, he leaned back in his chair, raising his glass. "In vodka veritas," he said.

"In vodka shit," Jude replied.

"Well, that's just typical of you, isn't it?" Klein's words slurred. "As soon as you're fucking beaten you start the insults."

She turned from him, shaking her head dismissively. But he still had a barb in his armory.

"Is that how you drive the Bastard Boy crazy?" he said.

She turned back on him, stung. "Keep him out of this," she snapped.

"You want to see *sealed up?*" Klein said. "There's your example. He's out of his head, you know that?"

"Who cares?" she said. "If he wants to have a nervous breakdown, he can have one."

"How very humanitarian of you."

She stood up at this juncture, knowing she was perilously close to losing her temper completely.

"I know the Bastard Boy's excuse," Klein went on. "He's anemic. He's only got enough blood for his brain or his prick. If he gets a hard-on, he can't remember his own name."

"I wouldn't know," Jude said, swilling the ice around in her glass.

"Is that your excuse too?" Klein went on. "Have you got something down there you haven't been telling us about?"

"If I had," she said, "you'd be the last to know."

And so saying, she deposited her drink, ice and all, down the front of his open shirt.

She regretted it afterwards, of course, and she drove

home trying to invent some way of making peace with him without apologizing. Unable to think of any, she decided to let it lie. She'd had arguments with Klein before, drunk and sober. They were forgotten after a month; two at most.

She got in to find more messages from Estabrook awaiting her. He wasn't sobbing any more. His voice was a colorless dirge, delivered from what was clearly genuine despair. The first call was filled with the same pleas she'd heard before. He told her he was losing his mind without her and needed her with him. Wouldn't she at least talk to him, let him explain himself? The second call was less coherent. He said she didn't understand how many secrets he had, how he was smothered in secrets and it was killing him. Wouldn't she come back to see him, he said, even if it was just to collect her clothes?

That was probably the only part of her exit scene she would rewrite if she could play it over again. In her rage she'd left a goodly collection of personal items, jewelry and clothes, in Estabrook's possession. Now she imagined him sobbing over them, sniffing them; God knows, even wearing them. But peeved as she was not to have taken them with her, she was not about to bargain for them now. There would come a time when she felt calm enough to go back and empty the cupboards and the drawers, but not quite yet.

There were no further calls after that night. With the New Year almost upon her, it was time to turn her attention to the challenge of earning a crust come January. She'd given up her job at Vandenburgh's when Estabrook had proposed marriage, and she'd enjoyed his money freely while they were together, trusting—naïvely, no doubt—that if they ever broke up he'd deal with her in an honorable fashion. She hadn't anticipated either the profound unease that had finally driven her from his side (the sense that she was almost owned, and that if she stayed with him a moment longer she'd never unshackle herself) or the vehemence of his revenge. Again, there'd come a time when she felt able to deal with the mutual mud-slinging of a divorce, but, like the business with the clothes, she wasn't ready for that turmoil yet, even though she could hope for some monies from such a settlement. In the meanwhile, she had to think about employment.

Then, on December thirtieth, she received a call from Estabrook's lawyer, Lewis Leader, a man she'd met only once but who was memorable for his loquaciousness. It was not in evidence on this occasion, however. He signaled what she assumed was his distaste for her desertion of his client with a manner that teetered on the rude. Did she know, he asked her, that Estabrook had been hospitalized? When she told him she didn't, he replied that though he was sure she didn't give a damn, he'd been charged with the duty of informing her. She asked him what had happened. He briskly explained that Estabrook had been found in the street in the early hours of the twenty-eighth, wearing only one item of clothing. He didn't specify what.

"Is he hurt?" she asked.

"Not physically," Leader replied. "But mentally he's in a bad state. I thought you ought to know, even though I'm sure he wouldn't want to see you."

"I'm sure you're right," Jude said.

"For what it's worth," Leader said, "he deserved better than this."

He signed off with that platitude, leaving Jude to ponder on why it was that the men she mated with turned out to be crazy. Just two days earlier she'd been predicting that Gentle would soon be in the throes of a nervous breakdown. Now it was Estabrook who was under sedation. Was it her presence in their lives that drove them to it, or was the lunacy in their blood? She contemplated calling Gentle at the studio, to see that he was all right, but decided against it. He had his painting to make love to, and she was damned if she was going to compete for his attention with a piece of canvas.

One useful possibility did spring from the news Leader had brought. With Estabrook in the hospital, there was nothing to stop her from visiting the house and picking up her belongings. It was an apt project for the last day of December. She'd gather the remnants of her life from the lair of her husband and prepare to begin the New Year alone.

2

He hadn't changed the lock, perhaps in the hope that she'd come back one night and slip into bed beside him. But as she entered the house she couldn't shake the feeling of being a burglar. It was gloomy outside, and she switched on all the lights, but the rooms seemed to resist illumination, as though the smell of spoiled food, which was pungent, was thickening the air. She braved the kitchen in search of something to drink, before she began her packing, and found plates of rotting food stacked on every surface, most of them barely picked at. She opened first a window and then the refrigerator, where there were further rancid goods. There was also ice and water. She put both into a clean glass and got about her work.

There was as much disarray upstairs as down. Estabrook had apparently lived in squalor since her departure: the bed they'd shared a swamp of filthy sheets, the floor littered with soiled linen. There was no sign of any of her clothes among these heaps, however, and when she went through to the adjacent dressing room she found them all hanging in place, untouched. Determined to be done with this distasteful business in as short a time as possible, she found herself a set of suitcases and proceeded to pack. It didn't take long. With that labor performed she emptied her belongings from the drawers and packed those. Her jewelry was in the safe downstairs, and it was there she went once she'd finished in the bedroom, leaving the cases by the front door to be picked up as she left. Though she knew where Estabrook kept the key to the safe, she'd never opened it herself. It was a ritual he'd demanded be rigorously observed that on a night when she was to wear one of the pieces he'd given her he'd first ask her which she favored, then go and get it from the safe and put it around her neck, or wrist, or slip it through the lobe of her ear himself. With hindsight, a blatant power play. She wondered what kind of fugue state she'd been in when sharing his company, that she'd endured such idiocies for so long. Certainly the luxuries he'd bestowed upon her had been pleasurable, but why had she played his game so passively? It was grotesque.

The key to the safe was where she'd expected it to be, secreted at the back of the desk drawer in his study. The safe itself was behind an architectural drawing on the study wall, several elevations of a pseudoclassical folly the artist had simply marked as *The Retreat.* It was far more elaborately framed than its merit deserved, and she had some difficulty lifting it. But she eventually succeeded and got into the safe it had concealed.

There were two shelves, the lower crammed with papers, the upper with small parcels, among which she assumed she would find her belongings. She took everything out and laid it all on the desk, curiosity overtaking the desire to have what was hers and be gone. Two of the packages clearly contained her jewelry, but the other three were far more intriguing, not least because they were wrapped in a fabric as fine as silk and smelled not of the safe's must but of a sweet, almost sickly, spice. She opened the largest of them first. It contained a manuscript, made up of vellum pages sewn together with an elaborate stitch. It had no cover to speak of but seemed to be an arbitrarily arrayed collection of sheets, their subject an anatomical treatise, or at least so she first assumed. On second glance she realized it was not a surgeon's manual at all but a pillow book, depicting lovemaking positions and techniques. Leafing through it she sincerely hoped the artist was locked up where he could not attempt to put these fantasies into practice. Human flesh was neither malleable nor protean enough to re-create what his brush and ink had set on the pages. There were couples intertwined like quarreling squid; others who seemed to have been blessed (or cursed) with organs and orifices of such strangeness and in such profusion they were barely recognizable as human.

She flicked back and forth through the sheets, her interest returning her to the double-page illustration at the center, which was laid out sequentially. The first picture showed a naked man and woman of perfectly normal appearance, the woman lying with her head on a pillow while the man knelt between her legs, applying his tongue to the underside of her foot. From that innocent beginning, a cannibalistic union ensued, the male beginning to devour the woman, starting with her legs, while his partner obliged him with the same act of devotion. Their antics defied both physics and physique, of course, but the artist had succeeded in rendering the act without grotesquerie, but rather in the manner of instructions for some extraordinary magical illusion. It was only when she closed the book, and found the images lingering in her head, that they distressed her, and to sluice them out she turned her distress into a righteous rage that Estabrook would not only purchase such bizarrenesses but hide them from her. Another reason to be well out of his company.

The second package contained a much more innocent item: what appeared to be a fragment of statuary the size of her fist. One facet had been crudely marked with what could have been a weeping eye, a lactating nipple, or a bud seeping sap. The other facets revealed the structure of the block from which the image had been carved. It was predominantly a milky blue, but shot through with fine seams of black and red. She liked the feel of it in her hand and only reluctantly put it down to pick up the third parcel. The contents of this were the prettiest find: half a dozen pea-sized beads, which had been obsessively carved. She'd seen oriental ivories worked with this level of care, but they'd always been behind museum glass. She took one of them to the window to study more closely. The artist had carved the bead to give the impression that it was in fact a ball of gossamer thread, wound upon itself. Curious, and oddly inviting. As she turned it over in her fingers, and over, and over, she found her concentration narrowing, focusing on the exquisite interweaving of threads, almost as though there were an end to be found in the ball, and if she could only grasp it with her mind she might unravel it and discover some mystery inside. She had to force herself to look away, or she was certain the bead's will would have overwhelmed her own, and she'd have ended up staring at its detail until she collapsed.

She returned to the desk and put the bead back among its fellows. Staring at it so intently had upset her equilibrium somewhat. She felt slightly dizzy, the litter she'd left on the desk slipping out of focus as she rifled through it. Her hands knew what she wanted, however, even if her conscious thought didn't. One of them picked up the fragment of blue stone, while her other strayed back to the bead she'd relinquished. Two souvenirs: why not? A piece of stone and a bead. Who could blame her for dispossessing Estabrook of such minor items when he'd intended her so much harm? She pocketed them both without further hesitation and set about wrapping up the book and the remaining beads, returning them to the safe and closing it, and replacing drawing and key. Then she picked up the cloth in which the fragment had been wrapped, pocketed that, took the jewelry, and returned to the front door, turning off the lights as she went. At the door she remembered she'd opened the kitchen window and headed back to close it. She didn't want the place burglarized in her absence. There was only one thief who had right of trespass here, and that was her.

3

She felt well satisfied with the morning's work and treated herself to a glass of wine with her spartan lunch, then started unpacking her loot. As she laid her hostage clothes out on the bed, her thoughts returned to the pillow book. She regretted leaving it now; it would have been the perfect gift for Gentle, who doubtless imagined he'd indulged every physical excess known to man. No matter. She'd find an opportunity to describe its contents to him one of these days and astonish him with her memory for depravity.

A call from Clem interrupted her work. He spoke so

softly she had to strain to hear. The news was grim. Taylor was at death's door, he said, having two days before succumbed to another sudden bout of pneumonia. He refused to be hospitalized, however. His last wish, he'd said, was to die where he had lived.

"He keeps asking for Gentle," Clem explained. "And I've tried to telephone him but he doesn't answer. Do you know if he's gone away?"

"I don't think so," she said. "But I haven't spoken to him since Christmas Night."

"Could you try and find him for me? Or rather for Taylor? If you could maybe go round to the studio and rouse him? I'd go myself but I daren't leave the house. I'm afraid as soon as I step outside . . ." He faltered, tears in his breath. "I want to be here if anything happens."

"Of course you do. And of course I'll go. Right now."

"Thanks. I don't think there's much time, Judy."

Before she left she tried calling Gentle, but as Clem had already warned her, nobody answered. She gave up after two attempts, put on her jacket, and headed out to the car. As she reached into her pocket for the keys she realized she'd brought the stone and the bead with her, and some superstition made her hesitate, wondering if she should deposit them back inside. But time was of the essence. As long as they remained in her pocket, who was going to see them? And even if they did, what did it matter? With death in the air who was going to care about a few purloined bits and pieces?

She had discovered the night she'd left Gentle at the studio that he could be seen through the window if she stood on the opposite side of the street, so when he failed to answer the door, that was where she went to spy him. The room seemed to be empty, but the bare bulb was burning. She waited a minute or so and he stepped into view, shirtless and bedraggled. She had powerful lungs and used them now, hollering his name. He didn't seem to hear at first. But she tried again, and this time he looked in her direction, crossing to the window.

"Let me in!" she yelled. "It's an emergency."

The same reluctance she read in his retreat from the window was on his face when he opened the door. If he had looked bad at the party, he looked considerably worse now.

"What's the problem?" he said.

"Taylor's very sick, and Clem says he keeps asking for you."

Gentle looked bemused, as though he was having difficulty remembering who Taylor and Clem were.

"You have to get cleaned up and dressed," she said. "Furie, are you listening to me?"

She'd always called him Furie when she was irritated with him, and that name seemed to work its magic now. Though she'd expected some objection from him, given his phobia where sickness was concerned, she got none. He looked too drained to argue, his stare somehow unfinished, as though it had a place it wanted to rest but couldn't find. She followed him up the stairs into the studio.

"I'd better clean up," he said, leaving her in the midst of the chaos and going into the bathroom.

She heard the shower run. As ever, he'd left the bathroom door wide open. There was no bodily function, to the most fundamental, he'd ever shown the least embarrassment about, an attitude which had shocked her at first but which she'd taken for granted after a time, so that she'd had to relearn the laws of propriety when she'd gone to live with Estabrook.

"Will you find a clean shirt for me?" he called through to her. "And some underwear?"

It seemed to be a day for going through other people's belongings. By the time she'd found a denim shirt and a pair of overwashed boxer shorts, he was out of the shower, standing in front of the bathroom mirror combing his wet hair back from his brow. His body hadn't changed since she'd last looked at it naked. He was as lean as ever, his buttocks and belly tight, his chest smooth. His hooded prick drew her eye: the part that truly gave the lie to Gentle's name. It was no great size in this passive state, but it was pretty even so. If he knew he was being scrutinized he made no sign of it. He peered at himself in the mirror without affection, then shook his head.

"Should I shave?" he said.

"I wouldn't worry about it," she said. "Here's your clothes."

He dressed quickly, repairing to his bedroom to find a pair of boots, leaving her to idle in the studio while he did so. The painting of the couple she'd seen on Christmas Night had gone, and his equipment—paints, easel, and primed canvases—had been unceremoniously dumped in a corner. In their place, newspapers, many of their pages bearing reports on a tragedy she had only noted in passing: the death by fire of twenty-one men, women, and children in an arson attack in South London. She didn't give the reports close scrutiny. There was enough to mourn this gloomy afternoon.

Clem was pale but tearless. He embraced them both at the front door, then ushered them into the house. The Christmas decorations were still up, awaiting Twelfth Night, the perfume of pine needles sharpening the air.

"Before you see him, Gentle," Clem said. "I should explain that he's got a lot of drugs in his system, so he drifts in and out. But he wanted to see you so badly."

"Did he say why?" Gentle asked.

"He doesn't need a reason, does he?" Clem said softly. "Will you stay, Judy? If you want to see him when Gentle's been in . . ."

"I'd like that."

While Clem took Gentle up to the bedroom, Jude went through to the kitchen to make a cup of tea, wishing as she did so that she'd had the foresight to tell Gentle as they drove about how Taylor had talked of him the week before, particularly the tale about his speaking in tongues. It might have provided Gentle with some sense of what Taylor needed to know from him now. The solving of mysteries had been much on Taylor's mind on Christmas Night. Perhaps now, whether drugged or not, he hoped to win some last reprieve from his confusion. She doubted Gentle would have any answers. The look she'd seen him give the bathroom mirror had been that of a man to whom even his own reflection was a mystery.

Bedrooms were only ever this hot for sickness or love, Gentle thought as Clem ushered him in: for the sweating out of obsession or contagion. It didn't always work, of course, in either case, but at least in love failure had its satisfactions. He'd eaten very little since he'd departed the scene in Streatham, and the stale heat made him feel lightheaded. He had to scan the room twice before his eyes settled on the bed in which Taylor lay, so nearly enveloped was it by the soulless attendants of modern death: an oxygen tank with its tubes and mask; a table loaded with dressings and towels; another, with a vomit bowl, bedpan, and towels; and beside them a third, carrying medication and ointments. In the midst of this panoply was the magnet that had drawn them here, who now seemed very like their prisoner. Taylor was propped up on plastic-covered pillows, with his eyes closed. He looked like an ancient. His hair was thin, his frame thinner still, the inner life of his body—bone, nerve, and vein—painfully visible through skin the color of his sheet. It was all Gentle could do not to turn and flee before the man's eyes flickered open. Death was here again, so soon. A different heat this time, and a different scene, but he was assailed by the same mixture of fear and ineptitude he'd felt in Streatham.

He hung back at the door, leaving Clem to approach the bed first and softly wake the sleeper.

Taylor stirred, an irritated look on his face until his gaze found Gentle. Then the anger at being called back into pain went from his brow, and he said, "You found him."

"It was Judy, not me," Clem said.

"Oh, Judy. She's a wonder," Taylor murmured.

He tried to reposition himself on the pillow, but the effort was beyond him. His breathing became instantly arduous, and he flinched at some discomfort the motion brought.

"Do you want a painkiller?" Clem asked him.

"No, thanks," he said. "I want to be clearheaded, so Gentle and I can talk." He looked across at his visitor, who was still lingering at the door. "Will you talk to me for a while, John?" he said. "Just the two of us?"

"Of course," Gentle said.

Clem moved from beside the bed and beckoned Gentle across. There was a chair, but Taylor patted the bed, and it was there Gentle sat, hearing the crackle of the plastic undersheet as he did so.

"Call if you need anything," Clem said, the remark directed not at Taylor but at Gentle. Then he left them alone.

"Could you pour me a glass of water?" Taylor asked.

Gentle did so, realizing as he passed it to Taylor that his friend lacked the strength to hold it for himself. He put it to Taylor's lips. There was a salve on them, which moistened them lightly, but they were still split, and puffy with sores. After a few sips Taylor murmured something.

"Enough?" Gentle said.

"Yes, thanks," Taylor replied. Gentle set the glass down. "I've had just about enough of everything. It's time it was all over."

"You'll get strong again."

"I didn't want to see you so we could sit and lie to each other," Taylor said. "I wanted you here so I could tell you how much I've been thinking about you. Night and day, Gentle."

"I'm sure I don't deserve that."

"My subconscious thinks you do," Taylor replied. "And, while we're being honest, the rest of me too. You don't look as if you're getting enough sleep, Gentle."

"I've been working, that's all."

"Painting?"

"Some of the time. Looking for inspiration, you know."

"I've got a confession to make," Taylor said. "But first, you've got to promise you won't be angry with me."

"What have you done?"

"I told Judy about the night we got together," Taylor said. He stared at Gentle as if expecting there to be some eruption. When there was none, he went on, "I know it was no big deal to you," he said. "But it's been on my mind a lot. You don't mind, do you?"

Gentle shrugged. "I'm sure it didn't come as any big surprise to her."

Taylor turned his hand palm up on the sheet, and Gentle took it. There was no power in Taylor's fingers, but he closed them round Gentle's hand with what little strength he had. His grip was cold.

"You're shaking," Taylor said.

"I haven't eaten in a while," Gentle said.

"You should keep your strength up. You're a busy man."

"Sometimes I need to float a little bit," Gentle replied.

Taylor smiled, and there in his wasted features was a phantom glimpse of the beauty he'd had.

"Oh, yes," he said. "I float all the time. I've been all over the room. I've even been outside the window, looking in at myself. That's the way it'll be when I go, Gentle. I'll float off, only that one time I won't come back. I know Clem's going to miss me—we've had half a lifetime together—but you and Judy will be kind to him, won't you? Make him understand how things are, if you can. Tell him how I floated off. He doesn't want to hear me talk that way, but you understand."

"I'm not sure I do."

"You're an artist," he said.

"I'm a faker."

"Not in my dreams, you're not. In my dreams you want to heal me, and you know what I say? I tell you I don't want to get well. I say I want to be out in the light."

"That sounds like a good place to be," Gentle said. "Maybe I'll join you."

"Are things so bad? Tell me. I want to hear."

"My whole life's fucked, Tay."

"You shouldn't be so hard on yourself. You're a good man."

"You said we wouldn't tell lies."

"That's no lie. You are. You just need someone to remind you once in a while. Everybody does. Otherwise we slip back into the mud, you know?"

Gentle took tighter hold of Taylor's hand. There was so much in him he had neither the form nor the comprehension to express. Here was Taylor pouring out his heart about love and dreams and how it was going to be when he died, and what did he, Gentle, have by way of contribution? At best, confusion and forgetfulness. Which of them was the sicker, then? he found himself thinking. Taylor, who was frail but able to speak his heart? Or himself, whole but silent? Determined he wouldn't part from this man without attempting to share something of what had happened to him, he fumbled for some words of explanation.

"I think I found somebody," he said. "Somebody to help me . . . remember myself."

"That's good."

"I'm not sure," he said, his voice gossamer. "I've seen some things in the last few weeks, Tay . . . things I didn't want to believe until I had no choice. Sometimes I think I'm going crazy."

"Tell me."

"There was someone in New York who tried to kill Jude."

"I know. She told me about it. What about him?" His eyes widened. "Is this the somebody?" he said.

"It's not a he."

"I thought Judy said it was a man."

"It's not a man," Gentle said. "It's not a woman, either. It's not even human, Tay."

"What is it then?"

"Wonderful," he said quietly.

He hadn't dared use a word like that, even to himself. But anything less was a lie, and lies weren't welcome here.

"I told you I was going crazy. But I swear if you had seen the way it changed . . . it was like nothing on earth."

"And where is it now?"

"I think it's dead," Gentle replied. "I wasted too long to find it. I tried to forget I'd ever set eyes on it. I was afraid of what it was stirring up in me. And then when that didn't work I tried to paint it out of my system. But it wouldn't go. *Of course,* it wouldn't go. It was *part* of me by that time. And then when I finally went to find it . . . it was too late."

"Are you sure?" Taylor said. Knots of discomfort had appeared on his face, as Gentle talked, and were tightening.

"Are you all right?"

"Yes, yes," he said. "I want to hear the rest."

"There's nothing else to hear. Maybe Pie's out there somewhere, but I don't know where."

"Is that why you want to float? Are you hoping—" He stopped, his breathing suddenly turning into gasps. "You know, maybe you *should* fetch Clem," he said.

"Of course."

Gentle went to the door, but before he reached it Taylor said, "You've got to understand, Gentle. Whatever the mystery is, you'll have to see it for us both."

With his hand on the door, and ample reason to beat a hasty retreat, Gentle knew he could still choose silence over a reply, could take his leave of the ancient without accepting the quest. But if he answered, and took it, he was bound.

"I'm going to understand," he said, meeting Taylor's despairing gaze. "We both are. I swear."

Taylor managed to smile in response, but it was fleeting. Gentle opened the door and headed out onto the landing. Clem was waiting.

"He needs you," Gentle said.

Clem stepped inside and closed the bedroom door. Feeling suddenly exiled, Gentle headed downstairs. Jude was sitting at the kitchen table, playing with a piece of rock.

"How is he?" she wanted to know.

"Not good," Gentle said. "Clem's gone in to look after him."

"Do you want some tea?"

"No, thanks. What I really need's some fresh air. I think I'll take a walk around the block."

There was a fine drizzle falling when he stepped outside, which was welcome after the suffocating heat of the sickroom. He knew the neighborhood scarcely at all, so he decided to stay close to the house, but his distraction soon got the better of that plan and he wandered aimlessly, lost in thought and the maze of streets. There was a freshness in the wind that made him sigh for escape. This was no place to solve mysteries. After the turn of the year everybody would be stepping up to a new round of resolutions and ambitions, plotting their futures like well-oiled farces. He wanted none of it.

As he began the trek back to the house he remembered that Jude had asked him to pick up milk and cigarettes on his journey, and that he was returning empty-handed. He turned and went in search of both, which took him longer than he expected. When he finally rounded the corner, goods in hand, there was an ambulance outside the house. The front door was open. Jude stood on the step, watching the drizzle. She had tears on her face.

"He's dead," she said.

He stood rooted to the spot a yard from her. "When?" he said, as if it mattered.

"Just after you left."

He didn't want to weep, not with her watching. There was too much else he didn't want to stumble over in her presence. Stony, he said, "Where's Clem?"

"With him upstairs. Don't go up. There's already too many people." She spied the cigarettes in his hand and reached for them. As her hand grazed his, their grief ran between them. Despite his intent, tears sprang to his eyes, and he went into her embrace, both of them sobbing freely, like enemies joined by a common loss or lovers about to be parted. Or else souls who could not remember whether they were lovers or enemies and were weeping at their own confusion.

16

I

Since the meeting at which the subject of the Tabula Rasa's library had first been raised, Bloxham had several times planned to perform the duty he'd volunteered himself for and go into the bowels of the tower to check on the security of the collection. But he'd twice put off the task, telling himself that there were more urgent claims on his time: specifically, the organization of the Society's Great Purge. He might have postponed a third time had the matter not been raised again, this in a casual aside from Charlotte Feaver, who'd been equally vociferous about the safety of the books at that first gathering and now offered to accompany him on the investigation. Women baffled Bloxham, and the attraction they exercised over him had always to be set beside the discomfort he felt in their company, but in recent days he'd felt an intensity of sexual need he'd seldom, if ever, experienced before. Not even in the privacy of his own prayers did he dare confess the reason. The Purge excited him—it roused his blood and his manhood—and he had no doubt that Charlotte had responded to this heat, even though he'd made no outward show of it. He promptly accepted her offer, and at her suggestion they agreed to meet at the tower on the last evening of the old year. He brought a bottle of champagne.

"We may as well enjoy ourselves," he said, as they headed down through the remains of Roxborough's original house, a floor of which had been preserved and concealed within the plainer walls of the tower.

Neither of them had ventured into this underworld for many years. It was more primitive than either of them remembered. Electric light had been crudely installed—cables from which bare bulbs hung looped along the passages—but otherwise the place was just as it had been in the first years of the Tabula Rasa. The cellars had been built for the express purpose of housing the Society's collection; thus for the millennium. A fan of identical corridors spread from the bottom stairs, lined on both sides with shelves that rose up the brick walls to the curve of the ceilings. The intersections were elaborately vaulted, but otherwise there was no decoration.

"Shall we break open the bottle before we start?" Bloxham suggested.

"Why not? What are we drinking from?"

His reply was to bring two fluted glasses from his pocket. She claimed them from him while he opened the bottle, its cork coming with no more than a decorous sigh, the sound of which carried away through the labyrinth and failed to return. Glasses filled, they drank to the Purge.

"Now we're here," Charlotte said, pulling her furs up around her, "what are we looking for?"

"Any sign of tampering or theft," Bloxham said. "Shall we split up or go together?"

"Oh, together," she replied.

It had been Roxborough's claim that these shelves carried every single volume of any significance in the hemisphere, and as they wandered together, surveying the tens of thousands of manuscripts and books, it was easy to believe the boast.

"How in hell's name do you suppose they gathered all this stuff up?" Charlotte wondered as they walked.

"I daresay the world was smaller then," Bloxham remarked. "They all knew each other, didn't they? Casanova, Sartori, the Comte de Saint-Germain. All fakes and buggers together."

"Fakes? Do you really think so?"

"Most of them," Bloxham said, wallowing in the ill-deserved role of expert. "There may have been one or two, I suppose, who knew what they were doing."

"Have you ever been tempted?" Charlotte asked him, slipping her arm through the crook of his as they went.

"To do what?"

"To see if any of it's worth a damn. To try raising a familiar or crossing into the Dominions."

He looked at her with genuine astonishment. "That's against every precept of the Society," he said.

"That's not what I asked," she replied, almost curtly. "I said, Have you ever been tempted?"

"My father taught me that any dealings with the Imajica would put my soul in jeopardy."

"Mine said the same. But I think he regretted not finding out for himself at the end. I mean, if there's no truth in it, then there's no harm."

"Oh, I believe there's truth in it," Bloxham said.

"You believe there are other Dominions?"

"You saw that damn creature Godolphin cut up in front of us."

"I saw a species I hadn't seen before, that's all." She stopped and arbitrarily plucked a book from the shelves. "But I wonder sometimes if the fortress we're guarding isn't empty." She opened the book, and a lock of hair fell from it. "Maybe it's all invention," she said. "Drug dreams and fancy." She put the book back on the shelf and turned to face Bloxham. "Did you really invite me down here to check the security?" she murmured. "I'm going to be damn disappointed if you did."

"Not entirely," he said.

"Good," she replied, and wandered on, deeper into the maze.

2

Though Jude had been invited to a number of New Year's Eve parties, she'd made no firm commitment to attend any of them, for which fact, after the sorrows the day had brought, she was thankful. She'd offered to stay with Clem once Taylor's body had been taken from the house, but he'd quietly declined, saying that he needed the time alone. He was comforted to know she'd be at the other end of the telephone if he needed her, however, and said he'd call if he got too maudlin.

One of the parties she'd been invited to was at the house opposite her flat, and on the evidence of past years it would raise quite a din. She'd several times been one of the celebrants there herself, but it was no great hardship to be alone tonight. She was in no mood to trust the future, if what the New Year brought was more of what the old had offered.

She closed the curtains in the hope that her presence would go undetected, lit some candles, put on a flute concerto, and started to prepare something light for supper. As she washed her hands, she found that her fingers and palms had taken on a light dusting of color from the stone. She'd caught herself toying with it several times during the afternoon, and pocketed it, only to find minutes later that it was once again in her hands. Why the color it had left behind had escaped her until now, she didn't know. She rubbed her hands briskly beneath the tap to wash the dust off, but when she came to dry them found the color was actually brighter. She went into the bathroom to study the phenomenon under a more intense light. It wasn't, as she'd first thought, dust. The pigment seemed to be in her skin, like a henna stain. Nor was it confined to her palms. It had spread to her wrists, where she was sure her flesh hadn't come in contact with the stone. She took off her blouse and to her shock discovered there were irregular patches of color at her elbows as well. She started talking to herself, which she always did when she was confounded by something.

"What the hell is this? I'm turning blue? This is ridiculous."

Ridiculous, maybe, but none too funny. There was a crawl of panic in her stomach. Had she caught some disease from the stone? Was that why Estabrook had wrapped it up so carefully and hidden it away?

She turned on the shower and stripped. There were no further stains on her body that she could find, which was some small comfort. With the water seething hot she stepped into the bath, working up a lather and rubbing at the color. The combination of heat and the panic in her belly was dizzying her, and halfway through scrubbing at her skin she feared she was going to faint and had to step out of the bath again, reaching to open the bathroom door and let in some cooler air. Her slick hand slid on the door-knob, however, and cursing she reeled around for a towel to wipe the soap off. As she did so she caught sight of herself in the mirror. Her neck was blue. The skin around her eyes was blue. Her brow was blue, all the way up into her hairline. She backed away from this grotesquerie, flattening herself against the steam-wetted tiles.

"This isn't real," she said aloud.

She reached for the handle a second time and wrenched at it with sufficient force to open the door. The cold brought gooseflesh from head to foot, but she was glad of the chill. Perhaps it would slap this self-deceit out of her. Shuddering with cold she fled the reflection, heading back into the candle-lit haven of the living room. There in the middle of the coffee table lay the piece of blue stone, its eye looking back at her. She didn't even remember taking it out of her pocket, much less setting it on the table in this studied fashion, surrounded by candles. Its presence made her hang back at the door. She was suddenly superstitious of it, as though its gaze had a basilisk's power and could turn her to similar stuff. If that was its business she was too late to undo it. Every time she'd turned the stone over she'd met its glance. Made bold by fatalism, she went to the table and picked the stone up, not giving it time to obsess her again but flinging it against the wall with all the power she possessed.

As it flew from her hand it granted her the luxury of knowing her error. It had taken possession of the room in her absence, had become more real than the hand that had thrown it or the wall it was about to strike. Time was its plaything, and place its toy, and in seeking its destruction she would unknit both.

It was too late to undo the error now. The stone struck the wall with a loud hard sound, and in that moment she was thrown out of herself, as surely as if somebody had reached into her head, plucked out her consciousness, and pitched it through the window. Her body remained in the room she'd left, irrelevant to the journey she was about to undertake. All she had of its senses was sight. That was

enough. She floated out over the bleak street, shining wet
in the lamplight, towards the step of the house opposite
hers. A quartet of party-goers—three young men with a
tipsy girl in their midst—was waiting there, one of the
youths rapping impatiently on the door. While they waited
the burliest of the trio pressed kisses on the girl, kneading
her breasts covertly as he did so. Jude caught glimpses of
the discomfort that surfaced between the girl's giggles; saw
her hands make vain little fists when her suitor pushed his
tongue against her lips, then saw her open her mouth to
him, more in resignation than lust. As the door opened and
the four stumbled into the din of celebration, she moved
away, rising over the rooftops as she flew and dropping
down again to catch glimpses of other dramas unfolding in
the houses she passed.

They were all, like the stone that had sent her on this
mission, fragments: slivers of dramas she could only guess
at. A woman in an upper room, staring down at a dress laid
on a stripped bed; another at a window, tears falling from
beneath her closed lids as she swayed to music Jude
couldn't hear; yet another rising from a table of glittering
guests, sickened by something. None of them women she
knew, but all quite familiar. Even in her short remembered
life she'd felt like all of them at some time or other: forsaken, powerless, yearning. She began to see the scheme
here. She was going from glimpse to glimpse as if to moments of her life, meeting her reflection in women of every
class and kind.

In a dark street behind King's Cross she saw a woman
servicing a man in the front seat of his car, bending to take
his hard pink prick between lips the color of menstrual
blood. She'd done that too, or its like, because she'd
wanted to be loved. And the woman driving past, seeing
the whores on parade and righteously sickened by them:
that was her. And the beauty taunting her lover out in the
rain, and the virago applauding drunkenly above: she'd
been in those lives just as surely, or they in hers.

Her journey was nearing its end. She'd reached a bridge
from which there would perhaps have been a panoramic

view of the city, but that the rain in this region was heavier than it had been in Notting Hill, and the distance was shrouded. Her mind didn't linger but moved on through the downpour—unchilled, unwetted—towards a lightless tower that lay all but concealed behind a row of trees. Her speed had dropped, and she wove between the foliage like a drunken bird, dropping down to the ground and sinking through it into a sodden and utter darkness.

There was a momentary terror that she was going to be buried alive in this place; then the darkness gave way to light, and she was dropping through the roof of some kind of cellar, its walls lined not with wine racks but with shelves. Lights hung along the passageways, but the air here was still dense, not with dust but with something she only understood vaguely. There was sanctity here, and there was power. She had felt nothing like it in her life: not in St. Peter's, or Chartres, or the Duomo. It made her want to be flesh again, instead of a roving mind. To walk here. To touch the books, the bricks; to smell the air. Dusty it would be, but *such* dust: every mote wise as a planet from floating in this holy space.

The motion of a shadow caught her eye, and she moved towards it along the passageway, wondering as she went what volumes these were, stacked on every side. The shadow up ahead, which she'd taken to be that of one person, was of two, erotically entangled. The woman had her back to the books, her arms grasping the shelf above her head. Her mate, his trousers around his ankles, was pressed against her, making short gasps to accompany the jabbing of his hips. Both had their eyes closed; the sight of each other was no great aphrodisiac. Was this coupling what she'd come here to see? God knows, there was nothing in their labors to either arouse or educate her. Surely the blue eye hadn't driven her across the city gathering tales of womanhood just to witness this joyless intercourse. There had to be something here she wasn't comprehending. Something hidden in their exchange, perhaps? But no. It was only gasps. In the books that rocked on the shelves behind them? Perhaps.

She drifted closer to scrutinize the titles, but her gaze ran beyond spines to the wall against which they stood. The bricks were the same plain stuff as all along the passages. The mortar between had a stain in it she recognized, however: an unmistakable blue. Excited now, she drove her mind on, past the lovers and the books and through the brick. It was dark on the other side, darker even than the ground she'd dropped through to enter this secret place. Nor was it simply a darkness made of light's absence, but of despair and sorrow. Her instinct was to retreat from it, but there was another presence here that made her linger: a form, barely distinguishable from the darkness, lying on the ground in this squalid cell. It was bound—almost cocooned—its face completely covered. The binding was as fine as thread, and had been wound around the body with obsessive care, but there was enough of its shape visible for her to be certain that this, like the ensnared spirits at every station along her route, was also a woman.

Her binders had been meticulous. They'd left not so much as a hair or toenail visible. Jude hovered over the body, studying it. They were almost complementary, like corpse and essence, eternally divided; except that she had flesh to return to. At least she hoped she did; hoped that now she'd completed this bizarre pilgrimage, and had seen the relic in the wall, she'd be allowed to return to her tainted skin. But something still held her here. Not the darkness, not the walls, but some sense of unfinished business. Was a sign of veneration required of her? If so, what? She lacked the knees for genuflection, and the lips for hosannas; she couldn't stoop; she couldn't touch the relic. What was there left to do? Unless—God help her—she had to *enter* the thing.

She knew the instant she'd formed the thought that this was precisely why she'd been brought here. She'd left her living flesh to enter this prisoner of brick, cord, and decay, a thrice-bounded carcass from which she might never emerge again. The thought revolted her, but had she come this far only to turn back because this last rite distressed her too much? Even assuming she could defy the forces that had brought her here, and return to the house of her body against their will, wouldn't she wonder forever what adventure she'd turned her back on? She was no coward; she would enter the relic and take the consequences.

No sooner thought than done. Her mind sank towards the binding and slipped between the threads into the body's maze. She had expected darkness, but there was light here, the forms of the body's innards delineated by the milk-blue she'd come to know as the color of this mystery. There was no foulness, no corruption. It was less a charnel house than a cathedral, the source, she now suspected, of the sacredness that permeated this underground. But, like a cathedral, its substance was quite dead. No blood ran in these veins, no heart pumped, no lungs drew breath. She spread her intention through the stilled anatomy, to feel its length and breadth. The dead woman had been large in life, her hips substantial, her breasts heavy. But the binding bit into her ripeness everywhere, perverting the swell and sweep of her. What terrible last moments she must have known, lying blind in this filth, hearing the wall of her mausoleum being built brick by brick. What kind of crime hung on her, Jude wondered, that she'd been condemned to such a death? And who were her executioners, the builders of that wall? Had they sung as they worked, their voices growing dimmer as the brick blotted them out? Or had they been silent, half ashamed of their cruelty?

There was so much she wished she knew, and none of it answerable. She'd finished her journey as she'd begun it, in fear and confusion. It was time to be gone from the relic, and home. She willed herself to rise out of the dead blue flesh. To her horror, nothing happened. She was bound here, a prisoner within a prisoner. God help her, what had she done? Instructing herself not to panic, she concentrated her mind on the problem, picturing the cell beyond the binding, and the wall she'd passed so effortlessly through, and the lovers, and the passageway that led out to the open sky. But imagining was not enough. She had let her curiosity overtake her, spreading her spirit through the corpse, and now it had claimed that spirit for itself.

A rage began in her, and she let it come. It was as recognizable a part of her as the nose on her face, and she needed all that she was, every particular, to empower her. If she'd had her own body around her it would have been flushing as her heartbeat caught the rhythm of her fury. She even seemed to hear it—the first sound she'd been aware of since leaving the house—the pump at its hectic work. It was not imagined. She felt it in the body around her, a tremor passing through the long-stilled system as her rage ignited it afresh. In the throne room of its head a sleeping mind woke and knew it was invaded.

For Jude there was an exquisite moment of shared consciousness, when a mind new to her—yet sweetly familiar—grazed her own. Then she was expelled by its wakefulness. She heard it scream in horror behind her, a sound of mind rather than throat, which went with her as she sped from the cell, out through the wall, past the lovers shaken from their intercourse by falls of dust, out and up, into the rain, and into a night not blue but bitterest black. The din of the woman's terror accompanied her all the way back to the house, where, to her infinite relief, she found her own body still standing in the candle-lit room. She slid into it with ease, and stood in the middle of the room for a minute or two, sobbing, until she began to shudder with cold. She found her dressing gown and, as she put it on, realized that her wrists and elbows were no longer stained. She went into the bathroom and consulted the mirror. Her face was similarly cleansed.

Still shivering, she returned to the living room to look for the blue stone. There was a substantial hole in the wall where its impact had gouged out the plaster. The stone itself was unharmed, lying on the rug in front of the hearth. She didn't pick it up. She'd had enough of its delirium for one night. Avoiding its baleful glance as best she could, she threw a cushion over it. Tomorrow she'd plan some way of ridding herself of the thing. Tonight she needed to tell somebody what she'd experienced, before she began to doubt it. Someone a little crazy, who'd not dismiss her account out of hand; someone already half believing. Gentle, of course.

17

TOWARDS MIDNIGHT, THE TRAFFIC outside Gentle's studio dwindled to almost nothing. Anybody who was going to a party tonight had arrived. They were deep in drink, debate, or seduction, determined as they celebrated to have in the coming year what the going had denied them.

Content with his solitude, Gentle sat cross-legged on the floor, a bottle of bourbon between his legs and canvases propped up against the furniture all around him. Most of them were blank, but that suited his meditation. So was the future.

He'd been sitting in this ring of emptiness for about two hours, drinking from the bottle, and now his bladder needed emptying. He got up and went to the bathroom, using the light from the lounge to go by rather than face his reflection. As he shook the last drops into the bowl, that light went off. He zipped himself up and went back into the studio. The rain lashed against the window, but there was sufficient illumination from the street for him to see that the door out onto the landing stood inches ajar.

"Who's there?" he said.

The room was still for a moment; then he glimpsed a form against the window, and the smell of something burned and cold pricked his nostrils. The whistler! My God, it had found him!

Fear made him fleet. He broke from his frozen posture and raced to the door. He would have been through it and away down the stairs had he not almost tripped on the dog waiting obediently on the other side. It wagged its tail in pleasure at the sight of him and halted his flight. The whistler was no dog lover. So who was here?

Turning back, he reached for the light switch and was

about to flip it on when the unmistakable voice of Pie 'oh' pah said, "Please don't. I prefer the dark."

Gentle's finger dropped from the switch, his heart hammering for a different reason. "Pie? Is that you?"

"Yes, it's me," came the reply. "I heard you wanted to see me, from a friend of yours."

"I thought you were dead."

"I was *with* the dead. Theresa and the children."

"Oh, God. Oh, God."

"You lost somebody too," Pie 'oh' pah said.

It was wise, Gentle now understood, to have this exchange in darkness: to talk, in shadow, of the grave and the lambs it had claimed.

"I was with the spirits of my children for a time. Your friend found me in the mourning place, spoke to me, told me you wanted to see me again. This surprises me, Gentle."

"As much as you talking to Taylor surprises me," Gentle replied, though after their conversation it shouldn't have done. "Is he happy?" he asked, knowing the question might be viewed as a banality, but wanting reassurance.

"No spirit is happy," Pie replied. "There's no release for them. Not in this Dominion or any other. They haunt the doors, waiting to leave, but there's nowhere for them to go."

"Why?"

"That's a question that's been asked for many generations, Gentle. And unanswered. As a child I was taught that before the Unbeheld went into the First Dominion there was a place there into which all spirits were received. My people lived in that Dominion then, and watched over that place, but the Unbeheld drove both the spirits and my people out."

"So the spirits have nowhere to go?"

"Exactly. Their numbers swell, and so does their grief."

He thought of Taylor, lying on his deathbed, dreaming of release, of the final flight into the Absolute. Instead, if Pie was to be believed, his spirit had entered a place of lost

souls, denied both flesh and revelation. What price understanding now, when the end of everything was limbo?

"Who is this Unbeheld?" Gentle said.

"Hapexamendios, the God of the Imajica."

"Is He a God of this world too?"

"He was once. But He went out of the Fifth Dominion,
through the other worlds, laying their divinities waste, until
He reached the Place of Spirits. Then He drew a veil across
that Dominion—"

"And became Unbeheld."

"That's what I was taught."

The formality and plainness of Pie 'oh' pah's account
lent the story authority, but for all its elegance it was still a
tale of gods and other worlds, very far from this dark room
and the cold rain running on the glass.

"How do I know any of this is true?" Gentle said.

"You don't, unless you see it with your own eyes," Pie
'oh' pah replied. His voice when he said this was almost sul-
try. He spoke like a seducer.

"And how do I do that?"

"You must ask me direct questions, and I'll try to answer them. I can't reply to generalities."

"All right, answer this: Can you take me to the Dominions?"

"That I can do."

"I want to follow in the footsteps of Hapexamendios.
Can we do that?"

"We can try."

"I want to see the Unbeheld, Pie 'oh' pah. I want to
know why Taylor and your children are in Purgatory. I
want to *understand* why they're suffering."

There was no question in this speech, therefore no reply
except the other's quickening breath.

"Can you take us now?" Gentle said.

"If that's what you want."

"It's what I want, Pie. Prove what you've said is true, or
leave me alone forever."

———

It was eighteen minutes to midnight when Jude got into her car to start her journey to Gentle's house. It was an easy drive, with the roads so clear, and she was several times tempted to jump red lights, but the police were especially vigilant on this night, and any infringement might bring them out of hiding. Though she had no alcohol in her system, she was by no means sure it was innocent of alien influences. She therefore drove as cautiously as at noon, and it took fully fifteen minutes to reach the studio. When she did she found the upper windows dark. Had Gentle decided to drown his sorrows in a night of high life, she wondered, or was he already fast asleep? If the latter, she had news worth waking him for.

"There are some things you should understand before we leave," Pie said, tying their wrists together, left to right, with a belt. "This is no easy journey, Gentle. This Dominion, the Fifth, is unreconciled, which means that getting to the Fourth involves risk. It's not like crossing a bridge. Passing over requires considerable power. And if anything goes wrong, the consequences will be dire."

"Tell me the worst."

"In between the Reconciled Dominions and the Fifth is a state called the In Ovo. It's an ether, in which things that have ventured from their worlds are imprisoned. Some of them are innocent. They're there by accident. Some were dispatched there as a judgment. They're lethal. I'm hoping we'll pass through the In Ovo before any of them even notice we're there. But if we were to become separated—"

"I get the picture. You'd better tighten that knot. It could still work loose."

Pie bent to the task, with Gentle fumbling to help in the darkness.

"Let's assume we get through the In Ovo," Gentle said. "What's on the other side?"

"The Fourth Dominion," Pie replied. "If I'm accurate in my bearings, we'll arrive near the city of Patashoqua."

"And if not?"

"Who knows? The sea. A swamp."

"Shit."

"Don't worry. I've got a good sense of direction. And there's plenty of power between us. I couldn't do this on my own. But together . . ."

"Is this the only way to cross over?"

"Not at all. There are a number of passing places here in the Fifth: stone circles, hidden away. But most of them were created to carry travelers to some particular location. We want to go as free agents. Unseen, unsuspected."

"So why have you chosen Patashoqua?"

"It has . . . sentimental associations," Pie replied. "You'll see for yourself, very soon." The mystif paused. "You *do* still want to go?"

"Of course."

"This is as tight as I can get the knot without stopping our blood."

"Then why are we delaying?"

Pie's fingers touched Gentle's face. "Close your eyes."

Gentle did so. Pie's fingers sought out Gentle's free hand and raised it between them.

"You have to help me," the mystif said.

"Tell me what to do."

"Make a fist. Lightly. Leave enough room for a breath to pass through. Good. Good. All magic proceeds from breath. Remember that."

He did, from somewhere.

"Now," Pie went on. "Put your hand to your face, with your thumb against your chin. There are very few incantations in our workings. No pretty words. Just pneuma like this, and the will behind them."

"I've got the will, if that's what you're asking," Gentle said.

"Then one solid breath is all we need. Exhale until it hurts. I'll do the rest."

"Can I take another breath afterwards?"

"Not in this Dominion."

With that reply the enormity of what they were undertaking struck Gentle. They were leaving Earth. Stepping off the edge of the only reality he'd ever known into another state entirely. He grinned in the darkness, the hand bound to Pie's taking hold of his deliverer's fingers.

"Shall we?" he said.

In the murk ahead of him Pie's teeth gleamed in a matching smile.

"Why not?"

Gentle drew breath.

Somewhere in the house, he heard a door slamming and footsteps on the stairs leading up to the studio. But it was too late for interruptions. He exhaled through his hand, one solid breath which Pie 'oh' pah seemed to snatch from the air between them. Something ignited in the fist the mystif made, bright enough to burn between its clenched fingers. . . .

At the door, Jude saw Gentle's painting almost made flesh: two figures, almost nose to nose, with their faces illuminated by some unnatural source, swelling like a slow explosion between them. She had time to recognize them both—to see the smiles on their faces as they met each other's gaze—then, to her horror, they seemed to turn inside out. She glimpsed wet red surfaces, which folded upon themselves not once but three times in quick succession, each fold diminishing their bodies, until they were slivers of stuff, still folding, and folding, and finally gone.

She sank back against the doorjamb, shock making her nerves cavort. The dog she'd found waiting at the top of the stairs went fearlessly to the place where they'd stood. There was no further magic there, to snatch him after them. The place was dead. They'd gone, the bastards, wherever such avenues led.

The realization drew a yell of rage from her, sufficient to send the dog scurrying for cover. She dearly hoped Gentle heard her, wherever he was. Hadn't she come here to share her revelations with him, so that they could investigate the great unknown together? And all the time he was preparing for his departure without her. Without her!

"How dare you?" she yelled at the empty space.

The dog whined in fear, and the sight of its terror mellowed her. She went down on her haunches.

"I'm sorry," she said to it. "Come here. I'm not cross with you. It's that little fucker Gentle."

The dog was reluctant at first but came to her after a time, its tail wagging intermittently as it grew more confident of her sanity. She rubbed its head, the contact soothing. All was not lost. What Gentle could do, she could do. He didn't have the copyright on adventuring. She'd find a way to go where he'd gone, if she had to eat the blue eye grain by grain to do so.

Church bells began to ring as she sat chewing this over, announcing in their ragged peals the arrival of midnight. Their clamor was accompanied by car horns in the street outside and cheers from a party in an adjacent house.

"Whoopee," she said quietly, on her face the distracted look that had obsessed so many of the opposite sex over the years. She'd forgotten most of them. The ones who'd fought over her, the ones who'd lost their wives in their pursuit of her, even those who'd sold their sanity to find her equal: all were forgotten. History had never much engaged her. It was the future that glittered in her mind's eye, now more than ever.

The past had been written by men. But the future—pregnant with possibilities—the future was a woman.

18

I

Until the rise of Yzordderrex, a rise engineered by the Autarch for reasons more political than geographical, the city of Patashoqua, which lay on the edge of the Fourth Dominion, close to where the In Ovo marked the perimeter of the Reconciled worlds, had just claim to be the preeminent city of the Dominions. Its proud inhabitants called it *casje au casje,* simply meaning the hive of hives, a place of intense and fruitful labor. Its proximity to the Fifth made it particularly prone to influences from that source, and even after Yzordderrex had became the center of power across the Dominions it was to Patashoqua that those at the cutting edge of style and invention looked for the coming thing. Patashoqua had a variation on the motor vehicle in its streets long before Yzordderrex. It had rock and roll in its clubs long before Yzordderrex. It had hamburgers, cinemas, blue jeans, and countless other proofs of modernity long before the great city of the Second. Nor was it simply the trivialities of fashion that Patashoqua reinvented from Fifth Dominion models. It was philosophies and belief systems. Indeed, it was said in Patashoqua that you knew a native of Yzordderrex because he looked like you did yesterday and believed what you'd believed the day before.

As with most cities in love with the modern, however, Patashoqua had deeply conservative roots. Whereas Yzordderrex was a sinful city, notorious for the excesses of its darker Kesparates, the streets of Patashoqua were quiet after nightfall, its occupants in their own beds with their own spouses, plotting vogues. This mingling of chic and conservatism was nowhere more apparent than in architecture. Built as it was in a temperate region, unlike the semitropical Yzordderrex, the buildings did not have to be designed with any climatic extreme in mind. They were either elegantly classical, and built to remain standing until Doomsday, or else functions of some current craze, and likely to be demolished within a week.

But it was on the borders of the city where the most extraordinary sights were to be seen, because it was here that a second, parasitical city had been created, peopled by inhabitants of the Four Dominions who had fled persecution and had looked to Patashoqua as a place where liberty of thought and action were still possible. How much longer this would remain the case was a debate that dominated every social gathering in the city. The Autarch had moved against other towns, cities, and states which he and his councils judged hotbeds of revolutionary thought. Some of those cities had been razed; others had come under Yzordderrexian edict and all sign of independent thought crushed. The university city of Hezoir, for instance, had been reduced to rubble, the brains of its students literally scooped out of their skulls and heaped up in the streets. In the Azzimulto the inhabitants of an entire province had been decimated, so rumor went, by a disease introduced into that region by the Autarch's representatives. There were tales of atrocity from so many sources that people became almost blasé about the newest horror, until, of course, somebody asked how long it would be until the Autarch turned his unforgiving eyes on the hive of hives. Then their faces drained of color, and people talked in whispers of how they planned to escape or defend themselves if that day ever came; and they looked around at their exquisite city, built to stand until Doomsday, and wondered just how near that day was.

2

Though Pie 'oh' pah had briefly described the forces that haunted the In Ovo, Gentle had only the vaguest impression of the dark protean state between the Dominions, occupied as he was by a spectacle much closer to his heart, that of the change that overtook both travelers as their bodies were translated into the common currency of passage.

Dizzied by lack of oxygen, he wasn't certain whether these were real phenomena or not. Could bodies open like flowers, and the seeds of an essential self fly from them the way his mind told him they did? And could those same bodies be remade at the other end of the journey, arriving whole despite the trauma they'd undergone? So it seemed. The world Pie had called the Fifth folded up before the travelers' eyes, and they went like transported dreams into another place entirely. As soon as he saw the light, Gentle fell to his knees on the hard rock, drinking the air of this Dominion with gratitude.

"Not bad at all," he heard Pie say. "We did it, Gentle. I

didn't think we were going to make it for a moment, but we did it!''

Gentle raised his head, as Pie pulled him to his feet by the strap that joined them.

"Up! Up!" the mystif said. "It's not good to start a journey on your knees."

It was a bright day here, Gentle saw, the sky above his head cloudless, and brilliant as the green-gold sheen of a peacock's tail. There was neither sun nor moon in it, but the very air seemed lucid, and by it Gentle had his first true sight of Pie since they'd met in the fire. Perhaps out of remembrance for those it had lost, the mystif was still wearing the clothes it had worn that night, scorched and bloodied though they were. But it had washed the dirt from its face, and its skin gleamed in the clear light.

"Good to see you," Gentle said.

"You too."

Pie started to untie the belt that bound them, while Gentle turned his gaze on the Dominion. They were standing close to the summit of a hill, a quarter of a mile from the perimeters of a sprawling shantytown, from which a din of activity rose. It spread beyond the foot of the hill and halfway across a flat and treeless plain of ocher earth, crossed by a thronged highway that led his eye to the domes and spires of a glittering city.

"Patashoqua?" he said.

"Where else?"

"You were accurate, then."

"More than I dared hope. The hill we're standing on is supposed to be the place where Hapexamendios first rested when He came through from the Fifth. It's called the Mount of Lipper Bayak. Don't ask me why."

"Is the city under siege?" Gentle said.

"I don't think so. The gates look open to me."

Gentle scanned the distant walls, and indeed the gates were open wide. "So who are all these people? Refugees?"

"We'll ask in a while," Pie said.

The knot had come undone. Gentle rubbed his wrist, which was indented by the belt, staring down the hill as he did so. Moving between the makeshift dwellings below he glimpsed forms of being that didn't much resemble humanity. And, mingling freely with them, many who did. It wouldn't be difficult to pass as a local, at least.

"You're going to have to teach me, Pie," he said. "I need to know who's who and what's what. Do they speak English here?"

"It used to be quite a popular language," Pie replied. "I can't believe it's fallen out of fashion. But before we go any farther, I think you should know what you're traveling with. The way people respond to me may confound you otherwise."

"Tell me as we go," Gentle said, eager to see the strangers below up close.

"As you wish." They began to descend. "I'm a mystif; my name's Pie 'oh' pah. That much you know. My gender you don't."

"I've made a guess," Gentle said.

"Oh?" said Pie, smiling. "And what's your guess?"

"You're an androgyne. Am I right?"

"That's part of it, certainly."

"But you've got a talent for illusion. I saw that in New York."

"I don't like the word *illusion*. It makes me a guiser, and I'm not that."

"What then?"

"In New York you wanted Judith, and that's what you saw. It was *your* invention, not mine."

"But you played along."

"Because I wanted to be with you."

"And are you playing along now?"

"I'm not deceiving you, if that's what you mean. What you see is what I am, to you."

"But to other people?"

"I may be something different. A man sometimes. A woman others."

"Could you be white?"

"I might manage it for a moment or two. But if I'd tried to come to your bed in daylight, you'd have known I wasn't

Judith. Or if you'd been in love with an eight-year-old, or a dog. I couldn't have accommodated that, except . . ."—the creature glanced around at him—". . . under very particular circumstances."

Gentle wrestled with this notion, questions biological, philosophical, and libidinous filling his head. He stopped walking for a moment and turned to Pie.

"Let me tell you what I see," he said. "Just so you know."

"Good."

"If I passed you on the street I believe I'd think you were a woman"—he cocked his head—"though maybe not. I suppose it'd depend on the light, and how fast you were walking." He laughed. "Oh, shit," he said. "The more I look at you the more I see, and the more I see—"

"The less you know."

"That's right. You're not a man. That's plain enough. But then . . ." He shook his head. "Am I seeing you the way you really are? I mean, is this the final version?"

"Of course not. There's stranger sights inside us both. You know that."

"Not until now."

"We can't go too naked in the world. We'd burn out each other's eyes."

"But this *is* you."

"For the time being."

"For what it's worth, I like it," Gentle said. "I don't know what I'd call you if I saw you in the street, but I'd turn my head. How's that?"

"What more could I ask for?"

"Will I meet others like you?"

"A few, maybe," Pie said. "But mystifs aren't common. When one is born, it's an occasion for great celebration among my people."

"Who are your people?"

"The Eurhetemec."

"Will they be here?" Gentle said, nodding towards the throng below.

"I doubt it. But in Yzordderrex, certainly. They have a Kesparate there."

"What's a Kesparate?"

"A district. My people have a city within the city. Or at least they had one. It's two hundred and twenty-one years since I was there."

"My God. How old are you?"

"Half that again. I know that sounds like an extraordinary span, but time works slowly on flesh touched by feits."

"Feits?"

"Magical workings. Feits, wantons, sways. They work their miracles even on a whore like me."

"Whoa!" said Gentle.

"Oh, yes. That's something else you should know about me. I was told—a long time ago—that I should spend my life as a whore or an assassin, and that's what I've done."

"Until now, maybe. But that's over."

"What will I be from now on?"

"My friend," Gentle said, without hesitation.

The mystif smiled. "Thank you for that."

The round of questions ended there, and side by side they wandered on down the slope.

"Don't make your interest too apparent," Pie advised as they approached the edge of this makeshift conurbation. "Pretend you see this sort of sight daily."

"That's going to be difficult," Gentle predicted.

So it was. Walking through the narrow spaces between the shanties was like passing through a country in which the very air had evolutionary ambition, and to breathe was to change. A hundred kinds of eye gazed out at them from doorways and windows, while a hundred forms of limb got about the business of the day—cooking, nursing, crafting, conniving, making fires and deals and love—and all glimpsed so briefly that after a few paces Gentle was obliged to look away, to study the muddy gutter they were walking in, lest his mind be overwhelmed by the sheer profusion of sights. Smells, too: aromatic, sickly, sour and sweet; and sounds that made his skull shake and his gut quiver.

There had been nothing in his life to date, either waking or sleeping, to prepare him for this. He'd studied the masterworks of great imaginers—he'd painted a passable Goya, once, and sold an Ensor for a little fortune—but the difference between paint and reality was vast, a gap whose scale he could not by definition have known until now, when he had around him the other half of the equation. This wasn't an invented place, its inhabitants variations on experienced phenomena. It was independent of his terms of reference: a place unto and of itself.

When he looked up again, daring the assault of the strange, he was grateful that he and Pie were now in a quarter occupied by more human entities, though even here there were surprises. What seemed to be a three-legged child skipped across their path only to look back with a face wizened as a desert corpse, its third leg a tail. A woman sitting in a doorway, her hair being combed by her consort, drew her robes around her as Gentle looked her way, but not fast enough to conceal the fact that a second consort, with the skin of a herring and an eye that ran all the way around its skull, was kneeling in front of her, inscribing hieroglyphics on her belly with the sharpened heel of its hand. He heard a range of tongues being spoken, but English seemed to be the commonest parlance, albeit heavily accented or corrupted by the labial anatomy of the speaker. Some seemed to sing their speech; some almost to vomit it up.

But the voice that called to them from one of the crowded alleyways off to their right might have been heard on any street in London: a lisping, pompous holler demanding they halt in their tracks. They looked in its direction. The throng had divided to allow the speaker and his party of three easy passage.

"Play dumb," Pie muttered to Gentle as the lisper, an overfed gargoyle, bald but for an absurd wreath of oiled kiss curls, approached.

He was finely dressed, his high black boots polished and his canary yellow jacket densely embroidered after what Gentle would come to know as the present Patashoquan fashion. A man much less showily garbed followed, an eye covered by a patch that trailed the tail feathers of a scarlet bird as if echoing the moment of his mutilation. On his shoulders he carried a woman in black, with silvery scales for skin and a cane in her tiny hands with which she tapped her mount's head to speed him on his way. Still farther behind came the oddest of the four.

"A Nullianac," Gentle heard Pie murmur.

He didn't need to ask if this was good news or bad. The creature was its own best advertisement, and it was selling harm. Its head resembled nothing so much as praying hands, the thumbs leading and tipped with lobster's eyes, the gap between the palms wide enough for the sky to be seen through it, but flickering, as arcs of energy passed from side to side. It was without question the ugliest living thing Gentle had ever seen. If Pie had not suggested they obey the edict and halt, Gentle would have taken to his heels there and then, rather than let the Nullianac get one stride closer to them.

The lisper had halted and now addressed them afresh. "What business have you in Vanaeph?" he wanted to know.

"We're just passing through," Pie said, a reply somewhat lacking in invention, Gentle thought.

"Who are you?" the man demanded.

"Who are *you?*" Gentle returned.

The patch-eyed mount guffawed and got his head slapped for his troubles.

"Loitus Hammeryock," the lisper replied.

"My name's Zacharias," Gentle said, "and this is—"

"Casanova," Pie said, which earned him a quizzical glance from Gentle.

"Zooical!" the woman said. "D'yee speakat te gloss?"

"Sure," said Gentle. "I speakat te gloss."

"Be careful," Pie whispered at his side.

"Bone! Bone!" the woman went on, and proceeded to tell them, in a language which was two parts English, or a variant thereof, one part Latin, and one part some Fourth Dominion dialect that consisted of tongue clicks and teeth tappings, that all strangers to this town, Neo Vanaeph, had to register their origins and intentions before they were allowed access: or, indeed, the right to depart. For all its ramshackle appearance, Vanaeph was no lawless stew, it appeared, but a tightly policed township, and this woman—who introduced herself in this flurry of lexicons as Pontiff Farrow—was a significant authority here.

When she'd finished, Gentle cast a confounded look in Pie's direction. This was proving more difficult terrain by the moment. Unconcealed in the Pontiff's speech was threat of summary execution if they failed to answer their inquiries satisfactorily. The executioner among this party was not hard to spot: he of the prayerful head—the Nullianac—waiting in the rear for his instructions.

"So," said Hammeryock. "We need some identification."

"I don't have any," Gentle said.

"And you?" he asked the mystif, which also shook its head.

"Spies," the Pontiff hissed.

"No, we're just . . . tourists," Gentle said.

"Tourists?" said Hammeryock.

"We've come to see the sights of Patashoqua." He turned to Pie for support. "Whatever they are."

"The tombs of the Vehement Loki Lobb," Pie said, clearly scratching around for the glories Patashoqua had to offer, "and the Merrow Ti' Ti'."

That sounded pretty to Gentle's ears. He faked a broad smile of enthusiasm. "The Merrow Ti' Ti'!" he said. "Absolutely! I wouldn't miss the Merrow Ti' Ti' for all the tea in China."

"*China?*" said Hammeryock.

"Did I say China?"

"You did."

"Fifth Dominion," the Pontiff muttered. "Spiatits from the Fifth Dominion."

"I object strongly to that accusation," said Pie 'oh' pah.

"And so," said a voice behind the accused, "do I."

Both Pie and Gentle turned to take in the sight of a scabrous, bearded individual, dressed in what might generously have been described as motley and less generously as rags, standing on one leg and scraping shit off the heel of his other foot with a stick.

"It's the hypocrisy that turns my stomach, Hammeryock," he said, his expression a maze of wiles. "You two pontificate," he went on, eyeing his pun's target as he spoke, "about keeping the streets free from undesirables, but you do nothing about the dog shite!"

"This isn't your business, Tick Raw," Hammeryock said.

"Oh, but it is. These are my friends, and you've insulted them with your slurs and your suspicions."

"Friends, sayat?" the Pontiff murmured.

"Yes, ma'am. Friends. Some of us still know the difference between conversation and diatribe. I have friends, with whom I talk and exchange ideas. Remember *ideas?* They're what make life worth living."

Hammeryock could not disguise his unease, hearing his mistress thus addressed, but whoever Tick Raw was he wielded sufficient authority to silence any further objection.

"My dearlings," he said to Gentle and Pie, "shall we repair to my home?"

As a parting gesture he lobbed the stick in Hammeryock's direction. It landed in the mud between the man's legs.

"Clean up, Loitus," Tick Raw said. "We don't want the Autarch's heel sliding in shite, now, do we?"

The two parties then went their separate ways, Tick Raw leading Pie and Gentle off through the labyrinth.

"We want to thank you," Gentle said.

"What for?" Tick Raw asked him, aiming a kick at a goat that wandered across his path.

"Talking us out of trouble," Gentle replied. "We'll be on our way now."

"But you've got to come back with me," Tick Raw said.

"There's no need."

"Need? There's *every* need! Have I got this right?" he said to Pie. "Is there need or isn't there?"

"We'd certainly like the benefit of your insights," Pie said. "We're strangers here. Both of us." The mystif spoke in an oddly stilted fashion, as if it wanted to say more, but couldn't. "We need reeducating," it said.

"Oh?" said Tick Raw. "Really?"

"Who is this Autarch?" Gentle asked.

"He rules the Reconciled Dominions, from Yzordder-rex. He's the greatest power in the Imajica."

"And he's coming here?"

"That's the rumor. He's losing his grip in the Fourth, and he knows it. So he's decided to put in a personal appearance. Officially, he's visiting Patashoqua, but this is where the trouble's brewing."

"Do you think he'll definitely come?" Pie asked.

"If he doesn't, the whole of the Imajica's going to know he's afraid to show his face. Of course that's always been a part of his fascination, hasn't it? All these years he's ruled the Dominions without anybody really knowing what he looks like. But the glamour's worn off. If he wants to avoid revolution he's going to have to prove he's a charismatic."

"Are you going to get blamed for telling Hammeryock we were your friends?" Gentle asked.

"Probably, but I've been accused of worse. Besides, it's almost true. Any stranger here's a friend of mine." He cast a glance at Pie. "Even a mystif," he said. "The people in this dung heap have no poetry in them. I know I should be more sympathetic. They're refugees, most of them. They've lost their lands, their houses, their tribes. But they're so concerned with their itsy-bitsy little sorrows they don't see the broader picture."

"And what *is* the broader picture?" Gentle asked.

"I think that's better discussed behind closed doors," Tick Raw said, and would not be drawn any further on the subject until they were secure in his hut.

———

It was spartan in the extreme. Blankets on a board for a bed; another board for a table; some moth-eaten pillows to squat on.

"This is what I'm reduced to," Tick Raw said to Pie, as though the mystif understood, perhaps even shared, his sense of humiliation. "If I'd moved on it might have been different. But I couldn't, of course."

"Why not?" Gentle asked.

Tick Raw gave him a quizzical look, glancing over at Pie, then looking back at Gentle again.

"I'd have thought that was obvious," he said. "I've kept my post. I'm here until a better day dawns."

"And when will that be?" Gentle inquired.

"You tell me," Tick Raw replied, a certain bitterness entering his voice. "Tomorrow wouldn't be too soon. This is no frigging life for a great sway-worker. I mean, look at it!" He cast his eyes around the room. "And let me tell you, this is the lap of luxury compared with some of the hovels I could show you. People living in their own excrement, grubbing around for food. And all in sight of one of the richest cities in the Dominions. It's obscene. At least I've got food in my belly. And I get some respect, you know. Nobody crosses me. They know I'm an evocator, and they keep their distance. Even Hammeryock. He hates me with a passion, but he'd never dare send the Nullianac to kill me, in case it failed and I came after him. Which I would. Oh, yes. Gladly. Pompous little fuck."

"You should just leave," Gentle said. "Go and live in Patashoqua."

"Please," Tick Raw said, his tone vaguely pained. "Must we play games? Haven't I proved my integrity? I saved your lives."

"And we're grateful," Gentle said.

"I don't want gratitude," Tick Raw said.

"What do you want then? Money?"

At this, Tick Raw rose from his cushion, his face reddening, not with blushes but with rage.

"I don't deserve this," he said.

"Deserve *what?*" said Gentle.

"I've lived in shite," Tick Raw said, "but I'm damned if I'm going to eat it! All right, so I'm not a great Maestro. I wish I were! I wish Uter Musky was still alive, and he could have waited here all these years instead of me. But he's gone, and I'm all that's left! Take me or leave me!"

The outburst completely befuddled Gentle. He glanced across at Pie, looking for some guidance, but the mystif had hung its head.

"Maybe we'd better leave," Gentle said.

"Yes! Why don't you do that?" Tick Raw yelled. "Get the fuck out of here. Maybe you can find Musky's grave and resurrect him. He's out there on the mount. I buried him with these two hands!" His voice was close to cracking now. There was grief in it as well as rage. "You can dig him up the same way!"

Gentle started to get to his feet, sensing that any further words from him would only push Tick Raw closer to an eruption or a breakdown, neither of which he wanted to witness. But the mystif reached up and took hold of Gentle's arm.

"Wait," Pie said.

"The man wants us out," Gentle replied.

"Let me talk to Tick for a few moments," Pie said.

The evocator glared fiercely at the mystif.

"I'm in no mood for seductions," he warned.

The mystif shook its head, glancing at Gentle. "Neither am I."

"You want me out of here?" he said.

"Not for long."

Gentle shrugged, though he felt rather less easy with the idea of leaving Pie in Tick Raw's company than his manner suggested. There was something about the way the two of them stared and studied each other that made him think there was some hidden agenda here. If so, it was surely sexual, despite their denials.

"I'll be outside," Gentle said, and left them to their debate.

He'd no sooner closed the door than he heard the two begin to talk inside. There was a good deal of din from the shack opposite—a baby bawling, a mother attempting to hush it with an off-key lullaby—but he caught fragments of the exchange. Tick Raw was still in a fury.

"Is this some kind of punishment?" he demanded at one point; then, a few moments later: "Patient? How much more frigging patient do I have to be?"

The lullaby blotted out much of what followed, and when it quieted again, the conversation inside Raw's shack had taken another turn entirely.

"We've got a long way to go," Gentle heard Pie saying, "and a lot to learn." Tick Raw made some inaudible reply, to which Pie said, "He's a stranger here."

Again Tick murmured something.

"I can't do that," Pie replied. "He's my responsibility."

Now Tick Raw's persuasions grew loud enough for Gentle to hear.

"You're wasting your time," the evocator said. "Stay here with me. I miss a warm body at night."

At this Pie's voice dropped to a whisper. Gentle took a half step back towards the door and managed to catch a few of the mystif's words. It said *heartbroken*, he was sure; then something about faith. But the rest was a murmur too soft to be interpreted. Deciding he'd given the two of them long enough alone, he announced that he was coming back in and entered. Both looked up at him: somewhat guiltily, he thought.

"I want to get out of here," he announced.

Tick Raw's hand was at Pie's neck and remained there, like a staked claim.

"If you go," Tick told the mystif, "I can't guarantee your safety. Hammeryock will be wanting your blood."

"We can defend ourselves," Gentle said, somewhat surprised by his own certainty.

"Maybe we shouldn't be quite so hasty," Pie put in.

"We've got a journey to make," Gentle replied.

"Let her make up her own mind," Tick Raw suggested. "She's not your property."

At this remark, a curious look crossed Pie 'oh' pah's face. Not guilt now, but a troubled expression, softening into resignation. The mystif's hand went up to its neck and brushed off Tick Raw's hold.

"He's right," it said to Tick. "We do have a journey ahead of us."

The evocator pursed his lips, as if making up his mind whether to pursue this business any further or not. Then he said, "Well then. You'd better go."

He turned a sour eye on Gentle.

"May everything be as it seems, stranger."

"Thank you," said Gentle, and escorted Pie out of the hut into the mud and flurry of Vanaeph.

"Strange thing to say," Gentle observed as they trudged away from Tick Raw's hut. *"May everything be as it seems."*

"It's the profoundest curse a sway-worker knows," Pie replied.

"I see."

"On the contrary," Pie said, "I don't think you see very much."

There was a note of accusation in Pie's words which Gentle rose to.

"I certainly saw what you were up to," he said. "You had half a mind to stay with him. Batting your eyes like a—" He stopped himself.

"Go on," Pie replied. "Say it. Like a *whore.*"

"That wasn't what I meant."

"No, please." Pie went on, bitterly. "You can lay on the insults. Why not? It can be very arousing."

Gentle shot Pie a look of disgust.

"You said you wanted education, Gentle. Well, let's start with *May everything be as it seems*. It's a curse, because if that were the case we'd all be living just to die, and mud would be king of the Dominions."

"I get it," Gentle said. "And you'd be just a whore."

"And you'd be just a faker, working for—"

Before the rest of the sentence was out of his mouth, a pack of animals ran out between two of the dwellings, squealing like pigs, though they looked more like tiny llamas. Gentle looked in the direction from which they'd

come, and saw—advancing between the shanties—a sight
to bring shudders.

"The Nullianac!"

"I see it!" Pie said.

As the executioner approached, the praying hands of its
head opened and closed, as though kindling the energies
between the palms to a lethal heat. There were cries of
alarm from the houses around. Doors slammed. Shutters
closed. A child was snatched from a step, bawling as it
went. Gentle had time to see the executioner draw two
weapons, with blades that caught the livid light of the arcs;
then he was obeying Pie's instruction to run, the mystif
leading the way.

The street they'd been on was no more than a narrow
gutter, but it was a well-lit highway by comparison with the
narrow alley they ducked into. Pie was light-footed; Gentle
was not. Twice the mystif made a turn and Gentle overshot
it. The second time he lost Pie entirely in the murk and dirt
and was about to retrace his steps when he heard the executioner's blade slice through something behind him and
glanced back to see one of the frailer houses folding up in a
cloud of dust and screams, its demolisher's shape, light-
ning-headed, appearing from the chaos and fixing its gaze
upon him. Its target sighted, it advanced with a sudden
speed, and Gentle darted for cover at the first turn, a route
that took him into a swamp of sewage which he barely
crossed without falling, and thence into even narrower passages.

It would only be a matter of time before he chanced
upon a cul-de-sac, he knew. When he did, the game would
be up. He felt an itch at the nape of his neck, as though the
blades were already there. This wasn't right! He'd barely
been out of the Fifth an hour and he was seconds from
death. He glanced back. The Nullianac had closed the distance between them. He picked up his pace, pitching himself around a corner and into a tunnel of corrugated iron,
with no way out at the other end.

"Shite!" he said, taking Tick Raw's favorite word for his
complaint. "Furie, you've killed yourself!"

The walls of the cul-de-sac were slick with filth, and high. Knowing he'd never scale them, he ran to the far end and threw himself against the wall there, hoping it might crack. But its builders (damn them!) had been better craftsmen than most in the vicinity. The wall rocked, and pieces of its fetid mortar fell about him, but all his efforts did was bring the Nullianac straight to him, drawn by the sound of his effort.

Seeing his executioner approaching, he pitched his body against the wall afresh, hoping for some last-minute reprieve. But all he got was bruises. The itch at his nape was an ache now, but through its pain he formed the despairing thought that this was surely the most ignominious of deaths, to be sliced up amid sewage. What had he done to deserve it? He asked it aloud.

"What have I done? What the fuck have I done?"

The question went unanswered; or did it? As his yells ceased he found himself raising his hand to his face, not knowing—even as he did so—why. There was simply an inner compulsion to open his palm and spit upon it. The spittle felt cold, or else his palm was hot. Now a yard away, the Nullianac raised its twin blades above its head. Gentle made a fist, lightly, and put it to his mouth. As the blades reached the top of their arc, he exhaled.

He felt his breath blaze against his palm, and in the instant before the blades reached his head the pneuma went from his fist like a bullet. It struck the Nullianac in the neck with such force it was thrown backwards, a livid spurt of energy breaking from the gap in its head and rising like earth-born lightning into the sky. The creature fell in the filth, its hands dropping the blades to reach for the wound. They never touched the place. Its life went out of it in a spasm, and its prayerful head was permanently silenced.

At least as shaken by the other's death as by the proximity of his own, Gentle got to his feet, his gaze going from the body in the dirt to his fist. He opened it. The spittle had gone, transformed into some lethal dart. A seam of discoloration ran from the ball of his thumb to the other side of his hand. That was the only sign of the pneuma's passing.

"Holy shite," he said.

A small crowd had already gathered at the end of the cul-de-sac, and heads appeared over the wall behind him. From every side came an agitated buzz that wouldn't, he guessed, take long to reach Hammeryock and Pontiff Farrow. It would be naïve to suppose they ruled Vanaeph with only one executioner in their squad. There'd be others; and here, soon. He stepped over the body, not caring to look too closely at the damage he'd done, but aware with only a passing glance that it was substantial.

The crowd, seeing the conquerer approach, parted. Some bowed, others fled. One said, "Bravo!" and tried to kiss his hand. He pressed his admirer away and scanned the alleys in every direction, hoping for some sign of Pie 'oh' pah. Finding none, he debated his options. Where would Pie go? Not to the top of the mount. Though that was a visible rendezvous, their enemies would spot them there. Where else? The gates of Patashoqua, perhaps, that the mystif had pointed out when they'd first arrived? It was as good a place as any, he thought, and started off, down through teeming Vanaeph towards the glorious city.

His worst expectations—that news of his crime had reached the Pontiff and her league—were soon confirmed. He was almost at the edge of the township, and within sight of the open ground that lay between its borders and the walls of Patashoqua, when a hue and cry from the streets behind announced a pursuing party. In his Fifth Dominion garb, jeans and shirt, he would be easily recognized if he started towards the gates, but if he attempted to stay within the confines of Vanaeph it would be only a matter of time before he was hunted down. Better to take the chance of running now, he decided, while he still had a lead. Even if he didn't make it to the gates before they came after him, they surely wouldn't dispatch him within sight of Patashoqua's gleaming walls.

He put on a fair turn of speed and was out of the township in less than a minute, the commotion behind him gathering volume. Though it was difficult to judge the distance to the gates in a light that lent such iridescence to the ground between, it was certainly no less than a mile; perhaps twice that. He'd not got far when the first of his pursuers appeared from the outskirts of Vanaeph, runners fresher and lighter than he, who rapidly closed the distance between them. There were plenty of travelers coming and going along the straight road to the gates. Some pedestrians, most in groups and dressed like pilgrims; other, finer figures, mounted on horses whose flanks and heads were painted with gaudy designs; still others riding on shaggy derivatives of the mule. Most envied however, and most rare, were those in motor vehicles, which, though they basically resembled their equivalents in the Fifth—a chassis riding on wheels—were in every other regard fresh inventions. Some were as elaborate as baroque altarpieces, every inch of their bodywork chased and filigreed. Others, with spindly wheels twice the height of their roofs, had the preposterous delicacy of tropical insects. Still others, mounted on a dozen or more tiny wheels, their exhausts giving off a dense, bitter fume, looked like speeding wreckage, asymmetrical and inelegant farragoes of glass and metalwork. Risking death by hoof and wheel, Gentle joined the traffic and put on a new spurt as he dodged between the vehicles. The leaders of the pack behind him had also reached the road. They were armed, he saw, and had no compunction about displaying their weapons. His belief that they wouldn't attempt to kill him among witnesses suddenly seemed frail. Perhaps the law of Vanaeph was good to the very gates of Patashoqua. If so, he was dead. They would overtake him long before he reached sanctuary.

But now, above the din of the highway, another sound reached him, and he dared a glance off to his left, to see a small, plain vehicle, its engine badly tuned, careering in his direction. It was open-topped, its driver visible: Pie 'oh' pah, God love him, driving like a man—or mystif—possessed. Gentle changed direction instantly, veering off the road and dividing a herd of pilgrims as he did so, and raced towards Pie's noisy chariot.

A chorus of whoops at his back told him the pursuers had also changed direction, but the sight of Pie had given

heat to Gentle's heels. His turn of speed was wasted, however. Rather than slowing to let Gentle aboard, Pie drove
on past, heading towards the hunters. The leaders scattered
as the vehicle bore down upon them, but it was a figure
Gentle had missed, being carried in a sedan chair, who was
Pie's true target. Hammeryock, sitting on high, ready to
watch the execution, was suddenly a target in his turn. He
yelled to his bearers to retreat, but in their panic they failed
to agree on a direction. Two pulled left, two right. One of
the chair's arms splintered, and Hammeryock was pitched
out, hitting the ground hard. He didn't get up. The sedan
chair was discarded, and its bearers fled, leaving Pie to veer
around and head back towards Gentle. With their leader
felled, the scattered pursuers, most likely coerced into serving the Pontiffs in the first place, had lost heart. They were
not sufficiently inspired to risk Hammeryock's fate and so
kept their distance, while Pie drove back and picked up his
gasping passenger.

"I thought maybe you'd gone back to Tick Raw," Gentle said, once he was aboard.

"He wouldn't have wanted me," Pie said. "I've had congress with a murderer."

"Who's that?"

"You, my friend, *you!* We're both assassins now."

"I suppose we are."

"And not much welcome in this region, I think."

"Where did you find the vehicle?"

"There's a few of them parked on the outskirts. They'll
be in them soon enough, and after us."

"The sooner we're in the city the better, then."

"I don't think we'd be safe there for long," the mystif
replied.

It had maneuvered the vehicle so that its snub nose
faced the highway. The choice lay before them. Left, to the
gates of Patashoqua. Right, down a highway which ran on
past the Mount of Lipper Bayak to a horizon that rose, at
the farthest limit of the eye, to a mountain range.

"It's up to you," Pie said.

Gentle looked longingly towards the city, tempted by its spires. But he knew there was wisdom in Pie's advice.

"We'll come back someday, won't we?" he said.

"Certainly, if that's what you want."

"Then let's head the other way."

The mystif turned the vehicle onto the highway, against the predominant flow of traffic, and with the city behind them they soon picked up speed.

"So much for Patashoqua," Gentle said as the walls became a mirage.

"No great loss," Pie remarked.

"But I wanted to see the Merrow Ti' Ti'," Gentle said.

"No chance," Pie returned.

"Why?"

"It was pure invention," Pie said. "Like all my favorite things, including myself. Pure invention!"

19

I

Though Jude had made an oath, in all sobriety, to follow Gentle wherever she'd seen him go, her plans for pursuit were stymied by a number of claims upon her energies, the most pressing of which was Clem's. He needed her advice, comfort, and organizational skills in the dreary, rainy days that followed New Year, and despite the urgency of her agenda she could scarcely turn her back on him. Taylor's funeral took place on January ninth, with a memorial service which Clem took great pains to perfect. It was a melancholy triumph: a time for Taylor's friends and relations to mingle and express their affections for the departed man. Jude met people she'd not seen in many years, and few, if any, failed to comment on the one conspicuous absentee: Gentle. She told everybody what she'd told Clem. That Gentle had been going through a bad time, and the last she'd heard he was planning to leave on holiday. Clem, of course, would not be fobbed off with such vague excuses. Gentle had left knowing that Taylor was dead, and Clem viewed his departure as a kind of cowardice. Jude didn't attempt to defend the wanderer. She simply tried to make as little mention of Gentle in Clem's presence as she could.

But the subject would keep coming up, one way or another. Sorting through Taylor's belongings after the funeral, Clem came upon three watercolors, painted by Gentle in the style of Samuel Palmer, but signed with his own name and dedicated to Taylor. Pictures of idealized landscapes, they couldn't help but turn Clem's thoughts back to Taylor's unrequited love for the vanished man, and Jude's to the place he had vanished for. They were among the few items that Clem, perhaps vengefully, wanted to destroy, but Jude persuaded him otherwise. He kept one in memory of Taylor, gave one to Klein, and gave the third to Jude.

Her duty to Clem not only took its toll upon her time but upon her focus. When, in the middle of the month, he suddenly announced that he was going to leave the next day for Tenerife, there to tan his troubles away for a fortnight, she was glad to be released from the daily duties of friend and comforter but found herself unable to rekindle the heat of ambition that had flared in her at the month's first hour. She had one unlikely touchstone, however: the dog. She only had to look at the mutt and she remembered—as though it were an hour ago—standing at the door of Gentle's flat and seeing the pair dissolving in front of her astonished eyes. And on the heels of that memory came thoughts of the news she had been carrying to Gentle that night: the dream journey induced by the stone that was now wrapped up and hidden from sight and seeing in her wardrobe. She was not a great lover of dogs, but she'd taken the mongrel home that night, knowing it would perish if she didn't. It quickly ingratiated itself, wagging a furious welcome when she returned home each night after being with Clem; sneaking into her bedroom in the early hours and making a nest for itself in her soiled clothes. She called it Skin, because it had so little fur, and while she didn't dote on it the way it doted on her, she was still glad of its company. More than once she found herself talking to it at great length, while it licked its paws or its balls, these monologues a means to refocus her thoughts without worrying that she was losing her mind. Three days after Clem's departure for sunnier climes, discussing with Skin how she should best proceed, Estabrook's name came up.

"You haven't met Estabrook," she told Skin. "But I'll guarantee you won't like him. He tried to have me killed, you know?"

The dog looked up from its toilet.

"Yes, I was amazed too," she said. "I mean, that's worse than an animal, right? No disrespect, but it is. I was his wife. I *am* his wife. And he tried to have me killed. What would you do, if you were me? Yes, I know, I should see him. He had the blue eye in his safe. And that book! Remind me to tell you about the book sometime. No, maybe I shouldn't. It'll give you ideas."

Skin settled his head on his crossed paws, gave a small sigh of contentment, and started to doze.

"You're a big help," she said. "I need some advice here. What do you say to a man who tried to have you murdered?"

Skin's eyes were closed, so she was obliged to furnish her own reply.

"I say: Hello, Charlie, why don't you tell me the story of your life?"

2

She called Lewis Leader the next day to find out whether Estabrook was still hospitalized. She was told he was, but that he'd been moved to a private clinic in Hampstead. Leader supplied details of his whereabouts, and Jude called to inquire both about Estabrook's condition and visiting hours. She was told he was still under close scrutiny but seemed to be in better spirits than he'd been, and she was welcome to come and see him at any time. There seemed little purpose in delaying the meeting. She drove up to

Hampstead that very evening, through another tumultuous rainstorm, arriving to a welcome from the psychiatric nurse in charge of Estabrook's case, a chatty young man called Maurice who lost his top lip when he smiled, which was often, and talked with an almost indiscreet enthusiasm about the state of his patient's mind.

"He has good days," Maurice said brightly. Then, just as brightly: "But not many. He's severely depressed. He made one attempt to kill himself before he came to us, but he's settled down a lot."

"Is he sedated?"

"We help keep the anxiety controllable, but he's not drugged senseless. We can't help him get to the root of the problem if he is."

"Has he told you what that is?" she said, expecting accusations to be tossed in her direction.

"It's pretty obscure," Maurice said. "He talks about you very fondly, and I'm sure your coming will do him a great deal of good. But the problem's obviously with his blood relatives. I've got him to talk a little about his father and his brother, but he's very cagey. The father's dead, of course, but maybe you can shed some light on the brother."

"I never met him."

"That's a pity. Charles clearly feels a great deal of anger towards his brother, but I haven't got to the root of why. I will. It'll just take time. He's very good at keeping his secrets to himself, isn't he? But then you probably know that. Shall I take you along to see him? I *did* tell him you'd telephoned, so I think he's expecting you."

Jude was irritated that the element of surprise had been removed, that Estabrook would have had time to prepare his feints and fabrications. But what was done was done, and rather than snap at the gleeful Maurice for his indiscretion she kept her displeasure to herself. She might need the man's smiling assistance in the fullness of time.

Estabrook's room was pleasant enough. Spacious and comfortable, its walls adorned with reproductions of Monet and Renoir, it was a soothing space. Even the piano concerto that played softly in the background seemed composed to placate a troubled mind. Estabrook was not in bed but sitting by the window, one of the curtains drawn aside so he could watch the rain. He was dressed in pajamas and his best dressing gown, smoking. As Maurice had said, he was clearly awaiting his visitor. There was no flicker of surprise when she appeared at the door. And, as she'd anticipated, he had his welcome ready.

"At last, a familiar face."

He didn't open his arms to embrace her, but she went to him and kissed him lightly on both cheeks.

"One of the nurses will get you something to drink, if you'd like," he said.

"Yes, I'd like some coffee. It's bitter out there."

"Maybe Maurice'll get it, if I promise to unburden my soul."

"Do you?" said Maurice.

"I do. I promise. You'll know the secrets of my potty training by this time tomorrow."

"Milk and sugar?" Maurice asked.

"Just milk," Charlie said. "Unless her tastes have changed."

"No," she told him.

"Of course not. Judith doesn't change. Judith's eternal."

Maurice withdrew, leaving them to talk. There was no embarrassed silence. He had his spiel ready, and while he delivered it—a speech about how glad he was that she'd come, and how much he hoped it meant she would begin to forgive him—she studied his changed face. He'd lost weight and was without his toupée, which revealed in his physiognomy qualities she'd never seen before. His large nose and tugged-down mouth, with jutting over-large lower lip, lent him the look of an aristocrat fallen on hard times. She doubted that she'd ever find it in her heart to love him again, but she could certainly manage a twinge of pity, seeing him so reduced.

"I suppose you want a divorce," he said.

"We can talk about that another time."

"Do you need money?"

"Not at the moment."

"If you do——"

"I'll ask."

A male nurse appeared with coffee for Jude, hot chocolate for Estabrook, and biscuits. When he'd gone, she plunged into a confession. One from her, she reasoned, might elicit one from him.

"I went to the house," she said. "To collect my jewelry."

"And you couldn't get into the safe."

"Oh, no, I got in."

He didn't look at her, but sipped his chocolate noisily.

"And I found some very strange things, Charlie. I'd like to talk about them."

"I don't know what you mean."

"Some souvenirs. A piece of a statute. A book."

"No," he said, still not looking her way. "Those aren't mine. I don't know what they are. Oscar gave them to me to look after."

Here was an intriguing connection. "Where did Oscar get them?" she asked him.

"I didn't inquire," Estabrook said with a detached air. "He travels a lot, you know."

"I'd like to meet him."

"No, you wouldn't," he said hurriedly. "You wouldn't like him at all."

"Globe-trotters are always interesting," she said, attempting to preserve a lightness in her tone.

"I told you," he said. "You wouldn't like him."

"Has he been to see you?"

"No. And I wouldn't see him if he did. Why are you asking me these questions? You've never cared about Oscar before."

"He *is* your brother," she said. "He has some filial responsibility."

"Oscar? He doesn't care for anybody but himself. He only gave me those presents as a sop."

"So they *were* gifts. I thought you were just looking after them."

"Does it matter?" he said, raising his voice a little. "Just don't touch them, they're dangerous. You put them back, yes?"

She lied and told him she had, realizing any more discussion on the matter would only infuriate him further.

"Is there a view out of the window?" she asked him.

"Of the heath," he said. "It's very pretty on sunny days, apparently. They found a body there on Monday. A woman, strangled. I watched them combing the bushes all day yesterday and all day today: looking for clues, I suppose. In this weather. Horrible, to be out in this weather, digging around looking for soiled underwear or some such. Can you imagine? I thought: I'm damn lucky I'm in here, warm and cosy."

If there was any indication of a change in his mental processes it was here, in this strange digression. An earlier Estabrook would have had no patience with any conversation that was not serving a clear purpose. Gossip and its purveyors had drawn his contempt like little else, especially when he knew he was the subject of the tittle-tattle. As to gazing out of a window and wondering how others were faring in the cold, that would have been literally unthinkable two months before. She liked the change, just as she liked the newfound nobility in his profile. Seeing the hidden man revealed gave her faith in her own judgment. Perhaps it was this Estabrook she'd loved all along.

They spoke for a while more, without returning to any of the personal matters between them, and parted on friendly terms, with an embrace that was genuinely warm.

"When will you come again?" he asked her.

"In the next couple of days," she told him.

"I'll be waiting."

So the gifts she'd found in the safe had come from Oscar Godolphin. Oscar the mysterious, who'd kept the family name while brother Charles disowned it; Oscar the enigmatic; Oscar the globe-trotter. How far afield had he gone, she wondered, to have returned with such outré trophies? Somewhere out of this world, perhaps, into the same remoteness to which she'd seen Gentle and Pie 'oh' pah dispatch themselves? She began to suspect that there was some conspiracy abroad. If two men who had no knowledge of each other, Oscar Godolphin and John Zacharias, knew about this other world and how to remove themselves there, how many others in her circle also knew? Was it information only available to men? Did it come with the penis and a mother fixation, as part of the male apparatus? Had Taylor known? Did Clem? Or was this some kind of family secret, and the part of the puzzle she was missing was the link between a Godolphin and a Zacharias?

Whatever the explanation, it was certain she would not get answers from Gentle, which meant she had to seek out brother Oscar. She tried by the most direct route first: the telephone directory. He wasn't listed. She then tried via Lewis Leader, but he claimed to have no knowledge of the man's whereabouts or fortunes, telling her that the affairs of the two brothers were quite separate, and he had never been called to deal with any matter involving Oscar Godolphin.

"For all I know," he said, "the man could be dead."

Having drawn a blank with the direct routes, she was thrown back upon the indirect. She returned to Estabrook's house and scoured it thoroughly, looking for Oscar's address or telephone number. She found neither, but she did turn up a photograph album Charlie had never shown to her, in which pictures of what she took to be the two brothers appeared. It wasn't difficult to distinguish one from the other. Even in those early pictures Charlie had the troubled look the camera always found in him, whereas Oscar, younger by a few years, was nevertheless the more confident of the pair: a little overweight, but carrying it easily, smiling an easy smile as he hooked his arm around his brother's shoulders. She removed the most recent of the photographs from the album which pictured Charles at puberty or thereabouts, and kept it. Repetition, she found, made theft easier. But it was the only information about Oscar she took away with her. If she was to get to the traveler and find out in what world he'd bought his souvenirs, she'd have to work on Estabrook to do so. It would take time, and her impatience grew with every short and rainy day. Even though she had the freedom to buy a ticket anywhere on the planet, a kind of claustrophobia was upon her. There was another world to which she wanted access. Until she got it, Earth itself would be a prison.

3

Leader called Oscar on the morning of January seventeenth with the news that his brother's estranged wife was asking for information on his whereabouts.

"Did she say why?"

"No, not precisely. But she's very clearly sniffing after something. She's apparently seen Estabrook three times in the last week."

"Thank you, Lewis. I appreciate this."

"Appreciate it in hard cash, Oscar," Leader replied. "I've had a very expensive Christmas."

"When have you ever gone empty-handed?" Oscar said. "Keep me posted."

The lawyer promised to do so, but Oscar doubted he'd provide much more by way of useful information. Only truly despairing souls confided in lawyers, and he doubted Judith was the despairing type. He'd never met her— Charlie had seen to that—but if she'd survived his company for any time at all she had to have a will of iron. Which begged the question: Why would a woman who knew (presuming she did) that her husband had conspired to kill her, seek out his company, unless she had an ulterior motive? And was it conceivable that said motive was finding brother Oscar? If so, such curiosity had to be nipped in the bud. There were already enough variables at play, what with the Society's purge now under way, and the inevitable police investigation on its heels, not to mention his new majordomo Augustine (né Dowd), who was behaving in altogether too snotty a fashion. And of course, most volatile of these variables, sitting in his asylum beside the heath, Charlie himself, probably crazy, certainly unpredictable, with all manner of tidbits in his head which could do Oscar a lot of harm. It could be only a matter of time before he started to become talkative, and when he did, what better ear to drop his discretions into than that of his inquiring wife?

That evening he sent Dowd (he couldn't get used to that saintly Augustine) up to the clinic, with a basket of fruit for his brother.

"Find a friend there, if you can," he told Dowd. "I need to know what Charlie babbles about when he's being bathed."

"Why don't you ask him directly?"

"He hates me, that's why. He thinks I stole his mess of pottage when Papa introduced me into the Tabula Rasa instead of Charlie."

"Why did your father do that?"

"Because he knew Charlie was unstable, and he'd do the Society more harm than good. I've had him under control until now. He's had his little gifts from the Dominions. He's had you fawn upon him when he needed something out of the ordinary, like his assassin. This all started with that fucking assassin! Why couldn't you have just killed the woman yourself?"

"What do you take me for?" Dowd said with distaste. "I couldn't lay hands on a woman. Especially not a beauty."

"How do you know she's a beauty?"

"I've heard her talked about."

"Well, I don't care what she looks like. I don't want her meddling in my business. Find out what she's up to. Then we'll work out our response."

Dowd came back a few hours later, with alarming news. "Apparently she's persuaded him to take her to the estate."

"What? What?" Oscar bounded from his chair. The parrots rose up squawking in sympathy. "She knows more than she should. Shit! All that heartache to keep the Society out of our hair, and now this bitch comes along and we're in worse trouble than ever."

"Nothing's happened yet."

"But it will, it will! She'll wind him around her little finger, and he'll tell her everything."

"What do you want to do about it?"

Oscar went to hush the parrots. "Ideally?" he said, as he smoothed their ruffled wings. "Ideally I'd have Charlie vanish off the face of the earth."

"He had much the same ambition for her," Dowd observed.

"Meaning what?"

"Just that you're both quite capable of murder."

Oscar made a contemptuous grunt. "Charlie was only playing at it," he said. "He's got no balls! He's got no vision!" He returned to his high-backed chair, his expression sullen. "It's not going to hold, damn it," he said. "I can feel it in my gut. We've kept things neat and tidy so far, but it's not going to hold. Charlie has to be taken out of the equation."

"He's your brother."

"He's a burden."

"What I mean is: he's *your* brother. You should be the one to dispatch him."

Oscar's eyes widened. "Oh, my Lord," he said.

"Think what they'd say in Yzorderrex, if you were to tell them."

"What? That I killed my own brother? I don't see much charm in that."

"But that you did what you had to do, however unpalatable, to keep the secret safe." Dowd paused to let the idea blossom. "That sounds heroic to me. Think what they'll say."

"I'm thinking."

"It's your reputation in Yzorderrex you care about, isn't it, not what happens in the Fifth? You've said before that this world's getting duller all the time."

Oscar pondered this for a while. "Maybe I *should* slip away. Kill them both to make sure nobody ever knows where I've gone—"

"Where *we've* gone."

"—then slip away and pass into legend. Oscar Godolphin, who left his crazy brother dead beside his wife and disappeared. Oh, yes. That'd make quite a headline in Patashoqua." He mused a few moments more. "What's the classic sibling murder weapon?" he finally asked.

"The jawbone of an ass."

"Ridiculous."

"You'll think of something better."

"So I will. Make me a drink, Dowdie. And have one yourself. We'll drink to escape."

"Doesn't everybody?" Dowd replied, but the remark was lost on Godolphin, who was already plunged deep into murderous thought.

20

I

Gentle and Pie were six days on the Patashoquan Highway, days measured not by the watch on Pie's wrist but by the brightening and darkening of the peacock sky. On the fifth day the watch gave up the ghost anyway, maddened, Pie supposed, by the magnetic field surrounding a city of pyramids they passed. Thereafter, even though Gentle wanted to preserve some sense of how time was proceeding in the Dominion they'd left, it was virtually impossible. Within a few days their bodies were accommodating the rhythm of their new world, and he let his curiosity feast on more pertinent matters: chiefly, the landscape through which they were traveling.

It was diverse. In that first week they passed out of the plain into a region of lagoons—the Cosacosa—which took two days to cross, and thence into tracts of ancient conifers so tall that clouds hung in their topmost branches like the nests of ethereal birds. On the other side of this stupendous forest, the mountains Gentle had glimpsed days before came plainly into view. The range was called the Jokalaylau, Pie informed him, and legend had it that after the

Mount of Lipper Bayak these heights had been Hapexa-mendios' next resting place as He'd crossed through the Dominions. It was no accident, it seemed, that the landscapes they passed through recalled those of the Fifth; they had been chosen for that similarity. The Unbeheld had strode the Imajica dropping seeds of humanity as He went—even to the very edge of His sanctum—in order to give the species He favored new challenges, and like any good gardener He'd dispersed them where they had the best hope of prospering. Where the native crop could be conquered or accommodated; where the living was hard enough to make sure only the most resilient survived, but the land fertile enough to feed their children; where rain came; where light came; where all the vicissitudes that strengthened a species by occasional calamity—tempest, earthquake, flood—were to hand.

But while there was much that any terrestrial traveler would have recognized, nothing, not the smallest pebble underfoot, was quite like its counterpart in the Fifth. Some of these disparities were too vast to be missed: the green-gold of the heavens, for instance, or the elephantine snails that grazed beneath the cloud-nested trees. Others were smaller but equally bizarre, like the wild dogs that ran along the highway now and then, hairless and shiny as patent leather; or grotesque, like the horned kites that swooped on any animal dead or near-dead on the road and only rose from their meals, purple wings opening like cloaks, when the vehicle was almost upon them; or absurd, like the bone-white lizards that congregated in their thousands along the edge of the lagoons, the urge to turn somersaults passing through their colonies in waves.

Perhaps finding some new response to these experiences was out of the question when the sheer proliferation of travelers' tales had all but exhausted the lexicon of discovery. But it nevertheless irritated Gentle to hear himself responding in clichés. The traveler moved by unspoilt beauty or appalled by native barbarism. The traveler touched by primitive wisdom or caught breathless by undreamt-of modernities. The traveler condescending; the traveler humbled; the traveler hungry for the next horizon or pining miserably for home. Of all these, perhaps only the last response never passed Gentle's lips. He thought of the Fifth only when it came up in conversation between himself and Pie, and that happened less and less as the practicalities of the moment pressed more heavily upon them. Food and sleeping quarters were easily come by at first, as was fuel for the car. There were small villages and hostelries along the highway, where Pie, despite an absence of hard cash, always managed to secure them sustenance and beds to sleep in. The mystif had a host of minor feits at its disposal, Gentle realized: ways to use its powers of seduction to make even the most rapacious hostelier pliant. But once they got beyond the forest, matters became more problematical. The bulk of the vehicles had turned off at the intersections, and the highway had degenerated from a well-serviced thoroughfare to a two-lane road, with more potholes than traffic. The vehicle Pie had stolen had not been designed for the rigors of long-distance travel. It started to show signs of fatigue, and with the mountains looming ahead it was decided they should stop at the next village and attempt to trade it in for a more reliable model.

"Perhaps something with breath in its body," Pie suggested.

"Speaking of which," Gentle said, "you never asked me about the Nullianac."

"What was there to ask?"

"How I killed it."

"I presumed you used a pneuma."

"You don't sound very surprised."

"How else would you have done it?" Pie said, quite reasonably. "You had the will, and you had the power."

"But where did I get it from?" Gentle said.

"You've always had it," Pie replied, which left Gentle nursing as many questions, or more, as he'd begun with. He started to formulate one, but something in the motion of the car began to nauseate him as he did so. "I think we'd better stop for a few minutes," he said. "I think I'm going to puke."

Pie brought the vehicle to a halt, and Gentle stepped out. The sky was darkening, and some night-blooming flower spiced the cooling air. On the slopes above them herds of pale-flanked beasts, relations of the yak but here called doeki, moved down through the twilight to their dormitory pastures, lowing as they came. The dangers of Vanaeph and the thronged highway outside Patashoqua seemed very remote. Gentle breathed deeply, and the nausea, like his questions, no longer vexed him. He looked up at the first stars. Some were red here, like Mars; others gold: fragments of the noonday sky that refused to be extinguished.

"Is this Dominion another planet?" he asked Pie. "Are we in some other galaxy?"

"No. It's not space that separates the Fifth from the rest of the Dominions, it's the In Ovo."

"So, is the whole of planet Earth the Fifth Dominion, or just part of it?"

"I don't know," Pie said. "*All,* I assume. But everyone has a different theory."

"What's yours?"

"Well, when we move between the Reconciled Dominions, you'll see it's very easy. There are countless passing places between the Fourth and the Third, the Third and the Second. We'll walk into a mist, and we'll come out into another world. Simple. But I don't think the borders are fixed. I think they move over the centuries, and the shapes of the Dominions change. So maybe it'll be the same with the Fifth. If it's reconciled, the borders will spread, until the whole planet has access to the rest of the Dominions. The truth is, nobody really knows what the Imajica looks like, because nobody's ever made a map."

"Somebody should try."

"Maybe you're the man to do it," Pie said. "You were an artist before you were a traveler."

"I was a faker, not an artist."

"But your hands are clever," Pie replied.

"Clever," Gentle said softly, "but never inspired."

This melancholy thought took him back, momentarily,

to Klein, and to the rest of the circle he'd left in the Fifth: to Jude, Clem, Estabrook, Vanessa, and the rest. What were they doing this fine night? Had they even noticed his departure? He doubted it.

"Are you feeling any better?" Pie inquired. "I see some lights down the road a little way. It may be the last outpost before the mountains."

"I'm in good shape," Gentle said, climbing back into the car.

They'd proceeded perhaps a quarter of a mile, and were in sight of the village, when their progress was brought to a halt by a young girl who appeared from the dusk to herd her doeki across the road. She was in every way a normal thirteen-year-old child but for one: her face, and those parts of her body revealed by her simple dress, were sleek with fawny down. It was plaited where it grew long at her elbows, and her temples, and tied in a row of ribbons at her nape.

"What village is this?" Pie asked, as the last of the doeki lingered in the road.

"Beatrix," she said, and without prompting added, "There is no better place in any heaven." Then, shooing the last beast on its way, she vanished into the twilight.

2

The streets of Beatrix weren't as narrow as those of Vanaeph, nor were they designed for motor vehicles. Pie parked the car close to the outskirts, and the two of them ambled into the village from there. The houses were unpretentious affairs, raised of an ocher stone and surrounded by stands of vegetation that were a cross between silver birch and bamboo. The lights Pie had spotted from a distance weren't those that burned in the windows, but lanterns that hung in these trees, throwing their mellow light across the streets. Just about every copse boasted its lantern trimmers—shaggy-faced children like the herder—some squatting beneath the trees, others perched precariously in their branches. The doors of almost all the houses stood open, and music drifted from several, tunes caught by the lantern trimmers and danced to in the dapple. Asked to guess, Gentle would have said life was good here. Slow, perhaps, but good.

"We can't cheat these people," Gentle said. "It wouldn't be honorable."

"Agreed," Pie replied.

"So what do we do for money?"

"Maybe they'll agree to cannibalize the vehicle for a good meal and a horse or two."

"I don't see any horses."

"A doeki would be fine."

"They look slow."

Pie directed Gentle's gaze up the heights of the Jokalay-lau. The last traces of day still lingered on the snowfields, but for all their beauty the mountains were vast and uninviting.

"Slow and certain is safer up there," Pie said. Gentle took Pie's point. "I'm going to see if I can find somebody in charge," the mystif went on, and left Gentle's side to go and question one of the lantern trimmers.

Drawn by the sound of raucous laughter, Gentle wandered on a little farther, and turning a corner he found two dozen of the villagers, mostly men and boys, standing in front of a marionette theater that had been set up in the lee of one of the houses. The show they were watching contrasted violently with the benign atmosphere of the village. To judge by the spires painted on the backdrop the story was set in Patashoqua, and as Gentle joined the audience two characters, one a grossly fat woman, the other a man with the proportions of a fetus and the endowment of a donkey, were in the middle of a domestic tiff so frenzied the spires were shaking. The puppeteers, three slim young men with identical mustaches, were plainly visible above the booth and provided both the dialogue and the sound effects, the former larded with baroque obscenities. Now another character entered—this a hunchbacked sibling of Pulcinella—and summarily beheaded Donkey Dick. The head flew to the ground, where the fat woman knelt to sob over it. As she did so, cherubic wings unfolded from behind its ears and it floated up into the sky, accompanied by a falsetto din from the puppeteers. This earned applause from the audience, during which Gentle caught sight of Pie in the street. At the mystif's side was a jug-eared adolescent with hair down to the middle of his back. Gentle went to join them.

"This is Efreet Splendid," Pie said. "He tells me—wait for this—he tells me his mother has dreams about white furless men and would like to meet you."

The grin that broke through Efreet's facial thatch was crooked but beguiling.

"She'll like you," he announced.

"Are you sure?" Gentle said.

"Certainly!"

"Will she feed us?"

"For a furless whitey, anything," Efreet replied.

Gentle threw the mystif a doubtful glance. "I hope you know what we're doing," he said.

Efreet led the way, chattering as he went, asking mostly about Patashoqua. It was, he said, his ambition to see the great city. Rather than disappoint the boy by admitting that he hadn't stepped inside the gates, Gentle informed him that it was a place of untold magnificence.

"Especially the Merrow Ti' Ti'," he said.

The boy grinned and said he'd tell everybody he knew that he'd met a hairless white man who'd seen the Merrow Ti' Ti'. From such innocent lies, Gentle mused, legends came.

At the door of the house, Efreet stood aside, to let Gentle be first over the threshold. He startled the woman inside with his appearance. She dropped the cat she was combing and instantly fell to her knees. Embarrassed, Gentle asked her to stand, but it was only after much persuasion that she did so, and even then she kept her head bowed, watching him furtively from the corners of her small dark eyes. She was short—barely taller than her son, in fact—her face fine-boned beneath its down. Her name was Larumday, she said, and she would very happily extend to Gentle and his lady (as she assumed Pie to be) the hospitality of her house. Her younger son, Emblem, was coerced into helping her prepare food while Efreet talked about where they could find a buyer for the car. Nobody in the village had any use for such a vehicle, he said, but in the hills was a man who might. His name was Coaxial Tasko, and it came as a considerable shock to Efreet that neither Gentle nor Pie had heard of the man.

"Everybody knows Wretched Tasko," he said. "He used to be a king in the Third Dominion, but his tribe's extinct."

"Will you introduce me to him in the morning?" Pie asked.

"That's a long time off," Efreet said.

"Tonight then," Pie replied, and it was thus agreed between them.

The food, when it came, was simpler than the fare they'd been served along the highway but no less tasty for that: doeki meat marinated in a root wine, accompanied by bread, a selection of pickled goods—including eggs the size of small loaves—and a broth which stung the throat like chili, bringing tears to Gentle's eyes, much to Efreet's undisguised amusement. While they ate and drank—the wine strong, but downed by the boys like water—Gentle asked about the marionette show he'd seen. Ever eager to parade his knowledge, Efreet explained that the puppeteers were on their way to Patashoqua ahead of the Autarch's host, who were coming over the mountains in the next few days. The puppeteers were very famous in Yzordderrex, he said, at which point Larumday hushed him.

"But, Mams—" he began.

"I said *hush*. I won't have talk of that place in this house. Your father went there and never came back. Remember that."

"I want to go there when I've seen the Merrow Ti' Ti', like Mr. Gentle," Efreet replied defiantly, and earned a sharp slap on the head for his troubles.

"Enough," Larumday said. "We've had too much talk tonight. A little silence would be welcome."

The conversation dwindled thereafter, and it wasn't

until the meal was finished and Efreet was preparing to take Pie up the hill to meet Wretched Tasko, that the boy's mood brightened and his spring of enthusiasms burst forth afresh. Gentle was ready to join them, but Efreet explained that his mother—who was presently out of the room—wanted him to stay.

"You should accommodate her," Pie remarked when the boy had headed out. "If Tasko doesn't want the car we may have to sell your body."

"I thought you were the expert on that, not me," Gentle replied.

"Now, now," Pie said, with a grin. "I thought we'd agreed not to mention my dubious past."

"So go," Gentle said. "Leave me to her tender mercies. But you'll have to pick the fluff from between my teeth."

He found Mother Splendid in the kitchen, kneading dough for the morrow's bread.

"You've honored our home, coming here and sharing our table," she said as she worked. "And please, don't think badly of me for asking, but . . ."—her voice became a frightened whisper—"what do you want?"

"Nothing," Gentle replied. "You've already been more than generous."

She looked at him balefully, as though he was being cruel, teasing her in this fashion.

"I've dreamt about somebody coming here," she said. "White and furless, like you. I wasn't sure whether it was a man or a woman, but now you're here, sitting at the table, I know it was you."

First Tick Raw, he thought, now Mother Splendid. What was it about his face that made people think they knew him? Did he have a doppelgänger wandering around the Fourth?

"Who do you think I am?" he said.

"I don't know," she replied. "But I knew that when you came everything would change."

Her eyes suddenly filled with tears as she spoke, and they ran down the silky fur on her cheeks. The sight of her distress in turn distressed him, not least because he knew he was the cause of it, but he didn't know why. Undoubtedly she had dreamt of him—the look of shocked recognition on her face when he'd first stepped over the threshold was ample evidence of that—but what did that fact signify? He and Pie were here by chance. They'd be gone again by morning, passing through the millpond of Beatrix leaving nary a ripple. He had no significance in the life of the Splendid household, except as a subject of conversation when he'd gone.

"I hope your life doesn't change," he said to her. "It seems very pleasant here."

"It is," she said, wiping the tears away. "This is a safe place. It's good to raise children here. I know Efreet will leave soon. He wants to see Patashoqua, and I won't be able to stop him. But Emblem will stay. He likes the hills, and tending the doeki."

"And you'll stay too?"

"Oh, yes. I've done my wandering," she said. "I lived in Yzordderrex, near the Oke T'Noon, when I was young. That's where I met Eloign. We moved away as soon as we were married. It's a terrible city, Mr. Gentle."

"If it's so bad, why did he go back there?"

"His brother joined the Autarch's army, and when Eloign heard he went back to try and make him desert. He said it brought shame on the family to have a brother taking a wage from an orphan-maker."

"A man of principle."

"Oh, yes," said Larumday, with fondness in her voice. "He's a fine man. Quiet, like Emblem, but with Efreet's curiosity. All the books in this house are his. There's nothing he won't read."

"How long has he been away?"

"Too long," she said. "I'm afraid perhaps his brother's killed him."

"A brother kill a brother?" Gentle said. "No. I can't believe that."

"Yzordderrex does strange things to people, Mr. Gentle. Even good men lose their way."

"Only men?" Gentle said.

"It's men who make this world," she said. "The Goddesses have gone, and men have their way everywhere."

There was no accusation in this. She simply stated it as fact, and he had no evidence to contradict it with. She asked him if he'd like her to brew tea, but he declined, saying he wanted to go out and take the air, perhaps find Pie 'oh' pah.

"She's very beautiful," Larumday said. "Is she wise as well?"

"Oh, yes," he said. "She's wise."

"That's not usually the way with beauties, is it?" she said. "It's strange that I didn't dream her at the table too."

"Maybe you did, and you've forgotten."

She shook her head. "Oh, no, I've had the dream too many times, and it's always the same: a white furless someone sitting at my table, eating with me and my sons."

"I wish I could have been a more sparkling guest," he said.

"But you're just the beginning, aren't you?" she said. "What comes after?"

"I don't know," he said. "Maybe your husband, home from Yzordderrex."

She looked doubtful. "Something," she said. "Something that'll change us all."

3

Efreet had said the climb would be easy, and measuring it in terms of incline, so it was. But the darkness made an easy route difficult, even for one as light-footed as Pie 'oh' pah. Efreet was an accommodating guide, however, slowing his pace when he realized Pie was lagging behind and warning of places where the ground was uncertain. After a time they were high above the village, with the snow-clad peaks of the Jokalaylau visible above the backs of the hills in which Beatrix slept. High and majestic as those mountains were, the lower slopes of peaks yet more monumental were visible beyond them, their heads lost in cumulus. Not far now, the boy said, and this time his promises were good.

Within a few yards Pie spotted a building silhouetted against the sky, with a light burning on its porch.

"Hey, Wretched!" Efreet started to call. "Someone to see you! Someone to see you!"

There was no reply forthcoming, however, and when they reached the house itself the only living occupant was the flame in the lamp. The door stood open; there was food on the table. But of Wretched Tasko there was no sign. Efreet went out to search around, leaving Pie on the porch. Animals corralled behind the house stamped and muttered in the darkness; there was a palpable unease.

Efreet came back moments later. "I see him up the hill! He's almost at the top."

"What's he doing there?" Pie asked.

"Watching the sky, maybe. We'll go up. He won't mind."

They continued to climb, their presence now noticed by the figure standing on the hill's higher reaches. "Who is this?" he called down.

"It's only Efreet, Mr. Tasko. I'm with a friend."

"Your voice is too loud, boy," the man returned. "Keep it low, will you?"

"He wants us to keep quiet," Efreet whispered.

"I understand."

There was a wind blowing on these heights, and its chill put the mystif in mind of the fact that neither Gentle nor itself had clothes appropriate to the journey that lay ahead of them. Coaxial clearly climbed here regularly; he was wearing a shaggy coat and a hat with fur ear warmers. He was very clearly not a local man. It would have taken three of the villagers to equal his mass or strength, and his skin was almost as dark as Pie's.

"This is my friend Pie 'oh' pah," Efreet whispered to him when they were at his side.

"Mystif," Tasko said instantly.

"Yes."

"Ah. So you're a stranger?"

"Yes."

"From Yzordderrex?"

"No."

"That's to the good, at least. But so many strangers, and all on the same night. What are we to make of it?"

"Are there others?" said Efreet.

"Listen," Tasko said, casting his gaze over the valley to the darkened slopes beyond. "Don't you hear the machines?"

"No. Just the wind."

Tasko's response was to pick the boy up and physically point him in the direction of the sound.

"Now *listen!*" he said fiercely.

The wind carried a low rumble that might have been distant thunder, but that it was unbroken. Its source was certainly not the village below, nor did it seem likely there were earthworks in the hills. This was the sound of engines, moving through the night.

"They're coming towards the valley."

Efreet made a whoop of pleasure, which was cut short by Tasko slapping his hand over the boy's mouth.

"Why so happy, child?" he said. "Have you never learned fear? No, I don't suppose you have. Well, learn it now." He held Efreet so tightly the boy struggled to be free. "Those machines are from Yzordderrex. From the Autarch. Do you understand?"

Growling his displeasure he let go, and Efreet backed away from him, at least as nervous of Tasko now as of the distant machines. The man hawked up a wad of phlegm and spat it in the direction of the sound.

"Maybe they'll pass us by," he said. "There are other valleys they could choose. They may not come through ours." He spat again. "Ach, well, there's no purpose in staying up here. If they come, they come." He turned to Efreet. "I'm sorry if I was rough, boy," he said. "But I've heard these machines before. They're the same that killed my people. Take it from me, they're nothing to whoop about. Do you understand?"

"Yes," Efreet said, though Pie doubted he did. The prospect of a visitation from these thundering things held no horror for him, only exhilaration.

"So tell me what you want, mystif," Tasko said as he started back down the hill. "You didn't climb all the way up here to watch the stars. Or maybe you did. Are you in love?"

Efreet tittered in the darkness behind them.

"If I were I wouldn't talk about it," Pie replied.

"So what, then?"

"I came here with a friend, from . . . some considerable distance, and our vehicle's nearly defunct. We need to trade it in for animals."

"Where are you heading?"

"Up into the mountains."

"Are you prepared for that journey?"

"No. But it has to be taken."

"The faster you're out of the valley the safer we'll be, I think. Strangers attract strangers."

"Will you help us?"

"Here's my offer, mystif," Tasko said. "If you leave Beatrix now, I'll see they give you supplies and two doeki. But you must be quick."

"I understand."

"If you go now, maybe the machines will pass us by."

4

Without anyone to lead him, Gentle had soon lost his way on the dark hill. But rather than turning around and heading back to await Pie in Beatrix, he continued to climb, drawn by the promise of a view from the heights and a wind to clear his head. Both took his breath away: the wind with its chill, the panorama with its sweep. Ahead, range upon range receded into mist and distance, the farthest heights so vast he doubted the Fifth Dominion could boast their equal. Behind him, just visible between the softer silhouettes of the foothills, were the forests which they'd driven through.

Once again, he wished he had a map of the territory, so that he could begin to grasp the scale of the journey they were undertaking. He tried to lay the landscape out on a page in his mind, like a sketch for a painting, with this vista of mountains, hills, and plain as the subject. But the fact of the scene before him overwhelmed his attempt to make symbols of it; to reduce it and set it down. He let the problem go and turned his eyes back towards the Jokalaylau. Before his gaze reached its destination, it came to rest on the hill slopes directly across from him. He was suddenly aware of the valley's symmetry, hills rising to the same height, left and right. He studied the slopes opposite. It was a nonsensical quest, seeking a sign of life at such a distance, but the more he squinted at the hill's face the more certain he became that it was a dark mirror, and that somebody as yet unseen was studying the shadows in which he stood, looking for some sign of him as he in his turn searched for them. The notion intrigued him at first, but then it began to make him afraid. The chill in his skin worked its way into his innards. He began to shiver inside, afraid to move for fear that this other, whoever or whatever it was, would see him and, in the seeing, bring calamity. He remained motionless for a long time, the wind coming in frigid gusts and bringing with it sounds he hadn't heard until now: the rumble of machinery; the complaint of unfed animals; sobbing. The sounds and the seeker on the mirror hill belonged together, he knew. This other had not come alone. It had engines and beasts. It brought tears.

As the cold reached his marrow, he heard Pie 'oh' pah calling his name, way down the hill. He prayed the wind wouldn't veer and carry the call, and thus his whereabouts, in the direction of the watcher. Pie continued to call for him, the voice getting nearer as the mystif climbed through the darkness. He endured five terrible minutes of this, his system racked by contrary desires: part of him desperately wanting Pie here with him, embracing him, telling him that the fear upon him was ridiculous; the other part in terror that Pie would find him and thus reveal his whereabouts to the creature on the other hill.

At last, the mystif gave up its search and retraced its steps down into the secure streets of Beatrix. Gentle didn't break cover, however. He waited another quarter of an hour until his aching eyes discovered a motion on the opposite slope. The watcher was giving up his post, it seemed, moving around the back of the hill. Gentle caught a glimpse of his silhouette as he disappeared over the brow, just enough to confirm that the other had indeed been human, at least in shape if not in spirit. He waited another minute, then started down the slope. His extremities were numb, his teeth chattering, his torso rigid with cold, but he went quickly, falling and descending several yards on his buttocks, much to the startlement of dozing doeki. Pie was below, waiting at the door of Mother Splendid's house. Two saddled and bridled beasts stood in the street, one being fed a palmful of fodder by Efreet.

"Where did you go?" Pie wanted to know. "I came looking for you."

"Later," Gentle said. "I have to get warm."

"No time," Pie replied. "The deal is we get the doeki, food, and coats if we go immediately."

"They're very eager to get rid of us suddenly."

"Yes, we are," said a voice from beneath the trees opposite the house. A black man with pale, mesmeric eyes stepped into view. "You're Zacharias?"

"I am."

"I'm Coaxial Tasko, called the Wretched. The doeki are yours. I've given the mystif some supplies to set you on your way, but please . . . tell nobody you've been here."

"He thinks we're bad luck," Pie said.

"He could be right," said Gentle. "Am I allowed to shake your hand, Mr. Tasko, or is that bad luck too?"

"You may shake my hand," the man said.

"Thank you for the transport. I swear we'll tell nobody we were here. But I may want to mention you in my memoirs."

A smile broke over Tasko's stern features.

"You may do that too," he said, shaking Gentle's hand. "But not till I'm dead, huh? I don't like scrutiny."

"That's fair."

"Now, please . . . the sooner you're gone the sooner we can pretend we never saw you."

Efreet came forward, bearing a coat, which Gentle put on. It reached to his shins and smelled strongly of the animal who'd been born in it, but it was welcome.

"Mother says goodbye," the boy told Gentle. "She won't come out and see you." He lowered his voice to an embarrassed whisper. "She's crying a lot."

Gentle made a move towards the door, but Tasko checked him. "Please, Mr. Zacharias, no delays," he said. "Go now, with our blessing, or not at all."

"He means it," Pie said, climbing up onto his doeki, the animal casting a backward glance at its rider as it was mounted. "We have to go."

"Don't we even discuss the route?"

"Tasko has given me a compass and directions." The mystif pointed to a narrow trail that led up out of the village. "That's the way we take."

Reluctantly, Gentle put his foot in the doeki's leather stirrup and hoisted himself into the saddle. Only Efreet managed a goodbye, daring Tasko's wrath to press his hand into Gentle's.

"I'll see you in Patashoqua one day," he said.

"I hope so," Gentle replied.

That being the full sum of their farewells, Gentle was left with the sense of an exchange broken in midsentence, and now permanently unfinished. But they were at least going on from the village better equipped for the terrain ahead than they'd been when they entered.

"What was all that about?" Gentle asked Pie, when they were on the ridge above Beatrix, and the trail was about to turn and take its tranquil lamp-lit streets from sight.

"A battalion of the Autarch's army is passing through the hills, on its way to Patashoqua. Tasko was afraid the presence of strangers in the village would give the soldiers an excuse for marauding."

"So that's what I heard on the hill."

"That's what you heard."

"And I saw somebody on the other hill. I swear he was looking for me. No, that's not right. Not me, but somebody.

That's why I didn't answer when you came looking for me."

"Any idea who it was?"

Gentle shook his head. "I just felt his stare. Then I got a glimpse of somebody on the ridge. Who knows? It sounds absurd now I say it."

"There was nothing absurd about the noises I heard. The best thing we can do is get out of this region as fast as possible."

"Agreed."

"Tasko said there was a place to the northeast of here, where the border of the Third reaches into this Dominion a good distance—maybe a thousand miles. We could shorten our journey if we made for it."

"That sounds good."

"But it means taking the High Pass."

"That sounds bad."

"It'll be faster."

"It'll be fatal," Gentle said. "I want to see Yzordderrex. I don't want to die frozen stiff in the Jokalaylau."

"Then we go the long way?"

"That's my vote."

"It'll add two or three weeks to the journey."

"And years to our lives," Gentle replied.

"As if we haven't lived long enough," Pie remarked.

"I've always held to the belief," Gentle said, "that you can never live too long or love too many women."

5

The doeki were obedient and surefooted mounts, negotiating the track whether it was churned mud or dust and pebbles, seemingly indifferent to the ravines that gaped inches from their hooves at one moment and the white waters that wound beside them the next. All this in the dark, for although the hours passed, and it seemed dawn should have crept up over the hills, the peacock sky hid its glory in a starless gloom.

"Is it possible the nights are longer up here than they were down on the highway?" Gentle wondered.

"It seems so," Pie said. "My bowels tell me the sun should have been up hours ago."

"Do you always calculate the passage of time by your bowels?"

"They're more reliable than your beard," Pie replied.

"Which direction is the light going to come from when it comes?" Gentle asked, turning in his saddle to scan the horizon. As he craned around to look back the way they'd come, a murmur of distress escaped his lips.

"What is it?" the mystif said, bringing its beast to a halt and following Gentle's gaze.

It didn't need telling. A column of black smoke was rising from the cradle of the hills, its lower plumes tinged with fire. Gentle was already slipping from his saddle, and now he scrambled up the rock face at their side to get a better sense of the fire's location. He lingered only seconds at the top before scrambling down, sweating and panting.

"We have to turn back," he said.

"Why?"

"Beatrix is burning."

"How can you tell from this distance?" Pie said.

"I know, damn it! Beatrix is burning! We have to go back." He climbed onto his doeki and started to haul it around on the narrow path.

"Wait," said Pie. "Wait, for God's sake!"

"We have to help them," Gentle said, against the rock face. "They were good to us."

"Only because they wanted us out!" Pie replied.

"Well, now the worst's happened, and we have to do what we can."

"You used to be more rational than this."

"What do you mean, *used to be?* You don't know anything about me, so don't start making judgments. If you won't come with me, fuck you!"

The doeki was fully turned now, and Gentle dug his heels into its flanks to make it pick up speed. There had only been three or four places along the route where the road had divided. He was certain he could retrace their steps back to Beatrix without much problem. And if he was right, and it was the town that was burning up ahead, he would have the column of smoke as a grim marker.

The mystif followed, after a time, as Gentle knew it must. It was happy to be called a friend, but somewhere in its soul it was a slave.

They didn't speak as they traveled, which was not surprising given their last exchange. Only once, as they mounted a ridge that laid the vista of foothills before them, with the valley in which Beatrix nestled still out of sight but unequivocally the source of the smoke, did Pie 'oh' pah murmur, "Why is it always fire?" and Gentle realized how insensitive he'd been to his companion's reluctance to return. The devastation that undoubtedly lay before them was an echo of the fire in which its adopted family had perished—a matter that had gone undiscussed between them since.

"Shall I go from here without you?" he asked.

The mystif shook its head. "Together, or not at all," it said.

The route became easier to negotiate from there on. The inclines were mellower and the track itself better kept, but there was also light in the sky, as the long-delayed dawn finally came. By the time they finally laid their eyes on the remains of Beatrix, the peacock-tail glory Gentle had first admired in the heavens over Patashoqua was overhead, its glamour making grimmer still the scene laid below. Beatrix was still burning fitfully, but the fire had consumed most of the houses and their birch-bamboo arbors. He brought his doeki to a halt and scoured the place from this vantage point. There was no sign of Beatrix's destroyers.

"On foot from here?" Gentle said.

"I think so."

They tethered the beasts and descended into the village. The sound of lamentation reached them before they were within its perimeters, the sobbing, emerging as it did from the murk of the smoke, reminding Gentle of the sounds he'd heard while keeping his vigil on the hill. The destruction around them now was somehow a consequence of that sightless encounter, he knew. Though he'd avoided the eye of the watcher in the darkness, his presence had been suspected, and that had been enough to bring this calamity upon Beatrix.

"I'm responsible," he said. "God help me . . . I'm responsible."

He turned to the mystif, who was standing in the middle of the street, its features drained of blood and expression.

"Stay here," Gentle said. "I'm going to find the family."

Pie didn't register any response, but Gentle assumed what he'd said had been understood and headed off in the direction of the Splendids' house. It wasn't simply fire that had undone Beatrix. Some of the houses had been toppled unburned, the copses around them uprooted. There was no sign of fatalities, however, and Gentle began to hope that Coaxial Tasko had persuaded the villagers to take to the hills before Beatrix's violators had appeared out of the night. That hope was dashed when he came to the place where the Splendids' home had stood. It was rubble, like the others, and the smoke from its burning timbers had concealed from him until now the horror heaped in front of it. Here were the good people of Beatrix, shoveled together in a bleeding pile higher than his head. There were a few sobbing survivors at the heap, looking for their loved ones in the confusion of broken bodies, some clutching at limbs they thought they recognized, others simply kneeling in the bloody dirt, keening.

Gentle walked around the pile, searching among the mourners for a face he knew. One fellow he'd seen laughing at the show was cradling in his arms a wife or sister whose body was as lifeless as the puppets he'd taken such pleasure in. Another, a woman, was burrowing in among the bodies, yelling somebody's name. He went to help her, but she screamed at him to stay away. As he retreated he caught sight of Efreet. The boy was in the heap, his eyes open, his mouth—which had been the vehicle for such unalloyed enthusiasms—beaten in by a rifle butt or a boot. At that moment Gentle wanted nothing—not life itself—as much as he wanted the bastard who'd done this, standing in his sights. He felt the killing breath hot in his throat, itching to be merciless.

He turned from the heap, looking for some target, even if it wasn't the murderer himself. Someone with a gun or a uniform, a man he could call the enemy. He couldn't remember ever feeling this way before, but then he'd never possessed the power he had now—or rather, if Pie was to be believed, he'd had it without recognizing the fact—and agonizing as these horrors were, it was salve to his distress, knowing there was such a capacity for cleansing in him: that his lungs, throat, and palm could take the guilty out of life with such ease. He headed away from the cairn of flesh, ready to be an executioner at the first invitation.

The street twisted, and he followed its convolutions, turning a corner to find the way ahead blocked by one of the invaders' war machines. He stopped in his tracks, expecting it to turn its steel eyes upon him. It was a perfect death-bringer, armored as a crab, its wheels bristling with bloodied scythes, its turret with armaments. But death had found the bringer. Smoke rose from the turret, and the driver lay where the fire had found him, in the act of scrabbling from the machine's stomach. A small victory, but one that at least proved the machines had frailties. Come another day, that knowledge might be the difference between hope and despair. He was turning his back on the machine when he heard his name called, and Tasko appeared from behind the smoking carcass. Wretched he was, his face bloodied, his clothes filthy with dust.

"Bad timing, Zacharias," he said. "You left too late and now you come back, too late again."

"Why did they do this?"

"The Autarch doesn't need reasons."

"He was here?" Gentle said. The thought that the Butcher of Yzordderrex had stood in Beatrix made his heart beat faster.

But Tasko said, "Who knows? Nobody's ever seen his face. Maybe he was here yesterday, counting the children, and nobody even noticed him."

"Do you know where Mother Splendid is?"

"In the heap somewhere."

"Jesus . . ."

"She wouldn't have made a very good witness. She was too crazy with grief. They left alive the ones who'd tell the story best. Atrocities need witnesses, Zacharias. People to spread the word."

"They did this as a warning?" Gentle said.

Tasko shook his huge head. "I don't know how their minds work," he said.

"Maybe we have to learn, so we can stop them."

"I'd prefer to die," the man replied, "than understand filth like that. If you've got the appetite, then go to Yzord-derrex. You'll get your education there."

"I want to help here," Gentle said. "There must be something I can do."

"You can leave us to mourn."

If there was any profounder dismissal, Gentle didn't know it. He searched for some word of comfort or apology, but in the face of such devastation only silence seemed appropriate. He bowed his head, and left Tasko to the burden of being a witness, returning up the street past the heap of corpses to where Pie 'oh' pah was standing. The mystif hadn't moved an inch, and even when Gentle came abreast of it, and quietly told it they should go, it was a long time before it looked round at him.

"We shouldn't have come back," it said.

"Every day we waste, this is going to happen again. . . ."

"You think you can stop it?" Pie said, with a trace of sarcasm.

"We won't go the long way around, we'll go through the mountains. Save ourselves three weeks."

"You *do*, don't you?" Pie said. "You think you can stop this."

"We won't die," Gentle said, putting his arms around Pie 'oh' pah. "I won't let us. I came here to understand, and I will."

"How much more of this can you take?"

"As much as I have to."

"I may remind you of that."

"I'll remember," Gentle said. "After this, I'll remember everything."

I

The Retreat at the Godolphin estate had been built in an age of follies, when the oldest sons of the rich and mighty, having no wars to distract them, amused themselves spending the gains of generations on buildings whose only function was to flatter their egos. Most of these lunacies, designed without care for basic architectural principles, were dust before their designers. A few, however, became noteworthy even in neglect, either because somebody associated with them had lived or died in notoriety or because they were the scene of some drama.

The Retreat fell into both categories. Its architect, Geoffrey Light, had died within six months of its completion, choked by a bull's pizzle in the wilds of West Riding, a grotesquerie which attracted some attention—as did the retirement from the public eye of Light's patron, Lord Joshua Godolphin, whose decline into insanity was the talk of court and coffeehouse for many years. Even at his zenith he'd attracted gossip, mainly because he kept the company of magicians. Cagliostro, the Comte de St. Germain, and even Casanova (reputedly no mean thaumaturgist) had spent time on the estate, as well as a host of lesser-known practitioners.

His Lordship had made no secret of his occult investigations, though the work he was truly undertaking was never known to the gossips. They assumed he kept company with these mountebanks for their entertainment value. Whatever his reasons, the fact that he retired from sight so suddenly drew further attention to his last indulgence, the folly

Light had built for him. A diary purporting to have belonged to the choked architect appeared a year after his demise, containing an account of the Retreat's construction. Whether it was the genuine article or not, it made bizarre reading. The foundations had been laid, it said, under stars calculated to be particularly propitious; the masons—sought and hired in a dozen cities—had been sworn to silence with an oath of Arabic ferocity. The stones themselves had been individually baptized in a mixture of milk and frankincense, and a lamb had been allowed to wander through the half-completed building three times, the altar and font placed where it had laid its innocent head.

Of course these details were soon corrupted by repetition, and Satanic purpose ascribed to the building. It became babies' blood that was used to anoint the stone, and a mad dog's grave that marked the spot where the altar was built. Sealed up behind the high walls of his sanctum, it was doubtful that Lord Godolphin even knew that such rumors were circulating until, two Septembers after his withdrawal, the inhabitants of Yoke, the village closest to the estate, needing a scapegoat to blame the poor harvest upon and inflamed by a passage from Ezekiel delivered from the pulpit of the parish church, used the Sunday afternoon to mount a crusade against the Devil's work and climbed the gates of the estate to raze the Retreat. They found none of the promised blasphemies: no inverted cross, no altar stained with virginal blood. But having trespassed they did what damage they could inflict out of sheer frustration, finally setting a bonfire of baled hay in the middle of the great mosaic. All the flames did was lick the place black, and the Retreat earned its nickname from that afternoon: the Black Chapel; or, Godolphin's Sin.

2

If Jude had known anything about the history of Yoke, she might well have looked for signs of its echoes in the village as she drove through. She would have had to look hard, but the signs were there to be found. There was scarcely a house within its bounds that didn't have a cross carved into the keystone above the door or a horseshoe cemented into the doorstep. If she'd had time to linger in the churchyard she would have found, inscribed on the stones there, entreaties to the good Lord that He keep the Devil from the living even as he gathered the dead to His Bosom, and on the board beside the gate a notice announcing that next Sunday's sermon would be "The Lamb in Our Lives," as though to banish any lingering thought of the infernal goat.

She saw none of these signs, however. It was the road and the man at her side—with occasional words of comfort directed towards the dog on the back seat—that consumed her attention. Getting Estabrook to bring her here had been a spur-of-the-moment inspiration, but there was sound logic behind it. She would be his freedom for a day, taking him out of the clinic's stale heat into the bracing January air. It was her hope that out in the open he might talk more freely about his family, and more particularly about brother Oscar. What better place to innocently inquire about the Godolphins and their history than in the grounds of the house Charlie's forefathers had built?

The estate lay half a mile beyond the village, along a private road that led to a gateway besieged, even in this sterile season, by a green army of bushes and creepers. The gates themselves had long ago been removed and a less elegant defense against trespasses raised: boards and corrugated iron covered with barbed wire. The storms of early December had brought down much of this barricade, however, and once the car was parked, and they both approached the gateway—Skin bounding ahead, yapping joyously—it became apparent that as long as they were willing to brave brambles and nettles, access could be readily gained.

"It's a sad sight," she remarked. "It must have been magnificent."

"Not in my time," Estabrook said.

"Shall I beat the way through?" she suggested, picking up a fallen branch and stripping off the twigs to do so.

"No, let me," he replied, relieving her of the switch and clearing a path for them by flaying the nettles mercilessly.

Jude followed in his green wake, a kind of exhilaration seizing her as she drew closer to stepping between the gate-posts, a feeling she ascribed to the sight of Estabrook so heartily engaged in this adventure. He was a very different man to the husk she'd seen slumped in a chair two weeks before. As she clambered through the debris of fallen timbers he offered her his hand, and like lovers in search of some trysting place they slipped through the broken barrier into the estate beyond.

She was expecting an open vista: a driveway leading the eye to the house itself. Indeed, once she might have enjoyed just such a view. But two hundred years of ancestral insanities, mismanagement, and neglect had given symmetry over to chaos, parkland to pampas. What had once been artfully placed copses, built for shady dalliance, had spread and become choked woods. Lawns once leveled to perfection were wildernesses now. Several other members of England's landed gentry, finding themselves unable to sustain the family manse, had turned their estates into safari parks, importing the fauna of lost empire to wander where deer had grazed in better-heeled times. To Jude's eye the effect of such efforts was always bathetic. The parks were always too tended, the oaks and sycamores an inappropriate backdrop for lion or baboon. But here, she thought, it was possible to imagine wild beasts roaming. It was like a foreign landscape, dropped in the middle of England.

It was a long walk to the house, but Estabrook was already leading the way, with Skin as scout. What visions were in Charlie's mind's eye, Jude wondered, that drove him on with such gusto? The past, perhaps: childhood visits here? Or further back still, to the days of High Yoke's glory, when the route they were taking had been raked gravel, and the house ahead a gathering place for the wealthy and the influential?

"Did you come here a lot when you were little?" she asked him as they plowed through the grass.

He looked around at her with a moment's bewilderment, as though he'd forgotten she was with him.

"Not often," he said. "I liked it, though. It was like a

playground. Later on, I thought about selling it, but Oscar would never let me. He had his reasons, of course. . . ."

"What were they?" she asked him lightly.

"Frankly, I'm glad we left it to run to seed. It's prettier this way."

He marched on, wielding his branch like a machete. As they drew closer to the house, Jude could see what a pitiful state it was in. The windows were gone, the roof was reduced to a timber lattice, the doors teetered on their hinges like drunks. All sad enough in any house, but near tragic in a structure that had once been so magnificent. The sunlight was getting stronger as the clouds cleared, and by the time they stepped through the porch it was pouring through the lattice overhead, its geometry a perfect foil for the scene below. The staircase, albeit rubble-strewn, still rose in a sweep to a half landing, which had once been dominated by a window fit for a cathedral. It was smashed now, by a tree toppled many winters before, the withered extremities of which lay on the spot where the lord and lady would have paused before descending to greet their guests. The paneling of the hallway and the corridors that led off it was still intact, and the boards solid beneath their feet. Despite the decay of the roof, the structure didn't look unsound. It had been built to serve Godolphins in perpetuity, the fertility of land and loin preserving the name until the sun went out. It was flesh that had failed it, not the other way about.

Estabrook and Skin wandered off in the direction of the dining room, which was the size of a restaurant. Jude followed a little way, but found herself drawn back to the staircase. All she knew about the period in which the house had flourished she'd culled from films and television, but her imagination rose to the challenge with astonishing ardor, painting mind pictures so intense they all but displaced the dispiriting truth. When she climbed the stairs, indulging, somewhat guiltily, her dreams of aristocracy, she could see the hallway below lit with the glow of candles, could hear laughter on the landing above and—as she descended—the sigh of silk as her skirts brushed the carpet.

Somebody called to her from a doorway, and she turned expecting to see Estabrook, but the caller was imagined, and the name too. Nobody had ever called her Peachplum.

The moment unsettled her slightly, and she went after Estabrook, as much to reacquaint herself with solid reality as for his company. He was in what had surely been a ballroom, one wall of which was a line of ceiling-high windows, offering a view across terraces and formal gardens to a ruined gazebo. She went to his side and put her arm through his. Their breaths became a common cloud, gilded by the sun through the shattered glass.

"It must have been so beautiful," she said.

"I'm sure it was." He sniffed hard. "But it's gone forever."

"It could be restored."

"For a fortune."

"You've got a fortune."

"Not that big."

"What about Oscar?"

"No. This is mine. He can come and go, but it's mine. That was part of the deal."

"What deal?" she said. He didn't reply. She pressed him, with words and proximity. "Tell me," she said. "Share it with me."

He took a deep breath. "I'm older than Oscar, and there's a family tradition—it goes back to the time when this house was intact—which says the oldest son, or daughter if there are no sons, becomes a member of a society called the Tabula Rasa."

"I've never heard of it."

"That's the way they'd like it to stay, I'm sure. I shouldn't be telling you any of this, but what the hell? I don't care any more. It's all ancient history. So . . . I was supposed to join the Tabula Rasa, but I was passed over by Papa in favor of Oscar."

"Why?"

Charlie made a little smile. "Believe it or not, they thought I was unstable. Me? Can you imagine? They were afraid I'd be indiscreet." The smile became a laugh. "Well, fuck them all. I'll *be* indiscreet."

"What does the Society do?"

"It was founded to prevent . . . let me remember the words exactly . . . to prevent *the tainting of England's soil.* Joshua loved England."

"Joshua?"

"The Godolphin who built this house."

"What did he think this taint was?"

"Who knows? Catholics? The French? He was crazy, and so were most of his friends. Secret societies were in vogue back then—"

"And it's still in operation?"

"I suppose so. I don't talk to Oscar very often, and when I do it's not about the Tabula Rasa. He's a strange man. In fact, he's a lot crazier than me. He just hides it better."

"You used to hide it very well, Charlie," she reminded him.

"More fool me. I should have let it out. I might have kept you." He put his hand up to her face. "I was stupid, Judith. I can't believe my luck that you've forgiven me."

She felt a pang of guilt, hearing him so moved by her manipulations. But they'd at least borne fruit. She had two new pieces for the puzzle: the Tabula Rasa and its raison d'être.

"Do you believe in magic?" she asked him.

"Do you want the old Charlie or the new one?"

"The new. The crazy."

"Then yes, I think I do. When Oscar used to bring his little presents round, he'd say to me, 'Have a piece of the miracle.' I used to throw most of them out, except for the bits and pieces you found. I didn't want to know where he got them."

"You never asked him?" she said.

"I did, finally. One night when you were away and I was drunk, he came round with that book you found in the safe, and I asked him outright where he got this smut from. I wasn't ready to believe what he told me. You know what made me ready?"

"No. What?"

"The body on the heath. I told you about it, didn't I? I watched them digging around in the muck and the rain for two days and I kept thinking, What a fucking life this is! No way out except feet first. I was ready to slit my wrists, and I probably would have done it except that you appeared, and I remembered the way I felt about you when I first saw you. I remembered feeling as though something miraculous was happening, as though I was reclaiming something I'd lost. And I thought, If I believe in one miracle I may as well believe in them all. Even Oscar's. Even his talk about the Imajica, and the Dominions in the Imajica, and the people there, and the cities. I just thought, Why not . . . embrace it all before I lose the chance? Before I'm a body lying out in the rain."

"You won't die in the rain."

"I don't care where I die, Jude, I care where I live, and I want to live in some kind of hope. I want to live with you."

"Charlie," she chided softly, "we shouldn't talk about that now."

"Why not? What better time? I know you brought me here because you've got questions of your own you want answering, and I don't blame you. If I'd seen that damn assassin come after me, I'd be asking questions too. But think about it, Judy, that's all I'm asking. Think about whether the new Charlie's worth a little bit of your time. Will you do that?"

"I'll do that."

"Thank you," he said, and taking the hand she'd tucked through his arm, he kissed her fingers.

"You've heard most of Oscar's secrets now," he said. "You may as well know them all. See the little wood way over towards the wall? That's his little railway station, where he takes the train to wherever he goes."

"I'd like to see it."

"Shall we stroll over there, ma'am?" he said. "Where did the dog go?" He whistled, and Skin came pounding in, raising golden dust. "Perfect. Let's take the air."

3

The afternoon was so bright it was easy to imagine what bliss this place would be, even in its present decay, come spring or high summer, with dandelion seeds and birdsong in the air and the evenings long and balmy. Though she was eager to see the place Estabrook had described as Oscar's railway station, she didn't force the pace. They strolled, just as Charlie had suggested, taking time to cast an appreciative glance back towards the house. It looked even grander from this aspect, with the terraces rising to the row of ballroom windows. Though the wood ahead was not large, the undergrowth and the sheer density of trees kept their destination from sight until they were under the canopy and treading the damp rot of last September's fall. Only then did she realize what building this was. She'd seen it countless times before, drawn in elevation and hanging in front of the safe.

"The Retreat," she said.

"You recognize it?"

"Of course."

Birds sang in the branches overhead, misled by the warmth and tuning up for courtship. When she looked up it seemed to her the branches formed a fretted vault above the Retreat, as if echoing its dome. Between the two, vault and song, the place felt almost sacred.

"Oscar calls it the Black Chapel," Charlie said. "Don't ask me why."

It had no windows and, from this side, no door. They had to walk around it a few yards before the entrance came in sight. Skin was panting at the step, but when Charlie opened the door the dog declined to enter.

"Coward," Charlie said, preceding Jude over the threshold. "It's quite safe."

The sense of the numinous she'd felt outside was stronger still inside, but despite all that she'd experienced since Pie 'oh' pah had come for her life, she was still ill prepared for mystery. Her modernity burdened her. She wished there was some forgotten self she could dredge from her crippled history, better equipped for this. Charlie had his bloodline even if he'd denied his name. The thrushes in the trees outside resembled absolutely the thrushes who'd sung here since these boughs had been strong enough to bear them. But she was adrift, resembling nobody; not even the woman she'd been six weeks ago.

"Don't be nervous," Charlie said, beckoning her in.

He spoke too loudly for the place; his voice carried around the vast bare circle and came back to meet him magnified. He seemed not to notice. Perhaps it was simply familiarity that bred this indifference, but she thought not. For all his talk of embracing the miraculous, Charlie was still a pragmatist, fixed in the particular. Whatever forces moved here, and she felt them strongly, he was dead to their presence.

Approaching the Retreat she'd thought the place windowless, but she'd been wrong. At the intersection of wall and dome ran a ring of windows, like a halo fitted to the chapel's skull. Small though they were, they let in sufficient light to strike the floor and rise up into the middle of the space, where the luminescence converged above the mosaic. If this was indeed a place of departure, that rarefied spot was the platform.

"It's nothing special, is it?" Charlie observed.

She was about to disagree, searching for a way to express what she was feeling, when Skin began barking outside. This wasn't the excited yapping with which he'd announced each new pissing place along the way, but a sound of alarm. She started towards the door, but the hold the chapel had on her slowed her response, and Charlie was out before she'd reached the step, calling to the dog to be quiet. He stopped barking suddenly.

"Charlie?" she said.

There was no reply. With the dog quieted she heard a greater quiet. The birds had stopped singing.

Again she said, "Charlie?" and as she did so somebody stepped into the doorway. It was not Charlie; this man, bearded and heavy, was a stranger. But her system responded to the sight of him with a shock of recognition, as though he was some long lost comrade. She might have thought herself crazy, except that what she felt was echoed on his face. He looked at her with narrowed eyes, turning his head a little to the side.

"You're Judith?"

"Yes. Who are you?"

"Oscar Godolphin."

She let her shallow breaths go, in favor of a deeper draft.

"Oh . . . thank God," she said. "You startled me. I thought . . . I don't know what I thought. Did the dog try and attack you?"

"Forget the dog," he said, stepping into the chapel. "Have we met before?"

"I don't believe so," she said. "Where's Charlie? Is he all right?"

Godolphin continued to approach her, his step steady. "This confuses things," he said.

"What does?"

"Me . . . knowing you. You being whoever you are. It confuses things."

"I don't see why," she said. "I'd wanted to meet you, and I asked Charlie several times if he'd introduce us, but he always seemed reluctant. . . ." She kept chattering, as much to defend herself from his appraisal as for communication's sake. She felt if she fell silent she'd forget herself utterly, become his object. "I'm very pleased we finally get to talk."

He was close enough to touch her now. She put out her hand to shake his.

"It really is a pleasure," she said.

Outside, the dog began barking again, and this time its din was followed by a shout.

"Oh, God, he's bitten somebody," Jude said, and started towards the door.

Oscar took hold of her arm, and the contact, light but proprietorial, checked her. She looked back towards him, and all the laughable clichés of romantic fiction were suddenly real and deadly serious. Her heart was beating in her throat; her cheeks were beacons; the ground seemed uncertain beneath her feet. There was no pleasure in this, only a sickening powerlessness she could do nothing to defend herself against. Her only comfort—and it was small—was the fact that her partner in this dance of desire seemed almost as distressed by their mutual fixation as she.

The dog's din was abruptly cut short, and she heard Charlie yell her name. Oscar's glance went to the door, and hers went with it, to see Estabrook, armed with a cudgel of wood, gasping at the threshold. Behind him, an abomination: a half-burned creature, its face caved in (Charlie's doing, she saw; there were scraps of its blackened flesh on the cudgel) reaching blindly for him.

She cried out at the sight, and he stepped aside as it lurched forward. It lost its balance on the step and fell. One hand, fingers burned to the bone, reached for the doorjamb, but Charlie brought his weapon down on its wounded head. Skull shards flew; silvery blood preceded its head to the step, as its hand missed its purchase and it collapsed on the threshold.

She heard Oscar quietly moan.

"You fuckhead!" Charlie said.

He was panting and sweaty, but there was a gleam of purpose in his eye she'd never seen the like of.

"Let her go," he said.

She felt Oscar's grip go from her arm and mourned its departure. What she'd felt for Charlie had been only a prophecy of what she felt now; as if she'd loved him in remembrance of a man she'd never met. And now that she had, now that she'd heard the true voice and not its echo, Estabrook seemed like a poor substitute, for all his tardy heroism.

Where these feelings came from she didn't know, but they had the force of instinct, and she would not be gainsaid. She stared at Oscar. He was overweight, overdressed, and doubtless overbearing: not the kind of individual she'd have sought out, given the choice. But for some reason she didn't yet comprehend, she'd had that choice denied. Some urge profounder than conscious desire had claimed her will. The fears she had for Charlie's safety, and indeed for her own, were suddenly remote: almost abstractions.

"Take no notice of him," Charlie said. "He's not going to hurt you."

She glanced his way. He looked like a husk beside his brother, beset by tics and tremors. How had she ever loved him?

"Come here," he said, beckoning to her.

She didn't move, until Oscar said, "Go on."

More out of obedience to his instruction than any wish to go, she started to walk towards Charlie.

As she did so another shadow fell across the threshold. A severely dressed young man with dyed blond hair appeared at the door, the lines of his face perfect to the point of banality.

"Stay away, Dowd," Oscar said. "This is just Charlie and me."

Dowd looked down at the body on the step, then back at Oscar, offering two words of warning: "He's dangerous."

"I know what he is," Oscar said. "Judith, why don't you step outside with Dowd?"

"Don't go near that little fucker," Charlie told her. "He killed Skin. And there's another of those things out there."

"They're called voiders, Charles," Oscar said. "And they're not going to harm a hair on her beautiful head. Judith. Look at me." She looked around at him. "You're not in danger. You understand? Nobody's going to hurt you."

She understood and believed him. Without looking back at Charlie, she went to the door. The dog killer moved aside, offering her a hand to help her over the voider's corpse, but she ignored it and went out into the sun with a shameful lightness in her heart and step. Dowd followed her as she walked from the chapel. She felt his stare.

"Judith . . ." he said, as if astonished.

"That's me," she replied, knowing that to lay claim to that identity was somehow momentous.

Squatting in the humus a little way from them she saw the other voider. It was idly perusing the body of Skin, running its fingers over the dog's flank. She looked away, unwilling to have the strange joy she felt soured by morbidity.

She and Dowd had reached the edge of the wood, where she had an unhindered view of the sky. The sun was sinking, gaining color as it fell and lending a new glamour to the vista of park, terraces, and house.

"I feel as though I've been here before," she said.

The thought was strangely soothing. Like the feelings she had towards Oscar, it rose from some place in her she didn't remember owning, and identifying its source was not for now as important as accepting its presence. That she did, gladly. She'd spent so much of her recent life in the grip of events that lay outside her power to control, it was a pleasure to touch a source of feeling that was so deep, so instinctive, she didn't need to analyze its intentions. It was part of her, and therefore good. Tomorrow, maybe, or the day after, she'd question its significance more closely.

"Do you remember anything specific about this place?" Dowd asked her.

She mused on this for a time, then said, "No. It's just a feeling of . . . belonging."

"Then maybe it's better not to remember," came the reply. "You know memory. It can be very treacherous."

She didn't like this man, but there was merit in his observation. She could barely remember ten years of her own span; thinking back beyond that would be near impossible. If the recollections came, in the fullness of time, she'd welcome them. But for now she had a brimming cup of feelings, and perhaps they were all the more attractive for their mystery.

There were raised voices from the chapel, though the echo within and the distance without made comprehension impossible.

"A little sibling rivalry," Dowd remarked. "How does it feel being a woman contested over?"

"There's no contest," she replied.

"They don't seem to think so," he said.

The voices were shouts now, rising to a pitch, then suddenly subdued. One of them went on talking—Oscar, she thought—interrupted by exhortations from the other. Were they bargaining over her, throwing their bids back and forth? She started to think she should intervene. Go back to the chapel and make her allegiance, irrational as it was, quite plain. Better to tell the truth now than let Charlie bargain away his goods and chattels only to discover the prize wasn't his to have. She turned and began to walk towards the chapel.

"What are you doing?" said Dowd.

"I have to talk to them."

"Mr. Godolphin told you—"

"I heard him. I have to talk to them."

Off to her right she saw the voider rise from its haunches, its eyes not on her but on the open door. It sniffed the air, then let out a whistle as plaintive as a whine and started toward the building with a loping, almost bestial, gait. It reached the door before Jude, stepping on its dead brother in its haste to be inside. As she came within a couple of yards of the door she caught the scent that had set it whining. A breeze—too warm for the season and carrying perfumes too strange for this world—came to meet her out of the chapel, and to her horror she realized that history was repeating itself. The train between the Dominions was being boarded inside, and the wind she smelled was blowing along the track from its destination.

"*Oscar!*" she yelled, stumbling over the body as she threw herself inside.

The travelers were already dispatched. She saw them passing from view like Gentle and Pie 'oh' pah, except that the voider, desperate to go with them, was pitching itself into the flux of passage. She might have done the same, but that its error was evident. Caught in the flux, but too late to be taken where the travelers had gone, its whistle became a screech as it was unknitted. Its arms and head, thrust into the knot of power which marked the place of departure, began to turn inside out. Its lower half, untouched by the power, convulsed, its legs scrambling for purchase on the mosaic as it tried to retrieve itself. Too late. She saw its head and torso unveiled, saw the skin of its arms stripped and sucked away.

The power that trapped it quickly died. But it was not so lucky. With its arms still clutching at the world it had perhaps glimpsed as its eyes went from its head, it dropped to the ground, the blue-black stew of its innards spilling across the mosaic. Even then, gutted and blind, its body refused to cease. It thrashed in its coils like the victims of a *grand mal*.

Dowd stepped past her, approached the passing place cautiously for fear the flux had left an echo, but, finding none, drew a gun from inside his jacket and, eyeing some vulnerable place in the mess at his feet, fired twice. The voider's throes slowed, then stopped. Sighing heavily, Dowd stepped away from the body and returned to where Jude stood.

"You shouldn't be here," he said. "None of this is for your eyes."

"Why not? I know where they've gone."

"Oh, do you?" he said, raising a quizzical eyebrow. "And where's that?"

"To the Imajica," she said, affecting complete familiarity with the notion, though it still astonished her.

He made a tiny smile, though she wasn't sure whether it was one of acceptance or subtle mockery. He watched her study him, almost basking in her scrutiny, taking it, perhaps, for simple admiration.

"And how do you know about the Imajica?" he inquired.

"Doesn't everybody?"

"I think you know better than that," he replied. "Though how *much* better, I'm not entirely sure."

She was something of an enigma to him, she suspected, and, as long as she remained so, might hope to keep him friendly.

"Do you think they made it?" she asked.

"Who knows? The voider may have spoilt their passage by trying to tag along. They may not have reached Yzordderrex."

"So where will they be?"

"In the In Ovo, of course. Somewhere between here and the Second Dominion."

"And how will they get back?"

"Simple," he said. "They won't."

4

So they waited. Or, rather, she waited, watching the sun disappear behind trees blotted with rookeries, and the evening stars appearing as light bringers in its place. Dowd busied himself dealing with the bodies of the voiders, dragging them out of the chapel, making a simple pyre of dead wood, and burning them upon it. He showed not the least concern that she was witnessing this, which was a lesson and perhaps a warning to her. He apparently assumed she was part of the secret world he and the voiders occupied, not subject to the laws and moralities the rest of the world was bounded by. In seeing all she'd seen, and passing herself off as expert in the ways of the Imajica, she had become a conspirator. There was no way back after this, to the company she'd kept and the life she'd known; she belonged to the secret, every bit as much as the secret belonged to her.

That of itself would be no great loss if Godolphin returned. He would help her find her way through the mysteries. If he didn't return, the consequences were less palatable. To be obliged to keep Dowd's company, simply because they were fellow marginals, would be unbearable. She would surely wither and die. But then if Godolphin was not in her life, what could that matter? From ecstasy to despair in the space of an hour. Was it too much to hope the pendulum would swing back the other way before the day was out?

The chill was adding to her misery, and—having no other source of warmth—she went over to the pyre, preparing to retreat if the scent or the sight was too offensive. But the smoke, which she'd expected to smell of burning meat, was almost aromatic, and the forms in the fire unrecognizable. Dowd offered her a cigarette, which she accepted, lighting it from a branch plucked from the edge of the fire.

"What were they?" she asked him, eyeing the remains.

"You've never heard of voiders?" he said. "They're the lowest of the low. I brought them through from the In Ovo myself, and I'm no Maestro, so that gives an idea of how gullible they are."

"When it smelled the wind—"

"Yes, that was rather touching, wasn't it?" Dowd said. "It smelled Yzordderrex."

"Maybe it was born there."

"Very possibly. I've heard it said they're made of collective desire, but that's not true. They're revenge children. Got on women who were working the Way for themselves."

"Working the Way isn't good?"

"Not for your sex, it isn't. It's strictly forbidden."

"So somebody who breaks the law's made pregnant as revenge?"

"Exactly. You can't abort voiders, you see. They're stupid, but they fight, even in the womb. And killing something you gave birth to is strictly against the women's codes. So they pay to have the voiders thrown into the In Ovo. They can survive there longer than just about anything. They feed on whatever they can find, including each other. And eventually, if they're lucky, they get summoned by someone in this Dominion."

So much to learn, she thought. Perhaps she should cultivate Dowd's friendship, however charmless he was. He seemed to enjoy parading his knowledge, and the more she knew the better prepared she'd be when she finally stepped through the door into Yzordderrex. She was about to ask him something more about the city when a gust of wind, blowing from out of the chapel, threw a flurry of sparks up between them.

"They're coming back," she said, and started towards the building.

"Be careful," Dowd said. "You don't know it's them."

His warning went unheeded. She went to the door at a

run, and reached it as the spicy summer wind died away. The interior of the chapel was gloomy, but she could see a single figure standing in the middle of the mosaic. It staggered towards her, its breathing ragged. The light from the fire caught it as it came within two yards of her. It was Oscar Godolphin, his hand up to his bleeding nose.

"That bastard," he said.

"Where is he?"

"Dead," he said plainly. "I had to do it, Judith. He was crazy. God alone knows what he might have said or done. . . ." He put his arm towards her. "Will you help me? He damn near broke my nose."

"I'll take him," Dowd said possessively. He stepped past her, fetching a handkerchief from his pocket to put to Oscar's nose. It was waved away.

"I'll survive," Oscar said. "Let's just get home." They were out of the chapel now, and Oscar was eyeing the fire.

"The voiders," Dowd explained.

Oscar threw a glance at Judith. "He made you pyrewatch with him?" he said. "I'm so sorry." He looked back at Dowd, pained. "That's no way to treat a lady," he said. "We're going to have to do better in future."

"What do you mean?"

"She's coming to live with us. Aren't you, Judith?"

She hesitated a shamelessly short time; then she said, "Yes, I am."

Satisfied, he went over to look at the pyre.

"Come back tomorrow," she heard him tell Dowd. "Scatter the ashes and bury the bones. I've got a little prayer book Peccable gave me. We'll find something appropriate in there."

While he spoke she stared into the murk of the chapel, trying to imagine the journey that had been taken from here, and the city at the other end from which that tantalizing wind had blown. She would be there one day. She'd lost a husband in pursuit of passage, but from her present perspective that seemed like a negligible loss. There was a new order of feeling in her, founded at the sight of Oscar Godolphin. She didn't yet know what he would come to mean to her, but perhaps she could persuade him to take her away with him, someday soon.

Eager as she was to create in her mind's eye the mysteries that lay beyond the veil of the Fifth, Jude's imagination, for all its fever, could never have conjured the reality of that journey. Inspired by a few clues from Dowd, she had imagined the In Ovo as a kind of wasteland, where voiders hung like drowned men in deep-sea trenches, and creatures the sun would never see crawled towards her, their paths lit by their own sickly luminescence. But the inhabitants of the In Ovo beggared the bizarreness of any ocean floor. They had forms and appetites that no book had ever set down. They had rages and frustrations that were centuries old.

And the scenes she'd imagined awaiting her on the other side of that prison were also very different from those she'd created. If she'd traveled on the Yzordderrexian Express she'd would not have been delivered into the middle of a summer city but into a dampish cellar, lined with the merchant Peccable's forbidden cache of charms and petrifications. In order to reach the open air, she would have had to climb the stairs and pass through the house itself. Once she'd reached the street, she'd have found some of her expectations satisfied at least. The air was warm and spicy there, and the sky was bright. But it was not a sun that blazed overhead, it was a comet, trailing its glory across the Second Dominion. And if she stared at it a moment, then looked down at the street, she'd have found its reflection glittering in a pool of blood. Here was the spot where the brawl between Oscar and Charlie had ended, and where the defeated brother had been left.

He had not remained there for very long. News of a man dressed in foreign garb and dumped in the gutter had soon spread, and before the last of his blood had drained from his body three individuals never before seen in this Kesparate had come to claim him. They were Dearthers, to judge by their tattoos, and had Jude been standing on Peccable's step watching the scene, she would have been touched to see how reverently they treated their burden as they spirited it away. How they smiled down at that bruised and lolling face. How one of them wept. She might also have noticed—though in the flurry of the street this detail might have escaped her eye—that though the defeated man lay quite still in the cradle his bearers made of their limbs, his eyes closed, his arms trailing until they were folded across his chest, said chest was not entirely motionless.

Charles Estabrook, abandoned for dead in the filth of Yzordderrex, left its streets with enough health in his body to be dubbed a loser, not a corpse.

22

I

The days following Pie and Gentle's second departure from Beatrix seemed to shorten as they climbed, supporting the suspicion that the nights in the Jokalaylau were longer than those in the lowlands. It was impossible to confirm that this was so, because their two timekeepers—Gentle's beard and Pie's bowels—became increasingly unreliable as they climbed, the former because Gentle ceased to shave, the latter because the travelers' desire to eat, and thus their need to defecate, dwindled the higher they went. Far from inspiring appetite, the rarefied air became a feast in itself, and they traveled for hour upon hour without their thoughts once turning to physical need. They had each other's company, of course, to keep them from completely forgetting their bodies and their purpose, but more reliable still were the beasts on whose shaggy backs they rode. When the doeki grew hungry they simply stopped, and would not be bullied or coaxed into moving from whatever bush or piece of pasture they'd found until they were sated. At first, this was an irritation, and the riders cursed as they slipped from their saddles on such occasions, knowing they had an idling hour ahead while the animals grazed. But as the days passed and the air grew thinner, they came to de-

pend upon the rhythm of the doekis' digestive tracts and
made such stopping places mealtimes for themselves.

It soon became apparent that Pie's calculations as to the
length of this journey had been hopelessly optimistic. The
only part of the mystif's predictions that experience was
confirming was the hardship. Even before they reached the
snow line, both riders and mounts were showing signs of
fatigue, and the track they were following became less visible by the mile as the soft earth chilled and froze, refusing
the traces of those who had preceded them. With the prospect of snowfields and glaciers ahead, they rested the doeki
for a day and encouraged the beasts to gorge themselves on
what would be the last available pasture until they reached
the other side of the range.

Gentle had called his mount Chester, after dear old
Klein, with whom it shared a certain ruminative charm. Pie
declined to name the other beast, however, claiming it was
bad luck to eat anything you knew by name, and circumstances might very well oblige them to dine on doeki meat
before they reached the borders of the Third Dominion.
That small disagreement aside, they kept their exchanges
frictionless when they set off again, both consciously skirt-
ing any discussion of the events in Beatrix or their significance. The cold soon became aggressive, the coats they'd
been given barely adequate defense against the assault of
winds that blew up walls of dusty snow so dense they often
obliterated the way ahead. When that happened Pie pulled
out the compass—the face of which looked more like a star
map to Gentle's untutored eye—and assessed their direction from that. Only once did Gentle remark that he hoped
the mystif knew what it was doing, earning such a withering
glance for his troubles it silenced him utterly on the matter
thereafter.

Despite weather that was worsening by the day—making Gentle think wistfully of an English January—good fortune did not entirely desert them. On the fifth day beyond
the snow line, in a lull between gusts, Gentle heard bells
ringing, and following the sound they discovered a group of
half a dozen mountain men, tending to a flock of a hundred

or more cousins to the terrestrial goat, these shaggier by far and purple as crocuses. The herders spoke no English, and only one of them, whose name was Kuthuss and who boasted a beard as shaggy and as purple as his beasts (leading Gentle to wonder what marriages of convenience had occurred in these lonely uplands), had any words in his vocabulary that Pie could comprehend. What he told was grim. The herders were bringing their herds down from the High Pass early because the snow had covered ground the beasts would have grazed for another twenty days in a normal season. This was not, he repeated several times, a normal season. He had never known the snow to come so early or fall so copiously; never known the winds to be so bitter. In essence, he advised them not to attempt the route ahead. It would be tantamount to suicide. Pie and Gentle talked this advice over. The journey was already taking far longer than they'd anticipated. If they went back down below the snow line, tempting as the prospect of relative warmth and fresh food was, they were wasting yet more time. Days when all manner of horrors could be unfolding: a hundred villages like Beatrix destroyed, and countless lives lost.

"Remember what I said when we left Beatrix?" Gentle said.

"No, to be honest, I don't."

"I said we wouldn't die, and I meant it. We'll find a way through."

"I'm not sure I like this messianic conviction," Pie said. "People with the best intentions die, Gentle. Come to think of it, they're often the first to go."

"What are you saying? That you won't come with me?"

"I said I'd go wherever you go, and I will. But good intentions won't impress the cold."

"How much money have we got?"

"Not much."

"Enough to buy some goatskins off these men? And maybe some meat?"

A complex exchange ensued in three languages—with Pie translating Gentle's words into the language Kuthuss understood and Kuthuss in turn translating for his fellow herders. A deal was rapidly struck; the herders seemed much persuaded by the prospect of hard cash. Rather than give over their own coats, however, two of them got about the business of slaughtering and skinning four of the animals. The meat, they cooked and shared among the group. It was fatty and underdone, but neither Gentle nor Pie declined, and it was washed down with a beverage they brewed from boiled snow, dried leaves, and a dash of liquor which Pie understood Kuthuss to have called the piss of the goat. They tasted it in spite of this. It was potent, and after a shot of it—downed like vodka—Gentle remarked that if this made him a piss-drinker, so be it.

The next day, having been supplied with skins, meat, and the makings of several pots of the herders' beverage, plus a pan and two glasses, they made their inarticulate farewells and parted company. The weather closed in soon after, and once again they were lost in a white wilderness. But their spirits had been buoyed up by the meeting, and they made steady progress for the next two and a half days, until, as twilight approached on the third, the animal Gentle was riding started to show signs of exhaustion, its head drooping, its hooves barely able to clear the snow they were trudging through.

"I think we'd better rest him," Gentle said.

They found a niche between boulders so large they were almost hills in themselves, and lit a fire to brew up some of the herders' liquor. It, more than the meat, was what had sustained them through the most demanding portions of the journey so far, but try as they might to use it sparingly, they had almost consumed their modest supply. As they drank they talked about what lay ahead. Kuthuss' predictions were proving correct. The weather was worsening all the time, and the chances of encountering another living soul up here if they were to get into difficulty were surely zero. Pie took a moment to remind Gentle of his conviction that they weren't going to die; come blizzard, come hurricane, come the echo of Hapexamendios Himself, down from the mountain.

"And I meant what I said," Gentle replied. "But I can

still fret about it, can't I?" He put his hands closer to the fire. "Any more in the piss pot?"

"I'm afraid not."

"I tell you, when we come back this way"—Pie made a wry face—"we will, we will. When we come back this way we've got to get the recipe. Then we can brew it back on earth."

They'd left the doeki a little distance away and heard now a lowing sound.

"Chester!" Gentle said, and went to the beasts.

Chester was lying on its side, its flank heaving. Blood streamed from its mouth and nose, melting the snow it poured upon.

"Oh, shit, Chester," Gentle implored, "don't die."

But he'd no sooner put what he hoped was a comforting hand on the doeki's flank than it turned its glossy brown eye towards him, let out one final moan, and stopped breathing.

"We just lost fifty percent of our transport," he said to Pie.

"Look on the bright side. We gained ourselves a week of meat."

Gentle glanced back towards the dead animal, wishing he'd taken Pie's advice and never named the beast. Now when he sucked its bones he'd be thinking of Klein.

"Will you do it or should I?" he said. "I suppose it should be me. I named him, I should skin him."

The mystif didn't argue, only suggested that it should move the other animal out of sight of the scene, in case it too lost all will to live, seeing its comrade disemboweled. Gentle agreed, and watched while Pie led the fretting creature away. Wielding the blade they'd been given as they left Beatrix, he then set about his butchering. He rapidly discovered that neither he nor the knife were equal to the task. The doeki's hide was thick, its fat rubbery, its meat tough. After an hour of hacking and tearing he'd only managed to strip the hide from the upper half of its back leg and a small portion of its flank. He was sticky with its blood and sweating inside his coat of furs.

"Shall I take over?" Pie suggested.

"No," Gentle snapped, "I can do it," and continued to labor in the same inept fashion, the blade dulled by now and the muscles driving it weary.

He waited a decent interval, then got up and went back to the fire where Pie was sitting, gazing into the flames. Disgruntled by his defeat, he tossed the knife down in the melting snow beside the fire.

"I give up," he said. "It's all yours."

Somewhat reluctantly, Pie picked up the knife, proceeded to sharpen it on the rock face, then went to work. Gentle didn't watch. Repulsed by the blood that had spattered him, he elected to brave the cold and wash it off. He found a place a little way from the fire where the ground was untrammeled, removed his coat and shirt, and knelt down to bathe in the snow. His skin crawled at the chill, but some urge to self-mortification was satisfied by this testing of will and flesh, and when he'd cleaned his hands and face he rubbed the pricking snow into his chest and belly, though the doeki's fluids hadn't stained him there. The wind had dropped in the last little while, and the sky visible between the rocks was more gold than green. He was seized by the need to stand unencumbered in its light, and without putting his coat back on he clambered up over the rocks to do so. His hands were numb, and the climb was more arduous than he'd anticipated, but the scene above and below him when he reached the top of the rock was worth the effort. No wonder Hapexamendios had come here on His way to His resting place. Even gods might be inspired by such grandeur. The peaks of the Jokalaylau receded in apparently infinite procession, their white slopes faintly gilded by the heavens they reached for. The silence could not have been more utter.

This vantage point served a practical as well as an aesthetic purpose. The High Pass was plainly visible. And so, some distance off to the right, was a sight perplexing enough for him to call the mystif up from its work. A glacier, its surface shimmering, lay a mile or more from the rock. But it wasn't the spectacle of such frozen enormity that claimed Gentle's eye, it was the presence within the ice of a litter of darker forms.

"You want to go and find out what they are?" the mystif said, washing its bloodied hands in the snow.

"I think we should," Gentle replied. "If we're walking in the Unbeheld's footsteps, we should make it our business to see what He saw."

"Or what He caused," Pie said.

They descended, and Gentle put his shirt and coat back on. The clothes were warm, having been left beside the fire, and he was glad of that comfort, but they also stank of his sweat and of the animals whose backs they'd been stripped from, and he half wished he could go naked, rather than be burdened by another hide.

"Have you finished with the skinning?" Gentle asked Pie as they set off, going by foot rather than waste the energies of their remaining vehicle.

"I've done what I can," Pie replied, "but it's crude. I'm no butcher."

"Are you a cook?" Gentle asked.

"Not really. Why'd you ask?"

"I've been thinking about food a lot, that's all. You know, after this trip I may never eat meat again. The fat! The gristle! It turns my stomach thinking about it."

"You've got a sweet tooth."

"You noticed. I'd kill for a plate of profiteroles right now, swimming in chocolate sauce." He laughed. "Listen to me. The glories of Jokalaylau laid before us and I'm obsessing on profiteroles." Then again, deadly serious. "Do they have chocolate in Yzorderrex?"

"By now, I'm sure they do. But my people eat plainly, so I never got an addiction for sugar. Fish, on the other hand—"

"Fish?" said Gentle. "I've no taste for it."

"You'll get one in Yzorderrex. There's restaurants down by the harbor . . ." The mystif's talk turned into a smile. "Now I'm sounding like you. We must both be sick of doeki meat."

"Go on," Gentle said. "I want to see you salivate."

"There are restaurants down by the harbor where the fish is so fresh it's still flapping when they take it into the kitchen."

"That's a recommendation?"

"There's nothing in the world as good as fresh fish," Pie said. "If the catch is good you've got a choice of forty, maybe fifty, dishes. From tiny jepas to squeffah my size and bigger."

"Is there anything I'd recognize?"

"A few species. But why travel all this way for a cod steak when you could have squeffah? Or better, there's a dish I have to order for you. It's a fish called an ugichee, which is almost as small as a jepas, and it lives in the belly of another fish."

"That sounds suicidal."

"Wait, there's more. The second fish is often eaten whole by a bloater called a coliacic. They're ugly, but the meat melts like butter. So if you're lucky, they'll grill all three of them together, just the way they were caught—"

"One inside the other?"

"Head, tail, the whole caboodle."

"That's disgusting."

"And if you're very lucky—"

"Pie—"

"—the ugichee's a female, and you find, when you cut through all three layers of fish—"

"—her belly's full of caviar."

"You guessed it. Doesn't that sound tempting?"

"I'll stay with my chocolate mousse and ice cream."

"How is it you're not fat?"

"Vanessa used to say I had the palate of a child, the libido of an adolescent, and the—well, you can guess the rest. I sweat it out making love. Or at least I used to."

They were close to the edge of the glacier now, and their talk of fish and chocolate ceased, replaced by a grim silence, as the identity of the forms encased in the ice became apparent. They were human bodies, a dozen or more. Ice-locked around them, a collection of debris: fragments of blue stone; immense bowls of beaten metal; the remnants of garments, the blood on them still bright. Gentle clambered and skidded across the top of the glacier until the bodies were directly beneath him. Some were buried too deeply to be studied, but those closer to the surface—faces upturned, limbs fixed in attitudes of desperation—were almost too visible. They were all women, the youngest barely out of childhood, the oldest a naked many-breasted hag who'd perished with her eyes still open, her stare preserved for the millennium. Some massacre had occurred here, or farther up the mountain, and the evidence been thrown into this river while it still flowed. Then, apparently, it had frozen around the victims and their belongings.

"Who are they?" Gentle asked. "Any idea?" Though they were dead, the past tense didn't seem appropriate for corpses so perfectly preserved.

"When the Unbeheld passed through the Dominions, He overthrew all the cults He deemed unworthy. Most of them were sacred to Goddesses. Their oracles and devotees were women."

"So you think Hapexamendios did this?"

"If not him, then His agents, His Righteous. Though on second thought He's supposed to have walked here alone, so maybe this is His handiwork."

"Then whoever He is," Gentle said, looking down at the child in the ice, "He's a murderer. No better than you or me."

"I wouldn't say that too loudly," Pie advised.

"Why not? He's not here."

"If this *is* His doing, He may have left entities to watch over it."

Gentle looked around. The air could not have been clearer. There was no sign of motion on the peaks or the snow-fields gleaming below. "If they're here I don't see 'em," he said.

"The worst are the ones you can't see," Pie replied. "Shall we go back to the fire?"

2

They were weighed down by what they'd seen, and the return journey took longer than the outward. By the time they made the safety of their niche in the rocks, to welcoming grunts from the surviving doeki, the sky was losing its golden sheen and dusk was on its way. They debated whether to proceed in darkness and decided against it. Though the air was calm at present, they knew from past experience that conditions on these heights were unpredictable. If they attempted to move by night, and a storm descended from the peaks, they'd be twice blinded and in danger of losing their way. With the High Pass so close, and the journey easier, they hoped, once they were through it, the risk was not worth taking.

Having used up the supply of wood they'd collected below the snow line, they were obliged to fuel the fire with the dead doeki's saddle and harness. It made for a smoky, pungent, and fitful blaze, but it was better than nothing. They cooked some of the fresh meat, Gentle observing as he chewed that he had less compunction about eating something he'd named than he thought, and brewed up a small serving of the herders' piss liquor. As they drank, Gentle returned the conversation to the women in the ice.

"Why would a God as powerful as Hapexamendios slaughter defenseless women?"

"Whoever said they were defenseless?" Pie replied. "I think they were probably very powerful. Their oracles must have sensed what was coming, so they had their armies ready—"

"Armies of women?"

"Certainly. Warriors in their tens of thousands. There are places to the north of the Lenten Way where the earth used to move every fifty years or so and uncover one of their war graves."

"They were all slaughtered? The armies, the oracles—"

"Or driven so deep into hiding they forgot who they

were after a few generations. Don't look so surprised. It happens."

"One God defeats how many Goddesses? Ten, twenty—"

"Innumerable."

"How?"

"He was One, and simple. They were many, and diverse."

"Singularity is strength—"

"At least in the short term. Who told you that?"

"I'm trying to remember. Somebody I didn't like much: Klein, maybe."

"Whoever said it, it's true. Hapexamendios came into the Dominions with a seductive idea: that wherever you went, whatever misfortune attended you, you needed only one name on your lips, one prayer, one altar, and you'd be in His care. And He brought a species to maintain that order once He'd established it. Yours."

"Those women back there looked human enough to me."

"So do I," Pie reminded him. "But I'm not."

"No . . . you're pretty diverse, aren't you?"

"I was once. . . ."

"So that puts you on the side of the Goddesses, doesn't it?" Gentle whispered.

The mystif put its finger to his lips.

Gentle mouthed one word by way of response: "Heretic."

It was very dark now, and they both settled to studying the fire. It was steadily diminishing as the last of Chester's saddle was consumed.

"Maybe we should burn some fur," Gentle suggested.

"No," said Pie. "Let it dwindle. But keep looking."

"At what?"

"Anything."

"There's only you to look at."

"Then look at me."

He did so. The privations of the last many days had seemingly taken little toll on the mystif. It had no facial hair to disfigure the symmetry of its features, nor had their spartan diet pinched its cheeks or hollowed its eyes. Studying its face was like returning to a favorite painting in a museum. There it was: a thing of calm and beauty. But, unlike the painting, the face before him, which presently seemed so solid, had the capacity for infinite change. It was months since the night when he'd first seen that phenomenon. But now, as the fire burned itself out and the shadows deepened around them, he realized the same sweet miracle was imminent. The flicker of dying flame made the symmetry swim; the flesh before him seemed to lose its fixedness as he stared and stirred it.

"I want to watch," he murmured.

"Then watch."

"But the fire's going out. . . ."

"We don't need light to see each other," the mystif whispered. "Hold on to the sight."

Gentle concentrated, studying the face before him. His eyes ached as he tried to hold onto it, but they were no competition for the swelling darkness.

"Stop looking," Pie said, in a voice that seemed to rise from the decay of the embers. "Stop looking, and *see.*"

Gentle fought for the sense of this, but it was no more susceptible to analysis than the darkness in front of him. Two senses were failing him here—one physical, one linguistic—two ways to embrace the world slipping from him at the same moment. It was like a little death, and a panic seized him, like the fear he'd felt some midnights waking in his bed and body and knowing neither: his bones a cage, his blood a gruel, his dissolution the only certainty. At such times he'd turned on all the lights, for their comfort. But there were no lights here. Only bodies, growing colder as the fire died.

"Help me," he said. The mystif didn't speak. "Are you there, Pie? I'm afraid. Touch me, will you? *Pie?*"

The mystif didn't move. Gentle started to reach out in the darkness, remembering as he did so the sight of Taylor lying on a pillow from which they'd both known he'd never rise again, asking for Gentle to hold his hand. With that memory, the panic became sorrow: for Taylor, for Clem, for every soul sealed from its loved ones by senses born to failure, himself included. He wanted what the child wanted: knowledge of another presence, proved in touch. But he knew it was no real solution. He might find the mystif in the darkness, but he could no more hold on to its flesh forever than he could hold the senses he'd already lost. Nerves decayed, and fingers slipped from fingers at the last.

Knowing this little solace was as hopeless as any other, he withdrew his hand and instead said, "I love you."

Or did he simply think it? Perhaps it was thought, because it was the idea rather than the syllables that formed in front of him, the iridescence he remembered from Pie's transforming self shimmering in a darkness that was not, he vaguely understood, the darkness of the starless night but his mind's darkness; and this seeing not the business of eye and object but his exchange with a creature he loved, and who loved him back.

He let his feelings go to Pie, if there was indeed a going, which he doubted. Space, like time, belonged to the other tale—to the tragedy of separation they'd left behind. Stripped of his senses and their necessities, almost unborn again, he knew the mystif's comfort as it knew his, and that dissolution he'd woken in terror of so many times stood revealed as the beginning of bliss.

A gust of wind, blowing between the rocks, caught the embers at their side, and their glow became a momentary flame. It brightened the face in front of him, and the sight summoned him back from his unborn state. It was no great hardship to return. The place they'd found together was out of time and could not decay, and the face in front of him, for all its frailty (or perhaps because of it), was beautiful to look at. Pie smiled at him but said nothing.

"We should sleep," Gentle said. "We've got a long way to go tomorrow."

Another gust came along, and there were flecks of snow in it, stinging Gentle's face. He pulled the hood of his coat up over his head and got up to check on the welfare of the doeki. It had made a shallow bed for itself in the snow and was asleep. By the time he got back to the fire, which had found some combustible morsel and was devouring it brightly, the mystif was also asleep, its hood pulled up around its head. As he stared down at the visible crescent of Pie's face, a simple thought came: that though the wind was moaning at the rock, ready to bury them, and there was death in the valley behind and a city of atrocities ahead, he was happy. He lay down on the hard ground beside the mystif. His last thought as sleep came was of Taylor, lying on a pillow which was becoming a snowfield as he drew his final breaths, his face growing translucent and finally disappearing, so that when Gentle slipped from consciousness, it was not into darkness but into the whiteness of that death-bed, turned to untrodden snow.

23

I

Gentle dreamed that the wind grew harsher and brought snow down off the peaks, fresh minted. He nevertheless rose from the relative comfort of his place beside the ashes, and took off his coat and shirt, took off his boots and socks, took off his trousers and underwear, and naked walked down the narrow corridor of rock, past the sleeping doeki, to face the blast. Even in dreams, the wind threatened to freeze his marrow, but he had his sights set on the glacier, and he had to go to it in all humility, bare-loined, bare-backed, to show due respect for those souls who suffered there. They had endured centuries of pain, the crime against them unrevenged. Beside theirs, his suffering was a minor thing.

There was sufficient light in the wide sky to show him his way, but the wastes seemed endless, and the gusts worsened as he went, several times throwing him over into the snow. His muscles cramped and his breath shortened, coming from between his numbed lips in hard, small clouds. He wanted to weep for the pain of it, but the tears crystallized on the ledge of his eye and would not fall.

Twice he stopped, because he sensed that there was something more than snow on the storm's back. He remembered Pie's talk of agents left in this wilderness to guard the murder site and, though he was only dreaming and knew it, he was still afraid. If these entities were charged to keep witnesses from the glacier, they would not simply drive the wakeful off but the sleeping too; and those who came as he came, in reverence, would earn their special ire. He studied the spattered air, looking for some sign of them, and once thought he glimpsed a form overhead that would have been invisible but that it displaced the snow: an eel's body with a tiny ball of a head. But it was come and gone too quickly for him to be certain he'd even seen it.

The glacier was in sight, however, and his will drove his limbs to motion, until he was standing at its edge. He raised his hands to his face and wiped the snow from his cheeks and forehead, then stepped onto the ice. The women gazed up at him as they had when he'd stood here with Pie 'oh' pah, but now, through the dust of snow blowing across the ice, they saw him naked, his manhood shrunk, his body trembling; on his face and lips a question he had half an answer to. Why, if this was indeed the work of Hapexamendios, had the Unbeheld, with all His powers of destruction, not obliterated every last sign of His victims? Was it because they were women or, more particularly, women of power? Had He brought them to ruin as best He could— overturning their altars and unseating their temples—but at the last been unable to wipe them away? And if so, was this ice a grave or merely a prison?

He dropped to his knees and laid his palms on the glacier. This time he definitely heard a sound in the wind, a raw howl somewhere overhead. The invisibles had entertained his dreaming presence long enough. They saw his purpose and were circling in preparation for descent. He blew against his palm and made a fist before the breath could slip, then raised his arm and slammed his hand against the ice, opening it as he did so.

The pneuma went off like a thunderclap. Before the tremors had died he snatched a second breath and broke it against the ice; then a third and fourth in quick succession, striking the steely surface so hard that had the pneuma not cushioned the blow he'd have broken every bone from wrist to fingertip. But his efforts had effect. There were hairline cracks spreading from the point of impact.

Encouraged, he began a second round of blows, but he'd delivered only three when he felt something take hold of his hair, wrenching his head back. A second grip instantly seized his raised arm. He had time to feel the ice splintering beneath his legs; then he was hauled up off the glacier by wrist and hair. He struggled against the claim, knowing that if his assaulters carried him too high death was assured; they'd either tear him apart in the clouds or simply drop him. The hold on his head was the less secure of the two, and his gyrations were sufficient to slip it, though blood ran down his brow.

Freed, he looked up at the entities. There were two, six feet long, their bodies scantily fleshed spines sprouting innumerable ribs, their limbs twelvefold and bereft of bone, their heads vestigial. Only their motion had beauty: a sinuous knotting and unknotting. He reached up and snatched at the closer of the two heads. Though it had no discernible features, it looked tender, and his hand had sufficient echo of the pneumas it had discharged to do harm. He dug his fingers into the flesh of the thing, and it instantly began to writhe, coiling its length around its companion for support, its limbs flailing wildly. He twisted his body to the left and right, the motion violent enough to wrench him free. Then he fell, a mere six feet but hard, onto slivered ice. The breath went from him as the pain came. He had time to see the agents descending upon him, but none in which to escape. Waking or sleeping, this was the end of him, he knew; death by these limbs had jurisdiction in both states.

But before they could find his flesh, and blind him, and unman him, he felt the shattered glacier beneath him shudder, and with a roar it rose, throwing him off its back into the snow. Shards pelted down upon him, but he peered up through their hail to see that the women were emerging from their graves, clothed in ice. He hauled himself to his feet as the tremors increased, the din of this unshackling echoing off the mountains. Then he turned and ran.

The storm was discreet and quickly drew its veil over the resurrection, so that he fled not knowing how the events he'd begun had finished. Certainly the agents of Hapexamendios made no pursuit; or, if they did, they failed to find him. Their absence comforted him only a little. His adventures had done him harm, and the distance he had to cover to get back to the camp was substantial. His run soon deteriorated into stumbling and staggering, blood marking his route. It was time to be done with this dream of endurance, he thought, and open his eyes; to roll over and put his arms around Pie 'oh' pah; to kiss the mystif's cheek and share this vision with it. But his thoughts were too confounded to take hold of wakefulness long enough for him to rouse himself, and he dared not lie down in the snow in case a dreamed death came to him before morning woke him. All he could do was push himself on, weaker by the step, putting out of his head the possibility that he'd lost his way and that the camp didn't lie ahead but off in another direction entirely.

He was looking down at his feet when he heard the shout, and his first instinct was to peer up into the snow above him, expecting one of the Unbeheld's creatures. But before his eyes reached his zenith they found the shape approaching him from his left. He stopped and studied the figure. It was shaggy and hooded, but its arms were outspread in invitation. He didn't waste what little energy he had calling Pie's name. He simply changed his direction and headed towards the mystif as it came to meet him. It was the faster of the two, and as it came it shrugged off its coat and held it open, so that he fell into its luxury. He couldn't feel it; indeed he could feel little, except relief. Borne up by the mystif he let all conscious thought go, the rest of the journey becoming a blur of snow and snow, and

Pie's voice sometimes, at his side, telling him that it would be over soon.

"Am I awake?" He opened his eyes and sat up, grasping hold of Pie's coat to do so. "Am I awake?"

"Yes."

"Thank God! Thank God! I thought I was going to freeze to death."

He let his head sink back. The fire was burning, fed with fur, and he could feel its warmth on his face and body. It took a few seconds to realize the significance of this. Then he sat up again and realized he was naked: naked and covered with cuts.

"I'm not awake," he said. "Shit! I'm not awake!"

Pie took the pot of herders' brew from the fire, and poured a cup.

"You didn't dream it," the mystif said. It handed the cup over to Gentle. "You went to the glacier, and you almost didn't make it back."

Gentle took the cup in raw fingers. "I must have been out of my mind," he said. "I remember thinking: I'm dreaming this, then taking off my coat and my clothes . . . why the hell did I do that?"

He could still recall struggling through the snow and reaching the glacier. He remembered pain, and splintering ice, but the rest had receded so far he couldn't grasp it. Pie read his perplexed look.

"Don't try and remember now," the mystif said. "It'll come back when the moment's right. Push too hard and you'll break your heart. You should sleep for a while."

"I don't fancy sleeping," he said. "It's a little too much like dying."

"I'll be here," Pie told him. "Your body needs rest. Let it do what it needs to do."

The mystif had been warming Gentle's shirt in front of the fire, and now helped him put it on, a delicate business. Gentle's joints were already stiffening. He pulled on his trousers without Pie's help, however, up over limbs that were a mass of bruises and abrasions.

"Whatever I did out there I certainly made a mess of myself," he remarked.

"You heal quickly," Pie said. This was true, though Gentle couldn't remember sharing that information with the mystif. "Lie down. I'll wake you when it's light."

Gentle put his head on the small heap of hides Pie had made as a pillow and let the mystif pull his coat up over him.

"Dream of sleeping," Pie said, laying a hand on Gentle's face. "And wake whole."

2

When Pie shook him awake, what seemed mere minutes later, the sky visible between the rock faces was still dark, but it was the gloom of snow-bearing cloud rather than the purple black of a Jokalaylaurian night. He sat up feeling wretched, aching in every bone.

"I'd kill for coffee," he said, resisting the urge to torture his joints by stretching. "And warm *pain au chocolat.*"

"If they don't have it in Yzordderrex, we'll invent it," Pie said.

"Did you brew up?"

"There's nothing left to burn."

"And what's the weather like?"

"Don't ask."

"That bad?"

"We should get a move on. The thicker the snow gets, the more difficult it'll be to find the pass."

They roused the doeki, which made plain its disgruntlement at having to breakfast on words of encouragement rather than hay, and, with the meat Pie had prepared the day before loaded, left the shelter of the rock and headed out into the snow. There had been a short debate before they left as to whether they should ride or not, Pie insisting that Gentle should do so, given his present delicacy, but he'd argued that they might need the doeki's strength to carry them both if they got into worse difficulties, and they should preserve such energies as it still possessed for such an emergency. But he soon began to stumble in snow that was waist high in places, his body, though somewhat healed by sleep, not equal to the demands upon it.

"We'll go more quickly if you ride," Pie told him.

He needed little persuasion and mounted the doeki, his fatigue such that he could barely sit upright with the wind so strong, and instead slumped against the beast's neck. He only occasionally raised himself from that posture, and when he did the scene had scarcely changed.

"Shouldn't we be in the pass by now?" he murmured to Pie at one point, and the look on the mystif's face was answer enough. They were lost. Gentle pushed himself into an upright position and, squinting against the gale, looked for some sign of shelter, however small. The world was white in every direction but for them, and even they were being steadily erased as ice clogged the fur of their coats and the snow they were trudging through deepened. Until now, however arduous the journey had become, he hadn't countenanced the possibility of failure. He'd been his own best convert to the gospel of their indestructibility. But now such confidence seemed self-deception. The white world would strip all color from them, to get to the purity of their bones.

He reached to take hold of Pie's shoulder, but misjudged the distance and slid from the doeki's back. Relieved of its burden the beast slumped, its front legs buckling. Had Pie not been swift and pulled Gentle out of harm's way, he might have been crushed beneath the creature's bulk. Hauling back his hood and swiping the snow from the back of his neck, he got to his feet and found Pie's exhausted gaze there to meet him.

"I thought I was leading us right," the mystif said.

"Of course you did."

"But we've missed the pass somehow. The slope's getting steeper. I don't know where the fuck we are, Gentle."

"In trouble is where we are, and too tired to think our way out of it. We have to rest."

"Where?"

"Here," Gentle said. "This blizzard can't go on forever.

There's only so much snow in the sky, and most of it's already fallen, right? *Right?* So if we can just hold on till the storm's over, and we can see where we are—"

"Suppose by that time it's night again? We'll freeze, my friend."

"Do we have any other choice?" Gentle said. "If we go on we'll kill the beast and probably ourselves. We could march right over a gorge and never know it. But if we stay here . . . *together* . . . maybe we're in with a chance."

"I thought I knew our direction."

"Maybe you did. Maybe the storm'll blow over, and we'll find ourselves on the other side of the mountain." Gentle put his hands on Pie's shoulders, sliding them around the back of the mystif's neck. "We have no choice," he said slowly.

Pie nodded, and together they settled as best they could in the dubious shelter of the doeki's body. The beast was still breathing, but not, Gentle thought, for long. He tried to put from his mind what would happen if it died and the storm failed to abate, but what was the use of leaving such plans to the last? If death seemed inevitable, would it not be better for him and Pie to meet it together—to slit their wrists and bleed to death side by side—rather than slowly freeze, pretending to the end that survival was plausible? He was ready to voice that suggestion now, while he still had the energy and focus to do so, but as he turned to the mystif some tremor reached him that was not the wind's tirade but a voice beneath its harangue, calling him to stand up. He did so.

The gusts would have blown him over had Pie not stood up with him, and his eyes would have missed the figures in the drifts but that the mystif caught his arm and, putting its head close to Gentle's, said, "How the hell did they get out?"

The women stood a hundred yards from them. Their feet were touching the snow but not impressing themselves upon it. Their bodies were wound with cloth brought from the ice, which billowed around them as the wind filled it. Some held treasures, claimed from the glacier: pieces of their temple, and ark, and altar. One, the young girl whose corpse had moved Gentle so much, held in her arms the head of a Goddess carved in blue stone. It had been badly vandalized. There were cracks in its cheeks, and parts of its nose, and an eye, were missing. But it found light from somewhere and gave off a serene radiance.

"What do they want?" Gentle said.

"You, maybe?" Pie ventured.

The woman standing closest to them, her hair rising half her height again above her head, courtesy of the wind, beckoned.

"I think they want us both to go," Gentle said.

"That's the way it looks," Pie said, not moving a muscle.

"What are we waiting for?"

"I thought they were dead," the mystif said.

"Maybe they were."

"So we take the lead from phantoms? I'm not sure that's wise."

"They came to find us, Pie," Gentle said.

Having beckoned, the woman was turning slowly on her toe tips, like a mechanical Madonna that Clem had once given Gentle, which had played "Ave Maria" as it turned.

"We're going to lose them if we don't hurry. What's your problem, Pie? You've talked with spirits before."

"Not like these," Pie said. "The Goddesses weren't all forgiving mothers, you know. And their rites weren't all milk and honey. Some of them were cruel. They sacrificed men."

"You think that's why they want us?"

"It's possible."

"So we weigh that possibility against the absolute certainty of freezing to death where we stand," Gentle said.

"It's your decision."

"No, this one we make together. You've got fifty percent of the vote and fifty percent of the responsibility."

"What do you want to do?"

"There you go again. Make up your own mind for once."

Pie looked at the departing women, their forms already

disappearing behind a veil of snow. Then at Gentle. Then at the doeki. Then back at Gentle. "I heard they eat men's balls."

"So what are you worried about?"

"All right!" the mystif growled, "I vote we go."

"Then it's unanimous."

Pie started to haul the doeki to its feet. It didn't want to move, but the mystif had a fine turn of threat when pressed, and began to berate it ripely.

"Quick, or we'll lose them!" Gentle said.

The beast was up now, and tugging on its bridle Pie led it in pursuit of Gentle, who was forging ahead to keep their guides in sight. The snow obliterated the women completely at times, but he saw the beckoner glance back several times, and knew that she'd not let her foundlings get lost again. After a time, their destination came in sight. A rock face, slate-gray and sheer, loomed from the murk, its summit lost in mist.

"If they want us to climb, they can think again," Pie yelled through the wind.

"No, there's a door," Gentle shouted over his shoulder. "See it?"

The word rather flattered what was no more than a jagged crack, like a bolt of black lightning burned into the face of the cliff. But it represented some hope of shelter, if nothing else.

Gentle turned back to Pie. "Do you see it, Pie?"

"I see it," came the response. "But I don't see the women."

One sweeping glance along the rock face confirmed the mystif's observation. They'd either entered the cliff or floated up its face into the clouds. Whichever, they'd removed themselves quickly.

"Phantoms," Pie said, fretfully.

"What if they are?" Gentle replied. "They brought us to shelter."

He took the doeki's rein from Pie's hands and coaxed the animal on, saying, "See that hole in the wall? It's going to be warm inside. Remember warm?"

The snow thickened as they covered the last hundred yards, until it was almost waist deep again. But all three—man, animal, and mystif—made the crack alive. There was more than shelter inside; there was light. A narrow passageway presented itself, its black walls encased in ice, with a fire flickering somewhere out of sight in the cavern's depths.

Gentle had let slip the doeki's reins, and the wise animal was already heading away down the passage, the sound of its hooves echoing against the glittering walls. By the time Gentle and Pie caught up with it, a slight bend in the passage had revealed the source of the light and warmth it was heading towards. A broad but shallow bowl of beaten brass was set in a place where the passage widened, and the fire was burning vigorously in its center. There were two curiosities, however: one, that the flame was not gold but blue; two, that it burned without fuel, the flames hovering six inches above the bottom of the bowl. But oh, it was warm. The cobs of ice in Gentle's beard melted and dropped off; the snowflakes became beads on Pie's smooth brow and cheek. The warmth brought a whoop of pure pleasure to Gentle's lips, and he opened his aching arms to Pie 'oh' pah.

"We're not going to die!" he said. "Didn't I tell you? We're not going to die!"

The mystif hugged him in return, its lips first pressed to Gentle's neck, then to his face.

"All right, I was wrong," it said. "There! I admit it!"

"So we go on and find the women, yes?"

"Yes!" it said.

A sound was waiting for them when the echoes of their enthusiasm died. A tinkling, as of ice bells.

"They're calling us," Gentle said.

The doeki had found a little paradise by the fire and was not about to move, for all Pie's attempts to tug it to its feet.

"Leave it awhile," Gentle said, before the mystif began a fresh round of profanities. "It's given good service. Let it rest. We can come back and fetch it later."

The passage they now followed not only curved but divided many times, the routes all lit by fire bowls. They chose between them by listening for the sound of the bells, which didn't seem to be getting any closer. Each choice, of course, made the likelihood of finding their way back to the doeki more uncertain.

"This place is a maze," Pie said, with a touch of the old unease creeping back into its voice. "I think we should stop and assess exactly what we're doing."

"Finding the Goddesses."

"And losing our transport while we do it. We're neither of us in any state to go much farther on foot."

"I don't feel so bad. Except for my hands." He raised them in front of his face, palm up. They were puffy and bruised, the lacerations livid. "I suppose I look like that all over. Did you hear the bells? They're just around the corner, I swear!"

"They've been just around the corner for the last three quarters of an hour. They're not getting any closer, Gentle. It's some kind of trick. We should go back for the animal before it's slaughtered."

"I don't think they'd shed blood in here," Gentle replied. The bells came again. "Listen to that. They *are* closer." He went to the next corner, sliding on the ice. "Pie. Come look."

Pie joined him at the corner. Ahead of them the passageway narrowed to a doorway.

"What did I tell you?" Gentle said, and headed on to the door and through it.

The sanctum on the other side wasn't vast—the size of a modest church, no more—but it had been hewn with such cunning it gave the impression of magnificence. It had sustained great damage, however. Despite its myriad pillars, chased by the finest craft, and its vaults of ice-sleek stone, its walls were pitted, its floor gouged. Nor did it take great wit to see that the objects that had been buried in the glacier had once been part of its furniture. The altar lay in hammered ruins at its center, and among the wreckage were fragments of blue stone, matching that of the statue the girl had carried. Now, more certainly than ever, they were standing in a place that carried the marks of Hapexa-mendios' passing.

"In His footsteps," Gentle murmured.

"Oh, yes," Pie murmured. "He was here."

"And so were the women," Gentle said. "But I don't think they ate men's balls. I think their ceremonies were more loving than that." He went down on his haunches, running his fingers over the carved fragments. "I wonder what they did? I'd like to have seen the rites."

"They'd have ripped you limb from limb."

"Why?"

"Because their devotions weren't for men's eyes."

"You could have got in, though, couldn't you?" Gentle said. "You would have been a perfect spy. You could have seen it."

"It's not the seeing," Pie said softly, "it's the feeling."

Gentle stood up, gazing at the mystif with new comprehension. "I think I envy you, Pie," he said. "You know what it feels like to be both, don't you? I never thought of that before. Will you tell me how it feels, one of these days?"

"You'd be better off finding out for yourself," Pie said.

"And how do I do that?"

"This isn't the time—"

"Tell me."

"Well, mystifs have their rites, just like men and women. Don't worry, I won't make you spy on me. You'll be *invited,* if that's what you want."

The remotest twinge of fear touched Gentle as he listened to this. He'd become almost blasé about the many wonders they'd witnessed as they traveled, but the creature that had been at his side these many days remained, he realized, undiscovered. He had never seen it naked since that first encounter in New York; nor kissed it the way a lover might kiss; nor allowed himself to feel sexual towards it. Perhaps it was because he'd been thinking of the women here, and their secret rites, but now, like it or not, he was looking at Pie 'oh' pah and was aroused.

Pain diverted him from these thoughts, and he looked

down at his hands to see that in his unease he'd made fists of them and reopened the cuts in his palms. Blood dropped onto the ice underfoot, shockingly red. With the sight of it came a memory he'd consigned to the back of his head.

"What's wrong?" Pie said.

But Gentle didn't have the breath to reply. He could hear the frozen river cracking beneath him, and the howl of the Unbeheld's agents wheeling overhead. He could feel his hand slamming, slamming, slamming against the glacier and the thorns of ice flying up into his face.

The mystif had come to his side. "Gentle," it said, anxious now. "Speak to me, will you? What's wrong?"

It put its arms around Gentle's shoulders, and at its touch Gentle drew breath.

"The women . . ." he said.

"What about them?"

"It was me who freed them."

"How?"

"Pneuma. How else?"

"You *undid* the Unbeheld's handiwork?" the mystif said, its voice barely audible. "For our sake I hope the women were the only witnesses."

"There were agents, just as you said there'd be. They almost killed me. But I hurt them back."

"This is bad news."

"Why? If I'm going to bleed, let *Him* bleed a little too."

"Hapexamendios doesn't bleed."

"Everything bleeds, Pie. Even God. Maybe especially God. Or else why did He hide Himself away?"

As he spoke the tinkling bells sounded again, closer than ever, and glancing over Gentle's shoulder Pie said, "She must have been waiting for that little heresy."

Gentle turned to see the beckoning woman standing halfway in shadow at the end of the sanctum. The ice that still clung to her body hadn't melted, suggesting that, like the walls, the flesh it was encrusted upon was still below zero. There were cobs of ice in her hair, and when she moved her head a little, as she did now, they struck each other and tinkled like tiny bells.

"I brought you out of the ice," Gentle said, stepping past Pie to approach her.

The woman said nothing.

"Do you understand me?" Gentle went on. "Will you lead us out of here? We want to find a way through the mountain."

The woman took a step backwards, retreating into the shadows.

"Don't be afraid of me," Gentle said. "Pie! Help me out here."

"How?"

"Maybe she doesn't understand English."

"She understands you well enough."

"Just talk to her, will you?" Gentle said.

Ever obedient, Pie began to speak in a tongue Gentle hadn't heard before, its musicality reassuring even if the words were unintelligible. But neither music nor sense seemed to impress the woman. She continued to retreat into the darkness, Gentle pursuing cautiously, fearful of startling her but more fearful still of losing her entirely. His additions to Pie's persuasions had dwindled to the basest bargaining.

"One favor deserves another," he said.

Pie was right, she did indeed understand. Even though she stood in shadow, he could see that a little smile was playing on her sealed lips. Damn her, he thought, why wouldn't she answer him? The bells still rang in her hair, however, and he kept following them even when the shadows became so heavy she was virtually lost among them. He glanced back towards the mystif, who had by now given up any attempt to communicate with the woman and instead addressed Gentle.

"Don't go any further," it said.

Though he was no more than fifty yards from where the mystif stood, its voice sounded unnaturally remote, as though another law besides that of distance and light held sway in the space between them.

"I'm still here. Can you see me?" he called back, and,

gratified to hear the mystif reply that it could, he returned his gaze to the shadows.

The woman had disappeared however. Cursing, he plunged on towards the place where she'd last stood, his sense that this was equivocal terrain intensifying. The darkness had a nervous quality, like a bad liar attempting to shoo him off with shrugs. He wouldn't go. The more it trembled, the more eager he became to see what it was hiding. Sightless though he was, he wasn't blind to the risk he was taking. Minutes before he'd told Pie that everything was vulnerable. But nobody, not even the Unbeheld, could make darkness bleed. If it closed on him he could claw at it forever and not make a mark on its hideless back.

He heard Pie calling behind him now: "Where the hell are you?"

The mystif was following him into the shadows, he saw.

"Don't come any further," he told it.

"Why not?"

"I may need a marker to find my way back."

"Just turn around."

"Not till I find her," Gentle said, forging on with his arms outstretched.

The floor was slick beneath him, and he had to proceed with extreme caution. But without the woman to guide them through the mountain, this maze might prove as fatal as the snows they'd escaped. He had to find her.

"Can you still hear me?" he called back to Pie.

The voice that told him *yes* was as faint as a long-distance call on a failing line.

"Keep talking," he yelled.

"What do you want me to say?"

"Anything. Sing a song."

"I'm tone deaf."

"Talk about food, then."

"All right," said Pie, "I already told you about the ugi-chee and the bellyful of eggs—"

"It's the foulest thing I ever heard," Gentle replied.

"You'll like it once you taste it."

"As the actress said to the bishop."

He heard Pie's muted laughter come his way. Then the mystif said, "You hated me almost as much as you hated fish, remember? And I converted you."

"I never hated you."

"In New York you did."

"Not even then. I was just confused. I'd never slept with a mystif before."

"How did you like it?"

"It's better than fish but not as good as chocolate."

"What did you say?"

"I said—"

"Gentle? I can hardly hear you."

"I'm still here!" he replied, shouting now. "I'd like to do it again sometime, Pie."

"Do what?"

"Sleep with you."

"I'll have to think about it."

"What do you want, a proposal of marriage?"

"That might do it."

"All right!" Gentle called back. "So marry me!"

There was silence behind him. He stopped and turned. Pie's form was a blurred shadow against the distant light of the sanctum.

"Did you hear me?" he yelled.

"I'm thinking it over."

Gentle laughed, despite the darkness and the unease it had wrung from him. "You can't take forever, Pie," he hollered. "I need an answer in—" He stopped as his outstretched fingers made contact with something frozen and solid. "Oh, *shit.*"

"What's wrong?"

"It's a fucking dead end!" he said, stepping right up to the surface he'd encountered and running his palms over the ice. "Just a blank wall."

But that wasn't the whole story. The suspicion he'd had that this was nebulous territory was stronger than ever. There was something on the other side of this wall, if he could only reach it.

"Make your way back," he heard Pie entreating.

"Not yet," he said to himself, knowing the words wouldn't reach the mystif. He raised his hand to his mouth and snatched an expelled breath.

"Did you hear me, Gentle?" Pie called.

Without replying he slammed the pneuma against the wall, a technique his palm was now expert in. The sound of the blow was swallowed by the murk, but the force he unleashed shook a freezing hail down from the roof. He didn't wait for the reverberations to settle but delivered a second blow, and a third, each impact opening further the wounds in his hand, adding blood to the violence of his blows. Perhaps it fueled them. If his breath and spittle did such service, what power might his blood contain, or his semen?

As he stopped to draw a fresh lungful, he heard the mystif yelling, and turned to see it moving towards him across a gulf of frantic shadow. It wasn't just the wall and the roof above that was shaken by his assault: the very air was in a furor, shaking Pie's silhouette into fragments. As his eyes fought to fix the image, a vast spear of ice divided the space between them, hitting the ground and shattering. He had time to raise his arms over his face before the shards struck him, but their impact threw him back against the wall.

"You'll bring the whole place down!" he heard Pie yell as new spears fell.

"It's too late to change our minds!" Gentle replied. *Move, Pie!*

Light-footed, even on this lethal ground, the mystif dodged through the ice towards Gentle's voice. Before it was even at his side, he turned to attack the wall afresh, knowing that if it didn't capitulate very soon they'd be buried where they stood. Snatching another breath from his lips he delivered it against the wall, and this time the shadows failed to swallow the sound. It rang out like a thunderous bell. The shock wave would have pitched him to the floor had the mystif's arms not been there to catch him.

"This is a passing place!" it yelled.

"What does that mean?"

"Two breaths this time," was its reply. "Mine as well as yours, in one hand. Do you understand me?"

"Yes."

He couldn't see the mystif, but he felt it raise his hand to its mouth.

"On a count of three," Pie said. *"One."*

Gentle drew a breathful of furious air.

"Two."

He drew again, deeper still.

"Three!"

And he expelled it, mingled with Pie's, into his hand. Human flesh wasn't designed to govern such force. Had Pie not been beside him to brace his shoulder and wrist, the power would have erupted from his palm and taken his hand with it. But they flung themselves forward in unison, and he opened his hand the instant before it struck the wall.

The roar from above redoubled, but it was drowned out moments later by the havoc they'd wrought ahead of them. Had there been room to retreat they'd have done so, but the roof was pitching down a fusillade of stalactites, and all they could do was shield their bare heads and stand their ground as the wall stoned them for their crime, knocking them to their knees as it split and fell. The commotion went on for what seemed like minutes, the ground shuddering so violently they were thrown down yet again, this time to their faces. Then, by degrees, the convulsions slowed. The hail of stone and ice became a drizzle, and stopped, and a miraculous gust brought warm wind to their faces.

They looked up. The air was murky, but light was catching glints off the daggers they lay on, and its source was somewhere up ahead. The mystif was first to its feet, hauling Gentle up beside it.

"A passing place," it said again.

It put its arm around Gentle's shoulders, and together they stumbled towards the warmth that had roused them. Though the gloom was still deep, they could make out the vague presence of the wall. For all the scale of the upheaval, the fissure they'd made was scarcely more than a man's height. On the other side it was foggy, but each step took them closer to the light. As they went, their feet sinking into a soft sand that was the color of the fog, they heard the ice bells again and looked back, expecting to see the women following. But the fog already obscured the fissure and the sanctum beyond, and when the bells stopped, as they did moments later, they lost all sense of its direction.

"We've come out into the Third Dominion," Pie said.

"No more mountains? No more snow?"

"Not unless you want to find your way back to thank them."

Gentle peered ahead into the fog. "Is this the only way out of the Fourth?"

"Lord, no," said Pie. "If we'd gone the scenic route we'd have had the choice of a hundred places to cross. But this must have been their secret way, before the ice sealed it up."

The light showed Gentle the mystif's face now, and it bore a wide smile.

"You did fine work," Pie said. "I thought you'd gone crazy."

"I think I did, a little," Gentle replied. "I must have a destructive streak. Hapexamendios would be proud of me." He halted to give his body a moment's rest. "I hope there's more than fog in the Third."

"Oh, believe me, there is. It's the Dominion I've longed to see more than any other, while I've been in the Fifth. It's full of light and fertility. We'll rest, and we'll feed, and we'll get strong again. Maybe go to L'Himby and see my friend Scopique. We deserve to indulge ourselves for a few days before we head for the Second and join the Lenten Way."

"Will that take us to Yzordderrex?"

"Indeed it will," Pie said, coaxing Gentle into motion again. "The Lenten Way's the longest road in the Imajica. It must be the length of the Americas, and more."

"A map!" said Gentle. "I *must* start making that map."

The fog was beginning to thin, and with the growing light came plants: the first greenery they'd seen since the foothills of the Jokalaylau. They picked up their pace as the vegetation became lusher and scented, calling them on to the sun.

"Remember, Gentle," Pie said, when they'd gone a little way, "I accepted."

"Accepted what?" Gentle asked.

The fog was wispy now; they could see a warm new world awaiting them.

"You proposed, my friend, don't you remember?"

"I didn't hear you accept."

"But I did," the mystif replied, as the verdant landscape was unveiled before them. "If we do nothing else in this Dominion, we should at the very least get married!"

24

I

England saw an early spring that year, with the days becoming balmy at the end of February and, by the middle of March, warm enough to have coaxed April and May flowers forth. The pundits were opining that if no further frosts came along to kill the blooms and chill the chicks in their nests, there would be a surge of new life by May, as parents let their fledglings fly and set about a second brood for June. More pessimistic souls were already predicting drought, their divining dampened when, at the beginning of March, the heavens opened over the island.

When—on that first day of rain—Jude looked back over the weeks since she'd left the Godolphin estate with Oscar and Dowd, they seemed well occupied; but the details of what had filled that time were at best sketchy. She had been made welcome in the house from the beginning and was allowed to come and go whenever it pleased her to do so, which was not often. The sense of belonging she'd discovered when she'd set eyes on Oscar had not faded, though she had yet to uncover its true source. He was a generous host, to be sure, but she'd been treated well by many men and not felt the devotion she felt now. That devotion was not returned, at least not overtly, which was something of a fresh experience for her. There was a certain reserve in Oscar's manner—and a consequent formality in their exchanges—which merely intensified her feelings for him. When they were alone together she felt like a long-lost mistress miraculously returned to his side, each with sufficient knowledge of the other that overt expressions of affection were superfluous; when she was with him in company—at the theater or at dinner with his friends—she was mostly silent, and happily so. This too was odd for her. She was accustomed to volubility, to handing out opinions on whatever subject was at issue, whether said opinions were requested or even seriously held. But now it didn't trouble her not to speak. She listened to the tittle-tattle and the chat (politics, finance, social gossip) as to the dialogue of a play. It wasn't her drama. She *had* no drama, just the ease of being where she wanted to be. And with such contentment to be had from simply witnessing, there seemed little reason to demand more.

Godolphin was a busy man, and though they spent some portion of every day together, she was more often than not alone. When she was, a pleasant languor overcame her, which contrasted forcibly with the confusion that had preceded her coming to stay with him. In fact she tried hard to put thoughts of that time out of her mind, and it was only when she went back to her flat to pick up belongings or bills (which, on Oscar's instruction, Dowd paid) that she was reminded of friends whose company she was at present not disposed to keep. There were telephone messages left for her, of course, from Klein, Clem, and half a dozen others. Later, there were even letters—some of them concerned for her health—and notes pushed through her door asking her to make contact. In the case of Clem she did so, guilty that she'd not spoken to him since the funeral. They lunched near his office in Marylebone, and she told him that she'd met a man and had gone to live with him on a temporary basis. Inevitably, Clem was curious. Who was this lucky individual? Anyone he knew? How was the sex:

sublime or merely wonderful? And was it love? Most of all, was it love? She answered as best she could: named the man and described him; explained that there was nothing sexual between them as yet, though the thought had passed through her mind on several occasions; and as to love, it was too soon to tell. She knew Clem well and could be certain that this account would be public knowledge in twenty-four hours, which suited her fine. At least with this telling she'd allayed her friends' fears for her health.

"So when do we get to meet this paragon?" Clem asked her as they parted.

"In a while," she said.

"He's certainly had quite an effect on you, hasn't he?"

"Has he?"

"You're so—I don't know the word exactly—tranquil, maybe? I've never seen you this way before."

"I'm not sure I've ever felt this way before."

"Well, just make sure we don't lose the Judy we all know and love, huh?" Clem said. "Too much serenity's bad for the circulation. Everybody needs a good rage once in a while."

The significance of this exchange didn't really strike her until the evening after, when—sitting downstairs in the quiet of the house, waiting for Oscar to come home—she realized how passive she'd become. It was almost as if the woman she'd been, the Jude of furies and opinions, had been shed like a dead skin, and now, tender and new, she had entered a time of waiting. Instruction would come, she assumed; she couldn't live the rest of her life so becalmed. And she knew to whom she had to look for that instruction: the man whose voice in the hall made her heart rise and her head light, Oscar Godolphin.

If Oscar was the good news that those weeks brought, Kuttner Dowd was the bad. He was astute enough to realize after a very short time that she knew far less about the Dominions and their mysteries than their conversation at the Retreat had suggested, and far from being the source of information she'd hoped he'd prove, he was taciturn, suspicious, and on occasion rude, though never the last in

Oscar's company. Indeed, when all three of them were together he lavished her with respect, its irony lost on Oscar, who was so used to Dowd's obsequious presence he barely seemed to notice the man.

Jude soon learned to match suspicion with suspicion, and several times verged on discussing Dowd with Oscar. That she didn't was a consequence of what she'd seen at the Retreat. Dowd had dealt almost casually with the problem of the corpses, dispatching them with the efficiency of one who had covered for his employer in similar circumstances before. Nor had he sought commendation for his labor, at least not within earshot of her. When the relationship between master and servant was so ingrained that a criminal act—the disposal of murdered flesh—was passed over as an unremarkable duty, it was best, she thought, not to come between them. It was *she* who was the interloper here, the new girl who dreamed she'd belonged to the master forever. She couldn't hope to have Oscar's ear the way Dowd did, and any attempt to sow mistrust might easily rebound upon her. She kept her silence, and things went on their smooth way. Until the day of rain.

2

A trip to the opera had been planned for March second, and she had spent the latter half of the afternoon in leisurely preparation for the evening, idling over her choice of dress and shoes, luxuriating in indecision. Dowd had gone out at lunchtime, on urgent business for Oscar which she knew better than to inquire about. She'd been told upon her arrival at the house that any questions as to Oscar's business would not be welcomed, and she'd never challenged that edict: it was not the place of mistresses to do so. But today, with Dowd uncharacteristically flustered as he left, she found herself wondering, as she bathed and dressed, what work Godolphin was about. Was he off in Yzordderrex, the city whose streets she assumed Gentle now walked with his soul mate the assassin? A mere two months before, with the bells of London pealing in the New

Year, she'd sworn to go to Yzordderrex after him. But she'd been distracted from that ambition by the very man whose company she'd sought to take her there. Though her thoughts returned to that mysterious city now, it was without her former appetite. She'd have liked to know if Gentle was safe in those summer streets—and might have enjoyed a description of its seamier quarter—but the fact that she'd once sworn an oath to get there now seemed almost absurd. She had all that she needed here.

It wasn't only her curiosity about the other Dominions that had been dulled by contentment; her curiosity about events in her own planet was similarly cool. Though the television burbled constantly in the corner of her bedroom, its presence soporific, she attended to its details scarcely at all and would not have noticed the midafternoon news bulletin, but that an item she caught in passing put her in mind of Charlie.

Three bodies had been found in a shallow grave on Hampstead Heath, the condition of the mutilated corpses implying, the report said, some kind of ritualistic murder. Preliminary investigations further suggested that the deceased had been known to the community of cultists and black magic practitioners in the city, some of whom, in the light of other deaths or disappearances among their number, believed that a vendetta against them was under way. To round the piece off, there was footage of the police searching the bushes and undergrowth of Hampstead Heath, while the rain fell and compounded their misery. The report distressed her for two reasons, each related to one of the brothers. The first, that it brought back memories of Charlie, sitting in that stuffy little room in the clinic, watching the heath and contemplating suicide. The second, that perhaps this vendetta might endanger Oscar, who was as involved in occult practices as any man alive.

She fretted about this for the rest of the afternoon, her concern deepening still further when Oscar failed to return home by six. She put off dressing for the opera and waited for him downstairs, the front door open, the rain beating the bushes around the step. He returned at six-forty with

Dowd, who had barely stepped through the door before he pronounced that there would be no opera visit tonight. Godolphin contradicted him immediately, much to his chagrin, telling Jude to go and get ready; they'd be leaving in twenty minutes.

As she dutifully headed upstairs, she heard Dowd say, "You know McGann wants to see you?"

"We can do both," Oscar replied. "Did you put out the black suit? No? What have you been doing all day? No, don't tell me. Not on an empty stomach."

Oscar looked handsome in black, and she told him so when, twenty-five minutes later, he came downstairs. In response to the compliment, he smiled and made a small bow.

"And you were never lovelier," he replied. "You know, I don't have a photograph of you? I'd like one, for my wallet. We'll have Dowd organize it."

By now, Dowd was conspicuous by his absence. Most evenings he would play chauffeur, but tonight he apparently had other business.

"We're going to have to miss the first act," Oscar said as they drove. "I've got a little errand to run in Highgate, if you'll bear with me."

"I don't mind," she said.

He patted her hand. "It won't take long," he said.

Perhaps because he didn't often take the wheel himself he concentrated hard as he drove, and though the news item she'd seen was still very much in her mind she was loath to distract him with talk. They made good time, threading their way through the back streets to avoid thoroughfares clogged by rain-slowed traffic, and arriving in a veritable cloudburst.

"Here we are," he said, though the windshield was so awash she could barely see ten yards ahead. "You stay in the warm. I won't be long."

He left her in the car and sprinted across a courtyard towards an anonymous building. Nobody came to the front door. It opened automatically and closed after him. Only when he'd disappeared, and the thunderous drumming of the rain on the roof had diminished somewhat, did she lean forward to peer out through the watery windshield at the building itself. Despite the rain, she recognized instantly the tower from the dream of blue eye. Without conscious instruction her hand went to the door and opened it, as her breath quickened with denials.

"Oh, no. Oh, no. . . ."

She got out of the car and turned her face up to the cold rain and to an even colder memory. She'd let this place— and indeed the journey that had brought her here, her mind moving through the streets touching this woman's grief and that woman's rage—slip into the dubious territory that lay between recollections of the real and those of the dreamed. In essence, she'd allowed herself to believe it had never happened. But here was the very place, to the window, to the brick. And if the exterior was so exactly as she'd seen it, why should she doubt that the interior would be any different?

There'd been a labyrinthine cellar, she remembered, lined with shelves piled high with books and manuscripts. There'd been a wall (lovers coupling against it) and, behind it, hidden from every sight but hers, a cell in which a bound woman had lain in darkness for a suffering age. She heard the prisoner's scream now, in her mind's ear: that howl of madness that had driven her up out of the ground and back through the dark streets to the safety of her own house and head. Was the woman still screaming, she wondered, or had she sunk back into the comatose state from which she'd been so unkindly woken? The thought of her pain brought tears to Jude's eyes, mingling with the rain.

"What are you doing?"

Oscar had reappeared from the tower and was hurrying across the gravel towards her, his jacket raised and tented over his head.

"My dear, you'll freeze to death. Get in the car. Please, *please.* Get in the car."

She did as he suggested, the rain running down her neck.

"I'm sorry," she said. "I . . . I wondered where you'd

gone, that was all. Then . . . I don't know . . . the place seemed familiar."

"It's a place of no importance," he said. "You're shivering. Would you prefer we didn't go to the opera?"

"Would you mind?"

"Not in the least. Pleasure shouldn't be a trial. You're wet and cold, and we can't have you getting a chill. One sickly individual's enough."

She didn't question this last remark; there was too much else on her mind. She wanted to sob, though whether out of joy or sorrow she wasn't sure. The dream she'd come to dismiss as fancy was founded in solid fact, and this solid fact beside her—Godolphin—was in turn touched by something momentous. She'd been persuaded by his practiced understatement: the way he talked of traveling to the Dominions as he would of boarding a train, and his expeditions in Yzordderrex as a form of tourism as yet unavailable to the great unwashed. But his reductionism was a screen—whether he was aware of the fact or not—a ploy to conceal the greater significance of his business. His ignorance, or arrogance, might well kill him, she began to suspect: which thought was the sorrow in her. And the joy? That she might save him, and he learn to love her out of gratitude.

Back at the house they both changed out of their formal attire. When she emerged from her room on the top floor she found him on the stairs, waiting for her.

"I wonder . . . perhaps we should talk?"

They went downstairs into the tasteful clutter of the lounge. The rain beat against the window. He drew the curtains and poured them brandies to fortify them against the cold. Then he sat down opposite her.

"We have a problem, you and I."

"We do?"

"There's so much we have to say to each other. At least . . . here am I presuming it's reciprocal, but for myself, certainly . . . certainly I've got a good deal I want to say, and I'm damned if I know where to begin. I'm aware that I owe you explanations, about what you saw at the estate, about Dowd and the voiders, about what I did to Charlie. The list goes on. And I've tried, really I have, to find some way to make it all clear to you. But the truth is, I'm not sure of the truth myself. Memory plays such tricks"—she made a murmur of agreement—"especially when you're dealing with places and people who seem to belong half in your dreams. Or in your nightmares." He drained his glass and reached for the bottle he'd set on the table beside him.

"I don't like Dowd," she said suddenly. "And I don't trust him."

He looked up from refilling his glass. "That's perceptive," he said. "You want some more brandy?" She proffered her glass, and he poured her an ample measure. "I agree with you," he said. "He's a dangerous creature, for a number of reasons."

"Can't you get rid of him?"

"He knows too much, I'm afraid. He'd be more dangerous out of my employ than in it."

"Has he got something to do with these murders? Just today, I saw the news—"

He waved her inquiry away. "You don't need to know about any of that, my dear," he said.

"But if you're at risk—"

"I'm not. I'm not. At least be reassured about that."

"So you know all about it?"

"Yes," he said heavily. "I know a little something. And so does Dowd. In fact, he knows more about this whole situation than you and I put together."

She wondered about this. Did Dowd know about the prisoner behind the wall, for instance, or was that a secret she had entirely to herself? If so, perhaps she'd be wise to keep it that way. When so many players in this game had information she lacked, sharing anything—even with Oscar—might weaken her position; perhaps threaten her life. Some part of her nature not susceptible to the blandishments of luxury or the need for love was lodged behind that wall with the woman she'd woken. She would leave it there, safe in the darkness. The rest—anything else she knew—she'd share.

"You're not the only one who crosses over," she said. "A friend of mine went."

"Really?" he said. "Who?"

"His name's Gentle. Actually, his real name's Zacharias. John Furie Zacharias. Charlie knew him a little."

"Charlie. . . ." Oscar shook his head. "Poor Charlie." Then he said, "Tell me about Gentle."

"It's complicated," she said. "When I left Charlie he got very vengeful. He hired somebody to kill me. . . ."

She went on to tell Oscar about the murder attempt in New York and Gentle's later intervention; then about the events of New Year's Eve. As she related this she had the distinct impression that at least some of what she was telling him he already knew, a suspicion confirmed when she'd finished her description of Gentle's removal from this Dominion.

"The mystif took him?" he said. "My God, that's a risk!"

"What's a mystif?" she asked.

"A very rare creature indeed. One would be born into the Eurhetemec tribe once in a generation. They're reputedly extraordinary lovers. As I understand it, they have no sexual identity, except as a function of their partner's desire."

"That sounds like Gentle's idea of paradise."

"As long as you know what you want," Oscar said. "If you don't I daresay it could get very confusing."

She laughed. "He knows what he wants, believe me."

"You speak from experience?"

"Bitter experience."

"He may have bitten off more than he can chew, so to speak, keeping the company of a mystif. My friend in Yzordderrex—Peccable—had a mistress for a while who'd been a madam. She'd had a very plush establishment in Patashoqua, and she and I got on famously. She kept telling me I should become a white slaver and bring her girls from the Fifth, so she could start a new business in Yzordderrex.

She reckoned we'd have made a fortune. We never did it, of course. But we both enjoyed talking about things venereal. It's a pity that word's so tainted, isn't it? You say *venereal,* and people immediately think of disease, instead of Venus. . . ." He paused, seeming to have lost his way, then said, "Anyway, she told me once that she'd employed a mystif for a while in her bordello, and it caused her no end of problems. She'd almost had to close her place, because of the reputation she got. You'd think a creature like that would make the ultimate whore, wouldn't you? But apparently a lot of customers just didn't want to see their desires made flesh." He watched her as he spoke, a smile playing around his lips. "I can't imagine why."

"Maybe they were afraid of what they were."

"You'd consider that foolish, I assume."

"Yes, of course. What you are, you are."

"That's a hard philosophy to live up to."

"No harder than running away."

"Oh, I don't know. I've thought about running away quite a lot of late. Disappearing forever."

"Really?" she said, trying to stifle any show of agitation. "Why?"

"Too many birds coming home to roost."

"But you're staying?"

"I vacillate. England's so pleasant in the spring. And I'd miss the cricket in the summer months."

"They play cricket everywhere, don't they?"

"Not in Yzordderrex they don't."

"You'd go there forever?"

"Why not? Nobody would find me, because nobody would ever guess where I'd gone."

"I'd know."

"Then maybe I'd have to take you with me," he said tentatively, almost as though he were making the proposal in all seriousness and was afraid of being refused. "Could you bear that thought?" he said. "Of leaving the Fifth, I mean."

"I could bear it."

He paused. Then: "I think it's about time I showed you

some of my treasures," he said, rising from his chair.
"Come on."

She'd known from oblique remarks of Dowd's that the
locked room on the second floor contained some kind of
collection, but its nature, when he finally unlocked the
door and ushered her in, astonished her.

"All this was collected in the Dominions," Oscar explained, "and brought back by hand."

He escorted her around the room, giving her a capsule
summary of what some of the stranger objects were and
bringing from hiding tiny items she might otherwise have
overlooked. Into the former category, among others, went
the Boston Bowl and Gaud Maybellome's *Encyclopedia of
Heavenly Signs;* into the latter a bracelet of beetles caught
by the killing jar in their daisy chain coupling—fourteen
generations, he explained, male entering female, and female in turn devouring the male in front, the circle joined
by the youngest female and the oldest male, who, by dint of
the latter's suicidal acrobatics, were face to face.

She had many questions, of course, and he was pleased
to play the teacher. But there were several inquiries he had
no answers to. Like the empire looters from whom he was
descended, he'd assembled the collection with commitment, taste, and ignorance in equal measure. Yet when he
spoke of the artifacts, even those whose function he had no
clue to, there was a touching fervor in his tone, familiar as
he was with the tiniest detail of the tiniest piece.

"You gave some objects to Charlie, didn't you?" she
said.

"Once in a while. Did you see them?"

"Yes, indeed," she said, the brandy tempting her tongue
to confess the dream of the blue eye, her brain resisting it.

"If things had been different," Oscar said, "Charlie
might have been the one wandering the Dominions. I owe
him a glimpse."

" 'A piece of the miracle,' " she quoted.

"That's right. But I'm sure he felt ambivalent about
them."

"That was Charlie."

"True, true. He was too English for his own good. He never had the courage of his feelings, except where you were concerned. And who could blame him?"

She looked up from the trinket she was studying to find that she too was a subject of study, the look on his face unequivocal.

"It's a family problem," he said. "When it comes to . . . matters of the heart."

This confession made, a look of discomfort crossed his face, and his hand went to his ribs. "I'll leave you to look around if you like," he said. "There's nothing in here that's really volatile."

"Thank you."

"Will you lock up after yourself?"

"Of course."

She watched him go, unable to think of anything to detain him, but feeling forsaken once he'd gone. She heard him go to his bedroom, which was down the hall on the same floor, and close the door behind him. Then she turned her attention back to the treasures on the shelves. It wouldn't stay there, however. She wanted to touch, and be touched by, something warmer than these relics. After a few moments of hesitation she left them in the dark, locking the door behind her. She would take the key back to him, she'd decided. If his words of admiration were not simply flattery—if he had bed on his mind—she'd know it soon enough. And if he rejected her, at least there'd be an end to this trial by doubt.

She knocked on the bedroom door. There was no reply. There was light seeping from under the door, however, so she knocked again and then turned the handle and, saying his name softly, entered. The lamp beside the bed was burning, illuminating an ancestral portrait that hung over it. Through its gilded window a severe and sallow individual gazed down on the empty sheets. Hearing the sound of running water from the adjacent bathroom, Jude crossed the bedroom, taking in a dozen details of this, his most private chamber, as she did so: the plushness of the pillows and the linen; the spirit decanter and glass beside the bed;

the cigarettes and ashtray on a small heap of well-thumbed paperbacks. Without declaring herself, she pushed the door open. Oscar was sitting on the edge of the bath in his undershorts, dabbing a washcloth to a partially healed wound in his side. Reddened water ran over the furry swell of his belly. Hearing her, he looked up. There was pain on his face.

She didn't attempt to offer an excuse for being there, nor did he request one. He simply said, "Charlie did it."

"You should see a doctor."

"I don't trust doctors. Besides, it's getting better." He tossed the washcloth into the sink. "Do you make a habit of walking into bathrooms unannounced?" he said. "You could have walked in on something even less—"

"Venereal?" she said.

"Don't mock me," he replied. "I'm a crude seducer, I know. It comes from years of buying company."

"Would you be more comfortable buying me?" she said.

"My God," he replied, his look appalled. "What do you take me for?"

"A lover," she said plainly. *"My* lover?"

"I wonder if you know what you're saying?"

"What I don't know I'll learn," she said. "I've been hiding from myself, Oscar. Putting everything out of my head so I wouldn't feel anything. But I feel a lot. And I want you to know that."

"I know," he said. "More than you can understand, I know. And it makes me afraid, Judith."

"There's nothing to be afraid of," she said, astonished that it was she who was mouthing these words of reassurance when he was the elder and presumably the stronger, the wiser. She reached out and put her palm flat against his massive chest. He bent forward to kiss her, his mouth closed until he met hers and found it open. One hand went around her back, the other to her breast, her murmur of pleasure smeared between their mouths. His touch moved down, over her stomach, past her groin, to hoist up her skirt and retrace its steps. His fingers found her sopping—she'd been wet since first stepping into the treasure room—and he slid his whole hand down into the hot pouch of her underwear, pressing the heel of his palm against the top of her sex while his long middle digit sought out her fundament, gently catching its flukes with his nail.

"Bed," she said.

He didn't let her go. They made an ungainly exit from the bathroom, with him guiding her backwards until she felt the edge of the bed behind her thighs. There she sat down, taking hold of the waistband of his blood-stained shorts and easing them down while she kissed his belly. Suddenly bashful, he reached to stop her, but she pulled them down until his penis appeared. It was a curiosity. Only a little engorged, it had been deprived of its foreskin, which made its outlandishly bulbous, carmine head look even more inflamed than the wound in its wielder's side. The stem was very considerably thinner and paler, its length knotted with veins bearing blood to its crown. If it was this disproportion that embarrassed him he had no need, and to prove her pleasure she put her lips against the head. His objecting hand was no longer in evidence. She heard him make a little moan above, and looked up to see him staring down at her with something very like awe on his face. Sliding her fingers beneath testicles and stem, she raised the curiosity to her mouth and took it inside; then she dropped both hands to her blouse and began to unbutton. But he'd no sooner started to harden in her mouth than he murmured a denial, withdrew his member, and stepped back from her, pulling up his underwear.

"Why are you doing this?" he said.

"I'm enjoying it."

He was genuinely agitated, she saw, shaking his head, covering the bulge in his underwear in a new fit of bashfulness.

"For whose sake?" he said. "You don't have to, you know."

"I know."

"I wonder?" he said, genuine puzzlement in his voice.

"I don't want to use you."

"I wouldn't let you."

"Maybe you wouldn't know."

This remark inflamed her. A rage rose such as she'd not felt in a long while. She stood up.

"I know what I want," she said, "but I'm not about to beg for it."

"That's not what I'm saying."

"What *are* you saying?"

"That I want you too."

"So do something about it," she said.

He seemed to find her fury freshly arousing and stepped towards her again, saying her name in a voice almost pained with feeling. "I'd like to undress you," he said. "Would you mind?"

"No."

"I don't want you to do anything—"

"Then I won't."

"—except lie down."

She did so. He turned off the bathroom light, then came to the edge of the bed and looked down at her. His bulk was emphasized by the light from the lamp, which threw his shadow up to the ceiling. Quantity had never seemed an arousing quality hitherto, but in him she found it intensely attractive, evidence as it was of his excesses and his appetites. Here was a man who would not be contained by one world, one set of experiences, but who was kneeling now like a slave in front of her, his expression that of one obsessed.

With consummate tenderness, he began to undress her. She'd known fetishists before—men to whom she was not an individual but a hook upon which some particular item was hung for worship. If there was any such particular in this man's head, it was the body he now began to uncover, proceeding to do so in an order and manner that made some fevered sense to him. First he slipped off her underpants; then he finished unbuttoning her blouse, without removing it. Next he teased her breasts from her bra, so that they were available to his toying, but then didn't play there but went to her shoes, removing them and setting them beside the bed before hoisting up her skirt so as to have a view of her sex. Here his eyes lingered, his fingers advancing up her thigh to the crease of her groin, then retreating. Not once did he look at her face. She looked at his, however, enjoying the zeal and veneration there. Finally he rewarded his own diligence with kisses. First on her lower legs, moving up towards her knees; then her stomach and her breasts, and finally returning to her thighs and up into the place he'd forbidden them both till now. She was ready for pleasure, and he supplied it, his huge hand caressing her breasts as he tongued her. She closed her eyes as he unfolded her, alive to every drop of moisture on her labia and legs. When he rose from this to finish undressing her—skirt first, then blouse and bra—her face was hot and her breath fast. He tossed the clothes onto the floor and stood up again, taking her knees and pushing them up and back, spreading her for his delectation, and holding her there, prettily exposed.

"Finger yourself," he said, not letting her go.

She put her hands between her legs and made a show for him. He'd slickened her well, but her fingers went deeper than his tongue, readying herself for the curiosity. He gorged on the sight, meanwhile, glancing up to her face several times, then returning to the spectacle below. All trace of his previous hesitation had gone. He encouraged her with his admiration, calling her a host of sweet names, his tented underwear proof—as if she needed it—of his arousal. She started to push her hips up from the bed to meet her fingers, and he took firmer grip of her knees as she moved, opening her wider still. Lifting his right hand to his mouth he licked his middle finger and put it down against her pucker of her other hole, rubbing it gently.

"Will you suck me now?" he asked her. "Just a little?"

"Show me it," she said.

He stepped away from her and took off his underwear. The curiosity was now fully risen and florid. She sat up and put it back between her lips, one hand holding it by its pulsing root while the other continued its dalliance with her own sex. She'd never been good at guessing the point at which the milk boiled over, so she took it from the heat of her mouth to cool him a little, glancing up at him as she did so. Either the extraction or her glance set him off, however.

"Damn!" he said. "Damn!", and started to step back from her, his hand going down to his groin to take the curiosity in a stranglehold.

It seemed he might have succeeded, as two desultory dribbles ran from its head. Then his testicles unleashed their flood, and it came forth in uncommon abundance. He moaned as it came, as much in self-admonishment as pleasure, she thought, that assumption confirmed when he'd emptied his sac upon the floor.

"I'm sorry . . ." he said, ". . . I'm sorry. . . ."

"There's no need," she said, standing up and putting her lips to his. He continued to murmur his apologies, however.

"I haven't done that in a long time," he said. "So adolescent."

She kept her silence, knowing anything she said would only begin a further round of self-reproach. He slipped away into the bathroom to find a towel. When he returned she was picking up her clothes.

"Are you going?" he said.

"Only to my room."

"Do you have to?" he said. "I know that wasn't much of a performance, but . . . the bed's big enough for us both. And I don't snore."

"The bed's enormous."

"So . . . would you stay?" he said.

"I'd like to."

He made a charming smile. "I'm honored," he said. "Will you excuse me a moment?"

He switched the bathroom light back on and disappeared inside, closing the door, leaving her to lie back on the bed and wonder at this whole turn of events. Its very oddness seemed appropriate. After all, this whole journey had begun with an act of misplaced love: love become murder. Now a new dislocation. Here she was, lying in the bed of a man with a body far from beautiful, whose bulk she longed to have upon her; whose hands were capable of fratricide but aroused her like none she'd ever known; who'd walked more worlds than an opium poet, but couldn't speak love without stumbling; who was a titan, and yet afraid. She made a nest among his duck-down pillows and waited there for him to come back and tell her a story of love.

He reappeared after a long while and slipped beneath the sheets beside her. True to her imaginings, he said he loved her at last, but only once he'd turned the light out, and his eyes were not available for study.

When she slept, it was deeply, and when she woke again, it was like sleeping, dark and pleasurable, the former because the drapes were still drawn, and between their cracks she could see that the sky was still benighted, the latter because Oscar was behind her, and inside. One of his hands was upon her breast, the other lifting her leg so that he could ease his upward stroke. He'd entered her with skill and discretion, she realized. Not only had he not stirred her until he was embedded, but he'd chosen the virgin passage, which—had he suggested it while she was awake—she'd have attempted to coax him from, fearing the discomfort. In truth, there was none, though the sensation was quite unlike anything she'd felt before. He kissed her neck and shoulder blade, light kisses, as though he was unaware of her wakefulness. She made it known with a sigh. His stroke slowed and stopped, but she pressed her buttocks back to meet his thrust, satisfying his curiosity as to the limit of its access, which was to say none. She was happy to accept him entirely, trapping his hand against her breast to press it to rougher service, while putting her own at the connecting place. He'd dutifully slipped on a condom before entering her, which, together with the fact that he'd already poured forth once tonight, made him a near perfect lover: slow and certain.

She didn't use the dark to reconfigure him. The man pressing his face into her hair, and biting at her shoulder, wasn't—like the mystif he'd described—a reflection of imagined ideals. It was Oscar Godolphin, paunch, curiosity, and all. What she *did* reconfigure was herself, so that she became in her mind's eye a glyph of sensation: a line dividing from the coil of her pierced core, up through her belly to the points of her breasts, then intersecting again at her nape, crossing and becoming woven spirals beneath the hood of her skull. Her imagination added a further refinement, inscribing a circle around this figure, which burned in the darkness behind her lips like a vision. Her rapture was perfected then: being an abstraction in his arms, yet pleasured like flesh. There was no greater luxury.

He asked if they might move, saying only, "The wound . . ." by way of explanation.

She went onto her hands and knees, he slipping from her for a tormenting moment while she did so, then putting the curiosity back to work. His rhythm instantly became more urgent, his fingers in her sex, his voice in her head, both expressing ecstasy. The glyph brightened in her mind's eye, fiery from end to end. She yelled out to him, first only *yes* and *yes,* then plainer demands, inflaming him to new invention. The glyph became blinding, burning away all thought of where she was, or what; all memory of conjunctions past subsumed in this perpetuity.

She was not even aware that he'd spent himself until she felt him withdrawing, and then she reached behind her to keep him inside a while longer. He obliged. She enjoyed the sensation of his softening inside her, and even, finally, his exiting, the tender muscle yielding its prisoner reluctantly. Then he rolled over onto the bed beside her and reached for the light. It was dim enough not to sting, but still too bright, and she was about to protest when she saw that he was putting his fingers to his injured side. Their congress had unknitted the wound. Blood was running from it in two directions: down towards the curiosity, still nestled in the condom, and down his side to the sheet.

"It's all right," he said as she made to get up. "It looks worse than it is."

"It still needs something to staunch it," she said.

"That's good Godolphin blood," he said, wincing and grinning at the same moment. His gaze went from her face to the portrait above the bed. "It's always flowed freely," he said.

"He doesn't look as though he approved of us," she said.

"On the contrary," Oscar replied. "I know for a fact he'd adore you. Joshua understood devotion."

She looked at the wound again. Blood was seeping between his fingers.

"Won't you let me cover that up?" she said. "It makes me queasy."

"For you . . . anything."

"Have you got any dressing?"

"Dowd's probably got some, but I don't want him knowing about us. At least, not yet. Let's keep it our secret."

"You, me, and Joshua," she said.

"Even Joshua doesn't know what we got up to," Oscar said, without a trace of irony audible in his voice. "Why do you think I turned the light out?"

In lieu of fresh dressing she went through to the bathroom to find a towel. While she was doing so he spoke to her through the open door.

"I meant what I said, by the way," he told her.

"About what?"

"That I'll do anything for you. At least, anything that's in my power to do or give. I want you to stay with me, Judith. I'm no Adonis, I know that. But I learned a lot from Joshua . . . about devotion, I mean." She emerged with the towel to be greeted by the same offer. "Anything you want."

"That's very generous."

"The pleasure's in the giving," he said.

"I think you know what I'd like most."

He shook his head. "I'm no good at guessing games. Only cricket. Just tell me."

She sat down on the edge of the bed and gently tugged his hand from the wound in his side, wiping the blood from between his fingers.

"Say it," he told her.

"Very well," she said. "I want you to take me out of this Dominion. I want you to show me Yzordderrex."

25

I

Twenty-two days after emerging from the icy wastes of the Jokalaylau into the balmier climes of the Third Dominion—days which had seen Pie and Gentle's fortunes rise dramatically as they journeyed through the Third's diverse territories—the wanderers were standing on a station platform outside the tiny town of Mai-ké, waiting for the train that once a week came through on its way from the city of Iahmandhas, in the northeast, to L'Himby, half a day's journey to the south.

They were eager to be departing. Of all the towns and villages they'd visited in the past three weeks, Mai-ké had been the least welcoming. It had its reasons. It was a community under siege from the Dominion's two suns, the rains which brought the region its crops having failed to materialize for six consecutive years. Terraces and fields that should have been bright with shoots were virtually dust bowls, stocks hoarded against this eventuality critically depleted. Famine was imminent, and the village was in no mood to entertain strangers. The previous night the entire populace had been out in the drab streets praying aloud, these imprecations led by their spiritual leaders, who had about them the air of men whose invention was nearing its end. The noise, so unmusical Gentle had observed that it would irritate the most sympathetic of deities, had gone on until first light, making sleep impossible. As a consequence, exchanges between Pie and Gentle were somewhat tense this morning.

They were not the only travelers waiting for the train. A farmer from Mai-ké had brought a herd of sheep onto the platform, some of them so emaciated it was a wonder they could stand, and the flock had brought with them clouds of the local pest: an insect called a zarzi, that had the wingspan of a dragonfly and a body as fat and furred as a bee. It fed on sheep ticks, unless it could find something more tempting. Gentle's blood fell into this latter category, and the lazy whine of the zarzi was never far from his ears as he waited in the midday heat. Their one informant in Mai-ké, a woman called Hairstone Banty, had predicted that the train would be on time, but it was already well overdue, which didn't augur well for the hundred other pieces of advice she'd offered them the night before.

Swatting zarzi to left and right, Gentle emerged from the shade of the platform building to peer down the track. It ran without crook or bend to its vanishing point, empty every mile of the way. On the rails a few yards from where he stood, rats, a gangrenous variety called graveolents, toed and fro-ed, gathering dead grasses for the nests they were constructing between the rails and the gravel the rails were set upon. Their industry only served to irritate Gentle further.

"We're stuck here forever," he said to Pie, who was squatting on the platform making marks on the stone with a sharp pebble. "This is Hairstone's revenge on a couple of hoopreo."

He'd heard this term whispered in their presence countless times. It meant anything from exotic stranger to repugnant leper, depending on the facial expression of the speaker. The people of Mai-ké were keen face-pullers, and when they'd used the word in Gentle's company there was little doubt which end of the scale of affections they had in mind.

"It'll come," said Pie. "We're not the only ones waiting."

Two more groups of travelers had appeared on the platform in the last few minutes: a family of Mai'kéacs, three generations represented, who had lugged everything they owned down to the station; and three women in voluminous robes, their heads shaved and plastered with white mud, nuns of the Goetic Kicaranki, an order as despised in Mai-ké as any well-fed hoopreo. Gentle took some comfort from the appearance of these fellow travelers, but the track was still empty, the graveolents, who would surely be the first to sense any disturbance in the rails, going about their nest building unperturbed. He wearied of watching them very quickly and turned his attention to Pie's scrawlings.

"What are you doing?"

"I'm trying to work out how long we've been here."

"Two days in Mai-ké, a day and a half on the road from Attaboy—"

"No, no," said the mystif, "I'm trying to work it out in Earth days. Right from first arriving in the Dominions."

"We tried that in the mountains, and we didn't get anywhere."

"That's because our brains were frozen stiff."

"So have you done it?"

"Give me a little time."

"Time, we've got," Gentle said, returning his gaze to the antics of graveolents. "These little buggers'll have grandchildren by the time the damn train arrives."

The mystif went on with its calculations, leaving Gentle to wander back into the comparative comfort of the waiting room, which, to judge by the sheep droppings on the floor, had been used to pen entire flocks in the recent past. The zarzi followed him, buzzing around his brow. He pulled from his ill-fitting jacket (bought with money he and Pie had won gambling in Attaboy) a dog-eared copy of *Fanny Hill*—the only volume in English, besides *Pilgrim's Progress,* which he'd been able to purchase—and used it to flail at the insects, then gave up. They'd tire of him eventually, or else he'd become immune to their attacks. Whichever; he didn't care.

He leaned against the graffiti-covered wall and yawned. He was bored. Of all things, bored! If, when they'd first arrived in Vanaeph, Pie had suggested that a few weeks later the wonders of the Reconciled Dominions would have become tedious, Gentle would have laughed the thought off as nonsense. With a gold-green sky above and the spires of Patashoqua gleaming in the distance, the scope for adventure had seemed endless. But by the time he'd reached Beatrix—the fond memories of which had not been entirely erased by images of its ruin—he was traveling like any man in a foreign land, prepared for occasional revelations but persuaded that the nature of conscious, curious bipeds was a constant under any heaven. They'd seen a great deal in the last few days, to be sure, but nothing he might not have imagined had he not stayed at home and got seriously drunk.

Yes, there had been glorious sights. But there had also been hours of discomfort, boredom, and banality. On their way to Mai-ké, for instance, they'd been exhorted to stay in some nameless hamlet to witness the community's festival: the annual donkey drowning. The origins of this ritual were, they were told, shrouded in fabulous mystery. They declined, Gentle remarking that this surely marked the nadir of their journey, and traveled on in the back of a wagon whose driver informed them that the vehicle had served his family for six generations as a dung carrier. He then proceeded to explain at great length the life cycle of his family's ancient foe, the pensanu, or shite rooster, a beast that with one turd could render an entire wagonload of dung inedible. They didn't press the man as to who in the region dined thusly, but they peered closely at their plates for many days following.

As he sat rolling the hard pellets of sheep dung under his heel, Gentle turned his thoughts to the one high point in their journey across the Third. That was the town of Effatoi, which Gentle had rechristened Attaboy. It wasn't that large—the size of Amsterdam, perhaps, and with that city's charm—but it was a gambler's paradise, drawing souls addicted to chance from across the Dominion. Here every game in the Imajica could be played. If your credit wasn't good in the casinos or the cock pits, you could always find a desperate man somewhere who'd bet on the color of your next piss if it was the only game on offer. Working together with what was surely telepathic efficiency, Gentle and the mystif had made a small fortune in the city—in eight currencies, no less—enough to keep them in clothes, food, and train tickets until they reached Yzord-derrex. It wasn't profit that had almost seduced Gentle into setting up house there, however. It was a local delicacy: a cake of strudel pastry and the honey-softened seeds of a marriage between peach and pomegranate, which he ate before they gambled to give him vim, then while they gambled to calm his nerves, and then again in celebration when they'd won. It was only when Pie assured him that the confection would be available elsewhere (and if it wasn't they now had sufficient funds to hire their own pastry chef to make it) that Gentle was persuaded to depart. L'Himby called.

"We have to move on," the mystif had said. "Scopique will be waiting."

"You make it sound like he's expecting us."

"I'm always expected," Pie said.

"How long since you were in L'Himby?"

"At least . . . two hundred and thirty years."

"Then he'll be dead."

"Not Scopique," Pie said. "It's important you see him, Gentle. Especially now, with so many changes in the air."

"If that's what you want to do, then we'll do it," Gentle had replied. "How far is L'Himby?"

"A day's journey, if we take the train."

That had been the first mention Gentle had heard of the iron road that joined the city of Iahmandhas and L'Himby: the city of furnaces and the city of temples.

"You'll like L'Himby," Pie had said. "It's a place of meditation."

Rested and funded, they'd left Attaboy the following morning, traveling along the River Fefer for a day, then, via Happi and Omootajive, into the province called the Ched Lo Ched, the Flowering Place (now bloomless), and finally to Mai-ké, caught in the twin pincers of poverty and puritanism.

On the platform outside, Gentle heard Pie say, "Good."

He raised himself from the comfort of the wall and stepped out into the sunshine again. "The train?" he said.

"No. The calculations. I've finished them." The mystif stared down at the marks on the platform at its feet. "This is only an approximation, of course, but I think it's sound within a day or two. Three at the most."

"So what day is it?"

"Take a guess."

"March . . . the tenth."

"Way off," said Pie. "By these calculations, and remember this is only an approximation, it's the seventeenth of May."

"Impossible."

"It's true."

"Spring's almost over."

"Are you wishing you were back there?" Pie asked.

Gentle chewed on this for a while, then said, "Not particularly. I just wish the fucking trains ran on time."

He wandered to the edge of the platform and stared down the line.

"There's no sign," Pie said. "We'd be quicker going by doeki."

"You keep doing that—"

"Doing what?"

"Saying what's on the tip of my tongue. Are you reading my mind?"

"No," said the mystif, rubbing out its calculation with its sole.

"So how did we win all that in Attaboy?"

"You don't need teaching," Pie replied.

"Don't tell me it comes naturally," Gentle said. "I've got through my entire life without winning a thing, and suddenly, when you're with me, I can do no wrong. That's no coincidence. Tell me the truth."

"That *is* the truth. You don't need teaching. *Reminding,* maybe. . . ." Pie gave a little smile.

"And that's another thing," Gentle said, snatching at one of the zarzi as he spoke.

Much to his surprise, he actually caught it. He opened his palm. He'd cracked its casing, and the blue mush of its innards was oozing out, but it was still alive. Disgusted, he flicked his wrist, depositing the body on the platform at his feet. He didn't scrutinize the remains, but pulled up a fistful of the sickly grass that sprouted between the slabs of the platform and set about scrubbing his palm with it.

"What were we talking about?" he said. Pie didn't reply. "Oh, yes . . . things I'd forgotten." He looked down at his clean hand. "Pneuma," he said. "Why would I ever forget having a power like the pneuma?"

"Either because it wasn't important to you any longer—"

"Which is doubtful."

"—or you forgot because you wanted to forget."

There was an oddness in the way the mystif pronounced its reply which grated on Gentle's ear, but he pursued the argument anyway.

"Why would I want to forget?" he said.

Pie looked back along the line. The distance was obscured by dust, but there were glimpses through it of a clear sky.

"Well?" said Gentle.

"Maybe because remembering hurts too much," it said, without looking around.

The words were even uglier to Gentle's ear than the reply that had preceded it. He caught the sense, but only with difficulty.

"Stop this," he said.

"Stop what?"

"Talking in that damn-fool way. It turns my gut."

"I'm not doing anything," the mystif said, its voice still distorted, but now more subtly. "Trust me. I'm doing nothing."

"So tell me about the pneuma," Gentle said. "I want to know how I came by a power like that."

Pie started to reply, but this time the words were so badly disfigured, and the sound itself so ugly, it was like a fist in Gentle's stomach, stirring the stew there.

"Jesus!" he said, rubbing his belly in a vain attempt to soothe the churning. "Whatever you're playing at—"

"It's not me," Pie protested. "It's you. You don't want to hear what I'm saying."

"*Yes, I do,*" Gentle said, wiping beads of chilly sweat from around his mouth. "I want answers. I want straight answers!"

Grimly, Pie started to speak again, but immediately the waves of nausea climbed Gentle's gut with fresh zeal. The pain in his belly was sufficient to bend him double, but he was damned if the mystif was going to keep anything from him. It was a matter of principle now. He studied Pie's lips through narrowed eyes, but after a few words the mystif stopped speaking.

"Tell me!" Gentle said, determined to have Pie obey him even if he could make no sense of the words. "What have I done that I want to forget so badly? *Tell me!*"

Its face all reluctance, the mystif once again opened its mouth. The words, when they came, were so hopelessly corrupted Gentle could barely grasp a fraction of their sense. Something about power. Something about death.

Point proved, he waved the source of this excremental din away and turned his eyes in search of a sight to calm his belly. But the scene around him was a convention of little horrors: a graveolent making its wretched nest beneath the rails; the perspective of the track, snatching his eye into the dust; the dead zarzi at his feet, its egg sac split, spattering its unborn onto the stone. This last image, vile as it was, brought food to mind. The harbor meal in Yzordderrex: fish within fish within fish, the littlest filled with eggs. The thought defeated him. He tottered to the edge of the platform and vomited onto the rails, his gut convulsing. He didn't have that much in his belly, but the heaves went on and on until his abdomen ached and tears of pain ran from his eyes. At last he stepped back from the platform edge, shuddering. The smell of his stomach was still in his nostrils, but the spasms were steadily diminishing. From the corner of his eye he saw Pie approach.

"Don't come near me!" he said. "I don't want you touching me!"

He turned his back on the vomit and its cause and retired to the shade of the waiting room, sitting down on the hard wood bench, putting his head against the wall, and closing his eyes. As the pain eased and finally disappeared, his thoughts turned to the purpose behind Pie's assault. He'd quizzed the mystif several times over the past four and a half months about the problem of power: how it was come by and—more particularly—how he, Gentle, had come to possess it. Pie's replies had been oblique in the extreme, but Gentle hadn't felt any great urge to get to the bottom of the question. Perhaps subconsciously he hadn't really wanted to know. Classically, such gifts had consequences, and he was enjoying his role as getter and wielder of power too much to want it spoiled with talk of hubris. He'd been content to be fobbed off with hints and equivocation, and he might have continued to be content, if he hadn't been irritated by the zarzi and the lateness of the L'Himby train, bored and ready for an argument. But that was only half the issue. He'd pressed the mystif, certainly, but he'd scarcely goaded it. The attack seemed out of all proportion to the offense. He'd asked an innocent question and been turned inside out for doing so. So much for all that loving talk in the mountains.

"Gentle . . ."

"Fuck you."

"The train, Gentle . . ."

"What about it?"

"It's coming."

He opened his eyes. The mystif was standing in the doorway, looking forlorn.

"I'm sorry that had to happen," it said.

"It didn't have to," Gentle said. "You made it happen."

"Truly I didn't."

"What was it then? Something I ate?"

"No. But there are some questions—"

"That make me sick."

"—that have answers you don't want to hear."

"What do you take me for?" Gentle said, his tone all quiet contempt. "I ask a question, you fill my head with so much shit for an answer that I throw up, and then it's my fault for asking in the first place? What kind of fucked-up logic is that?"

The mystif raised its hands in mock surrender. "I'm not going to argue," it said.

"Damn right," Gentle replied.

Any further exchange would have been impractical anyway, with the sound of the train's approach steadily getting louder, and its arrival being greeted by cheers and clapping from an audience that had gathered on the platform. Still feeling delicate when he stood, Gentle followed Pie out into the crowd.

It seemed half the inhabitants of Mai-ké had come down to the station. Most, he assumed, were sightseers rather than potential travelers; the train a distraction from hunger and unanswered prayers. There were some families here who planned to board, however, pressing through the crowd with their luggage. What privations they'd endured to purchase their escape from Mai-ké could only be imagined. There was much sobbing as they embraced those they were leaving behind, most of whom were old folk, who to judge by their grief did not expect to see their children and grandchildren again. The journey to L'Himby, which for Gentle and Pie was little more than a jaunt, was for them a departure into memory.

That said, there could be few more spectacular means of departure in the Imajica than the massive locomotive which was only now emerging from a cloud of evaporating steam. Whoever had made blueprints for this roaring, glistening machine knew its earth counterpart—the kind of locomotives outdated in the West but still serving in China and India—very well. Their imitation was not so slavish as to suppress a certain decorative joie de vivre—it had been painted so gaudily it looked like the male of the species in search of a mate—but beneath the daubings was a machine that might have steamed into King's Cross or Marylebone in the years following the Great War. It drew six carriages and as many freight vehicles again, two of the latter being loaded with the flock of sheep.

Pie had already been down the line of carriages and was now coming back towards Gentle.

"The second. It's fuller down the other end."

They got in. The interiors had once been lush, but usage had taken its toll. Most of the seats had been stripped of both padding and headrests, and some were missing backs entirely. The floor was dusty, and the walls—which had once been decorated in the same riot as the engine—were in dire need of a fresh coat of paint. There were only two other occupants, both male, both grotesquely fat, and both wearing frock coats from which elaborately bound limbs emerged, lending them the look of clerics who'd escaped from an accident ward. Their features were minuscule, crowded in the center of each face as if clinging together for fear of drowning in fat. Both were eating nuts, cracking them in their pudgy fists and dropping little rains of pulverized shell on the floor between them.

"Brothers of the Boulevard," Pie remarked as Gentle took a seat, as far from the nut-crackers as possible.

Pie sat across the aisle from him, the bag containing what few belongings they'd accrued to date alongside. There was then a long delay, while recalcitrant animals were beaten and cajoled into boarding for what they perhaps knew was a ride to the slaughterhouse and those on the platform made their final farewells. It wasn't just the vows and tears that came in through the windows. So did the stench of the animals, and the inevitable zarzi, though with the Brothers and their meal to attract them the insects were uninterested in Gentle's flesh.

Wearied by the hours of waiting and wrung out by his nausea, Gentle dozed and finally fell into so deep a sleep that the train's long-delayed departure didn't stir him, and when he woke two hours of their journey had already passed. Very little had changed outside the window. Here were the same expanses of gray-brown earth that had stretched around Mai-ké, clusters of dwellings, built from mud in times of water and barely distinguishable from the ground they stood upon, dotted here and there. Occasionally they would pass a plot of land—either blessed with a spring or better irrigated than the ground around it—from which life was rising; even more occasionally saw workers bending to reap a healthy crop. But generally the scene was just as Hairstone Banty had predicted. There would be many hours of dead land, she'd said; then they would travel through the Steppes, and over the Three Rivers, to the province of Bem, of which L'Himby was the capital city. Gentle had doubted her competence at the time (she'd been smoking a weed too pungent to be simply pleasurable, and wearing something unseen elsewhere in the town: a smile) but dope fiend or no, she knew her geography.

As they traveled, Gentle's thoughts turned once again to the origins of the power Pie had somehow awakened in him. If, as he suspected, the mystif had touched a hitherto passive portion of his mind and given him access to capabilities dormant in all human beings, why was it so damned reluctant to admit the fact? Hadn't Gentle proved in the mountains that he was more than willing to accept the notion of mind embracing mind? Or was that co-mingling now an embarrassment to the mystif, and its assault on the platform a way to reestablish a distance between them? If so, it had succeeded. They traveled half a day without exchanging a single word.

In the heat of the afternoon, the train stopped at a small town and lingered there while the flock from Mai-ké disembarked. No less than four suppliers of refreshments came through the train while it waited, one exclusively carrying pastries and candies, among which Gentle found a variation on the honey and seed cake that had almost kept him in Attaboy. He bought three slices, and then two cups of well-sweetened coffee from another merchant, the combination of which soon enlivened his torpid system. For its part, the mystif bought and ate dried fish, the smell of which drove Gentle even farther from its side.

As the shout came announcing their imminent departure, Pie suddenly sprang up and darted to the door. The thought went through Gentle's head that the mystif intended to desert him, but it had spotted newspapers for sale on the platform and, having made a hurried purchase, clambered aboard again as the train began to move off. Then it sat down beside the remains of its fish dinner and had no sooner unfolded the paper than it let out a low whistle.

"Gentle. You'd better look at this."

It passed the newspaper across the aisle. The banner

headline was in a language Gentle neither understood nor even recognized, but that scarcely mattered. The photographs below were plain enough. Here was a gallows, with six bodies hanging from it, and, inset, the death portraits of the executed individuals: among them, Hammeryock and Pontiff Farrow, the lawgivers of Vanaeph. Below this rogues' gallery a finely rendered etching of Tick Raw, the crazy evocator.

"So," Gentle said, "they got their comeuppance. It's the best news I've had in days."

"No, it's not," Pie replied.

"They tried to kill us, remember?" Gentle said reasonably, determined not to be infuriated by Pie's contentiousness. "If they got hanged I'm not going to mourn 'em! What did they do, try and steal the Merrow Ti' Ti'?"

"The Merrow Ti' Ti' doesn't exist."

"That was a joke, Pie," Gentle said, dead pan.

"I missed the humor of it, I'm sorry," the mystif said, unsmiling. "Their crime—" It stopped and crossed the aisle to sit opposite Gentle, claiming the paper from his hands before continuing. "Their crime is far more significant," it went on, its voice lowered. It began to read in the same whisper, précising the text of the paper. "They were executed a week ago for making an attempt on the Autarch's life while he and his entourage were on their peace mission in Vanaeph—"

"Are you kidding?"

"No joke. That's what it says."

"Did they succeed?"

"Of course not." The mystif fell silent while it scanned the columns. "It says they killed three of his advisers with a bomb and injured eleven soldiers. The device was . . . wait, my Omootajivac is rusty . . . the device was smuggled into his presence by Pontiff Farrow. They were all caught alive, it says, but hanged dead, which means they died under torture but the Autarch made a show of the execution anyway."

"That's fucking barbaric."

"It's very common, particularly in political trials."

"What about Tick Raw? Why's his picture in there?"

"He was named as a co-conspirator, but apparently he escaped. The damn fool!"

"Why'd you call him that?"

"Getting involved in politics when there's so much more at stake. It's not the first time, of course, and won't be the last—"

"I'm not following."

"People get frustrated with waiting and they end up stooping to politics. But it's so shortsighted. Stupid sod."

"How well do you know him?"

"Who? Tick Raw?" The placid features were momentarily confounded. Then Pie said, "He has . . . a certain reputation, shall we say? They'll find him for certain. There isn't a sewer in the Dominions he'll be able to hide his head in."

"Why should you care?"

"Keep your voice down."

"Answer the question," Gentle replied, dropping his volume as he spoke.

"He was a Maestro, Gentle. He called himself an evocator, but it amounts to the same thing: he had power."

"Then why was he living in the middle of a shithole like Vanaeph?"

"Not everybody cares about wealth and women, Gentle. Some souls have higher ambition."

"Such as?"

"Wisdom. Remember why we came on this journey? To understand. That's a fine ambition." Pie looked at Gentle, making eye-to-eye contact for the first time since the episode on the platform. *"Your* ambition, my friend. You and Tick Raw had a lot in common."

"And he knew it?"

"Oh, yes. . . ."

"Is that why he was so riled when I wouldn't sit down and talk with him?"

"I'd say so."

"Shit!"

"Hammeryock and Farrow must have taken us for spies, come to wheedle out plots laid against the Autarch."

"But Tick Raw saw the truth."

"He did. He was once a great man, Gentle. At least . . . that was the rumor. Now I suppose he's dead or being tortured. Which is grim news for us."

"You think he'll name us?"

"Who knows? Maestros have ways of protecting themselves from torture, but even the strongest man can break under the right kind of pressure."

"Are you saying we've got the Autarch on our tails?"

"I think we'd know it if we had. We've come a long way from Vanaeph. The trail's probably cold by now."

"And maybe they didn't arrest Tick, eh? Maybe he escaped."

"They still caught Hammeryock and the Pontiff. I think we can assume they've got a hair-by-hair description of us."

Gentle laid his head back against the seat. "Shit," he said. "We're not making many friends, are we?"

"All the more reason that we don't lose each other," the mystif replied. The shadows of passing bamboo flickered on its face, but it looked at him unblinking. "Whatever harm you believe I may have done you, now or in the past, I apologize for it. I'd never wish you any hurt, Gentle. Please believe that. Not the slightest."

"I know," Gentle murmured, "and I'm sorry too, truly."

"Shall we agree to postpone our argument until the only opponents we've got left in the Imajica are each other?"

"That may be a very long time."

"All the better."

Gentle laughed. "Agreed," he said, leaning forward and taking the mystif's hand. "We've seen some amazing sights together, haven't we?"

"Indeed we have."

"Back there in Mai-ké I was losing my sense of how marvelous all this is."

"We've got a lot more wonders to see."

"Just promise me one thing?"

"Ask it."

"Don't eat raw fish in eyeshot of me again. It's more than a man can take."

2

From the yearning way that Hairstone Banty had described L'Himby, Gentle had been expecting some kind of Khatmandu—a city of temples, pilgrims, and free dope. Perhaps it had been that way once, in Banty's long-lost youth. But when, a few minutes after night had fallen, Gentle and Pie stepped off the train, it was not into an atmosphere of spiritual calm. There were soldiers at the station gates, most of them standing idle, smoking and talking, but a few casting their eyes over the disembarking passengers. As luck had it, however, another train had arrived at an adjacent platform minutes before, and the gateway was choked with passengers, many hugging their life's belongings. It wasn't difficult for Pie and Gentle to dig their way through to the densest part of the crowd and pass unnoticed through the turnstiles and out of the station.

There were many more troops in the wide lamplit streets, their presence no less disturbing for the air of lassitude that hung about them. The uncommissioned ranks wore a drab gray, but the officers wore white, which suited the subtropical night. All were conspicuously armed. Gentle made certain not to study either men or weaponry too closely for fear of attracting unwelcome attention, but it was clear from even a furtive glance that both the armaments and the vehicles parked in every other alleyway were of the same elaborately intimidating design as he'd seen in Beatrix. The warlords of Yzordderrex were clearly past masters in the crafts of death, their technology several generations beyond that of the locomotive that had brought the travelers here.

To Gentle's eye the most fascinating sight was not the tanks or the machine guns, however, it was the presence among these troops of a subspecies he'd not encountered hitherto. Oethacs, Pie called them. They stood no taller than their fellows, but their heads made up a third or more of that height, their squat bodies grotesquely broad to bear the weight of such a massive load of bone. Easy targets, Gentle remarked, but Pie whispered that their brains were small, their skulls thick, and their tolerance for pain heroic, the latter evidenced by the extraordinary array of livid scars and disfigurements they all bore on skin that was as white as the bone it concealed.

It seemed this substantial military presence had been in place for some time, because the populace went about their evening business as if these men and their killing machines were completely commonplace. There was little sign of fraternization, but there was no harassment either.

"Where do we go from here?" Gentle asked Pie once they were clear of the crowds around the station.

"Scopique lives in the northeast part of the city, close to the temples. He's a doctor. Very well respected."

"You think he may be still practicing?"

"He doesn't mend bones, Gentle. He's a doctor of theology. He used to like the city because it was so sleepy."

"It's changed, then."

"It certainly has. It looks as though it's got rich."

There was evidence of L'Himby's newfound wealth everywhere: in the gleaming buildings, many of them looking as though the paint on their doors was barely dry; in the proliferation of styles among the pedestrians and in the number of elegant automobiles on the street. There were a few signs still remaining of the culture that had existed here before the city's fortunes had boomed: beasts of burden still wove among the traffic, honked at and cursed; a smattering of façades had been preserved from older buildings and incorporated—usually crudely—into the designs of the newer. And then there were the living façades, the faces of the people Gentle and Pie were mingling with. The natives had a physical peculiarity unique to the region: clusters of small crystalline growths, yellow and purple, on their heads, sometimes arranged like crowns or coxcombs but just as often erupting from the middle of the forehead or irregularly placed around the mouth. To Pie's knowledge, they had no particular function, but they were clearly viewed as a disfigurement by the sophisticates, many of whom went to extraordinary lengths to disguise their commonality of stock with the undecorated peasants. Some of these stylists wore hats, veils, and makeup to conceal the evidence; others had tried surgery to remove the growths and went proudly about unhatted, wearing their scars as proof of their wealth.

"It's grotesque," Pie said when Gentle remarked upon this. "But that's the pernicious influence of fashion for you. These people want to look like the models they see in the magazines from Patashoqua, and the stylists in Patashoqua have always looked to the Fifth for their inspiration. Damn fools! Look at them! I swear if we were to spread the rumor that everyone in Paris is cutting off their right arms these days, we'd be tripping over hacked-off limbs all the way to Scopique's house."

"It wasn't like this when you were here?"

"Not in L'Himby. As I said, it was a place of meditation. But in Patashoqua, yes, always, because it's so close to the Fifth, so the influence is very strong. And there's always been a few minor Maestros, you know, traveling back and forth, bringing styles, bringing ideas. A few of them made a kind of business of it, crossing the In Ovo every few months to get news of the Fifth and selling it to the fashion houses, the architects, and so on. So damn decadent. It revolts me."

"But you did the same thing, didn't you? You became part of the Fifth Dominion."

"Never here," the mystif said, its fist to its chest. "Never in my heart. My mistake was getting lost in the In Ovo and letting myself be summoned to earth. When I was there I played the human game, but only as much as I had to."

Despite their baggy and by now well-crumpled clothes, both Pie and Gentle were bare-headed and smooth-skulled, so they attracted a good deal of attention from envious posers parading on the pavement. It was far from welcome, of course. If Pie's theory was correct and Hammeryock or Pontiff Farrow had described them to the Autarch's torturers, their likenesses might very well have appeared in the broadsheets of L'Himby. If so, an envious dandy might have them removed from the competition with a few words in a soldier's ear. Would it not be wiser, Gentle suggested, if they hailed a taxi, and traveled a little more discreetly? The mystif was reluctant to do so, explaining that it could not remember Scopique's address, and their only hope of finding it was to go on foot, while Pie followed its nose. They made a point of avoiding the busier parts of the street, however, where café customers were outside enjoying the evening air or, less frequently, where soldiers gathered. Though they continued to attract interest and admiration, nobody challenged them, and after twenty minutes they turned off the main thoroughfare, the well-tended buildings giving way within a couple of blocks to grimier structures, the fops to grimmer souls.

"This feels safer," Gentle said, a paradoxical remark given that the streets they were wandering through now were the kind they would have instinctively avoided in any city of the Fifth: ill-lit backwaters, where many of the houses had fallen into severe disrepair. Lamps burned in even the most dilapidated, however, and children played in the gloomy streets despite the lateness of the hour. Their games were those of earth, give or take a detail—not filched, but invented by young minds from the same basic materials: a ball and a bat, some chalk and a pavement, a rope and a rhyme. Gentle found it reassuring to walk among them and hear their laughter, which was indistinguishable from that of human children.

Eventually the tenanted houses gave way to total dereliction, and it was clear from the mystif's disgruntlement that it was no longer sure of its whereabouts. Then, a little noise of pleasure, as it caught sight of a distant structure.

"That's the temple." Pie pointed to a monolith some miles from where they stood. It was unlit and seemed forsaken, the ground in its vicinity leveled. "Scopique had that view from his toilet window, I remember. On fine days he said he used to throw open the window and contemplate and defecate simultaneously."

Smiling at the memory, the mystif turned its back on the sight.

"The bathroom faced the temple, and there were no more streets between the house and the temple. It was common land, for the pilgrims to pitch their tents."

"So we're walking in the right direction," Gentle said. "We just need the last street on our right."

"That seems logical," Pie said. "I was beginning to doubt my memory."

They didn't have much farther to look. Two more blocks, and the rubble-strewn streets came to an abrupt end.

"This is it."

There was no triumph in Pie's voice, which was not surprising, given the scene of devastation before them. While it was time that had undone the splendor of the streets they'd passed through, this last had been prey to more systematic assault. Fires had been set in several of the houses. Others looked as though they'd been used for target practice by a Panzer division.

"Somebody got here before us," Gentle said.

"So it seems," Pie replied. "I must say I'm not altogether surprised."

"So why the hell did you bring us here?"

"I had to see for myself," Pie said. "Don't worry, the trail doesn't end here. He'll have left a message."

Gentle didn't remark on how unlikely he thought this, but followed the mystif along the street until it stopped in front of a building that, while not reduced to a heap of blackened stones, looked ready to succumb. Fire had eaten out its eyes, and the once-fine door had been replaced with partially rotted timbers; all this illuminated not by lamplight (the street had none) but by a scattering of stars.

"Better you stay out here," Pie 'oh' pah said. "Scopique may have left defenses."

"Like what?"

"The Unbeheld isn't the only one who can conjure guardians," Pie replied. "Please, Gentle . . . I'd prefer to do this alone."

Gentle shrugged. "Do as you wish," he said. Then, as an afterthought, "You usually do."

He watched Pie climb the debris-covered steps, pull several of the timbers off the door, and slip out of sight. Rather than wait at the threshold, Gentle wandered farther along the row to get another view of the temple, musing as he went that this Dominion, like the Fourth, had confounded not only his expectations but those of Pie as well. The safe haven of Vanaeph had almost seen their execution, while the murderous wastes of the mountains had offered resurrections. And now L'Himby, a sometime city of meditation, reduced to gaud and rubble. What next? He wondered. Would they arrive in Yzordderrex only to find it had spurned its reputation as the Babylon of the Dominions and become a New Jerusalem?

He stared across at the shadowy temple, his mind straying back to a subject that had occupied him several times on their journey through the Third: how best to address the challenge of making a map of the Dominions, so that when they finally returned to the Fifth Dominion he could give his friends some sense of how the lands lay. They'd traveled on all kinds of roads, from the Patashoquan Highway to the dirt tracks between Happi and Mai-ké; they'd wound through verdant valleys and scaled heights where even the hardiest moss would perish; they'd had the luxury of chariots and the loyalty of doeki; they'd sweated and frozen and gone dreamily, like poets into some place of fancy, doubting their senses and themselves. All this needed setting down: the routes, the cities, the ranges, and the plains all needed laying in two dimensions, to be pored over at leisure. In time, he thought, putting the challenge off yet again; in time.

He looked back towards Scopique's house. There was no sign of Pie emerging, and he began to wonder if some harm had befallen the mystif inside. He walked back to the steps, climbed them, and—feeling a little guilty—slid through the gap between the timbers. The starlight had more difficulty getting in than he did, and his blindness put a chill in him, bringing to mind the measureless darkness of the ice cathedral. On that occasion the mystif had been behind him; this time, in front. He waited a few seconds at the door, until his eyes began to make out the interior. It was a narrow house, full of narrow places, but there was a voice in its depths, barely above a whisper, which he pursued, stumbling through the murk. After only a few paces he realized it was not Pie speaking but someone hoarse and panicked. Scopique, perhaps, still taking refuge in the ruins?

A glimmer of light, no brighter than the dimmest star, led him to a door through which he had sight of the speaker. Pie was standing in the middle of the blackened room, turned from Gentle. Over the mystif's shoulder Gentle saw the light's fading source: a shape hanging in the air, like a web woven by a spider that aspired to portraiture, and held aloft by the merest breeze. Its motion was not arbitrary, however. The gossamer face opened its mouth and whispered its wisdom.

"—no better proof than in these cataclysms. We must hold to that, my friend, hold to it and pray . . . no, better not pray . . . I doubt every God now, especially the Aboriginal. If the children are any measure of the Father, then He's no lover of justice or goodness."

"Children?" said Gentle.

The breath the word came upon seemed to flutter in the threads. The face grew long, the mouth tearing.

The mystif glanced behind and shook its head to silence the trespasser. Scopique—for this was surely his message— was talking again.

"Believe me when I say we know only the tenth part of a tenth part of the plots laid in this. Long before the Reconciliation, forces were at work to undo it; that's my firm belief. And it's reasonable to assume that those forces have not perished. They're working in this Dominion, and the Dominion from which you've come. They strategize not in terms of decades, but centuries, just as we've had to. And they've buried their agents deeply. Trust nobody, Pie 'oh' pah, not even yourself. Their plots go back before we were born. We could either one of us have been conceived to serve them in some oblique fashion and not know it. They're coming for me very soon, probably with voiders. If I'm dead you'll know it. If I can convince them I'm just a harmless lunatic, they'll take me off to the Cradle, put me in the *maison de santé*. Find me there, Pie 'oh' pah. Or if you have more pressing business, then forget me; I won't blame you. But, friend, whether you come for me or not, know that when I think of you I still smile, and in these days that is the rarest comfort."

Even before he'd finished speaking the gossamer was losing its power to capture his likeness, the features softening, the form sinking in upon itself, until, by the time the last of his message had been uttered, there was little left for it to do but flutter to the ground.

The mystif went down on its haunches and ran its fingers through the inert threads. "Scopique," it murmured.

"What's the cradle he talked about?"

"The Cradle of Chzercemit. It's an inland sea, two or three days' journey from here."

"You've been there?"

"No. It's a place of exile. There's an island in the Cradle which was used as a prison. Mostly for criminals who'd committed atrocities but were too dangerous to execute."

"I don't follow that."

"Ask me another time. The point is, it sounds like it's been turned into an asylum." Pie stood up. "Poor Scopique. He always had a terror of insanity—"

"I know the feeling," Gentle remarked.

"—and now they've put him in a madhouse."

"So we must get him out," Gentle said very simply.

He couldn't see Pie's expression, but he saw the mystif's hands go up to its face and heard a sob from behind its palms.

"Hey," Gentle said softly, embracing Pie. "We'll find him. I know I shouldn't have come spying like that, but I thought maybe something had happened to you."

"At least you've heard him for yourself. You know it's not a lie."

"Why would I think that?"

"Because you don't trust me," Pie said.

"I thought we'd agreed," Gentle said. "We've got each other and that's our best hope of staying alive and sane. Didn't we agree to that?"

"Yes."

"So let's hold to it."

"It may not be so easy. If Scopique's suspicions are correct, either one of us could be working for the enemy and not know it."

"By enemy you mean the Autarch?"

"He's one, certainly. But I think he's just a sign of some greater corruption. The Imajica's sick, Gentle, from end to end. Coming here and seeing the way L'Himby's changed makes me want to despair."

"You know, you should have forced me to sit down and talk with Tick Raw. He might have given us a few clues."

"It's not my place to force you to do anything. Besides, I'm not sure he'd have been any wiser than Scopique."

"Maybe he'll know more by the time we speak with him."

"Let's hope so."

"And this time I won't take umbrage and waltz off like an idiot."

"If we get to the island, there'll be nowhere to waltz *to.*"

"True enough. So now we need a means of transport."

"Something anonymous."

"Something fast."

"Something easy to steal."

"Do you know how to get to the Cradle?" Gentle asked.

"No, but I can inquire around while you steal the car."

"Good enough. Oh, and Pie? Buy some booze and cigarettes while you're at it, will you?"

"You'll make a decadent of me yet."

"My mistake. I thought it was the other way round."

3

They left L'Himby well before dawn, in a car that Gentle chose for its color (gray) and its total lack of distinction. It served them well. For two days they traveled without incident, on roads that were less trafficked the farther from the temple city and its spreading suburbs they went. There was some military presence beyond the city perimeters, but it was discreet, and no attempt was made to stop them. Only once did they glimpse a contingent at work in a distant field, vehicles maneuvering heavy artillery into position behind barricades, pointing back towards L'Himby, the work just public enough to let the citizens know whose clemency their lives were conditional upon.

By the middle of the third day, however, the road they were traveling was almost entirely deserted, and the flatlands in which L'Himby was set had given way to rolling hills. Along with this change of landscape came a change of weather. The skies clouded; and with no wind to press them on, the clouds thickened. A landscape that might have been enlivened by sun and shadow became drear, almost dank. Signs of habitation dwindled. Once in a while they'd pass a homestead, long since fallen into ruin; more infrequently still they'd catch sight of a living soul, usually unkempt, always alone, as though the territory had been given over to the lost.

And then, the Cradle. It appeared suddenly, the road taking them up over a headland which presented them with a sudden panorama of gray shore and silver sea. Gentle had not realized how oppressed he'd been by the hills until this vista opened in front of them. He felt his spirits rise at the sight.

There were peculiarities, however, most particularly the thousands of silent birds on the stony beach below, all sitting like an audience awaiting some spectacle to appear from the arena of the sea, not one in the air or on the water.

It wasn't until Pie and Gentle reached the perimeter of this roosting multitude and got out of the car that the reason for their inactivity became apparent. Not only were they and the sky above them immobile, so was the Cradle itself. Gentle made his way through the mingled nations of birds—a close relation of the gull predominated, but there were also geese, oyster catchers, and a smattering of parrots—to the edge, testing it first with his foot, then with his fingers. It wasn't frozen—he knew what ice felt like from bitter experience—it was simply solidified, the last wave still plainly visible, every curl and eddy fixed as it broke against the shore.

"At least we won't have to swim," the mystif said.

It was already scanning the horizon, looking for Scopique's prison. The far shore wasn't visible, but the island was, a sharp gray rock rising from the sea several miles from where they stood, the *maison de santé,* as Scopique had called it, a cluster of buildings teetering on its heights.

"Do we go now or wait until dark?" Gentle asked.

"We'll never find it after dark," Pie said. "We have to go now."

They returned to the car and drove down through the birds, who were no more inclined to move for wheels than they'd been for feet. A few took to the air briefly, only to flutter down again; many more stood their ground and died for their stoicism.

The sea made the best road they'd traveled since the Patashoquan Highway; it had apparently been as calm as a millpond when it had solidified. They passed the corpses of several birds who'd been caught in the process, and there was still meat and feathers on their bones, suggesting that the solidification had occurred recently.

"I've heard of walking on water," Gentle said as they drove. "But *driving* . . . that's a whole other miracle."

"Have you any idea of what we're going to do when we get to the island?" Pie said.

"We ask to see Scopique, and when we've found him we leave with him. If they refuse to let us see him, we use force. It's simple as that."

"They may have armed guards."

"See these hands?" Gentle said, taking them off the wheel and thrusting them at Pie. "These hands are lethal." He laughed at the expression on the mystif's face. "Don't worry, I won't be indiscriminate." He seized the wheel again. "I like having the power, though. I really like it. The idea of using it sort of arouses me. Hey, will you look at that? The suns are coming out."

The parting clouds allowed a few beams through, and they lit the island, which was within half a mile of them now. The visitors' approach had been noticed. Guards had appeared on the cliff top and along the prison's parapet. Figures could be seen hurrying down the steps that wound down the cliff face, heading for the boats moored at its base. From the shore behind them rose the clamor of birds.

"They finally woke up," Gentle said.

Pie looked around. Sunlight was lighting the beach, and the wings of the birds as they rose in a squalling cloud.

"Oh, Jesu," Pie said.

"What's wrong?"

"The sea—"

Pie didn't need to explain, for the same phenomenon that was crossing the Cradle's surface behind them was now coming to meet them from the island: a slow shock wave, changing the nature of the matter it passed through. Gentle picked up speed, closing the gap between the vehicle and solid ground, but the road had already liquified completely at the island's shore, and the message of transformation was spreading at speed.

"Stop the car!" Pie yelled. "If we don't get out we'll go down in it."

Gentle brought the car to a skidding halt, and they flung themselves out. The ground beneath them was still solid enough to run on, but they could feel tremors in it as they went, prophesying dissolution.

"Can you swim?" Gentle called to Pie.

"If I have to," the mystif replied, its eyes on the approaching tide. The water looked mercurial, and seemed to be full of thrashing fish. "But I don't think this is something we want to bathe in, Gentle."

"I don't think we're going to have any choice."

There was at least some hope of rescue. Boats were being launched off the island's shore, the sound of the oars and the rhythmical shouts of the oarsmen rising above the churning of the silver water. The mystif wasn't looking for hope from that source, however. Its eyes had found a narrow causeway, like a path of softening ice, between where they stood and the land. Grabbing Gentle's arm, it pointed the way.

"I see it!" Gentle replied, and they headed off along this zigzag route, checking on the position of the two boats as they went. The oarsmen had comprehended their strategy and changed direction to intercept them. Though the flood was eating at their causeway from either side, the possibility of escape had just seemed plausible when the sound of the car upending and slipping into the waters distracted Gentle from his dash. He turned and collided with Pie as he did so. The mystif went down, falling on its face. Gentle hauled it back onto its feet, but it was momentarily too dazed to know their jeopardy.

There were shouts of alarm coming from the boats now, and the frenzy of water yards from their heels. Gentle half hoisted Pie onto his shoulders and picked up the race again. Precious seconds had been lost, however. The lead boat was within twenty yards of them, but the tide was half that distance behind, and half again between his feet and the bow. If he stood still, the floe beneath him would go before the boat reached them. If he tried to run, burdened with the semiconscious mystif, he'd miss his rendezvous with his rescuers.

As it was, the choice was taken from him. The ground beneath the combined weight of man and mystif fractured, and the silver waters of the Chzercemit bubbled up between his feet. He heard a shout of alarm from the creature in the nearest boat—an Oethac, huge-headed and scarred—then felt his right leg lose six inches as his foot plunged through the brittle floe. It was Pie's turn to haul him up now, but it was a lost cause: the ground would support neither of them.

In desperation he looked down at the waters that he was going to have to swim in. The creatures he'd seen thrashing were not *in* the sea but *of* the sea. The wavelets had backs and necks; the glitter of the spume was the glitter of countless tiny eyes. The boat was still speeding in their direction, and for an instant it seemed they might bridge the gap with a lunge.

"Go!" he yelled to Pie, pushing as he did so.

Though the mystif flailed, there was sufficient power in its legs to turn the fall into a jump. Its fingers caught the edge of the boat, but the violence of its leap threw Gentle from his precarious perch. He had time to see the mystif being hauled onto the rocking boat, and time too to think he might reach the hands outstretched in his direction. But the sea was not about to be denied both its morsels. As he dropped into the silver spume, which pressed around him like a living thing, he threw his hands up above his head in the hope that the Oethac would catch hold of him. All in vain. Consciousness went from him, and, uncaptained, he sank.

26

I

Gentle woke to the sound of a prayer. He knew before sight came to join the sound that the words were a beseechment, though the language was foreign to him. The voices rose and fell in the same unmelodious fashion as did earth congregations, one or two of the half dozen speakers lagging a syllable behind, leaving the verses ragged. But it was nevertheless a welcome sound. He'd gone down thinking he'd never rise again.

Light touched his eyes, but whatever lay in front of him was murky. There was a vague texture to the gloom, however, and he tried to focus upon it. It wasn't until his brow, cheeks, and chin reported their irritation to his brain that he realized why his eyes couldn't make sense of the scene. He was lying on his back, and there was a cloth over his face. He told his arm to rise and pluck it away, but the limb just lay stupid at his side. He concentrated, demanding it obey, his irritation growing as the timber of the supplications changed and a distressing urgency came into them. He felt the bed he was lying on jostled, and tried to call out in alarm, but there was something in his throat that prevented him from making a sound. Irritation became unease. What was wrong with him? Be calm, he told himself. It'll come clear; just be calm. But damn it, the bed was being lifted up! Where was he being taken? To hell with calm. He couldn't just lie still while he was paraded around. He wasn't dead, for God's sake!

Or was he? The thought shredded every hope of equilibrium. He was being lifted up, and carried, lying inert on a hard board with his face beneath a shroud. What was *that,* if it wasn't dead? They were saying prayers for his soul, hoping to waft it heavenward, meanwhile carrying his remains to what dispatch? A hole in the ground? A pyre? He had to stop them: raise a hand, a moan, anything to signal that this leave-taking was premature. As he was concentrating on making a sign, however primitive, a voice cut through the prayers. Both prayers and bier bearers stumbled to a halt and the same voice—it was Pie!—came again.

"Not yet!" it said.

Somebody off to Gentle's right murmured something in a language Gentle didn't recognize: words of consolation, perhaps. The mystif responded in the same tongue, its voice fractured with grief.

A third speaker now entered the exchange, his purpose undoubtedly the same as his compatriot's: coaxing Pie to leave the body alone. What were they saying? That the corpse was just a husk; an empty shadow of a man whose spirit was gone into a better place? Gentle willed Pie not to listen. The spirit was here! *Here!*

Then—joy of joys!—the shroud was pulled back from

his face, and Pie appeared in his field of vision, staring down at him. The mystif looked half dead itself, its eyes raw, its beauty bruised with sorrow.

I'm saved, Gentle thought. Pie sees that my eyes are open, and there's more than putrefaction going on in my skull. But no such comprehension came into Pie's face. The sight simply brought a new burst of tears. A man came to Pie's side, his head a cluster of crystalline growths, and laid his hands on the mystif's shoulders, whispering something in its ear and gently tugging it away. Pie's fingers went to Gentle's face and lay for a few seconds close to his lips. But his breath—which he'd used to shatter the wall between Dominions—was so piffling now it went unfelt, and the fingers were withdrawn by the hand of Pie's consoler, who then reached down and drew the shroud back over Gentle's face.

The prayer sayers picked up their dirge, and the bearers their burden. Blinded again, Gentle felt the spark of hope extinguished, replaced with panic and anger. Pie had always claimed such sensitivity. How was it possible that *now,* when empathy was essential, the mystif could be immune to the jeopardy of the man it claimed as a friend? More than that: a soul mate; someone it had reconfigured its flesh for.

Gentle's panic slowed for an instant. Was there some half hope buried amid these rebukes? He scoured them for a clue. Soul mate? Reconfigured flesh? Yes, of course: as long as he had *thought* he had *desire,* and desire could touch the mystif; *change* the mystif. If he could put death from his mind and turn his thoughts to sex he might still touch Pie's protean core: bring about some metamorphosis, however small, that would signal his sentience.

As if to confound him, a remark of Klein's drifted into his head, recalled from another world. "All that time wasted," Klein had said, "meditating on death to keep yourself from coming too soon. . . ."

The memory seemed mere distraction, until he realized that it was precisely the mirror of his present plight. Desire was now his only defense against premature extinction. He turned his thoughts to the little details that were always a stimulus to his erotic imagination: a nape bared by lifted curls, lips rewetted by a slow tongue, looks, touches, dares. But thanatos had eros by the neck. His terror drove arousal away. How could he hold a sexual thought in his head long enough to influence Pie when either the flame or the grave was waiting at his feet? He was ready for neither. One was too hot, the other too cold; one bright, the other so very dark. What he wanted was a few more weeks, days—hours, even; he'd be grateful for hours—in the space between such poles. Where flesh was; where love was.

Knowing the death thoughts couldn't be mastered, he attempted one final gambit: to embrace them, to fold them into the texture of his sexual imaginings. Flame? Let that be the heat of the mystif's body as it was pressed against him, and cold the sweat on his back as they coupled. Let the darkness be a night that concealed their excesses, and the pyre blaze like their mutual consumption. He could feel the trick working as he thought this through. Why should death be so unerotic? If they blistered or rotted together, mightn't their dissolution show them new ways to love, uncovering them layer by layer and joining their moistures and their marrows until they were utterly mingled?

He'd proposed marriage to Pie and been accepted. The creature was his to have and hold, to make over and over, in the image of his fondness and most forbidden desires. He did so now. He saw the creature naked and astride him, changing even as he touched it, throwing off skins like clothes. Jude was one of those skins, and Vanessa another, and Martine another still. They were all riding him high: the beauty of the world impaled on his prick.

Lost in this fantasy, he wasn't even aware that the prayers had stopped until the bier was halted once again. There were whispers all around him, and in the middle of the whispers soft and astonished laughter. The shroud was snatched away, and his beloved was looking down at him, grinning through features blurred by tears and Gentle's influence.

"He's alive! Jesu, he's *alive!*"

There were doubting voices raised, but the mystif laughed them down.

"I feel him in me!" it said. "I swear it! He's still with us. Put him down! *Put him down!*"

The pallbearers did as they were instructed, and Gentle had his first glimpse of the strangers who'd almost bade him farewell. Not a happy bunch, even now. They stared down at the body, still disbelieving. But the danger was over, at least for the time being. The mystif leaned over Gentle and kissed his lips. Its face was fixed once more, its features exquisite in their joy.

"I love you," it murmured to Gentle. "I'll love you until the death of love."

2

Alive he was; but not healed. He was moved to a small room of gray brick and laid on a bed only marginally more comfortable than the boards they'd laid him on as a corpse. There was a window, but being unable to move he had to rely upon Pie 'oh' pah to lift him up and show him the view through it, which was scarcely more interesting than the walls, being simply an expanse of sea—solid once again— under a cloudy sky.

"The sea only changes when the suns come out," Pie explained. "Which isn't very often. We were unlucky. But everyone is amazed that you survived. Nobody who fell into the Cradle ever came out alive before."

That he was something of a curiosity was evidenced by the number of visitors he had, both guards and prisoners. The regime seemed to be fairly relaxed, from what little he could judge. There were bars on the windows, and the door was unbolted and bolted up again when anybody came or went, but the officers, particularly the Oethac who ran the asylum, named Vigor N'ashap, and his number two—a military peacock named Aping, whose buttons and boots shone a good deal more brightly than his eyes, and whose features drooped on his head as though sodden—were polite enough.

"They get no news out here," Pie explained. "They just get sent prisoners to look after. N'ashap knows there was a plot against the Autarch, but I don't believe he knows whether it's been successful or not. They've quizzed me for hours, but they haven't really asked about us. I just told them we were friends of Scopique's, and we'd heard he'd lost his sanity, so we came to visit him. All innocence, in other words. And they seemed to swallow it. But they get supplies of food, magazines, and newspapers every eight or nine days—always out of date, Aping says—so our luck may not hold out too long. Meanwhile I'm doing what I can to keep them both happy. They get very lonely."

The significance of this last remark wasn't lost on Gentle, but all he could do was listen and hope his healing wouldn't take too long. There was some easing in his muscles, allowing him to open and close his eyes, swallow, and even move his hands a little, but his torso was still completely rigid.

His other regular visitor, and by far the most entertaining of those who came to gawk, was Scopique, who had an opinion on everything, including the patient's rigidity. He was a tiny man, with the perpetual squint of a watchmaker and a nose so upturned and so tiny his nostrils were virtually two holes in the middle of his face, which was already gouged with laugh lines deep enough to plant in. Every day he would come and sit on the edge of Gentle's bed, his gray asylum clothes as crumpled as his features, his glossy black wig never in the same place on his pate from hour to hour. Sitting, sipping coffee, he'd pontificate: on politics, on the various psychoses of his fellow inmates; on the subjugation of L'Himby by commerce; on the deaths of his friends, mostly by what he called despair's slow sword; and, of course, on Gentle's condition. He had seen people made rigid in such a fashion before, he claimed. The reason was not physiological but psychological, a theory which seemed to carry weight with Pie. Once, when Scopique had left after a session of theorizing, leaving Pie and Gentle alone, the mystif poured out its guilt. None of this would have come about, it said, if it had been sensitive to Gentle's situation from the beginning. Instead, it had been crude and unkind. The incident on the platform at Mai-ké was a case in point. Would Gentle ever forgive it? Ever believe that its actions were the product of ineptitude, not cruelty? Over the years it had wondered what would happen if they ever took the journey they were taking, and had tried to rehearse its responses, but it had been alone in the Fifth Dominion, unable to confess its fears or share its hopes, and the circumstances of their meeting and departure had been so haphazard that those few rules it had set itself had been thrown to the wind.

"Forgive me," it said over and over. "I love you and I've hurt you, but please, forgive me."

Gentle expressed what little he could with his eyes, wishing his fingers had the strength to hold a pen, so that he could simply write *I do,* but the small advances he'd made since his resurrection seemed to be the limit of his healing, and though he was fed and bathed by Pie, and his muscles massaged, there was no sign of further improvement. Despite the mystif's constant words of encouragement, there was no doubt that death still had its finger in him. In them both, in fact, for Pie's devotion seemed to be taking its own toll, and more than once Gentle wondered if the mystif's dwindling was simply fatigue, or whether they were symbiotically linked after their time together. If so, his demise would surely take them both to oblivion.

He was alone in his cell the day the suns came out again, but Pie had left him sitting up, with a view through the bars, and he was able to watch the slow unfurling of the clouds and the appearance of the subtlest beams, falling on the solid sea. This was the first time since their arrival that the suns had broken over the Chzercemit, and he heard a chorus of welcome from other cells, then the sound of running feet as guards went to the parapet to watch the transformation. He could see the surface of the Cradle from where he was sitting, and felt a kind of exhilaration at the imminent spectacle, but as the beams brightened he felt a tremor climbing through his body from his toes, gathering force as it went until by the time it reached his head it had force enough to throw his senses from his skull. At first he thought he'd stood up and run to the window—he was peering out through the bars at the sea below—but a noise at the door drew his gaze around to meet the sight of Scopique, with Aping at his side, crossing the cell to the sallow, bearded derelict sitting with a glazed expression against the far wall. He was that man.

"You have to come and see, Zacharias!" Scopique was enthusing, putting his arm beneath the derelict and hoisting him up.

Aping lent a hand, and together they began to carry Gentle to the window, from which his mind was already departing. He left them to their kindness, the exhilaration he'd felt like an engine in him. Out and along the dreary corridor he went, passing cells in which prisoners were clamoring to be released to see the suns. He had no sense of the building's geography, and for a few moments his speeding soul lost its way in the maze of gray brick, until he encountered two guards hurrying up a flight of stone stairs and went with them, an invisible mind, into a brighter suite of rooms. There were more guards here, forsaking games of cards to head out into the open air.

"Where's Captain N'ashap?" one of them said.

"I'll go and tell him," another said, and broke from his comrades towards a closed door, only to be called back by another, who told him, "He's in conference—with the mystif," the reply winning a ribald laugh from his fellows.

Turning his spirit's back on the open air, Gentle flew towards the door, passing through it without harm or hesitation. The room beyond was not, as he'd expected, N'ashap's office but an antechamber, occupied by two empty chairs and a bare table. On the wall behind the table hung a painting of a small child, so wretchedly rendered the subject's sex was indeterminate. To the left of the picture, which was signed *Aping,* lay another door, as securely closed as the one he'd just passed through. But there was a voice audible from the far side: Vigor N'ashap, in a little ecstasy.

"Again! Again!" he was saying, then an outpouring in a foreign tongue, followed by cries of "Yes!" and "There! There!"

Gentle went to the door too quickly to prepare himself for what lay on the other side. Even if he had—even if he'd conjured the sight of N'ashap with his breeches down and his Oethac prick purple—he could not have imagined Pie 'oh' pah's condition, given that in all their months together he had never once seen the mystif naked. Now he did, and the shock of its beauty was second only to that of its humiliation. It had a body as serene as its face, and as ambiguous, even in plain sight. There was no hair on any part of it; nor nipples; nor navel. Between its legs, however, which were presently spread as it knelt in front of N'ashap, was the source of its transforming self, the core its couplers touched with thought. It was neither phallic nor vaginal, but a third genital form entirely, fluttering at its groin like an agitated dove and with every flutter reconfiguring its glistening heart, so that Gentle, mesmerized, found a fresh echo in each motion. His own flesh was mirrored there, unfolding as it passed between Dominions. So was the sky above Patashoqua and the sea beyond the shuttered window, turning its solid back to living water. And breath, blown into a closed fist; and the power breaking from it: all there, all there.

N'ashap was disdainful of the sight. Perhaps, in his heat, he didn't even see it. He had the mystif's head clamped between his scarred hands and was pushing the sharp tip of his member into its mouth. The mystif made no objection. Its hands hung by its sides, until N'ashap demanded their attention upon his shaft. Gentle could bear the sight no longer. He pitched his mind across the room towards the Oethac's back. Hadn't he heard Scopique say that thought was power? If so, Gentle thought, I'm a mote, diamond hard. Gentle heard N'ashap gasp with pleasure as he pierced the mystif's throat; then he struck the Oethac's skull. The room disappeared, and hot meat pressed on him from all sides, but his momentum carried him out the other side, and he turned to see N'ashap's hands go from the mystif's head to his own, a shriek of pain coming from his lipless mouth.

Pie's face, slack until now, filled with alarm as blood poured from N'ashap's nostrils. Gentle felt a thrill of satisfaction at the sight, but the mystif rose and went to the officer's assistance, picking up a piece of its own discarded clothing to help staunch the flow. N'ashap twice waved its help away at first, but Pie's pliant voice softened him, and after a time the captain sank back in his cushioned chair and allowed himself to be tended. The mystif's cooings and caresses were almost as distressing to Gentle as the scene he'd just interrupted, and he retreated, confounded and repulsed, first to the door, then through it into the antechamber.

There he lingered, his sight fixed upon Aping's picture. In the room behind him, N'ashap had begun to moan again. The sound drove Gentle out, through the labyrinth and back to his room. Scopique and Aping had laid his body back on the bed. His face was devoid of expression, and one of his arms had slid from his chest and hung off the edge of the boards. He looked dead already. Was it any wonder Pie's devotion had become so mechanical, when all it had before it to inspire hope of recovery was this gaunt mannequin, day in, day out? He drew closer to the body, half tempted never to enter it again, to let it wither and die. But there was too much risk in that. Suppose his present state was conditional upon the continuance of his physical self? Thought without flesh was certainly possible—he'd heard Scopique pronounce on the subject in this very cell— but not, he guessed, for spirits so unevolved as his. Skin, blood, and bone were the school in which the soul learned flight, and he was still too much a fledgling to dare truancy. He had to go, vile as that notion was, back behind the eyes.

He went one more time to the window and looked out at the glittering sea. The sight of its waves beating at the rocks below brought back the terror of his drowning. He felt the living waters squirming around him, pressing at his lips like N'ashap's prick, demanding he open up and swallow. In horror, he turned from the sight and crossed the room at speed, striking his brow like a bullet. Returning into his substance with the images of N'ashap and sea on his mind, he comprehended instantly the nature of his sickness. Scopique had been wrong, all wrong! There was a solid—oh, *so* solid—physiological reason for his inertia. He felt it in his belly now, wretchedly real. He'd swallowed some of the waters and they were still inside him, living, prospering at his expense.

Before intellect could caution him he let his revulsion loose upon his body; threw his demands into each extremity. Move! he told them, move! He fueled his rage with the thought of N'ashap using him as he'd used Pie, imagining the Oethac's semen in his belly. His left hand found power enough to take hold of the bed board, its purchase sufficient to pull him over. He toppled onto his side, then off the bed entirely, hitting the floor hard. The impact dislodged something in the base of his belly. He felt it scrabble to catch hold of his innards again, its motion violent enough to throw him around like a sack full of thrashing fish, each twist unseating the parasite a little more and in turn releasing his body from its tyranny. His joints cracked like walnut shells; his sinews stretched and shortened. It was agony, and he longed to shriek his complaint, but all he could manage was a retching sound. It was still music: the first sound he'd made since the yell he'd given as the Cradle swallowed him up. It was short-lived, however. His wracked system was pushing the parasite up from his stomach. He felt it in his chest, like a meal of hooks he longed to vomit up but could not, for fear he'd turn himself inside out in the attempt. It seemed to know they'd reached an impasse, because its flailing slowed, and he had time to draw a desperate breath through pipes half clogged by its presence. With his lungs as full as he had hope of getting them, he hauled himself up off the ground by clinging to the bed, and before the parasite had time to incapacitate him with a fresh assault he stood to his full height, then threw himself face down. As he hit the ground the thing came up into his throat and mouth in a surge, and he reached between his teeth to snatch it out of him. It came with two pulls, fighting to the end to crawl back down his gullet. It was followed immediately by his last meal.

Gasping for air he dragged himself upright and leaned against the bed, strings of puke hanging from his chin. The thing on the floor flapped and flailed, and he let it suffer. Though it had felt huge when inside him, it was no bigger than his hand: a formless scrap of milky flesh and silver vein with limbs no thicker than string but fully twenty in number. It made no sound, except for the slap its spasms made in the bilious mess on the cell floor.

Too weak to move, Gentle was still slumped against the bed when, some minutes later, Scopique came back to look for Pie. Scopique's astonishment knew no bounds. He called for help, then hoisted Gentle back onto the bed, question following question so fast Gentle barely had breath or energy to answer. But sufficient was communicated for Scopique to berate himself for not grasping the problem earlier.

"I thought it was in your *head*, Zacharias, and all the time—all the time it was in your *belly*. This bastard thing!"

Aping arrived, and there was a new round of questions, answered this time by Scopique, who then went off in search of Pie, leaving the guard to arrange for the filth on the floor to be cleaned up and the patient brought fresh water and clean clothes.

"Is there anything else you need?" Aping wanted to know.

"Food," Gentle said. His belly had never felt emptier.

"It'll be arranged. It's strange to hear your voice and see you move. I got used to you the other way." He smiled. "When you're feeling stronger," he said, "we must find some time to talk. I hear from the mystif you're a painter."

"I was, yes," said Gentle, adding an innocent inquiry. "Why? Are you?"

Aping beamed. "I am," he said.

"Then we must talk," Gentle said. "What do you paint?"

"Landscapes. Some figures."

"Nudes? Portraits?"

"Children."

"Ah, children . . . do you have any yourself?"

A trace of anxiety crossed Aping's face. "Later," he said, glancing out towards the corridor, then back at Gentle. "In private."

"I'm at your disposal," Gentle replied.

There were voices outside the room. Scopique returning with N'ashap, who glanced down into the bucket containing the parasite as he entered. There were more questions, or rather the same rephrased, and answered on this third occasion by both Scopique and Aping. N'ashap listened with only half an ear, studying Gentle as the drama was recounted, then congratulating him with a curious formality. Gentle noted with satisfaction the plugs of dried blood in his nose.

"We must make a full account of this incident to Yzordderrex," N'ashap said. "I'm sure it will intrigue them as much as it does me."

So saying, he left, with an order to Aping that he follow immediately.

"Our commander looked less than well," Scopique observed. "I wonder why."

Gentle allowed himself a smile, but it went from his face at the sight of his final visitor. Pie 'oh' pah had appeared in the door.

"Ah, well!" said Scopique. "Here you are. I'll leave you two alone."

He withdrew, closing the door behind him. The mystif didn't move to embrace Gentle, or even take his hand. Instead it went to the window and gazed out over the sea, upon which the suns were still shining.

"Now we know why they call this the Cradle," it said.

"What do you mean?"

"Where else could a man give birth?"

"That wasn't birth," Gentle said. "Don't flatter it."

"Maybe not to us," Pie said. "But who knows how children were made here in ancient times? Maybe the men immersed themselves, drank the water, let it grow—"

"I saw you," Gentle said.

"I know," Pie replied, not turning from the window. "And you almost lost us both an ally."

"N'ashap? An ally?"

"He's the power here."

"He's an Oethac. And he's scum. And I'm going to have the satisfaction of killing him."

"Are you my champion now?" Pie said, finally looking back at Gentle.

"I saw what he was doing to you."

"That was nothing," Pie replied. "I knew what I was doing. Why do you think we've had the treatment we've had? I've been allowed to see Scopique whenever I want. You've been fed and watered. And N'ashap was asking no questions, about either of us. Now he will. Now he'll be suspicious. We'll have to move quickly before he gets his questions answered."

"Better that than you having to service him."

"I told you, it was nothing."

"It was to me," Gentle said, the words scraping in his bruised throat.

It took some effort, but he got to his feet so as to meet the mystif, eye to eye.

"At the beginning, you talked to me about how you thought you'd hurt me, remember? You kept talking about the station at Mai-ké, and saying you wanted me to forgive you, and I kept thinking there would never be anything between us that couldn't be forgiven or forgotten, and that when I had the words again I'd say so. But now I don't know. He saw you naked, Pie. Why him and not me? I think that's maybe unforgivable, that you granted him the mystery but not me."

"He saw no mystery," Pie replied. "He looked at me, and he saw a woman he'd loved and lost in Yzorddderrex. A woman who looked like his mother, in fact. That's what he was obsessing on. An echo of his mother's echo. And as long as I kept supplying the illusion, discreetly, he was compliant. That seemed more important than my dignity."

"Not any more," Gentle said. "If we're to go from here—together—then I want whatever you are to be mine.

I won't share you, Pie. Not for compliance. Not for life it-self."

"I didn't know you felt like this. If you'd told me—"

"I couldn't. Even before we came here, I felt it, but I couldn't bring myself to say anything."

"For what it's worth, I apologize."

"I don't want an apology."

"What then?"

"A promise. An oath." He paused. "A marriage."

The mystif smiled. "Really?"

"More than anything. I asked you once, and you ac-cepted. Do I need to ask again? I will if you want me to."

"No need," Pie said. "Nothing would honor me more. But here? Here, of all places?" The mystif's frown became a grin. "Scopique told me about a Dearther who's locked up in the basement. He could do the honors."

"What's his religion?"

"He's here because he thinks he's Jesus Christ."

"Then he can prove it with a miracle."

"What miracle's that?"

"He can make an honest man of John Furie Zacharias."

3

The marriage of the Eurhetemec mystif and the fugitive John Furie Zacharias, called Gentle, took place that night in the depths of the asylum. Happily, their priest was pass-ing through a period of lucidity and was willing to be ad-dressed by his real name, Father Athanasius. He bore the evidence of his dementia, however: scars on his forehead, where the crowns of thorns he repeatedly fashioned and wore had dug deep, and scabs on his hands where he'd driven nails into his flesh. He was as fond of the frown as Scopique of the grin, though the look of a philosopher sat badly on a face better suited to a comedian: with its blob nose that perpetually ran, its teeth too widely spread, and eyebrows, like hairy caterpillars, that concertinaed when he furrowed his forehead. He was kept, along with twenty or so other prisoners judged exceptionally seditious, in the deepest part of the asylum, his windowless cell guarded more vigorously than those of the prisoners on higher floors. It had thus taken some fancy maneuvering on Scopique's part to get access to him, and the bribed guard, an Oethac, was only willing to turn a hooded eye for a few minutes. The ceremony was therefore short, conducted in an ad hoc mixture of Latin and English, with a few phrases pronounced in the language of Athanasius' Second Dominion order, the Dearthers, the music of which more than compensated for its unintelligibility. The oaths themselves were necessarily spare, given the constraints of time and the redundance of most of the conventional vocabulary.

"This isn't done in the sight of Hapexamendios," Athanasius said, "nor in the sight of any God, or the agent of any God. We pray that the presence of our Lady may however touch this union with Her infinite compassion, and that you go together into the great union at some higher time. Until then, I can only be as a glass held up to your sacrament, which is performed in your sight for your sake."

The full significance of these words didn't strike Gentle until later, when, with the oaths made and the ceremony done, he lay down in his cell beside his partner.

"I always said I'd never marry," he whispered to the mystif.

"Regretting it already?"

"Not at all. But it's strange to be married and not have a wife."

"You can call me wife. You can call me whatever you want. Reinvent me. That's what I'm for."

"I didn't marry you to use you, Pie."

"That's part of it, though. We must be functions of each other. Mirrors, maybe." It touched Gentle's face. "I'll use *you*, believe me."

"For what?"

"For everything. Comfort, argument, pleasure."

"I do want to learn from you."

"About what?"

"How to fly out of my head again, the way I did this afternoon. How to travel by mind."

"By mote," Pie said, echoing the way Gentle had felt as he'd driven his thoughts through N'ashap's skull. "Meaning: a particle of thought, as seen in sunlight."

"It can only be done in sunlight?"

"No. It's just easier that way. Almost everything's easier in sunlight."

"Except this," Gentle said, kissing the mystif. "I've always preferred the night for this. . . ."

He had come to their marriage bed determined that he would make love with the mystif as it truly was, allowing no fantasy to intrude between his senses and the vision he'd glimpsed in N'ashap's office. That oath made him as nervous as a virgin groom, demanding as it did a double unveiling. Just as he unbuttoned and discarded the clothes that concealed the mystif's essential sex, so he had to tear from his eyes the comfort of the illusions that lay between his sight and its object. What would he feel then? It was easy to be aroused by a creature so totally reconfigured by desire that it was indistinguishable from the thing desired. But what of the configurer itself, seen naked by naked eyes?

In the shadows its body was almost feminine, its planes serene, its surface smooth, but there was an austerity in its sinew he couldn't pretend was womanly; nor were its buttocks lush, or its chest ripe. It was not his wife, and though it was happy to be imagined that way, and his mind teetered over and over on the edge of giving in to such invention, he resisted, demanding his eyes hold to their focus and his fingers to the facts. He began to wish it were lighter in the cell, so as not to give ease to ambiguity. When he put his hand into the shadow between its legs and felt the heat and motion there, he said, "I want to see," and Pie dutifully stood up in the light from the window so that Gentle could have a plainer view. His heart was pumping furiously, but none of the blood was reaching his groin. It was filling his head, making his face burn. He was glad he sat in shadow, where his discomfort was less visible, though he knew that shadow concealed only the outward show, and the mystif was perfectly aware of the fear he felt. He took a deep breath and got up from the bed, crossing to within touching distance of this enigma.

"Why are you doing this to yourself?" Pie asked softly. "Why not let the dreams come?"

"Because I don't want to dream you," he said. "I came on this journey to understand. How can I understand anything if all I look at is illusions?"

"Maybe that's all there is."

"That isn't true," he said simply.

"Tomorrow, then," Pie said, temptingly. "Look plainly tomorrow. Just enjoy yourself tonight. I'm not the reason we're in the Imajica. I'm not the puzzle you came to solve."

"On the contrary," Gentle said, a smile creeping into his voice. "I think maybe you *are* the reason. And the puzzle. I think if we stayed here, locked up together, we could heal the Imajica from what's between us." The smile appeared on his face now. "I never realized that till now. That's why I want to see you clearly, Pie, so there're no lies between us." He put his hand against the mystif's sex. "You could fuck or be fucked with this, right?"

"Yes."

"And you could give birth?"

"I haven't. But it's been known."

"And fertilize?"

"Yes."

"That's wonderful. And is there something else you can do?"

"Like what?"

"It isn't all doer or done to, is it? I know it isn't. There's something else."

"Yes, there is."

"A third way."

"Yes."

"Do it with me, then."

"I can't. You're male, Gentle. You're a fixed sex. It's a physical fact." The mystif put its hand on Gentle's prick, still soft in his trousers. "I can't take this away. You wouldn't want me to." It frowned. "Would you?"

"I don't know. Maybe."

"You don't mean that."

"If it meant finding a way, maybe I do. I've used my dick every way I know how. Maybe it's redundant."

Now it was Pie's turn to smile, but such a fragile smile, as though the unease Gentle had felt now burdened the mystif instead. It narrowed its shining eyes.

"What are you thinking?" Gentle said.

"How you make me a little afraid."

"Of what?"

"Of the pain ahead. Of losing you."

"You're not going to lose me," Gentle said, putting his hand around the back of Pie's neck and stroking the nape with his thumb. "I told you, we could heal the Imajica from here. We're strong, Pie."

The anxiety didn't go from the mystif's face, so Gentle coaxed its face towards his and kissed it, first discreetly, then with an ardor it seemed reluctant to match. Only moments before, sitting on the bed, he'd been the tentative one. Now it was the other way around. He put his hand down to its groin, hoping to distract it from its sadness with caresses. The flesh came to meet his fingers, warm and fluted, trickling into the shallow cup of his palm a moisture his skin drank like liquor. He pressed deeper, feeling the elaboration grow at his touch. There was no hesitation here; no shame or sorrow in this flesh, to keep it from displaying its need, and need had never failed to arouse him. Seeing it on a woman's face was a sure aphrodisiac, and it was no less so now.

He reached up from this play to his belt, unbuckling it with one hand. But before he could take hold of his prick, which was becoming painfully hard, the mystif did so, guiding him inside it with an urgency its face still failed to betray. The bath of its sex soothed his ache, immersing him balls and all. He let out a long sigh of pleasure, his nerve endings—starved of this sensation for months—rioting. The mystif had closed its eyes, its mouth open. He put his tongue hard between its lips, and it responded with a passion he had never seen it manifest before. Its hands wrapped around his shoulders, and in possession of them both it fell back against the wall, so hard the breath went from it into Gentle's throat. He drew it down into his lungs, inciting a hunger for more, which the mystif understood without need of words, inhaling from the heated air between them and filling Gentle's chest as though he were a just-drowned man being pumped back to life. He answered its gift with thrusts, its fluids running freely down the inside of his thighs. It gave him another breath, and another. He drank them all, eating the pleasure off its face in the moments between, the breath received as his prick was given. In this exchange they were both entered and enterer: a hint, perhaps, of the third way Pie had spoken of, the coupling between unfixed forces that could not occur until his manhood had been taken from him. Now, as he worked his prick against the warmth of the mystif's sex, the thought of relinquishing it in pursuit of another sensation seemed ludicrous. There could be nothing better than this; only different.

He closed his eyes, no longer afraid that his imagination would put a memory, or some invented perfection, in Pie's place, only that if he looked at the mystif's bliss too much longer he'd lose all control. What his mind's eye pictured, however, was more potent still: the image of them locked together as they were, inside each other, breath and prick swelling inside each other's skins until they could swell no further. He wanted to warn the mystif that he could hold on no longer, but it seemed to have that news already. It grasped his hair, pulling him off its face, the sting of it just another spur now, and the sobs too, coming out of them both. He let his eyes open, wanting to see its face as he came, and in the time it took for his lashes to unknit, the beauty in front of him became a mirror. It was *his* face he was seeing, *his* body he was holding. The illusion didn't cool him. Quite the reverse. Before the mirror softened into flesh, its glass becoming the sweat on Pie's sweet face, he passed the point of no return, and it was with that image in his eye—his face mingled with the mystif's—that his body unleashed its little torrent. It was, as ever, exquisite and racking, a short delirium followed by a sense of loss he'd never made peace with.

The mystif began to laugh almost before he was finished, and when Gentle drew his first clear breath it was to ask, "What's so funny?"

"The silence," Pie said, suppressing the music so that Gentle could share the joke.

He'd lain here in this cell hour after hour, unable to make a moan, but he'd never heard a silence such as this. The whole asylum was listening, from the depths where Father Athanasius wove his piercing crowns to N'ashap's office, its carpet indelibly marked with the blood his nose had shed. There was not a waking soul who'd not heard their coupling.

"Such a silence," the mystif said.

As it spoke, the hush was broken by the sound of someone yelling in his cell, a rage of loss and loneliness that went on unchecked for the rest of the night, as if to cleanse the gray stone of the joy that had momentarily tainted it.

27

I

If pressed, Jude could have named a dozen men—lovers, suitors, slaves—who'd offered her any prize she set her heart on in return for her affections. She'd taken several up on their largesse. But her requests, extravagant as some of them had been, were as nothing beside the gift she'd asked of Oscar Godolphin. *Show me Yzorderrex,* she'd said, and watched his face fill with trepidation. He'd not refused her out of hand. To have done so would have crushed in a moment the affection growing between them, and he would never have forgiven himself that loss. He listened to her request, then made no further mention of it, hoping, no doubt, she'd let the subject lie.

She didn't, however. The blossoming of a physical relationship between them had cured her of the strange passivity that had afflicted her when they'd first met. She had knowledge of his vulnerability now. She'd seen him wounded. She'd seen him ashamed of his lack of self-control. She'd seen him in the act of love, tender and sweetly perverse. Though her feelings for him remained strong, this new perspective removed the veil of unthinking acceptance from her eyes. Now, when she saw the desire he felt for her—and he several times displayed that desire in the days following their consummation—it was the old Judith, self-reliant and fearless, who watched from behind her smiles; watched and waited, knowing that his devotion empowered her more by the day. The tension between these two selves—the remnants of the compliant mistress his presence had first conjured and the willful, focused woman she'd been (and now was again)—scourged the last dregs of dreaminess from her system, and her appetite for Dominion-hopping returned with fresh intensity. She didn't shrink from reminding him of his promise to her as the days went by, but on the first two occasions he made some polite but spurious excuse so as to avoid talking further about it.

On the third occasion her insistence won her a sigh, and eyes cast to heaven.

"Why is this so important to you?" he asked. "Yzord-derrex is an overpopulated cesspit. I don't know a decent man or woman there who wouldn't prefer to be here in England."

"A week ago you were talking about disappearing there forever. But you couldn't you said, because you'd miss the cricket."

"You've got a good memory."

"I hang on your every word," she said, not without a certain sourness.

"Well, the situation's changed. There's most likely going to be revolution. If we went now, we'd probably be executed on sight."

"You've come and gone often enough in the past," she pointed out. "So have hundreds of others, haven't they? You're not the only one. That's what magic is for: passing between Dominions."

He didn't reply.

"I want to see Yzordderrex, Oscar," she said, "and if you won't take me I'll find a magician who will."

"Don't even joke about it."

"I mean it," she said fiercely. "You can't be the only one who knows the way."

"Near enough."

"There are others. I'll find them if I have to."

"They're all crazy," he told her. "Or dead."

"Murdered?" she said, the word out of her mouth before she'd fully grasped its implication.

The look on his face, however (or rather its absence: the willed blankness), was enough to confirm her suspicion. The bodies she'd seen on the news being carted away from their games were not those of burned-out hippies and sex-crazed satanists. They were possessors of true power, men and women who'd maybe walked where she longed to walk: in the Imajica.

"Who's doing it, Oscar? It's somebody you know, isn't it?"

He got up and crossed to where she sat, his motion so swift she thought for an instant he meant to strike her. But instead he dropped to his knees in front of her, holding her hands tight and staring up at her with almost hypnotic intensity.

"Listen to me carefully," he said. "I have certain familial duties, which I wish to God I didn't have. They make demands upon me I'd willingly shrug off if I could—"

"This is all to do with the tower, isn't it?"

"I'd prefer not to discuss that."

"We *are* discussing it, Oscar."

"It's a very private and a very delicate business. I'm dealing with individuals quite without any sense of morality. If they were to know that I've said even this much to you, both our lives would be in the direst jeopardy. I beg you, never utter another word about this to anyone. I should never have taken you up to the tower."

If its occupants were half as murderous as he was suggesting, she thought, how much more lethal would they be if they knew how many of the tower's secrets she'd seen?

"Promise me you'll let this subject alone," he went on.

"I want to see Yzordderrex, Oscar."

"Promise me. No more talk about the tower, in this house or out of it. *Say it,* Judith."

"All right. I won't talk about the tower."

"In this house—"

"—or out of it. But Oscar—"

"What, sweet?"

"I still want to see Yzordderrex."

2

The morning after this exchange she went up to Highgate. It was another rainy day, and failing to find an unoccupied cab she braved the Underground. It was a mistake. She'd never liked traveling by tube at the best of times—it brought out her latent claustrophobia—but she recalled as she rode that two of those murdered in the spate of killings had died in these tunnels: one pushed in front of a crowded train as it drew into Piccadilly station, the other stabbed to death at midnight, somewhere on the Jubilee Line. This was not a safe way to travel for someone who had even the slightest inkling of the prodigies half hidden in the world; and she was one of those few. So it was with no little relief she stepped out into the open air at Archway station (the clouds had cleared) and started up Highgate Hill on foot. She had no difficulty finding the tower itself, though the banality of its design, together with the shield of trees in full leaf in front of it, meant few eyes were likely to look its way.

Despite the dire warnings issued by Oscar it was difficult to find much intimidating about the place, with the spring sunshine warm enough to make her slip off her jacket, and the grass busy with sparrows quarreling over worms raised by the rain. She scanned the windows, looking for some sign of occupation, but saw none. Avoiding the front door, with its camera trained on the step, she headed down the side of the building, her progress unimpeded by walls or barbed wire. The owners had clearly decided the tower's best defense lay in its utter lack of character, and the less they did to keep trespassers out the fewer would be attracted in the first place. There was even less to see from the back than the front. There were blinds down over most of the windows, and those few that were not covered let onto empty rooms. She made a complete circuit of the tower, looking for some other way into it, but there was none.

As she returned to the front of the building she tried to imagine the passageways buried beneath her feet—the books piled in the darkness, and the imprisoned soul lying in a deeper darkness still—hoping her mind might be able to go where her body could not. But that exercise proved as fruitless as her window-watching. The real world was implacable; it wouldn't shift a particle of soil to let her through. Discouraged, she made one final circuit of the tower, then decided to give up. Maybe she'd come back here at night, she thought, when solid reality didn't insist on her senses so brutally. Or maybe seek another journey under the influence of the blue eye, though this option made her nervous. She had no real grasp of the mechanism by which the eye induced such flights, and she feared giving it power over her. Oscar already had enough of that.

She put her jacket back on and headed away from the tower. To judge by the absence of traffic on Hornsey Lane, the hill—which had been clogged with traffic—was still blocked, preventing drivers from making their way in this direction. The gulf usually filled with the din of vehicles was not empty, however. There were footsteps close behind her; and a voice.

"Who are you?"

She glanced around, not assuming the question was directed at her, but finding that she and the questioner—a woman in her sixties, shabbily dressed and sickly—were the only people in sight. Moreover, the woman's stare was fixed upon her with a near manic intensity. Again, the question, coming from a mouth that had about it a spittle-flecked asymmetry that suggested the speaker had suffered a stroke in the past.

"Who are you?"

Already irritated by her failure at the tower, Judith was in no mood to humor what was plainly the local schizophrenic and was turning on her heel to walk away when the woman spoke again.

"Don't you know they'll hurt you?"

"Who will?" she said.

"The people in the tower. The Tabula Rasa. What were you looking for?"

"Nothing."

"You were looking very hard for nothing."

"Are you spying for them?"

The woman made an ugly sound that Judith took to be a laugh. "They don't even know I'm alive," she said. Then, for the third time, "Who are you?"

"My name's Judith."

"I'm Clara Leash," the woman said. She cast a glance back in the direction of the tower. "Walk on," she said. "There's a church halfway up the hill. I'll meet you there."

"What is all this about?"

"At the church, not here."

So saying, she turned her back on Judith and walked off, her agitation enough to dissuade Judith from following. Two words in their short exchange convinced her she should wait at the church and find out what Clara Leash had to say, however. Those words were *Tabula Rasa*. She hadn't heard them spoken since her conversation with Charlie at the estate, when he'd told her how he'd been passed over for membership in favor of Oscar. He'd made light of it at the time, and much of what he'd said had been blotted from her mind by the violence and the revelations that followed. Now she found herself digging for recollections of what he'd said about the organization. Something about the tainted soil of England, and her saying tainted by what?, and Charlie making some comical reply. Now she knew what that taint was: magic. In that bland tower the lives of the men and women whose bodies had been found in shallow graves or scraped from the rails of the Piccadilly Line had been judged and found corrupt. No wonder Oscar was losing weight and sobbing in his sleep. He was a member of a Society formed for the express purpose of eradicating a second, and diminishing, society, to which he also belonged. For all his self-possession he was the servant of two masters: magic and its despoiler. It fell to her to help him by whatever means she could. She was his lover, and without her aid he would eventually be crushed between contrary imperatives. And he in his turn was her ticket to Yzordderrex, without whom she would never see the glories of the Imajica. They needed each other, alive and sane.

She waited at the church for half an hour before Clara Leash appeared, looking fretful.

"Out here's no good," she said. "Inside."

They stepped into the gloomy building and sat close to the altar so as not to be overheard by the three noontime supplicants who were at their prayers towards the back. It was not an ideal place in which to have a whispered conversation; their sibilance carried even if the sense did not, its echoes coming back to meet them off the bare walls. Nor was there much trust between them to begin with. To defend herself from Clara's glare, Judith spent the early part of their exchange with her back half turned to the woman, only facing her fully when they'd disposed of the circumlocutions and she felt confident enough to ask the question most on her mind.

"What do you know about the Tabula Rasa?"

"Everything there is to know," Clara replied. "I was a member of the Society for many years."

"But they think you're dead?"

"They're not far wrong. I haven't got more than a few months left, which is why it's important I pass along what I know."

"To me?"

"That depends," she said. "First I want to know what
you were doing at the tower."

"I was looking for a way in."

"Have you ever been inside?"

"Yes and no."

"Meaning what?"

"My mind's been inside even though my body hasn't,"
Judith said, fully expecting a repeat of Clara's weird little
laugh in response.

Instead, the woman said, "On the night of December
the thirty-first."

"How the hell did you know that?"

Clara put her hand up to Judith's face. Her fingers were
icy cold. "First, you should know how I departed the
Tabula Rasa."

Though she told her story without embellishments, it
took some time, given that so much of what she was explaining required footnotes for Judith to fully comprehend
its significance. Clara, like Oscar, was the descendant of
one of the Society's founding members and had been
brought up to believe in its basic principles: England,
tainted by magic—indeed, almost destroyed by it—had to
be protected from any cult or individual who sought to educate new generations in its corrupt practices. When Judith
asked how this near destruction had come about, Clara's
answer was a story in itself. Two hundred years ago this
coming midsummer, she explained, a ritual had been attempted that had gone tragically awry. Its purpose had
been to reconcile the reality of earth with those of four
other dimensions.

"The Dominions," Judith said, dropping her voice,
which was already low, lower still.

"Say it out loud," Clara replied. "Dominions! Dominions!" She only raised her voice to speaking volume, but
after such a time whispering it was shockingly loud. "It's
been a secret for too long," she said. "And that gives the
enemy power."

"Who is the enemy?"

"There are so many," she said. "In this Dominion, the

Tabula Rasa and its servants. And it's got plenty of those, believe me, in the very highest places."

"How?"

"It's not difficult, when your members are the descendants of kingmakers. And if influence fails, you can always buy your way past democracy. It's going on all the time."

"And in the other Dominions?"

"Getting information's more difficult, especially now. I knew two women who regularly passed between here and the Reconciled Dominions. One of them was found dead a week ago, the other's disappeared. She may also have been murdered—"

"By the Tabula Rasa."

"You know a good deal, don't you? What's your source?"

Judith had known Clara would ask that question eventually and had been trying to decide how she would answer it. Her belief in Clara Leash's integrity grew apace, but wouldn't it be precipitous to share with a woman she'd taken for a bag lady only two hours before a secret that could be Oscar's death warrant if known to the Tabula Rasa?

"I can't tell you my source," she said. "This person's in great danger as it is."

"And you don't trust me." She raised her hand to ward off any protest. "Don't sweet-talk me!" she said. "You don't trust me, and why should I blame you? But let me ask this: Is this source of yours a man?"

"Yes. Why?"

"You asked me before who the enemy was, and I said the Tabula Rasa. But we've got a more obvious enemy: the opposite sex."

"What?"

"Men, Judith. The destroyers."

"Oh, now wait—"

"There used to be Goddesses throughout the Dominions. Powers that took our sex's part in the cosmic drama. They're all dead, Judith. They didn't just die of old age. They were systematically eradicated by the enemy."

"Ordinary men don't kill Goddesses."

"Ordinary men serve extraordinary men. Extraordinary men get their visions from the Gods. And Gods kill Goddesses."

"That's too simple. It sounds like a school lesson."

"Learn it, then. And if you can, disprove it. I'd like that, truly I would. I'd like to discover that the Goddesses are all in hiding somewhere—"

"Like the woman under the tower?"

For the first time in this dialogue, Clara was lost for words. She simply stared, leaving Jude to fill the silence of her astonishment.

"When I said I've been into the tower in my mind, that isn't strictly true," Jude said. "I've only been *under* the tower. There's a cellar there, like a maze. It's full of books. And behind one of the walls there's a woman. I thought she was dead at first, but she isn't. She's maybe close to it, but she's holding on."

Clara was visibly shaken by this account. "I thought I was the only one who knew she was there," she said.

"More to the point, do you know who she is?"

"I've got a pretty good idea," Clara said, and picked up the story she'd been diverted from earlier: the tale of how she'd come to leave the Tabula Rasa.

The library beneath the tower, she explained, was the most comprehensive collection of manuscripts dealing with the occult sciences—but more particularly the legends and lore of the Imajica—in the world. It had been gathered by the men who'd founded the Society, led by Roxborough and Godolphin, to keep from the hands and minds of innocent Englishmen the stain of things Imajical; but rather than cataloguing the collection—making an index of these forbidden books—generations of the Tabula Rasa had simply left them to fester.

"I took it upon myself to sort through the collection. Believe it or not, I was once a very ordered woman. I got it from my father. He was in the military. At first I was watched by two other members of the Society. That's the law. No member of the Society is allowed into the library alone, and if any one judges either of the other two to be in any way unduly interested or influenced by the volumes, they can be tried by the Society and executed. I don't think it's ever been done. Half the books are in Latin, and who reads Latin? The other half—you've seen for yourself— they're rotting on their spines, like all of us. But I wanted order, the way Daddy would have liked it. Everything neat and tidy.

"My companions soon got tired of my obsession and left me to it. And in the middle of the night I felt something . . . or somebody . . . pulling at my thoughts, plucking them out of my scalp one by one, like hairs. Of course I thought it was the books, at first. I thought the words had got some power over me. I tried to leave, but you know I really didn't want to. I'd been Daddy's repressed little daughter for fifty years, and I was about ready to crack. Celestine knew it too—"

"Celestine is the woman in the wall?"

"I believe it's her, yes."

"But you don't know who she is?"

"I'm coming to that," Clara said. "Roxborough's house stood on the land where the tower now stands. The cellar is the cellar of that house. Celestine was—indeed, still is— Roxborough's prisoner. He walled her up because he didn't dare kill her. She'd seen the face of Hapexamendios, the God of Gods. She was insane, but she'd been touched by divinity, and even Roxborough didn't dare lay a finger on her."

"How do you know all this?"

"Roxborough wrote a confession, a few days before he died. He knew the woman he'd walled up would outlive him by centuries, and I suppose he also knew that sooner or later somebody would find her. So the confession was also a warning to whatever poor, victimized man came along, telling him that she was not to be touched. *Bury her again,* he said, I remember that very clearly. *Bury her again, in the deepest abyss your wits may devise—*"

"Where did you find this confession?"

"In the wall, that night when I was alone. I believe

Celestine led me to it, by plucking thoughts out of my head and putting new ones in. But she plucked too hard. My mind gave up. I had a stroke down there. I wasn't found for three days."

"That's horrible—"

"My suffering's nothing compared to hers. Roxborough had found this woman in London, or his spies had, and he knew she was a creature of immense power. He probably realized it more clearly than she did, in fact, because he says in the confession she was a stranger to herself. But she'd seen sights no other human being had ever witnessed. She'd been snatched from the Fifth Dominion, escorted across the Imajica, and taken into the presence of Hapexamendios."

"Why?"

"It gets stranger. When he interrogated her, she told him she'd been brought back into the Fifth Dominion pregnant."

"She was having God's child?"

"That's what she told Roxborough."

"She could have been inventing it all, just to keep him from hurting her."

"I don't think he'd have done that. In fact I think he was half in love with her. He said in the confession he felt like his friend Godolphin. *I'm broken by a woman's eye,* he wrote."

"That's an odd phrase," Jude thought, thinking of the stone as she did so: its stare, its authority.

"Well, Godolphin died obsessing on some mistress he'd loved and lost, claiming he'd been destroyed by her. The men were always the innocents, you see. Victims of female connivings. I daresay Roxborough'd persuaded himself that walling Celestine up was an act of love. Keeping her under his thumb forever."

"What happened to the child?" Judith said.

"Maybe she can tell us herself," Clara replied.

"Then we have to get her out."

"Indeed."

"Do you have any idea how?"

"Not yet," Clara said. "Until you appeared I was ready to despair. But between the two of us we'll find some way to save her."

It was getting late, and Jude was anxious that her absence not be noted, so the plans they laid were sketchy in the extreme. A further examination of the tower was clearly in order, this time—Clara proposed—under cover of darkness.

"Tonight," she suggested.

"No, that's too soon. Give me a day to make up some excuse for being out for the night."

"Who's the watchdog?" Clara said.

"Just a man."

"Suspicious?"

"Sometimes."

"Well, Celestine's waited a long time to be set free. She can wait another twenty-four hours. But please, no longer. I'm not a well woman."

Jude put her hand over Clara's hand, the first contact between them since the woman had touched her icy fingers to Jude's cheek. "You're not going to die," she said.

"Oh, yes, I am. It's no great hardship. But I want to see Celestine's face before I leave."

"We will," Judith said. "If not tomorrow night, soon after."

3

She didn't believe what Clara had said about men pertained to Oscar. He was no destroyer of Goddesses, either by hand or proxy. But Dowd was another matter entirely. Though his façade was civilized—almost prissy at times—she would never forget the casual way he'd disposed of the voiders' bodies, warming his hands at the pyre as though they were branches, not bones, that were cracking in the flames. And, as bad luck would have it, Dowd was back at the house when she returned, and Oscar was not, so it was his questions she was obliged to answer if she wasn't to arouse his suspicions with silence. When he asked her what she'd done with the day, she told him she'd gone out for a long walk along the Embankment. He then inquired as to whether the tube had been crowded, though she'd not told him she'd traveled that way. She said it was. You should take a cab next time, he said. Or, better still, allow me to drive you. I'm certain Mr. Godolphin would prefer you to travel in comfort, he said. She thanked him for his kindness. Will you be planning other trips soon? he asked. She had her story for the following evening already prepared, but Dowd's manner never failed to throw her off balance, and she was certain any lie she told now would be instantly spotted, so she said she didn't know, and he let the subject drop.

Oscar didn't come home until the middle of the night, slipping into bed beside her as gently as his bulk allowed. She pretended to wake. He murmured a few words of apology for stirring her, and then some of love. Feigning a sleepy tone, she told him she was going to see her friend Clem tomorrow night, and did he mind? He told her she should do whatever she wanted, but keep her beautiful body for him. Then he kissed her shoulder and neck and fell asleep.

She had arranged to meet Clara at eight in the evening, outside the church, but she left for that rendezvous two hours before in order to go via her old flat. She didn't know what place in the scheme of things the carved blue eye had, but she'd decided the night before that it should be with her when they made their attempt to liberate Celestine.

The flat felt cold and neglected, and she spent only a few minutes there, first retrieving the eye from her wardrobe, then quickly leafing through the mail—most of it junk— that had arrived since she'd last visited. These tasks completed, she set out for Highgate, taking Dowd's advice and hailing a taxi to do so. It delivered her to the church twenty-five minutes early, only to find that Clara was already there.

"Have you eaten, my girl?" Clara wanted to know.

Jude told her she had.

"Good," Clara said. "We'll need all our strength tonight."

"Before we go any further," Jude said, "I want to show you something. I don't know what use it can be to us, but I think you ought to see it." She brought the parcel of cloth out of her bag. "Remember what you said about Celestine plucking the thoughts out of your head?"

"Of course."

"This is what did the same to me."

She began to unwrap the eye, a subtle tremor in her fingers as she did so. Four months and more had passed since she'd hidden it away with such superstitious care but her memory of its effect was undimmed, and she half expected it to exercise some power now. It did nothing, though; it lay in the folds of its covering, looking so unremarkable she was almost embarrassed to have made such a show of unveiling it. Clara, however, stared at it with a smile on her lips.

"Where did you get this?" she said.

"I'd rather not say."

"This is no time for secrets," Clara snapped. "How did you come by it?"

"It was given to my husband. My ex-husband."

"Who by?"

"His brother."

"And who's his brother?"

She took a deep breath, undecided even as she drew it whether she'd expel it again as truth or fabrication.

"His name's Oscar Godolphin," she said.

At this reply Clara physically retreated from Judith, almost as though this name was proof of the plague.

"Do you *know* Oscar Godolphin?" she said, her tone appalled.

"Yes, I do."

"Is he the watchdog?" she said.

"Yes, he is."

"Cover it up," she said, shunning the eye now. "Cover it up and put it away." She turned her back on Judith, running her crabbed hands through her hair. "You and Godolphin?'' she said, half to herself. "What does that mean? What does that mean?"

"It doesn't mean anything," Jude said. "What I feel for him and what we're doing now are completely different issues."

"Don't be naïve," Clara replied, glancing back at Jude. "Godolphin's a member of the Tabula Rasa, and a man. You and Celestine are both women, and his prisoners—"

"I'm not his prisoner," Jude said, infuriated by Clara's condescension. "I do what I want when I want."

"Until you defy history," Clara said. "Then you'll see how much he thinks he owns you." She approached Jude again, taking her voice down to a pained whisper. "Understand this," she said. "You can't save Celestine and keep his affections. You're going to be digging at the very foundations—literally, the foundations—of his family and his faith, and when he finds out—and he will, when the Tabula Rasa starts to crumble—whatever's between you will mean nothing. We're not another sex, Judith, we're another species. What's going on in our bodies and our heads isn't remotely like what's going on in theirs. Our hells are different. So are our heavens. We're *enemies,* and you can't be on both sides in a war."

"It isn't war," Jude said. "If it was war I'd be angry, and I've never been calmer."

"We'll see how calm you are, when you see how things really stand."

Jude took another deep breath. "Maybe we should stop arguing and do what we came to do," she said. Clara looked at her balefully. "I think stubborn bitch is the phrase you're looking for," Jude remarked.

"I never trust the passive ones," Clara said, betraying a trace of admiration.

"I'll remember that."

The tower was in darkness, and the trees clogged the lamplight from the street, leaving the forecourt shadowy and the route down the flank of the building virtually lightless. Clara had obviously wandered here by night many times, however, because she went with confidence, leaving Jude to trail, snared by the brambles and stung by the nettles it had been easy to avoid in the sunshine. By the time she reached the back of the tower, her eyes were better accustomed to the murk and found Clara standing twenty yards from the building, staring at the ground.

"What are you doing back here?" Jude said. "We know there's only one way in."

"Barred and bolted," she said. "I'm thinking there may be some other entrance to the cellar under the turf, even if it's only a ventilation pipe. The first thing we should do is locate Celestine's cell."

"How do we do that?"

"We use the eye that took you traveling," Clara said. "Come on, come on, give it over."

"I thought it was too tainted to be touched."

"Not at all."

"The way you looked at it . . ."

"It's loot, my girl. That's what repulsed me. It's a piece of women's history traded between two men."

"I'm sure Oscar didn't know what it was," she said, thinking even as she defended him that this was probably untrue.

"It belongs to a great temple—"

"He certainly doesn't loot temples," Jude said, taking the contentious item from her pocket.

"I'm not saying he does," Clara replied. "The temples were brought down long before the line of the Godolphins was even founded. Well, are you going to hand it over or not?"

Jude unwrapped the eye, discovering in herself a reluctance to share it she hadn't anticipated. It was no longer as unremarkable as it had been. It gave off a subtle luminescence, blue and steady, by which she and Clara could see each other, albeit faintly.

Their gazes met, the eye's light gleaming between them like the glance of a third conspirator, a woman wiser than them both, whose presence—despite the dull murmur of traffic, and jets droning through the clouds above—exalted the moment. Jude found herself wondering how many women had gathered in the glow of this light or its like down the ages: gathered to pray, or make sacrifice, or shelter from the destroyer. Countless numbers, no doubt, dead and forgotten but, in this brief time out of time, reclaimed from anonymity; not named, but at least acknowledged by these new acolytes. She looked away from Clara, towards the eye. The solid world around her suddenly seemed irrelevant—at best a game of veils, at worst a trap in which the spirit struggled and, struggling, gave credence to the lie. There was no need to be bound by its rules. She could fly beyond it with a thought. She looked up again to confirm that Clara was also ready to move, but her companion was glancing out of the circle, towards the corner of the tower.

"What is it?" Jude said, following the direction of Clara's gaze. Somebody was approaching them through the darkness, in the walk a nonchalance she could name in a syllable: "Dowd."

"You know him?" Clara said.

"A little," Dowd said, his voice as casual as his gait. "But really, there's so much she doesn't know."

Clara's hands dropped from Jude's, breaking the charm of three.

"Don't come any closer," Clara said.

Surprisingly, Dowd stopped dead in his tracks, a few yards from the women. There was sufficient light from the eye for Jude to pick out his face. Something, or things, seemed to be crawling around his mouth, as though he'd just eaten a handful of ants and a few had escaped from between his lips.

"I would so love to kill you both," he said, and with the words further mites escaped and ran over his cheeks and chin. "But your time will come, Judith. Very soon. For now, it's just Clara. . . . It *is* Clara, isn't it?"

"Go to hell, Dowd," Jude said.

"Step away from the old woman," Dowd replied.

Jude's response was to take hold of Clara's arm. "You're not going to hurt anybody, you little shit," she said.

There was a fury rising in her the like of which she'd not felt in months. The eye was heavy in her hand; she was ready to brain the bastard with it if he took a step towards them.

"Did you not understand me, whore?" he said, moving towards her as he did so. "I told you: Step *away!*"

In her rage she went to meet his approach, raising her weighted hand as she did so, but in the instant that she let go of Clara he sidestepped her, and she lost sight of him. Realizing that she'd done exactly as he'd planned, she reeled around, intending to take hold of Clara again. But he was there before her. She heard a shout of horror and saw Clara staggering away from her attacker. The mites were at her face already, blinding her. Jude ran to catch hold of her before she fell, but this time Dowd moved towards her, not away, and with a single blow struck the stone from Jude's hand. She didn't turn to reclaim it but went to Clara's aid. The woman's moans were terrible; so were the tremors in her body.

"What have you done to her?" she yelled at Dowd.

"Undone, lovely, undone. Let her be. You can't help her now."

Clara's body was light, but when her legs buckled she carried Jude down with her. Her moans had become howls now, as she reached up to her face as if to scratch out her eyes, for there the mites were at some agonizing work. In desperation Jude tried to feel for the creatures in the darkness, but either they were too fast for her fingers or they'd gone where fingers couldn't follow. All she could do was beg for a reprieve.

"Make them stop," she said to Dowd. "Whatever you want, I'll do, but *please* make them stop."

"They're voracious little sods, aren't they?" he said.

He was crouching in front of the eye, the blue light illuminating his face, which wore a mask of chilling serenity. As she watched he picked mites from around his mouth and let them drop to the ground.

"I'm afraid they've got no ears, so I can't call them back," he said. "They only know how to *unmake*. And they'll unmake anything but their maker. In this case, that's me. So I'd leave her alone, if I were you. They're indiscriminate."

She turned her attention back to the woman in her arms. Clara had given up scratching at her eyes, and the tremors in her body were rapidly diminishing.

"Speak to me," Jude said. She reached for Clara's face, a little ashamed of how tentative Dowd's warning had made her.

There was no answer from the body, unless there were words in Clara's dying moans. Jude listened, hoping to find some vestigial sense there, but there was none. She felt a single spasm pass down Clara's spine, as though something in her head had snapped, and then the whole system stopped dead. From the moment when Dowd had first appeared, perhaps ninety seconds had passed. In that time every hope that had gathered here had been undone. She wondered if Celestine had heard this tragedy unfold, another's suffering adding to her own sum.

"Dead, then, lovey," Dowd said.

Jude let Clara's body slip from her arms into the grass.

"We should be going," he went on, his tone so bland they might have been forsaking a picnic instead of a corpse. "Don't worry about Clara. I'll fetch what's left of her later."

She heard the sound of his feet behind her and stood up, rather than be touched by him. Overhead, another jet was roaring in the clouds. She looked towards the eye, but it too had been unmade.

"Destroyer," she said.

28

I

Gentle had forgotten his short exchange with Aping about their shared enthusiasm for painting, but Aping had not. The morning after the wedding in Athanasius' cell, the sergeant came to fetch Gentle and escorted him to a room at the other end of the building, which he had turned into a studio. It had plenty of windows, so the light was as good as this region was ever likely to supply, and he had gathered over the months of his posting here an enviable selection of materials. The products of this workplace were, however, those of the most uninspired dilettante. Designed without compositional skill and painted without sense of color, their only real point of interest lay in their obsessiveness. There were, Aping proudly told Gentle, one hundred and fifty-three pictures, and their subject was unchanging: his child, Huzzah, the merest mention of whom had caused the loving portraitist such unease. Now, in the privacy of his place of inspiration, he explained why. His daughter was young, he said, and her mother dead; he'd been obliged to bring her with him when orders from Iahmandhas moved him to the Cradle.

"I could have left her in L'Himby," he told Gentle. "But who knows what kind of harm she'd have come to if I'd done that? She's a child."

"So she's here on the island?"

"Yes, she is. But she won't step out of her room in the daytime. She's afraid of catching the madness, she says. I love her very much. And as you can see"—he indicated the paintings—"she's very beautiful."

Gentle was obliged to take the man's word for it. "Where is she now?" he asked.

"Where she always is," Aping said. "In her room. She has very strange dreams."

"I know how she feels," Gentle said.

"Do you?" Aping replied, with a fervor in his voice that suggested that art was not, after all, the subject Gentle had been brought here to debate. "You dream too, then?"

"Everybody does."

"That's what my wife used to tell me." He lowered his voice. "She had prophetic dreams. She knew when she was going to die, to the very hour. But I don't dream at all. So I can't share what Huzzah feels."

"Are you suggesting that maybe I could?"

"This is a very delicate matter," Aping said. "Yzordderrexian law prohibits all prophetics."

"I didn't know that."

"Especially women, of course," Aping went on. "That's the real reason I keep her out of sight. It's true, she fears the madness, but I'm afraid for what's inside her even more."

"Why?"

"I'm afraid if she keeps company with anyone but me she'll say something out of turn, and N'ashap will realize she has visions like her mother."

"And that would be—"

"Disastrous! My career would be in tatters. I should never have brought her." He looked up at Gentle. "I'm only telling you this because we're both artists, and artists have to trust each other, like brothers, isn't that right?"

"That's right," said Gentle. Aping's large hands were trembling, he saw. The man looked to be on the verge of collapse. "Do you want me to speak to your daughter?" he asked.

"More than that . . ."

"Tell me."

"I want you to take her with you, when you and the mystif leave. Take her to Yzordderrex."

"What makes you think we're going there—or anywhere, come to that?"

"I have my spies, and so does N'ashap. Your plans are better known than you'd like. Take her with you, Mr. Zacharias. Her mother's parents are still alive. They'll look after her."

"It's a big responsibility to take a child all that way."

Aping pursed his lips. "I would of course be able to ease your departure from the island, if you were to take her."

"Suppose she won't go?" Gentle said.

"You must persuade her," he said simply, as though he knew Gentle had long experience of persuading little girls to do what he wanted.

Nature had played Huzzah Aping three cruel tricks. One, it had lent her powers that were expressly forbidden under the Autarch's regime; two, it had given her a father who, despite his sentimental dotings, cared more for his military career than for her; and, three, it had given her a face that only a father could ever have described as beautiful. She was a thin, troubled creature of nine or ten, her black hair cut comically, her mouth tiny and tight. When, after much cajoling, those lips deigned to speak, her voice was wan and despairing. It was only when Aping told her that her visitor was the man who'd fallen into the sea and almost died that her interest was sparked.

"You went down into the Cradle?" she said.

"Yes, I did," Gentle replied, coming to the bed on which she sat, her arms wrapped around her knees.

"Did you see the Cradle Lady?" the girl said.

"See who?" Aping started to hush her, but Gentle waved him into silence. "See who?" he said again.

"She lives in the sea," Huzzah said. "I dream about her—and I hear her sometimes—but I haven't seen her yet. I want to see her."

"Does she have a name?" Gentle asked.

"Tishalullé," Huzzah replied, pronouncing the run of the syllables without hesitation. "That's the sound the waves made when she was born," she explained. "Ti-shalullé."

"That's a lovely name."

"I think so," the girl said gravely. "Better than Huzzah."

"Huzzah's pretty too," Gentle replied. "Where I come

from, Huzzah's the noise people make when they're happy."

She looked at him as though the idea of happiness was utterly alien to her, which Gentle could believe. Now he saw Aping in his daughter's presence, he better understood the paradox of the man's response to her. He was frightened of the girl. Her illegal powers upset him for his reputation's sake, certainly, but they also reminded him of a power he had no real mastery over. The man painted Huzzah's fragile face over and over as an act of perverse devotion, perhaps, but also of exorcism. Nor was the child much better served by her gift. Her dreams condemned her to this cell and filled her with obscure longings. She was more their victim than their celebrant.

Gentle did his best to draw from her a little more information on this woman Tishalullé, but she either knew very little or was unprepared to vouchsafe further insights in her father's presence. Gentle suspected the latter. As he left, however, she asked him quietly if he would come and visit her again, and he said he would.

He found Pie in their cell, with a guard on the door. The mystif looked grim.

"N'ashap's revenge," it said, nodding towards the guard. "I think we've outstayed our welcome."

Gentle recounted his conversation with Aping and the meeting with Huzzah.

"So the law prohibits prophetics, does it? That's a piece of legislation I hadn't heard about."

"The way she talked about the Cradle Lady—"

"Her mother, presumably."

"Why do you say that?"

"She's frightened and she wants her mother. Who can blame her? And what's a Cradle Lady if not a mother?"

"I hadn't thought of it that way," Gentle said. "I'd supposed there might be some literal truth to what she was saying."

"I doubt it."

"Are we going to take her with us or not?"

"It's your choice, of course, but I say absolutely not."

"Aping said he'd help us if we took her."

"What's his help worth, if we're burdened with a child? Remember, we're not going alone. We've got to get Scopique out too, and he's confined to his cell the way we are. N'ashap has ordered a general clamp-down."

"He must be pining for you."

Pie made a sour face. "I'm certain our descriptions are on their way to his headquarters even now. And when he gets an answer he's going to be a very happy Oethac, knowing he's got a couple of desperadoes under lock and key. We'll *never* get out once he knows who we are."

"So we have to escape before he realizes. I just thank God the telephone never made it to this Dominion."

"Maybe the Autarch banned it. The less people talk, the less they can plot. You know, I think maybe I should try and get access to N'ashap. I'm sure I could persuade him to give us a freer rein, if I could just talk with him for a few minutes."

"He's not interested in conversation, Pie," Gentle said. "He'd prefer to keep your mouth busy some other way."

"So you simply want to fight your way out?" Pie replied. "Use pneuma against N'ashap's men?"

Gentle paused to think this option through. "I don't think that'd be too clever," he said. "Not with me still weak. In a couple of days, maybe we could take them on. But not yet."

"We don't have that long."

"I realize that."

"And even if we did, we'd be better avoiding a face-to-face conflict. N'ashap's troops may be lethargic, but there's a good number of them."

"Perhaps you *should* see him, then, and try to mellow him a little. I'll talk to Aping and praise his pictures some more."

"Is he any good?"

"Put it this way: As a painter he makes a damn fine father. But he trusts me, with us being fellow artists and all."

The mystif got up and called to the guard, requesting a

private interview with Captain N'ashap. The man mumbled something smutty and left his post, having first beaten the bolts on the door with his rifle butt to be certain they were firmly in place. The sound drove Gentle to the window, to stare out at the open air. There was a brightness in the cloud layer that suggested the suns might be on their way through. The mystif joined him, slipping its arms around his neck.

"What are you thinking?" it said.

"Remember Efreet's mother, in Beatrix?"

"Of course."

"She told me she'd dreamt about me coming to sit at her table, though she wasn't certain whether I'd be a man or a woman."

"Naturally you were deeply offended."

"I would have been once," Gentle said. "But it didn't mean that much when she said it. After a few weeks with you, I didn't give a shit what sex I was. See how you've corrupted me?"

"My pleasure. Is there any more to this story, or is that it?"

"No, there's more. She started talking about Goddesses, I remember. About how they were hidden away. . . ."

"And you think Huzzah's found one?"

"We saw acolytes in the mountains, didn't we? Why not a Deity? Maybe Huzzah did go dreaming for her mother . . ."

". . . but instead she found a Goddess."

"Yes. Tishalullé, out there in the Cradle, waiting to rise."

"You like the idea, don't you?"

"Of hidden Goddesses? Oh, yes. Maybe it's just the woman chaser in me. Or maybe I'm like Huzzah, waiting for someone I can't remember, wanting to see some face or other, come to fetch me away."

"I'm already here," Pie said, kissing the back of Gentle's neck. "Every face you ever wanted."

"Even a Goddess?"

"Ah—"

The sound of the bolts being drawn aside silenced them. The guard had returned with the news that Captain N'ashap had consented to see the mystif.

"If you see Aping," Gentle said as it left, "will you tell him I'd love to sit and talk painting with him?"

"I'll do that."

They parted, and Gentle returned to the window. The clouds had thickened their defenses against the suns, and the Cradle lay still and empty again beneath their blanket. Gentle said again the name Huzzah had shared with him, the word that was shaped like a breaking wave.

"Tishalullé."

The sea remained motionless. Goddesses didn't come at a call. At least, not his.

He was just estimating the time that Pie had been away—and deciding it was an hour or more—when Aping appeared at the cell door, dismissing the guard from his post while he talked.

"Since when have you been under lock and key?" he asked Gentle.

"Since this morning."

"But why? I understood from the captain that you and the mystif were guests, after a fashion."

"We were."

A twitch of anxiety passed over Aping's features. "If you're a prisoner here," he said stiffly, "then of course the situation's changed."

"You mean we won't be able to debate painting?"

"I mean you won't be leaving."

"What about your daughter?"

"That's academic now."

"You'll let her languish, will you? You'll let her die?"

"She won't die."

"I think she will."

Aping turned his back on his tempter. "The law is the law," he said.

"I understand," Gentle replied softly. "Even artists have to bow to that master, I suppose."

"I understand what you're doing," Aping said. "Don't think I don't."

"She's a child, Aping."

"Yes. I know. But I'll have to tend to her as best I can."

"Why don't you ask her whether she's seen her own death?"

"Oh, Jesu," Aping said, stricken. He began to shake his head. "Why must this happen to me?"

"It needn't. You can save her."

"It isn't so clear-cut," Aping said, giving Gentle a harried look. "I have my duty."

He took a handkerchief from his trouser pocket and wiped hard at his mouth, back and forth, as though a residue of guilt clung there and he was afraid it would give him away.

"I have to think," he said, going back to the door. "It seemed so easy. But now . . . I have to think."

The guard was at his post again when the door opened, and Gentle was obliged to let the sergeant go without having the chance to broach the subject of Scopique.

There was further frustration when Pie returned. N'ashap had kept the mystif waiting two hours and had finally decided not to grant the promised interview.

"I heard him even if I didn't see him," Pie said. "He sounded to be roaring drunk."

"So both of us were out of luck. I don't think Aping's going to help us. If the choice is between his daughter and his duty he'll choose his duty."

"So we're stuck here."

"Until we plot another plot."

"Shit."

2

Night fell without the suns appearing again, the only sound throughout the building that of the guards proceeding up and down the corridors, bringing food to the cells, then slamming and locking the doors until dawn. Not a single voice was raised to protest the fact that the privileges of the evening—games of Horsebone, recitations of scenes from Quexos, and Malbaker's *Numbubo,* works many here knew by heart—had been withdrawn. There was a universal reluctance to make a peep, as if each man, alone in his cell, was prepared to forgo every comfort, even that of praying aloud, to keep themselves from being noticed.

"N'ashap must be dangerous when drunk," Pie said, by way of explanation for this breathless hush.

"Maybe he's fond of midnight executions."

"I'd take a bet on who's top of his list."

"I wish I felt stronger. If they come for us, we'll fight, right?"

"Of course," Pie said. "But until they do, why don't you sleep for a while?"

"You must be kidding."

"At least stop pacing about."

"I've never been locked up by anybody before. It makes me claustrophobic."

"One pneuma and you could be out of here," Pie reminded him.

"Maybe that's what we should be doing."

"If we're pressed. But we're not yet. For Christ's sake, lie down."

Reluctantly, Gentle did so, and despite the anxieties that lay down beside him to whisper in his ear, his body was more interested in rest than their company, and he quickly fell asleep.

He was woken by Pie, who murmured, "You've got a visitor."

He sat up. The cell's light had been turned off, and had it not been for the smell of oil paint he'd not have known the identity of the man at the door.

"Zacharias. I need your help."

"What's wrong?"

"Huzzah is . . . I think she's going crazy. You've got to come." His whispering voice trembled. So did the hand he laid on Gentle's arm. "I think she's dying," he said.

"If I go, Pie comes too."

"No, I can't take that risk."

"And I can't take the risk of leaving my friend here," Gentle said.

"And I can't take the risk of being found out. If there isn't somebody in the cell when the guard passes—"

"He's right," said Pie. "Go on. Help the child."

"Is that wise?"

"Compassion's always wise."

"All right. But stay awake. We haven't said our prayers yet. We need both our breaths for that."

"I understand."

Gentle slipped out into the passage with Aping, who winced at every click the key made as he locked the door. So did Gentle. The thought of leaving Pie alone in the cell sickened him. But there seemed to be no other choice.

"We may need a doctor's help," Gentle said as they crept down the darkened corridors. "I suggest you fetch Scopique from his cell."

"Is he a doctor?"

"He certainly is."

"It's you she's asking for," Aping said. "I don't know why. She just woke up, sobbing and begging me to fetch you. She's so cold!"

With Aping's knowledge of how regularly each floor and passageway was patrolled to aid them, they reached Huzzah's cell without encountering a single guard. The girl wasn't lying on her bed, as Gentle had expected, but was crouched on the floor, with her head and hands pressed against one of the walls. A single wick burned in a bowl in the middle of the cell, her face unwarmed by its light. Though she registered their appearance with a glance, she didn't move from the wall, so Gentle went to where she was crouching and did the same. Shudders passed through her body, though her bangs were plastered to her brow with sweat.

"What can you hear?" Gentle asked her.

"She's not in my dreams any more, Mr. Zacharias," she said, pronouncing his name with precision, as though the proper naming of the forces around her would offer her some little control over them.

"Where is she?" Gentle inquired.

"She's outside. I can hear her. Listen."

He put his head to the wall. There was indeed a murmur in the stone, though he guessed its source was either the asylum's generator or its furnace rather than the Cradle Lady.

"Do you hear?"

"Yes, I hear."

"She wants to come in," Huzzah said. "She tried to come in through my dreams, but she couldn't, so now she's coming through the wall."

"Maybe . . . we should move away then," Gentle said, reaching to put his hand on the girl's shoulder. She was icy. "Come on, let me take you back to bed. You're cold."

"I was in the sea," she said, allowing Gentle to put his arms around her and draw her to her feet.

He looked towards Aping and mouthed the word *Scopique*. Seeing his daughter's frailty, the sergeant went from the door as obediently as a dog, leaving his Huzzah clinging to Gentle. He set her down on the bed and wrapped a blanket around her.

"The Cradle Lady knows you're here," Huzzah said.

"Does she?"

"She told me she almost drowned you, but you wouldn't let her."

"Why would she want to do that?"

"I don't know. You'll have to ask her, when she comes in."

"You're not afraid of her?"

"Oh, no. Are you?"

"Well, if she tried to drown me—"

"She won't do that again, if you stay with me. She likes me, and if she knows I like you she won't hurt you."

"That's good to know," Gentle said. "What would she think if we were to leave here tonight?"

"We can't do that."

"Why not?"

"I don't want to go up there," she said. "I don't like it."

"Everybody's asleep," he said. "We could just tiptoe

away. You and me and my friends. That wouldn't be so bad, would it?" She looked unpersuaded. "I think your papa would like us to go to Yzordderrex. Have you ever been there?"

"When I was very little."

"We could go again."

Huzzah shook her head. "The Cradle Lady won't let us," she said.

"She might, if she knew that was what you wanted. Why don't we go up and have a look?"

Huzzah glanced back towards the wall, as if she was expecting Tishalullé's tide to crack the stone there and then. When nothing happened, she said, "Yzordderrex is a very long way, isn't it?"

"It's quite a journey, yes."

"I've read about it in my books."

"Why don't you put on some warm clothes?" Gentle said.

Her doubts banished by the tacit approval of the Goddess, Huzzah got up and went to select some clothes from her meager wardrobe, which hung from hooks on the opposite wall. Gentle took the opportunity to glance through the small stack of books at the end of the bed. Several were entertainments for children, keepsakes, perhaps, of happier times; one was a hefty encyclopedia by someone called Maybellome, which might have made informative reading under other circumstances but was too densely printed to be skimmed and too heavy to be taken along. There was a volume of poems that read like nonsense rhymes, and what appeared to be a novel, Huzzah's place in it marked with a slip of paper. He pocketed it when her back was turned, as much for himself as her, then went to the door in the hope that Aping and Scopique were within sighting distance. There was no sign. Huzzah had meanwhile finished dressing.

"I'm ready," she said. "Shall we go? Papa will find us."

"I hope so," Gentle replied.

Certainly remaining in the cell was a waste of valuable time. Huzzah asked if she could take Gentle's hand, to which he said of course, and together they began to thread their way through the passageways, all of which looked bewilderingly alike in the semidarkness. Their progress was halted several times when the sound of boots on stone announced the proximity of guards, but Huzzah was as alive to their danger as Gentle and twice saved them from discovery.

And then, as they climbed the final flight of stairs that would bring them out into the open air, a din erupted not far from them. They both froze, drawing back into the shadows, but they weren't the cause of the commotion. It was N'ashap's voice that came echoing along the corridor, accompanied by a dreadful hammering. Gentle's first thought was of Pie, and before common sense could intervene he'd broken cover and was heading towards the source of the sound, glancing back once to signal that Huzzah should stay where she was, only to find that she was already on his heels. He recognized the passageway ahead. The open door twenty yards from where he stood was the door of the cell he'd left Pie in. And it was from there that the sound of N'ashap's voice emerged, a garbled stream of insults and accusations that was already bringing guards running. Gentle drew a deep breath, preparing for the violence that was surely inevitable now.

"No further," he told Huzzah, then raced towards the open door.

Three guards, two of them Oethacs, were approaching from the opposite direction, but only one of the two had his eyes on Gentle. The man shouted an order which Gentle didn't catch over N'ashap's cacophony, but Gentle raised his arms, open-palmed, fearful that the man would be trigger-happy, and at the same time slowed his run to a walk. He was within ten paces of the door, but the guards were there ahead of him. There was a brief exchange with N'ashap, during which Gentle had time to halve the distance between himself and the door, but a second order—this time plainly a demand that he stand still, backed up by the guard's training his weapon at Gentle's heart—brought him to a halt.

He'd no sooner done so than N'ashap emerged from the cell, with one hand in Pie's ringlets and the other holding his sword, a gleaming sweep of steel, to the mystif's belly. The scars on N'ashap's swollen head were inflamed by the drink in his system; the rest of his skin was dead white, almost waxen. He reeled as he stood in the doorway, all the more dangerous for his lack of equilibrium. The mystif had proved in New York it could survive traumas that would have laid any human dead in the gutter. But N'ashap's blade was ready to gut it like a fish, and there'd be no surviving that. The commander's tiny eyes fixed as best they could on Gentle.

"Your mystif's very faithful all of a sudden," he said, panting. "Why's that? First it comes looking for me, then it won't let me near it. Maybe it needs your permission, is that it? So give it." He pushed the blade against Pie's belly. *"Go on.* Tell it to be friendly, or it's dead."

Gentle lowered his hands a little, very slowly, as if in an attempt to appeal to Pie. "I don't think we have much choice," he said, his eyes going between the mystif's impassive face and the sword poised at its belly, putting the time it would take for a pneuma to blow N'ashap's head off against the speed of the captain's blade.

N'ashap was not the only player in the scene, of course. There were three guards already here, all armed, and doubtless more on their way.

"You'd better do what he wants," Gentle said, drawing a deep breath as he finished speaking.

N'ashap saw him do so, and saw too his hand going to his mouth. Even drunk, he sensed his danger and loosed a shout to the men in the passageway behind him, stepping out of their line of fire, and Gentle's, as he did so.

Denied one target, Gentle unleashed his breath against the other. The pneuma flew at the guards as their trigger fingers tightened, striking the nearest with such violence his chest erupted. The force of the blow threw the body back against the other two. One went down immediately, his weapon flying from his hand. The other was momentarily blinded by blood and a shrapnel of innards but was quick to regain his balance, and would have blown Gentle's head off had his target not been on the move, flinging himself towards the corpse. The guard fired once wildly, but before he could fire again Gentle had snatched up the dropped weapon and answered the fire with his own. The guard had enough Oethac blood to be indifferent to the bullets that came his way, till one found his spattered eye and blew it out. He shrieked and fell back, dropping his gun to clamp both hands to the wound.

Ignoring the third man, still moaning on the floor, Gentle went to the cell door. Inside, Captain N'ashap stood face to face with Pie 'oh' pah. The mystif's hand was on the blade. Blood ran from the sliced palm, but the commander was making no attempt to do further damage. He was staring at Pie's face, his own expression perplexed.

Gentle halted, knowing any intervention on his part would snap N'ashap out of his distracted state. Whoever he was seeing in Pie's place—the whore who resembled his mother, perhaps; another echo of Tishalullé, in this place of lost mamas?—it was sufficient to keep the blade from removing the mystif's fingers.

Tears began to well in N'ashap's eyes. The mystif didn't move, nor did its gaze flicker from the captain's face for an instant. It seemed to be winning the battle between N'ashap's desire and his murderous intention. His hand unknotted from around the sword. The mystif opened its own fingers, and the weight of the sword carried it out of the captain's grip to the ground. The noise it made striking the stone was too loud to go unheard by N'ashap, however entranced he was, and he shook his head violently, his gaze going instantly from Pie's face to the weapon that had fallen between them.

The mystif was quick: at the door in two strides. Gentle drew breath, but as his hand went to his mouth he heard a shriek from Huzzah. He glanced down the corridor towards the child, who was retreating before two more guards, both Oethacs, one snatching at her as she fled, the other with his sights on Gentle. Pie seized his arm and dragged him back from the door as N'ashap, still rising as he came, ran at them with his sword. The time to dispatch him with a pneuma had passed. All Gentle had space to do was seize the door handle and slam the cell closed. The key was in the lock, and he turned it as N'ashap's bulk slammed against the other side.

Huzzah was running now, her pursuer between the second guard and his target. Tossing the gun to Pie, Gentle went to snatch Huzzah up before the Oethac took her. She was in his arms with a stride to spare, and he flung them both aside to give Pie a clear line of fire. The pursuing Oethac realized his jeopardy and went for his own weapon. Gentle looked around at Pie.

"Kill the fuckers!" he yelled, but the mystif was staring at the gun in its hand as though it had found shite there.

"Pie! For Christ's sake! Kill them!"

Now the mystif raised the gun, but still it seemed incapable of pulling the trigger.

"Do it!" Gentle yelled.

The mystif shook its head, however, and would have lost them all their lives had two clean shots not struck the back of the guards' necks, dropping them both to the ground.

"Papa!" Huzzah said.

It was indeed the sergeant, with Scopique in tow, who emerged through the smoke. His eyes weren't on his daughter, whom he'd just saved from death. They were on the soldiers he'd dispatched to do so. He looked traumatized by the deed. Even when Huzzah went to him, sobbing with relief and fear, he barely noticed her. It wasn't until Gentle shook him from his daze of guilt, saying they should get going while they had half a chance, that he spoke.

"They were my men," he said.

"And this is your daughter," Gentle replied. "You made the right choice."

N'ashap was still battering at the cell door, yelling for help. It could only be moments before he got it.

"What's the quickest way out?" Gentle asked Scopique.

"I want to let the others out first," Scopique replied. "Father Athanasius, Izaak, Squalling—"

"There's no time," Gentle said. "Tell him, Pie! We have to go now or not at all. Pie? Are you with us?"

"Yes. . . ."

"Then stop dreaming and let's get going."

Still protesting that they couldn't leave the rest under lock and key, Scopique led the quintet up by a back way into the night air. They came out not onto the parapet but onto bare rock.

"Which way now?" Gentle asked.

There was already a proliferation of shouts from below. N'ashap had doubtless been liberated and would be ordering a full alert.

"We have to head for the nearest landfall."

"That's the peninsula," Scopique said, redirecting Gentle's gaze across the Cradle towards an arm of low-lying land that was barely discernible in the murk of the night.

That murk was their best ally now. If they moved fast enough it would cloak them before their pursuers even knew which direction they'd headed in. There was a beetling pathway down the island's face to the shore, and Gentle led the way, aware that every one of the four who were following was a liability: Huzzah a child, her father still racked by guilt, Scopique casting backwards glances, and Pie still dazed by the bloodshed. This last was odd in a creature he'd first encountered in the guise of assassin, but then this journey had changed them both.

As they reached the shore, Scopique said, "I'm sorry. I can't go. You all head on. I'm going to try and get back in and let the others out."

Gentle didn't attempt to persuade him otherwise. "If that's what you want to do, good luck," he said. "We have to go."

"Of course you do! Pie, I'm sorry, my friend, but I couldn't live with myself if I turned my back on the others. We've suffered too long together." He took the mystif's hand. "Before you say it, I'll stay alive. I know my duty, and I'll be ready when the time comes."

"I know you will," the mystif replied, drawing the handshake into an embrace.

"It will be soon," Scopique said.

"Sooner than I'd wish," Pie replied; then, leaving Scopique to head back up the cliff face, the mystif joined Gentle, Huzzah, and Aping, who were already ten yards from the shore.

The exchange between Pie and Scopique—with its intimation of a shared agenda hitherto kept secret—had not gone unnoted by Gentle; nor would it go unquestioned. But this was not the time. They had at least half a dozen miles to travel before they reached the peninsula, and there was already a swell of noise from behind them, signaling pursuit. Torch beams raked the shore as the first of N'ashap's troops emerged to give chase, and from within the walls of the asylum rose the din of the prisoners, finally giving voice to their rage. That, like the murk, might confound the hounds, but not for long.

The torches had found Scopique, and the beams now scanned the shore he'd been ascending from, each sweep wider than the one that preceded it. Aping was carrying Huzzah, which speeded their progress somewhat, and Gentle was just beginning to think that they might stand a chance of survival when one of the torches caught them. It was weak at such a distance, but strong enough that its light picked them out. Gunfire followed immediately. They were difficult targets, however, and the bullets went well wide.

"They'll catch us now," Aping gasped. "We should surrender." He set his daughter down and threw his gun to the ground, turning to spit his accusations in Gentle's face. "Why did I ever listen to you? I was *crazy*."

"If we stay here they'll shoot us on the spot," Gentle replied. "Huzzah as well. Do you want that?"

"They won't shoot us," he said, taking hold of Huzzah with one hand and raising the other to catch the beams. "Don't shoot!" he yelled. "Don't shoot! Captain? Captain! Sir! We surrender!"

"Fuck this," Gentle said, and reached to haul Huzzah from her father's grip.

She went into Gentle's arms readily, but Aping wasn't

about to relinquish her so easily. He turned to snatch her back, and as he did so a bullet struck the ice at their feet. He let Huzzah go and turned to attempt a second appeal. Two shots cut him short, the first striking his leg, the second his chest. Huzzah let out a shriek and wrenched herself from Gentle's hold, dropping to the ground at her father's head.

The seconds they'd lost in Aping's surrender and death were the difference between the slimmest hope of escape and none. Any one of the twenty or so troops advancing upon them now could pick them off at this distance. Even N'ashap, who was leading the group, his walk still unsteady, could scarcely have failed to bring them down.

"What now?" said Pie.

"We have to stand our ground," Gentle replied. "We've got no choice."

That very ground, however, was no steadier than N'ashap's walk. Though this Dominion's suns were in another hemisphere and there was only midnight from horizon to horizon, a tremor was moving through the frozen sea that both Pie and Gentle recognized from almost fatal experience. Huzzah felt it too. She raised her head, her sobs quieting.

"The Lady," she murmured.

"What about her?" said Gentle.

"She's near us."

Gentle put out his hand, and Huzzah took it. As she got up she scanned the ground. So did he. His heart had started to pound furiously, as the memories of the Cradle's liquification flooded back.

"Can you stop her?" he murmured to Huzzah.

"She's not come for us," the girl said, and her gaze went from the still solid ground beneath their feet to the group that N'ashap was still leading in their direction.

"Oh, Goddess . . ." Gentle said.

A cry of alarm was rising from the middle of the approaching pack. One of the torch beams went wild, then another, and another, as one by one the soldiers realized their jeopardy. N'ashap let out a shout himself: a demand for order among his troops that went unobeyed. It was difficult to see precisely what was going on, but Gentle could imagine it well enough. The ground was softening, and the Cradle's silver waters were bubbling up around their feet. One of the men fired into the air as the sea's shell broke beneath him; another two or three started back towards the island, only to find their panic excited a quicker dissolution. They went down as if snatched by sharks, silver spume fountaining where they'd stood. N'ashap was still attempting to preserve some measure of command, but it was a lost cause. Realizing this, he began to fire towards the trio, but with the ground rocking beneath him, and the beams no longer trained on his targets, he was virtually shooting blind.

"We should get out of here," Gentle said, but Huzzah had better advice.

"She won't hurt us if we're not afraid," she said.

Gentle was half tempted to reply that he was indeed afraid, but he kept his silence and his place, despite the fact that the evidence of his eyes suggested the Goddess had no patience with dividing the bad from the misguided or the unrepentant from the prayerful. All but four of their pursuers—N'ashap numbered among them—had already been claimed by the sea, some gone beneath the tide entirely, others still struggling to reach some solid place. Gentle saw one man scrambling up out of the water, only to have the ground he was crawling upon liquify beneath him with such speed the Cradle had closed over him before he had time to scream. Another went down shouting at the water that was bubbling up around him, the last sight of him his gun, held high and still firing.

All the torch carriers had succumbed now, and the only illumination was from the cliff top, where soldiers who'd had the luck to be left behind were training their beams on the massacre, throwing into silhouette the figures of N'ashap and the other three survivors, one of whom was making an attempt to race towards the solid ground where Gentle, Pie, and Huzzah stood. His panic undid him. He'd only run five strides when silvery foam bubbled up in front of him. He turned to retrace his steps, but the route had already gone to seething silver. In desperation he flung away his weapons and attempted to leap to safety, but fell short and went from sight in an instant.

One of the remaining trio, an Oethac, had fallen to his knees to pray, which merely brought him closer to his executioner, who drew him down in the throes of his imprecation, giving him time only to snatch at his comrade's leg and pull him down at the same time. The place where they'd vanished did not cease to seethe but redoubled its fury now. N'ashap, the last alive, turned to face it, and as he did so the sea rose up like a fountain, until it was half his height again.

"Lady," Huzzah said.

It was. Carved in water, a breasted body, and a face dancing with glints and glimmers: the Goddess, or her image, made of her native stuff, then gone the same instant as it broke and dropped upon N'ashap. He was borne down so quickly, and the Cradle left rocking so placidly the instant after, it was as though his mother had never made him.

Slowly, Huzzah turned to Gentle. Though her father was dead at her feet, she was smiling in the gloom, the first open smile Gentle had seen on her face.

"The Cradle Lady came," she said.

They waited awhile, but there were no further visitations. What the Goddess had done—whether it was to save the child, as Huzzah would always believe, or because circumstance had put within her reach the forces that had tainted Her Cradle with their cruelty—She had done with an economy She wasn't about to spoil with gloating or sentiment. She closed the sea with the same efficiency She'd employed to open it, leaving the place unmarked.

There was no further attempt at pursuit from the guards left on the cliff, though they kept their places, torches piercing the murk.

"We've got a lot of sea to cross before dawn," Pie said.

"We don't want the suns coming up before we reach the peninsula."

Huzzah took Gentle's hand. "Did Papa ever tell you where we're going in Yzordderrex?"

"No," he said. "But we'll find the house."

She didn't look back at her father's body, but fixed her eyes on the gray bulk of the distant headland and went without complaint, sometimes smiling to herself, as she remembered that the night had brought her a glimpse of a parent that would never again desert her.

29

I

The territory that lay between the shores of the Cradle and the limits of the Third Dominion had been, until the Autarch's intervention, the site of a natural wonder universally held to mark the center of the Imajica: a column of perfectly hewn and polished rock to which as many names and powers had been ascribed as there were shamans, poets, and storytellers to be moved by it. There was no community within the Reconciled Dominions that had not enshrined it in their mythology and found an epithet to mark it as their own. But its truest name was also perhaps its plainest: the Pivot. Controversy had raged for centuries about whether the Unbeheld had set it down in the smoky wastes of the Kwem to mark the midpoint between the perimeters of the Imajica, or whether a forest of such columns had once stood in the area, and some later hand (moved, perhaps, by Hapexamendios' wisdom) had leveled all but this one.

Whatever the arguments about its origins, however, nobody had ever contested the power that it had accrued standing at the center of the Dominions. Lines of thought had passed across the Kwem for centuries, carrying a freight of force which the Pivot had drawn to itself with a

magnetism that was virtually irresistible. By the time the
Autarch came into the Third Dominion, having already established his particular brand of dictatorship in Yzordderrex, the Pivot was the single most powerful object in the
Imajica. He laid his plans for it brilliantly, returning to the
palace he was still building in Yzordderrex and adding several features, though their purpose did not become apparent until almost two years later, when, acting with the kind
of speed that usually attends a coup, he had the Pivot toppled, transported, and set in a tower in his palace before
the blood of those who might have raised objections to this
sacrilege was dry.

Overnight, the geography of the Imajica was transformed. Yzordderrex became the heart of the Dominions.
Thereafter, there would be no power, either secular or sacred, that did not originate in that city; there would be no
crossroads sign in any of the Reconciled Dominions that
did not carry its name, nor any highway that did not have
upon it somewhere a petitioner or penitent who'd turned
his eyes towards Yzordderrex in hope of salvation. Prayers
were still uttered in the name of the Unbeheld, and bless-
ings murmured in the forbidden names of the Goddesses,
but Yzordderrex was the true Lord now, the Autarch its
mind and the Pivot its phallus.

One hundred and seventy-nine years had passed since the
day the Kwem had lost its great wonder, but the Autarch
still made pilgrimages into the wastes when he felt the need
for solitude. Some years after the removal of the Pivot he'd
had a small palace built close to the place where it had
stood, spartan by comparison with the architectural excesses of the folly that crowned Yzordderrex. This was his
retreat in confounding times, where he could meditate
upon the sorrows of absolute power, leaving his Military
High Command, the generals who ruled the Dominions on
his behalf, to do so under the eye of his once-beloved
Queen, Quaisoir. Lately she had developed a taste for repression that was waning in him, and he'd several times
thought of retiring to the palace in the Kwem permanently

and leaving her to rule in his stead, given that she took so much more pleasure from it than he. But such dreams were an indulgence, and he knew it. Though he ruled the Imajica invisibly—not one soul, outside the circle of twenty or so who dealt with him daily, would have known him from any other white man with good taste in clothes—his vision had shaped the rise of Yzordderrex, and no other would ever competently replace it.

On days like this, however, with the cold air off the Lenten Way whining in the spires of the Kwem Palace, he wished he could send the mirror he met in the morning back to Yzordderrex in his place and let his reflection rule. Then he could stay here and think about the distant past: England in midsummer. The streets of London bright with rain when he woke, the fields outside the city peaceful and buzzing with bees. Scenes he pictured longingly when he was in elegiac mood. Such moods seldom lasted long, however. He was too much of a realist, and he demanded truth from his memory. Yes, there had been rain, but it had come with such venom it had bruised every fruit it hadn't beaten from the bough. And the hush of those fields had been a battlefield's hush, the murmur not trees but flies, come to find laying places.

His life had begun that summer, and his early days had been filled with signs not of love and fruitfulness but of Apocalypse. There wasn't a preacher in the park who didn't have Revelation by heart that year, nor a whore in Drury Lane who wouldn't have told you she'd seen the Devil dancing on the midnight roofs. How could those days not have influenced him: filled him with a horror of imminent destruction, given him an appetite for order, for law, for Empire? He was a child of his times, and if they'd made him cruel in his pursuit of system, was that *his* fault or that of the *age*?

The tragedy lay not in the suffering that was an inevitable consequence of any social movement, but in the fact that his achievements were now in jeopardy from forces that—if they won the day—would return the Imajica to the chaos from which he had brought it, undoing his work in a fraction of the time it had taken for it to be achieved. If he was to suppress these subversive elements he had a limited number of options, and after the events in Patashoqua, and the uncovering of plots against him, he had retreated to the quiet of the Kwem Palace to decide between them. He could continue to treat the rebellions, strikes, and uprisings as minor irritations, limiting his reprisals to small but eloquent acts of suppression, such as the burning of the village of Beatrix and the trials and executions at Vanaeph. This route had two significant disadvantages. The most recent attempt upon his life, though still inept, was too close for comfort, and until every last radical and revolutionary had been silenced or dissuaded, he would be in danger. Furthermore, when his whole reign had been dotted with episodes that had required some measured brutalities, would this new spate of purges and suppressions make any significant mark? Perhaps it was time for a more ambitious vision: cities put under martial law, tetrarchs imprisoned so that their corruptions could be exposed in the name of a just Yzordderrex, governments toppled, and resistance met with the full might of the Second Dominion's armies. Maybe Patashoqua would have to burn the way Beatrix had. Or L'Himby and its wretched temples.

If such a route were followed successfully, the slate would be wiped clean. If not—if his advisers had underestimated the scale of unrest or the quality of leaders among the rabble—he might find the circle closing and the Apocalypse into which he'd been born that faraway summer coming around again, here in the heart of his promised land.

What then, if Yzordderrex burned instead of Patashoqua? Where would he go for comfort? Back to England, perhaps? Did the house in Clerkenwell still stand, he wondered, and if so were its rooms still sacred to the workings of desire, or had the Maestro's undoing scoured them to the last board and nail? The questions tantalized him. As he sat and pondered them he found a curiosity in his core— no, more than curiosity, an appetite—to discover what the Unreconciled Dominion was like almost two centuries after his creation.

His musings were interrupted by Rosengarten, a name he'd bequeathed to the man in the spirit of irony, for a more infertile thing never walked. Piebald from a disease caught in the swamps of Loquiot in the throes of which he had unmanned himself, Rosengarten lived for duty. Among the generals, he was the only one who didn't sin with some excess against the austerity of these rooms. He spoke and moved quietly; he didn't stink of perfumes; he never drank; he never ate kreauchee. He was a perfect emptiness, and the only man the Autarch completely trusted.

He had come with news and told it plainly. The asylum on the Cradle of Chzercemit had been the scene of a rebellion. Almost all the garrison had been killed, under circumstances which were still under investigation, and the bulk of the prisoners had escaped, led by an individual called Scopique.

"How many were there?" the Autarch asked.

"I have a list, sir," Rosengarten replied, opening the file he'd brought with him. "There are fifty-one individuals unaccounted for, most of them religious dissidents."

"Women?"

"None."

"We should have had them executed, not locked them away."

"Several of them would have welcomed martyrdom, sir. The decision to incarcerate them was taken with that in mind."

"So now they'll return to their flocks and preach revolution all over again. This we must stop. How many of them were active in Yzorddderrex?"

"Nine. Including Father Athanasius."

"Athanasius? Who was he?"

"The Dearther who claimed he was the Christos. He had a congregation near the harbor."

"Then that's where he'll return, presumably."

"It seems likely."

"All of them'll go back to their flocks, sooner or later.

We must be ready for them. No arrests. No trials. Just have them quietly dispatched."

"Yes, sir."

"I don't want Quaisoir informed of this."

"I think she already knows, sir."

"Then she must be prevented from anything showy."

"I understand."

"Let's do this discreetly."

"There *is* something else, sir."

"What's that?"

"There were two other individuals on the island before the rebellion—"

"What about them?"

"It's difficult to know exactly what to make of the report. One of them appears to have been a mystif. The description of the other may be of interest."

He passed the report to the Autarch, who scanned it quickly at first, then more intently.

"How reliable is this?" he asked Rosengarten.

"At this juncture I don't know. The descriptions were corroborated, but I haven't interrogated the men personally."

"Do so."

"Yes, sir."

He handed the report back to Rosengarten. "How many people have seen this?"

"I had all other copies destroyed as soon as I read it. I believe only the interrogating officers, their commander, and myself have been party to this information."

"I want every one of the survivors from the garrison silenced. Court-martial them all and throw away the key. The officers and the commander must be instructed that they will be held accountable for any leakage of this information, from any source. Such leakage to be punishable by death."

"Yes, sir."

"As for the mystif and the stranger, we must assume they're making way to the Second Dominion. First Beatrix,

now the Cradle. Their destination must be Yzordderrex.
How many days since this uprising?''

"Eleven, sir.''

"Then they'll be in Yzordderrex in a matter of days,
even if they're traveling on foot. Track them. I'd like to
know as much about them as I can.''

He looked out the window at the wastes of the Kwem.

"They probably took the Lenten Way. Probably passed
within a few miles of here.'' There was a subtle agitation in
his voice. "That's twice now our paths have come close to
crossing. And now the witnesses, describing him so well.
What does it mean, Rosengarten? What does it mean?''

When the commander had no answers, as now, he kept
his silence: an admirable trait.

"I don't know either,'' the Autarch said. "Perhaps I
should go out and take the air. I feel old today.''

The hole from which the Pivot had been uprooted was still
visible, though the driving winds of the region had almost
healed the scar. Standing on the lips of the hole was a fine
place to meditate on absence, the Autarch had discovered.
He tried to do so now, his face swathed in silk to keep the
stinging gust from his mouth and nostrils, his long fur coat
closely buttoned, and his gloved hands driven into his
pockets. But the calm he'd always derived from such medi-
tations escaped him now. Absence was a fine discipline for
the spirit when the world's bounty was a step away, and
boundless. Not so now. Now it reminded him of an emptiness that he both feared and feared to be filled, like the
haunted place at the shoulder of a twin who'd lost its other
in the womb. However high he built his fortress walls, however tightly he sealed his soul, there was one who would
always have access, and that thought brought palpitations.
This other knew him as well as he knew himself: his frailties, his desires, his highest ambition. Their business together—most of it bloody—had remained unrevealed and
unrevenged for two centuries, but he had never persuaded
himself that it would remain so forever. It would be finished at last, and soon.

Though the cold could not reach his flesh through his coat, the Autarch shuddered at the prospect. He had lived for so long like a man who walks perpetually in the noonday sun, his shadow falling neither in front of him nor behind. Prophets could not predict him, nor accusers catch his crimes. He was inviolate. But that would change now. When he and his shadow met—as they inevitably would—the weight of a thousand prophecies and accusations would fall upon them both.

He pulled the silk from his face and let the eroding wind assault him. There was no purpose in staying here any longer. By the time the wind had remade his features he would have lost Yzordderrex, and even though that seemed like a small forfeit now, in the space of hours it might be the only prize he'd be able to preserve from destruction.

2

If the divine engineers who had raised the Jokalaylau had one night set their most ambitious peak between a desert and an ocean, and returned the next night and for a century of nights thereafter to carve its steeps and sheers from foothills to clouded heights with lowly habitations and magnificent plazas, with streets, bastions, and pavilions—and if, having carved, they had set in the core of that mountain a fire that smoldered but never burned—then their handiwork, when filled to overflowing with every manner of life, might have deserved comparison with Yzordderrex. But given that no such masterwork had ever been devised, the city stood without parallel throughout the Imajica.

The travelers' first sight of it came as they crossed the causeway that skipped like a well-aimed stone across the delta of the River Noy, rushing in twelve white torrents to meet the sea. It was early morning when they arrived, the fog off the river conspiring with the uneasy light of dawn to keep the city from sight until they were so close to it that when the fog was snatched the sky was barely visible, the desert and the sea no more than marginal, and all the world was suddenly Yzordderrex.

As they'd walked the Lenten Way, passing from the Third Dominion into the Second, Huzzah had recited all she'd read about the city from her father's books. One of the writers had described Yzordderrex as a god, she reported, a notion Gentle had thought ludicrous until he set eyes upon it. Then he understood what the urban theologian had been about, deifying this termite hill. Yzordderrex was worthy of worship; and millions were daily performing the ultimate act of veneration, living on or within the body of their Lord. Their dwellings clung like a million panicked climbers to the cliffs above the harbor and teetered on the plateaus that rose, tier on tier, towards the summit, many so crammed with houses that those closest to the edge had to be buttressed from below, the buttresses in turn encrusted with nests of life, winged, perhaps, or else suicidal. Everywhere, the mountain teemed, its streets of steps, lethally precipitous, leading the eye from one brimming shelf to another: from leafless boulevards lined with fine mansions to gates that let onto shadowy arcades, then up to the city's six summits, on the highest of which stood the palace of the Autarch of the Imajica. There was an abundance of a different order here, for the palace had more domes and towers than Rome, their obsessive elaboration visible even at this distance. Rising above them all was the Pivot Tower, as plain as its fellows were baroque. And high above that again, hanging in the white sky above the city, the comet that brought the Dominion's long days and languid dusks: Yzordderrex's star, called Giess, the Witherer.

They stood for only a minute or so to admire the sight. The daily traffic of workers who, having found no place of residence on the back or in the bowels of the city, commuted in and out daily, had begun, and by the time the newcomers reached the other end of the causeway they were lost in a dusty throng of vehicles, bicycles, rickshaws, and pedestrians all making their way into Yzordderrex. Three among tens of thousands: a scrawny young girl wearing a wide smile; a white man, perhaps once handsome but sickly now, his pale face half lost behind a ragged brown beard; and a Eurhetemec mystif, its eyes, like so many of its breed, barely concealing a private grief. The crowd bore them forward, and they went unresisting where countless multitudes had gone before: into the belly of the city-god Yzordderrex.

30

I

When Dowd brought Judith back to Godolphin's house after the murder of Clara Leash, it was not as a free agent but as a prisoner. She was confined to the bedroom she'd first occupied, and there she waited for Oscar's return. When he came in to see her it was after a half-hour conversation with Dowd (she heard the murmur of their exchange, but not its substance), and he told her as soon as he appeared that he had no wish to debate what had happened. She'd acted against his best interests, which were finally—did she not realize this yet?—against her own too, and he would need time to think about the consequences for them both.

"I trusted you," he said, "more than I've ever trusted any woman in my life. You betrayed me, exactly the way Dowd predicted you would. I feel foolish, and I feel hurt."

"Let me explain," she said.

He raised his hands to hush her. "I don't want to hear," he said. "Maybe in a few days we'll talk, but not now."

Her sense of loss at his retreat was almost overwhelmed by the anger she felt at his dismissal of her. Did he believe her feelings for him were so trivial she'd not concerned herself with the consequences of her actions on them both? Or worse: had Dowd convinced him that she'd been planning to betray him from the outset, and she'd calculated everything—the seduction, the confessions of devotion—in order to weaken him? This latter scenario was the likelier of the two, but it didn't clear Oscar of guilt. He had still failed to give her a chance to justify herself.

She didn't see him for three days. Her food was served in her room by Dowd, and there she waited, hearing Oscar come and go, and on occasion hints of conversation on the stairs, enough to gather the impression that the Tabula Rasa's purge was reaching a critical point. More than once she contemplated the possibility that what she'd been up to with Clara Leash made her a potential victim, and that day by day Dowd was eroding Oscar's reluctance to dispatch her. Paranoia, perhaps; but if he had any scrap of feeling for her why didn't he come and see her? Didn't he pine, the way she did? Didn't he want her in his bed, for the animal comfort of it if nothing else? Several times she asked Dowd to tell Oscar she needed to speak with him, and Dowd—who affected the detachment of a jailer with a thousand other such prisoners to deal with daily—had said he'd do his best, but he doubted that Mr. Godolphin would want to have any dealings with her. Whether the message was communicated or not, Oscar left her solitary in her confinement, and she realized that unless she took more forcible action she might never see daylight again.

Her escape plan was simple. She forced the lock on her bedroom door with a knife unreturned after one of her meals—it wasn't the lock that kept her from straying, it was Dowd's warning that the mites which had murdered Clara were ready to claim her if she attempted to leave—and slipped out onto the landing. She'd deliberately waited until Oscar was home before she made the attempt, believing, perhaps naïvely, that despite his withdrawal of affection he'd protect her from Dowd if her life was threatened. She was sorely tempted to seek him out there and then. But perhaps it would be easier to treat with him when she was away from the house and felt more like a mistress of her own destiny. If, once she was safely away from the house, he chose to have no further contact with her, then her fear that Dowd had soured his feelings towards her permanently would be confirmed, and she would have to look for another way to get to Yzordderrex.

She made her way down the stairs with the utmost caution and, hearing voices at the front of the house, decided to make her exit through the kitchen. The lights were burning everywhere, as usual. The kitchen was deserted. She crossed quickly to the door, which was bolted top and bottom, crouching to slide the lower bolt aside.

As she stood up Dowd said, "You won't get out that way."

She turned to see him standing at the kitchen table, bearing a tray of supper dishes. His laden condition gave her hope that she might yet outmaneuver him, and she made a dash for the hallway. But he was faster than she'd anticipated, setting down his burden and moving to stop her so quickly she had to retreat again, her hand catching one of the glasses on the table. It fell, smashing musically.

"Now look what you've done," he said, with what seemed to be genuine distress. He crossed to the shards and bent down to gather them up. "That glass had been in the family for generations. I'd have thought you'd have had some fellow feeling for it."

Though she was in no temper to talk about broken glasses, she replied nevertheless, knowing her only hope lay in alerting Godolphin to her presence.

"Why should I give a damn about a glass?" she said.

Dowd picked up a piece of the bowl, holding it to the light.

"You've got so much in common, lovey," he said. "Both made in ignorance of yourselves. Beautiful, but fragile." He stood up. "You've *always* been beautiful. Fashions come and go, but Judith is always beautiful."

"You don't know a damn thing about me," she said.

He put the shards on the table beside the rest of the dirty plates and cutlery. "Oh, but I do," he said. "We're more alike than you realize."

He'd kept a glittering fragment back, and as he spoke he put it to his wrist. She only just had time to register what he was about to do before he cut into his own flesh. She looked away, but then—hearing the piece of glass dropped among the litter—glanced back. The wound gaped, but there was no blood forthcoming, just an ooze of brackish sap. Nor was the expression on Dowd's face pained. It was simply intent.

"You have a piffling recall of the past," he said; "I have too much. You have heat; I have none. You're in love; I've never understood the word. But Judith: *we are the same.* Both slaves."

She looked from his face to the cut to his face to the cut to his face, and with every move of her pupils her panic increased. She didn't want to hear any more from him. She despised him. She closed her eyes and conjured him at the voider's pyre, and in the shadow of the tower, crawling with mites, but however many horrors she put between them his words won through. She'd given up attempting to solve the puzzle of herself a long time ago, but here he was, spilling pieces she couldn't help but pick up.

"Who are you?" she said to him.

"More to the point, who are you?"

"We're not the same," she said. "Not even a little. I bleed. You don't. I'm human. You're not."

"But is it *your* blood you bleed?" he said. "Ask yourself that."

"It comes out of my veins. Of course it's mine."

"Then who are you?" he said.

The inquiry was made without overt malice, but she didn't doubt its subversive purpose. Somehow Dowd knew she was forgetful of her past and was pricking her to a confession.

"I know what I'm *not,*" she said, earning herself the time to invent an answer. "I'm not a glass. I'm not fragile or ignorant. And I'm not—"

What was the other quality he'd mentioned besides beauty and fragility? He'd been stopping to pick up the pieces of broken glass, and he described her some way or other.

"You're not what?" he said, watching her wrestle with her own reluctance to seize the memory.

She pictured him crossing the kitchen. Now look what you've done, he'd said. Then he'd stooped (she saw him do so, in her mind's eye) and as he'd begun to pick up the pieces, the words had come to his lips. And now to her memory too.

"That glass had been in the family for generations," he'd said. "I'd have thought you'd have had some fellow feeling for it."

"No," she said aloud, shaking her head to keep the sense of this from congealing there. But the motion only shook up other memories: of her trip to the estate with Charlie, when that pleasurable sense of belonging had suffused her and voices had called her sweet names from the past; of meeting Oscar on the threshold of the Retreat and knowing instantly she belonged at his side, without question, or care to question; of the portrait above Oscar's bed, gazing down on the bed with such a possessive stare he had turned off the light before they made love.

As these thoughts came, the shaking of her head grew wilder, the motion possessing her like a fit. Tears spat from her eyes. Her hands went out for help even as the power to request it went from her throat. Through a blur of motion she was just able to see Dowd standing beside the table, his hand covering his wounded wrist, watching her impassively. She turned from him, terrified that she'd choke on her tongue or break her head open if she fell, and knowing he'd do nothing to help her. She wanted to cry out for Oscar, but all that came was a wretched gargling sound. She stumbled forward, her head still thrashing, and as she did so saw Oscar in the hallway, coming towards her. She pitched her arms in his direction and felt his hands upon her, to pull her up out of her collapse. He failed.

2

He was beside her when she woke. She wasn't lying in the narrow bed she'd been consigned to for the last few nights but in the wide four-poster in Oscar's room, the bed she'd come to think of as theirs. It wasn't, of course. Its true owner was the man whose image in oils had come back to her in the throes of her fit: the Mad Lord Godolphin, hanging above the pillows on which she lay and sitting beside her in a later variation, caressing her hand and telling her how much he loved her. As soon as she came to consciousness and felt his touch, she withdrew from it.

"I'm . . . not a pet," she struggled to say. "You can't just . . . stroke me when . . . it suits you."

He looked appalled. "I apologize unconditionally," he said in his gravest manner. "I have no excuse. I let the Society's business take precedence over understanding you and caring for you. That was unforgivable. Then Dowd, of course, whispering in my ear. . . . Was he very cruel?"

"You're the one who's been cruel."

"I've done nothing intentionally. Please believe that, at least."

"You've lied to me over and over again," she said, struggling to sit up in bed. "You know things about me that I don't. Why didn't you share them with me? I'm not a child."

"You've just had a fit," Oscar said. "Have you ever had a fit before?"

"No."

"Some things are better left alone, you see."

"Too late," she said. "I've had my fit, and I survived it. I'm ready to hear the secret, whatever it is." She glanced up at Joshua. "It's something to do with him, isn't it? He's got a hold on you."

"Not on me—"

"You liar! You liar!" she said, throwing the sheets aside and getting onto her knees, so that she was face to face with the deceiver. "Why do you tell me you love me one moment and lie to me the next? Why don't you trust me?"

"I've told you more than I've ever told anybody. But then I find you've plotted against the Society."

"I've done more than plot," she said, thinking of her journey into the cellars of the tower.

Once again, she teetered on the edge of telling him what she'd seen, but Clara's advice was there to keep her from falling. *You can't save Celestine and keep his affections,* she'd said, *you're digging at the foundations of his family and his faith.* It was true. She understood that more clearly than ever. And if she told him all she knew, pleasurable as that unburdening would be, could she be absolutely certain that he wouldn't cleave to his history, at the last, and use what he knew against her? What would Clara's death and Celestine's suffering have been worth then? She was now their only agent in the living world, and she had no right to gamble with their sacrifices.

"What have you done," Oscar said, "besides plot? What have you done?"

"You haven't been honest with me," she replied. "Why should I tell you anything?"

"Because I can still take you to Yzordderrex," he said.

"Bribes now?"

"Don't you want to go any longer?"

"I want to know the truth about myself more."

He looked faintly saddened by this. "Ah." He sighed. "I've been lying for so long I'm not sure I'd know the truth if I tripped over it. Except . . ."

"Yes?"

"What we felt for each other," he murmured, "at least, what I feel for you . . . that was *true,* wasn't it?"

"It can't be much," Jude said. "You locked me away. You left me to Dowd—"

"I've already explained—"

"Yes, you were distracted. You had other business. So you forgot me."

"No," he protested, "I never forgot. Never, I swear."

"What then?"

"I was afraid."

"Of me?"

"Of everything. You, Dowd, the Society. I started to see plots everywhere. Suddenly the idea of your being in my bed seemed too much of a risk. I was afraid you'd smother me, or—"

"That's ridiculous."

"Is it? How can I be sure who you belong to?"

"I belong to myself."

He shook his head, his gaze going from her face up to the painting of Joshua Godolphin that hung above the bed.

"How can you know that?" he said. "How can you be certain that what you feel for me comes from your heart?"

"What does it matter where it comes from? It's there. Look at me."

He refused her demand, his eyes still fixed on the Mad Lord.

"He's dead," she said.

"But his legacy—"

"Fuck his legacy!" she said, and suddenly got to her feet, taking hold of the portrait by its heavy, gilded frame and wrenching it from the wall.

Oscar rose to protest, but her vehemence carried the day. The picture came from its hooks with a single pull, and she summarily pitched it across the room. Then she dropped back onto the bed in front of Oscar.

"He's dead and gone," she said. "He can't judge us. He can't control us. Whatever it is we feel for each other—and I don't pretend to know what it is—it's *ours.*" She put her hands to his face, her fingers woven with his beard. "Let go of the fears," she said. "Take hold of me instead."

He put his arms around her.

"You're going to take me to Yzordderrex, Oscar. Not in a week's time, not in a few days: tomorrow. I want to go tomorrow. Or else"—her hands dropped from his face—"let me go now. Out of here. Out of your life. I won't be your prisoner, Oscar. Maybe *his* mistresses put up with that, but I won't. I'll kill myself before I'll let you lock me up again."

She said all of this dry-eyed. Simple sentiments, simply put. He took hold of her hands and raised them to his cheeks again, as if inviting her to possess him. His face was full of tiny creases she'd not seen before, and they were wet with tears.

"We'll go," he said.

3

There was a balmy rain falling as they left London the next day, but by the time they'd reached the estate the sun was breaking through, and the parkland gleamed around them as they entered. They didn't make any detours to the house but headed straight to the copse that concealed the Retreat. There was a breeze in the branches, and they flickered with light leaves. The smell of life was everywhere, stirring her blood for the journey ahead.

Oscar had advised her to dress with an eye to practicality and warmth. The city, he said, was subject to rapid and radical shifts in temperature, depending on the direction of the wind. If it came off the desert, the heat in the streets could bake the flesh like unleavened bread. And if it swung and came off the ocean, it brought marrow-chilling fogs and sudden frosts. None of this daunted her, of course. She was ready for this adventure as for no other in her life.

"I know I've gone on endlessly about how dangerous the city's become," Oscar said as they ducked beneath the low-slung branches, "and you're tired of hearing about it, but this isn't a civilized city, Judith. About the only man I trust there is Peccable. If for any reason we were to be separated—or if anything were to happen to me—you can rely upon him for help."

"I understand."

Oscar stopped to admire the pretty scene ahead, dappled sunlight falling on the pale walls and dome of the Retreat. "You know, I used only to come here at night," he said. "I thought that was the sacred time, when magic had the strongest hold. But it's not true. Midnight Mass and moonlight is fine, but miracles are here at noon as well; just as strong, just as strange."

He looked up at the canopy of trees.

"Sometimes you have to go away from the world to see the world," he said. "I went to Yzordderrex a few years back and stayed—oh, I don't know, two months, maybe two and a half, and when I came back to the Fifth I saw it like a child. I swear, like a child. This trip won't just show you other Dominions. If we get back safe and sound—"

"We will."

"Such faith. If we do, this world will be different too. Everything changes after this, because you'll be changed."

"So be it," she said.

She took hold of his hand, and they started towards the Retreat. Something made her uneasy, however. Not his words—his talk of change had only excited her—but the hush between them, perhaps, which was suddenly deep.

"Is there something wrong?" he said, feeling her grip tighten.

"The silence. . . ."

"There's always an odd atmosphere here. I've felt it before. A lot of fine souls died here, of course."

"At the Reconciliation?"

"You know about that, do you?"

"From Clara. It was two hundred years ago this midsummer, she said. Perhaps the spirits are coming back to see if someone's going to try again."

He stopped, tugging on her arm. "Don't talk about it, even in jest. Please. There'll be no Reconciliation, this summer or any other. The Maestros are dead. The whole thing's—"

"All right," she said. "Calm down. I won't mention it again."

"After this summer it'll be academic anyway," he said, with a feigned lightness, "at least for another couple of centuries. I'll be dead and buried long before this hoopla starts again. I've got my plot, you know? I chose it with Peccable. It's on the edge of the desert, with a fine view of Yzordderrex."

His nervous babble concealed the quiet until they reached the door; then he let it drop. She was glad he was silent. The place deserved reverence. Standing at the step, it wasn't difficult to believe phantoms gathered here, the dead of centuries past mingling with those she'd last seen living on this very spot: Charlie for one, of course, coaxing her inside, telling her with a smile that the place was nothing special, just stone; and the voiders too, one burned, one skinned, both haunting the threshold.

"Unless you see any just impediment," Oscar said, "I think we should do this."

He led her inside, to the middle of the mosaic.

"When the time comes," he said. "We have to hold on to each other. Even if you think there's nothing to hold on to, there is; it's just changed for a time. I don't want to lose you between here and there. The In Ovo's no place to go wandering."

"You won't lose me," she said.

He went down on his haunches and dug into the mosaic, pulling from the pattern a dozen or so pieces of pyramidal stone the size of two fists, which had been so designed as to be virtually invisible when set in their places.

"I don't fully understand the mechanisms that carry us over," he said as he worked. "I'm not sure anybody does completely. But according to Peccable there's a sort of common language into which anybody can be translated. And all the processes of magic involve this translation."

He was laying the stones around the edge of the circle as he spoke, the arrangement seemingly arbitrary.

"Once matter and spirit are in the same language, one can influence the other in any number of ways. Flesh and bone can be transformed, transcended—"

"Or transported?"

"Exactly."

Jude remembered how the removal of a traveler from this world into another looked from the outside: the flesh folding upon itself, the body distorted out of all recognition.

"Does it hurt?" she said.

"At the beginning, but not badly."

"When will it begin?" she said.

He stood up. "It already has," he said.

She felt it, as he spoke: a pressure in her bowels and bladder, a tightness in her chest that made her catch her breath.

"Breathe slowly," he said, putting his palm against her breastbone. "Don't fight it. Just let it happen. There's no harm going to come to you."

She looked down at his hand, then beyond it to the circle that enclosed them, and out through the door of the Retreat to the sunlit grass that lay just a few paces from where she stood. Close as it was, she couldn't return there. The train she'd boarded was gathering speed around her. It was too late for doubts or second thoughts. She was trapped.

"It's all right," she heard Oscar say, but it didn't feel that way at all.

There was a pain in her belly so sharp it felt as though she'd been poisoned, and an ache in her head, and an itch too deep in her skin to be scratched. She looked at Oscar. Was he enduring the same discomforts? If so he was bearing them with remarkable fortitude, smiling at her like an anesthetist.

"It'll be over soon," he was saying. "Just hold on . . . it'll be over soon."

He drew her closer to him, and as he did so she felt a tingling pass through her cells, as though a rainstorm was breaking inside her, sluicing the pain away.

"Better?" he said, the word more shape than sound.

"Yes," she told him and, smiling, put her lips to his, closing her eyes with pleasure as their tongues touched.

The darkness behind her lids was suddenly brightened by gleaming lines, falling like meteors across her mind's eye. She lifted her lids again, but the spectacle came out of her skull, daubing Oscar's face with streaks of brightness. A dozen vivid hues picked out the furrows and creases of his skin; another dozen, the geology of bone beneath; and another, the lineaments of nerves and veins and vessels, to the tiniest detail. Then, as though the mind interpreting them had done with its literal translation and could now rise to poetry, the layered maps of his flesh simplified. Redundancies and repetitions were discarded, the forms that emerged so simple and so absolute that the matter they represented seemed wan by comparison, and receded before them. Seeing this show, she remembered the glyph

she'd imagined when she and Oscar had first made love:
the spiral and curve of her pleasure laid on the velvet behind her eyes. Here was the same process again, only the
mind imagining them was the circle's mind, empowered by
the stones and by the travelers' demand for passage.

A motion at the door distracted her gaze momentarily.
The air around them was close to dropping its sham of
sights altogether, and the scene beyond the circle was
blurred. But there was enough color in the suit of the man
at the threshold for her to know him even though she
couldn't make out his face. Who else but Dowd wore that
absurd shade of apricot? She said his name, and though she
heard no sound from her throat, Oscar understood her
alarm and turned towards the door.

Dowd was approaching the circle at speed, his intention
perfectly clear: to hitch a ride to the Second Dominion.
She'd seen the gruesome consequences of such interfer-
ence before, on this very spot, and she braced herself
against Oscar for the coming shock. Instead of trusting to
the circle to dispatch the hanger-on, however, Oscar turned
from her and went to strike Dowd. The circle's flux multi-
plied his violence tenfold, and the glyph of his body became an illegible scrawl, the colors dirtied in an instant.
The pain she'd thought washed away swept back over her.
Blood ran from her nose and into her open mouth. Her
skin itched so violently she'd have brought blood to that
too had the pain in her joints not kept her from moving.

She could make no sense of the scribble in front of her
until her glance caught sight of Oscar's face, smeared and
raw, screaming back at her as he toppled from the circle.
She reached to haul him back, despite the searing pain her
motion brought, and took hold of an arm, determined that
wherever they were delivered, to Yzordderrex or death,
they'd go there together. He returned her grasp, seizing her
outstretched arms and dragging himself back onto the Express. As his face emerged from the blur beyond the smile
she realized her error. It was Dowd she'd hauled aboard.

She let go of her hold, in revulsion more than rage. His
face was horribly contorted, blood streaming from eyes,

ears, and nose. But the mind of passage was already working on this fresh text, preparing to translate and transport it. She had no way of braking the process, and to leave the circle now would be certain suicide. Beyond it, the scene was blurred and darkening, but she caught sight of Oscar, rising from the ground, and thanked whatever deities protected these circles that he was at least alive. He was moving towards the circle again, she saw, as though to dare its flux a second time, but it seemed he judged the train to be moving too swiftly now, because he retreated, arms up over his face. Seconds later the whole scene disappeared, the sunlight at the threshold burning on for a heartbeat longer than the rest, then that too folding away into obscurity.

The only sight left to her now was the matrix of lines which were the translator's rendering of her fellow traveler, and though she despised him beyond words she kept her eyes fixed upon them, having no other point of reference. All bodily sensation had disappeared. She didn't know if she was floating, falling, or even breathing, though she suspected she was doing none of these things. She had become a sign, transmitted between Dominions, encoded in the mind of passage. The sight before her—Dowd's shimmering glyph—was not secured by sight but by thought, which was the only currency valid on this trip. And now, as if her powers to purchase were increasing with familiarity, the absence around her began to gain detail. The In Ovo, Oscar had called this place. Its darkness swelled in a million places, their skins stretching until they gleamed and split, glutinous forms breaking out and in their turn swelling and splitting, like fruit whose seeds were sown inside each other and nourished to corruption by their predecessors' decay. Repulsive as this was, there was worse to come, as new entities appeared, these no more than scraps from a cannibal's table, sucked bloodless and gnawed: idiot doodles of life that didn't bear translation into any material form. Primitive though they were, they sensed the presence of finished life forms in their midst and rose towards the travelers like the damned to passing angels. But they swarmed too late. The visitors moved on and away, the darknesses sealing up their tenants and receding.

Jude could see Dowd's body in the midst of his glyph, still insubstantial but brightening by the moment. With the sight, the agonies of ferriage returned, though not as sharply as those that had pained her at the outset of the journey. She was glad to have them if they proved her nerves were hers again; surely it meant the journey was almost over. The horrors of the In Ovo had almost disappeared entirely when she felt the faint heat on her face. But the scent this heat raised to her nostrils brought more certain proof that the city was near: a mingling of the sweets and sours she'd first smelled on the wind that had issued from the Retreat months before.

She saw a smile come over Dowd's face, cracking the blood already dried on it: a smile which became a laugh in a beat or two, ringing off the walls of the merchant Peccable's cellar as it grew solid around them. She didn't want to share his pleasure, after all the harms he'd devised, but she couldn't help herself. Relief that the journey hadn't killed her, and sheer exhilaration that after all this time she was here, brought laughter onto her face and, with every breath between, the air of the Second Dominion into her lungs.

I

Five miles up the mountainside from the house in which Jude and Dowd were taking their first gasps of Yzordderrexian air, the Autarch of the Reconciled Dominions sat in one of his watchtowers and surveyed the city he had inspired to such notorious excess. It was three days since his return from the Kwem Palace, and almost every hour somebody—it was usually Rosengarten—had brought news of further acts of civil defiance, some in regions of the Imajica so remote that word of the mutinies had been weeks in coming, some—these more disturbing—barely beyond the palace walls. As he mused he chewed on kreau-chee, a drug to which he'd been addicted for some seventy years. Its side effects were severe and unpredictable for those unused to it. Periods of lethargy alternated with bouts of priapism and psychotic hallucination. Sometimes the fingers and toes swelled to grotesque proportions. But the Autarch's system had been steeped in kreauchee for so many years the drug no longer assaulted either his phy-sique or his faculties, and he could enjoy its capacity to lift him from dolor without having to endure its discomforts.

Or at least such had been the case until recently. Now, as if in league with the forces that were destroying his dream below, the drug refused to give him relief. He'd demanded a fresh supply while meditating at the place of the Pivot, only to get back to Yzordderrex to find that his procurers in the Scoriae Kesparate had been murdered. Their killers were reputedly members of the Dearth, an order of rene-gade shammists—worshipers of the Madonna, he'd heard it rumored—who'd been fulmigating revolution for years and had until now presented so little threat to the status quo that he'd let them be for entertainment's sake. Their pamphlets—a mingling of castration fantasies and bad the-ology—had made farcical reading, and with their leader Athanasius in prison many of them had retreated to the desert to worship at the margins of the First Dominion, the so-called Erasure, where the solid reality of the Second paled and faded. But Athanasius had escaped his custody and returned to Yzordderrex with fresh calls to arms. His first act of defiance, it seemed, had been the slaughter of the kreauchee pushers. A small deed, but the man was wily enough to know what an inconvenience he'd caused with it. No doubt he was touting it as an act of civil healing, per-formed in the name of the Madonna.

The Autarch spat out the wad of kreauchee he was chewing and vacated the watchtower, heading off through the monumental labyrinth of the palace towards Quaisoir's quarters in the hope that she had some small supply he could filch. To left and right of him were corridors so im-mense no human voice would carry along them, each lined with dozens of chambers—all exquisitely finished, all exquisitely empty—the ceilings of many so high that thin clouds formed there. Though his architectural endeavors had once been the wonder of the Dominions, the enormity of his ambition, and indeed of his achievement, mocked him now. He'd wasted his energies with these follies, when he should have been concerning himself with the shock waves his empire building had sent through the Imajica.

It wasn't the pogroms he'd instigated that were causing these troubles, his analysts informed him. The present unrest was a consequence of less violent changes in the fabric of the Dominions, the rise of Yzordderrex and its companion cities being one of those changes, and perhaps its most significant. All eyes had been turned towards the tinsel glories of those cities, and a new pantheon had been created for tribes and communities that had long since lost faith in the deities of rock and tree. Peasants had left their dust bowls in their hundreds of thousands to claim their slice of this miracle, only to end up fermenting their envy and despair in hellholes like Vanaeph.

That was one way revolutionaries were made, the analysts said: not out of ideologies but out of frustration and rage. Then there were those who saw a chance to profit by anarchy, like the new species of nomads that were making portions of the Lenten Way impassable—crazed and merciless bandits who took pleasure in their own notoriety. And finally, there were the new rich, the dynasties created by the boom in consumption that had come with Yzordderrex's rise. In the early days they'd repeatedly turned to the regime for protection against the acquisitive poor. But the Autarch had been too busy building his palace, and the help had not been forthcoming, so the dynasties had formed private armies to police their lands, swearing their continued allegiance to the Empire even as they plotted against it. Now those plots were no longer theory. With their armies primed to defend their estates, the boom barons were announcing themselves independent of Yzordderrex and its taxes.

There was, the analysts said, no evidence of collusion

among these elements. How could there be? They didn't have a single philosophical notion in common. They were neo-feudalists, neo-communists, neo-anarchists, all enemies of the others. It was purely coincidence that had roused them to rebellion at the same moment. Either that, or unfortuitous stars.

The Autarch barely listened to such assessments. What little pleasure he'd taken in politics at the beginning of his regime had quickly staled. It wasn't the craft he'd been born to, and he found it tiresome and dull. He'd appointed his Tetrarchs to rule over the four Reconciled Dominions—the Tetrarch of the First doing so *in absentia,* of course—leaving him to obsess upon making Yzordderrex the city to end all cities, and the palace its glorious crown. What he'd in fact created was a monument to purposelessness, which, when he was under the influence of kreauchee, he would rail against as at some enemy.

One day, for instance, in visionary mood, he'd had all the windows in the chambers facing the desert smashed, and great tonnages of rancid meat laid on the mosaics. Within a day, flocks of carrion birds had forsaken the hot high winds above the sands and were feasting and breeding on tables and beds prepared for the royalty of the Dominions. In another such mood he'd had fishes brought up from the delta and housed in the baths. The water was warm, the food plentiful, and they proved so fecund he could have walked on their backs within weeks. Then they became overcrowded, and he spent many hours watching the consequences: patricide, fratricide, infanticide. But the cruelest revenge he wreaked against his folly was the most private. One by one he was using the high halls with their drizzling clouds as stages for dramas in which nothing was feigned, not even death; and when the final act had been performed he had each theater sealed as elaborately as a king's tomb and moved on to another chamber. Little by little, the glorious palace of Yzordderrex was becoming a mausoleum.

The suite of chambers he was entering now was exempt from this process, however. Quaisoir's bathrooms, bedrooms, lounges, and chapel were a state unto themselves, and he'd long ago sworn to her he would never violate them. She'd decorated the rooms with any lush or luxurious item that pleased her eclectic eye. It was an aesthetic he himself had favored, before his present melancholia. He'd filled the bedrooms now nested by carrion birds with immaculate copies of baroque and rococo furniture, had commissioned the walls to be mirrored like Versailles, and had the toilets gilded. But he'd long since lost his taste for such extravagances, and now the very sight of Quaisoir's rooms nauseated him so much that if he hadn't been driven by need he'd have retreated, appalled by their opulence.

He called his wife's name as he went. First through the lounges, strewn with the leavings of a dozen meals; all were empty. Then into the state room, which was appointed even more grandly than the lounges, but also empty. Finally, to the bedroom. At its threshold, he heard the slap of feet on the marble floor, and Quaisoir's servant Concupiscentia paddled into view. She was naked, as always, her back a field of multicolored extremities each as agile as an ape's tail, her forelimbs withered and boneless things, bred to such vestigial condition over generations. Her large green eyes seeped constantly, the feathery fans to either side of her face dipping to brush the moisture from her rouged cheeks.

"Where's Quaisoir?" he demanded.

She drew a coquettish fan of her tails over her lower face and giggled behind them like a geisha. The Autarch had slept with her once, in a kreauchee fugue, and the creature never let him by without a show of flirtation.

"Not now, for Christ's sake," he said, disgusted at the display. "I want my wife! Where is she?"

Concupiscentia shook her head, retreating from his raised voice and fist. He pushed past her into the bedroom. If there was any tiny wad of kreauchee to be had, it would be here, in her boudoir, where she lazed away so many days, listening to Concupiscentia sing hymns and lullabies. The chamber smelled like a harbor bordello, a dozen sickly perfumes draping the air like the veils that hung around the bed.

"I want kreauchee!" he said. "Where is it?"

Again, a great shaking of the head from Concupiscentia, this time accompanied by whimpering.

"Where?" he shouted. *"Where?"*

The perfume and the veils sickened him, and he began to rip at the silks and gossamers in his rage. The creature didn't intervene until he picked up the Bible lying open on the pillows and threatened to rip out its onion-leaf pages.

"Pleas ep!" she squealed. "Please ep! Shellem beat I if ye taurat the Book. Quaisoir lovat the Book."

It wasn't often he heard the gloss, the pidgin English of the islands, and the sound of it—as misshapen as its source—infuriated him even more. He tore half a dozen pages from the Bible, just to make her squeal again. She obliged.

"I want kreauchee!" he said.

"I havat! I havat!" the creature said, and led him from the bedroom into the enormous dressing room that lay next door, where she began to search through the gilded boxes on Quaisoir's dressing table.

Catching sight of the Autarch's reflection in the mirror, she made a tiny smile, like a guilty child, before bringing a package out of the smallest of the boxes. He snatched it from her fingers before she had a chance to proffer it. He knew from the smell that stung his nostrils that this was good quality, and without hesitating he unwrapped it and put the whole wad into his mouth.

"Good girl," he told Concupiscentia. "Good girl. Now, do you know where your mistress got it?"

Concupiscentia shook her head. "She goallat alon unto the Kesparates, many nights. Sometimes shellem a goat beggar, sometimes shellem goat—"

"A whore."

"No, no. Quaisoir isem a whore."

"Is that where she is now?" the Autarch said. "Is she out whoring? It's a little early for that, isn't it, or is she cheaper in the afternoon?"

The kreauchee was better than he'd hoped; he felt it striking him as he spoke, lifting his melancholy and replacing it with a vehement buzz. Even though he'd not penetrated Quaisoir in four decades (nor had any desire to), in some moods news of her infidelities could still depress him. But the drug took all that pain away. She could sleep with fifty men a day, and it wouldn't take her an inch from his side. Whether they felt contempt or passion for each other was irrelevant. History had made them indivisible and would hold them together till the Apocalypse did them part.

"Shellem not whoring," Concupiscentia piped up, determined to defend her mistress's honor. "Shellem downer ta Scoriae."

"The Scoriae? Why?"

"Executions," Concupiscentia replied, pronouncing this word—learned from her mistress's lips—perfectly.

"Executions?" the Autarch said, a vague unease surfacing through the kreauchee's soothings. "What executions?"

Concupiscentia shook her head. "I dinnet knie," she said. "Jest executions. Allovat executions. She prayat to tem—"

"I'm sure she does."

"We all prayat far the sols, so ta go intat the presence of the Unbeheld washed—"

Here were more phrases repeated parrot fashion, the kind of Christian cant he found as sickening as the decor. And, like the decor, these were Quaisoir's work. She'd embraced the Man of Sorrows only a few months ago, but it hadn't taken her long to claim she was His bride. Another infidelity, less syphilitic than the hundreds that had gone before, but just as pathetic.

The Autarch left Concupiscentia to babble on and dispatched his bodyguard to locate Rosengarten. There were questions to be answered here, and quickly, or else it wouldn't only be the Scoriae where heads would roll.

2

Traveling the Lenten Way, Gentle had come to believe that, far from being the burden he'd expected her to be, Huzzah was a blessing. If she hadn't been with them in the Cradle he was certain the Goddess Tishalullé would not have intervened on their behalf; nor would hitchhiking along the highway have been so easy if they hadn't had a winsome child to thumb rides for them. Despite the months she'd spent hidden away in the depths of the asylum (or perhaps because of them), Huzzah was eager to engage everyone in conversation, and from the replies to her innocent inquiries he and Pie gleaned a good deal of information he doubted they'd have come by otherwise. Even as they'd crossed the causeway to the city, she'd struck up a dialogue with a woman who'd happily supplied a list of the Kesparates and even pointed out those that were visible from where they'd walked. There were too many names and directions for Gentle to hold in his head, but a glance towards Pie confirmed that the mystif was attending closely and would have all of them by heart by the time they reached the other side.

"Wonderful," Pie said to Huzzah when the woman had departed. "I wasn't sure I'd be able to find my way back to my people's Kesparate. Now I know the way."

"Up through the Oke T'Noon, to the Caramess, where they make the Autarch's sweetmeats," Huzzah said, repeating the directions as if she was reading them off a blackboard. "Follow the wall of the Caramess till we get to Smooke Street, then up to the Viaticum, and we'll be able to see the gates from there."

"How did you remember all that?" Gentle said, to which Huzzah somewhat disdainfully asked how he could have allowed himself to forget.

"We mustn't get lost," she said.

"We won't," Pie replied. "There'll be people in my Kesparate who'll help us find your grandparents."

"If they don't it doesn't matter," Huzzah said, looking gravely from Pie to Gentle. "I'll come with you to the First Dominion. I don't mind. I'd like to see the Unbeheld."

"How do you know that's where we're going?" Gentle said.

"I've heard you talking about it," she replied. "That's what you're going to do, isn't it? Don't worry, I'm not scared. We've seen a Goddess, haven't we? He'll be the same, only not as beautiful."

This unflattering notion amused Gentle mightily.

"You're an angel, you know that?" he said, going down on his haunches and sliding his arms around her.

She'd put on a few pounds in weight since they'd begun their journey together, and her hug, when she returned it, was strong.

"I'm hungry," she murmured in his ear.

"Then we'll find somewhere to eat," he replied. "We can't have our angel going hungry."

They walked up through the steep streets of the Oke T'Noon until they were clear of the throng of itinerants coming off the causeway. Here there were any number of establishments offering breakfast, from stalls selling barbecued fish to cafés that might have been transported from the streets of Paris, but that the customers sipping coffee were more extraordinary than even that city of exotics could boast. Many were species whose peculiarities he now took for granted: Oethacs and Heratea; distant relatives of Mother Splendid and Hammeryock; even a few who resembled the one-eyed croupier from Attaboy. But for every member of a tribe whose features he recognized, there were two or three he did not. As in Vanaeph, Pie had warned him that staring too hard would not be in their best interests, and he did his best not to enjoy too plainly the array of courtesies, humors, lunacies, gaits, skins, and cries that filled the streets. But it was difficult. After a time they found a small café from which the smell of food was particularly tempting, and Gentle sat down beside one of the windows, from which he could watch the parade without drawing too much attention.

"I had a friend called Klein," he said as they ate, "back in the Fifth Dominion. He liked to ask people what they'd do if they knew they only had three days to live."

"Why three?" Huzzah asked.

"I don't know. Why three anything? It's one of those numbers."

" 'In any fiction there's only ever room for three players,' " the mystif remarked. " 'The rest must be . . .' "—its flow faltered in mid-quotation—" 'agents,' something, and something else. That's a line from Pluthero Quexos."

"Who's he?"

"Never mind."

"Where was I?"

"Klein," said Huzzah.

"When he got around to asking me this question, I told him, If I had three days left I'd go to New York, because you've got more chance of living out your wildest dreams there than anywhere. But now I've seen Yzordderrex—"

"Not much of it," Huzzah pointed out.

"It's enough, angel. If he asks me again I'm going to tell him I'd like to die in Yzordderrex."

"Eating breakfast with Pie and Huzzah," she said.

"Perfect."

"Perfect," she replied, echoing his intonation precisely.

"Is there anything I couldn't find here if I looked hard enough?"

"Some peace and quiet," Pie remarked.

The hubbub from outside was certainly loud, even in the café.

"I'm sure we'll find some little courtyards up in the palace," Gentle said.

"Is that where we're going?" Huzzah asked.

"Now listen," said Pie. "For one thing, Mr. Zacharias doesn't know what the hell he's talking about—"

"Language, Pie," Gentle put in.

"And for another, we brought you here to find your grandparents, and that's our first priority. Right, Mr. Zacharias?"

"What if you can't find them?" Huzzah said.

"We will," Pie replied. "My people know this city from top to bottom."

"Is that possible?" Gentle said. "I somehow doubt it."

"When you've finished your coffee," Pie said, "I'll allow them to prove you wrong."

With their bellies filled, they headed on through the streets, following the route they'd had laid out for them: from the Oke T'Noon to the Caramess, following the wall until they reached Smooke Street. In fact the directions were not entirely reliable. Smooke Street, which was a narrow thoroughfare, and far emptier than those they'd left, did not lead them onto the Viaticum as they'd been told it would, but rather into a maze of buildings as plain as barracks. There were children playing in the dirt, and among them wild ragemy, an unfortunate cross between porcine and canine strains that Gentle had seen spitted and served in Mai-ké but which here seemed to be treated as pets. Either the mud, the children, or the ragemy stank, and their smell had attracted zarzi in large numbers.

"We must have missed a turning," the mystif said. "We'd be best to—"

It stopped in mid-sentence as the sound of shouting rose from nearby, bringing the children up out of the mud and sending them off in pursuit of its source. There was a high unmusical holler in the midst of the din, rising and falling like a warrior cry. Before either Pie or Gentle could remark on this, Huzzah was following the rest of the children, darting between the puddles and the rooting ragemy to do so. Gentle looked at Pie, who shrugged; then they both headed after Huzzah, the trail leading them down an alleyway into a broad and busy street, which was emptying at an astonishing rate as pedestrians and drivers alike sought cover from whatever was racing down the hill in their direction.

The hollerer came first: an armored man of fully twice Gentle's height, carrying in each fist scarlet flags that snaked behind him as he ran, the pitch and volume of his cry undimmed by the speed at which he moved. On his

heels came a battalion of similarly armored soldiers—
none, even in the troop, under eight feet tall—and behind
them again a vehicle which had clearly been designed to
mount and descent the ferocious slopes of the city with
minimum discomfort to its passengers. The wheels were
the height of the hollerer, the carriage itself low-slung between them, its bodywork sleek and dark, its windows
darker still. A gull had become caught between the spokes
of the wheels on the way down the hill, and it flapped and
bled there as the wheels turned, its screeches a wretched
but perfect complement to the cacophony of wheels, engine, and hollerer.

Gentle took hold of Huzzah as the vehicle raced past,
though she was in no danger of being struck. She looked
around at him, wearing a wide grin.

"Who was that?" she said.

"I don't know."

A woman sheltering in the doorway beside them furnished the answer. "Quaisoir," she said. "The Autarch's
woman. There's arrests being made down in the Scoriae.
More Dearthers."

She made a small gesture with her fingers, moving them
across her face from eye to eye, then down to her mouth,
pressing the knuckles of first and third fingers against her
nostrils while the middle digit tugged at her lower lip, all
this with the speed of one who made the sign countless
times in a day. Then she turned off down the street, keeping close to the wall as she went.

"Athanasius was a Dearther, wasn't he?" Gentle said.
"We should go down and see what's happening."

"It's a little too public," Pie said.

"We'll stay to the back of the crowd," Gentle said. "I
want to see how the enemy works."

Without giving Pie time to object, Gentle took Huzzah's
hand and headed after Quaisoir's troop. It wasn't a difficult
trail to follow. Everywhere along the route faces were once
more appearing at windows and doors, like anemones
showing themselves again after being brushed by the un-
derbelly of a shark: tentative, ready to hide their tender

heads again at the merest sign of a shadow. Only a couple of tots, not yet educated in terror, did as the three strangers were doing and took to the middle of the street, where the comet's light was brightest. They were quickly reclaimed for the relative safety of the doorways in which their guardians hovered.

The ocean came into view as the trio descended the hill, and the harbor was now visible between the houses, which were considerably older in this neighborhood than in the Oke T'Noon or up by the Caramess. The air was clean and quick here; it enlivened their step. After a short while the domestic dwellings gave way to docklands: warehouses, cranes, and silos reared around them. But the area was by no means deserted. The workers here were not so easily cowed as the occupants of the Kesparate above, and many were leaving off their labors to see what this rumpus was all about. They were a far more homogenized group than Gentle had seen elsewhere, most a cross between Oethac and *Homo sapiens,* massive, even brutish men who in sufficient numbers could certainly trounce Quaisoir's battalion. Gentle hoisted Huzzah up to ride on his back as they joined this congregation, fearful she'd be trampled if he didn't. A few of the dockers gave her a smile, and several stood aside to let her mount secure a better place in the crowd. By the time they came within sight of the troops again they were thoroughly concealed.

A small contingent of the soldiers had been charged to keep onlookers from straying too close to the field of action, and this they were attempting to do, but they were vastly outnumbered, and as the crowd swelled it steadily pushed the cordon towards the site of the hostilities, a warehouse some thirty yards down the street, which had apparently been laid siege to. Its walls were pitted with bullet strikes, and its lower windows smoked. The besieging troops—who were not dressed showily like Quaisoir's battalion, but in the monochrome Gentle had seen paraded in L'Himby—were presently hauling bodies out of the building. Some were on the second story, pitching dead men—and a couple who still had life in them—out of the windows onto the bleeding heap below. Gentle remembered Beatrix. Was this cairn building one of the marks of the Autarch's hand?

"You shouldn't be seeing this, angel," Gentle told Huzzah, and tried to lift her off his shoulders. But she held fast, taking fistfuls of his hair as security.

"I want to see," she said. "I've seen it with Daddy, lots of times."

"Just don't get sick on my head," Gentle warned.

"I won't," she said, outraged at the suggestion.

There were fresh brutalities unfolding below. A survivor had been dragged from the building and was kicked to the ground a few yards from Quaisoir's vehicle, the doors and windows of which were still closed. Another was defending himself as best he could from bayonet jabs, yelling in defiance as his tormentors encircled him. But everything came to a sudden halt with the appearance on the warehouse roof of a man wearing little more than ragged underwear, who opened his arms like a soul in search of martyrdom and proceeded to harangue the assembly below.

"That's Athanasius!" Pie murmured in astonishment.

The mystif was far sharper sighted than Gentle, who had to squint hard to confirm the identification. It was indeed Father Athanasius, his beard and hair longer than ever, his hands, brow, and flank running with blood.

"What the hell's he doing up there," Gentle said, "giving a sermon?"

Athanasius' address wasn't simply directed at the troops and their victims on the cobblestones below. He repeatedly turned his head towards the crowd, shouting in their direction too. Whether he was issuing accusations, prayers, or a call to arms, the words were lost to the wind, however. Soundless, his display looked faintly absurd and undoubtedly suicidal. Rifles were already being raised below, to put him in their sights.

But before a shot could be fired the first prisoner, who'd been kicked to his knees close to Quaisoir's vehicle, slipped custody. His captors, distracted by Athanasius' performance, were slow to respond, and by the time they did so their victim was already dashing towards the crowd, ignoring quicker escape routes to do so. The crowd began to part, anticipating the man's arrival in its midst, but the troops behind him were already turning their muzzles his way. Realizing they intended to fire in the direction of the crowd, Gentle dropped to his haunches, yelling for Huzzah to clamber down. This time she didn't protest. As she slipped from his shoulders several shots were fired. He glanced up and through the mesh of bodies caught sight of Athanasius falling back, as if struck, and disappearing behind the parapet around the roof.

"Damn fool," he said to himself, and was about to scoop Huzzah up and carry her away when a second round of shots froze him in his tracks.

A bullet caught one of the dockers a yard from where he crouched, and the man went down like felled timber. Gentle looked around for Pie, rising as he did so. The escaping Dearther had also been hit, but he was still staggering forward, heading towards a crowd that was now in confusion. Some were fleeing, some standing their ground in defiance, some going to the aid of the fallen docker.

It was doubtful the Dearther saw any of this. Though the momentum of his flight still carried him forward, his face—too young to boast a beard—was slack and expressionless, his pale eyes glazed. His lips worked as though to impart some final word, but a sharpshooter below denied him the comfort. Another bullet struck the back of his neck and appeared on the other side, where three fine blue lines were tattooed across his throat, the middle one bisecting his Adam's apple. He was thrown forward by the bullet's impact, the few men between him and Gentle parting as he fell. His body hit the ground a yard from Gentle, with only a few twitches of life left in it. Though his face was to the ground, his hands still moved, making their way through the dirt towards Gentle's feet as if they knew where they were going. His left arm ran out of power before it could reach its destination, but the right had sufficient will behind it to find the scuffed toe of Gentle's shoe.

He heard Pie murmuring to him from close by, coaxing

him to come away, but he couldn't forsake the man, not in these last seconds. He started to stoop, intending to clasp the dying fingers in his palm, but he was too late by seconds. The arm lost its power, and the hand dropped back to the ground lifeless.

"Now will you come?" Pie said.

Gentle tore his eyes from the corpse and looked up. The scene had gained him an audience, and there was a disturbing anticipation in their faces, puzzlement and respect mingled with the clear expectation of some pronouncement. Gentle had none to offer and opened his arms to show himself empty-handed. The assembly stared on, unblinking, and he half thought they might assault him if he didn't speak, but a further burst of gunfire from the siege site broke the moment, and the starers gave up their scrutiny, some shaking their heads as though waking from a trance. The second of the captives had been executed against the warehouse wall, and shots were now being fired into the pile of bodies to silence some survivor there. Troops had also appeared on the roof, presumably intending to pitch Athanasius' body down to crown the cairn. But they were denied that satisfaction. Either he'd faked being struck, or else he'd survived the wounding and crawled off to safety while the drama unfolded below. Whichever, he'd left his pursuers empty-handed.

Three of the cordon keepers, all of whom had fled for cover as their comrades fired on the crowd, now reappeared to claim the body of the escapee. They encountered a good deal of passive resistance, however, the crowd coming between them and the dead youth, jostling them. They forced their way through with well-aimed jabs from bayonets and rifle butts, but Gentle had time to retreat from in front of the corpse as they did so.

He had also had time to look back at the corpse-strewn stage visible beyond the heads of the crowd. The door of Quaisoir's vehicle had opened, and with her elite guard forming a shield around her she finally stepped out into the light of day. This was the consort of the Imajica's vilest tyrant, and Gentle lingered a dangerous moment to see what mark such intimacy with evil had made upon her.

When she came into view the sight of her, even with eyes that were far from perfect, was enough to snatch the breath from him. She was human, and a beauty. Nor was she simply *any* beauty. She was Judith.

Pie had hold of his arm, drawing him away, but he wouldn't go.

"Look at her. Jesus. Look at her, Pie. *Look!*"

The mystif glanced towards the woman.

"It's Judith," Gentle said.

"That's impossible."

"It is! It is! Use your fucking eyes! It's Judith!"

As if his raised voice was a spark to the bone-dry rage of the crowd all around, violence suddenly erupted, its focus the trio of soldiers who were still attempting to claim the dead youth. One was bludgeoned to the ground while another retreated, firing as he did so. Escalation was instantaneous. Knives were slid from their sheaths, machetes unhooked from belts. In the space of five seconds the crowd became an army and five seconds later claimed its first three lives. Judith was eclipsed by the battle, and Gentle had little choice but to go with Pie, more for the sake of Huzzah than for his own safety. He felt strangely inviolate here, as though that circle of expectant stares had lent him a charmed life.

"It was Judith, Pie," he said again, once they were far enough from the shouts and shots to hear each other speak.

Huzzah had taken firm hold of his hand and swung on his arm excitedly. "Who's Judith?" she said.

"A woman we know," Gentle said.

"How could that be her?" The mystif's tone was as fretful as it was exasperated. "Ask yourself: How could that be her? If you've got an answer, I'm happy to hear it. Truly I am. Tell me."

"I don't know how," Gentle said. "But I trust my eyes."

"We left her in the Fifth, Gentle."

"If *I* got through, why shouldn't she?"

"And in the space of two months she takes over as the

Autarch's wife? That's a meteoric rise, wouldn't you say?''

A fresh fusillade of shots rose from the siege site, followed by a roar of voices so profound it reverberated in the stone beneath their feet. Gentle stopped, walked, and looked back down the slope towards the harbor.

"There's going to be a revolution," he said simply.

"I think it's already begun," Pie replied.

"They'll kill her," he said, starting back down the hill.

"Where the hell are you going?" Pie said.

"I'm coming with you," Huzzah piped up, but the mystif took hold of her before she could follow.

"You're not going anywhere," Pie said, "except home to your grandparents. Gentle, will you listen to me? It's not Judith."

Gentle turned to face the mystif, attempting a reasoning tone. "If it's not her then it's her double; it's her echo. Some part *of* her, here in Yzordderrex."

The mystif didn't reply. It merely studied Gentle, as if coaxing him with its silence to articulate his theory more fully.

"Maybe people can be in two places at one time," Gentle said. Frustration made him grimace. "I *know* it was her, and nothing you can say's going to change my mind. You two go in to the Kesparate. Wait for me. I'll—"

Before he could finish his instructions, the holler that had first announced Quaisoir's descent from the heights of the city was raised again, this time at a higher pitch, to be drowned out almost instantly by a surge of celebratory cheering.

"That sounds like a retreat to me," Pie said, and was proved right twenty seconds later with the reappearance of Quaisoir's vehicle, surrounded by the tattered remnants of her retinue.

The trio had plenty of time to step out of the path of wheels and boots as they thundered up the slope, for the pace of the retreat was not as swift as that of the advance. Not only was the ascent steep but many of the elite had sustained wounds in defending the vehicle from assault and trailed blood as they ran.

"There's going to be such reprisals now," Pie said.

Gentle murmured his agreement as he stared up the slope where the vehicle had gone. "I have to see her again," he said.

"That's going to be difficult," Pie replied.

"She'll see me," Gentle said. "If I know who she is, then she's going to know who I am. I'll lay money on it."

The mystif didn't take up the bet. It simply said, "What now?"

"We go to your Kesparate, and we send out a search party to look for Huzzah's folks. Then we go up"—he nodded towards the palace—"and get a closer look at Quaisoir. I've got some questions to ask her. Whoever she is."

3

The wind veered as the trio retraced their steps, the relatively clear ocean breeze giving sudden way to a blisteringly hot assault off the desert. The citizens were well prepared for such climatic changes, and at the first hint of a shift in the wind, scenes of almost mechanical, and therefore comical, efficiency were to be seen high and low. Washing and potted plants were gathered from windowsills; ragemy and cats gave up their sun traps and headed inside; awnings were rolled up and windows shuttered. In a matter of minutes the street was emptied.

"I've been in these damn storms," the mystif said. "I don't think we want to be walking about in one."

Gentle told it not to fret, and hoisting Huzzah onto his shoulders, he set the pace as the storm scourged the streets. They'd asked for fresh directions a few minutes before the wind veered, and the shopkeeper who'd supplied them had known his geography. The directions were good even if walking conditions were not. The wind smelt like flatulence and carried a blinding freight of sand, along with ferocious heat. But they at least had the freedom of the streets. The only individuals they glimpsed were either felonious, crazy, or homeless, into all three of which categories they themselves fell.

They reached the Viaticum without error or incident, and from there the mystif knew its way. Two hours or more after they'd left the siege at the harbor they reached the Eurhetemec Kesparate. The storm was showing signs of fatigue, as were they, but Pie's voice fairly sang when it announced, "This is it. This is the place where I was born."

The Kesparate in front of them was walled, but the gates were open, swinging in the wind.

"Lead on," Gentle said, setting Huzzah down.

The mystif pushed the gate wide and led the way into streets the wind was unveiling before them as it fell, dropping sand underfoot. The streets rose towards the palace, as did almost every street in Yzordderrex, but the dwellings built upon it were very different from those elsewhere in the city. They stood discreet from one another, tall and burnished, each possessed of a single window that ran from above the door to the eaves, where the structure branched into four overhanging roofs, lending the buildings, when side by side, the look of a stand of petrified trees. In the street in front of the houses were the real thing: trees whose branches still swayed in the dying gusts like kelp in a tidal pool, their boughs so supple and their tight white blossoms so hardy the storm had done them no harm.

It wasn't until he caught the tremulous look on Pie's face that Gentle realized what a burden of feeling the mystif bore, stepping back into its birthplace after the passage of so many years. Having such a short memory, he'd never carried such luggage himself. There were no cherished recollections of childhood rites, no Christmas scenes or lullabies. His grasp of what Pie might be feeling had to be an intellectual construct and fell—he was sure—well shy of the real thing.

"My parents' home," the mystif said, "used to be between the chianculi"—it pointed off to its right, where the last remnants of sand-laden gusts still shrouded the distance—"and the hospice." It pointed to its left, a white-walled building.

"So somewhere near," Gentle said.

"I think so," Pie said, clearly pained by the tricks memory was playing.

"Why don't we ask somebody?" Huzzah suggested.

Pie acted upon the suggestion instantly, walking over to the nearest house and rapping on the door. There was no reply. It moved next door and tried again. This house was also vacated. Sensing Pie's unease, Gentle took Huzzah to join the mystif on the third step. The response was the same here, a silence made more palpable by the drop in the wind.

"There's nobody here," Pie said, remarking, Gentle knew, not simply on the empty houses but on the whole hushed vista.

The storm was completely exhausted now. People should have been appearing in their doorsteps to brush off the sand and peer at their roofs to see they were still secure. But there was nobody. The elegant streets, laid with such precision, were deserted from end to end.

"Maybe they've all gathered in one place," Gentle suggested. "Is there some kind of assembly place? A church or a senate?"

"The chianculi's the nearest thing," Pie said, pointing towards a quartet of pale yellow domes set amid trees shaped like cypresses but bearing Prussian blue foliage. Birds were rising from them into the clearing sky, their shadows the only motion on the streets below.

"What happens at the chianculi?" Gentle said as they started towards the domes.

"Ah! In my youth," the mystif said, attempting a lightness of tone it clearly didn't feel, "in my youth it was where we had the circuses."

"I didn't know you came from circus stock."

"They weren't like any Fifth Dominion circus," Pie replied. "They were ways we remembered the Dominion we'd been exiled from."

"No clowns and ponies?" Gentle said.

"No clowns and ponies," Pie replied, and would not be drawn on the subject any further.

Now that they were close to the chianculi, its scale—and that of the trees surrounding it—became apparent. It was

fully five stories high from the ground to the apex of its
largest dome. The birds, having made one celebratory circuit of the Kesparate, were now settling in the trees again,
chattering like myna birds that had been taught Japanese.

Gentle's attention was briefly claimed by the spectacle,
only to be grounded again when he heard Pie say, "They're
not all dead."

Emerging from between the Prussian blue trees were
four of the mystif's tribe, negroes wrapped in undyed robes
like desert nomads, some folds of which they held between
their teeth, covering their lower faces. Nothing about their
gait or garments offered any clue to their sex, but they were
evidently prepared to oust trespassers, for they came
armed with fine silver rods, three feet or so in length and
held across their hips.

"On no account move or even speak," the mystif said to
Gentle as the quartet came within ten yards of where they
stood.

"Why not?"

"This isn't a welcoming party."

"What is it then?"

"An execution squad."

So saying, the mystif raised its hands in front of its chest,
palms out, then—breaking its own edict—it stepped forward, addressing the squad as it did so. The language it
spoke was not English but had about it the same oriental
lilt Gentle had heard from the beaks of the settling birds.
Perhaps they'd indeed been speaking in their owners'
tongue.

One of the quartet now let the bitten veil drop, revealing
a woman in early middle age, her expression more puzzled
than aggressive. Having listened to Pie for a time, she murmured something to the individual at her right, winning
only a shaken head by way of response. The squad had continued to approach Pie as it talked, their stride steady; but
now, as Gentle heard the syllables *Pie 'oh' pah* appear in
the mystif's monologue, the woman called a halt. Two
more of the veils were dropped, revealing men as finely
boned as their leader. One was lightly mustached, but the

seeds of sexual ambiguity that blossomed so exquisitely in Pie were visible here. Without further word from the woman, her companion went on to reveal a second ambiguity, altogether less attractive. He let one hand drop from the silver rod he carried and the wind caught it, a ripple passing through its length as though it were made not of steel but of silk. He lifted it to his mouth and draped it over his tongue. It fell in soft loops from his lips and fingers, still glinting like a blade even though it folded and fluttered.

Whether this gesture was a threat or not Gentle couldn't know, but in response to it the mystif dropped to its knees and indicated with a wave of its hand that Gentle and Huzzah should do the same. The child cast a rueful glance in Gentle's direction, looking to him for endorsement. He shrugged and nodded, and they both knelt, though to Gentle's way of thinking this was the last position to adopt in front of an execution squad.

"Get ready to run," he whispered across to Huzzah, and she returned a nervous little nod.

The mustachioed man had now begun to address Pie, speaking in the same tongue the mystif had used. There was nothing in either his tone or attitude that was particularly threatening, though neither, Gentle knew, were foolproof indications. There was some comfort in the fact of dialogue, however, and at a certain point in the exchange the fourth veil was dropped. Another woman, younger than the leader and altogether less amiable, was taking over the conversation with a more strident tone, waving her ribbon blade in the air inches from Pie's inclined head. Its lethal capacity could not be in doubt. It whistled as it sliced and hummed as it rose again, its motion, for all its ripples, chillingly controlled. When she'd finished talking, the leader apparently ordered them to their feet. Pie obliged, glancing around at Gentle and Huzzah to indicate they should do the same.

"Are they going to kill us?" Huzzah murmured.

Gentle took her hand. "No, they're not," he said. "And if they try, I've got a trick or two in my lungs."

"Please, Gentle," Pie said. "Don't even—"

A word from the squad leader silenced the appeal, and the mystif answered the next question directed at it by naming its companions: Huzzah Aping and John Furie Zacharias. There then followed another short exchange between the members of the squad, during which time Pie snatched a moment to explain.

"This is a very delicate situation," Pie said.

"I think we've grasped that much."

"Most of my people have gone from the Kesparate."

"Where?"

"Some of them tortured and killed. Some taken as slave labor."

"But now the prodigal returns. Why aren't they happy to see you?"

"They think I'm probably a spy, or else I'm crazy. Either way, I'm a danger to them. They're going to keep me here to question me. It was either that or a summary execution."

"Some homecoming."

"At least there's a few of them left alive. When we first got here, I thought—"

"I know what you thought. So did I. Do they speak any English?"

"Of course. But it's a matter of pride that they don't."

"But they'll understand me?"

"Don't, Gentle."

"I want them to know we're not their enemies," Gentle said, and turned his address to the squad. "You already know my name," he said. "I'm here with Pie 'oh' pah because we thought we'd find friends here. We're not spies. We're not assassins."

"Let it alone, Gentle," Pie said.

"We came a long way to be here, Pie and me. All the way from the Fifth. And right from the beginning Pie's dreamed about seeing you people again. Do you understand? You're the dream Pie's come all this way to find."

"They don't care, Gentle," Pie said.

"They have to care."

"It's their Kesparate," Pie replied. "Let them do it their way."

Gentle mused on this a moment. "Pie's right," he said. "It's your Kesparate, and we're just visitors here. But I want you to understand something." He turned his gaze on the woman whose ribbon blade had danced so threateningly close to the mystif's pate. "Pie's my friend," he said. "I will protect my friend to the very last."

"You're doing more harm than good," the mystif said. "Please stop."

"I thought they'd welcome you with open arms," Gentle said, surveying the quartet's unmoved faces. "What's wrong with them?"

"They're protecting what little they've got left," Pie said. "The Autarch's sent in spies before. There've been purges and abductions. Children taken. Heads returned."

"Oh, Jesus." Gentle made a small, apologetic shrug. "I'm sorry," he said, not just to Pie but to them all. "I just wanted to say my piece."

"Well, it's said. Will you leave it to me now? Give me a few hours, and I can convince them we're sincere."

"Of course, if that's what it'll take. Huzzah and I can wait around until you've worked it all out."

"Not here," Pie said. "I don't think that would be wise."

"Why not?"

"I just don't," Pie said, softly insisting.

"You're afraid they're going to kill us all, aren't you?"

"There is . . . some doubt . . . yes."

"Then we'll all leave now."

"That's not an option. I stay and you leave. That's what they're offering. It's not up for negotiation."

"I see."

"I'll be all right, Gentle," Pie said. "Why don't you go back to the café where we had breakfast? Can you find it again?"

"I can," Huzzah said. She'd spent the time of this exchange with downcast eyes. Now that they were raised, they were full of tears.

"Wait for me there, angel," Pie said, conferring Gentle's epithet upon her for the first time. "Both of you angels."

"If you're not with us by twilight we'll come back and

find you," Gentle said. He threw his gaze wide as he said this, a smile on his lips and threat in his eyes.

Pie put out a hand to be shaken. Gentle took it, drawing the mystif closer.

"This is very proper," he said.

"Any more would be unwise," Pie replied. "Trust me."

"I always have. I always will."

"We're lucky, Gentle," Pie said.

"How so?"

"To have had this time together."

Gentle met the mystif's gaze, as it spoke, and realized there was a deeper farewell beneath this formality, which he didn't want to hear. For all its bright talk, the mystif was by no means certain they would be meeting again.

"I'm going to see you in a few hours, Pie," Gentle said. "I'm depending on that. Do you understand? We have vows."

The mystif nodded and let its hand slip from Gentle's grasp. Huzzah's smaller, warmer fingers were there, ready to take its place.

"We'd better go, angel," he said, and led Huzzah back towards the gate, leaving Pie in the custody of the squad.

She glanced back at the mystif twice as they walked, but Gentle resisted the temptation. It would do Pie no good to be sentimental at this juncture. Better just to proceed on the understanding that they'd be reunited in a matter of hours, drinking coffee in the Oke T'Noon. At the gate, however, he couldn't keep himself from glancing down the street of blossom-laden trees for one last glimpse of the creature he loved. But the execution squad had already disappeared into the chianculi, taking the prodigal with them.

32

I

With the long Yzordderrexian twilight still many hours from falling, the Autarch had found himself a chamber close to the Pivot Tower where the day could not come. Here the consolations brought by the kreauchee were not spoiled by light. It was easy to believe that everything was a dream and, being a dream, not worth mourning if—or rather when—it passed. In his unerring fashion Rosengarten had discovered the niche, however, and to it he brought news as disruptive as any light. A quiet attempt to eradicate the cell of Dearthers led by Father Athanasius had been turned into a public spectacle by Quaisoir's arrival. Violence had flared and was already spreading. The troops who had mounted the original siege were thought to have been massacred to a man, though this could not now be verified because the docklands had been sealed off by makeshift barricades.

"This is the signal the factions have been waiting for," Rosengarten opined. "If we don't stamp this out immediately, every little cult in the Dominion's going to tell its disciples that the Day's come."

"Time for judgment, eh?"

"That's what they'll say."

"Perhaps they're right," the Autarch replied. "Why don't we let them run riot for a while? None of them like each other. The Scintillants hate the Dearthers, the Dearthers hate the Zenetics. They can all slit each other's throats."

"But the city, sir."

"The city! The city! What about the frigging city? It's *forfeit*, Rosengarten. Don't you see that? I've been sitting here thinking, If I could call the comet down on top of it I would. Let it die the way it's lived: beautifully. Why so tragic, Rosengarten? There'll be other cities. I can build another Yzordderrex."

"Then maybe we should get you out now, before the riots spread."

"We're safe here, aren't we?" the Autarch said. A silence followed. "You're not so sure."

"There's such a swell of violence out there."

"And you say she started it?"

"It was in the air."

"But she was the inspiring spark?" He sighed. "Oh, damn her, damn her. You'd better fetch the generals."

"All of them?"

"Mattalaus and Racidio. They can turn this place into a fortress." He got to his feet. "I'm going to speak with my loving wife."

"Shall we come and find you there?"

"Not unless you want to witness murder, no."

As before, he found Quaisoir's chambers empty, but this time Concupiscentia—no longer flirtatious but trembling and dry-eyed, which was like tears to her seeping clan—knew where her mistress was: in her private chapel. He stormed in, to find Quaisoir lighting candles at the altar.

"I was calling for you," he said.

"Yes, I heard," she replied. Her voice, which had once made every word an incantation, was drab; as was she.

"Why didn't you answer?"

"I was praying," she said. She blew out the taper she'd lit the candles with and turned from him to face the altar. It was, like her chamber, a study in excess. A carved and painted Christ hung on a gilded cross, surrounded by cherubim and seraphim.

"Who were you praying for?" he asked her.

"For myself," she said simply.

He took hold of her shoulder, spinning her around. "What about the men who were torn apart by the mob? No prayers for them?"

"They've got people to pray for them. People who loved them. I've got nobody."

"My heart bleeds," he said.

"No, it doesn't," she replied. "But the Man of Sorrows bleeds for me."

"I doubt that, lady," he said, more amused by her piety than irritated.

"I saw Him today," she said.

This was a new conceit. He pandered to it. "Where was this?" he asked her, all sincerity.

"At the harbor. He appeared on a roof, right above me. They tried to shoot Him down, and He was struck. I saw Him struck. But when they looked for the body it had gone."

"You know you should go down to the Bastion with the rest of the madwomen," he told her. "You can wait for the Second Coming there. I'll have all this transported down there if you'd like."

"He'll come for me here," she said. "He's not afraid. *You're* the one who's afraid."

The Autarch looked at his palm. "Am I sweating? No. Am I on my knees begging Him to be kind? No. Accuse me of most crimes, and I'm probably guilty. But not fear. You know me better than that."

"He's here, in Yzordderrex."

"Then let Him come. I won't be leaving. He'll find me if He wants me so badly. He won't find me praying, you understand. Pissing maybe, if He could bear the sight." The Autarch took Quaisoir's hand and tugged it down between his legs. "He might find He's the one who's humbled." He laughed. "You used to pray to this fellow, lady. Remember? Say you remember."

"I confess it."

"It's not a crime. It's the way we were made. What are we to do but suffer it?" He suddenly drew close. "Don't think you can desert me for Him. We belong to each other. Whatever harm you do me, you do yourself. Think about that. If our dreams burn, we cook in them together."

His message was getting through. She didn't struggle in his embrace, but shook with terror.

"I don't want to take your comforts from you. Have

your Man of Sorrows if He helps you sleep. But remember how our flesh is joined. Whatever little sways you learned down in the Bastion, it doesn't change what you are."

"Prayers aren't enough," she said, half to herself.

"Prayers are useless."

"Then I have to find Him. Go to Him. Show Him my adoration."

"You're going nowhere."

"I have to. It's the only way. He's in the city, waiting for me."

She pressed him away from her.

"I'll go to Him in rags," she said, starting to tear at her robes. "Or naked! Better naked!"

The Autarch didn't attempt to catch hold of her again but withdrew from her, as though her lunacy were contagious, letting her tear at her clothes and draw blood with the violence of her revulsion. As she did so she started to pray aloud, her prayer full of promises to come to Him, on her knees, and beg His forgiveness. As she turned, delivering this exhortation to the altar, the Autarch lost patience with her hysteria and took her by the hair—twin fistfuls of it—drawing her back against him.

"You're not listening!" he said, both compassion and disgust overwhelmed by a rage even the kreauchee couldn't quell. "There's only one Lord in Yzordderrex!"

He threw her aside and mounted the steps of the altar in three strides, clearing the candles from it with one backward sweep of his arm. Then he clambered up onto the altar itself to drag down the crucifix. Quaisoir was on her feet to stop him, but neither her appeals nor her fists slowed him. The gilded seraphim came first, wrenched from their carved clouds and pitched behind him to the ground. Then he put his hands behind the Savior's head and pulled. The crown He wore was meticulously carved, and the thorns punctured his fingers and palms, but the sting only gave fire to his sinews, and a snarl of splintered wood announced his victory. The crucifix came away from the wall, and all he had to do was step aside to let gravity take it. For an instant he thought Quaisoir intended to fling herself beneath its weight, but a heartbeat before it toppled she stumbled back from the steps, and it fell amid the litter of dismembered seraphim, cracking as it struck the stone floor.

The commotion had of course brought witnesses. From his place on the altar the Autarch saw Rosengarten racing down the aisle, his weapon drawn.

"It's all right, Rosengarten!" he panted. "The worst is over."

"You're bleeding, sir."

The Autarch sucked at his hand. "Will you have my wife escorted to her chambers?" he said, spitting out the gold-flecked blood. "She's to be allowed no sharp instruments, nor any object with which she could do herself any harm. I'm afraid she's very sick. We'll have to watch over her night and day from now on."

Quaisoir was kneeling among the pieces of the crucifix, sobbing there.

"Please, lady," the Autarch said, jumping down from the altar to coax her up. "Why waste your tears on a dead man? Worship nothing, lady, except in adoration . . ." He stopped, puzzled by the words; then he took them up again. "In adoration of your True Self."

She raised her head, heeling away the tears with her hands to stare at him.

"I'll have some kreauchee found for you," he said. "To calm you a little."

"I don't want kreauchee," she murmured, her voice washed of all color. "I want forgiveness."

"Then I forgive you," he replied, with flawless sincerity.

"Not from you," she said.

He studied her grief for a time. "We were going to love and live forever," he said softly. "When did you become so *old?*"

She made no reply, so he left her there, kneeling in the debris. Rosengarten's underling, Seidux, had already arrived to take charge of her.

"Be considerate," he told Seidux as they crossed at the door. "She was once a great lady."

He didn't wait to watch her removal but went with Rosengarten to meet Generals Mattalaus and Racidio. He felt better for his exertion. Though like any great Maestro he was untouched by age, his system still became sluggish and needed an occasional stirring up. What better way to do it than by demolishing idols?

As they passed by a window which gave onto the city the spring went from his step, however, seeing the signs of destruction visible below. For all his defiant talk of building another Yzordderrex, it would be painful to watch this one torn apart, Kesparate by Kesparate. Half a dozen columns of smoke were already rising from conflagrations across the city. Ships were burning in the harbor, and there were bordellos aflame around Lickerish Street. As Rosengarten had predicted, all the apocalyptics in the city would fulfill their prophecies today. Those who'd said corruption came by sea were burning boats; those who railed against sex had lit their torches for the brothels. He glanced back towards Quaisoir's chapel as his consort's sobs were raised afresh.

"It's best we don't stop her weeping," he said. "She has good reason."

2

The full extent of the harm Dowd had done himself in his late boarding of the Yzordderrexian Express did not become apparent until their arrival in the icon-filled cellar beneath the merchant's house. Though he'd escaped being turned inside out, his trespass had wounded him considerably. He looked as though he'd been dragged face down over a freshly graveled road, the skin on his face and hands shredded and the sinew beneath oozing the meager filth he had in his veins. The last time Jude had seen him bleed, the wound had been self-inflicted and he'd seemed to suffer scarcely at all; but not so now. Though he held on to her wrist with an implacable grip and threatened her with a death that would make Clara's seem merciful if she attempted to escape him, he was a vulnerable captor, wincing as he hauled her up the stairs into the house above.

This was not the way she had imagined herself entering Yzorddderrex. But then the scene she met at the top of the stairs was not as she'd imagined either. Or rather, it was all too imaginable. The house—which was deserted—was large and bright, its design and decoration almost depressingly recognizable. She reminded herself that this was the house of Oscar's business partner Peccable, and the influence of Fifth Dominion aesthetics was likely to be strong in a dwelling that had a doorway to Earth in its cellar. But the vision of domestic bliss this interior conjured was depressingly bland. The only touch of exoticism was the parrot sulking on its perch by the window; otherwise this nest was irredeemably suburban, from the row of family photographs beside the clock on the mantelpiece to the drooping tulips in the vase on the well-polished dining room table.

She was sure there were more remarkable sights in the street outside, but Dowd was in no mood, or indeed condition, to go exploring. He told her they would wait here until he was feeling fitter, and if any of the family returned in the meanwhile she was to keep her silence. He'd do the talking, he said, or else she'd put not only her own life in jeopardy but that of the whole Peccable clan.

She believed him perfectly capable of such violence, especially in his present pain, which he demanded she help him ameliorate. She dutifully bathed his face, using water and towels from the kitchen. The damage was regrettably more superficial than she'd initially believed, and once the wounds were cleaned he rapidly began to show signs of recovery. She was now presented with a dilemma. Given that he was healing with superhuman speed, if she was going to exploit his vulnerability and escape it had to be soon. But if she did—if she fled the house there and then—she'd have turned her back on the only guide to the city she had. And, more importantly, she would be gone from the spot to which she still hoped Oscar would come, following her across the In Ovo. She couldn't afford to take the risk of his arriving and finding her gone into a city that from all reports was so vast they might search for each other ten lifetimes and never cross paths.

A wind began to get up after a while, and it carried a member of the Peccable family to the door. A gangling girl in her late teens or early twenties, dressed in a long coat and flower-print dress, who greeted the presence of two strangers in the house, one clearly recovering from injury, in a studiedly sanguine fashion.

"Are you friends of Papa's?" she asked, removing her spectacles to reveal eyes that were severely crossed.

Dowd said they were and began to explain how they'd come to be here, but she politely asked him if he'd hold off his story until the house had been shuttered against the coming storm. She turned to Jude for help in this, and Dowd made no objection, correctly assuming that his captive was not going to venture out into an unknown city as a storm came upon it. So, with the first gusts already rattling the door, Jude followed Hoi-Polloi around the house, locking any windows that were open even an inch, then closing the shutters in case the glass was blown in.

Even though the sandy wind was already obscuring the distance, Jude got a glimpse of the city outside. It was frustratingly brief, but sufficient to reassure her that when she finally got to walk the streets of Yzordderrex her months of waiting would be rewarded with wonders. There were myriad tiers of streets set on the slopes above the house, leading up to the monumental walls and towers of what Hoi-Polloi identified as the Autarch's palace, and just visible from the attic room window was the ocean, glittering through the thickening storm. But these were sights—ocean, rooftops, and towers—she might have seen in the Fifth. What marked this place as another Dominion was the people in the streets outside, some human, many not, all retreating from the wind or the commotions it carried. A creature, its head vast, stumbled up the street with what looked to be two sharp-snouted pigs, barking furiously, under each arm. A group of youths, bald and robed, ran in the other direction, swinging smoking censers above their heads like bolas. A man with a canary-yellow beard and china-doll skin was carried, wounded but yelling furiously, into a house opposite.

"There's riots everywhere," Hoi-Polloi said. "I wish Papa would come home."

"Where is he?" Jude asked.

"Down at the harbor. He had a shipment coming in from the islands."

"Can't you telephone him?"

"Telephone?" Hoi-Polloi said.

"Yes, you know, it's a—"

"I know what it is," Hoi-Polloi said testily. "Uncle Oscar showed me one. But they're against the law."

"Why?"

Hoi-Polloi shrugged. "The law's the law," she said. She peered out into the storm before shuttering the final window. "Papa will be sensible," she went on. "I'm always telling him, Be sensible, and he always is."

She led the way downstairs to find Dowd standing on the front step, with the door flung wide. Hot, gritty air blew in, smelling of spice and distance. Hoi-Polloi ordered Dowd back inside with a sharpness that made Jude fear for her, but Dowd seemed happy to play the erring guest and did as he was asked. She slammed the door and bolted it, then asked if anybody wanted tea. With the lights swinging in every room, and the wind rattling every loose shutter, it was hard to pretend nothing was amiss, but Hoi-Polloi did her best to keep the chat trivial while she brewed a pot of Darjeeling and passed around slices of Madeira cake. The sheer absurdity of the situation began to amuse Jude. Here they were having a tea party while a city of untold strangeness was racked by storm and revolution all around. If Oscar appears now, she thought, he'll be most entertained. He'll sit down, dunk his cake in his tea, and talk about cricket like a perfect Englishman.

"Where's the rest of your family?" Dowd asked Hoi-Polloi, when the conversation once more returned to her absentee father.

"Mama and my brothers have gone to the country," she said, "to be away from the troubles."

"Didn't you want to go with them?"

"Not with Papa here. Somebody has to look after him. He's sensible most of the time, but I have to remind him." A particularly vehement gust brought slates rattling off the roof like gunshots. Hoi-Polloi jumped. "If Papa was here," she said, "I think he'd suggest we had something to calm our nerves."

"What do you have, lovey?" Dowd said. "A little brandy, maybe? That's what Oscar brings, isn't it?"

She said it was and fetched a bottle, dispensing it to all three of them in tiny glasses.

"He brought us Dotterel too," she said.

"Who's Dotterel?" Jude inquired.

"The parrot. He was a present to me when I was little. He had a mate but she was eaten by the ragemy next door. The brute! Now Dotterel's on his own, and he's not happy. But Oscar's going to bring me another parrot soon. He said he would. He brought pearls for Mama once. And for Papa he always brings newspapers. Papa loves newspapers."

She babbled on in a similar vein with barely a break in the flow. Meanwhile, the three glasses were filled and emptied and filled again several times, the liquor steadily taking its toll on Jude's concentration. In fact she found the monologue, and the subtle motion of the light overhead, positively soporific and finally asked if she might lie down for a while. Again, Dowd made no objection and let Hoi-Polloi escort Jude up to the guest bedroom, offering only a slurred "sweet dreams, lovey" as she retired.

She laid her buzzing head down gratefully, thinking as she dozed that it made sense to sleep now, while the storm prevented her from taking to the streets. When it was over her expedition would begin, with or without Dowd. Oscar was not coming for her, that much seemed certain. Either he'd sustained too much injury to follow or else the Express had been somehow damaged by Dowd's late boarding. Whichever, she could not delay her adventures here any longer. When she woke, she'd emulate the forces rattling the shutters and take Yzordderrex by storm.

———

She dreamt she was in a place of great grief: a dark chamber, its shutters closed against the same storm that raged outside the room in which she slept and dreamt—and knew she slept and dreamt even as she did so—and in this chamber was the sound of a woman sobbing. The grief was so palpable it stung her, and she wanted to soothe it, as much for her own sake as that of the griever. She moved through the murk towards the sound, encountering curtain after curtain as she went, all gossamer thin, as though the trousseaus of a hundred brides had been hung in this chamber. Before she could reach the weeping woman, however, a figure moved through the darkness ahead of her, coming to the bed where the woman lay and whispering to her.

"Kreauchee . . ." the other said, and through the veils Jude glimpsed the lisping speaker.

No figure as bizarre as this had ever flitted through her dreams before. The creature was pale, even in the gloom, and naked, with a back from which sprawled a garden of tails. Jude advanced a little to see her better, and the creature in her turn saw her, or at least her effect upon the veils, for she looked around the chamber as if she knew there was a haunter here. Her voice carried alarm when it came again.

"There's som'ady here, ledy," it said.

"I'll see nobody. Especially Seidux."

"It's notat Seidux. I seeat no'ady, but I feelat som'ady here stell."

The weeping diminished. The woman looked up. There were still veils between Jude and the sleeper's face, and the chamber was indeed dark, but she knew her own features when she saw them, though her hair was plastered to her sweating scalp, and her eyes puffed up with tears. She didn't recoil at the sight, but stood as still as spirits were able amid gossamer, and watched the woman with her face rise up from the bed. There was bliss in her expression.

"He's sent an angel," she said to the creature at her side. "Concupiscentia . . . He's sent an angel to summon me."

"Yes?"

"Yes. For certain. This is a sign. I'm going to be forgiven."

A sound at the door drew the woman's attention. A man in uniform, his face lit only by the cigarette he drew upon, stood watching.

"Get out," the woman said.

"I came only to see that you were comfortable, Ma'am Quaisoir."

"I said get out, Seidux."

"If you should require anything—"

Quaisoir got up suddenly and pitched herself through the veils in Seidux's direction. The suddenness of this assault took Jude by surprise, as it did its target. Though Quaisoir was a head shorter than her captor, she had no fear of him. She slapped the cigarette from his lips.

"I don't want you watching me," she said. "Get out. Hear me? Or shall I scream rape?"

She began to tear at her already ragged clothes, exposing her breasts. Seidux retreated in confusion, averting his eyes.

"As you wish!" he said, heading out of the chamber. "As you wish!"

Quaisoir slammed the door on him and turned her attention back to the haunted room.

"Where are you, spirit?" she said, moving back through the veils. "Gone? No, not gone." She turned to Concupiscentia. "Do you feel its presence?" The creature seemed too frightened to speak. "I feel nothing," Quaisoir said, now standing still amid the shifting veils. "Damn Seidux! The spirit's been driven out!"

Without the means to contradict this, all Jude could do was wait beside the bed and hope that the effect of Seidux's interruption—which had seemingly blinded them to her presence—would wear off now that he'd been exiled from the chamber. She remembered as she waited how Clara had talked about men's power to destroy. Had she just witnessed an example of that, Seidux's mere presence enough to poison the contact between a dreaming spirit and a waking one? If so, he'd done it all unknowing: innocent of his power, but no more forgivable for that. How many times in any day did he and the rest of his kind—hadn't Clara said they were another species?—spoil and mutilate in their unwitting way, Jude wondered, preventing the union of subtler natures?

Quaisoir sank back down on the bed, giving Jude time to ponder the mystery her face represented. She hadn't doubted from the moment she'd entered this chamber that she was traveling here much as she'd first traveled to the tower, using the freedom of a dream state to move invisibly through the real world. That she no longer needed the blue eye to facilitate such movement was a puzzle for another time. What concerned her now was to find out how this woman came to have her face. Was this Dominion somehow a mirror of the world she'd left? And if not—if she was the only woman in the Fifth to have a perfect twin—what did that echo signify?

The wind was beginning to abate, and Quaisoir dispatched her servant to the window to remove the shutters. There was still a red dust hanging in the atmosphere, but, moving to the sill beside the creature, Jude was presented with a vista that, had she possessed breath in this state, would have taken it away. They were perched high above the city, in one of the towers she'd briefly glimpsed as she'd gone around the Peccable house with Hoi-Polloi, bolting and shuttering. It was not simply Yzordderrex that lay before her, but signs of the city's undoing. Fires were raging in a dozen places beyond the palace walls, and within those walls the Autarch's troops were mustering in the courtyards. Turning her dream gaze back towards Quaisoir, Jude saw for the first time the sumptuousness of the chamber in which she'd found the woman. The walls were tapestries, and there was no stick of furniture that did not compete in its gilding. If this was a prison, then it was fit for royalty.

Quaisoir now came to the window and looked out at the panorama of fires.

"I have to find Him," she said. "He sent an angel to

bring me to Him, and Seidux drove the angel out. So I'll
have to go to Him myself. Tonight . . ."

Jude listened, but distractedly, her mind more occupied
by the opulence of the chamber and what it revealed about
her twin. It seemed she shared a face with a woman of some
significance, a possessor of power, now dispossessed, and
planning to break the bonds set upon her. Romance
seemed to be her reason. There was a man in the city below
with whom she desperately wanted to be reunited, a lover
who sent angels to whisper sweet nothings in her ear. What
kind of man? she wondered. A Maestro, perhaps, a wielder
of magic?

Having studied the city for a time, Quaisoir left the window and went through to her dressing room.

"I mustn't go to Him like this," she said, starting to undress. "That would be shameful."

The woman caught sight of herself in one of the mirrors
and sat down in front of it, peering at her reflection with
distaste. Her tears had made mud of the kohl around her
eyes, and her cheeks and neck were blotchy. She took a
piece of linen from the dressing table, sprinkled some fra-
grant oil upon it, and began to roughly clean her face.

"I'll go to Him naked," she said, smiling in anticipation
of that pleasure. "He'll prefer me that way."

This mystery lover intrigued Jude more and more. Hearing her own voice musky with talk of nakedness, she was
tantalized. Would it not be a fine thing to see the consummation? The idea of watching herself couple with some
Yzordderrexian Maestro had not been among the wonder-
ments she'd anticipated discovering in this city, but the notion carried an erotic *frisson* she could not deny herself.
She studied the reflection of her reflection. Though there
were a few cosmetic differences, the essentials were hers, to
the last nick and mole. This was no approximation of her
face, but the thing exactly, which fact strangely excited her.
She had to find a way to speak with this woman tonight.
Even if their twinning was simply a freak of nature, they
would surely be able to illuminate each other's lives with an
exchange of histories. All she needed was a clue from her

doppelgänger as to where in the city she intended to go looking for her Maestro lover.

With her face cleansed, Quaisoir got up from in front of the mirror and went back into the bedroom. Concupiscentia was sitting by the window. Quaisoir waited until she was within inches of her servant before she spoke, and even then her words were barely audible.

"We'll need a knife," she said.

The creature shook her head. "They tookat em all," she said. "You seem how ey lookat and lookat."

"Then we must make one," Quaisoir replied. "Seidux will try to oppose our leaving."

"You wishat to kill em?"

"Yes, I do."

This talk chilled Jude. Though Seidux had retreated before Quaisoir when she'd threatened to cry rape, Jude doubted that he'd be so passive if challenged physically. Indeed, what more perfect excuse would he need to regain his dominance than her coming at him with a knife? If she'd had the means, she would have been Clara's mouthpiece now and echoed her sentiments on man the desolator, in the hope of keeping Quaisoir from harm. It would be an unbearable irony to lose this woman now, having found her way (surely not by accident, though at present it seemed so) across half the Imajica into her very chamber.

"I cet shapas te knife," Concupiscentia was saying.

"Then do it," Quaisoir replied, leaning still closer to her fellow conspirator.

Jude missed the next exchange, because somebody called her name. Startled, she looked around the room, but before she'd half scanned it she recognized the voice. It was Hoi-Polloi, and she was rousing the sleeper after the storm.

"Papa's here!" Jude heard her say. "Wake up, Papa's here!"

There was no time to bid farewell to the scene. It was there in front of her one moment, and replaced the next with the face of Peccable's daughter, leaning to shake her awake.

"Papa—" she said again.

"Yes, all right," Jude said brusquely, hoping the girl would leave without further exchanges coming between her and the sights sleep had brought. She knew she had scant moments to drag the dream into wakefulness with her, or it would subside and the details become hazy the deeper it sank.

She was in luck. Hoi-Polloi hurried back down to her father's side, leaving Jude to recite aloud all she'd seen and heard. Quaisoir and her servant Concupiscentia; Seidux and the plot against him. And the lover, of course. She shouldn't forget the lover, who was presumably somewhere in the city even now, pining for his mistress who was locked up in her gilded prison. With these facts fixed in her head, she ventured first to the bathroom, then down to meet Peccable.

Well dressed and better fed, Peccable had a face upon which his present ire sat badly. He looked slightly absurd in his fury, his features too round and his mouth too small for the rhetoric they were producing. Introductions were made, but there was no time for pleasantries. Peccable's fury needed venting, and he seemed not to care much who his audience was, as long as they sympathized. He had reason for fury. His warehouse near the harbor had been burned to the ground, and he himself had only narrowly escaped death at the hands of a mob that had already taken over three of the Kesparates and declared them independent city-states, thereby issuing a challenge to the Autarch. So far, he said, the palace had done little. Small contingents of troops had been dispatched to the Caramess, to the Oke T'Noon, and the seven Kesparates on the other side of the hill, to suppress any sign of uprisings there. But no offensive had been launched against the insurgents who had taken the harbor.

"They're nothing more than rabble," the merchant said. "They've no care for property or person. Indiscriminate destruction, that's all they're good for! I'm no great lover of the Autarch, but he's got to be the voice of decent people like me in times like this! I should have sold my business a year ago. I talked with Oscar about it. We planned to move away from this wretched city. But I hung on and hung on, because I believe in people. That's my mistake," he said, throwing his eyes up to the ceiling like a man martyred by his own decency. "I have too much faith." He looked at Hoi-Polloi. "Don't I?"

"You do, Papa, you do."

"Well, not any more. You go and pack our belongings, sweet. We're getting out tonight."

"What about the house?" Dowd said. "And all the collectibles downstairs?"

Peccable cast a glance at Hoi-Polloi. "Why don't you start packing now?" he said, clearly uncomfortable with the idea of debating his black market activities in front of his daughter.

He cast a similar glance at Jude, but she pretended not to comprehend its significance and remained seated. He began to talk anyway.

"When we leave this house we leave it forever," he said. "There'll be nothing left to come back to, I'm convinced of that." The outraged bourgeois of minutes before, appealing for civil stability, was now replaced by an apocalyptic. "It was bound to happen sooner or later. They couldn't control the cults in perpetuity."

"They?" said Jude.

"The Autarch. And Quaisoir."

The sound of the name was like a blow to her heart. "Quaisoir?" she said.

"His wife. The consort. Our lady of Yzordderrex: Ma'am Quaisoir. She's been his undoing, if you ask me. He always kept himself hidden away, which was wise; nobody thought about him much as long as trade was good and the streets were lit. The taxes, of course: the taxes have been a burden upon us all, especially family men like myself, but let me tell you we're better off here than they are in Patashoqua or Iahmandhas. No, I don't think he's done badly by us. The stories you hear about the state of things when he first took over: Chaos! Half the Kesparates at war with the other half. He brought stability. People prospered. No, it's not his policies, it's *her:* she's his undoing. Things were fine until she started to interfere. I suppose she thinks she's doing us a favor, deigning to appear in public."

"Have you . . . seen her then?" Jude asked.

"Not personally, no. She stays out of sight, even when she attends executions. Though I heard that she showed herself today, out in the open. Somebody said they'd actually seen her face. Ugly, they said. Brutish. I'm not surprised. All these executions were her idea. She enjoys them, apparently. Well, people don't like that. Taxes, yes. An occasional purge, some political trials—well, yes, those too; we can accept those. But you can't make the law into a public spectacle. That's a mockery, and we've never mocked the law in Yzordderrex."

He went on in much the same vein, but Jude wasn't listening. She was attempting to conceal the heady mixture of feelings that was coursing through her. Quaisoir, the woman with her face, was not some minor player in the life of Yzordderrex but one of its two potentates; by extension, therefore, one of the great rulers of the Imajica. Could she now doubt that there was purpose in her coming to this city? She had a face which owned power. A face that went in secret from the world, but that behind its veils had made the Autarch of Yzordderrex pliant. The question was: What did that mean? After so unremarkable a life on earth, had she been called into this Dominion to taste a little of the power that her other took for granted? Or was she here as a diversion, called to suffer in place of Quaisoir for the crimes she'd supposedly committed? And if so, who was the summoner? Clearly it had to be a Maestro with ready access to the Fifth Dominion and agents there to conspire with. Was Godolphin some part of this plot? Or Dowd, perhaps? That seemed more likely. And what about Quaisoir? Was she in ignorance of the plans being laid on her behalf or a fellow plotter?

Tonight would tell, Jude promised herself. Tonight she'd find some way to intercept Quaisoir as she went to meet her angel-dispatching lover, and before another day had gone by Jude would know whether she'd been brought from the Fifth to be a sister or a scapegoat.

33

GENTLE DID AS HE'D PROMISED PIE, and stayed with Huzzah at the café where they'd breakfasted until the comet's arc took it behind the mountain and the light of day gave way to twilight. Doing so tried not only his patience but his nerve, because as the afternoon wore on the unrest from the lower Kesparates spread up through the streets, and it became increasingly apparent that the establishment would stand in the middle of a battlefield by evening. Party by party, the customers vacated their tables as the sound of rioting and gunfire crept closer. A slow rain of smuts began to fall, spiraling from a sky which was intermittently darkened now by smoke rising from the burning Kesparates.

As the first wounded began to be carried up the street, indicating that the field of action was now very near, the owners of several nearby shops gathered in the café for a short council, debating, presumably, the best way to defend their property. It ended in accusation, the insults an education to both Gentle and Huzzah. Two of the owners returned with weapons a few minutes later, at which point the manager, who introduced himself as Bunyan Blew, asked Gentle if he and his daughter didn't have a home to go to. Gentle replied that they had promised to meet somebody here earlier in the day, and they would be most obliged if they could remain until their friend arrived.

"I remember you," Blew replied. "You came in this morning, didn't you, with a woman?"

"That's who we're waiting for."

"She put me in mind of somebody I used to know," Blew said. "I hope she's safe out there."

"So do we," Gentle replied.

"You'd better stay then. But you'll have to lend me a hand barricading the place."

Bunyan explained that he'd known this was going to happen sooner or later and was prepared for the eventuality. There were timbers to nail over the windows, and a supply of small arms should the mob try to loot his shelves.

In fact, his precautions proved unnecessary. The street became a conduit for ferrying the wounded army from the combat zone, which was moving up the hill one street east of the café. There were two nerve-racking hours, however, when the din of shouting and gunfire was coming from all compass points, and the bottles on Blew's shelves tinkled every time the ground shook, which was often. One of the shopkeepers who'd left in high dudgeon earlier came beating at the door during this siege, and stumbled over the threshold with blood streaming from his head and tales of destruction from his mouth. The army had called up heavy artillery in the last hour, he reported, and it had practically leveled the harbor and rendered the causeway impassable, thereby effectively sealing the city. This was all part of the Autarch's plan, he said. Why else were whole neighborhoods being allowed to burn unchecked? The Autarch was leaving the city to consume its own citizens, knowing the conflagration would not be able to break the palace walls.

"He's going to let the mob destroy the city," the man went on, "and he doesn't care what happens to us in the meantime. Selfish bastard! We're all going to burn, and he's not going to lift a finger to help us!"

This scenario certainly fitted the facts. When, at Gentle's suggestion, they went up onto the roof to get a better view of the situation, it seemed to be exactly as described. The ocean was obliterated by a wall of smoke climbing from the embers of the harbor; further flame-shot columns rose from two dozen neighborhoods, near and far; and through the dirty heat coming off the Oke T'Noon's pyre the causeway was just visible, its rubble damming the delta. Clogged by smoke, the comet shed a diminished light on the city, and even that was fading as the long twilight deepened.

"It's time to leave," Gentle told Huzzah.

"Where are we going to go?"

"Back to find Pie 'oh' pah," he replied. "While we still can."

———

It had been apparent from the roof that there was no safe route back to the mystif's Kesparate. The various factions warring in the streets were moving unpredictably. A street that was empty one moment might be thronged the next, and rubble the moment after that. They would have to go on instinct and a prayer, taking as direct a path back to where they'd left Pie 'oh' pah as circumstance allowed. Dusk in this Dominion usually lasted the length of an English midwinter day—five or six hours—the tail of the comet keeping traces of light in the sky long after its fiery head had dropped beneath the horizon. But the smoke thickened as Gentle and Huzzah traveled, eclipsing the languid light and plunging the city into a filthy gloom. There were still the fires to compensate, of course, but between the conflagration, in streets where the lamps hadn't been lit and the citizens had shuttered their windows and blocked their keyholes to keep any sign of occupation from showing, the darkness was almost impenetrable. In such thoroughfares Gentle hoisted Huzzah onto his shoulders, from which vantage point she was able to snatch sights to steer him by.

It was slow going, however, halting at each intersection to calculate the least dangerous route to follow, and taking refuge at the approach of both governmental and revolutionary troops. But for every soldier in this war there were half a dozen bystanders, people daring the tide of battle like beachcombers, retreating before each wave, only to return to their watching places when it receded: a sometimes lethal game. A similar dance was demanded of Gentle and Huzzah. Driven off course again and again, they were obliged to trust to instinct as to their direction, and inevitably instinct finally deserted them.

In an uncommon hush between clamors and bombardments, Gentle said, "Angel? I don't know where we are any more."

A comprehensive fusillade had brought down most of the Kesparate around them, and there were precious few places of refuge amid the rubble, but Huzzah insisted they find one: a call of nature that could be delayed no longer.

Gentle set her down, and she headed off for the dubious cover of a semidemolished house some yards up the street. He stood guard at the door, calling inside to her and telling her not to venture too far. He'd no sooner offered this warning than the appearance of a small band of armed men drove him back into the shadows of the doorway. But for their weapons, which had presumably been plucked from dead men, they looked ill suited to the role of revolutionaries. The eldest, a barrel of a man in late middle age, still wore the hat and tie he'd most likely gone to work in that morning, while two of his accomplices were barely older than Huzzah. Of the two remaining members, one was an Oethac woman, the other of the tribe to which the executioner in Vanaeph had belonged: a Nullianac, its head like hands joined in prayer.

Gentle glanced back into the darkness, hoping to hush Huzzah before she emerged, but there was no sign of her. He left the step and headed into the ruins. The floor was sticky underfoot, though he couldn't see with what. He did see Huzzah, however, or her silhouette, as she rose from relieving herself. She saw him too and made a little noise of protest, which he hushed as loudly as he dared. A fresh bombardment close by brought shock waves and bursts of light, by which he glimpsed their refuge: a domestic interior, with a table set for the evening meal, and its cook dead beneath it, her blood the stickiness under his heel.

Beckoning Huzzah to him and holding her tight, he ventured back towards the door as a second bombardment began. It drove the looters to the step for cover, and the Oethac caught sight of Gentle before he could retreat into shadow. She let out a shout, and one of the youths fired into the darkness where Gentle and Huzzah had stood, the bullets spattering plaster and wood splinters in all directions. Backing away from the door through which their attackers were bound to come, Gentle ushered Huzzah into the darkest corner and drew a breath. He barely had time to do so before the trigger-happy youth was at the doorway, firing indiscriminately. Gentle unleashed a pneuma from the darkness, and it flew towards the door. He'd underestimated his strength. The gunman was obliterated in an instant, but the pneuma took the door frame and much of the wall to either side of it at the same time.

Before the dust could clear and the survivors come after them, he went to find Huzzah, but the wall against which she'd been crouching was cracked and curling like a stone wave. He yelled her name as it broke. Her shriek answered him, off to his left. The Nullianac had snatched her up, and for a terrifying instant Gentle thought it intended to annihilate her, but instead it drew her to it like a doll and disappeared into the dust clouds.

He started in pursuit without a backward glance, an error that brought him to his knees before he'd covered two yards of ground, as the Oethac woman delivered a stabbing blow to the small of his back. The wound wasn't deep, but the shock drove his breath from him as he fell, and her second blow would have taken out the back of his skull had he not rolled out of its way. The small pick she was wielding, wet with his blood, buried itself in the ground, and before she could pull it free he hauled himself to his feet and started after Huzzah and her abductor. The second youth was moving after the Nullianac, squealing with drugged or drunken glee, and Gentle followed the sound when he lost the sight, the chase taking him out of the wasteland and into a Kesparate that had been left relatively untouched by the conflict.

There was good reason. The trade here was in sexual favors, and business was booming. Though the streets were narrower than in any other district Gentle had passed through, there was plenty of light spilling from the doorways and windows, the lamps and candles arranged to best illuminate the wares lolling on step and sill. Even a passing glance confirmed that there were anatomies and gratifications on offer here that beggared the most dissolute backwaters of Bangkok or Tangiers. Nor was there any paucity of customers. The imminence of death seemed to have whipped up the consensual libido. Even if the flesh pushers and pill pimps who offered their highs as Gentle passed never made it to morning, they'd die rich. Needless to say,

the sight of a Nullianac carrying a protesting child barely
warranted a look in a street sacred to depravity, and Gentle's calls for the abductor to be stopped went ignored.

The crowd thickened the farther down the street he ventured, and he finally lost both sight and sound of those he
was pursuing. There were alleyways off the main thoroughfare (its name—Lickerish Street—daubed on one of the
bordello walls), and the darkness of any of them might be
concealing the Nullianac. He started to yell Huzzah's
name, but in the come-ons and hagglings two shouted syllables were drowned out. He was about to run on when he
glimpsed a man backing out of one of the alleyways with
distress on his face. He pushed his way through to the man
and took hold of his arm, but he shrugged it off and fled
before Gentle could ask what he'd seen. Rather than call
Huzzah's name again, Gentle saved his breath and headed
down the alley.

There was a fire of mattresses burning twenty yards
down it, tended by a masked woman. Insects had nested in
the ticking and were being driven out by the flames, some
attempting to fly on burning wings, only to be swatted by
the fire maker. Ducking her wild swings, Gentle asked after
the Nullianac, and the woman directed him on down the
alley with a nod. The ground was seething with refugees
from the mattresses, and he broke a hundred shells with
every step until he was well clear of the fumigator's fire.
Lickerish Street was now too far behind him to shed any
light on the scene, but the bombardment which the crowd
behind him had been so indifferent to still continued all
around, and explosions farther up the city's slopes briefly
but garishly lit the alleyway. It was narrow and filthy, the
buildings blinded by brick or boarded up, the road between
scarcely more than a gutter, choked with trash and decaying vegetable matter. Its stench was sickening, but he
breathed it deeply, hoping the pneuma born of and on that
foetid air would be all the more potent for its foulness. The
theft of Huzzah had already earned her abductors their
deaths, but if they had done the least hurt to her he swore

to himself he'd return that hurt a hundredfold before he executed them.

The alleyway twisted and turned, narrowing to a man's width in some places, but the sense that he was closing on them was confirmed when he heard the youth whooping a little way ahead. He slowed his pace a little, advancing through shin-deep refuse, until he came in sight of a light. The alleyway ended a few yards from where he stood, and there, squatting with its back to the wall, was the Nullianac. The light source was neither lamp nor fire but the creature's head, between the sides of which arcs of energy passed back and forth.

By their flickers, Gentle saw his angel, lying on the ground in front of her captor. She was quite still, her body limp, her eyes closed, for which fact Gentle was grateful, given the Nullianac's present labors. It had stripped the lower half of her body, and its long, pale hands were busy upon her. The whooper was standing a little way off from the scene. He was unzipped, his gun in one hand, his half-hard member in the other. Every now and then he aimed the gun at the child's head, and another whoop came from his lips.

Nothing would have given Gentle more satisfaction at that moment than unleashing a pneuma against them both from where he stood, but he still wielded the power ineptly and feared that he'd do Huzzah some accidental harm, so he crept a little closer, another explosion on the hill throwing its brutal light down on the scene. By it he caught a glimpse of the Nullianac's work, and then, more stomach-turning still, heard Huzzah gasp. The light withered as she did so, leaving the Nullianac's head to shed its flickering gleam on her pain. The whooper was silent now, his eyes fixed on the violation. Looking up, the Nullianac uttered a few syllables shaped out of the chamber between its skulls, and reluctantly the youth obeyed its order, retreating from the scene a little way. Some crisis was near. The arcs in the Nullianac's head were flaring with fresh urgency, its fingers working as if to expose Huzzah to their discharge. Gentle drew breath, realizing he would have to risk hurting Huzzah if he was to prevent the certainty of worse harm. The whooper heard his intake and turned to peer into the darkness. As he did so another lethal brightness dropped around them from on high. By it, Gentle stood revealed.

The youth fired on the instant, but either his ineptitude or his arousal spoiled his aim. The shots went wide. Gentle didn't give him a second chance. Reserving his pneuma for the Nullianac, he threw himself at the youth, striking the weapon from his hand and kicking the legs from under him. The whooper went down within inches of his gun, but before he could reclaim it Gentle drove his foot down on the outstretched fingers, bringing a very different kind of whoop from the kid's throat.

Now he turned back on the Nullianac, in time to see it raising its fireful head, the arcs cracking like slapsticks. Gentle's fist went to his mouth, and he was discharging the pneuma when the whooper seized hold of his leg. The death warrant went from Gentle's hand, but it struck the Nullianac's flank rather than its head, wounding but not dispatching it. The kid hauled on Gentle's leg again, and this time he toppled, falling into the muck where he'd put the whooper seconds before, his punctured back striking the ground hard. The pain blinded him, and when sight returned the youth was up, and rummaging among the arsenal at his belt. Gentle glanced towards the Nullianac. It had dropped against the wall, its head thrown back and spitting darts of fire. Their light was little, but enough for Gentle to catch the gleam of the dropped gun at his side. He reached for it as the delinquent's hand fumbled with another weapon, and he had it leveled before the youth could get his cracked finger on the trigger. He pointed not at the youth's head or heart, but at his groin. A littler target, but one which made the kid drop his gun instantly.

"Don't do that, sirrah!" he said.

"The belt," Gentle said, getting to his feet as the youth unbuckled and unburdened himself of his filched arsenal.

By another blaze from above he saw the boy now full of tics and jitters, pitiful and powerless. There would be no honor in shooting him down, whatever crimes he'd been responsible for.

"Go home," he said. "If I see your face ever again—"

"You won't, sirrah!" the boy said. "I swear! I swear you won't!"

He didn't give Gentle time to change his mind, but fled as the light that had revealed his frailty faded. Gentle turned the gun and his gaze upon the Nullianac. It had raised itself from the ground and slid up the wall into a standing position, its fingers, their tips red with its deed, pressed to the place where the pneuma had struck it. Gentle hoped it was suffering, but he had no way of knowing until it spoke. When it did, when the words came from its wretched head, they were faltering and barely comprehensible.

"Which is it to be," it said, "you or her? I will kill one of you before I pass. Which is it to be?"

"I'll kill you first," Gentle said, the gun pointed at the Nullianac's head.

"You could," it said. "I know. You murdered a brother of mine outside Patashoqua."

"Your brother, huh?"

"We're rare, and know each other's lives," it said.

"So don't get any rarer," Gentle advised, taking a step towards Huzzah as he spoke, but keeping his eyes fixed on her violator.

"She's alive," it said. "I wouldn't kill a thing so young. Not quickly. Young deserves slow."

Gentle risked a glance away from the creature. Huzzah's eyes were indeed wide open and fixed upon him in her terror.

"It's all right, angel," he said, "nothing's going to happen to you. Can you move?"

He glanced back at the Nullianac as he spoke, wishing he had some way of interpreting the motions of its little fires. Was it more grievously wounded than he'd thought, and preserving its energies for healing? Or was it biding its time, waiting for its moment to strike?

Huzzah was pulling herself up into a sitting position, the

motion bringing little whimpers of pain from her. Gentle longed to cradle and soothe her, but all he'd dared do was drop to his haunches, his eyes fixed on her violator, and reach for the clothes she'd had torn from her.

"Can you walk, angel?"

"I don't know," she sobbed.

"Please try. I'll help you."

He put his hand out to do so but she avoided him, saying no through her tears and pulling herself to her feet.

"That's good, sweetheart," he said. There was a reawakening in the Nullianac's head, the arcs dancing again. "I want you to start walking, angel," Gentle said. "Don't worry about me, I'm coming with you."

She did as he instructed, slowly, the sobs still coming. The Nullianac started to speak again as she went.

"Ah, to see her like that. It makes me ache." The arcs had begun their din again, like distant firecrackers. "What would you do to save her little soul?" it said.

"Just about anything," Gentle replied.

"You deceive yourself," it said. "When you killed my brother, we inquired after you, my kin and I. We know how foul a savior you are. What's my crime beside yours? A small thing, done because my appetite demands it. But you—*you*—you've laid waste the hopes of generations. You've destroyed the fruit of great men's trees. And *still* you claim you would give yourself to save her little soul?"

This eloquence startled Gentle, but its essence startled him more. Where had the creature plucked these conceits from, that it could so easily spill them now? They were inventions, of course, but they confounded him nevertheless, and his thoughts strayed from his present jeopardy for a vital moment. The creature saw him drop his guard and acted on the instant. Though it was no more than two yards from him, he heard the sliver of silence between the light and its report, a void confirming how foul a savior he was. Death was on its way towards the child before his warning cry was even in his throat.

He turned to see his angel standing in the alleyway some distance from him. She had either turned in anticipation, or had been listening to the Nullianac's speech, because she stood full face to the blow coming at her. Still, time ran slow, and Gentle had several aching moments in which to see how her eyes were fixed upon him, her tears all dried, her gaze unblinking. Time too for that warning shout, in acknowledgment of which she closed her eyes, her face becoming a blank upon which he could inscribe any accusation his guilt wished to contrive.

Then the Nullianac's blow was upon her. The force struck her body at speed, but it didn't break her flesh, and for an instant he dared hope she had found some defense against it. But its hurt was more insidious than a bullet or a blow, its light spreading from the point of impact up to her face, where it entered by every means it could, and down to where its dispatcher's fingers had already pried.

He let out another shout, this time of revulsion, and turned back on the Nullianac, raising the gun its words had made him so forgetful of and firing at its heart. It fell back against the wall, its arms slack at its side, the space between its skulls still issuing its lethal light. Then he looked back at Huzzah, to see that it had eaten her away from the inside, and that she was flowing back along the line of her destroyer's gaze, into the chamber from which the stroke had been delivered. Even as he watched, her face collapsed, and her limbs, never substantial, decayed and went the same way. Before she was entirely consumed, however, the harm Gentle's bullet had done the Nullianac took its toll. The stream of power fractured and failed. When it did, darkness descended, and for a time Gentle couldn't even see the creature's body. Then the bombardment on the hill began afresh, its blaze brief but bright enough to show him the Nullianac's corpse, lying in the dirt where it had squatted.

He watched it, expecting some final act of retaliation, but none came. The light died, and left Gentle to retreat along the alleyway, weighed down not only by his failure to save Huzzah's life, but by his lack of comprehension of what had just happened. In plain terms, a child in his care had been slaughtered by her molester, and he'd failed to prevent that slaughter. But he'd been wandering in the Dominions too long to be content with simple assessments. There was more here than stymied lust and sudden death. Words had been uttered more appropriate to pulpit than gutter. Hadn't he himself called Huzzah his angel? Hadn't he seen her grow seraphic at the end, knowing she was about to die and accepting that fate? And hadn't he in his turn been dubbed a deficient savior—and proved that accusation true by failing to deliver her? These were high-flown words, but he badly needed to believe them apt, not so that he could indulge messianic fantasies, but so that the grief welling in him might be softened by the hope that there was a higher purpose here, which in the fullness of time he'd come to know and understand.

A burst of fire threw light down the alleyway, and Gentle's shadow fell across something twitching in the filth. It took him a moment to comprehend what he was seeing, but when he did he loosed a shout. Huzzah had not quite gone. Small scraps of her skin and sinew, dropped when the Nullianac's claim upon her was cut short, moved here in the rot. None were recognizable; indeed, had they not been moving in the folds of her bloodied clothes he'd not even have known them as her flesh. He reached down to touch them, tears stinging his eyes, but before his fingers could make contact, what little life the scraps had owned went out.

He rose raging; rose in horror at the filth beneath his feet, and the dead, empty houses that channeled it, and in disgust at himself, for surviving when his angel had not. Turning his gaze on the nearest wall, he drew breath and put not one hand but two against his lips, intending to do what little he could to bury these remains.

But rage and revulsion were fueling his pneuma, and when it went from him it brought down not one wall but several, passing through the teetering houses like a bullet through a pack of cards. Shards of pulverized stone flew as the houses toppled, the collapse of one initiating the fall of the next, the dust cloud growing in scale as each house added to its sum.

He started up the alleyway in pursuit of the pneuma, fearing that his disgust had given it more purpose than he'd intended. It was heading towards Lickerish Street, where the crowds were still milling, oblivious to its approach. They were not wandering that street innocent of its corruption, of course, but neither did their presence there deserve death. He wished he could draw the breath as he exhaled it, call the pneuma back into himself. But it had its head, and all he could do was run after it as it brought down house after house, hoping it would spend its power before it reached the crowd.

He could see the lights of Lickerish Street through the hail of demolition. He picked up his pace, to try and outrun the pneuma, and was a little ahead of it when he set eyes on the throng itself, thicker than ever. Some had interrupted their window-shopping to watch the spectacle of destruction. He saw their gawking faces, their little smiles, their shaking heads: saw they didn't comprehend for an instant what was coming their way. Knowing any attempt to warn them verbally would be lost in the furor, he raced to the end of the alleyway and flung himself into their midst, intending to scatter them, but his antics only drew a larger audience, who were in turn intrigued by the alleyway's capitulation. One or two had grasped their jeopardy now, their expressions of curiosity become looks of fear; finally, too late, their unease spread to the rest, and a general retreat began.

The pneuma was too quick, however. It broke through the last of the walls in a devastating shower of rock shards and splinters, striking the crowd at its densest place. Had Hapexamendios, in a fit of cleansing ire, delivered a judgment on Lickerish Street He could scarcely have scoured it better. What had seconds before been a crowd of puzzled sightseers was blood and bone in a heartbeat.

Though he stood in the midst of this devastation, Gentle remained unharmed. He was able to watch his terrible weapon at work, its power apparently undecayed despite the fact that it had demolished a string of houses. Nor, having cut a swath through the crowd, was it following the trajectory set at his lips. It had found flesh and clearly intended to busy itself in the midst of living stuff until there was none left to undo.

He was appalled at the prospect. This hadn't been his intention, or anything like it. There seemed to be only one option available to him, and that he instantly took: he stood in the pneuma's path. He'd used the power in his lungs many times now—first against the Nullianac's brother in Vanaeph, then twice in the mountains, and finally on the island, when they were making their escape from Vigor N'ashap's asylum—but in all that time he'd only had the vaguest impression of its appearance. Was it like a fire-breather's belch, or like a bullet made of will and air, nearly invisible until it did its deed?

Perhaps it had been the latter once, but now, as he set himself in its path, he saw that it had gathered dust and blood along its route, and from those essential elements it had made itself a likeness of its maker. It was *his* face that was coming at him, albeit roughly sculpted: his brow, his eyes, his open mouth, expelling the very breath it had begun with. It didn't slow as it approached its maker, but struck Gentle's chest the way it had struck so many before him. He felt the blow but was not felled by it. Instead the power, knowing its source, discharged itself through his system, running to his fingertips and coursing across his scalp. Its shock was come and gone in a moment, and he was left standing in the middle of the devastation with his arms spread wide and the dust falling around him.

Silence followed. Distantly, he could hear the wounded sobbing, and half-demolished walls going to rubble, but he was encircled by a hush that was almost reverential. Somebody dropped to his knees nearby, to tend, he thought, to one of the wounded. Then he heard the hallelujahs the man was uttering and saw his hands reaching up towards him. Another of the crowd followed suit, and then another, as though this scene of their deliverance was a sign they'd been waiting for and a long-suppressed flood of devotion was breaking from each of their hearts.

Sickened, Gentle turned his gaze away from their grate-

ful faces, up the dusty length of Lickerish Street. He had
only one ambition now: to find Pie and take comfort from
this insanity in the mystif's arms. He broke from his ring of
devotees and started up the street, ignoring their clinging
hands and cries of adoration. He wanted to berate them for
their naïveté, but what good would that do? Any pronouncement he made now, however self-deprecatory,
would probably be taken as the jotting for some gospel. Instead he kept his silence and picked his way over the stones
and corpses, his head down. The hosannas followed him,
but he didn't once acknowledge them, knowing even as he
went that his reluctance might seem like divine humility,
but unable to escape the trap circumstance had set.

The wasteland at the head of the street was as daunting
as ever, but he started across it not caring what fires might
come. Its terrors were nothing beside the memory of Huzzah's scrap, twitching in the muck, or the hallelujahs he
could still hear behind him, raised in ignorance of the fact
that he—the savior of Lickerish Street—was also its destroyer, but no less tempting for that.

34

I

Every trace of the joy that the vast halls of the chianculi
had once seen—no clowns or ponies, but circuses such as
any showman in the Fifth would have wept to own—had
gone. The echoing halls had become places of mourning
and of judgment. Today, the accused was the mystif Pie
'oh' pah; its accuser one of the few lawyers in Yzordderrex
the Autarch's purges had left alive, an asthmatic and
pinched individual called Thes 'reh' ot. He had an audience
of two for his prosecution—Pie 'oh' pah, and the judge—
but he delivered his litany of crimes as if the hall were full
to the rafters. The mystif was guilty enough to warrant a
dozen executions, he said. It was at very least a traitor and

coward, but probably also an informant and a spy. Worse, perhaps, it had abandoned this Dominion for another without the consent of its family or its teachers, denying its people the benefit of its rarity. Had it forgotten in its arrogance that its condition was sacred, and that to prostitute itself in another world (the Fifth, of all places, a mire of unmiraculous souls!) was not only a sin upon itself but upon its species? It had gone from this place clean and dared to return debauched and corrupted, bringing a creature of the Fifth with it and then freely confessing that said creature was its husband.

Pie had expected to be met with some recriminations upon return—the memories of Eurhetemec were long, and they clung strongly to tradition as the only contact they had with the First Dominion—but the vehemence of this catalogue was still astonishing. The judge, Culus 'su' erai, was a woman of great age but diminished physique, who sat bundled in robes as colorless as her skin, listening to the litany of accusations without once looking at either accuser or accused. When Thes 'reh' ot had finished, she offered the mystif the chance to defend itself, and it did what it could.

"I admit I've made many errors," Pie said. "Not least leaving my family—and my people were my family—without telling them where I was going or why. But the simple fact is: I didn't know. I fully intended to return, after maybe a year or so. I thought it'd be fine to have traveler's tales to tell. Now, when I finally return, I find there's nobody to tell them to."

"What possessed you to go into the Fifth?" Culus asked.

"Another error," Pie said. "I went to Patashoqua and I met a theurgist there who said he could take me over to the Fifth. Just for a jaunt. We'd be back in a day, he said. A day! I thought this was a fine idea. I'd come home having walked in the Fifth Dominion. So I paid him—"

"In what currency?" said Thes 'reh' ot.

"Cash. And some little favors. I didn't prostitute myself, if that's what you're suggesting. If I had, maybe he'd have kept his promises. Instead, his ritual delivered me into the In Ovo."

"And how long were you there?" Culus 'su' erai inquired.

"I don't know," the mystif replied. "The suffering there seemed endless and unendurable, but it was perhaps only days."

Thes 'reh' ot snorted at this. "Its *sufferings* were of its own making, ma'am. Are they strictly relevant?"

"Probably not," Culus 'su' erai, conceded. "But you were claimed out of the In Ovo by a Maestro of the Fifth, am I right?"

"Yes, ma'am. His name was Sartori. He was the Fifth's representative in the Synod preparing for the Reconciliation."

"And you served him?"

"I did."

"In what capacity?"

"In any way he chose to request. I was his familiar."

Thes 'reh' ot made a sound of disgust. His response was not feigned, Pie thought. He was genuinely appalled at the thought of one of his people—especially a creature so blessed as a mystif—serving the will of a *Homo sapiens*.

"Was Sartori, in your estimation, a good man?" Culus asked Pie.

"He was the usual paradox. Compassion when it was least expected. Cruelty the same. He had an extraordinary ego, but then I don't believe he could have carried the responsibility of the Reconciliation without one."

"Was he cruel to you?" Culus inquired.

"Ma'am?"

"Do you not understand the question?"

"Yes. But not its relevance."

Culus growled with displeasure. "This court may be much reduced in pomp and ceremony," she said, "and its officers a little withered, but the authority of both remains undiminished. Do you understand me, mystif? When I ask a question I expect it answered, promptly and truthfully."

Pie murmured apologies.

"So," said Culus. "I will repeat the question. Was Sartori cruel to you?"

"Sometimes," Pie replied.

"And yet when the Reconciliation failed you didn't forsake his company and return to this Dominion?"

"He'd summoned me out of the In Ovo. He'd bound me to him. I had no jurisdiction."

"Unlikely," Thes 'reh' ot remarked. "Are you asking us to believe—"

"Did I hear you ask permission to question the accused again?" Culus snapped.

"No, ma'am."

"Do you request such permission?"

"Yes, ma'am."

"Denied," Culus replied and turned her eye back upon Pie. "I think you learned a great deal in the Fifth Dominion, mystif," she said. "And you're the worse for it. You're arrogant. You're sly. And you're probably just as cruel as your Maestro. But I don't believe you're a spy. You're something worse than that. You're a fool. You turned your back on people who loved you and let yourself be enslaved by a man responsible for the deaths of a great many fine souls across the Imajica. I can tell you've got something to say, Thes 'reh' ot. Spit it out, before I give judgment."

"Only that the mystif isn't here simply charged with spying, ma'am. In denying its people the benefits of its birthright, it committed a grievous crime against us."

"I don't doubt that," Culus said. "And it frankly sickens me to look on something so tainted that once had perfectibility within its grasp. But, may I remind you, Thes 'reh' ot, how few we are? The tribe is diminished to almost nothing. And this mystif, whose breed was always rare, is the last of its line."

"The last?" said Pie.

"Yes, the last!" Culus replied, her voice trembling as it rose. "While you were at play in the Fifth Dominion our people have been systematically decimated. There are now fewer than fifty souls here in the city. The rest are either dead or scattered. Your own line is destroyed, Pie 'oh' pah. Every last one of your clan is murdered or dead of grief."

The mystif covered its face with its hands, but Culus didn't spare it the rest of her report.

"Two other mystifs survived the purges," she went on, "until just a year ago. One was murdered here in the chiancula, while it was healing a child. The other went into the desert—the Dearth are there, at the edge of the First, and the Autarch's troops don't like to go so near to the Erasure—but they caught up with it before it reached the tents. They brought its body back and hung it on the gates."

She stepped down from her chair and approached Pie, who was sobbing now.

"So you see, it may be that you did the right thing for the wrong reasons. If you'd stayed you'd be dead by now."

"Ma'am, I protest," Thes 'reh' ot said.

"What would you prefer I did?" Culus said. "Add this foolish creature's blood to the sea already spilt? No. Better we try and turn its taint to our advantage."

Pie looked up, puzzled.

"Perhaps we've been too pure. Too predictable. Our stratagems foreseen, our plots easily uncovered. But you're from another world, mystif, and maybe that makes you potent." She paused for breath. Then she said, "This is my judgment. Take whomsoever you can find among our number and use your tainted ways to murder our enemy. If none will go with you, go alone. But don't return here, mystif, while the Autarch is still breathing."

Thes 'reh' ot let out a laugh that rang around the chamber. "Perfect!" he said. "Perfect!"

"I'm glad my judgment amuses you," Culus replied. "Remove yourself, Thes 'reh' ot." He made to protest but she brought forth such a shout he flinched as if struck. "I said, *remove yourself!*"

The laughter fell from his face. He made a small formal bow, murmuring some chilly words of parting as he did so, and left the chamber. She watched him go.

"We have all become cruel," she said. "You in your way. Us in ours." She looked back at Pie 'oh' pah. "Do you know why he laughed, mystif?"

"Because he thinks your judgment is execution by another name?"

"Yes, that's precisely what he thinks. And, who knows, perhaps that's what it is. But this may be the last night of the Dominion, and last things have power tonight they never had before."

"And I'm a last thing."

"Yes, you are."

The mystif nodded. "I understand," it said. "And it seems just."

"Good," she said. Though the trial was over, neither moved. "You have a question?" Culus asked.

"Yes, I do."

"Better ask it now."

"Do you know if a shaman called Arae 'ke' gei is still alive?"

Culus made a little smile. "I wondered when you'd get to him," she said. "He was one of the survivors of the Reconciliation, wasn't he?"

"Yes."

"I didn't know him that well, but I heard him speak of you. He held on to life long after most people would have given up, because he said you'd come back eventually. He didn't realize you were bound to your Maestro, of course."

She said all this disingenuously, but there was a penetrating look in her rheumy eyes throughout.

"Why didn't you come back, mystif?" she said. "And don't spin me some story about jurisdiction. You could have slipped your bondage if you'd put your mind to it, especially in the confusion after the failure of the Reconciliation. But you didn't. You chose to stay with your wretched Sartori, even though members of your own tribe had been victims of his ineptitude."

"He was a broken man. And I was more than his familiar, I was his friend. How could I leave him?"

"That's not all," Culus said. She'd been a judge too long to let such simplifications pass unchallenged. "What else, mystif? This is the night of last things, remember. Tell it now or run the risk of not telling it at all."

"Very well," said Pie. "I always nurtured the hope that there would be another attempt at Reconciliation. And I wasn't the only one who nurtured such a hope."

"Arae 'ke' gei indulged it too, huh?"

"Yes, he did."

"So that's why he kept your name alive. And himself too, waiting for you to come back." She shook her head. "Why do you wallow in these fantasies? There'll be no Reconciliation. If anything, it'll be the other way about. The Imajica'll come apart at the seams, and every Dominion will be sealed up in its own little misery."

"That's a grim vision."

"It's an honest one. And a rational one."

"There are still people in every Dominion willing to try again. They've waited two hundred years, and they're not going to let go of their hope now."

"Arae 'ke' gei let go," Culus said. "He died two years ago."

"I was . . . prepared for that eventuality," Pie said. "He was old when I knew him last."

"If it's any comfort, your name was on his lips at the very end. He never gave up believing."

"There are others who can perform the ceremonies in his place."

"I was right," Culus said. "You are a fool, mystif." She started towards the door. "Do you do this in memory of your Maestro?"

Pie went with her, opening the door and stepping out into a twilight sharp with smoke. "Why would I do that?" Pie said.

"Because you loved him," Culus said, her gaze accusatory. "And that's the real reason why you never came back here. You loved him more than your own people."

"Perhaps that's true," Pie said. "But why would I do anything in memory of the living?"

"The living?"

The mystif smiled, bowing to its judge as it retreated

from the light at the door, fading into the gloom like a phantom. "I told you Sartori was a broken man, not a dead one," it said as it went. "The dream is still alive, Culus 'su' erai. And so is my Maestro."

2

Quaisoir was waiting behind the veils when Seidux came in. The windows were open, and within the warm dusk came a din aphrodisiacal to a soldier like Seidux. He peered at the veils, trying to make out the figure behind them. Was she naked? It seemed so.

"I have an apology to make," she said to him.

"There's no need."

"There's every need. You were doing your duty, watching me." She paused. When she spoke again, her voice was sinuous. "I like to be watched, Seidux. . . ."

He murmured: "You do?"

"Certainly. As long as my audience is appreciative."

"I'm appreciative," he said, surreptitiously dropping his cigarette and grinding it out beneath the heel of his boot.

"Then why don't you close the door?" she said to him. "In case we get noisy. Maybe you should tell the guards to go and get drunk?"

He did so. When he returned to the veils he saw that she was kneeling up on the bed, her hand between her legs. And, yes, she was naked. When she moved the veils moved with her, some of them sticking momentarily to the oiled gloss of her skin. He could see how her breasts rode up as she raised her arms, inviting his kisses there. He put his hand out to part the veils, but they were too abundant, and he could find no break in them, so he simply pressed on towards her, half blinded by their luxury.

Her hand went down once more between her legs, and he couldn't conceal a moan of anticipation at the thought of replacing it with his own. There was swelling in her fingers, he thought: some device she'd been pleasuring herself with, most likely, anticipating his arrival, easing herself open to accommodate his every inch. Thoughtful, pliant thing that she was, she was even handing it to him now, as though in confession of her little sin; thinking perhaps that he'd want to feel its warmth and wetness. She pushed it through the veils towards him, as he in turn pressed towards her, murmuring as he went a few promises that ladies liked to hear.

Between those promises he caught the sound of tearing fabric, and assuming that she was clawing her way through the veils in her hunger to reach him, began to do the same himself, until he felt a sharp pain in his belly. He looked down through the layers that clung about his face and saw a stain spreading through the weave. He let out a cry and started to disentangle himself, catching sight of her pleasuring device buried deep in him as he wrestled to be out of her way. She withdrew the blade, only to plunge it into him a second time, and a third, leaving it in his heart as he fell backwards, his fingers dragging the veils down with him.

Standing at one of the upper windows of Peccable's house, watching the fires that raged in every direction, Jude shuddered, and looking down at her hands saw them glistening, wet with blood. The vision lasted only the briefest time, but she had no doubt of what she'd seen, nor what it signified. Quaisoir had committed the crime she'd been plotting.

"It's quite a sight, isn't it?" she heard Dowd say, and turned to look at him, momentarily disoriented. Had he seen the blood too? No, no. He was talking about the fires.

"Yes, it is," she said.

He came to join her at the glass, which rattled with each fusillade. "The Peccables are almost ready to leave. I suggest we do the same. I'm feeling much renewed." He had indeed healed with astonishing speed. The wounds on his face were barely visible now.

"Where will we go?" she said.

"Around the other side of the city," he said. "To where I first trod the boards. According to Peccable the theater is still standing. The Ipse, it's called. Built by Pluthero Quexos himself. I'd like to see it again."

"You want to be a tourist on a night like this?"

"The theater may not be standing tomorrow. In fact, the whole of Yzordderrex could be in ruins by daybreak. I thought you were the one who was so hungry to see it."

"If it's a sentimental visit," she said, "maybe you should go alone."

"Why, have you got some other agenda?" he asked her. "You have, haven't you?"

"How could I have?" she protested lightly. "I've never set foot here before."

He studied her, his face all suspicion. "But you always wanted to come here, didn't you? Right from the start. Godolphin used to wonder where you got the obsession from. Now I'm wondering the same." He followed her gaze through the window. "What's out there, Judith?"

"You can see for yourself," she replied. "We'll probably get killed before we reach the top of the street."

"No," he said. "Not us. We're blessed."

"Are we?"

"We're the same, remember? Perfect partners."

"I remember," she replied.

"Ten minutes, then we'll go."

"I'll be ready."

She heard the door close behind her, then looked down at her hands again. All trace of the vision had faded. She glanced back towards the door, to be certain that Dowd had gone, then put her hands to the glass and closed her eyes. She had ten minutes to find the woman who shared her face, ten minutes before she and Dowd were out in the tumult of the streets and all hope of contact would be dashed.

"Quaisoir," she murmured.

She felt the glass vibrate against her palms and heard the din of the dying across the roofs. She said her double's name a second time, turning her thoughts to the towers that would have been visible from this very window if the air between hadn't been so thick with smoke. The image of that smoke filled her head, though she hadn't consciously conjured it, and she felt her thoughts rise in its clouds, wafted on the heat of destruction.

It was difficult for Quaisoir to find something discreet to wear among garments she had acquired for their immodesty, but by tearing all the decoration from one of her simpler robes she had achieved something like seemliness. Now she left her chambers and prepared for her final journey through the palace. She had already plotted her route once she was out of the gates: back down to the harbor, where she'd first seen the Man of Sorrows, standing on the roof. If He wasn't there, she would find somebody who knew His whereabouts. He hadn't come into Yzordderrex simply to disappear again. He would leave trails for His acolytes to follow, and trials, no doubt, for them to endure, proving in their endurance how much they desired to come into His presence. But first, she had to get out of the palace, and to do so she took corridors and stairways that had not been used in decades, familiar only to her, the Autarch, and the masons who'd laid these cold stones, cold themselves now. Only Maestros and their mistresses preserved their youth, and doing so was no longer the bliss it had been. She would have liked the years to show on her face when she knelt before the Nazarene, so that He would know that she'd suffered, and that she deserved His forgiveness. But she would have to trust that He would see through the veil of her perfection to the pain beneath.

Her feet were bare, and the chill rose through her soles, so that by the time she reached the humid air outside, her teeth were chattering. She halted for a moment, to orient herself in the maze of courtyards that surrounded the palace, and as she turned her thoughts from the practical to the abstract she met another thought, waiting at the back of her skull for just such a turn. She didn't doubt its source for a moment. The angel that Seidux had driven from her chamber that afternoon had waited at the threshold all this time, knowing she would come at last, seeking guidance. Tears started to her eyes when she realized she'd not been forsaken. The Son of David knew her agony and sent this messenger to whisper in her head.

Ipse, it said. *Ipse.*

She knew what the word meant. She'd patronized the Ipse many times, masked, as were all the women of the *haut monde* when visiting places of moral dubiety. She'd seen all the works of Quexos performed there; and translations of Flotter; even, on occasion, Koppocovi's farces, crude as they were. That the Man of Sorrows should have chosen such a place was certainly strange, but who was she to question His purposes?

"I hear," she said aloud.

Even before the voice in her had faded, she was making her way through the courtyards to the gate by which she would be delivered most readily into the Deliquium Kesparate, where Pluthero Quexos had built his shrine to artifice, soon to be reconsecrated in the name of Truth.

Jude took her hands from the window and opened her eyes. There had been none of the clarity she'd experienced when asleep in this contact—in truth she was not even certain she'd made it—but there was no time left to try again. Dowd was calling her, and so were the streets of Yzordderrex, blazing though they were. She'd seen blood spilt from her place by the window; numerous assaults and beatings; troop charges and retreats; civilians warring in rabid packs, and others marching in brigades, armed and ordered. In such a chaos of factions she had no way of judging the legitimacy of any cause; nor, in truth, did she much care. Her mission was seek out her sister in this maelstrom, and hope that she in her turn was seeking out Jude.

Quaisoir would be disappointed, of course, if and when they finally met. Jude was not the messenger of the Lord she was hurrying to find. But then lords divine or secular were not the redeemers and salvers of the world legend made them out to be. They were spoilers; they were destroyers. The evidence of that was out there, in the very streets Jude was about to tread, and if she could only make Quaisoir share and understand that vision, perhaps the promise of sisterhood would not be so unwelcome a gift to bring to this meeting, which she could not help but think of as a reunion.

35

I

Demanding directions as he went, usually from wounded men, Gentle took several hours to get from the hosannas of Lickerish Street to the mystif's Kesparate, during which period the city's decline into chaos quickened, so that he went half expecting that the streets of straight houses and blossom-clad trees would be ashes and rubble by the time he arrived. But when he finally came to the city-within-a-city he found it untouched by looters or demolishers, either because they knew there was little of worth to them here or—more likely—because the lingering superstition about a people who'd once occupied the Unbeheld's Dominion kept them from doing their worst.

Entering, he went first to the chiancula, prepared to do whatever was necessary—threaten, beg, cajole—in order to be returned into the mystif's company. The chiancula and all the adjacent buildings were deserted, however, so he began a systematic search of the streets. They, like the chiancula, were empty, and as his desperation grew his discretion fled, until he was shouting Pie's name to the empty streets like a midnight drunkard.

Eventually, these tactics earned him a response. One of the quartet who'd appeared to offer such chilly welcome when he'd first come here appeared: the mustached young man. His robes were not held between his teeth this time, and when he spoke he deigned to do so in English. But the lethal ribbon still fluttered in his hands, its threat undisguised.

"You came back," he said.

"Where's Pie?"

"Where's the girl child?"

"Dead. Where's Pie?"

"You seem different."

"I am. Where's Pie?"

"Not here."

"Where then?"

"The mystif's gone up to the palace," the man replied.

"Why?"

"That was the judgment upon it."

"Just to go?" Gentle said, taking a step towards the man. "There must have been more to it than that."

Though the silk sword protected the man, Gentle came with a burden of power that beggared his own, and sensing this he answered less obliquely.

"The judgment was that it kill the Autarch," he said.

"So it's been sent up there alone?"

"No. It took some of our tribe with it and left a few of us to guard the Kesparate."

"How long ago since they went?"

"Not very long. But you won't get into the palace. Neither will they. It's suicide."

Gentle didn't linger to argue but headed back towards the entrance, leaving the man to guard the blossoms and the empty streets. As he approached the gate, however, he saw that two individuals, a man and a woman, had just entered and were looking his way. Both were naked from the waist up, their throats painted with the blue triple stripe he remembered from the siege at the harbor, marking them as members of the Dearth. At his approach, both acknowledged him by putting palm to palm and inclining their heads. The woman was half as big again as her companion, her body a glorious machine, her head—shaved but for a ponytail—set on a neck wider than her cranium and, like her arms and belly, so elaborately muscled the merest twitch was a spectacle.

"I said he'd be here!" she told the world.

"I don't know what you want," he said, "but I can't supply it."

"You *are* John Furie Zacharias?"

"Yes."

"Called Gentle?"

"Yes. But—"

"Then you have to come. Please. Father Athanasius

sent us to find you. We heard what happened on Lickerish Street, and we knew it had to be you. I'm Nikaetomaas," the woman said. "This is Floccus Dado. We've been waiting for you since Estabrook arrived."

"Estabrook?" said Gentle. There was a man he hadn't given a thought to in many a month. "How do you know him?"

"We found him in the street. We thought he was the one. But he wasn't. He knew nothing."

"And you think I do?" Gentle said, exasperated. "Let me tell you, I know fuck-all! I don't know who you think I am, but I'm not your man."

"That's what Father Athanasius said. He said you were in ignorance—"

"Well, he was right."

"But you married the mystif."

"So what?" said Gentle. "I love it, and I don't care who knows it."

"We realize that," Nikaetomaas said, as though nothing could have been plainer. "That's how we tracked you."

"We knew it would come here," Floccus said. "And wherever it had gone, you would be."

"It isn't here," Gentle said. "It's up in the palace."

"In the palace?" said Nikaetomaas, turning her gaze up towards the lowering walls. "And you intend to follow it?"

"Yes."

"Then I'll come with you," she said. "Mr. Dado, go back to Athanasius. Tell him who we've found and where we've gone."

"I don't want company," Gentle said. "I don't even trust myself."

"How will you get into the palace without someone at your side?" Nikaetomaas said. "I know the gates. I know the courtyards."

Gentle turned the options over in his head. Part of him wanted to go as a rogue, carrying the chaos he'd brought to Lickerish Street as his emblem. But his ignorance of palace geography could indeed slow him, and minutes might make the difference between finding the mystif alive or dead. He nodded his consent, and the parties divided at the gate: Floccus Dado back to Father Athanasius, Gentle and Nika-etomaas up towards the Autarch's fortress.

The only subject he broached as they traveled was that of Estabrook. How was he, Gentle asked: still crazy?

"He was almost dead when we found him," Nika-etomaas said. "His brother left him here for dead. But we took him to our tents on the Erasure, and we healed him there. Or, more properly, his being there healed him."

"You did all this, thinking he was me?"

"We knew that somebody was going to come from the Fifth to begin the Reconciliation again. And of course we knew it had to be soon. We just didn't know what he looked like."

"Well, I'm sorry to disappoint you, but that's twice you've got it wrong. I'm no more your man than Esta-brook."

"Why did you come here, then?" she said.

That was an inquiry that deserved a serious reply, if not for her sake, then for his own.

"There were questions I wanted answered, that I couldn't answer on earth," he said. "A friend of mine died, very young. A woman I knew was almost murdered—"

"Judith."

"Yes, Judith."

"We've talked about her a great deal," Nikaetomaas said. "Estabrook was obsessed with her."

"Is he still?"

"I haven't spoken to him for a long time. But you know he was trying to bring her to Yzordderrex when his brother intervened."

"Did she come?"

"Apparently not," Nikaetomaas said. "But Athanasius believes she will eventually. He says she's part of the story of the Reconciliation."

"How does he work that out?"

"From Estabrook's obsession with her, I suppose. The

way he talked about her, it was though she was something holy, and Athanasius loves holy women."

"Let me tell you, I know Judith very well, and she's no Virgin."

"There are other kinds of sanctity among our sex," Nikaetomaas replied, a little testily.

"I'm sorry. I didn't mean any offense. But if there's one thing Jude's always hated it's being put on a pedestal."

"Then maybe it's not the idol we should be studying, but the worshiper. Athanasius says obsession is fire to our fortress."

"What does that mean?"

"That we have to burn down the walls around us, but it takes a very bright flame to do so."

"An obsession, in other words."

"That's one such flame, yes."

"Why would we want to burn down these walls in the first place? Don't they protect us?"

"Because if we don't, we die inside, kissing our own reflections," Nikaetomaas said, the reply too well turned to be improvised.

"Athanasius again?" Gentle said.

"No," said Nikaetomaas. "An aunt of mine. She's been locked up in the Bastion for years, but in here"—Nikaetomaas pointed to her temple—"she's free."

"And what about the Autarch?" Gentle said, turning his gaze up towards the fortress.

"What about him?"

"Is he up there, kissing his reflection?"

"Who knows? Maybe he's been dead for years, and the state's running itself."

"Do you seriously believe that?"

Nikaetomaas shook her head. "No. He's alive, behind his walls."

"What's he keeping out, I wonder?"

"Who knows? Whatever he's afraid of, I don't think it breathes the same air that we do."

Before they left the rubble-strewn thoroughfares of the Kesparate called Hittahitte, which lay between the gates of

the Eurhetemec Kesparate and the wide Roman streets of
Yzordderrex's bureaucratic district, Nikaetomaas dug
around in the ruins of a garret for some means of disguise.
She found a collection of filthy garments which she insisted
Gentle don, then found some equally disgusting for herself.
Their faces and physiques had to be concealed, she explained, so that they could mingle freely with the wretched
they'd find gathered at the gates. Then they headed on,
their climb bringing them into streets lined with buildings
of classical severity and scale, as yet unscorched by the
torches that were being passed from hand to hand, roof to
roof, in the Kesparates below. They would not remain pristine much longer, Nikaetomaas predicted. When the rebels' fire reached these edifices—the Taxation Courts and
the Bureaus of Justice—it would leave no pillar unblack-
ened. But for now the travelers moved between monoliths
as quiet as mausoleums.

On the other side, the reason for their donning of stink-
ing and louse-ridden clothes became apparent. Nikaetomaas had brought them not to one of the great gates of
the palace but to a minor opening, around which a group
dressed in motley indistinguishable from their own was
gathered. Some of them carried candles. By their fitful light
Gentle could see that there was not a single body that was
whole among them.

"Are they waiting to get in?" he asked his guide.

"No. This is the gate of Saint Creaze and Saint Evendown. Have you not heard of them in the Fifth? I thought
that's where they were martyred."

"Very possibly."

"They appear everywhere in Yzordderrex. Nursery
rhymes, puppet plays—"

"So what happens here? Do the saints make personal
appearances?"

"After a fashion."

"And what are these people hoping for?" Gentle asked,
casting a glance among the wretched assembly. "Healing?"

They were certainly in dire need of such miracles. Crippled and diseased, suppurating and broken, some of them looked so weak they'd not make it till morning.

"No," Nikaetomaas replied. "They're here for sustenance. I only hope the saints aren't too distracted by the revolution to put in an appearance."

She'd no sooner spoken than the sound of an engine chugging into life on the far side of the gates pitched the crowd into frenzy. Crutches became weapons, and diseased spittle flew, as the invalids fought for a place close to the bounty they knew was imminent. Nikaetomaas pushed Gentle forward into the brawl, where he was obliged to fight, though he felt ashamed to do so, or else have his limbs torn from their sockets by those who had fewer than he. Head down, arms flailing, he dug his way forward as the gates began to open.

What appeared on the other side drew gasps of devotion from all sides and one of incredulity from Gentle. Trundling forward to fill the breadth of the gates was a fifteen-foot study in kitsch: a sculpted representation of Saints Creaze and Evendown, standing shoulder to shoulder, their arms stretched out towards the yearning crowd, while their eyes rolled in their carved sockets like those of carnival dummies, looking down on their flock as if affrighted by them one moment and up to heaven the next. But it was their apparel that drew Gentle's appalled gaze. They were clothed in their largesse: dressed in food from throat to foot. Coats of meat, still smoking from the ovens, covered their torsos; sausages hung in steaming loops around their necks and wrists; at their groins hung sacks heavy with bread, while the layers of their skirts were of fruit and fish. The crowd instantly surged forward to denude them, the brawlers merciless in their hunger, beating each other as they climbed for their share.

The saints were not without defense, however; there were penalties for the gluttonous. Hooks and spikes, expressly designed to wound, were set among the bountiful folds of skirts and coats. The devotees seemed not to care, but climbed up over the statues, disdainful of fruit and fish, in order to reach the steaks and sausages above. Some fell, doing themselves bloody mischief on the way down; others—scrambling over the victims—reached their goals with shrieks of glee and set about loading the bags on their backs. Even then, in their triumph, they were not secure. Those behind either dragged them from their perches or pulled the bags from their backs and pitched them to accomplices in the crowd, where they in turn were set upon and robbed.

Nikaetomaas held on to Gentle's belt so that they wouldn't be separated in this mêlée, and after much maneuvering they reached the base of the statues. The machine had been designed to block the gates, but Nikaetomaas now squatted down in front of the plinth, and—her activities concealed from the guards watching from above the gate—tore at the casing that housed the vehicle's wheels. It was beaten metal, but it came away like cardboard beneath her assault, its rivets flying. Then she ducked into the gap she'd created. Gentle followed. Once below the saints, the din of the crowd became remoter, the thump of bodies punctuating the general hubbub. It was almost completely dark, but they shimmied forward on their stomachs, the engine—huge and hot—dripping its fluids on them as they went. As they reached the other side, and Nikaetomaas began to prize away the casing there, the sound of shouting became louder. Gentle looked around. Others had discovered Nikaetomaas' handiwork and, perhaps thinking there were new treasures to be discovered beneath the idols, were following: not two or three, now, but many. Gentle began to lend Nikaetomaas a hand, as the space filled up with bodies, new brawls erupting as the pursuers fought for access. The whole structure, enormous as it was, began to shudder, the combination of brawlers below and above conspiring to tip it. With the violence of the rocking increasing by the moment, Gentle had sight of escape. A sizable courtyard lay on the other side of the saints, scored by the tracks of the engine and littered with discarded food.

The instability of the machine had not gone unnoticed, and two guards were presently forsaking their meal of prime steak and raising the alarm with panicked shouts. Their retreat allowed Nikaetomaas to wriggle free unnoticed, then turn to haul Gentle after her. The juggernaut was now close to toppling, and shots were being fired on the other side as the guards above the gate sought to dissuade the crowd from further burrowings. Gentle felt hands grasping at his legs, but he kicked back at them, as Nikaetomaas dragged him forward, and slid out into the open air as several cracks, like sudden thunder, announced that the saints were tired of teetering and ready to fall. Backs bent, Gentle and Nikaetomaas darted across the rind- and crust-littered ground to the safety of the shadows as, with a great din the saints fell backwards like comic drunkards, a mass of their adherents still clinging to arms and coats and skirts. The structure came apart as it hit the ground, pitching pieces of carved, cooked, and crippled flesh in all directions.

The guards were descending from the ramparts now, to stem with bullets the flow of the crowd. Gentle and Nikaetomaas didn't linger to watch this fresh horror but took to their heels, up and away from the gates, the pleas and howls of those maimed by the fall following them through the darkness.

2

"What's the din, Rosengarten?"

"There's a minor problem at the Gate of Saints, sir."

"Are we under siege?"

"No. It was merely an unfortunate accident."

"Fatalities?"

"Nothing significant. The gate's now been sealed."

"And Quaisoir? How's she?"

"I haven't spoken with Seidux since early evening."

"Then find out."

"Of course."

Rosengarten withdrew, and the Autarch returned his attention to the man transfixed in the chair close by.

"These Yzordderrexian nights," he said to the fellow,

"they're so very long. In the Fifth, you know, they're half this length, and I used to complain they were over too soon. But now"—he sighed—"now I wonder if I wouldn't be better off going back there and founding a New Yzordderrex. What do you think?"

The man in the chair didn't reply. His cries had long since ceased, though the reverberations, more precious than the sound itself, and more tantalizing, continued to shake the air, even to the ceiling of this chamber, where clouds sometimes formed and shed delicate, cleansing rains.

The Autarch drew his own chair up closer to the man. A sac of living fluid the size of his head was clamped to the victim's chest, its limbs, fine as thread, puncturing him, and reaching into his body to touch his heart, lungs, liver, and lights. He'd summoned the entity, which was the shreds of a once much more fabulous beast, the renunciance, from the In Ovo, selecting it as a surgeon might choose some instrument from a tray, to perform a delicate and very particular task. Whatever the nature of such summoned beasts, he had no fear of them. Decades of such rituals had familiarized him with every species that haunted the In Ovo, and while there were certainly some he would never have dared bring into the living world, most had enough base instinct to know their master's voice and would obey him within the confines of their wit. This creature he'd called Abelove, after a lawyer he'd known briefly in the Fifth, who'd been as leechlike as this scrap of malice, and almost as foul smelling.

"How does it feel?" the Autarch asked, straining to catch the merest murmur of a reply. "The pain's passed, hasn't it? Didn't I say it would?"

The man's eyes flickered open, and he licked his lips. They made something very close to a smile.

"You feel a kind of union with Abelove, am I right? It's worked its way into every little part. Please speak, or I'll take it from you. You'll bleed from every hole it's made, but that pain won't be anything beside the loss you'll feel."

"Don't . . ." the man said.

"Then talk to me," the Autarch replied, all reason. "Do you know how difficult it is to find a leech like this? They're almost extinct. But I gave this one to you, didn't I? And all I'm asking is that you tell me how it feels."

"It feels . . . good."

"Is that Abelove talking, or you?"

"We're the same," came the reply.

"Like sex, is it?"

"No."

"Like love, then?"

"No. Like I'm unborn again."

"In the womb?"

"In the womb."

"Oh, God, how I envy you. I don't have that memory. I never floated in a mother."

The Autarch rose from his chair, his hand covering his mouth. It was always like this when the dregs of kreauchee moved in his veins. He became unbearably tender at such times, moved to expressions of grief and rage at the obscurest cue.

"To be joined with another soul," he said, "indivisibly. Consumed and made whole in the same moment. What a precious joy."

He turned back to his prisoner, whose eyes were closing again. The Autarch didn't notice.

"It's times like this," he said, "I wish I were a poet. I wish I had the words to express my yearning. I think that if I knew that one day—I don't care how many years from now, centuries even, I don't care—if I *knew* that one day I was going to be united, indivisibly, with another soul, I could begin to be a good man."

He sat down again beside the captive, whose eyes were completely closed.

"But it won't happen," he said, tears beginning to come. "We're too much ourselves. Afraid of letting go of what we are in case we're nothing, and holding on so tight we lose everything else." Agitation was shaking the tears out of his eyes now. "Are you listening to me?" he said.

He shook the man, whose mouth fell open, a trickle of saliva dribbling from one corner.

"Listen!" he raged. "I'm giving you my pain here!"

Receiving no response, he stood up and struck his captive across the face so hard the man toppled over, the chair to which he was bound falling with him. The creature clamped to his chest convulsed in sympathy with its host.

"I didn't bring you here to sleep!" the Autarch said. "I want you to share your pain with me."

He put his hands on the leech and began to tear it from the man's chest. The creature's panic flooded its host, and instantly the man began to writhe, the cords drawing blood as he fought to keep the leech from being stolen. Less than an hour before, when Abelove had been brought out of the shadows and displayed to the prisoner, he'd begged to be spared its touch. Now, finding his tongue again, he pleaded twice as hard not to be separated from it, his pleas swooping into screams when the parasite's filaments, barbed so as to prevent their removal, were wrenched from the organs they'd pierced. As soon as they broke surface they began to flail wildly, seeking to return to their host or find a new one. But the Autarch was unmoved by the panic of either lover and divided them like death itself, pitching Abelove across the chamber and taking the man's face in fingers sticky with his infatuate's blood.

"Now," he said. "How does it feel?"

"Give it back . . . *please* . . . give it back."

"Is this like being born?" the Autarch said.

"Whatever you say! Yes! Yes! Just give it back!"

The Autarch left the man's side and crossed the chamber to the spot where he'd made the summoning. He picked his way through the spirals of human gut he'd arranged on the floor as bait and snatched up the knife still lying in the blood beside the blindfolded head, returning at no more than an amble to where the victim was lying. There he cut the prisoner's bonds and stood back to watch the rest of the show. Though he was grievously wounded, his punctured lungs barely able to draw breath, the man fixed his eyes on the object of his desire and began to crawl towards it. Ashen, the Autarch let him crawl, knowing as he went that the distance was too great, and the scene must end in tragedy.

The lover had advanced no more than a couple of yards when there was a rapping on the door.

"Go away!" the Autarch said, but the rapping came again, this time accompanied by Rosengarten's voice.

"Quaisoir's gone, sir," he said.

The Autarch watched the crawling man's despair and despaired himself. Despite all his indulgences, the woman had deserted him for the Man of Sorrows.

"Come in!" he called.

Rosengarten entered and made his report. Seidux was dead, stabbed and thrown from a window. Quaisoir's quarters were empty, her servant vanished, her dressing room overturned. A search for her abductors was already under way.

"Abductors?" the Autarch said. "No, Rosengarten. There are no abductors. She's gone of her own accord."

Not once as he spoke did he take his eyes off the lover, who had covered a third of the distance between his chair and his darling but was weakening fast.

"It's over," the Autarch said. "She's gone to find her Redeemer, the poor bitch."

"Then shouldn't I dispatch troops to find her?" Rosengarten said. "The city's dangerous."

"So's she when she wants to be. The women in the Bastion taught her some unholy stuff."

"I hope that cesspit's been burned to the ground," Rosengarten said, with a rare passion.

"I doubt it is," the Autarch replied. "They've got ways of protecting themselves."

"Not from me, they haven't," Rosengarten boasted.

"Yes, even from you," the Autarch told him. "Even from me. The power of women can't be scoured away, however hard we try. The Unbeheld attempted it, but he didn't succeed. There's always some corner—"

"Just say the word," the commander broke in, "and I'll go down there now. Hang the bitches in the streets."

"No, you don't understand," the Autarch said, his voice almost monotonous, but all the more sorrowful for that. "The corner isn't out there, it's in here." He pointed to his skull. "It's in our minds. Their mysteries obsess us, even though we put them out of sight. Even me. God knows, I should be free of it. I wasn't cast out like the rest of you were. How can I yearn for something I never had? But I do." He sighed. "Oh, I do."

He looked around at Rosengarten, whose expression was uncomprehending.

"Look at him." The Autarch glanced back at the captive as he spoke. "He's got seconds left to live. But the leech gave him a taste and he wants it back again."

"A taste of what?"

"Of the womb, Rosengarten. He said it was like being in the womb. We're all *cast out*. Whatever we build, wherever we hide, we're cast out."

As he spoke the prisoner gave a last exhausted moan and lay still. The Autarch watched the body awhile, the only sound in the vastness of the chamber the weakening motions of the leech on the cold floor.

"Lock the doors and seal them up," the Autarch said, turning to leave without looking back at Rosengarten. "I'm going to the Pivot Tower."

"Yes, sir."

"Come and find me when it's light. These nights, they're too long. Too long. I wonder, sometimes . . ."

But what he wondered had gone from his head before it could reach his lips, and when he left the lovers' tomb it was in silence.

36

I

Gentle's thoughts had not often turned to Taylor as he and Pie journeyed, but when, in the streets outside the palace, Nikaetomaas had asked him why he'd come to the Imajica, it had been Taylor's death he'd spoken of first, and only then of Judith and the attempt upon her life. Now, as he and Nikaetomaas passed through the balmy, benighted courtyards and up into the palace itself, he thought of the man again, lying on his final pillow, talking about floating and charging Gentle to solve mysteries that he'd not had time to solve himself.

"I had a friend in the Fifth who would have loved this place," Gentle said. "He loved desolation."

It was here, in every courtyard. Gardens had been planted in many of them and left to riot. But riot took energy, and nature was weary here, the plants throttling themselves after a few spurts and withering back into earth the color of ash. The scene was not so different once they got inside, wandering mapless down galleries where the dust was as thick as the soil in the dead gardens, into forsaken annexes and chambers laid out for guests who had breathed their last decades before. Most of the walls, whether of chambers or galleries, were decorated: some with tapestries, many others with immense frescoes, and while there were scenes Gentle recognized from his travels—Patashoqua under a green-gold sky, with a flight of air balloons rising from the plain outside its walls; a festival at the L'Himby temples—the suspicion grew on him that the finest of these images were of earth; or, more particularly, of England. Doubtless the pastoral was a universal mode, and shepherds wooed nymphs in the Reconciled Dominions just as sonnets described them doing in the Fifth, but there were details of these scenes that were indisputably English: swallows swooping in mild summer skies; cattle drinking in water meadows while their herders slept; the Salisbury spire rising from a bank of oaks; the distant towers and domes of London, glimpsed from a slope on which maids and swains made dalliance; even Stonehenge, relocated for drama's sake to a hill and set against thunderheads.

"England," Gentle said as they went. "Somebody here remembers England."

Though they passed by these works too fast for him to scrutinize them carefully, he saw no signature on any. The artists who'd sketched England, and returned to depict it so lovingly, were apparently content to remain anonymous.

"I think we should start climbing," Nikaetomaas suggested when by chance their wanderings brought them to the foot of a monumental staircase. "The higher we are the more chance we'll have of grasping the geography."

The ascent was five flights long—more deserted galleries presenting themselves on every floor—but it finally delivered them onto a roof from which they were able to glimpse the scale of the labyrinth they were lost in. Towers twice and three times the height of the one they'd climbed loomed above them while, below, the courtyards were laid out in all directions, some crossed by battalions but most as deserted as every other corridor and chamber. Beyond them lay the palace walls, and beyond the walls themselves the smoke-shrouded city, the sound of its convulsions dim at such a distance.

Lulled by the remoteness of this aerie, both Gentle and Nikaetomaas were startled by a commotion that erupted much closer by. Almost grateful for signs of life in this mausoleum, even if it was the enemy, they headed in pursuit of the din makers, back down a flight of stairs and across an enclosed bridge between towers.

"Hoods!" Nikaetomaas said, tucking her ponytail back into her shirt and pulling the crude cowl over her head. Gentle did the same, though he doubted such a disguise would offer them much protection if they were discovered.

Orders were being given in the gallery ahead, and Gentle drew Nikaetomaas into hiding to listen. The officer had words of inspiration for his squad, promising every man who brought a Eurhetemec down a month's paid leave. Somebody asked him how many there were, and he replied that he'd heard six, but he didn't believe it because they'd slaughtered ten times that number. However many there are, he said—six, sixty, six hundred—they're outnumbered and trapped. They won't get out alive. So saying, he divided his contingent and told them to shoot on sight.

Three soldiers were dispatched in the direction of Nikaetomaas and Gentle's hiding place. They had no sooner passed than she stepped out of the shadows and brought two of the three down with single blows. The third turned to defend himself, but Gentle—lacking the mass or muscle power that made Nikaetomaas so effective—used momentum instead, flinging himself against the man with such force he threw both of them to the ground. The soldier raised his gun towards Gentle's skull, but Nikaetomaas took hold of both weapon and hand, hauling the man up by his arm until he was head to head with her, the gun pointing at the roof, the fingers around it too crushed to fire. Then she pulled his helmet off with her free hand and peered at him.

"Where's the Autarch?"

The man was too pained and too terrified to claim ignorance. "The Pivot Tower," he said.

"Which is where?"

"It's the tallest tower," he sobbed, scrabbling at the arm he was dangling by, down which blood was running.

"Take us there," Nikaetomaas said. "Please."

Teeth gritted, the man nodded his head, and she let him go. The gun went from his pulverized fingers as he struck the ground. She invited him to stand with a hooked finger.

"What's your name?" she asked him.

"Yark Lazarevich," he told her, nursing his hand in the crook of his arm.

"Well, Yark Lazarevich, if you make any attempt—or I choose to interpret any act of yours as an attempt—to alert help, I will swat the brains from your pan so fast they'll be in Patashoqua before your pants fill. Is that plain?"

"That's plain."

"Do you have children?"

"Yes. I've got two."

"Think of them fatherless and take care. You have a question?"

"No, I just wanted to explain that the tower's quite a way from here. I don't want you thinking I'm leading you astray."

"Be fast, then," she said, and Lazarevich took her at her word, leading them back across the bridge towards the stairs, explaining as he went that the quickest route to the tower was through the Cesscordium, and that was two floors down.

They had descended perhaps a dozen steps when shots were fired behind them, and one of Lazarevich's two comrades staggered into view, adding shouts to his gunfire to raise the alarm. Had he not been groggy he might have put a bullet in Nikaetomaas or Gentle, but they were away down the stairs before he'd even reached the top, Lazarevich protesting as he went that none of this was his doing, and he loved his children and all he wanted to do was see them again.

There was the sound of running in the lower gallery, and shouts answering those of the alarm raiser above. Nikaetomaas unleashed a series of expletives which could not have been fouler had Gentle understood them, and reached for Lazarevich, who hared off down the stairs before she could snatch hold of him, meeting a squad of his comrades at the bottom. Nikaetomaas' pursuit had taken her past Gentle, directly into their line of fire. They didn't hesitate. Four muzzles flared; four bullets found their mark. Her physique availed her nothing. She dropped where she stood, her body tumbling down the stairs and coming to a halt a few steps from the bottom. Watching her fall, three thoughts went through Gentle's head. One, that he'd have these bastards for this. Two, that stealth was irrelevant now. And three, that if he brought the roof down on their murderous heads, and word spread that there was another power in the palace besides the Autarch, that would be no bad thing. He'd regretted the deaths he'd caused in Lickerish Street, but he would not regret these. All he had to do was get his hand to his face to tear away the cloth before the bullets flew. There were more soldiers converging on the spot from several directions. Come on, he thought, raising his hands in feigned surrender as the others approached: come on, join the jubilee.

One of the gathering number was clearly a man of authority. Heels clicked together as he appeared, salutes were exchanged. He looked up the staircase towards his hooded prisoner.

"General Racidio," one of the captains said. "We have two of the rebels here."

"These aren't Eurhetemecs." His gaze went from Gentle to the body of Nikaetomaas, then back up to Gentle again. "I think we have two Dearthers here."

He started up the stairs towards Gentle, who was surreptitiously drawing breath through the open weave of the cloth around his face in preparation for his unveiling. He would have two or three seconds at best. Time perhaps to seize Racidio and use him as a hostage if the pneuma failed to kill every one of the gunmen.

"Let's see what you look like," the commander said, and tore the cloth from Gentle's face.

The instant that should have seen the pneuma loosed instead saw Racidio drop back in stupefaction from the features he'd uncovered. Whatever he saw was missed by the soldiers below, who kept their guns trained on Gentle until Racidio spat an order that they be lowered. Gentle was as confounded as they, but he wasn't about to question the reprieve. He dropped his hands and, stepping over the body of Nikaetomaas, came to the bottom of the stairs. Racidio retreated further, shaking his head as he did so, and wetting his lips, but apparently unable to find the words to express himself. He looked as though he was expecting the ground to open up beneath him; indeed, was silently willing it to do so. Rather than risk disabusing the man of his error by speaking, Gentle summoned his guide Lazarevich forward with the hooked finger Nikaetomaas had used minutes before. The man had taken refuge behind a shield of soldiers and only came out of hiding reluctantly, glancing at his captain and Racidio in the hope that Gentle's summons would be countermanded. It was not, however. Gentle went to meet him, and Racidio uttered the first words he'd been able to find since setting eyes on the trespasser's face.

"Forgive me," he said. "I'm mortified."

Gentle didn't give him the solace of a response but, with Lazarevich at his side, took a step towards the knot of soldiers at the top of the next flight of stairs. They parted without a word and he headed between their ranks, fighting the urge to pick up his pace, tempting though it was. And he regretted too not being able to say his farewells to Nikaetomaas. But neither impatience nor sentiment would profit him now. He'd been blessed, and maybe in the fullness of time he'd understand why. In the short term, he had to get to the Autarch and hope that the mystif was there also.

"You still want to go to the Pivot Tower?" Lazarevich said.

"Yes."

"When I get you there, will you let me go?"

Again he said, "Yes."

There was a pause, while Lazarevich oriented himself at the bottom of the stairs. Then he said, "Who are you?"

"Wouldn't you like to know," Gentle replied, his answer as much for his own benefit as that of his guide.

2

There had been six of them at the start. Now there were two. One of the casualties had been Thes 'reh' ot, shot down as he etched with a cross a corner they'd turned in the maze of courtyards. It had been his inspiration to mark their route and so facilitate a speedy exit when they'd finished their work.

"It's only the Autarch's will that holds these walls up," he'd said as they'd entered the palace. "Once he's down, they'll come too. We need to beat a quick retreat if we're not to get buried.''

That Thes 'reh' ot had volunteered for a mission his laughter had dubbed fatal was surprising enough, but this further show of optimism teetered on the schizophrenic. His sudden death not only robbed Pie of an unlooked-for ally, but also of the chance to ask him why he'd joined the assault. But then several such conundrums had accrued around this endeavor, not least the sense of inevitability that had attended every phase, as though this judgment had been laid down long before Pie and Gentle had ever appeared in Yzordderrex, and any attempt to flout it would defy the wisdom of greater magistrates than Culus. Such inevitability bred fatalism, of course, and though the mystif had encouraged Thes 'reh' ot to plot their route of return, it entertained few delusions about making that journey. It willfully kept from its mind the losses that extinction would bring until its remaining comrade, Lu 'chur' chem—a purebred Eurhetemec, his skin blue-black, his eyes double-irised—raised the subject. They were in a gallery lined with frescoes that evoked the city Pie had once called home: the painted streets of London, depicted as they'd been in the age into which the mystif had been born, replete with pigeon hawkers, mummers, and dandies.

Seeing the way Pie gazed at these sights, Lu 'chur' chem said, "Never again, eh?"

"Never again what?"

"Out in a street, seeing the way the world is some morning."

"No?"

"No," Lu 'chur' chem said. "We're not coming back this way, and we both know it."

"I don't mind," Pie replied. "I've seen a lot of things. I've felt even more. I've got no regrets."

"You've had a long life?"

"Yes, I have."

"And your Maestro? He had a long life too?"

"Yes, he did," Pie said, looking again at the scenes on the walls.

Though the renderings were relatively unsophisticated, they touched the mystif's memories awake, evoking the bustle and din of the crowded thoroughfares it and its Maestro had walked in the bright, hopeful days before the Reconciliation. Here were the fashionable streets of Mayfair, lined with fine shops and paraded by finer women, abroad to buy lavender water and mantua silk and snow-white muslin. Here was the throng of Oxford Street, where half a hundred vendors clamored for custom: purveyors of slippers, wildfowl, cherries, and gingerbread, all vying for a niche on the pavement and a space in the air to raise their cries. Here too was a fair, St. Bartholomew's most likely, where there was more sin to be had by daylight than Babylon ever boasted by dark.

"Who made these?" Pie wondered aloud as they proceeded.

"Diverse hands, by the look of 'em," Lu 'chur' chem replied. "You can see where one style stops and another starts."

"But somebody directed these painters, gave them the details, the colors. Unless the Autarch just stole artists from the Fifth Dominion."

"Perfectly possible," Lu 'chur' chem said. "He stole architects. He put tribes in chains to build the place."

"And nobody ever challenged him?"

"People tried to stir up revolutions over and over again, but he suppressed them. Burnt down the universities, hanged the theologians and the radicals. He had a stranglehold. *And* he had the Pivot, and most people believe that's the Unbeheld's seal of approval. If Hapexamendios didn't want the Autarch to rule Yzordderrex, why did He allow the Pivot to be moved here? That's what they said. And I don't—"

Lu 'chur' chem stopped in his tracks, seeing that Pie had already done so.

"What is it?" he asked.

The mystif stared up at the picture they had come abreast of, its breath quickened by shock.

"Is something wrong?" Lu 'chur' chem said.

It took a few moments to find the words. "I don't think we should go any further," it said.

"Why not?"

"Not together, at least. The judgment fell on me, and I should finish this alone."

"What's wrong with you? I've come this far. I want to have the satisfaction."

"What's more important?" the mystif asked him, turning from the painting it had been so fixated by. "Your satisfaction, or succeeding in what we came here to do?"

"You know my answer to that."

"Then trust me. I have to go on alone. Wait for me here if you like."

Lu 'chur' chem made a phlegm-hawking growl, like Culus' growl, only coarser. "I came here to kill the Autarch," he said.

"No. You came here to help me, and you've done that. It's my hands that have to dispatch him, not yours. That's the judgment."

"Suddenly it's the judgment, the judgment! I shit on the judgment! I want to see the Autarch dead. I want to look on his face."

"I'll bring you his eyes," Pie said. "That's the best I can do. I mean it, Lu 'chur' chem. We have to part here."

Lu 'chur' chem spat on the ground between them.

"You don't trust me, do you?" he said.

"If that's what you want to believe."

"Mystif shite!" he exploded. "If you come out of this alive, I'll kill you, I swear, I'll kill you!"

There was no further argument. He simply spat again and turned his back, stalking off down the gallery, leaving the mystif to return its gaze to the picture which had quickened its pulse and breath.

Though it was curious to see a rendering of Oxford Street and St. Bartholomew's Fair in this setting, so far in years and Dominions from the scene that had inspired them, Pie might have suppressed the suspicion—growing in its belly while Lu 'chur' chem talked of revolution—that this was no coincidence, had the final image in the cycle not been so unlike those that had preceded it. The rest had been public spectacles, rendered countless times in satirical prints and paintings. This last was not. The rest had been well-known sites and streets, famous across the world. This last was not. It was an unremarkable thoroughfare in Clerkenwell, almost a backwater, which Pie doubted any artist of the Fifth had ever turned his pen or brush to depicting. But here it was, represented in meticulous detail: Gamut Street, to the brick, to the leaf. And taking pride of place in the center of the picture, number 28, the Maestro Sartori's house.

It had been lovingly re-created. Birds courted on its roof; on its step, dogs fought. And in between the fighters and wooers stood the house itself, blessed by a dappled sunlight denied the others in the row. The front door was closed, but the upper windows were flung wide, and the artist had painted somebody watching from one of them, his face too deeply shadowed to be recognized. The object of his scrutiny was not in doubt, however: the girl in the window across the street, sitting at her mirror with her dog on her lap, her fingers teasing from its bow the ribbon that would presently unlace her bodice. In the street between this beauty and her doting voyeur were a dozen details that could only have come from firsthand experience. On the pavement beneath the girl's window a small procession of charity children passed, wards of the parish, dressed all in white and carrying their wands. They marched raggedly behind their beadle, a brute of a man called Willis, whom Sartori had once beaten senseless on that very spot for cruelty to his charges. Around the far corner came Roxborough's carriage, drawn by his favorite bay, Bellamarre, named in honor of the Comte de St. Germain, who had swindled half the women of Venice under that alias a few years before. A dragoon was being ushered out of number 32 by the mistress of that house, who entertained officers of the Prince of Wales regiment—the Tenth, and no other—whenever her husband was away. The widow opposite watched enviously from her step.

All these and a dozen other little dramas were being

played out in the picture, and there wasn't one Pie didn't remember seeing enacted countless times. But who was the unseen spectator who'd instructed the painters in their craft, so that carriage, girl, soldier, widow, dogs, birds, voyeurs, and all could be set down with such verisimilitude?

Having no solution to the puzzle, the mystif plucked its gaze from the picture and looked back along the immense length of the gallery. Lu 'chur' chem had disappeared, spitting as he went. The mystif was alone, the routes ahead and behind similarly deserted. It would miss Lu 'chur' chem's companionship and bitterly regretted that it had lacked the wit to persuade its comrade that it had to go on alone, without causing such offense. But the picture on the wall was proof of secrets here it had not yet fathomed, and when it did so it wanted no witnesses. They too easily became accusers, and Pie was weighed down with enough reproaches already. If the tyrannies of Yzordderrex were in some fashion linked with the house on Gamut Street—and if Pie, by extension, was an unwitting collaborator in those tyrannies—it was important to learn of this guilt unaccompanied.

As prepared as possible for such revelations, the mystif left its place in front of the painting, reminding itself as it went of the promise made to Lu 'chur' chem. If it survived this enterprise, it had to return with the eyes of the Autarch. Eyes which it now didn't doubt had once been laid on Gamut Street, studying it as obsessively as the watcher at the painted window studied his lady love, sitting across the street in thrall to her reflection.